THE
IMMORTALS

By the same author

Male Chauvinism
Power!
Success!
Charmed Lives
Worldly Goods
Queenie
The Fortune
Curtain

THE IMMORTALS

Michael Korda

CHAPMANS

Chapmans Publishers Ltd
141–143 Drury Lane
London WC2B 5TB

First published in the USA by Poseidon Press 1992
First published in Great Britain by Chapmans 1992

The right of Michael Korda to be identified
as the author of this work has been asserted.

Excerpt from Marilyn Monroe's 'Red Diary' as quoted in
Norma Jean: My Secret Life with Marilyn Monroe by Ted
Jordan. Copyright © 1989 by Ted Jordan. Reprinted by
permission of William Morrow & Company, Inc

A CIP catalogue record for this book is
available from the British Library

ISBN 1 85592 053 0

Printed and bound in Great Britain by
Butler & Tanner Ltd, Frome, Somerset

I would like to express my indebtedness to the major published sources on which I have relied.

Patricia Bosworth:	*Montgomery Clift*
Ben Bradlee:	*Conversations with Kennedy*
Steven Brill:	*The Teamsters*
Peter Collier and David Horowitz:	*The Kennedys*
Curt Gentry:	*J. Edgar Hoover*
Fred Lawrence Guiles:	*Legend*
Ted Jordan:	*Norma Jean*
Patricia Seaton Lawford:	*The Peter Lawford Story*
Dan E. Moldea:	*The Hoffa Wars*
Kenneth P. O'Donnell and David Powers:	*Johnny, We Hardly Knew Ye*
Lena Pepitone:	*Marilyn Monroe Confidential*
Arthur M. Schlesinger, Jr.:	*A Thousand Days*
Arthur M. Schlesinger, Jr.:	*Robert Kennedy and His Times*
William V. Shannon:	*The Heir Apparent*
Sandra Shevey:	*The Marilyn Scandal*
Anthony Summers:	*Goddess*
Maurice Zolotow:	*Marilyn Monroe*

For MARGARET

And in memory of
Jeanne Bernkopf

"I say to you, you will face pain in your life.
It is not aimed at anyone but it will come your way."
—TED ROSENTHAL

"Say a prayer for Norma Jean. She's dead."
—JIM DOUGHERTY

"The Kennedy story is about people who broke the
rules, and were ultimately broken by them."
—CHRIS LAWFORD

"Big tits, big ass, big deal."
—MARILYN MONROE

CONTENTS

PROLOGUE: CAMELOT, 15

PART ONE: THE BLONDE ON THE PHONE, 21

PART TWO: STRAWHEAD, 177

PART THREE: LANCER, 359

PART FOUR: LEGEND, 443

EPILOGUE: A PRAYER FOR NORMA JEAN, 551

PROLOGUE

CAMELOT

It was another late evening at the White House. They were serving coffee and liqueurs to the accompaniment of the Marine string orchestra playing selections from *Camelot,* when the President caught my eye. A naval aide in dress blues had just given him a message.

I knew the form. The President made his apologies, whispered something to Jackie, and left. I waited a few minutes, then slipped out discreetly to join him.

The same aide was waiting for me outside the Blue Room, and asked me to follow him. To my surprise, we didn't go upstairs to the family quarters where Jack had a study. Instead, we took a round-about route through the empty corridors to the Oval Office, where the aide knocked on the door and opened it for me.

Jack was making himself a drink—a strong one, from the color of it. He looked at me, and I nodded. He made another and handed it to me; then we sat down facing each other. He was sitting stiffly upright in his rocking chair, but he didn't rock it. His expression was remote and hard to read, even for someone who knew him as well as I did.

He had developed the face of a Roman emperor in the past few months. His jowls were heavier, the lines on his face deeper, his eyes sadder than I had ever seen them before. Power corrupts, as we are always being reminded by political commentators, but it also matures. The man before me looked as if he had been through the fires of hell—which, of course, like every president, he had.

"God, I hate *Camelot!*" He spoke wearily. "I've *begged* Jackie to tell them to play something else, but it's like talking to a goddamn brick wall. . . ."

17

He sipped his drink. Whatever he had on his mind, he seemed reluctant to approach it. "I just spoke to Peter," he said finally.

"Lawford?" I raised an eyebrow. I could not imagine why a call from the President's brother-in-law required an emergency meeting.

The distaste on Jack's face was evident as he nodded. I knew how deep his contempt for Lawford ran. Lawford had introduced him years ago to his circle of Hollywood friends—Sinatra and so on— had put his Malibu beach house more or less permanently at Jack's disposal as his West Coast "love nest" and set him up with innumerable starlets—made himself, in short, the presidential pimp, for which Jack roundly despised him.

Like his father, Jack hated people who could be bought, especially those who looked after his pleasures. In some ways he had a puritan sense of morality, though only about other people.

He gave me a look that made it clear I was about to hear bad news. "She's dead," he said brusquely.

I knew instantly whom he meant. "Dead?" I repeated numbly.

"Suicide, apparently. Pills. Booze." Jack shook his head in puzzlement. No Kennedy could ever understand suicide—they were all too fiercely attached to life.

"I see. Where's Bobby?"

"On his way back to San Francisco." Jack's voice was flat. "To Ethel and his loving family," he added savagely.

I nodded. If he didn't want to give me the details, I wasn't about to ask for them.

"Will you go to California?" he asked. He knew I wouldn't want to, so he put it on the line: "As a favor to me, David," he added.

"You can count on me, Mr. President." The moment seemed to call for the formality.

"Thank you." He hesitated. "I need someone I can trust. Someone who knows his way around out there. There may be a few brushfires to put out."

"The press."

"Yes." He sipped his drink. He looked exhausted now. "The police. The coroner." He paused. "And so on."

"I have good contacts in Los Angeles," I assured him. "And first-rate people working for me."

"I want you to handle this yourself, David."

"Of course." The thought of what had happened was becoming real to me. "Poor girl," I said.

"It's a hell of a thing," he said miserably. There were tears in his

18

eyes. He rubbed them, as if in fatigue, then turned back briskly to the business at hand. It was as much of a benediction as she was going to get from him—probably as much as anybody would ever get. He was not a man to dwell on grief, any more than his father was.

"I've got an Air Force plane waiting for you at Andrews," he said. "Can you leave right away?"

"Certainly, Mr. President," I was about to say—but then I realized that I could hardly even speak, for I had a sudden image of Marilyn standing in a doorway, and my own eyes filled with tears.

PART ONE

THE BLONDE
ON THE PHONE

1

The moment Jack and Marilyn set eyes on each other, I knew there was going to be trouble.

They met at Charlie Feldman's house in Beverly Hills, the summer of 1954. Jack had come out to "the Coast" (as he liked to call it, with an ironic grin) to breathe new life into the California Democrats with a display of Kennedy glamour—and more important, Kennedy vigor. Eisenhower had beaten Adlai Stevenson in '52 by a landslide, and given Ike's popularity, whoever ran against him in '56 was going to lose again, so while Jack's ostensible mission was to rally the faithful, his *real* purpose was to drop the hint that he'd be around to win in '60. That, and to get laid—since, then as now, LA was to sex what Washington is to politics.

I accompanied him because my old friend Joe Kennedy had asked me to—*asked,* not told; neither Jack nor his father was in a position to order me around. The Old Man and I (everybody, including Jack, called Ambassador Kennedy "the Old Man" behind his back) went back together a long way, and shared a lot of secrets, even though I was his junior by a generation.

We had met in Hollywood, when he was trying to beat Mayer, Cohn, Zanuck, and the Warner brothers at their own game, and I was trying to persuade them that there is a difference between the art of "public relations" and hiring a flack.

It was a lesson the studio bosses never learned, but Joe did. The maverick Irishman, with his ties to bootleggers, his notorious affairs, and his reputation for shady dealing as a Wall Street raider, was soon to emerge as FDR's head of the SEC, ambassador to the Court

23

of St. James's, would-be Democratic kingmaker, and paterfamilias of America's most photogenic political dynasty—a transformation, I must confess, that was partly my doing.

Joe owed me for that, and recognized the fact. I owed him too, and was grateful: without his help I would have found it difficult to raise enough money on Wall Street in the grim thirties to launch what was to become the largest international public relations company in the world. Besides that—and perhaps more important—we *liked* each other. I admired his toughness and unconcealed rough edges; I think *he* admired my smoothness and gift for conciliation. He was an old bully, Joe Kennedy, but he never tried to bully me.

I suppose this is as good a time as any to introduce myself. My name is David Arthur Leman. My father spelled the family name "Lehrman," but when I started out in business on my own, I thought it a good idea to simplify it for those clients—of whom there were still a good many then—who preferred to be represented by a Leman rather than a Lehrman. Nobody, by the way, in the interests of simplicity or otherwise, has ever presumed to call me Dave. David I have always been to everyone, including my mother, my wives, and Jack Kennedy.

I was born into the kind of wealthy New York German-Jewish family that discouraged informality—and affection: the beloved only son who is at once pampered and relentlessly pushed to achieve. My father—with whom I do not think I exchanged two intimate words in our life together—was the owner of a thriving art book publishing house, in whose footsteps I never had, from earliest childhood, the slightest intention of following.

I grew up in a big, antique-filled apartment on Central Park West, progressed through New York's then excellent public school system as an overachieving honor student, and did the same at Columbia. To my father's undisguised annoyance, I went to work after graduation as a publicity man for Jed Harris, the Broadway producer, though he should not have been surprised—my mother was hopelessly stagestruck, and the fondest memory of my childhood was going to the theater with her.

With hindsight, I know what I sought in my profession was something of the theater's glamour and excitement—an escape from respectability. I can also see now that what attracted me to Joe Kennedy was that he and his family represented the polar opposite of my father—they were brawling, aggressive, unashamedly sentimental, outspoken, and fiercely attached to one another.

Besides, for somebody like myself, whose secret passion was poli-

24

tics, Joe was a fascinating friend and mentor. Back then, in the thirties, he was as close to FDR as anybody ever got; more than anyone it was he who had brokered FDR's nomination in 1932. He still cherished the illusion then that one day he might be not just a kingmaker but the king himself. It wasn't until 1939, when his fierce isolationism and his pro-appeasement record put him at odds with history and FDR, that Joe turned his presidential ambitions toward his eldest son.

I'm an old man now, as I write this—older than anybody has the right to be. When I look at photographs taken then, I see a different person altogether, one I hardly even recognize. Before me is a snapshot of Marilyn and myself sitting on the famous zebra-skin banquette at El Morocco, smiling for the photographer. Marilyn's smile is dazzling, the kind only a movie star can put on at the sight of a photographer's flashgun, instantly radiating on command high-voltage happiness and sex appeal, though I seem to remember she was near tears a moment before. She is wearing a white evening gown—white was her favorite color, perhaps because of its associations with virginity. The neckline plunges unvirginally to her navel, exposing her shoulders and most of her breasts, and she is holding a glass of champagne in her right hand.

The man sitting beside her with a big grin on his face is a tall, well-built fellow, broad-shouldered without any suggestion of being athletic. The face, as I look at it now, is handsome, but slightly too self-satisfied, too smug—a powerful nose; a good, strong chin; a full head of hair, worn a bit on the long side, as if cut by an English barber; a brisk military mustache.

He wears a chalk-stripe suit of impeccable cut, this stranger, with a broad-striped shirt with a plain white collar and cuffs, a somber embroidered silk tie, and a white silk waistcoat with lapels and pearl buttons—clearly a personal sartorial trademark. In the lapel of his jacket is a miniature white carnation. Unmistakably, he fancies himself as a dandy.

That person has long since gone, alas. If Marilyn were alive today, I remind myself, she would be sixty-six. Jack would be seventy-five. I am over eighty myself, God help me.

Well, I've had a good life, as well as a long one, and looking back on it, my friendship with Joe—and his sons—was one of the best parts. I wouldn't have missed a minute of it, despite all the pain and the tragedy. It's taken me more than two decades to come to grips with the truth of it—and my role in what happened—but my age being what it is, it's now or never if I'm going to tell the story.

It's odd. If it hadn't been for Joe, I would have given up my business in the 1950s and moved to England and missed it all. I was rich, bored with my work, disgusted by the McCarthy era, recently remarried. I had always loved England—three of the best years of my life were spent there during the war as a public relations officer for the Air Force, with a colonel's eagles on my shoulders and a suite at Claridge's. It had always been my dream to live there. I already had my eye on a pretty little house in Wilton Mews, and was beginning to correspond with estate agents about Georgian manor houses in the country, when Joe got wind of my plans and took me to dinner at Le Pavillon to torpedo them. "Don't you do it to yourself, David!" he begged me.

"What are you talking about, Joe?" I said. "I've always wanted to live like an English gentleman."

"Horseshit. That's the point. You're *not* an English gentleman. Deep down where it counts, behind all that fucking politeness, the Limeys will hate your guts. Need I remind you I was our ambassador there? I *know* those people, David."

Joe leaned over and touched my hand, a surprisingly gentle gesture, at odds with the cold blue anger in his eyes. "Besides," he said softly, "don't jump ship when it's close to home, David. Jack's going to run, you have my word. When he does, he's going to win. I need you, David. *He* needs you. And once he's in the White House, who can say?" He shook his head. "Backstabbing old fraud that he was, I wouldn't have missed being in FDR's inner circle for any goddamn thing, David, let alone spending the rest of my life in a country where everybody talks through their noses and it rains six days out of seven."

Joe had me, of course, as he knew he would. The two things I most envied him were his relationship to FDR and his ambassadorship, badly as both had turned out for him. Besides, I knew he wasn't kidding. Jack did not seem like presidential material to me—or to anyone else except his father, so far as I knew—but if Joe said he was going to run, I was prepared to believe it. And he was right. Being an insider in a presidential race is the biggest adventure American life can offer, and we both knew I couldn't resist it.

Right there at Le Pavillon, over the rack of lamb, I knew I wasn't going to buy that mews house. I remember Joe's laughter when he realized he'd won, so loud that people looked up from their food all over the restaurant. He had laughed like that the first time I ever gave *him* a piece of advice, at a booth in the Brown Derby in Hollywood, after he asked me how he could go about changing his image —he was not thinking, even then, so much of himself as of his boys. I told him that Walter Ivy, the creator of "public relations" as a business, had been asked the same question by John D. Rockefeller, and came up with the brilliant suggestion that the old robber baron try giving away a dime to every child he met, accompanied by a little homily on the virtues of thrift—a strategy that worked so well John D. senior was practically canonized in his own lifetime. Joe Kennedy thought about it for a few moments, then leaned back, bared his big, uneven white teeth, and laughed. "The hell with it," he said. "I'm not giving *my* money away to strangers."

Lots of people liked to think of the Kennedys, father *and* sons, as if they were somehow imbued with the spirit of the old-time Irish politicians like Rose Kennedy's father, Honey Fitz, but I knew better. The old pols genuinely loved people—those who were on their side, at least. Their laughter was real and happy, but Joe's heartiest laughter was reserved for stories about other people's misfortunes. Even Jack, a far more attractive figure than his father, lacked the common touch of the born politician—he was never entirely able to hide the fact that he regarded most people as his inferiors.

I could hear Jack laughing then, in Feldman's enormous living room, with the big sliding glass doors opening out onto the pool and the obligatory collection of Impressionist paintings on the walls. Second-rate Impressionists, of course—the best ones seldom end up in the collections of Hollywood talent agents, however wealthy.

I could tell just by listening to Jack's laughter that he was no more impressed by Feldman and the Democrats assembled in his living room than I was by the paintings.

The truth was, a lot of the people in the room were old enough to still nurse bitter feelings about Joe Kennedy, who during his brief stay in Hollywood had been one of the most hated men in the history of the movie business, so not all of them were inclined to greet his son with open arms. In fact, Jack's first task here was to show that he wasn't anything like his father.

He was seated in the center of the room, stiffly upright—I could tell by the way he stretched out first one leg, then the other, that his back was giving him more pain than usual—drinking scotch, while Feldman, standing beside him, called people over one by one to introduce them to the Senator.

Feldman leaned over to say something, and Jack laughed again, even louder. Then there was a truly theatrical silence—and everybody except Jack turned toward the glass wall facing the pool. I did too, just in time to see Marilyn make her entrance.

It took Jack a moment to realize he had lost the attention of his audience—even here, among the richest and most powerful people in Hollywood, Marilyn Monroe's appearance brought an instant hush of amazement and excitement. Then he turned too, with some difficulty, to see who had eclipsed him, and rose to his feet, while Feldman abandoned his position beside the Senator to go over to the door and greet Marilyn, who looked woefully helpless and vulnerable, like a little girl who had wandered in on a grown-ups' party by mistake.

She was wearing a tight black dress of some shimmering material, which seemed to be several sizes too small for her, a white fox stole, costume jewelry earrings, and a cheap black patent-leather handbag. The whole outfit looked as if it might have been purchased from a thrift shop. Not that it mattered—Marilyn was beyond good taste, or bad. At this point in her life she was perhaps the biggest star in Hollywood: *River of No Return* had just been released, she had completed filming *There's No Business Like Show Business*, and she had been married to Joe DiMaggio for about six months.

I took the opportunity to move closer to Jack, whose expression resembled that of a man getting his first glimpse of the Grand Canyon or Mount Everest—some natural wonder of awesome proportions and reputation.

"Jesus *Christ!*" he whispered.

"Don't even *think* of it, Jack," I whispered back.

He grinned wickedly. "I don't know what you mean, David."

I ignored that. "She's the most visible woman in America," I warned him.

He nodded. "It's a challenge, certainly."

"She's married."

"So am I. So are you."

"There's a rumor she's having an affair with Charlie Feldman."

Jack looked at Feldman as if he had never seen his host before, then shook his head in puzzlement. Feldman was elderly and stout, his skin tanned to the color of crisp bacon. He wore a well-crafted hairpiece. "Why would she do that?" Jack asked. "He can't make her a star. She's *already* a star."

"Who knows what goes on in a woman's mind?"

That made sense to him. "Ah—who indeed?" he said.

Feldman had Marilyn by the elbow now, and was moving her in our direction, while she held back as if she were shy. I thought then that Marilyn was a better actress in everyday life than in front of the camera. Nothing that happened later was to change my mind.

Jack closed the distance, determined to reach Marilyn before I did, took her hand, squeezed it briefly rather than shaking it, and gave her his most dashing smile. She smiled back. "I can't *believe* you're a *senator?*" She cooed, in her tiny, breathless voice. She had a charming habit of ending every sentence as if it were a question. "I thought they were all old men?"

She hadn't removed her hand from his, and I could see that Feldman's face was a mixture of regret and dismay—he must have been wishing he'd never invited Jack here, or that he hadn't invited Marilyn. "Are you *sure* you're a senator?" she asked, giggling. "You look just like a *boy.*"

She could hardly have said anything more certain to charm him. He looked her over from top to toe, appreciatively, lingering on the full wonder of all that lush, incredible beauty. "Well," he said at last, "you look just like a girl."

I knew my cue. I asked Feldman to introduce me to a couple of important California Democrats who had just arrived, giving Jack and Marilyn a few moments to talk alone.

I didn't find out what happened until the next day—though I could have guessed.

———

I caught up with Jack the next morning at the pool of the Bel Air Hotel. I was on my way to my LA office, in our own building on Sunset Boulevard. He was lying in the sun, wearing swimming trunks and wraparound sunglasses, and smoking a cigar. He hated to be seen smoking cigars in public, partly because he was afraid it would lose him votes among women, partly because it seemed like a middle-aged, wealthy man's habit and he wanted to appeal to the young as long as he could, but no hotel was more private than the Bel Air in those days, which was why we were staying there instead of at the Beverly Hills.

I sat down beside him, and ordered breakfast. Jack had finished his and was sipping at his coffee, with the *Los Angeles Times* in his lap. Half a dozen papers were spread around his chaise. He devoured newspapers; no story was too trivial to escape his attention if he thought it was something he could put to use. "I lost you last night," I said. "How was the rest of your evening?"

"Ah—interesting. *Very* interesting." He gave me one of those smiles that always made me wonder how anybody could vote against him. "You were right about Feldman, by the way."

I raised an eyebrow.

"She *is* fucking him."

"She told you that?"

"She's a remarkably—ah—*frank* young woman."

"I see." I tried to imagine a good reason why Marilyn Monroe would tell Jack she was having an affair with Feldman on their first date—if you could describe whatever took place between them as that—but none came to mind.

"She wanted me to know," Jack said. "She didn't think there should be any secrets between us." He smiled. "I sat next to her at dinner—"

"I saw."

Jack did not take criticism—even implied criticism—easily, even from me. "I can't be expected to work for the party *all* the time, David," he snapped, very much his father's son. "This isn't Soviet Russia. . . . Anyway, as I was saying, I sat next to her at dinner, and I happened to put my hand on her leg. A friendly pat, you know. . . ."

"I know." I did not want to add that most of the more important Democrats in Hollywood had noticed that the Senator's right hand was under the tablecloth throughout the meal, obliging him to eat with his left.

"Well, I moved it up to her thigh—she didn't object, you know, didn't even appear to notice. Then finally she turned to me and said, 'Before you go any higher, Senator, you'd better know I never wear panties, just so you're not surprised.' She said it with the most innocent expression. . . ."

"And was it true?"

"Oh, yes. Absolutely true!"

"Is she still in the hotel?"

He shook his head. "She left early this morning, before anybody else was up."

I gave a silent prayer of thanks. The staff at the Bel Air was famous for its discretion, but Marilyn was not the kind of person about whom it was easy to be discreet.

"I take it you had a good time?"

He stared out across the pool, his expression hidden by cigar smoke. "She's a lot smarter than you'd think," he said at last, which didn't really answer my question.

"Not just a dumb blonde?"

"Not a dumb blonde at all. She's going to divorce DiMaggio, you know."

That was news. "They were only just married, surely?"

Jack shrugged. He had a jaundiced but tolerant view of other people's arrangements about life, his own being designed entirely to suit him. "DiMaggio's jealous." He recited what she had told him: "He wants her to have kids and give up her career. His idea of a good time is watching a ball game on TV, or sitting around with his cronies at Toots Shor's, talking sports. The sex was great at first, but now even that's no good." He took a contented puff on his cigar. "She says she's afraid of him."

"Women always say that in California when they're thinking about divorce. That's because 'physical cruelty' is the only sure-fire grounds the courts here accept."

"It sounded to me as if she was telling the truth. Of course, you never know, with women."

"The two of you certainly seem to have had a good chat," I said, trying to disguise my envy.

Jack took off his sunglasses, and gave me a wink. "Well, she's quite a talker."

"I'm sure she has other talents."

"I would say so, David. I would *certainly* say so." He chuckled. "Do you know what she told me? When she signed her first big contract with Twentieth Century–Fox, she looked Darryl Zanuck right in the eye, gave him a sweet smile, and said, 'Well, I guess I'll never have to suck Jewish cock again, will I?' "

His robust laughter rang out across the pool, drowning out the noise of the sprinklers and the faraway hum of traffic on Sunset Boulevard.

I let him get on with what he wanted to tell me, without asking why, if Marilyn's story was true, she was sleeping with Charlie Feldman.

Jack was as entitled to his illusions as the next man, I decided.

———

Later that day, Jack and I sat together in the first-class cabin of American's LA/Washington flight. Jack always reserved the window seat on the right side of the first row. He needed to be in row 1 so he could stretch his legs out, because of his back, but why he had to be on the far right, I don't know. Perhaps it was just a habit, perhaps he thought it was lucky. He was a great believer in luck.

Once he was settled in, his coat and shoes off and his tie loosened, he gave the stewardesses a professional once-over. One of them attracted his attention, and he flashed her the famous Kennedy smile. I guessed that before we landed, she would receive a small gold-edged card with blue engraved script reading "United States Senate" at the top and Jack's private telephone number penciled below it in his firm, sprawling hand. Jack was like a man who always needed to know where his next meal was coming from, even when he wasn't hungry.

"All those movie people," he said, getting back to business. "What do they think of me?"

"I think they were interested."

He stared at me coldly for a moment, the living image of his old man, as if he was thinking he didn't need me to tell him what he already knew. "The truth is, they like Adlai better," I said. "He reminds them of Jimmy Stewart in *Mr. Smith Goes to Washington.* A simple, honest country boy taking on the slick big-city pols. Movie people like to see things in movie story terms."

"Governor Stevenson isn't a country boy. He isn't honest or simple either. He's a wealthy man and a god-awful snob."

"I know that, Jack. You know it. But the rest of the world doesn't. Maybe it's the photo of him with the hole in the sole of his shoe."

"What else?" he said. "I may not be the most sensitive guy in the world, but I noticed a certain, ah, *reserve,* at Feldman's."

"Well, for a start, a lot of people there remember your father. . . ."

Jack's face hardened. "I'm not interested in that crap," he snapped. Jack had had a lifetime of dealing with the fact that he was Joe Kennedy's son, but he still wasn't good at it.

"Your other problem," I went on, happy enough to change direction, "is Joe McCarthy."

"That figures," Jack said with a sigh, and took a sip of his scotch —Ballantine, which he always asked for because his father owned the American distributorship.

Senator Joseph McCarthy's campaign against "Reds in high places" had brought him to the peak of his power. Exploiting the country's fear of the Cold War, McCarthy had made himself famous (or notorious, depending on how you felt about him) by searching out subversives and Communist sympathizers ("Comsymps," in the jargon of the day), real or imagined. Nowhere was he a more live issue than in Hollywood, where countless people had been made unemployable, and some even jailed, because of his accusations.

I happened to think (along with most "liberal" Democrats) that

McCarthy was the country's major problem, as opposed to its savior, but Jack's difficulty was that most of his constituents, not to speak of his father and his brother Bobby, stood foursquare behind the senator's "crusade." Bobby was counsel to McCarthy's subcommittee, locked in fierce rivalry with Roy Cohn, an equally ambitious New York lawyer, for the senator's attention. Bobby's loyalty to McCarthy was visceral, unwavering, absolute, and his pursuit of "subversives" was as unrelentingly vicious (in my view) as his mentor's.

Jack knew I stood to his left on this issue, and I knew he was trapped, so we didn't need to discuss it in detail. "You've got to get Bobby out of there," I said. "Before it's too late."

"I know. It's not easy. He likes the limelight. And he loves a good fight."

I knew all about Bobby's love of a good fight. He had once celebrated his birthday by hitting a man over the head with a beer bottle in a Boston bar for failing to sing "Happy Birthday" when asked to, then refused to apologize. He was not a young man you wanted to cross. "Find him something else to investigate," I suggested. "The SEC, for instance. Wall Street is full of crooks."

"A lot of them are friends of Dad's. Not a great idea, David." Jack stretched, his face creasing from the sudden pain. "The problem is, I need an issue myself—one that has nothing to do with anticommunism, preferably—before I go to the convention in '56."

"It ought to be something that plays on television," I suggested. "Look what the organized crime hearings did for Kefauver."

Estes Kefauver had been a virtually unknown senator until a long list of organized-crime hoodlums taking the Fifth on television before his subcommittee made him a national hero, as well as a much talked-about vice presidential candidate for '56.

As it happened, I knew some of those heavyset men with gravelly voices who had refused to answer questions on the grounds that they might incriminate themselves, and as I thought about them, it occurred to me that there *was* one issue tailor-made for Jack— and for Bobby as well. "You might think about labor corruption," I said.

Jack raised an eyebrow.

"It's a major issue. You take the Teamsters. They're shot through with corruption. . . ."

"David," Jack said patiently. "My constituents are blue-collar. They're union members. I want the AFL-CIO on my side."

"It's the AFL-CIO that wants the Teamsters cleaned up, Jack, believe me."

"I'll think about it." He spoke without much conviction. "I'd want a guarantee in blood from George Meany that he's in favor before I made a move."

"You might get it," I said.

"That'll be the day." The stewardesses were beginning to serve dinner. Jack looked at them as they bent over with their trays, his attention diverted to more pleasant thoughts than labor unions. "Well, whatever Feldman's friends thought of me," he said, "it was worth making the trip just to meet Marilyn."

I sipped my drink, feeling that peculiar combination of relaxation and good-fellowship that accompanies a long flight. "You never *did* tell me why she's having an affair with Feldman," I said.

He chuckled. "He asked her to."

"He *asked* her?"

"They were at a party. Feldman told her he wasn't a young man anymore, and if he had a last wish, one thing he could have in the world before he died, it would be to go to bed with her."

He looked pensive. "It's not a bad line, you know. I might try it myself. Leaving out the part about being old, of course."

"And it worked?"

"It worked fine. Marilyn was really touched. She told me it seemed like such an honest thing to say. I guess she thought it wasn't such a big deal. If that was his one wish in the world, ah, why not *give* it to him? So she did."

"And then?"

"And then, I guess, she couldn't find a good way to stop without hurting his feelings."

"She's quite a girl."

The stewardess asked Jack if he wanted her to freshen his drink. She was smiling brightly, her pretty young face as close to his as she could get it by leaning over me, but Jack had turned his head to look out the window at the darkening mountains of the Southwest below, and didn't seem to notice her.

"Why, yes, she's quite a girl," I heard him say, ever so softly, and from the tone of his voice I would have said he sounded like a man who had fallen in love, if I hadn't known him so well.

2

I'm a New Yorker, by birth and temperament, and Washington has never been one of my favorite cities. Like Beverly Hills, it's a one-industry town where people go to bed early and where it's difficult to eat a good meal. However, I had opened up an office in Washington early on in my career, since for many of my major clients "public relations" and "lobbying" were synonymous. I never took on politicians as clients—they pay late, if at all—but I did very well in that profitable gray area where politics and big business meet.

I went there often. I went everywhere, of course, in those days—travel was part of my business. Even before jet planes made travel easier, I was constantly on the move, to California, to Europe, back again seeking clients. Having created a worldwide organization with thousands of employees, I found my job was to bring in enough business to keep them busy, and if it meant flying from New York, to LA, to Tokyo, then back to New York all in the same week, so be it. This had led to considerable strain in my first marriage, and an eventual divorce. Luckily, there had been no children to complicate things, so my first wife and I had parted on reasonably amicable terms. My second marriage, distressingly, was beginning to show signs of the same strain. My wife Maria, I noticed, no longer objected as strongly as she had at first to the amount of time I was away on business—a bad sign, in my experience.

Whenever I was in Washington, I made a point of looking up Jack Kennedy, partly because we enjoyed each other's company, partly, as Jack knew, because his father was always after me to report back on how he was doing. Over the years, as Jack and I became close friends (despite the difference in our ages), he not only came to trust my advice—it had paid off for him, after all, again and again—but also began to trust that I wouldn't tell his father anything he didn't want him to know.

We had a lot in common, Jack and I, with enough differences to keep us interested in each other. Oddly enough, Maria bore a distinct resemblance to Jackie Kennedy, long before it became fashionable to resemble her—so much so that Jack once suggested, not entirely in jest, that it would be fun to try wife swapping, just to see, as he put it, if he could "tell the difference between them in bed." Maria was a great admirer of Jack's, and I suspect she would have been less shocked by the suggestion than I was—she might not have been all that difficult to persuade, as a matter of fact.

Maria and Jackie not only looked alike, they wore the same kind of clothes, used the same decorators and hairdressers, and had many friends in common. In later years, Maria complained that "the Jackie Kennedy look" was in fact *hers*—that Jackie had simply modeled herself after Maria. This may have been true, and was no doubt all the more galling because until Jackie became a national figure in 1960, Maria was a far more famous beauty.

Since we've been divorced for decades—Maria left me, shortly after Jack's assassination, for a Brazilian multimillionaire named D'Souza—I can admit freely that I've always suspected that Maria and Jack might have had an affair at some point. He was not above sleeping with the wives of his friends. Or the friends of his wife.

——

Jack's second-floor Senate office was a hangover from his even wilder days as a bachelor congressman—a friendly, noisy, chaotic place, full of pretty young secretaries and the kind of Boston Irish political followers who looked like either retired boxers or Jesuit priests, with names like Mugsy, Kenny, or Red. No sign of Jackie's taste for elegance was present—the fact is, I don't think she ever visited her husband's office, which was just as well, considering what went on there.

They weren't big on ceremony either. One of Jack's Irish watch-dogs—I think it was a huge ex–Boston cop named "Boom-Boom" Reardon—banged on the door of Jack's inner sanctum and hollered, "Wake up, Jack, yez got a visitor."

There was a muffled sound that might have been Jack's voice

asking me to wait a moment—the doors of the Old Senate Office Building had been made of solid oak back in the days when Americans built for the ages.

It did not seem to me likely that Jack was taking a nap. I went over to the window, looked out, and was not surprised to see a young woman emerge presently from an unmarked door into the parking lot below, where the Senator's car was waiting. I thought she looked familiar as she slipped into the back seat while Mugsy O'Leary held the door open for her; then I recognized her as the stewardess who had caught Jack's eye on the flight from LA a few days ago.

There was a click as Jack turned the lock, and Boom-Boom pushed the door open for me.

"Sorry to keep you waiting, David," Jack said, yawning. "I took a nap. This weather knocks the, ah, shit out of you, doesn't it?" He was buttoning his shirt. I recognized it as a custom-made one, from Lanvin in Paris, his favorite shirtmaker. One of the things I liked best about Jack was that while he could pretend to be one of the boys, and could certainly swear a blue streak when his Irish was up, he was in fact a rather fastidious man, with refined tastes— which he did his best to hide from most of his close followers, street-fighting veterans of Boston's bare-knuckle political wars to a man.

"Are you going home?" I asked.

He nodded warily. "Jackie's expecting me," he said. "At some point. Why?"

"You might want to think about changing your shirt, that's all. There's lipstick on the collar."

He flushed, then broke into a grin. The Kennys, Mugsys, and Boom-Booms of his world were not inclined to notice such details, either because they were hardened to that kind of thing or out of some deep-rooted Catholic determination to ignore what they didn't want to know. I was never certain whether their blindness to Jack's nonstop womanizing was innocence or guile. Given the nature of the Irish, I suppose it could have been both. "That's the best advice I've gotten all day," he said. "Thank you."

"It's the *next*-to-best advice, as a matter of fact," I told him firmly. "Listen to me, please."

He was sitting behind his desk in his shirtsleeves, his shoes off and his stockinged feet on a leather ottoman. He made a steeple of his hands and stared at me with that hard edge to his expression he always had when he knew he was about to get news or advice he didn't want to hear. "Well?" he asked.

I leaned forward. "The papers are going to carry a story tomorrow that Bobby took a swing at Roy Cohn outside the committee room."

"Oh, shit."

"Bobby should know better, Jack."

"That isn't what happened," he said. "Cohn took a swing at Bobby. Bobby walked away."

"Well, that's not the way it's being reported. My guess is, Cohn leaked his version to the press first. Or maybe McCarthy, as a way of putting Bobby in his place."

"Maybe. . . ."

"Nice people, Jack. All of this, you don't need."

"I'm not going to tell Bobby what to do. He's a big boy."

This was a lofty evasion. Jack was perfectly prepared to tell Bobby what to do when it suited him, and Bobby—though he sometimes smoldered with mutinous anger—eventually obeyed. The core belief of the Kennedys wasn't Catholicism, it was primogeniture. Besides, Kennedy family loyalties went beyond politics—anybody who took a swing at Bobby might as well have taken a swing at Jack.

"It bears out what I was saying on the way back from LA, Jack. You need an issue. And Bobby needs a new set of playmates."

"I *know* that," he said impatiently. "Why do you think I've been making speeches about getting the French out of Vietnam?"

"Nobody in this country gives two hoots about Vietnam, Jack. Outside Washington, people don't know where it is and couldn't care less whether the French are there or not. You're not going to get on TV with France and Vietnam, Jack. Now corruption in labor, that's another story. It's a pocketbook issue, a gut issue, there are villains and bad guys—bad guys, by the way, like you wouldn't believe. . . ."

"Yes, I can see that, but I still say—"

I rushed in. "I know what you said. George Meany has to sign up behind you. In blood. Well, I went to see Meany, Jack, and he gave me a message for you. He said, 'Tell Jack we're behind him one hundred percent. If he can get Dave Beck, and expose the Teamster leadership for the thugs they've become, he has our unconditional support. In blood, if you like.' That's what the man said, Jack."

Jack stared at me thoughtfully. "But not in writing, I suppose?" he asked.

"Not in writing, no. You'll have to make do with blood."

"We nail Beck and his gang to the wall for Meany and the AFL-CIO, and I get their support in '60, is that the idea?"

"That's the idea. They're scared of Beck and the Teamsters, Jack. They're giving organized labor a bad name, for one thing. For another, they're using their mob connections to grow faster than any other union."

"Why doesn't Meany do something about it, if he feels so strongly?"

"Dog don't eat dog. Labor leaders don't like attacking other labor leaders in public. Meany wants to get rid of the Beck crowd, but he'd like the United States Senate to do it for him. That's where you come in. That's where Bobby comes in. Let him take on Beck, Jack —Bobby's going to look like a hero, instead of a guy who hangs out with people like Cohn and McCarthy, persecuting file clerks who once subscribed to *The New Masses*."

Jack held up his hand. "*Stop* that!" he said firmly. "I won't have you making fun of Bobby, David. Some of those file clerks may be Communist spies. . . ."

He looked at me and sighed. This was a subject on which we were never going to see eye to eye, any more than his father and I did. On the other hand, Jack knew a lost cause when he saw one, and McCarthy was as lost as a cause could be. "How bad are things with the Teamsters?" he asked. "Really."

"Very. Corruption, sweetheart deals with mobsters, paper locals, even murder. It's a real horror story, Jack. I heard about it from a guy named Mollenhoff, who's made this something of a one-man crusade. . . ."

Jack stared out the window. Then he turned back to me. "All right," he said. "I'm willing to give it a try. Tell this fellow Mollenhoff to talk to Bobby, will you, David?"

He punched his right fist hard against the palm of his other hand, cheering up as he always did at the prospect of action. "Honest unions. That's a cause worth fighting for, isn't it?"

It would be seen that way by most people—certainly by the press. It was not, however, a cause worth *dying* for, I reminded myself, and decided to sound a note of caution. "It *could* get rough, Jack," I said. "That's the only thing."

He laughed. "They don't know what rough is until they've met Bobby," he said. "Let's have a drink." He called for Boom-Boom.

"Good enough." I congratulated myself on what seemed like a sensible change of course. I felt I'd earned my drink.

Boom-Boom shambled in, all three hundred pounds of him, a good deal of it muscle. Jack had told me that Boom-Boom had been a mounted cop until he put on too much weight, and that for years he was a fixture in Boston's Saint Patrick's Day parade, riding a white draft horse. I could believe it.

"You sure you want a drink, Jack?" the giant asked. "Shouldn't yez be gettin' home to herself?"

"When I need your marital advice, I'll ask for it," Jack said crisply, but without a trace of resentment. Boom-Boom mixed our drinks and handed them to us. I couldn't help feeling that if Jack had asked him to coldcock me with the butt of the police revolver he carried—illegally—under his jacket, Boom-Boom would have done it without any fuss. Jack's relationship to these Stone Age spear-carriers of his was feudal. He was their leader, boss, chief, and they were blindly loyal.

Boom-Boom left, slamming the door behind him. "Boom-Boom's got a point, Jack," I said.

"Don't *you* start on me too, David. That's all I hear from Bobby these days. You'd think he wanted me to run for 'Husband of the Year.'" He laughed. Jackie had never completely forgiven him for delaying the announcement of their engagement until after the *Saturday Evening Post* had run an article naming him "Bachelor of the Year."

"I'm just suggesting that you're putting too much trust in the goodwill of the press, that's all."

He gave a bark of derision. "I don't trust them an inch, David. There are simply certain kinds of stories they won't run. You know that as well as I do."

He was right, up to a point. In those innocent, pre-Watergate days, when the press still left the private lives of presidents alone, nobody had ever reported the well-known fact that Ike's wartime driver, Kay Summersby, was his mistress, or that FDR and Eleanor led separate lives. The Washington press corps knew all about Jack's womanizing, but there was very little chance they would print it. Of course, there were exceptions to this convention, and I thought I should remind him of the fact. "They won't run stories about you and any *ordinary* girl, that's true," I said. "What you have to be careful about is somebody who's so famous that her whole life is a news story. Or who just doesn't *care* about secrecy enough to bother."

He looked at me over the rim of his glass, his expression thoughtful. "Marilyn?" he asked.

"Marilyn."

There was a long silence; then he cleared his throat. "Tell me something, David," he said. "How did my father get away with having Gloria Swanson as his mistress all those years?"

It was a good question. In her time, Gloria Swanson had been as big a star as Marilyn. "To start with, he wasn't planning to run for the presidency when he and Gloria were—ah—together," I answered.

"Dad was a public figure."

The truth was, I didn't know myself how Joe had managed to get away with it. He even took Swanson and Rose to Europe on the same boat once, in adjoining staterooms, which certainly raised eyebrows. "I imagine your father got away with it mostly because he just didn't *give* a shit what people thought," I suggested. "That, and luck. And the fact that your mother is a saint."

"Well, *I* don't give a shit what people think either, David. And God knows, I'm lucky. I'm nearly forty. If I've learned one thing, it's take what you want while you can get it. You never know what's going to happen. . . ."

He had a faraway look in his eyes. Jack was no mystic, but I knew what was on his mind. Even ten years later, his brother Joe junior's death still haunted him. Joe junior had been the Kennedy heir apparent, the eldest son who was supposed to become the first Irish-Catholic president of the United States. Jack adored him, as everybody did. He had everything Jack later developed, in spades—charm, wit, dashing good looks, courage, astonishing success with women, all of it snuffed out in one bright burst of explosives when his bomber blew up over the English Channel.

I had been with the Old Man in Hyannis when they brought him the news, and I've never forgotten the look on his face. It wasn't grief—it was cold, hard, murderous rage. Joe Kennedy took everything personally; from the way he reacted to the news of his eldest son's death, I could tell that he held FDR personally responsible, as if Roosevelt had engineered America's entry into the war just to punish him. He even said as much, later that night, after he'd told Rose and had a couple of drinks. He had a telegram of condolence from FDR in his hand, which he crumpled into a ball and hurled out the window savagely. "He killed my boy, that crippled bastard!" he snarled, and went into his bedroom, slamming the door behind him.

That was part of the answer to Jack's question about how his father got away with his affair with Gloria Swanson—the part I didn't want to tell him. There were no gray areas in Joe Kennedy's soul; you were for him or against him, and that was that, and if you were against him, he would destroy you, even if it took a lifetime or cost him a fortune to do it. People were *afraid* of Joe, even FDR, and they were right to be. They weren't afraid of Jack, and I wasn't sure they ever would be.

Jack stood up. He was rail-thin. The Kennedys' most strictly guarded family secret was Jack's ill health, which Joe was determined to hide not only from the world, lest Jack be thought too sickly to be president, but more fiercely, from himself. Jack had suffered from asthma as a child, a football injury and a war wound had so damaged his back that he was in constant and acute pain—worse, the doctors feared that he might become paralyzed—and he had an adrenal deficiency that made any kind of operation dangerous.

The Kennedys had solved the problem of Jack's health by simply not talking about it, in much the same way that they denied, to themselves and to others, the very obvious fact that Jack's sister Rosemary was retarded. No matter how much Jack ate—and he was a notoriously finicky eater—he lost weight, a symptom of his adrenal disorder, which was regarded, by everyone but his family, as a fatal disease until the development of cortisone.

"Do you think going after the Teamsters will do it, David? Really?" He was clearly having second thoughts.

"So far as I can see, it's your best shot at an issue. It's red-hot, it's ready-made, and if you don't grab it fast, somebody else will. Stu Symington, maybe."

"Fuck Stu Symington. You're right."

Jack went into the bathroom to change his shirt, and I caught a glimpse of the *Daily News* on his desk. The front page was a photograph of Marilyn at Idlewild Airport—Joe DiMaggio glowering in the doorway of the plane behind her—arriving in New York to shoot *The Seven Year Itch*.

3

She had never liked New York much. It seemed to her a mean-spirited, hard-edged, noisy city, all steam and dirt, full of ugly people pushing each other out of the way in the crowded streets. She was used to wide, empty, palm-lined streets, to friendly people, to the glitter of chrome from a million cars.

Actually, the truth was, she was a little *afraid* of New York. She didn't seem to fit in, even as a visitor. She had the wrong clothes, the wrong look, the wrong attitude. She didn't like the fancy restaurants, or the big department stores, where everybody was so rude.

She hated the hotel, too. The studio had put everyone who mattered into the St. Regis, either because they got a deal or because it was Darryl Zanuck's favorite place to stay. It was okay for Joe, she thought—Toots Shor's, where he could sit and schmooze with his cronies, was only a five-minute walk away—but she couldn't even get through the narrow, cramped lobby without causing a near riot.

In Los Angeles, people took movie stars calmly, but New Yorkers mobbed her wherever she went. Her first day at the St. Regis, she had been unable to make her way through the crowd to the street, and had to take refuge in the dark, deserted King Cole Bar while a way was cleared for her; she had found herself suddenly alone there with the strangest man she had ever seen. He had mad, staring eyes, plastered-back dyed black hair, waxed mustaches that rose to sharp points ending at the level of his eyebrows, like tiny radio antennas at either side of his face. He wore huge rings on each finger, and by his side sat a cheetah with a jeweled collar, which he held by a gold chain. Thus she made the acquaintance of Salvador Dalí, who held her spellbound for nearly half an hour while Joe, the studio PR people, the hotel security men, and the cops tried to clear a passage for her to the front door.

She had never heard of Dalí, as it happened, but he wasn't shy about telling her that he was the greatest living painter in the world, Picasso included. With grave Spanish courtesy he told her he wanted to paint her as Venus rising from the sea, which was just about the nicest offer anybody had made to her since her arrival in New York. At first she had been afraid of the cheetah, but when she finally got up the nerve to stroke the back of its neck, it responded just like any other cat, with a deep, throaty purr.

When they came for her at last and guided her out to the canopy where Joe waited, scowling at the mob of fans, photographers, and curious passersby that now blocked Fifty-fifth Street completely, she told him about Dalí and the cheetah, but he wasn't interested, or maybe he just thought she was kidding.

"Dolly who?" he asked impatiently, pushing her into the waiting limousine so fast that she almost tripped.

———

Thinking about Joe gave her a headache, which wasn't improved by the fact that she had arrived in New York with cramps. Other women, most of them, seemed to cope with the problem easily enough, but like her mother she had world-class periods, so devastating and painful that she lived in fear of them. She was convinced they were part of the reason her mother had gone crazy and had to be institutionalized, which made her even more frightened that the same thing might happen to her one day.

The problem with Joe was that in her mind—in her *heart*, more important—she was already divorced from him. Yet here he was in New York, beside her as always (except when he ran off to Toots Shor's), telling her what to do and what to wear, an all-too-real, flesh-and-blood husband whom she had already dismissed from her mind—so much so that it sometimes puzzled her to wake up in the morning and find him in the bed next to her.

That was the way she was, she thought unapologetically—waiting, or going through long, slow formalities, was always intolerable to her. Years ago, when she made up her mind she no longer wanted to be married to Jim Dougherty, she had simply moved out of her in-laws' house and started dating again, as if Jim, who was still at sea somewhere in the Pacific, had ceased to exist—which, in her head, he had.

The Slugger was fading the same way, but so far she hadn't screwed up her courage to have a talk with him about it, so he had no idea—not being a particularly introspective soul—that so far as she was concerned, they were already divorced.

There were other things she hadn't told Joe—so many that her mind actually seemed to buzz with secrets, as if they were flying around inside her head. She had told him next to nothing about her plans—or rather, she had told him only what she supposed he wanted to hear.

Joe hated the "phonies" and the "movie big shots" whom he accused of exploiting her, so he wasn't unhappy that she was thinking of breaking her contract with 20th Century–Fox—particularly since he assumed, with a little help from her, that he would have her to himself for a while, playing the housewife, visiting with his family in San Francisco, perhaps even having that baby. . . .

She hadn't told him she had already agreed to form a company of her own with Milton Greene, the photographer, or that once she had jumped ship on Zanuck and Fox, she would be working harder than ever. Even in small things she had stored up a lot of trouble for herself. Joe had been incensed by the skirt-blowing scene when he read the script for *The Seven Year Itch*, not just because her panties would be exposed—though he wasn't actually too crazy about that —but because they would be exposed on location in New York City, "his town," where he had reigned as "the Yankee Clipper" for so many years.

Ordinary New Yorkers, he complained, *his* fans, would see *his* wife, in the flesh, showing her *tush* right there on Lexington Avenue! He went on about it for days, building up a head of steaming anger that threatened to erupt at any minute, until finally she promised that the scene would be toned down, that her skirt wouldn't rise above midthigh level—except that she hadn't mentioned a word of this to Billy Wilder, the director, who was going ahead with the scene as planned.

Meanwhile, here she was, "the biggest star since Garbo," as Wilder kept telling her—although it was really Harlow she identified with—trapped in her hotel suite like an animal in a cage!

She paced restlessly, drinking champagne and occasionally spilling it on the stained and tattered old terry-cloth robe she always wore while she was being made up. Whitey Snyder, her makeup man and best friend—she had insisted on his being given a room on the same floor of the hotel—had made her up hours ago, filling her in on the weather, the news, and the latest gossip, as he always did, but there was no way she could get out of the hotel quietly.

She pulled off the robe and let it fall to the floor, and continued pacing, naked. She always left her clothes on the floor—another little habit that enraged Joe. . . .

Joe liked everything clean and tidy, but in just two days, she had already made a shambles of the elegant suite. There were piles of magazines and newspapers on the floor, her clothes spread out on every piece of furniture, makeup spilled everywhere, room service trays and ice buckets piled up faster than they could be taken away. There were so many flowers that it gave her the creeps; they reminded her of a funeral—her old boyfriend Johnny Hyde's, to be exact. She hardly even bothered to look at the cards, but one modest bouquet of roses had caught her attention, since it bore a small card with gold edges and blue engraved script that read "United States Senate," below which, in a precise hand that was not his own, was the message, "Welcome to New York! Jack."

She had called him this morning, as soon as Joe had left, and been put through immediately by a secretary who seemed to take a call from Marilyn Monroe in her stride. Jack himself had been cordial, but guarded, as if there were other people in the room. He was late for a roll call, whatever that was, he had explained, but would call her back as soon as he was able.

She had asked him when he was going to be in New York, feeling that it ought to have been *his* job to bring up the subject, not hers, but all he said was, "Very soon," crisply, as if to cut off further discussion of the subject. When she told him how difficult it was for her to leave the hotel, he said, "I'll take care of *that*" decisively; then he hung up with a quick good-bye.

Well, what did she expect, she asked herself, after one night? Sir Galahad to the rescue? Jack Kennedy was a busy man, after all, doing whatever it was that senators did, which *had* to be a lot more important than what movie people—or former sports stars— did.

The house phone rang and she picked it up. She held it to her ear and said nothing—experience had taught her that even in a first-class hotel, the crazies sometimes got through to you. It was safer to let the caller speak first. There was a pause; then the desk clerk said, "I'm sorry to disturb you, Miss Monroe, but Mr. David Leman is in the lobby and wishes to speak to you." He sounded in awe of David Leman.

The name seemed vaguely familiar, but she couldn't place it. Anyway, she didn't put much trust in names. Reporters would pretend to be anyone to reach her—on her honeymoon with Joe she had once received an emergency call from her own beloved Aunt Ana, only to find, when she got on the line, that it was a stringer for Walter Winchell, wanting a few words on what it was like to be Mrs. DiMaggio.

"Mr. Leman says he's a friend of, ah, Jack's," the desk clerk added. It came back to her then—the memory of a tall, dark-haired, exquisitely tailored man with a Clark Gable mustache and a white waistcoat, Jack's companion at Charlie Feldman's party, who seemed to know everybody in the world.

"Send him up!" she said, slipping quickly back into her robe. Then something told her that David Leman wasn't the kind of man who would appreciate a dirty old terry-cloth robe, so she went into the bedroom and exchanged it for a silk wrapper and a pair of satin mules, feeling as if she was dressed up like Joan Crawford—that *bitch*—who she assumed was probably David Leman's idea of a movie star.

She wished there were time to tidy up the suite—now that she looked at it, it was a real *mess*—but she sprayed a little of her favorite Chanel No. 5 around and hoped for the best.

She gave him her biggest, happiest smile as she opened the door for him.

———

Years ago, I asked my old friend Aaron Diamond, the Hollywood superagent, why he gave up representing performers in favor of best-selling novelists and as-told-to celebrity autobiographers. "I decided I wanted to sleep nights," he growled. "I got tired of all those three a.m. phone calls."

I took the same view myself, even in the days when I was a young man in Hollywood. Few egos are more fragile than those of movie stars, or more insatiably demanding.

Marilyn was no exception, the only difference being that she did nothing to hide the fragility of *her* ego—it was right there on the surface for all to see, in the puzzled, self-absorbed eyes and the hands that were constantly in motion. I found myself staring at her hands. She wrung them, she picked at her nail polish, she plucked at the edge of her silk wrapper, pulling at loose threads as if she were intent on unraveling the whole thing. She sat hunched over, as if hugging herself, apparently unaware that her hands were leading a nervous, high-energy life of their own.

She had a kind of natural sexual grace, the like of which I had never encountered before—or since. Sitting there, in an armchair at the St. Regis, I could see her breasts clearly through the thin silk of her wrapper, but I never suspected, even for a moment, that she was putting on a display for my benefit, any more than when she slipped out of her satin mules and rubbed her toes, revealing a large expanse of thigh. Later on, I was to revise this naive judgment. Marilyn, I was to discover, always knew exactly what effect she had on men, and stage-managed it carefully. Her innocence was at once real and an act.

"Would you like some champagne?" she asked, in her breathy little voice.

I said I would, even though it was still a few minutes short of noon. Apart from an astonishing profusion of flowers, there were at least half a dozen champagne coolers around the room, each containing an open bottle on ice. Apparently, Marilyn had the waiter open each bottle as soon as it was delivered, then let it sit there until it went flat. There was a bottle at her feet, leaving a damp circular stain on the rug. She filled a glass, noticed that it wasn't bubbling, and gave a charming little shrug, part surprise, part irritation. She got up, kicking the satin mules out of her way, tried a couple of bottles, and eventually found one that was fresh enough to satisfy her. She brought the glass over to me and sat down again, exposing so much leg that it was impossible not to notice she wasn't wearing any panties. Jack, I told myself, had been telling the truth.

"I hate it when the fizz goes out of it?" she said, wrinkling her nose at the rising bubbles. "When I started drinking champagne," she went on, "somebody gave me one of those gold *swizzle* sticks?" She had a habit of emphasizing unexpected words, which gave her speech a curious rhythm all its own. "You're supposed to put it in your glass and twirl it *round* to get rid of the bubbles?" She demonstrated with her forefinger. "I couldn't see the point? I mean, the bubbles are *it* for me."

It occurred to me to wonder if Marilyn was drunk, but I saw no sign of it. She seemed to treat the champagne as a prop, judging from the fact that there were three or four glasses leaving rings on the furniture, each with her lipstick on the rim, and each very nearly full.

There were millions of men who would have given their right arm, no doubt, to be sitting where I was at that moment, but the truth was that Jack's call had come at an inopportune moment. As it happened, I had an officeful of people waiting for me, having interrupted a meeting with a group of senior Ford Motor Company executives to come over here only because Marilyn had told the switchboard not to put through any calls to her. "Jack told me you have a problem," I said. "He asked me to see if I could be of any help."

She frowned. "Oh *boy*, do I ever have a problem! I can't get *out* of here!"

I nodded sympathetically. "I saw the crowd downstairs."

"It's not just the crowd. It's the reporters. They follow me everywhere. It's like a whole convoy, with convertibles for the photographers?" She looked as if she was about to cry. I'd never met anybody, not even in show business, who looked more forlorn when she was sad.

"I have a business meeting," she said. "I mean, it's with somebody whose name I don't want to see in the papers? And how come the phones don't work? I can call out, but nobody can call me?"

"You asked the operator to hold your calls. She wouldn't put me through." I wondered whom she had planned to meet. I didn't yet know about her plans to walk out on Fox, or her partnership with Milton Greene.

"Hold my *calls?* That was last night."

"Well, you have to give her the okay in the morning to put them through again," I explained.

"Is that why you came in *person?*" She bit her lip, then buried her face in her hands. "Oh, God, I'm *sorry*," she wailed. "You had to leave home and run all the way over here. . . ."

"Look here, it's almost lunchtime. Honestly, I don't mind a bit."

"Really?" She uncovered her face.

"Absolutely."

She leaned over impulsively and gave me a quick kiss on the cheek, the kind a child might bestow on an elderly relative for a present that was slightly better than what she had expected. "You're a *dear*," she said. "I don't know why, but I just had this *picture* of you, sitting at home having breakfast, with your wife, and a dog at your feet. . . . Are you married?"

"Yes," I said. "And we *do* have a dog. Two, as a matter of fact."

"What kind?"

"Pugs. A male and female."

"Cute! What are they named?"

"Edward and Mrs. Simpson," I said, and since there was no reaction, I added, "After the duke and duchess of Windsor, you see."

Marilyn nodded vaguely, but she didn't smile. Clearly, the duke and duchess didn't mean much to her, if anything.

Her eyes misted over. "I had a dog when I was a *little* girl," she whispered. "In Hawthorne, when I was a foster child? His name was Tippy?"

"That's nice."

She nodded. "Our next-door neighbor shot him one night, because he was barking."

I wasn't sure how to handle that. "I'm so sorry," I said finally.

It seemed to be enough. "Thank you," Marilyn whispered, taking my hand in hers and clutching it. She had surprisingly strong fingers.

We sat for what seemed like a long time facing each other, hand in hand, meditating on Tippy's death. It was not how I had expected to spend the late morning.

I cleared my throat. "Well, as to your problem," I began.

Marilyn's enormous eyes stared blankly into mine. "What problem?" she asked, her mind apparently still back in Hawthorne with Tippy.

"Getting you out of the hotel."

"Oh," she said dreamily, still kneading my hand. I noticed that she was not wearing a wedding ring, and wondered if that had any significance. "Tell me," she said, "what is it you actually *do*?"

"I own a public relations firm."

I had Marilyn's full attention now. No stars are ever completely happy with their PR. "You mean, you do, like, *publicity?*"

I shook my head. It was a common mistake. I do *not* do publicity, and never have done—I create an *image* for my clients, shape the way they are perceived by the press and the public. Publicity is for foot soldiers; I have always been a strategist on the grand scale. "I don't do personal publicity," I explained. "I try to 'accentuate the positive' for my clients." I laughed, but Marilyn had apparently never heard the song. "My job is to ensure that their activities are seen in the best light."

"What *kind* of clients?"

"CBS. Israel. The Las Vegas Chamber of Commerce. Ford. The Joseph P. Kennedy Foundation. . . ."

Her eyes widened. "No kidding? Jack's dad?"

I nodded.

Marilyn was all business now, Tippy forgotten. "Joe Schenck," she said, "told me he was the biggest shit who ever owned a studio."

I had forgotten that she had been Schenck's girlfriend when she was an ambitious starlet in the 20th Century–Fox talent pool. Schenck must have been in his seventies then, at the losing end of his long, bitter feud with Darryl Zanuck for control of the studio, and just released from Danbury, Connecticut, Federal Correction Institute, pardoned by Truman after serving several months of a five-year sentence for making payoffs to union racketeers in exchange for labor peace, and perjuring himself on the subject.

"Oddly enough," I said, "Joe Kennedy holds much the same opinion of Schenck."

"Joe Schenck's a tough old guy," she said with a certain amount of admiration. "I was really *scared* of him at first, you know, but he had all this *energy*—more than anybody I'd ever met, until Johnny Hyde came along. . . ." Hyde had been her agent-mentor-lover in the early years. She sipped her champagne. "You know how I met him?"

I shook my head.

"He was in his car, leaving the studio. He'd just had a meeting with Zanuck about something, and he was really *angry* about it. I was on my way to the commissary for lunch. He took one look at me, told his chauffeur to stop, opened the door, and said, 'Get inna car, goilie!' "

She had the voice down perfectly, the guttural rasping accent, New York by way of Rybinsk-on-the-Volga, a growl deepened by a lifetime of smoking cigars and screaming at people. For the first time it occurred to me that Marilyn was a pretty good actress, or at least that she *could* have been, in the right hands.

"Is Jack like his father?" she asked.

It was a question that seemed to call for an honest answer. "Not yet," I said. "He may be, though, one day."

She raised an eyebrow.

"People think Jack's a lightweight," I explained. "He's not. But he's got *grace*, you see, which Joe never had. Some people mistake that for weakness. It isn't so."

She seemed to understand. "Is he like his father with women?" she asked.

"Jack's less cynical than his father," I said, taking a deep breath. "Joe loves winning much more than he's ever loved any woman. Jack *can* fall in love with a woman. He was in love with Inga Arvad, before the war, until his father broke it up."

"Oh dear. Why?"

51

"Well, for one thing, the FBI thought Inga was a German spy, so Joe may have done the right thing for once. . . ."

"Is Jack in love with Jackie?"

I told her the truth. "Not yet. But I think he will be, in time."

Marilyn sat quietly for a moment, apparently contemplating the future. Then she sighed. "You won't believe this," she said, "but when it comes to men, I've never had any regrets. Even when it was bad, it was good, if you see what I mean?"

"It's a healthy attitude," I said. "Joan Crawford once said something similar to me."

Her face tightened, and I could see anger in her eyes. *"Joan Crawford!"* she spat. "Are you a friend of hers?"

"Not at all," I said carefully, conscious that I was walking a tightrope. "Joan invited me out to dinner once, to sound me out about handling Pepsi-Cola's PR, got looped on vodka, and made a grotesque pass at me, right there at Chambord, for all the world to see."

"What did you do?"

"I said no gracefully, got her home, and handed her back to her husband, Alfred Steele. By way of thanks, she spread the rumor that I'm a homosexual. Which, as it happens, I am not. I just don't like going to bed with elderly women who make a public spectacle of themselves—or who want me to cut my fees."

"We have something in common," Marilyn said quietly, then began to giggle uncontrollably.

"We do?"

"Joan made a pass at *me,* too! Right after I made *Clash by Night,* she made friends with me, and I was really impressed—I mean, I was this nobody, and here was this big star being nice to me. . . . I didn't have too many clothes then, so she was always inviting me over to her house to lend me hers, but she was about half my size, you know, so nothing fit. Then, after a couple of months, she made this pass at me, right there in her walk-in closet while I was trying to squeeze into one of her dresses. Talk about *creepy?"*

"What did *you* do?"

"I ran. I drove home without my shoes—left them in the closet with hers. Then, when I won the *Photoplay* gold medal—as the best new actress of the year, in '53—she told a reporter, 'There's nothing wrong with my tits, but I don't go around throwing them in people's faces!' " Marilyn looked grim. "She really *stuck* it to me."

"What did you do then?"

She gave an angelic smile, sweet as honey. "I told Louella Parsons how sorry I was Joan had said that about me, because having been a homeless child, I admired her so much for taking four children in, and for being such a *wonderful* mother to them."

She laughed. "*That* shut her up, and she never spoke to me again. Or about me. Actually, I thought she had pretty scrawny tits, if you want to know the truth."

I was impressed by Marilyn's counterattack, a savage knockout punch delivered with wit and style. Joan Crawford's cruelty to her children was one of those unspoken facts of Hollywood life, something insiders knew but the public didn't. "You certainly got your revenge on *her*," I said.

Marilyn shrugged. "I was pissed off? It doesn't often happen, but when it does, oh *boy*, look *out!* Did you get *your* revenge?"

I nodded. "I would say so, yes. I took Coca-Cola on as a client."

Marilyn shrieked with laughter, and gave me a kiss—the real thing this time, leaving lipstick all over my mouth.

"Oh *my!*" she cried. "I can see we're going to be *friends*, David! Now call whoever it is you have to call and get me out of here. I've got things to *do!*"

———

She loved Milton Greene's studio almost as much as she loved Milton. It was like a grown-up's playground, perched on the roof of the big, old-fashioned office building, with a stone colonnade all the way around it. Outside, on the flagstone terrace, there was a grape arbor, a fountain, garden furniture, so that you could almost imagine you were in Italy, while inside, the big, high-ceilinged studio was full of dark shadows, vivid backdrops and strange props—pipe racks hung with old costumes, wicker baskets full of hats, odd pieces of furniture, bric-a-brac of every description as far as the eye could see.

Whenever she saw Milton, the phrase "bright as a button" came to her mind. He looked like a soulful child, with his sad dark eyes and his round face, but that was only at first glance. She could never explain, even to herself, why she had chosen Milton, of all people, to lead her out of Hollywood or help her break the contract with Fox.

At Fox, she was always going to be their "dumb blonde"—that was the way they saw her, and that was that. Zanuck *hated* her— not just because she had refused to let him fuck her, which he thought was his due, but because she had been Joe Schenck's girl, and Darryl hated Joe.

Since everybody in Hollywood knew how unhappy she was at Fox, and how much Zanuck hated her, she had been deluged with offers, many of them from people who had more money, more experience, and more clout than Milton—which wasn't saying much, since Milton had no money, very little experience, and no clout at all without the use of her name.

Maybe she trusted him precisely because he *wasn't* one of the big producers, or agents, or entertainment lawyers, who would have tried to make her do what *they* thought she should do, once she was free and clear of Fox. . . .

She shucked off her shoes, went into the dressing room, slipped out of her dress and put on a robe. Milton's friend and sidekick Joe Eula, dark, diminutive, and crackling with energy, put his head around the door and winked at her. "Try on these, baby doll," he said, tossing her a pair of black stockings. Joe was as volatile as Milton was calm, and Milton was the calmest person she had ever met, a man of so few words—and those so softly spoken—that you had to really concentrate to hear what he said. Milton seemed to have to think forever before saying even the most ordinary thing, which she hoped was a sign of intelligence, since she had more or less pledged her future to him. She came back out and told him she was ready.

Milton shoved some papers over to her. "Do I sign these?" she asked.

He thought about that—or something—for a long time. "Maybe you should get a lawyer to look at them first?" he suggested. Like her, he tended to end his sentences as if they were questions, even when they weren't. Maybe *that* was part of why she liked him, she thought. That and the fact that he had burst into tears when she told him about Tippy.

"The only lawyer I've got right now is Jerry Giesler?" she said.

"Jerry? He's a divorce lawyer."

"I know."

There was a long silence. Nobody looked gloomier than Milton when he wanted to look gloomy, she decided. "Did you talk to DiMaggio about our deal yet?" he asked at last.

She shook her head.

"Oy vey."

"It won't affect the deal," she said.

"Sure." His expression said it all—the knowledge that *everything* would have an effect on their deal: the weather, her periods, her love life, certainly her divorce. "You should wear paler makeup," he said, changing the subject—something he was an expert at. He waved at Joe, who came over carrying a bottle of champagne and a makeup box, put a towel around her, and got to work, occasionally glancing toward Milton, who either shrugged or nodded. "Giesler might not be the right man?" Milton suggested. "For this."

"I could get Ike Lublin? or Mickey Rudin?"

"Frank's lawyer? Yes. You could get Mickey . . ." Milton had a way of repeating what she'd said, which didn't tell her whether he was for or against whatever it was, or even if he had any opinion at all.

"So long as it's fifty-fifty," she said. "I don't care about anything else."

Milton picked up a Leica and looked at her through the finder. No matter what he was involved in, he never forgot he was a photographer first and foremost. "I don't know, Joe?" he whispered. "The hair."

"I *know.* Don't *nag,* baby! I've already *thought* about the hair." She felt Joe's fingers in her hair, pulling, shaping, undoing everything that Mr. Kenneth had wrought so carefully in the suite this morning.

"Yes," Milton said, clicking the camera a couple of times. "Yes." He repeated it quietly a few more times. Joe poured a couple of glasses of champagne, and they both stared at her.

"Try the stockings on, baby," Joe said. "You know, make a production of it." He reached overhead and adjusted some lights, then went behind her and lowered a black velvet backdrop.

Milton nodded glumly. "Not fifty-fifty," he said to her, picking up his camera.

She was leaning back in the bentwood Thonet chair, one leg pointing up at the ceiling as she pulled on a black stocking, and she froze. "What the hell are you talking about?" she asked, suddenly furious.

Milton grinned. "You get fifty-*one* percent, Marilyn," he said. "I want *you* to have control."

"Control of Monroe-Greene Productions?"

"It's going to be called Marilyn Monroe Productions. It's *your* company, Marilyn. That's what I'm trying to tell you."

She tilted her chair so far back that she almost tipped over, laughing with joy, not just at the fact that she had control of herself at last but because Milton had given it to her, because she had made the right choice when she picked him. She could hear the whir and the click of his camera, hear him whispering to himself, in his New York accent, "Bee-*you*-ti-ful!" and she already knew these were going to be the sexiest, *happiest* photographs anybody had ever taken of her.

"Pick up the phone," Joe told her. "Like one of those Vargas girls in *Esquire*."

She picked up the receiver and placed it against her ear obediently. Then, out of a spirit of mischief, she dialed the number Jack had given her. She heard the phone ring while Milton clicked his camera, and a deep voice, with an unmistakable Boston Irish accent, growled, "Senator Kennedy's office."

She asked to speak to the Senator, thinking that she could actually feel layers of Irish-Catholic disapproval for who and what she was coming over the telephone line from Washington, D.C. There was a heavy clunk as he put the receiver at his end down on the desk, and the subdued hum of conversation in the background—she thought she heard a woman's laughter—and then whoever it was shouted in a booming voice, "Jack, it's the blonde on the phone for yez."

The blonde on the phone? She felt a moment of indignation; then Jack himself came on the phone. "Did David get you out of the St. Regis?" he asked. He was whispering, so she had to strain to hear him.

"I'm out, thank you. Footloose, fancy-free, and on the town." She giggled. "Where are *you?*"

"It's been hectic here. . . ."

"Oh. I thought you told me back there in LA you'd drop everything the moment I got to New York? Well, I'm here?"

"I can get up tomorrow."

It was on the tip of her tongue to say that *this* particular "blonde on the phone" didn't wait for any man, that by tomorrow she might have found somebody else, that he needn't bother, but there was something about Jack that gave her pause. "Guess what I'm doing?" she asked, in her most sultry voice.

"Well, ah, I've no idea. . . ."

"I'm sitting on a chair, tilting it *way* back, with one leg stuck high up in the air, while I pull on a black nylon stocking and fasten it to my garter. I'm not wearing any panties either."

There was a long pause; she heard him swallow hard. "I'd like to see *that,*" he said.

"Well, you'd be looking right at it if you were here, smart guy."

"Perhaps you can, ah, replay the scene for me tomorrow?"

She made a wet, kissing noise into the receiver. "Oh, I hate to repeat myself, honey," she said. "Get it while it's hot, get it while it's going, that's my advice."

"Where the hell *are* you?" There was just enough irritation in the way he asked to assure her that she had hit home, had awakened whatever small sense of proprietorship he might feel over her. She would let him think about what he was missing—it would teach him not to take her quite so easily for granted next time.

"I'm sitting here with two divine men. Drinking champagne and having a *ball*."

"You're *what*?"

"I'm having a ball with two guys." She laughed. "It's okay, honey. I'm being photographed."

He laughed uneasily. "Of course. I should have guessed that."

If it had been anybody else, she would have resented the smug tone. Once or twice when she had *really* been angry at Joe, she had called him and said loving things to him on the phone while she was in bed with another man. It had given her a sense of being in control. She pictured him at the other end of the line, watching sports on television with the sound turned down as he talked to her about how his flight had been or what the hotel was like, unaware that as they spoke, there was a man in bed beside her. . . .

"Can you meet me for dinner tomorrow?" he asked, interrupting her thoughts. "At the Carlyle?"

"Sure." It was easy to arrange. She could tell Wilder that she needed to spend the evening with Joe, and tell Joe that she needed to have dinner with Wilder to talk about her role; the chance of their meeting each other was minimal. Once Wilder started to shoot the picture, though, it would be a lot more difficult.

"I've got to run," he said, still whispering. "I'll see you tomorrow."

She blew him another kiss. "I can hardly wait." She broke the connection, and gave Milton a big grin. "Where's the Carlyle?" she asked.

He contemplated the question for a moment as if it required heavy thinking. He changed lenses, reloaded, checked his exposure, then looked up. "Madison Avenue and Seventy-sixth Street," he said. The dark eyes glistened with sharp intelligence, like the dots of two exclamation marks. "Jack Kennedy's suite is on the twentieth floor," he added softly.

For a moment she was about to lose her temper with Mr. "Bright as a Button" for being a smart-ass. Then he gave her one of his sad, little-boy smiles and she began to laugh instead, happy with the way she was going to look in the photographs, with the prospect of this new affair, with the future.

Really, she thought, crossing her fingers—she was the luckiest girl in the world!

Love always made her an optimist, every time.

――――

She was in a hall, expensively furnished in the manner of a gentlemen's club—or what she imagined one to look like from the movies, for she had never been inside such a place in her life. The walls were decorated with old ship prints. The furniture was dark, polished mahogany and gleaming tufted leather, which reminded her of the banquettes in the Hollywood Brown Derby, where Johnny Hyde used to have a regular table for lunch.

There was a door open a crack at the far end. She went in, and found Jack Kennedy already in bed, reading the financial section of *The New York Times*. To her surprise, he was wearing glasses, which he instantly took off. There was a bottle of champagne in an ice bucket on the bedside table. He poured her a glass as she sat down beside him. "I guess I'm not going to get dinner?" she said sweetly. "I'd have ordered a club sandwich before I left if I'd known."

"Are you hungry?"

"A girl likes to get fed. I can remember when the only time I ever got a decent meal was on a date. I used to eat enough to last me for days!"

"Actually, there's food in the living room."

She went into the living room, where a table had been prepared, picked up a shrimp cocktail and brought it back to the bedroom. She sat down again on the bed beside Jack and ate the shrimps carefully, dipping each one in the cocktail sauce by its tail, leaning forward so as not to drip anything on her dress. She offered one to Jack, but he shook his head.

There was a part of her that would have preferred to start the evening with dinner, candlelight, and conversation, but she had been around long enough to know that some men had to fuck before they could eat or talk. Jack Kennedy was obviously one of them.

She emptied her champagne glass in one gulp, then leaned over and kissed him, driving her tongue deep into his mouth.

She felt his hands behind her, tugging at the zipper of her dress, but she pushed them away. She wanted things *her* way this time!

Pulling back the covers, she unfastened his robe; then, kicking off her shoes, she got up on the bed, pulled her dress up as far as it would go, and lowered herself onto him, her knees pressed against his slim waist. She held his wrists, so that all he could do was lie flat, while she controlled her own movements. It excited her, the feeling that *she* was fucking *him,* making love at her own pace, to satisfy her own needs, *using* him! All the more exciting somehow because he was naked while she was fully dressed, stockings, earrings, dress, fur stole, and all—the opposite of the days when she had to take off her clothes for men who didn't do more than unzip themselves, and sometimes insisted she do even that for them.

She heard him groan harshly, felt him throb inside her, and slowed down, holding him back. "Not yet, not yet," she told him, conscious that it was a command, not a plea—then, when she was ready, she plunged deeply down, felt him come, and let herself go, eyes closed, head back, with a cry that was like a howl of pain, and certainly audible all the way down the hall, if not to the lobby.

"*Jesus!*" he said. He sounded awestruck—as well he might be, she thought; nobody got sex like *that* every day, not even Jack Kennedy!

She stretched out her arms luxuriously. It had been even better than it was the first time, in California. She felt great—and *really* hungry now. Reluctantly she lifted herself off him. She stood up, unzipped her dress and let it fall to the floor, then went to the bathroom and slipped into one of the hotel's terry-cloth robes. She looked at herself in the full-length mirror, makeup a disaster, hair tousled, stockings wrinkled. "My God, I'm a mess!" she moaned.

Jack appeared in the doorway, wearing his silk robe, a drink in one hand, a glass of champagne for her in the other. "You don't look a mess to me," he said.

"You're sweet, but I know a mess when I see it."

"Tell me," he said. "When you closed your eyes, just before you came, what were you thinking about?"

She knew what he wanted to ask was, "*Who* were you thinking about?" which is what men always wanted to know, and women, too, if she was going to be honest about it. "I was thinking that you were the best, sugar," she said, looking him right in the eye.

The answer to the question he hadn't dared to ask would have surprised him, and a lot of other people as well. When she made love, it was, more often than not, her ex-husband, Jim Dougherty, she thought of. She had been the most virginal of brides, at sixteen appallingly innocent and uninstructed, but Jim, unimaginative as he was in most ways, took the time and trouble to arouse and awaken her on the hideaway bed in their tiny "studio" apartment in Sherman Oaks, until very shortly she couldn't get enough of him, and he nearly lost his job because he was always falling asleep at work. In the end, poor Jim was to discover that he had awakened more than he bargained for, but she was always grateful to him for the gift of her own sexuality.

"Do you do this kind of thing often?" she asked, figuring she'd earned the right to ask a few questions.

He hesitated. "I don't know about 'often.' That means different things to different people."

"Doesn't Jackie mind?"

He thought about it. "Jackie and I have, ah—an understanding." He did not say what it was.

"You mean she *doesn't* mind?" The idea puzzled her. She would have minded like hell if Joe fucked around with other women. It was unfair, considering her own behavior, but there it was.

"I didn't say Jackie doesn't *mind*." He searched for an explanation. "You know, almost everybody who's worth a damn is a bit of a fraud. Take me: I don't always feel like a senator . . ."

"I know just what you mean, honey. I don't always feel like Marilyn Monroe."

"There you are. Well, Jackie's an exception. She's the only person I know who's *exactly* what she seems to be." He paused reflectively for a moment. "No," he went on. "That's not true. My brother Bobby's another. He's a true believer."

"In what?"

"In me."

God, what she would have given to have somebody who believed in her like that! The people who loved her most always wanted her to be somebody else—like Joe, with his dream of her becoming a housewife . . . Still, it wasn't Bobby she was interested in. "What's Jackie like?" she asked.

"Well, the two of you are quite different. . . ."

She could tell he hoped that was the end of it, but she wasn't about to let him off the hook. "How?"

"She's—ah—slimmer than you."

"I meant in bed."

There was a long, unwilling silence. She could read in Jack's face that he had gone as far as he was willing to go—farther than he had wanted to, in fact. At any moment, he was going to start resenting her because he'd answered her questions, so she gave him a kiss on the cheek, then put her arms around him and held him tightly for a few moments until he relaxed again.

Having spent most of her childhood in houses where people hardly ever touched each other, she could never have enough kissing or hugging. They sat down at the table, facing each other. She rubbed her foot against his, enjoying the touch of flesh against flesh, picked up a piece of cold chicken with her fingers and bit into it as if she hadn't eaten in days, while Jack tore small pieces off his roll. He helped himself to a slice of ham, carefully trimmed off the fat, and cut it into small pieces, all exactly the same size. She wiped the mayonnaise off her mouth. "You're a picky eater," she said. "No wonder you're so thin."

"I'm not hungry. When I am, I eat, I promise you."

"I'll bet you don't. I'm an orphanage girl, see? I never wait for the next meal because I'm never sure there's going to *be* a next meal." She made herself a sandwich and bit into it with satisfaction. "It drives them *crazy* at Fox when they see me eat," she said between mouthfuls. "They're always afraid I'll get too fat to fit into my costumes! You know how I plan to spend my old age?"

He shook his head.

"I'm going to let myself *go*. Eat whatever I want, let myself get as fat as a pig. I'm going to be big, fat, and sloppy, and not a bit ashamed of it. I've got it all worked out, see—I'm going to have a *great* old age. How about you?"

"I haven't given it much thought, to tell you the truth."

"I think about it all the time." She finished her sandwich and took a pickle off his plate—she loved to eat off other people's plates, as if what they had must always taste better than what was on her own.

"I want a big house," she said. "Somewhere on the sea, Malibu, or maybe Santa Barbara. Oh, and lots of dogs. And a cook who can make great Mexican food, enchiladas, burritos, chicken mole, stuff like that. . . . I'm going to sit in the sun and read all the books I should have read before, or maybe take up painting, or something like that. . . ."

He laughed. "I can't imagine you that way."

"I can." She held out her glass so he could refill it. "Old age," she said. She sipped her champagne, wrinkling her nose at the bubbles. She leaned forward, chin resting on her fist, looking into his eyes adoringly from close up, as if she wanted to pretend that they were an ordinary couple, at breakfast perhaps, or eating dinner at home while he filled her in on his day. "Talk to me about something else. Talk to me about what *you're* doing. Talk to me about anything but the movie business." She shuddered briefly. "Or sports."

"Most of my time lately has been spent arguing with Bobby," he said. "And my father." He looked glum. "About Senator McCarthy." He put the full spin on the word "Senator," intoning it with a respect made more pronounced by his Harvard/Boston accent.

"*Joe* McCarthy? I *hate* that guy."

He looked a little pissed off. Clearly, he didn't want to waste his time talking politics with her. She pinched his leg hard with her toes —she had always been proud of the strength of her toes—and he winced. "Don't crap out on me, Jack," she said. "I'm not Jackie. I'm not some bimbo either."

He had the grace to look embarrassed. "I never said you were."

"No, but you *thought* it."

"Okay, okay," he said, holding up his hand in surrender. "Why don't you like Senator McCarthy?"

"Do you?"

He looked thoughtful, his handsome young face suddenly dark. "Not much, frankly. I know he's a drunk, and I suspect he's a fraud. And probably a homosexual as well. You didn't answer my question."

"He hurts people. I know plenty of people in Hollywood who have had their lives destroyed by McCarthy, or his followers. . . . *Good* people, a lot of them."

"Some of them may be Communists, you know."

"Oh, 'Communist,' that's just a word, Jack. The people who've lost their jobs weren't building bombs or anything. They were acting, or writing scripts, or composing music, and now they're finished. No jobs, no money, no hope."

She could tell this wasn't the way he had thought his evening was going to be, but she didn't care. In Hollywood, the anti-Communist witch hunt was led by men like Darryl Zanuck, Harry Cohn, Jack Warner—the bosses—who were not above using it to pay off old scores. Anticommunism, in her opinion, was just another way of tightening the screws on the workers, the little people, among whom she counted herself.

"You're wrong," he said. "Communism *is* a threat. I'm not crazy about Senator McCarthy personally, but that doesn't mean a real threat to freedom doesn't exist." He didn't seem comfortable with this piece of rhetoric. She wondered if he was quoting from his father.

"My father and my brother Bobby think he's fighting the good fight. So, ah, do most of the voters in the commonwealth of Massachusetts. Bobby would follow Senator McCarthy into the fires of hell. Which he may get a chance to do, since just between the two of us, McCarthy's through. My main concern, frankly, is to get Bobby off the McCarthy ship before it, ah, goes down."

"Bobby doesn't want to abandon ship?"

"Exactly. He wants to go down with the captain. A lousy idea. I should know. When PT-109 went down, I was in the water and swimming for my life as fast as everybody else. Of course, Bobby never saw action in the war, so he has a higher regard for heroism than I do."

She was surprised. "But you *were* a hero," she protested. "I read all about it in the *Reader's Digest.*"

He shrugged. "I was run over by a Jap destroyer. It was like a traffic accident between a sports car and a truck. When General MacArthur heard about it, he told the Navy to court-martial me. Then Dad got into the act, so I got a medal instead."

"You *did* save your men's lives."

"Yes. I'm not sure they *deserved* to be saved, frankly. We wouldn't have been rammed by the destroyer if they'd been on their toes. Well," he went on philosophically, "that's life, right? You get made a hero for doing something stupid; you get killed for doing something smart."

"You're not going to let Bobby go down with McCarthy, are you? Your own brother?"

Jack looked a little startled. He took family relationships seriously —they were perhaps the only thing he was serious about—but without sentimentality. "I'm going to persuade Bobby to jump ship," he said. "Counsel on the McClellan subcommittee is what I had in mind for him."

It was on the tip of her tongue to ask if the entire Senate was Irish, but she held herself back. She was curious about politics and didn't want to distract him. She nodded, and went on eating the potato salad with her fingers. "This McClellan subcommittee," she repeated dreamily, "what do they do?"

"They're, ah, going to be investigating labor unions. Hopefully, Bobby can make a name for himself there without being involved with people like Roy Cohn." The distaste on his face was evident—for a young man, she thought, he could look surprisingly patrician when he chose, and he was obviously more willing to show his contempt for Cohn than for a fellow senator.

"Gosh!" she said. "What's wrong with labor unions? Which ones is Bobby going after?"

"Does it matter?"

"It does to me. I bet you and your brother have never been in a union? I'm a Screen Actors Guild member myself. I probably know more about unions than Bobby does."

"Very likely. I'm sure he'd be happy to have you instruct him, though." He put his hand on her thigh. She noticed it was placed so that he could take a quick peek at his watch. She would have to find a way to get him to take his watch off in the future, she decided.

"I don't think SAG figures in Bobby's plans," he said. "It's the Teamsters he's after. These fellows Beck and Hoffa."

She shuddered, despite the warmth of his hand and the touch of his fingers moving up her thigh. "I know all about the Teamsters," she said.

He poured himself a demitasse. He stirred it, his eyes on her. "I know they're rough. David Leman warned me about that too. But the more Bobby tells me about them, the more I like it. I need an issue. This could be the one."

"Is David involved in this? I thought he did PR?"

"He does a lot of things. My father trusts him. So do I. He's a very bright guy, with extraordinary connections, not just here but in England. And Israel. . . ."

"David is a smart cookie," she said. "I *like* him."

He raised an eyebrow. "No kidding?" he asked, cheerful again. "How much?"

She gave a sultry look. "He's *very* sexy," she said, eyes half closed as if she were thinking about him. "I really *dig* guys with a mustache. . . ." She shivered in mock ecstasy, arms folded tightly across her breasts. "Clark Gable is my *ideal*."

"You think David looks like Clark Gable?"

"Mm."

"That's funny. Jackie's always saying the same thing. . . . I can't see it myself. Anyway, David's Jewish."

"Honey, some of the sexiest guys I've known were Jewish. Jewish is very sexy, believe me. A Jewish guy who looks like Clark Gable. . . ." She gave a little squeal of delight at the thought.

A look of frank annoyance crossed Jack's face. "I don't get the impression that Maria—*Mrs.* Leman—shares your opinion about David's sexiness."

"That's marriage for you." She giggled, then poked him in the ribs. "You're *jealous!*" she cried.

"The hell I am."

"You *are!* I'm surprised, you know? I didn't think you were the type."

"I'm not . . . well, maybe a bit . . . David and I go back a long time."

"Oh, sweetheart, don't worry. I *like* a man to be jealous."

"You *do?* What about Joe? You're always complaining about the fact that he's jealous."

"Hon-ee, he's my *husband!* A jealous *husband* is no fun at all. A jealous lover is a whole different story." She gave him a kiss. "Anyway, forget I told you David looks like Gable."

He put down the coffee cup. His hand had moved up her leg to the point where he could touch her pubic hair. He stroked it gently, while she played the game of resisting him as long as possible, pretending that she didn't feel a thing. "How late can you stay?" he asked.

"I ought to be back in my hotel by one. After that, my story for the evening wears kind of thin."

"And that matters?"

"It does to *me,*" she said firmly.

His fingers were deep inside her now, stroking gently, then harder, until she was so wet that he could slip three fingers into her cunt, while his index finger slowly penetrated her asshole. She still sat there, smiling like a proper little girl at a tea party (not that she had ever been to any tea parties as a child). Then, quite suddenly, her poise deserted her, and pulling off her robe, she dropped to her knees and took him in her mouth, groaning with excitement. He drew her to her feet, and for what seemed a very long time they stood pressed close against each other, naked, their robes at their feet.

They were kissing so hard that neither of them could speak, but he broke away from her at last to take a breath and said, "In the bedroom. I can't do it standing up, not with my back."

She followed him in, let him lie down and make himself comfortable, then lay down beside him, her legs entwined with his. "God, we fit beautifully," she said. "We were made for each other." She nibbled his ear, turning over on her side so he could enter her more comfortably, her hand on his prick, guiding him in but letting him do the work this time, at his pace. "I want to spend the night with you," she whispered. "I'll bet you look really cute when you're asleep, all curled up in bed."

"Listen," he said in a husky voice, his breath hot against her face, trying to get it right this time. "There'll be plenty of time for nights together. All the time in the world. We're going to have a long affair, you and I."

She laughed softly, settling into the rhythm of his lovemaking. He was holding her hard, his fingers dug deep into her flesh, and she knew he would leave bruises; she bruised easily. But the strange thing about husbands, she had long ago concluded, was that however jealous they were, they seldom noticed such things, presumably because they no longer bothered to look.

"A love affair?" she asked softly. "Is that what we're having?"

And in a voice that seemed almost surprised, as if it were the last thing he had expected to come of the evening, he said: "Why, yes, I think so."

She thought so too.

4

The King Cole Bar of the St. Regis was never my favorite place for lunch. It was as dark and claustral as Radames's tomb in *Aida*, and, on that summer Saturday afternoon, almost as empty. Marilyn had called me to ask if she could buy me lunch to thank me for having "rescued" her, though her real intention, I suspected, was to pump me about Jack. She had apparently had enough of hiding away upstairs in her suite, and somehow made the discovery that in the last booth, she was almost completely safe from prying eyes. That and the prevailing gloom were enough to protect her from her fans, or the merely curious, though she took the additional precaution of wearing sunglasses and a scarf over her hair.

Dalí was seated in solitary, eccentric splendor by the door, if a man accompanied by a pet cheetah can be described as "solitary," and to my surprise, Marilyn giggled as we walked past him. "Some great painter!" she whispered to me as we sat down. "A couple of days ago, he was telling me I was the most beautiful woman in the world and he was going to paint me as Venus; today he can't even tell it's *me* because I'm wearing a scarf on my head!" She looked glum. "The cheetah didn't recognize me either."

"Perhaps it did."

She shook her head. "No. It didn't even open its eyes."

For a moment I thought Marilyn was going to cry. Most of her sadder stories, I was to learn, involved animals—poor Tippy, or Mugsy, the part collie who pined away in sadness after the breakup of Marilyn's marriage to Jim Dougherty, or Johnny Hyde's Chihuahua, who was taken away from her after his death, or later Hugo, who stayed with Arthur Miller after the divorce.

"Forget about Dalí," I said. "Forget about the cat. I hear the picture is going to be great."

Admittedly, I was trying to cheer her up, but I was also telling her the truth. *The Seven Year Itch* had been a big hit on Broadway. Getting Wilder to direct it was a rare stroke of genius for the 20th Century–Fox management, as was casting Tom Ewell, who had played the part on stage, as Marilyn's male lead. After four years of mostly mediocre films and dumb-blonde roles in Hollywood musicals, she was at last getting a chance to do something good, and by all accounts her rushes had been terrific so far.

"The picture? Yeah, I think it's going to be pretty good. I mean, it's not a *total* piece of crap, like the last one."

I was about to say I had enjoyed *How to Marry a Millionaire,* but she put her index finger against my lips. "*Don't* tell me you liked it, please, David, or I'll lose my respect for you. Do you know what Bosley Crowther wrote about me? In *The New York Times?*" Her eyes misted over. " 'Miss Monroe's wriggling and squirming are embarrassing to behold.' "

I patted her hand. "The hell with him!" I said.

She shook her head. "He was right! I hated it as much as Mr. Crowther. Maybe more. But I knew *The Seven Year Itch* was right for me, I just *knew* it somehow. . . . Zanuck didn't want to let me have it, and Charlie Feldman wanted me to do another musical, so when I heard Charlie was going to produce it himself, I said to myself, 'Well, this is *it,* honey, you're going to change his mind for him if it's the *last* thing you do.' "

I stared at my menu as if it required my undivided attention. Jack had wondered why Marilyn was fucking Feldman, and when he asked her, she gave him a touching story about how she felt sorry for him. I suspected that she had just told me the truth. Feldman had had it in his power to give her the part of a lifetime, and she had been determined to do anything to make sure she got it. It is a tribute to Marilyn's charm and air of innocence that I was surprised—and faintly disappointed.

Even in the dim light, she glowed. She was wearing a pale blue dress with a small matching jacket thrown over her shoulders, a single row of pearls around her neck. There was nothing sexy about her outfit—indeed, it looked as if she might have chosen it to please Joe DiMaggio, whose demand that she wear more modest clothes with high necklines and full skirts had made the news several months ago, giving rise to jokes and cartoons that must have been a good deal more embarrassing to him than seeing his wife in public in low-cut dresses with bare shoulders. Not, of course, that any of this mattered. If DiMaggio supposed that Marilyn's sexuality could be concealed by anything short of a tarpaulin, he was, I thought, an even more deluded husband than most.

While we ate, Marilyn and I chatted happily about all the people we knew in Hollywood. Of course, as a beautiful blond photographer's model and, later, a starlet, she had been taken everywhere and met everyone, long before she was famous. She had been an acting pupil of Charles Laughton's, the mistress (briefly) of John Huston, a sometime date of A&P billionaire Huntington Hartford. In her brief stint at Columbia, she was perhaps the only beautiful starlet on the lot at whom Harry Cohn *didn't* make a pass, because he discovered, by accident, that Marilyn had been raised as a Christian Scientist, the religion to which his wife Rose had converted and in which he himself had become a believer.

Between the summer of 1945, when she was discovered by an army photographer on the production line of the Radio Plane Company in Van Nuys working as a dope sprayer on target drones, to the summer of 1952, when the news that she posed nude for the famous "Golden Girl" calendar made her nationally famous, Marilyn met practically everyone who mattered in and around the movie industry. The range of her acquaintanceship was astounding, from Groucho Marx, who had given her her first real break in *Love Happy* (and pinched her ass so hard one day on the set that she screamed), to Arthur Miller, who held her toe during a soulful late-night conversation in Charlie Feldman's living room, and urged her to read Carl Sandburg's biography of Lincoln.

"I've always thought Arthur was a good playwright, but a rather dull fellow."

She chewed her lip for a moment. "Well, maybe he's a *little* bit boring, okay," she admitted reluctantly, "but he's so brilliant, and *dignified*. I could really fall for a man like that, I think. . . ."

She sounded sincere. A baseball player, a United States senator, and a distinguished playwright! I wondered what on earth attracted Marilyn to three such different men; then it occurred to me that like her, each of them was a star in his own field.

"I tried to explain to Jack why I hate Joe McCarthy," she said. "I should have mentioned that it's people like Arthur that McCarthy's talking about when he rants and raves about Communists. I told him how much I hate everything McCarthy stands for."

It was on the tip of my tongue to say that Jack stood for many of the same things, only in a smoother way, but discretion was the better part of valor. "How did Jack take that?" I asked.

"Well, he *listened*. I think he sort of agrees, in a wishy-washy kind of way, you know? It's really his brother—Bobby?—he says, who's the witch hunter of the family."

"A word of advice," I warned her gently, becoming the first of many people who would instruct Marilyn over the years on how to please the Kennedy family and handle her role as Jack's mistress-in-chief. "If you're planning on seeing more of Jack, don't call Bobby a 'witch hunter.'"

"What should I call him?"

"A 'concerned patriot' would be okay. For practical purposes, just stick to 'Bobby' without any editorializing."

"Well, okay. Jack told me he's trying to get Bobby to aim for the Teamsters instead. Big mistake, I told him."

"Did you?" I looked at her more closely. Despite the wide-open, innocent eyes and the glamorous face, this was no dumb blonde. Of course, I reminded myself, she had been Joe Schenck's mistress, not to speak of Johnny Hyde's and Charlie Feldman's. These were hard, successful, self-made men—*ganze machers,* to use the phrase by which they would describe themselves. Marilyn's mentors had been tough guys, and there were few subjects they were more knowledgeable about than labor racketeering.

"I know the Teamsters are tough," I said. "But Jack's a senator. I don't think there's much real risk."

"I do." She shivered.

As it happens, this was an example of woman's intuition to which I should have paid attention. I saw my role, unfortunately, as calming down Marilyn, not carrying her warning to Jack. "His father knows all about the Teamsters," I pointed out. "The Old Man financed a lot of the liquor business during Prohibition. And who do you think drove the trucks? Teamsters. They don't scare him a bit. Believe me, if there was any real danger, Joe would be the first to warn Jack and Bobby off. The Old Man talks tough, but he loves his kids so much it's scary."

"God, I'd *love* to be a member of a family like that!" she said sadly. There were tears in her eyes.

"No you wouldn't," I said. "Tight families aren't necessarily happy ones."

"I'd settle for an *un*happy family, David."

"Surely not?"

"Oh, honey! Christmas at the orphanage! You had to be there. Believe me, I'd have taken any family that would have me. Who wants a Christmas stocking from the city of Los Angeles?"

We sat in companionable silence for a few moments, holding hands lightly. I would have given anything to fill Jack's place, and did not entirely rule out the possibility if I played my cards right, but in the meantime, I was content to be in Marilyn's company. She had a kind of genius for making even total strangers share her moods, particularly when she talked about her unhappy childhood. The fact that much of what she said was untrue didn't matter—you still had tears welling from your eyes to match her own.

She dabbed briefly at her eyes. "I bet Jack's father would like me."

"No doubt about it," I said. "Like" was not the word!

"I wish we'd met earlier." There was a wistful expression on her face. "Jack would have been a lot better off married to me than to Jackie," she said firmly. "Of course, it could still happen. . . . Think how beautiful our children would be. . . ."

Smart as she was on the subject of the Teamsters, this was clearly an area in which she suffered from delusions. "Marilyn," I said. "Jack's Catholic."

She looked at me blankly.

"Catholics don't get divorced."

"They don't?"

"Not if they want to stay in the Church. Certainly not if they're going to run for the presidency, which Jack is."

"Oh." She looked disappointed, but not heartbroken. She was a child of the movies, for whom illusion was substance, which explains, I think, why she so often stubbed her toe on the hard edges of life.

I glanced at my watch. She was beginning to show small signs of restlessness—the nervous plucking of her fingers at the seams of her dress, the quick looks toward the door as if she were expecting someone, or hoping to get away before someone came in. "Where's your husband?" I asked.

She looked at me vaguely. "Who?"

"Your husband. Joe."

"Oh, *Joe.*" She thought for a moment. "I think he went to Yankee Stadium for some kind of award."

It came to me that there was a major ceremony honoring Di-

Maggio taking place even as we spoke. "I'm surprised he didn't want you there," I said.

"He did." Her expression suggested that hell could have frozen over before she'd appear beside him in Yankee Stadium. "Actually, that reminds me of something I wanted to ask you. . . ." She put her face close to mine, lips slightly parted, a look of desperate, pleading need in her eyes.

"We have a location shot tonight," she said. "One in the morning? Outside the Trans-Lux, at Fifty-first and Lexington?"

I nodded. Everybody in New York knew this, since it had been on the front page of the *Daily News*.

"I'm supposed to be standing on a subway grating, you know? A train goes by and my skirt gets blown up?"

I had met Billy Wilder at "21" a couple of nights before and he had told me about his plans for the shot.

"The problem is," Marilyn went on, "I kind of promised Joe it wasn't going to happen."

I must have looked blank, because she gave me an irritable glance. "Well, he was upset, so I told him they had rewritten the scene so all that happens is my skirt gets blown about a little in the breeze. . . ."

"And that's *not* what's going to happen?"

She shook her head. "Billy's got a wind machine under the grating. My skirt's going to be above my shoulders when he turns it on. I'm going to be wearing a white pleated skirt and white panties. I had to give my bush a fresh platinum bleach job so it won't show through."

I sat silently for a moment, trying to picture this, then trying to put it out of my mind. "You think Joe is going to be angry then?" I asked in a strangled voice.

"Oh *boy!* Is he ever! I was counting on his not coming to see it, but now he's *insisting* on being there. . . . I guess I really screwed up this time."

"I'm not sure what I can do about it." I hoped Marilyn didn't have me in mind to play the peacemaker with DiMaggio. I didn't fancy the task of explaining that his wife had lied to him, or that he was going to be sharing his intimate knowledge of her crotch with millions of moviegoers, as well as photographers from every major daily and magazine.

"Billy promised me he'd keep the public away—that's why he's shooting at one a.m.—but I don't trust the studio PR people. They want a big media event, see, so I think they'll probably ignore Billy and let the public watch from real close. . . ."

Nothing was more certain. If I had worked for a studio, that's exactly what I would have done. I would have paid off the cops too, to move the police barriers closer to the action. What you wanted was a controlled riot, to make the headlines.

"The more people there, and the closer they are, the madder Joe will be," Marilyn said. "He's not going to be happy about his fans staring at my ass from close up."

"Not many husbands would be."

Her eyes turned cold. "Look, he has his profession, I have mine. *Fuck* what he thinks! Only I have to live with him, so what I want you to do is find a way to have the crowds keep a decent distance, okay?"

"That may not be easy."

"*Please*, David! Just do your *best*, all right? There must be *some-body* you can talk to?"

"The mayor. The police commissioner. And I shall, to both of them. But there are still going to be big crowds. I'll do what I can, I promise. I may need to spread some money to the cops, by the way. Not much, but some."

"Whatever," she said. "I've got to run. I've got to see Whitey Snyder, my makeup man."

She stood up and leaned over to give me a kiss on the lips. "Thank you, David," she said. "You're a sweetheart." She left the table, with that walk that made the modesty of her dress seem pointless.

She stopped and turned, a couple of tables away. "Whatever it costs," she called out, "send the bill to Milton Greene, at Marilyn Monroe Productions." Then she was on her way again, undulating past the row of banquettes in the complete silence that she could bring about in any public place.

It was the first time I had heard of "Marilyn Monroe Productions," or her connection to Milton Greene, and all of a sudden it occurred to me that she might have even bigger things in mind for the future than an affair with Jack Kennedy.

———

Because of his profession I had vaguely expected Whitey Snyder to be a homosexual, but to my surprise, he turned out to be a bulky, silver-haired, middle-aged family man, dressed in California casual clothes and wearing a massive brushed-gold ID bracelet that—he told me proudly—Marilyn had given him. He was friendly, easygoing, and ferociously protective of Marilyn—one of the first of that small group of employee-friends and loyalists who stuck up for her, and *with* her, to the very end.

And beyond, in Whitey's case. For it was poor Whitey who would go over to the mortuary the night before her funeral with a fifth of gin in his jacket pocket to see him through the ordeal of making her up to be laid out in her coffin in the pale lime-green Pucci dress she had bought for the last week in her life she was ever happy.

Whitey introduced himself to me as we were standing together near the camera, on Fifty-first Street, Marilyn having told him that I was "one of the good guys." I asked him how it was going. He shrugged. "Usually the director is ready and Marilyn ain't," he said. "This time, it's the opposite. Marilyn's ready and the director ain't. At the last minute the cops started to move the barriers back, because the crowd was too close."

The crowd still seemed to me to be pretty close, as well as huge and raucous, but I was glad to have wrought any improvement, however small. "Is it a tough picture?" I asked, conscious as I said it that I had been away from the movie business too long. It was like asking a combat infantryman if this was a tough war. All movies were hell—it was just a matter of degree.

Whitey gave me a nervous smile, showing big white teeth. "It beats *River of No Return*," he said. "We were on location way up north. It rained every day, Marilyn got a cold *and* broke a leg, and I had to do her makeup in a log cabin, while we both froze our asses off. Now *that* was a tough movie. Otto Preminger was the director, which says it all. . . ."

"Did he give you a hard time?"

"I'm a union man," Whitey said proudly. "He couldn't have given me a hard time if his life depended on it."

I wondered how much of Marilyn's knowledge about unions came from Whitey. "Tell me," I said, "no connection, but as a union man, what do you think of the Teamsters?"

Whitey looked at me a little suspiciously, wondering, I suppose, if I was some kind of fink. "They get results for their members. Nothing wrong with that, is there?"

"Nothing at all." It was a pity, I thought, that we couldn't introduce Whitey to Jack, who held the typical liberal view that labor unions were the blue-collar wing of the Democratic party.

We were standing shoulder to shoulder around the camera and the banks of lights; on three sides of us the crowds of onlookers and photographers pressed up against the police barricades and the broad, sweaty backs of the cops holding them in check. Only in New York City can you produce a crowd at one in the morning, as Wilder should have known. If *my* advice had been asked, I would have told him to shoot the scene at nine in the morning instead. New Yorkers never pay attention to anything, not even Marilyn with her skirt above her head, when they're on their way to work.

There was a stir down the street, where the stars' trailers were parked, the hum of their air conditioners almost drowned out by the roar of the big generators that powered the lights. Whitey noticed and made his way swiftly into the dark.

A moment later, Marilyn appeared in the bright pool of light in front of the camera, a figure so dazzling that to this day I can remember every detail—the white pleated skirt, the open-toe, sling-back, high-heeled white shoes, the gleaming platinum-blond hair.

She smiled at the crowd and waved timidly, as if to say, "Yes, it's me." There was a moment of silence, as if they couldn't believe their eyes; then the crowd went wild, cheering, whistling, shouting out her name, pushing and shoving against the barricades until the cops had to turn around to face them, swinging their nightsticks threateningly.

Yet the people weren't in any way hostile, you could sense that. Marilyn somehow represented their dream, the symbol of all the unattainable things that ordinary people want—sexiness, glamour, fame, money, happiness—or perhaps she was the living proof that an ordinary person could achieve all those things. Oh, sure, she was a sex symbol, but she was much *more* than that. Rita Hayworth was a sex symbol, Jean Harlow had been a sex symbol, but Marilyn was the girl-next-door who has grown up to be a star, the woman you've always wanted if you're a man, always dreamed of being if you're a woman. Marilyn's sexiness was only part of her appeal—she was, in her own way, a piece of that amorphous national yearning we call "the American Dream."

There was nothing phony about it either. Marilyn loved the crowd, the crowd loved Marilyn—symbiosis in its finest form. She pirouetted in the Klieg lights; because she was a big girl, people tended to forget how graceful she could be. She had worked hard to become a dancer, having no natural gift for it, and the fact that she had succeeded was one of the reasons why she never doubted that she could become a serious actress.

They gave her a round of applause. She blew a kiss out into the hot, sultry Manhattan night and they went wild.

Behind her in the shadows stood a few figures. I searched in vain for her husband, only to find him standing beside me, having been relegated to the area for privileged spectators. He looked angry and out of place, upset at being pushed aside. My heart did not bleed for him. After all, if he had been playing baseball, he would hardly have allowed Marilyn to stand beside him at bat during a game.

In the three years since his retirement, he had lost nothing of his athlete's build—it was easy to see why Marilyn had found him physically attractive—but he was trembling with anger at the size of the crowd. The muscles in his cheeks were working hard, as if he were chewing on his fury like a cud, his eyes flat, dark pools of anger. His muscular tension was so intense that his hands were shaking like an old man's. I moved a step farther away—if he was going to hit anyone, I didn't want it to be me.

To my surprise, I found myself standing next to a child, a boy of ten or eleven—I'm bad about children's ages, having none of my own. I couldn't help wondering what in God's name he was doing out in the street at this time of night, or how he managed to find his way into the space reserved for the privileged like DiMaggio and myself. He was a slightly built lad, his face at once innocent and intensely serious, wearing a baseball jacket with his name— "Timmy"—embroidered on the front. He carried a red notebook, and his eyes were fixed on Marilyn with an intensity that was, if anything, greater than DiMaggio's, and every bit as possessive.

Marilyn, notoriously a bundle of nerves at work, seemed relaxed, perhaps because showing her legs was a lot easier than remembering her lines. And of course, she was turned on by the crowd.

She stepped beyond the lights, turned as if she had just come out of the theater with Tom Ewell, hesitated for a second, found her mark on the first take, then burst into giggles as the breeze from the subway rose through the grating she was standing on and made her skirt billow above her knees. She pushed it down with a demure gesture. There was a chorus of whistles and cheers, fairly subdued, as if the fans had been expecting more. Beside me, DiMaggio breathed a sigh of relief.

There followed the usual interminable wait as Whitey repaired Marilyn's makeup and people talked to each other over walkie-talkies. The lights were killed, readjusted, tested, killed again, while Marilyn waited patiently. Wilder hovered over her, talking earnestly with his hands. Once or twice he acted out the movement he wanted —ending with her knees bent in a little crouch. Next to me, Timmy scribbled furiously in his notebook. I recognized in him—in juvenile form—the obsessive quality of the born "fan."

The lights came on, Marilyn and Ewell went back under the theater marquee, the clapper-boy held up his board, Wilder grinned mischievously from his seat beside the camera, and she swept through the scene again—only this time there was a gale-force wind from the grating.

She pirouetted quickly while her skirt, like a spinnaker that has been blown out of control, rose to shoulder height. She put her head back and laughed, fighting to pull the skirt down, but at the same time, sensualist that she was, obviously enjoying the rush of air on that breathlessly hot summer night.

The crowd went mad—cheers, frenzied whistling, applause. Marilyn responded to it, twirling like a ballerina, then crouching low to regain control over the skirt, just as Wilder had shown her. Caught up in the crowd's sexual excitement—and, who knows, her own as well, for she was not only at the center of it all but *creating* it—Marilyn whirled round and round in the light. Tom Ewell (who knew when he had been hopelessly upstaged) hovered beside her, bashful and admiring.

She was to repeat that shot more than thirty times that night—the last take was at 4:15 a.m.! Wilder had the wind machine cranked higher and higher, until Marilyn's skirt was lifted straight up. Whitey, it must be said, had done his work well and even in the glare of the Kliegs and the spots, you couldn't see the shadow of Marilyn's pubic triangle at all, though the cheeks of her ass were clearly defined, and from some angles—the rear particularly—she might as well have been naked.

This was the famous image that would be enlarged into a cutout figure one hundred feet high and hoisted above Loew's State Theater on Broadway, the life-sized one that Jack Kennedy would have placed on the ceiling above his hospital bed when he underwent his back operation a couple of months later, and the one that would appear over the years on T-shirts, mugs, and souvenir kitsch all over the world—probably the best-remembered photograph ever taken of Marilyn and a permanent symbol of the national libido.

At once symbol and hauntingly real, Marilyn managed to convey the notion that sex was innocent fun. Not many people can do that, and that night she put her heart and soul into it, right there in front of the camera on Lexington and Fifty-first. I couldn't take my eyes off her. The people in the crowd of spectators must have felt something similar, for gradually their rowdiness died down, as if they, too, were communicating with their most intimate fantasies. I knew at that moment that I was in love with her, and also knew it was hopeless.

By the time I turned around to look at DiMaggio's face, he was gone.

He had left before Marilyn really got into the swing of the thing, doing take after take for the camera with the abandon of a stripper.

DiMaggio missed the best takes.

I thought that was probably just as well.

———

It was nearly five in the morning when I finally returned home. I had told Maria that Billy Wilder had invited me to watch the shooting of his big scene with Marilyn—she had expressed no interest in accompanying me, which was just as well.

A light sleeper, she woke as I stretched out in bed, having dropped my sweat-sodden clothes on the floor. "What on earth time is it, darling?" she mumbled.

"Late." I was exhausted by the heat and the emotion, yet not at all sleepy. Without any conscious decision I put my arms around her and stroked her until she gave a small, sleepy moan, not so much of arousal, I suspect, as of surprise. Maria was a woman who liked— demanded—a certain routine to her life, even in its most intimate aspects. Sex at five in the morning was not part of the routine. I didn't care. I had seldom felt such an urgent need. My erection was so stiff that it was painful. I plunged it into her from behind with a sigh of relief.

"My goodness, David," Maria said with a certain amount of interest, "what's gotten *into* you?"

She moved farther over onto her side, to make herself more comfortable—we had been married long enough to know every curve of each other's bodies, every requirement of position, and to be bored by the knowledge. She began to moan more urgently, surrendering to her own feelings, or fantasies perhaps, of who knows whom, while in my mind, my eyes tightly closed even in the dark, I saw Marilyn's bright hair flashing in the lights as she pirouetted, her skirt flying, and imagined I felt in my hands her pale thighs and full buttocks. . . .

It was past ten when I woke to the ring of the telephone. Maria, I noticed, had picked my clothes up off the floor—a peace offering of some kind, for she did not usually bother with that kind of domestic detail. I assumed it was my secretary calling to ask where I was on a Monday morning, but a vaguely familiar voice—Whitey's, I realized—said, "You'd better get over here right away, Mr. Leman."

"What? Where?"

"The St. Regis. There's been a problem. Marilyn's asking for you."

———

Marilyn's suite looked as if a small tornado had struck it. A couple of chairs had been knocked over and there were shards of glass on the floor. Volume 1 of Carl Sandburg's *Abraham Lincoln* was propped on the windowsill, the pages open to dry, as if it had been soaked somehow. There was an emptiness to the room, the hard-to-define feeling one has when someone has moved out of a place. Without even knowing what had happened, I guessed that DiMaggio had walked out on her.

She came in from the bedroom looking so unlike the sexy, glamorous star she had been last night that it was hard to believe I was seeing the same person. Every trace of glamour was gone—even her hair had lost its dazzling, golden glow and looked drab, lifeless, bleached out. She had obviously been crying. Her face was pale and puffy, the lips swollen. I couldn't see her eyes, since she was wearing big sunglasses, with lenses that were so dark she had to feel her way into the room like a blind person. I wanted to put my arms around her, but she did not look as if she wanted to be touched, even for comforting. "I know," she said in a tiny voice. "I look like shit, don't I?"

"No you don't."

"Don't try to bullshit me, David."

"You put in a hard night's work. You should be asleep."

"I enjoyed the work. It didn't start getting hard until I came home." She was sipping what looked like iced tea. Every so often, she would pick out an ice cube and press it against her lips. I've seldom seen anybody look more miserable. "I never thanked you for getting the crowd moved back last night," she said. "Not that it did any good."

"I was standing next to Joe. He didn't look happy."

"No shit." She shook her head, then leaned over and gave me a quick peck on the cheek. "I'm sorry," she said. "It isn't your fault that Joe was pissed off." She stared into space for a moment. "It isn't mine either. I was just doing my job, just the way he did when he played ball. If he doesn't like it, the hell with him, right?"

"Right." The truth is that I wasn't entirely comfortable serving as Marilyn's version of Miss Lonelyhearts, and not only because I didn't want to make a habit of it. There are few roles more stressful than that of talking to a woman you desire about the men in her life.

"He's gone back to California, you know?" she said.

I nodded. "I guessed it was something of the sort."

"Is it going to hit the papers? That would make it worse."

"I can see that would be painful for you. . . ."

She shook her head. "I was thinking of the Slugger, David. I can take it. He's all muscle, but I'm a lot tougher than he is."

I believed her. "The story isn't out yet, that I know of. It's too soon. It would help if *you* vanished for a couple of days too. They might assume the two of you have gone off for some time together."

"That's exactly what I want," she said, something of her optimism returning. "Arthur Miller told me how beautiful Connecticut was— full of little villages and old inns. . . . Do you know any?"

"Lots."

"Could you get one of your people to reserve a double room for me somewhere? As 'Mr. and Mrs. DiMaggio'?"

"I'm sure I could, but somebody would leak that to the press right away. Wouldn't an assumed name—"

She cut me off. "No." Her tone was firm. "Just *do* it, please, David, the way I want it. As a favor to me. It's asking a lot, I know, but I don't want to use the studio people, and my own PR girl is from LA, so she couldn't find Connecticut on a map. . . ."

"Anything you say, Marilyn, but Walter Winchell will know what inn you're at in Connecticut an hour after I make that call." I don't know why it didn't occur to me that Marilyn was establishing an alibi and hoped to send the press off in the wrong direction. I hadn't learned yet how devious she could be when she wanted something badly enough.

There was a knock on the door. Whitey Snyder stuck his head in. "It's Milton Greene, Marilyn," he said. "He says he has an appointment to see you."

"Oh God, I forgot."

I got up to go, but she grabbed me by the wrist and pulled me back. "Stay," she said. "I need all the help I can get today."

I knew Greene and his bright, pretty young wife, Amy, slightly. By now I had learned that he and Marilyn were going into business together. Plenty of people in New York knew it was happening, since

Greene had been obliged to seek out financing from various people on Wall Street, including my old friend Robert Dowling, who loved dabbling in the motion picture business. He had told me something about their plans, as well as the intriguing news that Arthur Miller was taking a "personal" interest. The only people of importance who remained in complete ignorance were the executives of 20th Century–Fox, whose egos were such that they could not imagine the defection of a star in the middle of a contract renegotiation, unless to a rival studio.

Greene came in, looking like a world-weary schoolboy, and we greeted each other pleasantly enough. I had worked with him on various gala dinners or dances to raise money for the Democratic party or for Israel, and had always found him an agreeable companion. He had done a photo-essay on me for *Life* magazine with which I was surprisingly gratified. Except for the fact that he had no money and had never made a picture, Marilyn could not have placed herself in more sympathetic hands.

He looked a little nervous at my presence, and I could hardly blame him. Poor man! He was only at the beginning of the long succession of lawyers, accountants, advisers, and self-appointed protectors who would push and shove to get between him and Marilyn, and very nearly put him into bankruptcy before they were through.

He glanced around the room—Marilyn had gone off to get a fresh bottle of champagne, even in distress determined to be the perfect hostess. "Joe's not here?" he asked.

I shook my head. "He went back to California."

"Uh-oh." Milton's face turned a shade paler, his eyes darker and sadder, if that was possible. Marilyn's private life always seemed about to burst the levees and flood her professional life out of sight. Separation or divorce from DiMaggio would make it hard for her to concentrate on their new company, and turn the public's attention from Marilyn the actress to Marilyn the brokenhearted love goddess. There was even a chance that breaking up with DiMaggio might diminish her popularity.

"Did she talk to you about what we're doing?" he asked me anxiously.

"I've heard a little about it, but not from her."

"They're going to go crazy at Twentieth when they find out."

"No question. Zanuck is going to come after you with both barrels. Do you have a good lawyer?"

He shrugged as if to say that even the best lawyer in the world wasn't going to offer much protection. Greene's best bet was to hope that the studio would let Marilyn get away with it rather than risk a long legal battle with America's favorite blonde.

"If you need help . . ." I offered.

He nodded. "*Oy*, do I need help," he said quietly.

"This DiMaggio thing will blow over, don't you worry." I was willing to say anything, however foolish, to cheer him up.

"You think?" He looked incredulous, then sighed. "Well, it was coming, anybody could see that," he admitted. "Once she had a new man in her life, I mean."

I nodded.

"An intellectual," Greene mused. "Quite a jump from a ballplayer."

It was my turn to look incredulous. As a young man, Jack had written a book—ghosted for him by first-rate journalists whom Arthur Krock and I had selected—but nobody would have described him as "an intellectual."

"Don't get me wrong," Greene said. "I *like* him. But I think he might be a little too *serious* for Marilyn, you know?"

"Jack? Serious?"

He stared at me. "Jack? I was talking about Arthur Miller." He leaned forward and whispered. "They're having an affair, Arthur and Marilyn," he said, "which is okay. But she wants to *marry* him. I don't think that's such a hot idea, frankly."

I wondered if she had mentioned any of this to Jack. Miller was exactly the kind of self-righteous, left-wing Jewish intellectual that Jack, however discreetly, most despised.

Marilyn came in, wobbly on her bare feet, with the champagne, and handed it to Greene, who popped the cork. She had brought in three toothbrush glasses from the bathroom, and we sipped lukewarm champagne without much enthusiasm. Her face seemed to have sagged, and her eyes were unfocused. She was having a certain amount of trouble getting the glass to her mouth too. I wondered if she had been taking sedatives while she was out of the room—certainly she had the slow-motion gestures of somebody on pills.

Greene didn't appear to have noticed. "This won't take long," he said, in the soothing voice one might use with a child. "I just want to go over the points you ought to discuss with Mickey Rudin. . . ."

Marilyn blinked. "Mickey who?"

"Sinatra's lawyer. Remember? You were going to get him to look over the contracts for you, honey?"

"I *like* Frank," she said, as if one of us might be going to give her an argument.

"Me too," Greene said, taking the papers out of his briefcase.

"He's a lot more fun than Arthur."

"No doubt about that, baby."

"But Arthur's smarter."

"Maybe so. Frank's pretty smart himself." He rolled his eyes. "Marilyn honey, would you like to leave this to another day?"

"No. I want to get rid of everything. Got rid of the Slugger today." She giggled. "Got rid of Zanuck and the studio today. Start with a clean fucking slate, right, David?"

Marilyn's voice was slowing down, like a record played at the wrong speed, and her eyes were turning dull. I didn't want to get in Greene's way, but I felt somehow responsible for Marilyn. "You ought to be in bed," I said. "Milton and I are going to put you there."

"Not before I've signed these," she said, and before Greene could stop her, she took a pen, bent over the documents, found the places marked for her signature, and signed. "Whoopee!" she cried. "That does it!"

I could see that Greene was caught between conflicting emotions. He had Marilyn's signature on what was, for him, the deal of a lifetime, but being a cautious, orderly fellow in business, he knew this wasn't the way it should be done.

Greene surrendered glumly to the demands of self-interest, guiding her hand to the rest of the copies, marking with his finger the places for her to sign and initial. I had to sympathize with him—it was an opportunity not likely to be repeated, and surely beat months of negotiations.

Marilyn's eyes by now were glazed. I hoped I would never have to testify as to her condition when she signed. "We'd better get her to a doctor," I said to Greene.

She was sitting on the sofa, slumped against an arm, eyes half closed, hands on her lap. She still had on the false fingernails she had worn last night for filming, but several of them were already badly chipped. Her breathing was regular, but very slow and loud.

Greene listened to her breathing, his head bent over her chest. "No doctor," he said.

"She may need one. We don't know what she's taken. . . ."

"Look, take my word for it, David, I *know* about these things. Marilyn's taken a couple of downers, that's all, no big deal. She'll sleep this off."

His tone of voice was so calm, cool, and serious that I found myself believing him, despite my distrust of amateur diagnosticians. I certainly wasn't eager to take the risk that a doctor might remove Marilyn from the hotel in an ambulance and have her stomach pumped out in the Bellevue emergency room while several hundred reporters stood vigil outside.

"Let's get her to bed," Greene said, carefully gathering up his signed papers and putting them away.

It was easier said than done. Marilyn photographed bigger than she was—5 feet 5 1/2; 117 pounds; 37, 22, 36, statistics I remember to this day because for my fiftieth birthday she had them engraved on the lid of a silver cigarette box instead of her initials, an odd example of the way Marilyn's figure, even to her, seemed to have a greater reality than herself—but it isn't easy to pick up a woman who has passed out on a sofa behind a marble coffee table that's too heavy to move. Greene squeezed in between the sofa and the table to take her legs, while I leaned over the back of the sofa to take her shoulders.

"Heave!" he ordered, and we both heaved, eventually managing to lift Marilyn. I don't know why it didn't occur to either of us to ask Whitey Snyder to help—in Greene's case, I suspect it was a natural reluctance to let anybody near Marilyn now that she was his principal asset. In any event, we dragged her into the bedroom and put her down on the bed as gently as possible.

The room showed signs of DiMaggio's hasty departure, as well as Marilyn's habit of keeping all her possessions in torn shopping bags and bursting cardboard boxes. On the bedside table was a guidebook to Washington, D.C. I picked it up. Inside the front cover was a reservation slip for a suite at the Hay-Adams Hotel in the name of Mrs. James Dougherty—Marilyn's name in her first marriage. The suite was reserved for the weekend. I guessed that it was not Arthur Miller she was going to see.

I put the book back down on the night table. Marilyn had moved in her sleep. We had put her on her back, arms folded, but she had rolled over onto her side and curled up like a child, her head resting on her hands. Her gown had loosened, and I could see her breasts—couldn't take my eyes off them, in fact. They weren't particularly large, but they were perfectly shaped, the color of the palest pearly pink, so firm that there was not the slightest sag to them.

"Let's go," Greene said gently.

I shook my head, still overcome, my hands trembling from the touch of her skin.

I turned and followed him out of the room reluctantly. I knew now where she was going for the weekend, and why she had wanted me to make a reservation for her in Connecticut in her own name. Once the press found out, they would be combing the inns of Connecticut, not looking for her in Washington.

I caught one last look at her sleeping as I closed the bedroom door.

God, I thought to myself, but Jack was a lucky man!

———

Or was he? The question occurred to me the moment I arrived home to an irate telephone call from Jack's father. "What's all this about Jack and Marilyn Monroe?" he asked. "Did you know anything about it?"

I admitted that I did, as I sorted through my mail.

"You should have told me," Joe said.

"I don't think it's part of my job to keep you up to date on Jack's love life," I said.

"The hell it's not!" His voice was tight, rising in pitch with anger. "This isn't just another goddamn girl he's fucking, it's Marilyn Monroe."

"I've pointed out to Jack that there are risks involved—"

"To hell with pointing it out to *Jack!* You should have told *me!* I had to hear it from Bobby, who's worried sick over it."

I doubted that. Marilyn wasn't Jack's first movie star, even if she was the most famous, and Bobby had plenty else to worry about. Joe was just building up a case for himself, making it clear that he expected to know everything that went on in Jack's life—a task I had always refused to help him with.

"She's more sensible than people give her credit for," I said. "I'm pretty sure she wouldn't do anything to hurt Jack."

He snorted. "Movie stars are all crazy." He should know, I thought but didn't say—Gloria Swanson had led him a merry dance. His tone softened—a sure sign that he was going to ask me for a favor. "Look," he said, "I don't expect you to tell me every little thing Jack does, but keep your eye on the situation for me, will you? Jack is going to be president. He can't get mixed up in a scandal with a movie star."

"I'll do my best," I said. "I don't suppose it will last long. These things never do with Jack. Nor with Marilyn, I hear."

Joe chuckled. "Well, it can't do him any harm, so long as it isn't serious. I wouldn't mind meeting her myself."

"She says the same about you."

"Does she now? Well, well. . . ." Joe was not above making a play for Jack's girls, and sometimes he even succeeded, such was his determination to compete and win. Back in the days when his children were younger, Joe had a reputation for sleeping with the daughters of his friends and the friends of his daughters, but he didn't draw the line at the girlfriends of his sons either.

"You let me know if you think there's a problem, David," he said. "You owe me that, at least."

I acknowledged it, reluctantly.

"Christ, though, you've got to hand it to our Jack," he added—I could hear the satisfaction in his voice. "They can't say no to him, can they?"

I had never heard such parental pride from Joe, not even the day Jack won his first Senate race, defeating his rival, Henry Cabot Lodge —and Joe was a sworn enemy of the Lodges and all they stood for in Boston.

I wondered if Bobby had told his father that Jack was planning to go after the Teamsters as well. I guessed not, or I would have had an earful about that, too.

5

She held her guidebook in one hand. With the other she grasped Jack Kennedy's hand, twining her fingers with his, ignoring his embarrassment at this open display of intimacy. It was the first time she'd been to Washington, and she was overwhelmed.

They were standing on the floor of the Senate, on a Sunday morning—it had taken all of Jack's senatorial clout to persuade the usher to open it up for her.

She had dressed for the occasion in a white summer dress with tiny black polka dots and a jaunty straw hat with a matching polka-dot ribbon. The dress had a tight sash around her waist in reversed polka dots, white on black. There were an awful lot of polka dots, she thought when she saw herself in a mirror, and she wondered briefly if it had been the right choice for a figure like hers. She looked at the podium and sighed. "Just think," she said. "Lincoln spoke from there."

He frowned. "Ah, I don't think he did, you know, Marilyn. The president gives the State of the Union speeches in the House—still does." He sensed her disappointment. "Webster spoke here. Clay. Calhoun. There's enough history here."

"Oh, yes." She squeezed his fingers harder, smiling to disguise the fact that it wasn't the same without Lincoln. If only she had managed to get beyond the first pages of Sandburg's book, she might not have made a fool of herself, she thought. . . .

She had to hand it to Jack! He had assumed, naturally enough, that the only sight she wanted to see in Washington was him, but once she had him on his back in her bedroom at the Hay-Adams, he surrendered gracefully enough. She was touched by his willingness to show her the sights, for until they had spent some time together, she had not realized how bad his back was, how much pain even the simplest things, like climbing the steps of the Lincoln Memorial, cost him. There was a pair of crutches in the front seat of the car; whenever they stopped to get out and look at something, his driver-body-guard Boom-Boom offered them to Jack. Usually Jack just shook his head and limped off, his face drawn with pain, but where there were a lot of steps involved, he sometimes gave in and took them, with an expression that clearly signified fury at his own weakness.

He walked her over to his desk. She sat down, while he leaned against it, supporting his weight with his arms and shoulders. "This is where you work?" she asked.

"Most of the work is done in committee. Or by getting together over a drink. Half the business of the Senate is done in Lyndon Johnson's office after six o'clock by a pack of old farts sitting around over a bottle of bourbon, trading favors. . . ."

It was clear to her that Jack resented not being part of that. She noticed that his face had suddenly turned pale. His smile was fixed, but his knuckles were white as he pressed his hands hard against the desk. "Is it that bad?" she asked, reaching out to touch him. "The back?"

He shook his head, mouth set, as if the question irritated him. She wasn't fooled for a moment. The Slugger had his share of aches and pains after a lifetime of baseball, and even with a daily massage and hot baths there were still days when his expression was just like Jack's, and yet he wouldn't admit to her he was in pain until he was on the floor groaning, if then. Were all men stubborn and childish? she wondered.

"You ought to be lying down," she said. Then it occurred to her that the pain was really *her* fault, for making him drag himself around Washington when he was too proud to use his crutches, and she felt a stab of guilt.

He gave a crooked grin. "I *was* lying down, remember?"

They had spent the night together in her suite at the Hay-Adams. The sex between them had been as good as ever. Granted, she would have liked a little more variation, some of that muscle-stretching, high-voltage, athletic sex of the Slugger's that left her limp, but Jack was used to women pleasing *him*, which was kind of a turn-on in its own way. Besides, she couldn't help telling herself, when she slowly, carefully raised and lowered herself on his penis: I could be fucking *the next president of the United States!*

It had been disappointing, though, having at last spent a whole night with Jack, to discover that he was not any more "cuddleable" in bed than Joe. She had gone to the trouble of making sure the hotel put an extra-firm mattress and a board on the bed, but it was still too soft for Jack, who complained about it off and on all night.

She had dreamed of holding him tightly in her arms as they both slept, their limbs twined, their lips touching, of waking to see his face close to hers on the pillow. Instead, once he was finally asleep, he lay snoring gently while she tossed and turned beside him, having, at the end of their lovemaking, neglected to take her sleeping pills for fear of disturbing him by getting up.

"Is there anything else you'd like to see?" he asked.

"There is *one* thing more I'd like to see," she answered in a timid voice, like a little girl asking a grown-up for a favor—Norma Jean speaking! she thought.

"Whatever," he said, but she could tell his heart wasn't in it.

"I want to see your home."

She was delighted at the surprise on his face—dismay, really—for she had already learned that he set great store by never showing surprise. He cleared his throat. "I don't think that's such a great idea."

"I do." She pouted gracefully. "Anyway, you promised."

"I did not!"

"You said 'whatever.' That means whatever I want, doesn't it? Anyway, what's the problem? You told me that Jackie's in Hyannis Port and the servants have the day off?"

"That's true, but . . ."

"Well then." She stared at him unblinkingly. He blushed. "You're not *afraid,* are you? I mean, I came down here, didn't I? *I* didn't mind taking a risk."

She knew she had him now—he was the kind of man who could always be counted on to respond to a challenge.

He was glaring at her, his eyes icy; then he laughed. "Well, what are you waiting for?" he asked. "Let's go."

———

Boom-Boom was silent as they passed through the hot Virginia countryside, his disapproval evident in the way he drove in slow motion. Despite Jack's snapping at him to get a move on, he acted as if he were taking his driving test, braking a hundred feet before every intersection and looking in both directions with exaggerated care.

The landscape was alien to her, with its rolling, wooded hills shrouded in heat haze. She didn't like the look of it much. Woods, trees, and farmland frightened her, made her feel somehow *trapped* —she was a child of the far horizon, the Pacific Ocean or the desert, where you could see for miles and the sun burned everything clean.

"I've never seen so many farms in my life," she said.

Jack stared out the window on his side, as if the farms were new to him. There were few subjects that interested him less than farming. "Well, it's mostly gentleman farming," he said with contempt. "That's Ambassador McGee's farm." He pointed to a storybook red-brick Colonial house, set high on a hill, surrounded by huge, ancient oaks. "Texas oil and gas, then an ambassadorship, now the CIA. Has a famous herd of cattle. What are they, Boom-Boom?"

"Black Angus, boss."

"Black Angus, right. McGee paid, I think, a couple of hundred thousand dollars for a prize bull." He shook his head in wonder. "Jackie rides over there a lot, with his girls."

"She likes it here?"

"Loves it. It's the way she was brought up. Horses, hunting—all that sort of goddamned thing."

He looked out the window glumly. It was well known that his taste ran more toward the South of France than rural Virginia, but that was not the kind of signal he wanted to give the voters. For some reason, Jackie's fooling around with horses played well in the press—better, say, than sunbathing at Eden Roc, on the Cap d'Antibes—and anyway, it kept her busy and, for the most part, off his back.

"You don't like it?"

His expression turned, for an instant, sour and angry. She had clearly touched a raw nerve. "The house is too goddamned big," he snapped. "A fucking white elephant. And the commuting drives me crazy. Mornings and evenings, the rush hour traffic is unbelievable. . . . Of course, none of that makes any difference to Jackie."

"Why did you buy it, then?"

He sighed. "It's what Jackie wanted—the horses and all. And I figured we'd need a big house, for all the children!" He laughed harshly. "What an irony *that* turned out to be!"

"Jack," she said, "that isn't her fault." It was the one subject that could always arouse her sympathy for another woman. Nobody, she told herself, could have tried harder to give the Slugger the child he wanted, but she knew in the deep, private hollow of her guilt that it wasn't true.

"I didn't say it was Jackie's *fault*. It's hard for her, I know. When she had the miscarriage, the doctors told her she might never be able to have a child, ever. . . . And there's Ethel, popping kids out with Bobby, one after the other, no trouble at all. . . . That doesn't help. As you can imagine." His tone was bitter.

"I can imagine."

"It hasn't been a happy house for either of us. I can't seem to get Jackie to see that."

The car slowed. They turned up a long, twisting gravel drive, with big trees on either side, and pulled to a stop in front of a large, handsome old house—larger than she had imagined. She realized instantly that Jack was right—it was a house for a big, noisy family. Two people living here without children could only be unhappy; it must be Jackie's selfishness that made her unable to see that.

"It's so *old*," she whispered.

"It *was* the headquarters for the Army of the Potomac during the Civil War, so it's got some history. . . ."

Now that he was home, Jack took his crutches. He moved easily with them, using his powerful shoulders to swing himself up the steps to the front door.

She followed him into the big hallway as he closed the door on Boom-Boom's red, perspiring face. The house was furnished just as she had pictured it, full of antiques that had obviously been chosen by someone who knew and cared a lot about them. She knew nothing about antiques herself, but she was sure that these were the real thing.

She felt a twinge of envy, the familiar shame of coming from the wrong side of the tracks. Most of her adult life had been spent in borrowed rooms or apartments; even when she had finally forced Joe out of his family's house in San Francisco, they had rented a furnished house in Beverly Hills, near San Vicente Boulevard, with lots of bulky furniture in avocado and gold tweed and a Formica wet bar in the living room, pretty nice for North Palm Drive, but a world removed from this.

Every room seemed to have a big stone fireplace; the wide-board floors were covered in expensive Oriental rugs. Everywhere there was evidence of Jackie's pursuit—hunting prints, whips, boots, and hunt caps in the hall, foxes embroidered on cushions, ribbons hanging from beams, silver trophies. She ran her hand over the marble of the hall table. "Is this an old piece?" she asked.

He shrugged. "Eighteenth-century, I think. French. Cost a fortune. Tom Hoving—he's one of Jackie's friends in the art world—says it ought to be in the Metropolitan Museum, or the White House. Well, that's Jackie for you. She has an eye for these things."

"You must be very proud she has such good taste."

"Ah, yes." Something about the way he looked at the living room, with its exquisite pieces, arranged in perfect symmetry, seemed to suggest that he might have preferred furniture you could put your feet up on and didn't have to worry about leaving rings on with your drink.

"Satisfied?" he asked.

"Never, honey. Can we go upstairs?"

He hesitated. "Please," she asked. It was curiosity of the meanest sort, and she despised herself for it, but once she had brought him this far, there was no point in stopping. She could not explain it to herself, this need to *see* with her own eyes how her rival—already she thought of Jackie as that—lived and dressed, where they slept, as if without that intimate knowledge there would always be a part of him that remained hidden from her.

When she was twenty-one, and passionately in love with John Carroll, the actor, she had actually persuaded him to let her move into his house, and for a time she became "best friends" with Lucille, his wife, until she asked Lucille if she wouldn't mind divorcing John so *she* could marry him—at which point Carroll reluctantly piled her belongings into his station wagon and drove her to a rented apartment on Franklin Avenue. . . .

Was it just a question of wanting to know what she was up against, she wondered, or did it go deeper than that? Was it that she wanted to find out, if she could, *why* the husband was unfaithful?

She followed Jack up the narrow, elegant stairway to the bedroom. He seemed increasingly glum. He sat down on the bed with a groan, while she busied herself in the dressing room, glancing into Jackie's closets.

Oh, how she envied those neat rows of couture clothing, none of which she could have worn, for they were all designed with the kind of skinny, flat-chested women in mind that Joe Eula liked to call "fashion freaks." She couldn't see a single dress with polka dots. She pulled out an evening gown so plain and simple and expensive that she suddenly yearned to be a fashion freak herself. The label read "Oleg Cassini." She took it out to the bedroom and held it up for Jack to see. "How do you think I'd look in this?" she asked.

He lay stretched out with his feet on the silk counterpane—he had not bothered to take his shoes off. "Put it back!" he said sharply, his eyes suddenly cold.

She hung the dress up and went back to the bedroom, kicking off her shoes and reaching behind her to undo her zipper. "Sometimes I do things that aren't very nice," she said. "There's a possibility that I'm not a nice person, you know? The jury's still out."

"Who's on the jury?"

"My therapist. The Slugger." She paused. "You, I guess."

"You get my vote."

She wasn't sure he meant it. "Even after I made you bring me here? I mean, it's an awful thing to do to another woman, isn't it? I'd go crazy if anybody did it to *me*." She leaned over and kissed him on the mouth. "It's not the first time I've done it either. I mean, it's sort of a *habit*, you know? Like shoplifting."

She unzipped his trousers, and went down on him. He gave a groan of pleasure. She looked up at him from between his knees. "Does Jackie do this for you?" she wanted to ask, but there was something in his expression that stopped her. It wasn't that he looked threatening, or that his eyes flashed a warning, or anything like that—it was, instead, a look of infinite sadness that caught her attention, a shadow image of that pessimism she had seen so often in the mirror during her own childhood.

She took him in her mouth again, and slowly, expertly made him come. Oh, she had been taught by real connoisseurs of oral sex, and it was a knowledge that gave her power over men, not to be despised.

She slid up the bed until her head was next to his on the pillow. His eyes were closed, but his expression was not that of a man who has just had one of the great blow jobs of a lifetime. "What's up, honey?" she asked gently.

"Nothing."

She knew that tone of voice, all right. It was the same as the Slugger's when what he meant was, *Shut up and mind your own business!* She reached down and gave Jack's balls a squeeze, not painfully hard but just firm enough to show him who was boss in *this* situation. "Hey," she said, "this is *me!* Remember?"

He grunted, then gave in with a sigh, like any other man forced to talk about the things he didn't want to talk about. "All right. The pain's killing me," he said quietly. "The truth is, I'm going to have to have my back operated on finally, and that scares the shit out of me."

"But honey, lots of people have back operations. . . . I mean, it's not like cancer?"

"It's as bad, in my case. They've got to take out all the crushed bone fragments, repair the disks—if they can—then put in steel pins.

... If I don't have the operation, I'm probably going to be a cripple, certainly in pain for the rest of my life. If I do, I could end up paralyzed. Or dead. It's just my luck, but I happen to have another little problem"—he laughed bitterly—"an adrenal deficiency, which they say could make recovery, ah, impossible."

He closed his eyes, his expression stoic. "The odds stink. My doctor figures they're a lot less than fifty-fifty, and she's the god-damned *optimist!* They want to do it in two stages, but I won't let them. I'd rather get it all over with in one big operation—take my chances and the hell with it."

She wondered how many people knew—if he had even told it to Jackie. She loved him for telling *her*. She pressed close to him, squeezing him in her arms as if his life depended on keeping him next to her. "I'd *die* if anything happened to you, my darling," she said.

He started to laugh, but she smothered his laughter with kisses. "No, I *mean* it," she said. "But nothing's *going* to happen, trust me! It's going to be fine, I can *feel* it, baby. I'm never wrong."

"I believe you," he said.

"You'd *better!*"

She got on top of Jack, let her breasts rub against his face, took him inside her, used all those muscles that it took so much experience in the sack even to find, to squeeze the very last drop of pleasure out of him, then slowly, languorously fucked him in his own bed until the sadness left her.

"If *this* doesn't make your back feel better, sugar," she whispered in his ear as he came, "nothing will!"

6

"It's for you, honey," Amy Greene called from the far end of the big, low-beamed country kitchen.

Marilyn could read the faint note of irritation in Amy's voice over the fact that she tied the phone up for hours and made hundreds of calls a day.

She smiled sweetly at Amy and took the phone. She *liked* Amy well enough, but Amy behaved as if they were sisters, casting herself in the role of Big Sister.

It wasn't clear to her why she had decided to live with Milton and Amy after she'd divorced Joe D. and walked out on Fox. It had tickled her pink to make a double declaration of independence, but once she had done it, her capacity to make decisions seemed to ebb. She hadn't wanted to stay in California, but she couldn't face the problems of finding a place to live in New York.

In times of trouble, she had always sought refuge by moving in with somebody else's family, and the Greenes had been the logical choice. Milton, she had to confess, had come through so far: he'd made arrangements with Buddy Adler for her to star as Cherie in the movie version of Bill Inge's *Bus Stop,* with Josh Logan as the director, and even more surprisingly, he was negotiating a deal for her to star with Laurence Olivier, of all people, in *The Prince and the Showgirl.* She had mixed feelings about working with Olivier, but no more mixed than her feelings about Arthur Miller.

In the past months, her friendship with Arthur had ripened into a sort of love affair, despite what was going on between her and Jack. With Arthur, she felt like a college girl whose professor has fallen in love with her—a novel feeling for her.

With a fatal passivity that she was unable to prevent, she went along with Arthur's intention to marry her as if she shared it. Events were moving so quickly they left her dizzy: first her divorce, which, while it was amicable enough—Joe, despite his pain and anger, had been the perfect gentleman—turned into an excruciating media circus like everything else in her life; then the romance with Arthur, which was proceeding at breakneck speed. She had tried to slow it down by telling him that she couldn't even *begin* to think seriously about marriage as long as he was still married, but then he walked out on his family, horrifying his friends—and her too, to tell the truth.

She picked up the phone. There was no privacy in the Greene household, but she didn't really mind. She liked the fact that the whole house revolved around *her,* a kind of instant family, surrounding her with its warmth and protection.

"Ah, am I speaking to Marilyn Monroe?" The voice startled her. It was like Jack's, with the same nasal Boston Irish quality, overlaid with long Harvard vowels, and somewhere deep in the background a certain clipped quality that was unmistakably upper-class, except that this voice was higher than Jack's, with a rapid-fire, Bugs Bunny tempo to it.

She was startled, first of all, because she had been expecting a call from Arthur, then because she thought that Jack might be playing a joke on her, and jokes always made her anxious because she seldom "got" them. Then, too, there was the small problem that she had never told Arthur about Jack, which made her nervous. Arthur had urged that they be completely frank with each other about their pasts, but the truth was, his was on the dull side, and as hers was anything but, she had edited out most of it, including Jack.

"Jack?" she asked in a whisper, since Amy was standing right next to her.

"No. This is, ah, *Robert* Kennedy. Bobby. Jack's brother."

"Oh, gosh! Jack has told me so much about you. I mean, it's almost like we've met, you know? How *is* Jack?"

"Well, that's, ah, why I'm calling." Bobby Kennedy's voice was cautious. She could sense endless layers of Irish-Catholic disapproval behind the stilted politeness. What was it Jack had once said? "Bobby is the best hater I know." He had said it with a politician's appreciation of a useful virtue in a brother, but it had chilled her then, and perhaps as a result, she felt chilled now. "He's in the hospital, you know," Bobby said.

"I know." Jack had entered the Hospital for Special Surgery in New York for his back operation, which was reported to have been a success. She had sent him flowers, with her initials and her telephone number in Connecticut on the card, and was more than a little pissed off that she hadn't heard back from him yet. "How is he?"

"Not too good, frankly." There was a pause. "The truth is, he might not make it." Bobby could not conceal the emotion in his voice.

"Might not *make* it? You can't mean he's going to die!"

"I'm sorry, but that's exactly what I do mean, Miss Monroe."

"Marilyn, please." She shut her eyes, remembering Jack when she had seen him last, his handsome face below hers as he lay back on the bed. There was enough Christian Science left in her to believe that putting yourself in the hands of doctors was a form of weakness and lack of faith. "Is there anything I can do?" she asked.

Bobby cleared his throat. "Well, yes, I think so. Jack's spirits are really the problem, as much as anything else. I mean, the goddamned operation was a bust, and now he's got an infection they can't cure, and a hole in his back as big as a goddamned fist." He said "goddamned" exactly the way Jack did. There was a tremor in his voice now, as if he was about to cry. "He's pretty well played out," he said. "It's the first time I've ever seen Jack without hope. . . . That's why it's so important to cheer him up."

"How am I going to cheer him up, Bobby?" It was the first time she had used his name, and it made her feel part of the family.

"Ah," Bobby said, "I've already thought of a way."

When he explained, she burst out laughing.

She hung up the telephone. "Well, Miss Goldilocks," Amy said with a knowing wink. "And how's Arthur today?"

———

She entered the Hospital for Special Surgery with a scarf over her hair, dark glasses, and a belted raincoat.

Bobby and Boom-Boom were waiting in the lobby, Boom-Boom for once looking glad to see her. Bobby, for all his fearsome reputation and many children (four? she wondered, or was it already five?), looked like a shy teenager in a suit with pants that were too short for him, and a button-down shirt with a collar so big it made his neck seem scrawny. When she got closer to him, she could see that he was built like a bantamweight fighter, with a wiry toughness you couldn't miss. He wasn't as handsome as Jack, or as polished, but with his pale blue eyes, his sandy hair and trademark smile, he had a star quality of his own. He shook her hand firmly. "We've got the room next to Jack's for you," he said. "Everything's there." He ushered her into the elevator. "It's great of you to do this. You're a good sport."

"Nobody ever called me *that* before!"

He blushed, looking younger than ever. "Well, I meant it as a compliment, you know."

"How is he?"

He shook his head. A veil of sadness darkened his eyes. "The same." He sighed. "Father was here earlier today, but he didn't stay. He can't bear to see Jack like this. Not sick, I mean, but *defeated*. Father doesn't believe in failure or defeat, do you see?"

"Sort of. My granny was Christian Scientist. My mom too. *They* didn't believe in illness."

"Did it work for them?"

"No," she said curtly.

They left the elevator in silence. Bobby led her down the corridor and opened a door for her. She felt frightened and trapped, and fought to conceal it from him. She hated hospitals, loathed the strange smells and the presence of sickness and death.

The empty hospital room did nothing to ease her terror. On the bed her "costume" was laid out neatly—a nurse's uniform and cap, white shoes and stockings, all in the correct size. She had given the information to Bobby's secretary, who hadn't seemed at all surprised at being sent out to buy a nurse's uniform for Marilyn Monroe: apparently the Kennedy organization was trained to produce anything. She slipped behind a cloth screen, wiggled out of her clothes, and put on the uniform. It fit perfectly. She stepped out, shook her hair loose, and pinned on the cap. "Okay?"

Bobby grinned. It made him look a lot less forbidding, even suggested he might have some portion of Jack's charm. "If this doesn't make Jack smile, he's a goner for sure. Ready?"

"Not yet." She took her makeup out of her handbag and went to the mirror. She was Marilyn Monroe, after all, and this was a performance.

"You promise Jackie isn't going to turn up while I'm in there?" she asked.

"No way."

"Let's go, then," she said.

They walked into the corridor. Boom-Boom gave a thumbs-up

sign, indicating that there were no real nurses or doctors in sight. "You're on," Bobby said.

Nurse! she told herself. She knew she could play one if she put her mind to it. She rapped her knuckles against the door firmly—a nurse wouldn't have a hesitant knock; a nurse would know she *belonged* here, that *she* was in charge of things. She opened the door briskly, walked in, and suddenly gasped. "Oh my God, Jack!" she cried, stepping out of character. "What have they *done* to you?"

He didn't seem to hear. He was lying on his back in a maze of wires, pulleys, and counterweights, a cervical collar holding his head immobile. His face was so thin she could hardly recognize him. His skin, which was usually tanned, was an almost transparent white, stretched tightly over his bones. His hair was damp and matted, his cheeks deeply etched with lines of pain. Even his hands, folded over the hospital sheet on his chest, looked fragile and withered, like an old man's. Despite all the flowers, there was a smell of stale sweat and antiseptics, and the sickly sweet stench of an infected open wound.

Suddenly the joke no longer seemed funny, like a frat house prank that has somehow led to tragedy, leaving the jokers standing around looking shamefaced and guilty. She felt foolish in the face of his suffering, and helpless.

She started to cry, which wasn't in the script at all, the tears dropping onto the bosom of her starched white dress. She stood there for what felt like a long time, watching the dying man—for it was impossible for her to think of Jack as anything else. She loved him, she was sure of it, and because she loved him he would die, like everyone she loved.

She realized that Jack had opened his eyes. He stared at her as if he couldn't make sense of what he was seeing. At first his eyes seemed opaque, expressionless, dead, but very gradually they took on life again, the bright color returning. He was crying too—from pain, she thought, but then she saw they were tears of laughter: he smiled, as if it was unimaginably hard to do; the smile broadened, turned into the familiar grin, and with that, his face seemed to shed the marks of pain, defeat, and fear she had seen there. "Jesus!" he gasped through his laughter. "Whose idea was this?"

"Bobby's."

"Son of a bitch! There's hope for him yet! How did he get you in here?"

"How did *you* get into the Hay-Adams?"

"Ha!" He shook his head cautiously and winced with pain. "Well, I'm glad you're here."

He studied her carefully, still laughing silently, and winked. "You'd make a hell of a nurse, you know. You could bring Lazarus back to life, with a hard-on."

"Forget Lazarus. How about *you?*"

"It's been terrible. Still is. The goddamned doctors screwed up. The pain's bad too—worse than it was in the navy hospital, during the war, and I didn't think anything could be worse than that."

"Can't they give you anything?"

"They did. It didn't help a lot. They're not giving me much now. Father told the doctor, 'Don't give Jack too much for the pain—it's something he has to go through by himself.' " He grimaced, but she couldn't help noticing that he seemed to feel his father had been right.

"Sit down," he said, casting a glance at the chair beside his bed. "How's *your* life?"

"I'm sort of engaged."

"To?"

"Arthur Miller."

"I'd heard something about that. Congratulations are in order?"

"Maybe."

"That doesn't sound very enthusiastic."

"Oh, he's a wonderful man!" she cried out, as if she wanted to convince herself. "Really! He's such a *brain!* And so serious—*concerned,* I mean. I'm a lucky girl."

"I'm happy for you."

"Well, it's sure going to be different from being married to the Slugger, I guess."

"I would say." He closed his eyes. "If I ever get on my feet again —no thanks to the fucking doctors—let's go away someplace together. I'm going to think of that every time I get depressed here."

"Whenever, Jack. Wherever you like. Always, my darling."

"Even though you're a married lady?"

"I was a married lady before, remember?"

He smiled wearily, obviously tiring now. "Can you give me something to drink?"

She filled a glass with iced water and held the curved straw to his lips, just the way she had seen it done in the movies. He drank briefly. She put the glass back on the bed table. There was a small towel beside the Thermos; she dampened it with cold water and began to rub his brow and cheeks with it gently. He groaned quietly with satisfaction and grasped her free hand.

His breathing was soft and regular, and he was clearly falling asleep. He mumbled something in a groggy voice. She leaned close to his lips. "I love you," she thought she heard him mutter; then he was silent. She wondered if he had really said it, or she had just imagined it.

She sat there, wiping his face, her hand in his, until Bobby opened the door, worried no doubt about what had happened, and found her there in the twilight, tears streaming down her face.

———

"The Ambassador wants you to call him in Florida," Maria said as I entered her dressing room. She was getting ready for dinner, doing her face at her makeup table in her slip, a martini and a cigarette at her elbow. She did not turn around or look up from the mirror. That's marriage for you.

It was a shame, I thought, because she was a very beautiful woman, but we had long since reached that stage of marriage where sex seems likely to make things worse rather than better. A few years ago, I would have put my arms around her and made love to her on the dressing room floor—or at any rate felt tempted to—but I knew if I even leaned down to kiss her, she would only say, "*Don't,* darling, please, you'll smear my makeup and I'll have to start all over again—then we'll be late."

Of course, we were going out. I do not think I can remember our ever spending an evening at home, unless we were entertaining. Certainly that's part of my profession—being out in the world—in addition to which Maria was, in every sense of the phrase, a *femme du monde,* for whom an evening at home was an evening wasted. Still, I couldn't help thinking one of the reasons we were out every night was so as not to be alone with each other, as well as to make sure that by the time we got home, we were too tired to do anything more than take a sleeping pill and fall into bed. . . .

"Did he say what was on his mind?" I asked.

"Jack. What else?" She wasn't annoyed. Maria adored not only Jack but also his father, who flirted with her outrageously. "He sounded upset."

I went into the living room, poured myself a martini from the iced shaker, and dialed Joe Kennedy's unlisted number in Palm Beach.

He picked up on the first ring. "Where the hell have you been?" he growled.

"Creeping home from the office in rush hour traffic, Joe," I said. "What can I do for you?"

"I'm not complaining, mind you," he said. "I'd a lot rather talk to Maria than you. She's prettier and she knows more gossip."

Both of these things were true. Maria knew everything that was happening among the rich, the famous, and the notorious, and spent a good deal of time keeping Joe informed. "I can put her back on the line if you like," I said.

He laughed. "No, it's you I need, worse luck. The two of you are going to the Cassini party?"

"Yes."

"That son of a bitch sleeps with more beautiful women than Jack! And he's only a fucking dress designer!"

"That's probably one of the reasons they sleep with him, don't you think? Women will do anything for a man who can make them look good."

"I guess so. . . . Listen, have you seen all this crap about Jack? The papers are treating him as if he's *dying!*" His voice rose. *"They're writing my boy off!"*

It was true enough. The press had picked up on the seriousness of Jack's condition despite my efforts to gloss it over as a routine operation.

"I've told them it isn't true—"

"Fuck that! I want it *stopped,* do you hear me? What are you going to *do* about it?"

I could tell from the pitch of Joe's voice that he was about to go into one of his rages, which, while they didn't frighten me, didn't do *him* any good. "I'll think of something," I soothed. "He needs to get his teeth into something as soon as he can—a big issue, something that puts him in the public eye. . . ." I thought hard, grasping for an idea that would pacify Joe. "In the meantime, it wouldn't be a bad idea for him to write a book," I suggested.

"A book?"

Joe was silent for a moment. He had a great respect for books, though none at all for writers. He had discovered years ago that people paid attention to books, which was why he had gone to such lengths to get Jack's little book on England rewritten and published. "Having a book with his name on it will do young Jack a world of good," he had told me then, and he had been right. Even Eleanor

Roosevelt, whom Joe hated—a feeling he had passed on to Jack—had praised it. "What about?" he asked suspiciously.

"Maybe something inspirational. People who have overcome great handicaps and succeeded. DeWitt Wallace would love it—the *Reader's Digest* would run it for sure."

"No cripples!" Joe barked.

"What?"

"No *physical* handicaps. Nothing about FDR and his fucking wheelchair. We don't want readers thinking that Jack's writing about cripples because *he's* a cripple, don't you see?"

I saw. As usual Joe, in his blunt way, had a point. "Courage," I said. "That's what he should be writing about. People who stood up to be counted, and changed American history by doing so." It sounded like a blurb, I realized, but that was a hazard of the profession.

"Yes. I like it, David. Find him a publisher. That fellow, what's his name, Sorensen? The speechwriter Jack likes so much? He could write the goddamn thing for Jack, now couldn't he? So long as he doesn't put a goddamn liberal twist on it."

"He'll need to write it in a hurry."

"Well, tell him to get cracking," Joe said crisply, with the confidence of a man who was used to buying writers and telling them what to do without taking any crap from them. His friend Jack Warner had once said, talking of screenwriters, "Writers are schmucks with typewriters, a dime a dozen," and Joe took the same view.

"I'll make the arrangements," I said.

"Good. No need to tell Jack yet." He sounded more relaxed now that we had a plan. "I hear Marilyn Monroe visited him in the hospital there, disguised as a nurse!" He laughed.

I hadn't heard that, and it startled me. "Jesus," I said, "that's risky."

But Joe gave a snort of contempt. The Kennedys would take any risk when it came to women, and Joe was proud of it. "Lay off, David," he said. "Let the boy have his fun."

He paused. "It can't do any harm."

7

"Well, *my* hat's off to her. She brought our Jack round sooner than all the rest of us combined."

We were sitting by the pool of the Kennedy mansion in Palm Beach—the Ambassador, Bobby, and myself—after breakfast. Bobby was wearing a baggy pair of swim trunks, his hair wet and tousled from his first ocean swim of the day. Joe was dressed for his morning golf game, in the kind of white plus fours that had been fashionable before the war, with tartan socks and a cashmere pullover. Neither Bobby nor I had wanted to join Joe in a "strategy session," as it pleased him to call his morning grouse at the world, but we weren't in a position to argue the point. Joe had brought me down here to discuss Jack's future now that he was out of the hospital.

"Marilyn certainly brought him round," Bobby agreed. "But he's still pretty bad, you've got to face it."

"I don't have to face a damned thing, Bobby. Jack's on his feet now."

"He's on crutches," Bobby said, always the realist. "So far as anybody knows, he'll *always* be on crutches."

"He's alive. He's out of the hospital. If he has to be operated on again, he'll be operated on."

"I don't know if he can take another one."

"He's my son. He can take one if he has to. He's going to recover, Bobby. I don't want to hear any more pessimistic bullshit in my house. Not from you, not from anyone. What do you think, David?"

"I thought it was a mistake to try and do it all in one operation,"

I said. "So did the doctors. They let Jack talk them into it, and so did you. Don't let him be his own doctor next time."

Joe chuckled indulgently. "Jack always was the one who could charm the birds off the trees. He charmed the doctors, sure—and the nurses, too." He grinned wickedly. "I guess he's charmed Marilyn Monroe, all right."

"I guess he has," I said. The more I heard about her escapade in Jack's hospital room, the more I shuddered at the public relations problem it could have caused. Bobby and I had clashed about it, but he had been unrepentant, as usual. Everything Bobby did had to be right, even if he had to twist the facts to make it so.

"I hear she's marrying this kike playwright?" Joe said. "The one who's a pinko?"

Bobby and I exchanged looks. Bobby was too much in awe of his father to confront him about things like this, which he hated. As I was the only "kike" around, I suppose it was incumbent on me to object, but I had long since accepted that kind of thing as part of the Ambassador's vocabulary—he had once referred to his old friend Cardinal Leahy of Boston, during some dispute, as "a bog-stupid, lace-curtain Mick," and to Bernie Baruch as "FDR's ambassador to the Elders of Zion."

I didn't take it personally. Joe Kennedy was simply of a generation of American men that felt no embarrassment in calling a Jew a kike, a black person a nigger, or—which said it all in Joe's case—an Irishman a Mick. I was of the generation of American Jews that took for granted Otto Kahn's dictum that "a kike is a Jewish gentleman who has just left the room," so such things did not weigh as heavily on me as they did on Bobby, who was smoldering with impotent anger in his deck chair.

I knew that the Ambassador had probably said it just to get Bobby's goat, to pay him back for his pessimism about Jack's recovery —he was like that with his children. The only exception he made was with Jack, because Jack was going to run for the presidency and therefore, in Joe's view of things, had to be kept innocent of any taint of old-fashioned bigotry, even at home. In fact, Jack *was* unbigoted, largely because he took people as they were. What mattered to Jack was beauty, talent, and wit, not race or color.

"I can't see why she'd want to marry a fellow like that," Joe went on, warming to his theme. I guessed that the notion of Miller's being a "pinko" aggravated the Old Man more than the fact that he was Jewish.

"Maybe she's in love with him," Bobby said.

"She's in love with *Jack!*" he snapped back. "Or so I've been led to believe."

We sat for a few moments in silence while Joe contemplated human frailty—his only form of soul-searching, so far as I knew—and Bobby quietly seethed. Joe glanced at his watch. "Where the hell's Jack?" he asked.

"He probably had a bad night," Bobby said.

"Christ, it's nearly nine-thirty!" The Ambassador not only believed in early rising but was so insistent on punctuality that he had electric clocks in every room in his houses synchronized centrally, so nobody would have an excuse for being late.

Bobby shook his head. He did not often rebel against his father, but when it came to Jack, he was like a ferocious but faithful watchdog. "Let him sleep," he said gently.

"You're not doing Jack any favors by being soft on him, Bobby. He's not going to get better feeling sorry for himself."

"He needs time. He's *got* time. He's got a year before he needs to be in fighting shape."

"I told you before, Bobby. 'Fifty-six isn't going to be Jack's year."

"I know that," Bobby said impatiently. "But he's going to look like an amateur if he goes to the convention without control of the Massachusetts delegation. You know what people like McCormack are calling him? 'The playboy senator,' for God's sake!"

Joe's eyes were invisible behind his old-fashioned round tortoiseshell sunglasses, but his face flushed. Congressman John McCormack was one of his enemies. *"Fuck* McCormack!" he snarled. "Who gives a shit what he says?"

"Plenty of people in Massachusetts."

"Horseshit! I know what you want to do, Bobby, and I'm not having it, do you hear me? You're trying to get Jack tied up in a fight up there in Boston with a bunch of political bums and hacks like 'Onions' Burke and Freddy Blip. For Christ sake, can't you get it through your head he's running for president, not for alderman?"

I could see that he was dying to drag me into the argument, but I was saved by the appearance of Jack, hobbling out of the house on his crutches at last, in white shorts and an old tennis shirt, looking as thin as a Giacometti sculpture.

Jack eased himself gingerly into his chair—it had been specially made for him, with a straight wooden back and a flat seat—and stared blankly out to sea, as if it seemed so far away that he would never get there again, or swim in it.

"Did I hear the name Onions Burke taken in vain?" he asked, grinning weakly.

"I was just setting Bobby straight," the Ambassador said. He changed subjects quickly. "How's Jackie?"

Jack shrugged. "Sleeping late," he said curtly.

Jackie slept late whenever she was in Palm Beach or Hyannis, or stayed in her room "resting" in the afternoons, and it was tactfully recognized that this was her way of avoiding the rough games of the Kennedys, the fierce, competitive kidding of Jack's sisters and Ethel, the remote, chilling haughtiness of Rose Kennedy, and the Ambassador's energetic coarseness and heavy-handed inquisitions about pregnancy. Jackie, like me, wasn't afraid of the Old Man, which perhaps explains why he showed more respect for her than for anyone else around him, but she wasn't charmed by him either. She knew exactly how to handle him—hardly surprising, for in many ways he must have seemed like her own father, "Black Jack" Bouvier, except that Black Jack had a lot more charm and no gift for making money or even keeping it.

Joe made savage fun of Jackie's social pretensions, but never to her face. I think he felt that so long as she didn't make a fuss about Jack's women and produced an heir for him, Jack had made a pretty good choice in marrying her. Her discretion—in public, anyway—about Jack's affairs was beyond reproach, and not even Joe could complain that she wasn't doing her best to have a baby.

Jack gave Bobby a cold, hard, big brother's stare, indicating, I guessed, that Bobby should have kept his mouth shut. "Well," he said, "I'm not planning to get myself into a pissing match up there in Massachusetts."

"Goddamned right you're not!" Joe glanced at his watch. "I've said my piece. I guess I can watch from the sidelines while Jack takes on Onions Burke and Bobby takes on organized labor."

Bobby stared grimly at his father. "I'm not doing any such thing."

"I hear things, you know. I'm not out of touch. This fellow Mollenhoff's been filling your ears with fairy stories about the Teamsters."

"Maybe," Bobby conceded grudgingly.

"Mollenhoff's a bleeding heart. I'll tell you one thing about the Teamsters—they don't have any goddamned Reds in their union. And the Teamsters did more to get FDR reelected in '44 than the rest of the AFL and the CIO put together. He gave his Fala speech at their convention, you know. . . ."

Bobby knew and didn't care. "They're racketeers now," he snapped.

The Ambassador looked at me pleadingly. I shrugged. That the Teamsters were racketeers and worse, I knew. Beck was corrupt, vain, and pompous, ripe, I guessed, for the plucking, for his egomania and greed had long since made him careless. Hoffa was a different kind of man altogether, vicious, built like one of the Mack trucks his members drove, shrewd, gifted with a capacity for hatred that more than matched Bobby's. "Oh, the Teamsters are corrupt enough, all right," I said. "No doubt about that. I imagine people like George Meany will be happy to see them in the spotlight, whatever they say about union solidarity."

"You've thought it all out, have you?" Joe asked sarcastically.

"It's a good issue," Jack said. He sounded weary.

"Jack's going to get great mileage out of attacking Dave Beck," I went on. "Bobby too." The Ambassador gave me a look that said, *I've heard* that *before,* but I knew that at heart he didn't much care who Jack went after, so long as he went after *someone.* It was action and headlines he wanted just now—proof that Jack was alive and well. He set some store by my instincts, and a lot more by Bobby's, despite their argument about whether or not Jack should fight for control of the Massachusetts Democratic machine.

"God knows Beck's a big, fat target," Joe said, turning the idea over in his mind. "He'll fight back, though. This Hoffer fellow too."

Bobby didn't correct his father about Hoffa's name. "Let 'em," he said. "They don't know what a fight is yet."

"Mm." Joe looked sharply at Jack—a look that, from long experience, I could interpret as a warning to make sure Bobby didn't go too far. Ill as he was, Jack caught it and nodded.

Joe got up with a sigh. "So be it," he said. "On your head be it," he added, without indicating which one of us he meant. "I'm going to play golf." He walked toward the gate, where his car waited for him. "I'll probably have lunch at the club," he said. "Don't wait for me."

We sat silently for a few moments. Joe's departure always caused a kind of vacuum. "Lunch at the club," Jack said derisively. "He's got a girlfriend in Palm Beach. That's where he's going, after his game."

"Really?" I asked. "Who?" Bobby, I noticed, seemed to have gone into some kind of trance, his cheeks red with embarrassment. He idolized his father, and never cared to hear about the Ambassador's human failings.

Jack was more of a realist about such things. "She's a buxom blonde-from-the-bottle, on the right side of forty, with a nice secluded little house just past The Breakers. I believe she's, ah, separated from her husband. Good-looking lady, by the way. If she weren't fucking Dad, I wouldn't say no myself. . . . We should all be doing as well when we're sixty-seven."

He looked moody. He was housebound here at Palm Beach, with Jackie at his side most of the day. She had him to herself for once, and it was this enforced monogamy, I suspect, as much as anything, that got him started on writing his book, *Profiles in Courage,* which he worked at every day, taking the research and rough drafts done for him by Ted Sorensen and transforming them into his own prose. He turned to Bobby. "Dad's right," he said. "Beck will fight, you know."

Bobby looked mulish—a look that nobody did better. "Let him. He's scum. A bully who's sold out his own people to gangsters."

"Yes, you're right. But he's a tough nut to crack."

"I like tough nuts."

Jack smiled. He knew better than anybody how gutsy Bobby was, and what a mistake people made when they underrated him. "Well," he said after a pause, "if you're going to crack anybody's, I guess they may as well be Dave Beck's. Or Hoffa's."

Bobby rose and went into the house looking like a schoolboy, leaving the two of us together to listen to the sound of the lawn sprinklers. "What do you think, David?" Jack asked. "Just between us. I mean, you steered me onto the Teamsters in the first place."

"I warned you they were dangerous too. You don't get something for nothing."

"Spare me the wisdom, David. Exactly how dangerous *are* they?"

"I don't think they'd do anything to a United States senator, if that's what you're asking. Or his brother."

Looking back on it, I suppose I was naive, but so were we all then. It was a mistake, too, to have challenged Jack's courage. He stuck his chin out and his jaw muscles clenched automatically.

"I'm not afraid of Beck, or Hoffa, or their friends, David. Get *that* straight right away."

"I'm not suggesting you are."

"That doesn't mean I don't worry about where all this might lead.

I mean, here you've got this fellow Mollenhoff giving Bobby chapter and verse on every crime the Teamsters have committed, and now Bobby's worked up a real head of steam about it. . . . Maybe it's the issue I'm looking for, but what's the bottom line? Do we go after Beck? Do we go after Hoffa? What do we do about the mob guys? I want to know where we're headed before we haul anchor."

Jack had guts, but he was no fool. Bobby was the righteous crusader—Jack merely wanted to look good in the headlines, and for that he needed a goal, something that would allow him to announce that the good guys, i.e., the Kennedy brothers, had won.

"Put Beck behind bars," I said. "Do that and you're a hero to the public, to the AFL-CIO, and to George Meany. Get your name on some serious labor reform legislation while you're at it, and you can go to the '56 convention looking like a major contender for the vice presidency."

"I don't want to be vice president, for Christ's sake."

"Fine. Then turn it down when it's offered to you. That's even better."

He stared out toward the far horizon, looking thoughtful. It was an appealing script, but I could tell he was still suspicious. "Let's say we get Beck," he said. "What about Hoffa? By all accounts he's even worse."

"If you get Beck, you can decide what to do about Hoffa later. Maybe he can be somebody else's problem. Beck's the one who's building a mansion with his union's money. He's a sitting duck for Bobby."

"Mm." Jack still did not look completely reassured. "And the mob?"

I answered him truthfully. "I don't know the answer to that one, Jack."

"Can you find out?"

"Maybe."

"Try. For me. After all, this was your bright idea in the first place. I want a sure thing, David. No loose ends, no surprises. If there's going to be a lot of trouble, we can always do something else. Hell, we've got until '60, right? I want to know *exactly* what we're getting into, okay?"

"Okay. It may not be easy."

"I'll owe you one, David."

I waved my hand. I thought of myself as Jack's friend, as well as a friend of the family. I was willing to do him a favor anytime—God knows, the Ambassador had done *me* a lot of favors in the past. One day, when Jack was president, I might ask him for something in return, but not now. I had always dreamed of being ambassador to the Court of St. James's, like Jack's father, and thought I would make a pretty good one, but now was hardly the time to bring up the subject. Besides, I was sure Jack knew about it. He had the politician's nose for knowing what other men's secret ambitions were without asking.

"Do it discreetly, David," he said. "I don't want Bobby to hear what you're doing."

I suppose it's only fair to add that Jack's request didn't come from out of the blue. The art of public relations, after all, is making people and things look better than they are—if everyone were honest and virtuous, there would be no need for the services of people like myself. Over the years, my clients had included labor union leaders, casinos in Las Vegas and Cuba, big-time entertainers, and racetracks, and it was often necessary to put "a good face," as people are so fond of saying, on rumors of mob involvement or to conceal the fact of it. The mob itself, at its highest level, was concerned with its "image," and anxious to present gangsters as men of honor, respect, and old-fashioned virtue, though they never found a way until Mario Puzo did it for them.

I quickly won the respect of the mobsters I had to deal with from time to time, mostly by keeping my mouth shut when it was necessary, never promising anything I couldn't deliver, and not fawning over them. As a result, I became acquainted in time with many of the major mob figures—among them Luciano, whom I liked; Costello, whom I didn't; Lansky, whom I saw often in Florida (he was the smartest of the lot); and Moe Dalitz in Las Vegas, a real gentleman.

I do not apologize for this. They never asked me to do anything dishonest for them, nor would I have. The dividing line between business and crime is in any case a thin one, and many of the "legitimate" figures I dealt with, or had as clients, like Howard Hughes or J. Paul Getty, seem to me, in retrospect, more corrupt than the bosses of "the Mafia."

My connections in this area were well known to Jack's father, and a source of great curiosity to Jack, who was fascinated by mobsters and ascribed to them powers that went far beyond anything they really had. Joe knew them for what they were—streetwise thugs who preyed on the weak and exploited human weakness; Jack thought they were sinister and glamorous—a mistake I had done nothing to discourage, to my shame and Jack's subsequent misfortune.

"Believe me, Jack," I said, "if there's one thing these fellows understand, it's discretion. I'll see what I can do."

"Good. Thank you, David. You're a real pal."

"One thing, though—if we get involved, they'll want something in return."

He looked at me thoughtfully. "What?"

"I don't know."

"We can't pay them money if it ever comes to that. No way."

"They won't want money. These are straight shooters, in their own way, these big-time mob guys. If they say they'll deliver, whatever it is, they will. But they'll expect the same from you."

"Sure," he said, but I could see that he hadn't really taken my warning seriously. The only person in the world about whom Jack felt any fear at all was his father. And maybe Jackie. I should have borne down harder on him at this point, but he looked so frail and tired that I didn't, and anyway, he changed the subject. It was a fatal error on my part to let him. "Jesus," he said, "but I miss the action. . . ."

"What have you been doing with yourself down here?"

"Apart from going stir-crazy? I'm working on this goddamned book—thanks a lot for *that* bright idea, David! When I've finished it, I'm going to put myself back in the doctors' hands for another fucking operation."

He closed his eyes for a moment as if to shut out the thought of going through all that pain and immobility again, and who could blame him? "Marilyn called me yesterday," he said.

"Here?"

"Luckily, Jackie was swimming."

"How is she?"

"Well, you know Marilyn. Should she marry Miller, or shouldn't she? As if I could tell her. I mean, it's probably a mistake, but then again, most marriages are, don't you think?"

I nodded. I knew his feelings on the subject.

"She wanted to come down here, to, ah, see me."

"A mistake."

"Yes. A nice thought, though. I don't think she was too disappointed when I told her it wouldn't work. She told me all about the Actors Studio, and the fellow who runs it, what's his name?"

"Lee Strasberg."

"Right. She sounded pretty cheerful, as a matter of fact. About her career, anyway. She said she could have me back on my feet again in five minutes! Told me how she'd *do* it too!" He laughed.

I had an instant, white-hot flash of sexual envy, a mental image of those lush white thighs opening for Jack.

He gave me a curious glance. "You think Marilyn's going to be a problem?"

I cleared my throat. As a matter of fact, I did think that Marilyn was almost as dangerous for Jack as Beck and Hoffa were going to be for Bobby. "You know what they say, Jack—never fuck a woman who's got more problems than you do."

For a moment I thought Jack was angry at me, but then he threw his head back and laughed, happier than I had seen him for weeks. "Oh, David," he said, gasping for breath. "They're the only kind worth fucking!"

8

She was trying to concentrate on what Milton was telling her about Larry Olivier, whom she could only think of as Sir *Laurence* Olivier, the greatest actor in the English-speaking world.

Somehow she knew, no matter how rosy a picture Milton painted, that she and Laurence Olivier were not fated to be friends. Milton had screened some of Olivier's films for her, but they merely depressed her even more, since in most of them she could hardly understand a word he said.

She liked the idea of working with Joshua Logan on *Bus Stop,* which she was going to do first, a lot better. Cherie was a role she understood, and at least Logan, whom she had met, spoke the same language and was talked of with some respect at the Studio.

"You didn't tell me Sir Olivier was going to direct the picture himself," she said.

"Not Sir Olivier," Milton corrected her for the umpteenth time. "Sir Laurence. Listen, the whole *point* is that Larry wants to direct. That's how we got him."

"I thought we got him because he needed money."

He rolled his eyes. "That too. He's directed before, lots of times."

"He hasn't directed *me,* Milton. And it's *my* money we're paying him, isn't it?"

There were beads of sweat on Milton's forehead. "Well, ours, yes," he said.

"Mostly mine."

He sighed. "Mostly yours, okay."

"I was just trying to make a point, see? If it's my money, I want to be told everything. And I want things to be done *my* way, not Sir Olivier's. I'm the one who's paying him, after all, and he has to understand that? Right?"

"Right."

"Milton? Are you *sure* he understands?"

"I'll make sure, Marilyn. Don't worry."

But she *did* worry. She was already beginning to resent the way Milton and Amy talked these days about Larry this and Vivien that. It was Milton's job to worry about *her* feelings, not Olivier's, still less Vivien Leigh's, just because Vivien Leigh had played the role of Elsie in *The Prince and the Showgirl* opposite Olivier on stage—the same role she would play in the picture.

"One other thing," she said, staring right in his eyes so he knew she meant business. "I talked to Paula Strasberg about putting her on the payroll."

Milton pretended to look puzzled. "Paula? Strasberg?"

"From the Actors Studio."

"Oh, Lee's wife, sure. Uh, what's she going to *do*, Marilyn?"

"She's going to be my dramatic coach, babykins."

"Uh-huh. What does that *mean*, Marilyn?"

"She goes with me to help me with my performance. Listen, Milton, this is a very big deal. Lee and Paula have never done this before, not for *anyone*, not even Marlon or Monty. I couldn't believe Paula would do it, frankly. I mean, Lee's a *genius,* and Paula's like his interpreter, or disciple, see?" She could see he wasn't enthusiastic. "Paula's a professional," she continued. "She understands me better than I understand myself. If she told me to throw myself out the window, I'd do it and know I could fly."

She stretched out her arms to show what she meant, knocking several prints of herself off the wall. The walls of his workroom were covered with pictures of her, for despite his new role as her partner and producer, Milton still photographed her all the time.

"Uh, that's great," Milton mumbled, with the nervous look of somebody trapped in a small space with a lunatic. "Have you talked all this over with Dr. Kris?"

Marianne Kris was her new analyst. She had been recommended by Lee and Paula Strasberg, who felt that therapy was indispensable for anybody who wanted to understand the Method—a fact that she had neglected to mention to Milton. "Marianne's very supportive," she said curtly. "She's all for the idea."

"You're really planning to take Paula to *England?*"

"You bet your ass, honey. Where I go, Paula goes." She held two fingers together.

"Larry might not like that, you know?"

"So tell Larry who's paying the bills, Milton."

He shrugged. "And if he still doesn't like it?"

"Then tell him to shove it."

There was a long silence while Milton digested this new facet of her personality. "Okay," he said, accepting his fate. "Paula's part of the deal, I guess. How much are we paying her?"

She gave him a hard look. "How much are we paying for the antique furniture you charged to the company?"

He raised an eyebrow and gave her a sad smile.

"Milton, remember this: I may *look* like a dumb blonde, but I'm *not* a dumb blonde."

"Okay." He had once been a street kid from Brooklyn, smaller than all the rest and therefore obliged to be tougher. He knew all the angles, Milton did, but he also knew when he was beaten. "I'll make the arrangements with Paula," he said.

"I want it done right away, before I go back to LA. I want Paula on *Bus Stop.*" She looked him firmly in the eye. "Be generous, Milton," she said.

"*Vey iz mir.*"

"You bet." She looked at the clock and squealed—she seldom wore a watch because watches, however expensive, had a way of stopping dead the moment she put them on, as if there were some kind of magnetic force in her that jammed the movement. "I've got to run," she cried. "I'm going to be late."

"Late for what?"

She hesitated, on the verge of saying that she was going to meet Jack at the Carlyle. "Late for a hair appointment, in town," she said, wishing she were better at telling lies. "I've got to change. It's nearly two. Can I borrow your car?"

"Be my guest."

She laughed as she opened the door. "Milton, honey, I *am* your guest."

9

If you don't gamble, there's not much to do in Las Vegas, but I wasn't there for amusement. I was there to pump Moe Dalitz, on Jack's behalf.

Morris "Moe" Dalitz had made his mark and his money in the old Detroit "Purple Gang" during Prohibition, and had had the good sense to make a deal with the rising Sicilian mobsters instead of fighting them, unlike most of the other Jewish gangsters.

Way back then, Moe got some of his liquor from certain distilleries across the border in Canada that were owned, at arm's length, by Joe Kennedy, so when Moe moved to the warmer climate of the West Coast, about the same time that Joe took over RKO at a few pennies on the dollar, it was only natural that the two newcomers from the East would do each other a quiet favor occasionally, in which I was the go-between. Moe could intercede with Willie Bioff to ensure labor peace on the RKO lot, while Joe could make sure that his old pal William Randolph Hearst kept Moe Dalitz's name out of the papers.

In the end, Moe did better on the West Coast than Joe did and went on to become one of the founding fathers of Las Vegas. Unlike most of his fellow mobsters, he was a rich man with money of his own to invest. He had been the only major gang leader to boldly declare to the IRS his earnings as a bootlegger during Prohibition, shrewdly calculating that if he paid taxes on the profit from his illegal business, the government wouldn't send him to prison for doing it. He built the Desert Inn and swiftly became the dean of casino owners —"Mr. Las Vegas," as the local press called him. It was Moe who made the city build sidewalks (despite the opposition of his fellow casino owners, who didn't see any reason to encourage gamblers to walk outside), Moe who built, despite ridicule, the first golf course, arguing that the casinos had to become "more than just a few guys upstairs in a hotel room playing poker."

And it was Moe who put on the first floor show and brought in the big-name stars to add glamour to the simple business of giving people an air-conditioned place in which to lose their money. In the process, he became a kind of bridge between the new breed of gangsters back in Chicago and the Midwest—men like Tony Accardo, who had inherited Al Capone's empire, or Sam Giancana, who, after much bloodletting, succeeded Accardo—and the big entertainers, bankers, and politicians without whom the business couldn't grow.

Moe was no "dese, dem, and dose" hoodlum with a pinkie ring. He was a solid, handsome man in his fifties, with brooding, sensitive eyes, sharp features like those of Dick Tracy in profile, faultless conservative tailoring, and the fingers of a concert pianist. It was said that he had once strangled a man with those fingers in the storeroom of a bar and grill in suburban Detroit, but that was many decades ago, and most of the more prominent business figures in Vegas had done such things in their time. Some were still doing them.

He was waiting for me in the center banquette of the restaurant in the Desert Inn, to which I was ushered by the maître d', whose manner was that of a cardinal presenting a distinguished visitor to the pope. He offered me a dark red, gold-tasseled dinner menu the size of the *The New York Times* as I sat down, but Moe waved it away. "The chef knows what we're having, Frankie," Moe said. He was so soft-spoken that you had to listen hard to hear what he was saying. "Are they treating you right, David?" he asked.

"Fine," I said. Las Vegas had not yet reached the peak of vulgarity for which it was to become famous, but it was still plenty lush. I had a vast suite overlooking the desert, with a marble bathroom, a bed big enough for a Roman orgy, and fruit, champagne, and flowers as far as the eye could see.

"It's comped," Moe said. "I set up a tab for you too, in case you want to play."

"You didn't have to do all that."

"*Mi casa, su casa,* as they say out here, David. Enjoy." Lying on its side in a silver wine rack on the table was a bottle of Haut-Brion '47 uncorked and breathing—a favorite of mine, as Moe knew. He had become a wine connoisseur late in life, and even managed to hire the sommelier from Le Pavillon in New York away from Henri Soulé to look after his treasures.

He poured us both a glass, sniffed the bouquet approvingly, tasted it with satisfaction, then toasted me. "Life is good, my friend," he said. "And for you?"

"Also good."

"I hear your business prospers."

"I can't complain."

He nodded gravely. Good business was a serious matter, not to be spoken of lightly. "I ordered a simple meal," he said. "I told the chef to make us a Caesar salad, T-bone steaks—the best you ever tasted, take my word—and baked potatoes."

"That sounds perfect, Moe." I meant it too. Steaks are the one thing they know how to cook in Vegas, and Moe knew his meat, having at one point acquired control of the meatcutters union in Cleveland by murdering the opposition.

We chatted, rather circumspectly, about old times while our salad was served. The steaks—as good as Moe had promised—were on the table before he got around to asking what had brought me to Las Vegas.

"I need some information," I said.

Moe's eyes suddenly seemed a lot less soulful. Still, he gave me a nod—permission to continue.

"I need to ask a few questions about the Teamsters."

"The Teamsters?" He shook his head. "What kind of questions?"

I leaned closer. "You know Joe Kennedy's boy Jack?"

"The senator?"

"Right."

He nodded, his eyes very wary now. Moe had first-rate political connections, local and national, and a number of western senators were deeply beholden to him, including, it was rumored, Lyndon Johnson. And Moe had a memory like an elephant's when it came to politics. "What does Jack Kennedy want to know about the Teamsters that his father can't tell him?" Moe asked. "Leave them alone and they might vote for him. He's a Catholic, and so are a lot of them; he's Irish, which is okay too; and he's a war hero, which they like. He's no pinko either, not like this Stevenson character. . . . Hell, the Teamsters *used* to be Democrats."

"I know," I said quickly, before he told me about FDR and Fala too. "But Bobby's going to be chief counsel for the McClellan subcommittee, and Jack's on the committee himself, and all they hear is Beck this and Hoffa that. . . . These guys seem to be surrounded by snitches—"

I caught a look of disapproval on Moe's face. "No names," he whispered.

I apologized. Every profession has its own rules, and in Moe's they mattered more than most. "What I meant to say," I went on, "is that everybody's pointing Bobby in the direction of the Teamsters. Jack's worried. Is there anything there? And how's the leadership going to react to an investigation?"

Moe grimaced. "Anything *there?* What do *you* think? Sure there's stuff there."

Moe had finished his steak. He took a last sip of the wine and called for two espressos. He looked around the room, apparently pleased to see that almost every table was filled with high rollers and the kind of leggy blondes you couldn't help looking at twice. "If Joe's boy is going after the Teamsters, he'd better have balls as big as his father's. Bigger maybe."

"I don't think that's a problem," I said. I was a little chilled. Moe was usually clean-mouthed for a gangster. If he said that Bobby was going to need big balls, he must have meant it seriously.

I felt, for the first time, that I might be plunging into deeper water than Jack had supposed. From the expression on Moe's face I could tell, with a sinking heart, that my interest in the Teamsters wasn't going to be satisfied in an after-dinner conversation between two old friends.

The questions I asked had touched a live nerve. Now I wished I hadn't asked them, but, as we all know (and as Jack had yet to find out), you can't call back words once they are spoken. I should have flown back east on the next plane and told Jack to forget about it— warned him that he was dabbling in dangerous waters, full of man-eating sharks. If I had been with anyone but Moe Dalitz, I would have made my hasty apologies and left, but Moe was a person I really liked, and whose respect I valued, so I stayed.

On reflection decades later, I realize that I had trapped myself— and Jack. By asking questions about the Teamsters, I was stirring up the mob's interest in Jack Kennedy. Even if I had followed my instinct (or my fear) and taken the first flight out of Las Vegas I could get on, they would have come after me eventually, eager to find out what they could do for the junior senator from Massachusetts—and more important, what he could do for *them.*

"You want to know about the Teamsters, there's a guy you ought to meet," Moe said. "He's the man you want, not me."

"Where is he?"

"Here."

"Can you set it up for me?"

"Sure," he said, a little too casually. "Do you play golf?"

"Golf? A little."

"You ought to play more, David. Enjoy life! A young man like you, you shouldn't work so hard. Me, I swim, I play golf. Tennis, when it's not too hot. I wear the same size pants I did when I was twenty." He leaned across the table so close to me that I could feel the warmth of his breath on my face. "The party you should see will want to meet you on the golf course."

"Why?"

A look of mild exasperation crossed Moe's face. "Because he likes to talk to people out in the open, in the fresh air, understand? That way there aren't any hidden mikes or bugs, right?"

"How do I get in touch with him?"

Moe snapped his fingers at the maître d', who brought over two snifters of cognac and warmed them over a burner—something that seems to be part of the culture in Vegas and Miami. Moe took a couple of Montecruz #1 Individuales from his breast pocket and passed me one.

"He'll get in touch with *you*, David," he said. "Don't worry."

————

The voice on the telephone was of the old-fashioned, cement mixer variety, and instructed me to be downstairs in the lobby at ten-thirty next morning, where somebody would be waiting for me.

It didn't take me more than a second to spot the "somebody" standing next to the front desk—a short, pudgy young man in a baggy summer suit, wearing dark glasses and a fedora. He was sweating, despite the fierce air-conditioning. When he turned toward me, I saw the bulge of a small revolver under his coat. That didn't mean much. More people went armed than unarmed within the Las Vegas city limits in those days. Besides, he didn't look like serious muscle—more of the gofer type, I thought. His soft handshake confirmed that impression—soft *and* damp, so unpleasantly, in fact, that it was hard to resist wiping my fingers off on my handkerchief. "Mr. Leman?" he asked in a husky voice with a New York accent.

I nodded.

"You got no clubs?"

"None, I'm afraid." I had no golf clothes either. I wore a pair of gray flannel slacks, loafers, and a shirt with the sleeves rolled up and the collar unbuttoned.

We stepped outside into the blinding heat and glare. He opened the back door of a Cadillac for me, heaved himself into the driver's seat, and turned the air conditioner up to high. "It's a great climate, ain't it?" he asked.

I nodded. He had an irritating voice, whiny and high-pitched. I found the daily newspaper on the seat beside me and picked it up, to show I wasn't interested in conversation.

We drove through the desert for a few minutes, turned into a driveway, and entered Moe Dalitz's famous golf course, a triumph of man over nature. It could only be kept alive in this heat by twenty-four-hour-a-day watering—it was like building an eighteen-hole golf course in the middle of the Sahara. We parked and walked past the clubhouse and out onto the course, where a small, elderly, broad-shouldered man in leisure clothes waited, club in hand.

"Red," my driver said, "here's the guy you wanted."

I knew whom I was seeing now: Paul "Red" Dorfman, the most trusted associate of Sam Giancana and for years head of the Chicago scrap handlers union—a position Dorfman had taken over after its founder and secretary-treasurer was murdered.

Dorfman had been a featherweight champion way back in the twenties, and still carried himself in a boxer's crouch, but I remembered that he had been stripped of his title after he was accused of beating a rival union official unconscious with brass knuckles in the man's own office. The victim refused to make a complaint, of course, so it became just another of the dozens of felonies for which Dorfman had never been indicted, ranging from murder to rigging primary ballots in Cook County, Illinois.

As he swung the golf club back and forth, I couldn't help thinking that it wouldn't take much to make him aim it for my head. The famous red hair was shot with gray now, but his face had the flush of a man who wasn't by any means overjoyed to see me.

"You got no hat?" he growled. "In this sun, you gotta wear a hat." He turned to the man who had picked me up and said, "Go get him one, Jake, from the clubhouse."

He snapped his fingers at one of the caddies, standing carefully out of hearing, who handed me a club. "Play," Dorfman whispered, scanning the horizon. "If there's any FBI surveillance, you and me were playing golf, not standing around talking."

I took a few practice swings to warm up, then hit the ball about fifty yards, off course and into the desert.

Dorfman chuckled. "Try to make it look real, will you?" he said. "I shoulda bet you five bucks a stroke."

I would've liked to have him on the ski slopes with me, I thought, the son of a bitch! Or at the bridge table, except that he would probably have cheated.

"You oughta take some lessons," he said. He hit his ball straight down the fairway, while I asked myself why every mobster in Las Vegas apparently felt entitled to give me a lecture on sports and exercise. Personally, I thought I was in better shape than any of them. Certainly I have outlived them all.

"Great shot, Red!" my driver said, returning from the clubhouse at a trot and gasping like a gaffed fish in the surreal heat.

"Shut the fuck up, Jake. Who asked you? Give the man the hat."

Jake handed me a white one-size-fits-all baseball-style cap with a ventilated mesh top. Embroidered in gold thread on the front of it was the logo of the Teamsters, a wagon wheel surmounted by two horse's heads. Above it was the message: "Tony Pro Invitational Golf Tournament, Las Vegas"; below it, in red capitals: "N.J. TEAMSTER JOINT COUNCIL."

I put it on gingerly as we walked. "Moe says you're asking questions about the Teamsters," Dorfman said. "He says you're good people." He looked me up and down. "You don't look like no good people to me."

I ignored this, took another shot, and flubbed it.

"Putz!" Dorfman said, ever the good sport. He clapped me on the back, hard enough to make me wince. "I'm gonna *kill* you!" The word did not sound good, coming from him.

"Did Moe tell you what I wanted?"

He nodded. "Sure. Look, if the McClellan committee goes after the Teamsters, they're gonna hit pay dirt, they dig hard enough, no point denying *that*. When you're talking Teamsters, you're talking stuff that's hard to explain to civilians, you know what I mean? It's not an ordinary business. Different rules apply, you get my drift?"

I got his drift. Not every senator could be expected to understand the need for murder, extortion, racketeering, and thieving in the labor business. Most of the casinos in Vegas and half the new hotels in Miami Beach had been financed out of the Teamsters' Central States Pension Fund, brokered by Dorfman and his friends, and all the Teamsters' insurance was handled by Dorfman's stepson. Some of this was marginally legal, but even the part that was legal wouldn't look good once it was out in the open, and I strongly suspected that the part that was *illegal* was a bottomless abyss of horrors. "What happens if the committee starts digging hard, Mr. Dorfman?" I asked.

"Call me Red, okay?" He gave me a searching look. "A lot of guys could get mad. Dave Beck. Jimmy Hoffa." He paused. "Me."

"How mad?"

He shrugged. "Depends how far it goes, David. Listen, we're reasonable guys. We all understand how things work. If we gotta take some heat every once in a while, so be it. That comes with the territory, like the man says, am I right? Fine. A few guys get clipped maybe, a few go to the slammer, business gets fucked up for a while, the politicians get themselves reelected, life goes on. *Qué será, será.*" He looked at me. "What will be, will be," he added helpfully, in case I hadn't heard the song.

"Bobby Kennedy might not see it that way. '*Qué será, será*' is not exactly Bobby's philosophy of life."

Dorfman made a shot—another good one. He stared at me. "You want my advice, David, you tell Jack Kennedy and his little brother Bobby not to go too fucking far."

"Bobby's very tough, Red."

"Tough? Don't shit me. He's a college kid."

"Take my word for this, Red: Don't ever think of Bobby as 'a college kid.' He's tough as nails. And he's a Kennedy. He can't be bullied or bought. Neither can Jack."

"Who cares? They can be hit. If it comes to that."

I looked him square in the eye. "I doubt it."

He laughed. "Everybody can be hit, David, believe me." He said it with professional expertise. "Even a president. Hell, FDR nearly got hit in '32—only the mayor of Chicago, that scumbag Cermak, took the bullet instead. Truman almost got hit by those spics, right outside the White House, with the Secret Service all around him! You want somebody hit, my friend, whoever, there's always a way."

It seemed to me that we were getting off on the wrong foot, but I wasn't too worried. I'd heard this kind of bluster before, in the old days in Hollywood, from gangsters like Willie Bioff and Mickey Cohen who were always threatening to blow away people who annoyed them. In my experience, they only killed their own people, as a way of settling jurisdictional disputes, and by the time they settled down in LA or Vegas or Tahoe to enjoy their ill-gotten gains, they were mostly paper tigers, living off their reputation for violence.

"Nobody needs to get hurt," I said. "We're talking politics—and business."

Dorfman was gripping his clubs so hard that the knuckles on his big freckled hands were white. "Red," I went on soothingly, "listen to me, please. The Teamsters have got people leaking like sieves to the McClellan committee's investigators. Bobby can't ignore all that even if he wanted to, and Jack, who's on the committee himself, can't tell his brother to lay off, which he wouldn't do anyway, because it's not the Kennedy family tradition."

Dorfman still looked like a bull about to charge, if you can imagine a bull in tasseled golf shoes. But he was listening, particularly once he heard the word "leaking."

"Leaking like what?" he asked.

"Sieves. You know—those things you wash vegetables in."

"Yeah." Dorfman watched while I missed the ball a couple of times, but he had lost interest in my game. "Fucking stoolies." He sighed. "When I was running the scrap handlers, back in Chicago, nobody fucking leaked, believe you me. Look, if you wanna push the ball with your foot, go ahead, or we're gonna be here all fucking day."

Irritated, I took a wild swing at the ball—so wild that Dorfman jumped back—and sank it. I felt a glow of pride. If the FBI *was* filming us, J. Edgar Hoover, whom I knew and disliked, would at least see my moment of triumph. "Look, Red," I said, emboldened by my unexpected success, "all I'm trying to tell you is that there's going to be trouble—heat. Jack—Senator Kennedy—can't stop that, but he'd like to keep it within reasonable limits."

"We bend over backwards to make Bobby look good, while Jack makes like a labor statesman, that the deal?"

"Well, something like that," I said uncomfortably since it was exactly what Jack had in mind. "It's not a deal, by the way. It's more like a *suggestion*, for you to pass on to the right quarter."

He looked thoughtful. "It might work," he said. "But only if Bobby goes easy on Hoffa. And if Hoffa don't lose his temper at Bobby." He paused to choose his words. "Jimmy blows up easy, frankly. He's got a hell of a fucking temper."

I'd met Hoffa, who had reminded me of a hand grenade with the pin drawn, but I assumed, wrongly, that this was just a pose, one of those little tricks that leaders of men pick up along the way to power. I wondered too why Dorfman was more concerned with Hoffa's sensibilities than with Dave Beck's problems as the Teamsters' leader.

Dorfman moved close to me—closer than I found comfortable. "How about you offer Bobby and Jack a suggestion from *me?* We give you Beck and you leave Hoffa alone." He spoke in a whisper like sandpaper.

I couldn't believe my ears. Dorfman was offering up the president of the International Brotherhood—probably the most powerful union leader in the country—on a silver platter. I guessed that Dorfman and his Teamster pals would have no problem supplying enough documents and witnesses to send Beck to prison for life.

"Why Beck?" I asked.

Dorfman shrugged. "That's none of your goddamned business. Just tell the Kennedys, they want the fat fuck, they can have him, with enough evidence to sink a ship. But that's it, you understand? We'll throw in a few guys to make weight, but we get to choose them. Fair enough?"

It was more than fair—or would have been, if Jack were the only one concerned—but I wasn't so sure that even Jack could make Bobby swallow it. It would mean letting the Hoffa faction in the Teamsters use the McClellan committee to get rid of their own enemies while they went scot-free—exactly the kind of deal that Bobby hated.

Still, there was no question that putting Dave Beck behind bars would be a major coup. Everybody else in the labor movement, from George Meany on down, would be only too happy to see Beck in handcuffs, and grateful to Jack for doing what they didn't have the guts to do themselves.

"I'll pass it on," I said, trying not to show my excitement. "That's all I can say."

"You do that. Now let's play some golf."

———

I did my best, not so much because I wanted to put up a decent game against Dorfman as to get the whole damned thing over with as quickly as possible. It was brutally hot, and Dorfman's company wasn't anything I wanted to prolong now that we'd dealt with the essentials. He must have felt the same way, because he didn't offer me lunch at the club or even a drink, which was okay with me. I was so happy to get into the back of the air-conditioned Cadillac I didn't even notice I was still wearing the cap.

On the drive back to the hotel, the driver tried to be chatty. "He's quite a guy, Red, ain't he?" he said.

I nodded. The face reflected in the rearview mirror was pale, suety, and furtive; the hands on the steering wheel were fat and hairy, with stubby, uncared-for fingers.

"I learned a lot working for him."

Red Dorfman, no doubt, would have told him to "shut the fuck up," but I didn't. "I'm sure," I said curtly.

"You better believe it. He's been like a father to me, Red has."

I doubted that. Dorfman's attitude toward his driver was one of total contempt, so far as I could see.

"I got plans, you know? I'm more interested in the entertainment side of the business"—it came out "dabiznus," as if it were one word —"than the, uh, gaming side. Red's giving me a piece of action in Dallas—nightclubs, that kind of thing."

I guessed that this was probably Dorfman's way of getting rid of an employee who wasn't tough enough to be a bodyguard or serious muscle, or smart enough to handle the games. Pimping in Dallas wasn't my idea of a career advancement, but it clearly was his.

"If you're ever in Texas," he said, leaning back, "look me up, you want anything." He handed me a damp, crumpled pasteboard card that bore a drawing of a gartered woman's leg with a high-heeled pump dangling from the foot, embossed in gold against a brown ten-gallon Stetson. The words "The Golden Stripper" appeared above it in letters of twisted rope printed to look like a lariat.

I put it in my pocket and shook the sweaty hand that was offered to me across the front seat. "Jake Rubenstein, Mr. Leman," he said. "But my friends call me Jack Ruby."

10

The best thing about making *Bus Stop* was that it put the prospect of working with Olivier right out of her mind. Making a movie was never a happy experience for her—*Bus Stop* was no exception—but at least it took her back to California, which, she guessed, was still "home" to her, at some level. . . .

She had been surprised and touched when Josh Logan told her he was going to give her a big party for the completion of the picture, and attributed it to her new status as a star who owned herself and made her own decisions.

Only Logan, a Broadway director, an intellectual, a New Yorker, would have had the balls to ask Bill and Edie Goetz to host the wrap party for *Bus Stop,* a picture that hadn't been made by MGM—or taken everybody's breath away by inviting Sukarno, the president of Indonesia, who happened to be in Los Angeles on his way home from Washington after a frosty meeting with Ike and John Foster Dulles that would shortly place him in the Soviet camp.

Partly because Edie Goetz was "old Hollywood," Louis B. Mayer's daughter, *everybody* came—the crème de la crème, the biggest names and powers in the industry: Sam Goldwyn, Jack Warner, Dore Schary, as well as stars who hadn't even noticed her when she was a starlet—even her idol, Clark Gable.

It was a triumphant evening—her revenge, if you wanted to look at it that way, and she did. She had reached the top. She had the whole industry at her feet, her handprints in cement outside Grauman's Chinese Theater, a bronze star on the sidewalk at Hollywood and Vine, her home on the maps the little old ladies sold to tourists taking the tour of the homes of the stars.

All the same, despite the champagne, she felt a little depressed because she didn't have a date. Loneliness gradually filled her mind, and she retreated from the noise and the press of people to the side of the room, feeling her glow fade. Her new PR girl saw her and pushed through the crowd to her side. "Tyrone Power is here," she said, full of excitement. "He's dying to say hello to you."

She had always admired Tyrone Power more than any other big star except Gable. Normally she would have dropped everything just for the chance of meeting him, but crankiness was rising in her like sap. "The hell with Tyrone Power," she said. "All those years when I was a starlet on the Fox lot and he was a big-deal star, he never tried to fuck me once."

It was the kind of thing that when it was repeated—as it would be—would take on a humorous spin and be quoted as an example of her sense of humor, but she had said it bitterly, and the PR girl, who was no fool, noticed it and looked as if she was wondering what she had gotten herself into.

Before the girl could say anything, Logan pushed his way toward them with a small brown man, in a funny cap and kind of Nehru jacket, in tow. Behind them pressed a whole mob of small brown Orientals, jabbering and hissing. The man next to Josh was clearly their leader.

She had forgotten all about Logan's distinguished foreign guest: it was simply not the kind of thing that interested her. They were face-to-face now, surrounded by the great man's entourage, his body-guards, the Secret Service, reporters, photographers. It was clear that she was expected to do something. She flung her arms around him and gave him a kiss. "I've always wanted to meet the president of India!" she cried.

There was a sudden silence. A look of annoyance crossed the president's face, as if he suspected that he had been made the victim of some devious Western practical joke, played on him, worst of all, by a *woman*.

Logan cleared his throat nervously. "President Sukarno is the president of *Indonesia*, Marilyn," he said.

"I've never heard of it," she said. "But hi anyway, Mr. President."

There was a lot of murmuring, and all of a sudden, as if somebody had waved a magic wand, Sukarno and his people were gone. The look on his face as he turned away told her clearly enough that she had insulted him, and probably Logan as well, for now that she thought of it, he had been excited and honored by the prospect of having Sukarno as his guest and had briefed her carefully on what to say.

Feeling suddenly embarrassed and foolish, she opened a door and stepped into Bill Goetz's study—a large, dark room in the English style, with a lot of bookshelves and antique furniture—to find David Leman examining Goetz's collection of Degas bronzes.

David looked up quickly, as if he'd been caught reading Goetz's mail, and smiled. "Marilyn," he said. "I couldn't get close enough to you to say hello out there."

She gave him a kiss on the cheek. "I just insulted the president of Indonesia," she said. "I guess I've caused a diplomatic incident?"

They sat down on the sofa. He was holding a glass of champagne, which he handed to her. She took a drink and felt a little better.

"I wouldn't worry," he said. "Ike and Dulles already stepped on his corns in Washington. He'll have his people out in the streets burning American flags and stoning the windows of USIA libraries the moment he gets home."

David always had the inside scoop on everything. It was one of the things she liked about him.

"Jack met him in Washington," he went on, "and said all he wanted to know was whether Jack would give him a list of girls he could call when he got to LA."

She giggled. "I guess Jack didn't give him mine."

"I don't suppose he thinks of you as foreign aid. I hear the picture is great, by the way."

She nodded. If David was saying that, it probably reflected the opinion of the studio. He was as well connected in the movie business as he was in politics. All in all, she thought, he was a man she could be interested in, except for the fact that in her mind he was inextricably linked to Jack Kennedy. What the hell, she thought— she and Jack weren't married. She hadn't seen him in months. Anyway, Jack wasn't the kind of person you could possess exclusively any more than she was—that was one of his attractions, or at least she persuaded herself it was, for there was a tiny part of her that believed in old-fashioned, faithful love, and she wanted to believe she was capable of it with the right man, if she ever found him.

In the meantime, here was David, good-looking and clearly lusting after her—there was no mistaking *that*. She felt a sudden softening toward him, a kind of warm, liquid sensation deep inside, maybe just because she was alone and needed a man, or because in the subdued light of the library, he really did look like Gable. She leaned a little closer to him, her bosom almost hanging out of her low-cut dress, her lips parted, interested in a detached sort of way to see what would happen. "What brings *you* to the Coast, David?" she asked, a little more breathlessly than was necessary.

A furtive look crossed his face—she wondered why. "Business," he said. "I have an office here, you know."

"I know. Josh was in awe when I told him I knew you."

He laughed, but she could see he was pleased. How easy it was to flatter men, she thought, especially the smart ones. "I'm just back from Vegas," he said.

"Vegas? I didn't figure you for a gambler? I'm not, but I *like* Vegas. I went there when Frank opened at the Desert Inn. He had a table down front for his friends, and I just couldn't believe it—Liz Taylor, Cyd Charisse, Ava Gardner, and I were all at the same table. There wasn't a woman *there* Frank hadn't fucked!"

She caught the gleam in his eyes. Envy? Pain? *Go for it, David!* she said to herself, her lips only inches from his. She could tell that something was holding him back—perhaps his friendship with Jack, perhaps the fear of being discovered embracing her on the Goetzes' sofa—but that made it more of a challenge. She realized he was glancing toward the door, and it didn't take much to guess why. "Are you here by yourself?" she whispered.

He shook his head. His cheeks were red—was he blushing? "Ah, no," he stammered. "As it happens, Maria is with me."

Maria? She strained to remember who Maria was; then it came back to her. "Your wife!" she said. "She's here?"

He nodded toward the door, as if she were on the other side of it, or about to open it. "She's—ah—circulating. Maria has a lot of friends out here on the Coast."

"She was in Vegas with you?"

He shook his head again. "No, I was there strictly on business. . . . For Jack. . . ." He blushed more deeply this time, obviously regretting that he'd let it slip out. She wondered what kind of business Jack could have in Vegas. Given time, she was pretty sure she could squeeze the answer out of David, right here on the sofa.

There was a part of her that was willing to try. She had always enjoyed sex in unlikely places, the risk of discovery adding its own special excitement. She let her lips actually touch David's, very gently, almost as if by accident. She wondered if he had the guts to fuck her right now, with his wife next door circulating among her West Coast friends.

Focusing all her energy, she *challenged* him to, with an expression he could hardly mistake for anything else: *You wanted it, baby, here's your chance!* But she already guessed it wasn't going to happen—David simply wasn't the type to take that kind of risk, not even for *her. Fuck you!* she thought. *You had your chance!*

She pulled away slightly, still smiling at him. "I'm going to England, you know," she said, breaking the spell.

He gave a little sigh. Regret? Relief? "Yes, I know," he said. "I saw Larry Olivier in New York. He's thrilled that he's going to be working with you."

"The whole idea scares the shit out of me, frankly," she said. "England, Larry, Vivien, all that. . . ."

"You'll do fine."

"Maybe. I'm going to New York first."

"I heard. The word is, congratulations are in order for you and Arthur."

She nodded without enthusiasm. "I'm going to be there awhile, apartment hunting," she said.

"If I can be of any help . . ."

The door opened, and a lot of people came in, Pat Lawford, Josh and Nedda Logan, and a woman who looked just like Jacqueline Kennedy and whose expression made it clear that she was Maria Leman. Then she was pulled back into the party, and in a few minutes she hardly even remembered how close she had come to putting her arms around David and giving him what he wanted. . . .

11

When Jackie and Jack finally moved to Georgetown, selling Hickory Hill, their big country house in Virginia, to Bobby and Ethel —who had no problem filling it with their brood—journalists would turn it into Camelot on the Potomac, with nonstop parties of New Frontiersmen and their pretty ladies playing touch football and pushing each other into the swimming pool fully dressed, but I always found it a gloomy old place, full of rooms either too big or too small that even Jackie couldn't make cheerful. I never saw Jack at Hickory Hill when he didn't look as if he wanted to be elsewhere. Jackie too was anything but cheerful when I arrived.

I gave Jack the Tony Pro Invitational cap from Red Dorfman, which he put on with a big grin, but it didn't raise a laugh from Jackie.

He took the hat off and put it on the table as she went off to check on lunch. I added Jack Ruby's card, for a laugh. "In case you're ever in Dallas," I said.

"God forbid! I'll pass it on to Lyndon. How about a walk before lunch?"

"Can you?"

He nodded. "Not far. And you're going to carry my cane, in case I need it. But I've turned the corner. I've got a new doctor, Janet Travell, who's a miracle worker. She's given me some exercises— tough to do at first, but they make a world of difference. And I'm to keep walking, keep moving, as much as possible. I already feel like a new man."

"No pain?"

"Oh, plenty of pain, sure, but she gives me some injections for that—Novocaine, I think, straight into the muscles—and that helps."

We stepped out the French doors into the warmth of a perfect Virginia early summer's day. Jack walked slowly and with some difficulty, but it was a pleasure to see him on his feet again. We walked over to the pool. "I swim every morning too. The water has to be warmed to ninety-five degrees. Jackie complains it's like swimming in soup, but cold water just kills me. . . ."

He looked toward the horizon. "I thought it might be a good idea to get outside for this conversation," he said. "You never know."

So Jack and Red Dorfman had something in common! I wondered if Jack really thought somebody might have bugged Hickory Hill; then I thought of J. Edgar Hoover and realized that nothing was more possible. "Dorfman made me play golf in the desert sun because he was afraid of surveillance," I told him. "That's how I got the hat."

Jack nodded thoughtfully. "Then he's a smart fellow. Good. If we're going to do business with him, we don't want him behaving, ah, rashly. *Are* we going to do business?"

"Maybe, Jack. Maybe."

Jack's eyes focused on the far horizon at the rolling hills. Though he was listening to me with his full attention, he somehow managed to communicate that he was the one who would make any decisions. His illness and his two desperate operations had matured him, as a lot of people were soon to discover. "You didn't make them any promises, did you?" he asked.

"None. But they made us a serious proposition."

He nodded again. His eyes were hooded. We were walking round and round the pool at a slow pace, Jack with his hands behind his back, his face set with determination. "What do we get if we go for it?"

"Dave Beck."

He whistled. He glanced at me to see if I was joking. "Son of a bitch!" he said in awe. "They'd give him up?"

"Lock, stock, and barrel. Plus a reasonable number of his associates and all the evidence you'd need to get them sent away. Of course, there's a price."

He looked away, as if he weren't listening. "Yes?" He waited for me to tell him what it was.

"You lay off Hoffa," I said. I did not mention laying off Moe

Dalitz, Red Dorfman, and their friends. If Hoffa was safe, they would be too. Besides, Jack knew exactly who the people around Hoffa were, and what would be involved if the committee accepted Beck as their sacrificial goat. There would be headlines, praise for him from labor leaders, public approval—and business as usual for Jimmy Hoffa and the mob.

If he was shocked at the prospect, it didn't show. He looked at me thoughtfully. "To be perfectly honest with you, David," he said, "even though this was your idea, I wouldn't have taken a bet you could bring it off. I must say, I'm impressed."

"If you think politicians or gangsters are tough, wait until you have to deal with the CEO of any Fortune Five Hundred company —guys like Bob McNamara, or Roger Blough, or Tom Watson. I deal with them every day."

"That's what Dad is always saying about big business."

"He knows what he's talking about."

He was silent for a moment. "Our distinguished committee chairman, Senator McClellan, will be overjoyed. He's scared shitless that he's going to step out into the limelight and come back empty-handed. If we can guarantee he gets to bring back Beck as a trophy, he's going to be one happy hunter."

"What about Bobby?"

"Ah, what about him? It's a good question. He won't be happy. For some reason, he has a hair up his ass about your Mr. Hoffa. Beck seems to me just as good a catch—maybe better in some ways —but Bobby wants to see Hoffa doing time in Lewisburg or Atlanta, sewing mailbags or whatever it is they do these days." He sighed. "Well, I'll talk to him."

"Better you than me."

Jack frowned. "I know Bobby can be a pain, David, but he's my brother. And he's a team player. Of course, the amenities are going to have to be observed. Hoffa is going to have to appear before the committee and act suitably humble. He'll have to answer some tough questions—tough enough to show we mean business. We can't have him taking the Fifth for days on end either. He has to meet us halfway."

"But the questions Hoffa's asked needn't come as a total shock to him, need they? Couldn't they be *limited*—agreed upon mutually in advance, for example?"

Jack focused on the flowers around the pool as if he were judging a garden show. "There'll be details to be worked out," he murmured distantly. "You'll be wanting to talk to Kenny or Dave about that."

I didn't like the sound of that a bit. I made a mental note to get myself out of this particular loop as soon as possible.

Jack looked across the flat, unruffled surface of the pool. Jackie was standing in one of the French windows, waving at him. He did not wave back. "Lunch," he said. "You'll pass the message on?"

I nodded. I didn't think that could do any harm.

I could tell that Jack was torn between curiosity to know how and to whom I would signal his agreement to the deal and the realization that it was something he was better off not knowing. He loved details, Jack did—nothing pleased him more than to hear about the machinations of spies, gangsters, and all the rest of the mysterious characters who lived in the shadows of public life—but he had an acute sense of when it didn't pay to ask a question.

I waited, and he said nothing.

His father would have been proud of him, I thought.

———

Lunch was just the three of us, and the atmosphere between Jack and Jackie was so cold and thick that you could cut it with a knife. Clearly, Jack had gone too far somewhere.

Jackie asked after Maria, who was still in California, then chattered brightly to me as the meal was served. I may as well confess that I have always liked Jackie. She is good company, attractive, gifted with superb taste and a real talent for the kind of conversation and mild flirtation that appeals to men of all ages.

I think Jack seriously underestimated just how tough she was, when he married her. His sisters and Ethel made malicious fun of her pretensions (when she had pointed out to them that her name was pronounced "Jack-*leen*," they shouted: "Rhymes with 'queen,' of course!"), but she and her sister, Lee, were made of sterner stuff. After all, they were the daughters of one of the most notorious (and charming) womanizers and drunks of his generation, while their mother, Janet, had raised social climbing to such an art that she impressed even Joe Kennedy, no mean judge of social climbers himself. The Bouvier girls had earned their degrees in the school of emotional hard knocks.

"How is Los Angeles, David?" she asked me.

I told her about Joshua Logan's party at the Goetzes', described what Maria was wearing (Jackie always wanted to know), and filled her in on what was happening in the lives of her West Coast friends. Her sister-in-law Pat had married Peter Lawford the year before, over the ferocious objections of Joe Kennedy, who said that the only thing he hated worse than one of his daughters marrying an actor was having her marry an *English* actor.

Jackie, at the beginning, got along well with Lawford, who went out of his way to amuse her, until she began to suspect that he was providing a string of Hollywood starlets for Jack, at which point she turned against him. Still, he introduced her to a lot of the more socially presentable movie people, and Jackie was no more immune to that kind of glamour than anyone else.

I told her the story about Marilyn and President Sukarno (leaving out Sukarno's request for Jack's list of the local starlets, of course), since I knew it would amuse her, and she laughed—that breathy, tinkling little laugh which the Kennedy girls found false and affected, but which always seemed to me bewitchingly sexy. "Isn't that funny, darling?" she asked Jack, who was not laughing, his mind, perhaps, on what he was going to say to Bobby.

"Nobody ever said she was a diplomat," he said grumpily.

Jackie smiled at him sweetly. "Oh, Jack darling," she said, "that's not nice! I thought you were a great admirer of hers."

She turned to me. "Jack's seen every one of Marilyn Monroe's pictures at least twice, David. He's a real fan. Next time you're in Los Angeles, you ought to get her autograph for him. He'd be *thrilled,* wouldn't you, Jack?" It occurred to me too late that Jackie had somehow found out about Jack and Marilyn. I realized that I had put my foot in it.

Jack glowered at her, his mouth set in stubborn determination not to be provoked, particularly in front of me. "That would be great," he said through clenched teeth.

"There you are, David—a little commission for you. Maybe you could even find a way of introducing Jack to her?"

I coughed uneasily. "I imagine that's possible," I said, trying to keep the tone light.

"I'll *bet* it is!" Jackie snapped savagely.

We sat in uncomfortable silence while coffee was served. Jackie was certainly entitled to her anger, I thought, but it wouldn't do her much good. She had pursued Jack hard, though everybody around him—his father, the Ambassador; his old college chum and resident court jester, Lem Billings; even Rose Kennedy and His Eminence the archbishop-cardinal of Boston—had warned her about Jack's women and the fact that he was, as they tactfully put it, "too set in his bachelor ways" to give them up. Far from being a deterrent, the warnings merely increased Jack's attraction for her, and her determination to marry him. Jackie, I suspected, was only capable of loving the kind of dangerous man her father was, not the kind of "safe" man who might love her exclusively. She once told Maria that even as a schoolgirl she had always dreamed of marrying an "experienced" man, and God knows, that was what she got, twice.

Having made her decision, she received no sympathy from Jack's family. She had a certain respect, as I said, for the Ambassador, but she hated Rose Kennedy, whom she always referred to with acid emphasis as "*Belle Mère*," and whom she often caricatured savagely and accurately, to Jack's acute discomfort.

I looked at my watch. "I must be going," I said.

"Back to New York?" Jackie asked. "How I long to get back there"—she paused tellingly—"and have some fun of my own!"

"New York, yes. Then Miami, tomorrow. I have business there."

"Los Angeles, New York, Miami—you do lead an active life, David, in all the exciting places. I'm madly envious."

"It's all business, Jackie."

She smiled. "Of *course* it is. Isn't that *always* what men say, Jack?"

I breathed a sigh of relief as the driver took me back to National Airport.

———

Years before, one February when the temperature in New York hadn't risen above zero for a week, I flew to Miami to get warm and, not having much else to do there, ended up purchasing, pretty much on impulse, a house in Key Biscayne.

Maria said I wouldn't use it enough to make it worthwhile, and she turned out to be right, but once I took the Miami Beach Chamber of Commerce on as a client, it seemed a good idea to keep up a residence there.

Florida, I may say now that I no longer have Miami Beach as a client, is not one of my favorite places in the world—as compared to Cap d'Antibes, for example—but there's a certain pleasure to feeling the warmth and sun on one's body or lying on one's back in the pool looking up at a clear blue sky above the palm fronds, when only two or three hours away one's fellow New Yorkers are slipping and sliding on ice.

I came out of the pool, toweling myself, to find Red Dorfman sitting in the lanai, at my breakfast table. His bodyguard—real muscle this time, unlike Jack Ruby—lurked in the background against the bougainvillea. Dorfman was dressed for the golf course. "You found your way, I see," I said to him, feigning a calm I did not feel. I had been waiting for him to call and set up a meeting.

"Big deal! You think your place is hard to find, just because you got an unlisted fucking telephone number? Don't make me laugh." He pointed in the direction of my neighbor. "Nice location too— right next to Bebe's place. I been there lotsa times, to meet Nixon."

I raised an eyebrow. I was not surprised to learn that Nixon had what later came to be called a "back channel" to the Teamsters—I merely hoped that Dorfman was a little more discreet about using Jack's name than he was about Nixon's.

"You got a nice place, David." He examined my breakfast table and nodded his approval. "You live nice."

"I try, Red, I try." I poured him a cup of coffee and put a couple of slices of fresh papaya on my plate.

"You wanna go on trying, you better have good news for me."

I ate my papaya calmly, wiped my mouth, and stared at him. "I'm the messenger, Red. If you start threatening me, you're not going to get any messages, okay?" In my experience, you can't let people like Dorfman intimidate you, even for a moment, or you lose face.

He backed down sullenly. "Okay, okay," he muttered. "Whatsa matter? You can't take a joke?"

"Was that a joke? I didn't hear you or your friend over there with the shoulder holster laughing. Maybe I missed the punch line."

"Don't be a smart-ass, David."

"Red, just so we're clear about it, the two of us, I am not a smart-ass. I'm smart. I hope you're enjoying your stay in Miami?"

He shrugged. "It's okay. I like the track, the dogs, the jai alai. I'm staying at the Deauville, where they always treat me nice."

I'll bet they do, I said to myself. The Deauville Hotel was a home away from home for gangsters—you were consorting with known felons just by sitting beside the pool or entering the bar.

Dorfman helped himself to a slice of papaya. "So what's your guy say?" he asked.

"My guy is willing to go along, in principle."

"What the fuck does 'in principle' mean?"

"Well, your guy has to show up in Washington, as we discussed, and answer questions." I caught the look on his face. "Don't worry,"

I said. "We'll let him have the questions in advance. He'll have plenty of time to come up with answers."

"So it's just, like, window dressing, right?"

"Exactly. Well put. Of course, he—your guy—will have to be on his best behavior."

Dorfman's face was expressionless. It crossed my mind that his control over "his guy's" good behavior might be less reliable than Moe had given me to believe in Vegas. Hoffa's temper was certainly the first thing you noticed about him, along with his white athletic socks, although the one time I did business with him, he had held it in check and we had made a very reasonable deal.

Joe Kennedy had bought the Chicago Merchandise Mart before the war as an investment for his children—then, and for all I know, still, the biggest commercial building in the world—so its profitability was a continuing concern of his. He was therefore alarmed in the early fifties when he learned that the Teamsters were trying to organize the Merchandise Mart's employees. Since I knew my way around union politics, Joe asked me to go to Detroit, from which Hoffa was running his growing midwestern empire.

Oddly enough, Hoffa then had a reputation for being a left-wing labor leader. As I was to discover, he had in fact begun his career under the influence of Eugene Debs, and as a result, many people made the mistake of assuming he was a kind of midwestern Trotsky. I hadn't been in his office five minutes before I realized this was not the case. Hoffa was an idealist gone bad. His headquarters had much the same atmosphere of corruption and violence—and many of the same kind of thugs—as a Nazi gauleiter's; I could not help thinking, during my brief visit, that many of the faces I saw there would have looked right above brown uniforms with swastika armbands.

Nevertheless, Hoffa himself turned out to be unexpectedly reasonable, and not without a certain amount of gritty charm. He made a deal on the spot, and Joe Kennedy bought himself guaranteed labor peace in Chicago. Nothing else between Hoffa and the Kennedys was to go as smoothly.

"What do you mean by 'best behavior'?" Dorfman asked, as if the concept were unfamiliar to him.

"Tell him to think of it as a parole board hearing," I suggested.

Dorfman put his head back and laughed loud enough to startle the bodyguard. "I'll tell him that," he said. "He's never done time, but he'll get the picture."

He stood up and we shook hands. "I'll be in touch with you," he told me.

"Jack may want to have somebody else look after this from now on," I said. If I had anything to say about it, he would.

He didn't let go of my hand. Instead, he squeezed it hard and shook his head, still smiling but with hard, cold eyes. "You got it wrong, David," he said. "You're our boy. Moe vouched for you to me. I vouched for you to Hoffa and to my guys in Chicago, my *padroni*."

"I'm not sure I'm comfortable with that, Red."

He let go of my hand and gave me a big bear hug. "You got a sense of humor," he said. "I like a guy with a sense of humor. I always read that piece inna *Reader's Digest* every month—what is it, 'Laughter Is the Best Medicine'?" He laughed, as if to show he knew how. "You're in, *bubbi*, that's all there is to it. You don't wanna be found floating facedown in the pool, like the guy at the beginning of *Sunset Boulevard*, do you?"

I closed my eyes and thought about William Holden floating in Gloria Swanson's pool. "If that's the way you want it, Red," I said.

What have I done to Jack Kennedy? I wondered. Then, more realistically: What have I done to myself?

"Don't worry. It'll all work out," Dorfman said. "You'll see."

"I hope so," I said, suppressing a shiver.

"It had better!" He lingered a moment, flexing his shoulders like the boxer he had once been.

I looked him in the eye. I didn't have anything to lose, I thought. "Your ass is on the line as much as mine, Red," I said evenly.

He gave me the defiant look of a bully whose bluff has been called, but his heart wasn't in it.

I turned my attention back to my breakfast and buttered a piece of toast. By the time I'd put Cooper's Vintage Oxford marmalade on it, Dorfman and his shadow were gone, leaving behind only a faint aroma of pungent cologne, like the smell of brimstone that is said to accompany the devil.

I poured myself another cup of coffee and picked up the paper. On the front page was a photo of Marilyn arriving in London. She was smiling, but to anyone who knew her, the look in her eyes was one of stark terror. Next to her, looking distinctly uncomfortable, was Arthur Miller, holding her by the elbow as if he was afraid she might trip and fall.

They did not look to me like happy newlyweds.

12

She could hear Amy Greene knocking on the bathroom door again. "Marilyn honey," Amy whispered, "are you okay? Everybody's waiting for you."

She *wasn't* okay. She was sitting in the toilet of the first-class cabin on Pan American's overnight flight to London, trying to pretend that none of this was happening to her—that she wasn't about to be greeted by the Oliviers on their home ground, that she wasn't committed to make a picture in which she had to play exactly the kind of dumb blonde she didn't want to be, that this wasn't—just her luck!—day one of a monumental period that left her bloated, aching, seized by cramps and unstoppable bleeding.

The thought of getting out of the airplane paralyzed her. She sat on the toilet seat in a silver-gray silk ribbed-knit dress that had been "form-fitting" when she bought it at Bendel's but in her present shape was obscenely, uncomfortably tight. She had kicked off her white, high-heeled pumps. There was a pile of damp, crumpled Kleenex on the floor; she shredded another tissue and dropped it at her feet.

The last few months had been, in Dr. Kris's words, "traumatic and stressful," leaving her with the feeling that she was reaching the crest of a roller-coaster ride, and about to plunge downward. Of course, happiness always did that to her—the moment she felt happy, she began to worry about how she'd feel when it was over. Marriage always made her happy in the beginning because it was like joining a new family. She had managed to get herself embraced by Arthur's family at first meeting—nobody could have tried harder

142

than she did—and in his father, Isidore, a crusty, funny, outspoken Jewish patriarch, she found at once the father figure she was always searching for. She liked being a daughter, she decided, a lot more than she liked being a wife. . . .

"Marilyn!" It was Milton this time, his voice low but insistent, with an edge of panic to it. She had met Olivier in New York, and kept him waiting for over two hours. Olivier had been charming about it, on the surface, but she'd had no trouble reading the anger in his eyes—as well as a clouded look of doubt, as if he were saying to himself, Oh my God! What have I gotten myself into!

Whatever Olivier had expected, she had failed to deliver, and she knew it. Stiff, awkward, giggling nervously like a schoolgirl and hating herself for being in awe of him, she had projected about as much dazzle as a burned-out light bulb. He kept up a steady, desperate chatter about all the Hollywood friends they must have in common, while she smiled until her jaws ached. When he finally, mercifully, was ready to leave, he took her hand in his and begged her not to keep the press waiting in England. "It's different at home," he warned her. "They won't forgive you there, darling."

She had tried to talk to him about the Studio—the Method—the Strasbergs (she thought of them as a single entity, like Father—Son—Holy Ghost, Jack had joked when she tried to explain the whole thing to him), but Olivier had changed subjects with a superior smile that made it clear he didn't take the Strasbergs (or her) seriously.

Arthur wasn't any help when she talked to *him* about it. He couldn't conceal his admiration for Olivier—all she heard was Larry this and Larry that, until she began to suspect that he hoped "Larry" would perform in one of his plays one day, or that he had even discussed *writing* a play for him. . . .

Milton's worried voice interrupted her thoughts again. "Marilyn honey, do you want me to get Arthur?"

"No!" Arthur must already think she was crazy. Talking to him through a locked toilet door didn't seem a good way to improve matters between them. "Is it a mob scene out there?" she asked fearfully.

"This is England, Marilyn. Everything is under control."

"Is Mrs. Olivier there?"

"*Lady* Olivier, Marilyn. Vivien. Sure. She's waiting for you."

"What's she wearing?"

"A suit. Kind of pale mauve tweed, pleated skirt, jacket with a big open collar."

You had to hand it to Milton, she thought. How many men could describe a woman's clothes so accurately? "Glamorous?" she asked, leaning close to the door so she could whisper.

She could hear him sigh. "Sort of," he admitted. "More, like, *elegant,* but in a very English way—kind of like the Queen or Princess Margaret but better-looking, if you see what I mean."

Great! She cursed herself for having chosen a dress that rose to a high neckline in front, almost like a turtleneck sweater, showing none of what the British public wanted to see. She would be upstaged by Vivien Leigh, who had to be nearly twenty years older than she was! "Is she wearing a hat?"

There was a moment's pause. "Uh-huh. A matching hat, with a loose ribbon around it. Larry's wearing a dark suit, and he's smiling, but he doesn't look happy. Let's *go,* honey!"

A hat! She should have worn a hat! Why hadn't she realized that of *course* Vivien Leigh would be wearing a hat? She had decided to wear short white gloves to match her shoes, although she was afraid they made her hands look like Minnie Mouse's, but now she couldn't decide whether they were correct or not.

"Marilyn, Arthur's coming, and he looks really pissed off."

Whatever lay ahead, she wasn't up to another argument with Arthur, who—for all his simple, pipe-smoking calm and single-minded devotion to her—always needed to feel (and make *her* feel) he was in the right. She powdered her nose quickly, put on her goddamned, stupid white gloves, unlocked the door, and tottered out, with Milton and Amy supporting her on either side in the narrow corridor as if they were bodyguards. Arthur's tall figure was in the shadow, next to the door of the plane.

Milton gave her a desperate smile. "Arm in arm, honey," he said. "He's your *husband.* Remember? Knock 'em dead!"

"Tell Arthur not to be a stiff," she heard Amy whisper to her; then she was at the door, her arm thrust through Arthur's, and together they stepped out into the gray morning sunlight, pushed from behind by the Greenes. A roar went up—louder than anything she had heard since she entertained the troops in Korea in 1954— from a vast crowd of people only barely held in check by row after row of London bobbies. Reporters and photographers battled to get to the front of the crowd, passengers held their small children above their heads so they could see; everywhere there was pushing, shoving, and shouting. At the front of the mob, as small and neat as the figures on a wedding cake, stood the Oliviers, a nervous smile on his face, a look of fury on hers.

An airport official guided her toward them; another handed her a bouquet of flowers. Sir Laurence mumbled a greeting she couldn't hear above the noise and gave her a peck on the cheek, Lady Olivier shook her fingertips limply—she too wore gloves, though hers were long, pale mauve suede ones, as tight-fitting as a second skin—then the press broke through the barriers and swept around them like a storm. Hands plucked at her clothes and hair, flashbulbs popped in her face, questions were screamed at her. She pressed herself against Arthur's chest, while Sir Laurence and the airport security men cleared a path for her.

They plunged into the waiting Rolls-Royce like bank robbers making a getaway, Vivien Leigh sitting beside her on the back seat, Arthur and Olivier facing their wives on the jump seats. Vivien was smiling vaguely and waving to the crowd like a queen, which irritated her because the crowds had come to see *her*. Somehow she felt overshadowed by the Oliviers. She told herself that this was *her* movie, that she owned it, that she was paying Sir Laurence, but it did no good; he still looked as if *he* owned the world, sitting back elegantly in earnest conversation with Arthur—genius to genius, she thought bitterly.

She hadn't realized until she saw them together how badly dressed Arthur was in his off-the-rack seersucker jacket, baggy pants, and clodhopper shoes, in contrast to Olivier, with his florid complexion, his long hair carefully brushed in little wings above his ears, his superbly tailored double-breasted suit, his narrow, gleamingly polished shoes. He was sending about a zillion volts of English charm in Arthur's direction, while Arthur, clearly awed by his new pal "Larry," sat stiffly upright, his head grazing the roof of the car, nodding, smiling, and drinking in every word.

She and Vivien sat as far away from each other as they could, in silence, while their husbands were lost in their newfound mutual admiration society. "You played the part of Elsie on stage, didn't you?" she asked finally, hating the little-girl-being-nice-to-her-betters tone of voice.

Vivien—who had been chain-smoking ferociously ever since they left London airport—looked her in the eye for the first time. "Yes, I did," she snapped. "Larry and I did it together. It was a great success."

Vivien breathed smoke into her face and dismissed her with a grimace. "It's a shame you didn't see us—Miss Monroe." Her pronunciation was as sharp as the edge of a knife. "You would have known exactly how to play Elsie."

"I'll find my *own* way," she said, not bothering to hide her anger.

"Well, good luck to you, I'm sure."

She sat in tongue-tied rage during the rest of the trip, while Olivier, conscious at last that he had been avoiding her—or, she thought, more likely remembering that she was his meal ticket—rattled on and on about the cottage he had rented for her and Arthur. Then he stopped suddenly and peered out the window.

"The bloody press is following us," he said. "Damn! I'd hoped we'd get away from the buggers."

"Larry hates film journalists—particularly the columnists," Vivien explained. "He barred them from the studio when he was making *Henry the Fifth,* didn't you, darling? They've never forgiven it, Miss Monroe."

She herself had never felt that way about the press at all. Columnists and reporters were usually on her side back home, especially since the story was mostly Marilyn versus 20th Century–Fox, so she was cast as a kind of female David going up against Goliath.

"Paul Tandy is the one Larry hates most, Miss Monroe," Vivien said sweetly. "Isn't he, darling?" She smiled at him. "Tandy is on the *Mail,* you see. One of our most important newspapers—unfortunately for Larry. Larry got paid a lot of money to endorse a cigarette on television, and ever since then, Tandy calls him 'Sir Cork Tip' in his column." She laughed loudly. "I'm afraid Larry doesn't find it funny at all. Does *your* husband have a sense of humor, Miss Monroe?"

"Arthur? I guess so." The truth was, Arthur had no sense of humor at all about himself, nor had the Slugger, who thought of himself as a national institution, but she wasn't about to tell that to Vivien Leigh.

Vivien glanced briefly in Arthur's direction and shrugged. "How nice for you, darling," she said unbelievingly.

"Sir Cork Tip" glared balefully at his wife, but before he could say anything, they arrived at the rented house. He got out first, followed by Arthur, forgoing politeness so he could clear a path for her and Vivien through the crowd of reporters already ringing the car. She thought the two men looked like Mutt and Jeff. She could hear him pleading with them—"Marilyn's tired, give her a chance to freshen up, please, be reasonable, chaps. . . ."

Apparently, he reached some kind of understanding with them, for he turned and waved. Vivien stepped out of the car first like royalty, into a blaze of flashbulbs, a smile fixed on her face; then she followed, temporarily blinded by the flashes.

Vivien proceeded at a stately pace, and the mob parted. She wasn't sure whether it was the title that did it or simply the expression on Vivien's face, which seemed to convey that she didn't even *see* the press, that they were invisible to her, beneath her notice. Whatever it was, it worked, except for one tall, well-dressed man who blocked their way slightly. "Miss Leigh," he shouted, in one of those English upper-class voices that are so sharp they can cut glass, "how do you feel about Sir Laurence doing love scenes with Miss Monroe?"

Vivien didn't break stride. "Sir Laurence has done love scenes with *me,* Paul. I don't suppose he has anything new to learn about love scenes."

"Paul Tandy," Vivien explained as they forced their way past him. He was writing in his notebook, his face set in a quizzical smile.

She felt her face growing flushed. Vivien hadn't bothered to give *her* a chance to say something—had ensured she was going to be treated like the dumb blonde seductress and home breaker, just as she'd always been.

She rushed inside the house, where Arthur was standing in the hallway, looking out of place against the antique furniture and Oriental carpets. The "cottage" was a big country house, old, lavishly furnished, and elegant—like a movie set—with an elaborate formal garden stretching out toward the woods. "Charming view," Olivier said, "isn't it?" He drew her into the living room. "So comfortable, don't you think?"

Beads of sweat were showing on his forehead. He seemed to her to be suggesting that a dumb American movie star like herself might not understand how valuable all these things were, or how lucky she was to be here. She didn't feel lucky about it at all. Parkside House didn't look like the kind of place where she could walk around naked, or leave her champagne glass or coffee cup on the furniture without worrying, and besides, it was costing her an arm and a leg. She smiled back at him woodenly.

"Perhaps you'd like to see the rest?" Olivier asked. "The paneling in the master bedroom is superb. . . . I expect you'll want to go and, ah, wash up?"

She nodded, suddenly too tired to speak.

Vivien led the way upstairs to the master bedroom and pointed out the bathroom. As she opened the door, desperate to get inside, Vivien placed one gloved hand gently on the door, her dark smoky-gray eyes fixed on hers like a cobra's on a mongoose, and in a low, husky whisper, the words perfectly articulated, said: "When Larry tries to fuck you, darling—as I'm sure he will—do be kind, won't you? It's been ages since he's fucked *me,* but I do remember that he needs all the help he can get, poor dear!"

With that, Vivien closed the door, leaving her alone at last.

13

The dark gray '54 Ford sedan was just where Dorfman had been told it would be, in the parking lot behind the Acropolis Diner, half hidden by a Dempsey Dumpster overflowing with garbage.

Dorfman got out of his car, told his driver to go get himself a cup of coffee, walked over to the Ford, carefully avoiding the rain puddles, opened the back door, and sat down. Hoffa didn't look at him, or shake hands.

Dorfman lit a cigarette, studied the back of the driver's neck, and decided it was nobody he knew. "Anybody coulda gotten inna your car, Jimmy, blown you away before you knew what fucking happened," he chided. "You oughta lock the doors, have a couple guys around, keep an eye on things. You take too many fucking risks."

Hoffa laughed, a grating sound that merely expressed his savage contempt for the world at large. He was built like a concrete mixer, and although there was no fat on him and he wasn't tall, his muscular bulk seemed to take up most of the back seat, crowding Dorfman against the door on his side. Hoffa's face was the color of raw veal, his mouth like a surgical scar; his pale eyes were expressionless.

"Anybody tries it, I'll tear the piece outa his hand, shove it up his ass, and pull the fucking trigger. How are you, Red? What have you got for me?"

Hoffa turned his head enough to get a good look at Dorfman, just in case he might be harboring any ideas about trying it himself. He knew you didn't stay alive by trusting people, not even Dorfman, who knew as much about the Teamsters as any outsider did. He had a lot of respect for Dorfman, as it happened, but it was mingled with

149

a certain degree of contempt. Dorfman had arrived like some guinea in a brand-new metallic sky-blue Caddy, with sweeping, sculptured streaks of chrome ending in big tail fins like those of a rocketship in a cartoon—the kind of car Hoffa often gave away to people who had done him a favor, but would never dream of owning himself. Guys like Dorfman, Hoffa told himself, would rather get picked up by an FBI surveillance team than arrive in an old, beat-up car.

Hoffa bought his suits on sale at J. C. Penney, along with the short white athletic socks he always wore. Dorfman was dressed in a gray custom-tailored silk suit, a white-on-white shirt, a silver tie. Dorfman wore narrow Italian loafers and a natty hat with a band that matched the tie—he'd worked with the guineas so long he dressed like one. Some of the Teamster leaders were beginning to dress like that too, and Hoffa didn't like it.

Dorfman leaned close. Hoffa got a whiff of his cologne and frowned. He preferred the sweat of a real workingman. "We got a deal, Jimmy," Dorfman whispered, glancing at the driver.

Hoffa nodded. "Take a walk," he told the driver. "Stay close."

When the driver was gone, Dorfman told Hoffa the bare bones of the deal he had worked out with David Leman back in Key Biscayne, while Hoffa listened impassively, his eyes focused on the rain streaking the windshield.

After Dorfman had finished, Hoffa held up a meaty hand for silence and thought for a while. He had never doubted that the Kennedys would play—it was just a question of how to approach them. They were rich, and the rich were corrupt and lazy. The old man was capitalism at its greedy worst, which meant you could always deal with him, just as he had back in '52 over the Merchandise Mart thing. As for Jack, he was just a playboy, who'd make any deal to look good, and the kid brother, Bobby, was nothing more than a loudmouthed college punk. *Fuck 'em!* Hoffa simmered a little while in the warmth of his contempt for the rich. He was as firm an anti-Communist as J. Edgar Hoover, if not firmer, but the one thing you could say for the Russians was that they had cleared out all *their* rich parasites and put power in the hands of the workingmen.

The more he thought about the deal, the better he liked it. The idea of fat Dave Beck doing time in Atlanta or Lewisburg warmed his heart, but the important thing, he knew, was to give the Teamsters an in with the Democrats, just in case they won in '60. The Teamsters were the only union that regularly endorsed Republican candidates, which was okay so long as Ike was running, because Ike would always win. Nixon or Stassen or Rockefeller, or whoever it was going to be in '60, might lose, he thought, leaving the Teamsters sucking hind tit. A little insurance wouldn't hurt. Getting rid of Beck and his cronies was step number one, Hoffa reminded himself. After that, the target was George Meany.

He nodded at Dorfman. "You done good, Red."

"Thanks, Jimmy," Dorfman said in a tone that suggested he didn't need any praise from Hoffa.

A shadow of doubt crossed Hoffa's face. "But I don't like this shit about going to D.C., answering questions from Bobby. On that one, I say we tell them to fuck off, Red."

Dorfman cleared his throat. "It's part of the deal, Jimmy. Leman was a hundred percent clear on that. It's just 'window dressing,' Jimmy, to make Bobby look good, but it's gotta be. You'll get the questions in advance, with plenty of time to work out the answers with your lawyers. . . . It's no big deal, believe me, not compared to the fact they're gonna get rid of that fat putz Beck for us."

Hoffa shrugged his massive shoulders. Dorfman was right, but something still made him uneasy, some gut instinct told him it was a mistake. On the other hand, he was offering the Kennedys a terrific deal, and the old man owed him one for the Merchandise Mart, so maybe he was being too cautious. . . .

Fuck it, he told himself. I didn't get this far without taking risks! "Okay, Red," he said at last. "You tell them we'll go ahead. The questions have gotta be cleared with me and Edward Bennett Williams, and I don't want no surprises. On your head be it."

"That's the idea, Jimmy—no surprises for either side." He hesitated. "Of course, you gotta do your bit to make it all look kosher."

"Meaning?"

"Well, you gotta show some respect for the Senate committee, Jimmy."

"Respect?"

"You know. Like it was a grand jury hearing." He had planned to say "parole hearing," as David Leman had suggested, but you could never count on Hoffa's sense of humor. "You gotta be a little bit"—he sought the right word—"*humble.*"

Hoffa glared at him. "Are you telling me I gotta eat shit, right there in public, in front of the fucking TV cameras?"

"Eat shit, no, Jimmy. Just be polite, show a little respect, that kind of thing. . . ." Dorfman was sweating, sending out waves of cologne. He took off his hat—the same as Frank Sinatra's—and fanned it in front of his face. "You go there, you answer the questions, you make like the responsible labor leader the press is always saying you ain't, and act nice for the fucking senators. Is that such a big thing to ask?"

"Okay, okay," Hoffa conceded with a grimace. "It had better not go wrong, that's all I'm saying."

Dorfman held up both hands. Things could always go wrong, but this one seemed pretty foolproof to him, since both sides stood to gain. You could usually count on greed and ambition, he thought, both of which you had working here. He lit another cigarette with damp fingers, anxious to move on now that he had Hoffa's reluctant consent. "Guess who Jack Kennedy is boffing?" he said, anxious to change the subject. "Guy I know in LA, knows a guy says it's Marilyn Monroe."

"No shit? Who says?" Hoffa's voice betrayed no prurient interest because he had none. There was a deep streak of the puritan in him when it came to sex. He was never really comfortable when guys started swapping dirty stories. He didn't like sexual gossip either, unless it was something he could use as leverage against someone, in which case he listened carefully but without pleasure. Hoffa, Dorfman thought, was probably the only guy who had ever visited Vegas without getting laid.

Dorfman hummed a few bars of a song, imitating the familiar late-night, booze-and-cigarette voice of America's favorite singer. Even Hoffa, who was tone-deaf, recognized it. "Well," he said, "I guess if he's the one who said it, he oughta know."

"You bet he knows. You want me to put some guys on it? Get some pictures of Jack Kennedy and Marilyn together, maybe?"

Hoffa cracked his knuckles—a habit he had when he was thinking. "I might ask Bernie to see what he can do. If he needs any help on the West Coast, you give him what he wants, unnerstan'?"

Dorfman understood. Bernie Spindel was Hoffa's secret weapon, the best wireman in the country, a former consultant to the FBI and the CIA who had crossed over to work for Hoffa. Spindel reported only to Hoffa, and it was widely rumored that he had bugged not just the homes and offices of Hoffa's enemies but those of his Teamster colleagues as well.

Dorfman had heard countless stories about Spindel's prowess, and believed most of them: how Spindel had bugged the jury room during one of Hoffa's many trials for labor racketeering, so Hoffa knew exactly which jurors to put pressure on; how Spindel had deactivated all the bugs the FBI had placed in Hoffa's offices; how he had managed to record a conversation in a parked car between a rival of Hoffa's for the midwestern Teamster leadership and an FBI agent that resulted in the rival's subsequently being found hanging by the neck from a meat hook in the freezer of a meat-packing plant. Spindel was loyal only to Hoffa, and used only when Hoffa meant business.

Dorfman jumped at the opportunity to be of service to Spindel. "Anything Bernie wants," he said to Hoffa, maybe a couple of beats too fast, because Hoffa turned and stared at him, the pale eyes as hard as rock.

"Don't get any ideas, Red," he said. "Bernie is mine. Hands off, unnerstan'?"

Dorfman gave a grin, though his eyes reflected anger. He wasn't used to being talked to that way. "Hey, Jimmy, understood," he said. He shook hands—for a man of his strength, who liked to impress visitors to his office by cracking walnuts with his hands, Hoffa had a pretty limp handshake, by wiseguy standards anyway, but Dorfman had long since come to the conclusion that Hoffa simply didn't feel any need for the touching and feeling and firm handshakes that bound most men, criminal or otherwise.

Dorfman walked across the parking lot to his waiting car with a sense of relief—a feeling he always had when he left Hoffa. Hoffa seemed to think he was invulnerable, and Dorfman knew that was a dangerous idea for any man to have.

Hoffa not only thought he was bigger than the United States Senate—which he might turn out to be right about—but also thought he was tougher than Dorfman's people, men like Momo Giancana, who ran the Chicago mob.

Dorfman had seen the bodies of plenty of people who thought that. He got in his car and, without looking at the driver, said, "Momo's place, and step on it."

———

"They could hardly miss him in a metallic sky-blue '56 Cadillac Fleetwood. Top of the line. Nothing but the best for Red Dorfman!"

The Director didn't smile. His face was impassive as he sat motionless behind his big mahogany desk, hands joined on the spotless blotter in front of him, showing exactly one inch of starched white cuff at each wrist, his fingernails freshly manicured and clear-lacquered. Some thought the thin gold identification bracelet on his right wrist a little out of place for the country's top cop; others had remarked on the fact that his deputy director, close friend, and housemate, Clyde Tolson, wore an identical one, but the Director was untroubled by such innuendo.

Tolson, who was sitting at one side of the vast polished desk, exchanged a glance with him as Special Agent Kirkpatrick made his report. The Director used a '56 Cadillac Fleetwood himself, though of course, his was black.

He nodded ever so slightly to Kirkpatrick, who continued. "Surveillance from a distance established that Dorfman met with Hoffa in the parking lot of a diner. They sat in the back seat of Hoffa's car and talked for twenty-one minutes."

Hoover pursed his lips. He thought it was a criminal waste of manpower keeping watch on racketeers like Dorfman or crooked labor leaders like Hoffa. Of course people like that belonged behind bars—that went without saying—but the real enemy was godless communism; every agent engaged in the surveillance of organized crime was one man less in the more important battle to uncover Soviet spies and domestic traitors.

"Afterwards," Kirkpatrick went on, "Hoffa returned to his office, and Dorfman was driven to La Luna di Napoli restaurant, where he met with a known leader of the Chicago crime syndicate, Sam 'Momo' Giancana, over a cup of Italian coffee."

"They call it espresso," Tolson said helpfully.

Hoover stared into the middle distance, as if in touch with some deity floating invisibly at the far end of his big office. "Do we have any idea what Dorfman and Giancana were discussing?" he asked.

"No, sir. We had a bug in the restaurant at one time, but you'll remember that we had to abandon it when we moved most of our surveillance teams into the University of Chicago."

Hoover nodded. It had been done on his orders. The University of Chicago was even more undermined by Marxist agitators posing as professors than most places of higher education were. What was the point of keeping round-the-clock teams listening to Giancana and his pals fixing horse races and planning hijackings when in the University of Chicago common room, members of the faculty were actually discussing the overthrow of the United States government and the Constitution by force?

In an ideal world, he would have had the funding to do both, but since this clearly *wasn't* an ideal world—much of it being run by "liberals," even with a Republican in the White House—he had been obliged to choose, and had targeted the greater threat.

"Nothing from informants?" Hoover asked.

Tolson looked at the papers in his hand. He was wearing reading glasses. He and the Director were growing old together, like a married couple who had long since learned to live with each other's weaknesses and idiosyncrasies. "Not a lot, Director," he said—he always used Hoover's title when there was anyone else around. "Rumors that Hoffa's about to move in on Dave Beck, with mob support."

Hoover laughed. "We've heard that one before."

"I hear Bobby Kennedy's planning to subpoena Beck *and* Hoffa," Tolson said. "Probably Dorfman, too. My guess is that there's some kind of hanky-panky going on between the Kennedys and the Teamsters, maybe to make Jack and Bobby look good in the press."

Hoover sighed. Nothing was more likely, he thought glumly. He hadn't liked the idea of turning Bobby Kennedy loose on labor racketeers when he heard about it, and had told Joe Kennedy so. Bobby had fought the good fight as counsel on Senator McCarthy's committee, uncovering Communists in government, and he should have kept up the good work, in Hoover's opinion. The Ambassador had agreed, but in the end, he'd given in to his boys, as he always seemed to.

The Director had a guarded respect for Ambassador Kennedy, who had always known the score when it came to leftists, even in the days of the New Deal, when there were pinkos and fellow travelers at the very highest level of government. Kennedy had passed a lot of useful information on to the FBI then, and Hoover never forgot a favor—which was why, when young Jack became unsuitably involved in 1941 with Inga Arvad, a beautiful young Danish woman formerly married to a Hungarian flying ace, Hoover had been willing to do Jack's anxious father a favor and arranged to have her denounced as a German spy.

Hoover felt that he had thereby settled accounts with Ambassador Kennedy and owed him nothing more now than the polite respect he had for anyone who was white, wealthy, and conservative. He made no secret of the fact that he thought Bobby was ruthless and rude to his elders and betters—among them Hoover himself—and Jack merely a self-indulgent lightweight, whose personal immorality, carefully monitored by the Bureau, was bound to get him deep in hot water sooner or later. He looked forward to teaching them who was top dog in Washington, when Jack's time came, if it ever did.

Hoover prided himself on the sensitivity of his political antennae.

Decades of experience had honed all his political instincts toward a single goal: his own survival as director of the FBI, whoever was president. Indeed, he had a certain contempt for presidents—and not just because he knew all their dirty little secrets. Presidents came and went every four or eight years, but he, J. Edgar Hoover, remained. Coolidge had been president when he was appointed director of the Bureau, which he then re-formed in his own image, and in all those years, no president had ever dared to challenge him. About Jack Kennedy, however, he felt a nagging doubt.

Oh, Joe Kennedy called him regularly, with honeyed words about his son Jack's confidence in him, the boy's admiration for the Director's patriotic zeal, and so on, but Hoover listened to these blandishments with a mixture of indifference and fear—and not only because he knew Ambassador Kennedy to be a smooth-tongued flatterer.

He knew very well that Jack Kennedy cracked jokes about him—jokes about the director of the Federal Bureau of Investigation!—at Washington dinner parties, with journalists present, and counted among his friends and supporters many of Hoover's severest critics. The Director was sixty years old—only five years short of federal retirement age. Like an old wolf surrounded by younger rivals, he knew instinctively that he could expect little mercy from Jack Kennedy, still less from Bobby.

He therefore watched every move of the Kennedys with unwavering attention. The Ambassador's tax returns, cocktail party gossip, Jack's affairs with women, Bobby's struggle with Roy Cohn, the machinations by which David Leman, the New York–based PR magnate, was securing good reviews for Jack's book *Profiles in Courage,* or by which the Ambassador had obtained for his long-suffering wife a papal decoration—nothing was too small to capture the Director's interest. He surveyed the future as if standing on a mountaintop, and the only danger he saw on the horizon was from Jack Kennedy.

The truth was, though he didn't want his subordinates to know it, he didn't care whether Hoffa replaced Beck or not, with or without mob support. If you removed one crook from the leadership of the Teamsters, you would merely get another in his place. He knew there was no percentage in turning his agents loose on an organization that enjoyed the support of Vice President Nixon and a large number of senators and congressmen, thanks to the Teamsters' generous campaign fund contributions.

Dorfman and Hoffa's meeting in Chicago and Dorfman's subsequent meeting with Giancana—these things interested him only because Jack and Bobby were planning to take on the Teamsters. Dirt, as he was fond of saying, attracted dirt. "Is there any hard evidence of 'hanky-panky' between the Kennedys and the Teamsters, Mr. Tolson?" he asked.

"It's mostly just gut instinct, Director," Tolson admitted. "Jack and Bobby seem very confident that they're going to put Beck away. Too confident, maybe. . . . I'll tell you what's *really* interesting. David Leman was observed playing golf in Las Vegas with Dorfman recently. We have it on film."

Hoover paused. He knew David Leman both as a powerful, wealthy big-league public relations "mogul," as *Time* magazine always called him, and as one of the few people who enjoyed, if that was the right word, the confidence of Joe Kennedy. He flicked through his mental card file on Leman (Lehrman), David A., and decided that only a personal request from Joe or Jack Kennedy would have sent Leman to play golf with Dorfman.

"I wouldn't have thought Leman was much of a golfer," he said. "Those people seldom are." He sniffed. "More interested in making money." Hoover did not consider himself an anti-Semite, but he harbored certain firmly held ideas about the races, and for decades had quietly resisted recruiting Jewish FBI special agents.

"We can play the film for you, Director. Leman got in one good shot, as a matter of fact. Probably a fluke."

"Surely, Mr. Tolson, surely." Hoover frowned. "So it's reasonable to suppose that Jack Kennedy is dealing with the Teamsters—probably the Hoffa faction—and the mob, correct?"

"Correct, Director," Tolson and Kirkpatrick said in unison.

Hoover smiled. "Well, it's not a pretty thought, is it? For a United States senator to be in cahoots with racketeers like that."

"Not pretty at all," Tolson agreed. "It would look bad if it were leaked to the press—"

Hoover held up a pudgy hand in a majestic gesture of silence. "We shouldn't even *dream* of doing that," he said. "We should let things develop while we watch and wait. We have nothing to gain by making all this public, nothing at all. Keep your eye on the ball, Mr. Kirkpatrick. Leave no stone unturned."

Hoover was in the habit of giving cryptic orders. He had once scrawled "*Watch the borders!*" on a report because the margins weren't wide enough for him to write his comments, only to discover some weeks later that hundreds of agents were patrolling the Mexican and Canadian borders looking for they knew not what threat. Mindful of this, he cleared his throat and added: "I want all the facts of this sordid transaction, in case they should be useful later on. You've done good work, Kirkpatrick. Keep it up." He looked the young agent directly in the eye, man to man—he knew how much the agents valued the little personal touches that were so much a part of good leadership. "Anything else to report?"

Kirkpatrick closed his file. "An informant in Hollywood told one of our people out there that Senator Kennedy is having an affair with Marilyn Monroe."

"I thought he was having an affair with someone else," Hoover said.

Kirkpatrick blushed. "There's a whole list of women here. . . . It's hard to keep it up to date, as a matter of fact. Our informant—he's a well-known singer—seemed to feel this affair with the Monroe woman is more serious, or I wouldn't have mentioned it."

"You did right." Hoover stared glumly at his clean desktop. Normally he enjoyed hearing the gossip his agents picked up on the sex lives of the rich, the famous, and the politically powerful, but he had always had a soft spot in his heart for Marilyn Monroe, and it saddened him to think that she was behaving like a common tramp with a womanizer like Jack Kennedy. "This kind of thing wouldn't have happened in the old days," he said. "You could count on people like Louis Mayer to keep his stars in line." He sighed. "I suppose you could see it coming a mile away. I thought *The Seven Year Itch* was a piece of prurient trash, whatever the critics said. And I hear *Bus Stop* is worse."

"You liked *How to Marry a Millionaire,* Director," Tolson said soothingly.

"That's just my point. That was decent family entertainment. First she gets talked into making decadent motion pictures, then she actually *marries* a card-carrying Communist, now she's having an extramarital affair with Jack Kennedy. . . . You can see the pattern, all right. Subversion in its most insidious form."

Hoover stood up—a rare honor—and shook Kirkpatrick's hand. He prided himself on having a good, solid handshake. He believed you could judge a man's worth by the way he shook hands, and the belief had never let him down. He had once met Alger Hiss before the war, at a reception, and Hiss had a damp, flabby handshake, so it had come as no surprise to him when Hiss was uncovered as a traitor. "Put the best men you've got on it," he ordered.

Hoover caught what he took to be a look of hesitation on the agent's face. "You may feel, Kirkpatrick," he said, "that it's beneath us to be following the personal lives of people like Miss Monroe and Senator Kennedy. That it's not as important as fighting subversion and crime. But it *is*. Information like this is vital to national security. When you see the big picture, the way I do, it all fits in. Then you understand that what Miss Monroe does isn't just her private business—oh no, not at all. It has"—he paused dramatically, as if in search of the right word—"*ramifications*. It *matters*. Everything is to come directly to me. That will be all."

Kirkpatrick nodded and left the room, closing the door quietly behind him.

"A sad business," Tolson said as Hoover regained his seat.

"Sad indeed," Hoover said, but in truth he felt a certain lightening of his heart. Sexual peccadilloes would only take him so far in insuring himself against a future with Jack Kennedy in it, but a connection between a United States senator and mobsters, fully documented—that was heavy artillery!

Of course, you could hardly count Marilyn Monroe as a sexual peccadillo, he told himself. It occurred to him with a certain glee that Jack Kennedy was exposing himself to public scandal just the way his father had with Gloria Swanson.

He clasped his hands and gave Tolson a smile. "Let's move on, Clyde," he said.

14

London is a city I've always felt I could live in happily, which is one reason why I opened a branch office there early on in my career. I always told Joe Kennedy that the only thing I envied him was his appointment as United States ambassador to the Court of St. James's. "If I had one ambition, it would be that," I once said to him, over dinner at Le Pavillon, when he was still on speaking terms with Soulé.

"Forget it, David," he had replied. "It'll cost you a pisspotful of money, and nobody back home will listen to a word you say."

All the same, over the years, the ambition had become part of my life, nor did it seem like an impossible dream, since traditionally the only qualifications for the office of American ambassador to Great Britain were to be rich and a friend of the president's. I stared at the American embassy every time I drove past it on Grosvenor Square as if it were going to be mine one day.

The last person I expected to see in the bar of the Connaught was Buddy Adler—Hollywood people usually stayed at Claridge's or the Dorchester. He waved to me and I went over and sat down.

We exchanged Hollywood gossip for a few minutes; then I asked him about Marilyn. The only news I had read about her was that she had been badly mauled by the British reporters at a disastrous press conference held in her rented house the day she arrived—a big mistake on Olivier's part, or Milton Greene's, I thought. Marilyn's charm apparently hadn't come through to the British press at all—perhaps because, despite Olivier's pleas, she kept them waiting for nearly two hours. She had lost her temper with Paul Tandy when he challenged her to name the number of her favorite Beethoven symphony, and finally flounced out of the room in tears.

That was bad, but had nothing to do with the picture. I sipped my dry martini gratefully. "How are things going on *The Prince and the Showgirl?*" I asked.

Buddy rolled his eyes. "They're in bad trouble," he said.

People said that about all of Marilyn's pictures. You always heard horror stories about her lateness, her inability to remember lines, her reliance on Paula Strasberg or Natasha Lytess, her previous coach. Her costars were always rumored to be about to walk, the director on the verge of quitting, the studio making plans to close the production down, yet somehow the pictures always got completed successfully, and so far every one of them had made money at the box office.

"No, no," he said. "I know what you're thinking, but this time it's true. They're way behind schedule. Olivier ordered Paula off the set."

That caught my attention. If Larry had been forced to order Paula Strasberg off the set, he must be at his wit's end, since it amounted to a declaration of total war against Marilyn. In any case, Buddy wasn't a man with an ax to grind about Marilyn, unlike his fellow Fox executives. He had taken on the thankless task of producing *Bus Stop* for Fox, and although practically everyone there, from Zanuck down, wanted him to fail just to teach Marilyn a lesson, he had managed to hold things together somehow and bring off a far better picture than anything she had done before—so good, in fact, that Fox was obliged to give it major promotion and back it for an Oscar nomination.

"Is Marilyn okay?" I asked him.

Buddy shook his head. "Not too good, from what I saw. The funny thing is, everybody says she comes across better in the rushes than Olivier does, and he's going crazy trying to figure out why."

He laughed and I joined in. We both knew that it didn't matter how great an actor Larry was—the camera loved Marilyn, and that was that.

"How's she getting on with Arthur?" I asked. Marilyn had married Arthur Miller only a few weeks earlier. Miller had intended it to be a small private ceremony near his home, in Roxbury, Connecticut, thus making the same mistake that Joe DiMaggio had—for nothing about Marilyn was "private," nor, at heart, whatever she said, did she really want it so. She belonged to her fans, not her husbands, and she knew it.

Poor Miller! Instead of privacy, he found over five hundred reporters and photographers encamped in front of his house in the hot July sun! When he and Marilyn came out to talk to them after the wedding to make a plea to be left alone, Maria Sherbatoff, the pretty young correspondent from *Paris-Match,* was thrown through the windshield of a car in the confusion and hysteria. On the afternoon of her wedding day, Marilyn cradled the dying girl in her arms, and as she fled back to the house, her dress soaked in blood, photographers ran after her, trampling the lawns and flowers to get a better shot.

This would have seemed to anyone like an inauspicious way to begin a marriage, and Marilyn had been understandably down when I called her the day after the wedding—though not as down as one might have imagined, for she was used to that kind of bad luck and attracted it not only for herself but for others.

Buddy heaved a sigh, which said it all. I had hoped that a couple of weeks by themselves in the English countryside might do wonders for the newly wed Millers, but judging from his face, that had not been the case. "You wouldn't know they were on their honeymoon," he said. "I'll tell you *that.*"

Before I could pump him on the subject, his date arrived, and I drank up and went upstairs to change for dinner myself.

Despite a heavy schedule of appointments, I decided to call Marilyn in the morning.

"Hello, Arthur," I said.

Miller rose from what he was doing, and we shook hands. He looked thinner and gaunter than ever, with the lugubrious air of a man who has traded one difficult marriage for another. He was sitting in the library of the big—and to my eyes, rather vulgarly overfurnished—house Larry had rented for the happy new couple, working at a card table set up in one corner of the room, as his "study," I suppose. The tabletop was strewn with Marilyn's publicity clippings, which Miller—America's greatest playwright—was busy pasting in an album. I had seldom seen a more depressing sight.

There was a beautiful color photograph of Marilyn in a frame on his table, next to an open notebook. Her face had been photographed almost without makeup, while she was lying down, her head resting against her arms, her gloriously blond hair, worn loose and long, covering part of her face, her neck, and—barely—her breasts, one rosy nipple just showing through the tendrils. Her mouth was open, smiling, her eyes half closed, her expression one of such exquisite pleasure that it was almost orgiastic. "Nice photograph of Marilyn," I said.

He nodded his head glumly. "She had it taken here, a couple of weeks ago. I liked it so much that I asked for a print."

I could see why. It was the sexiest photograph I'd ever seen of her. I made my way up the stairs and knocked on the door of Marilyn's room. "Come in," she called. Her voice was dull.

She had taken over a bedroom for her own use. It was stripped of furniture and decoration to make room for a professional hair dryer, a makeup table with a brightly lit mirror, a massage table, several pipe racks to hold her clothes and costumes, and a telephone on a long cord so she could walk around the room while she talked on it. Everywhere, there was the clutter and mess without which Marilyn was never really at home. She was sitting on the floor, leaning against a stack of cushions removed from the sofa, reading a script. Her hair was in curlers, her face washed clean of makeup; she wore a white silk blouse and tight black pants of the kind that used to be called pedal pushers. I leaned over and gave her a kiss. "Jesus, David," she said, "you don't know how good it is to see you."

I moved a pile of magazines from a chair and sat down gingerly, for it was one of those spindly antique chairs meant to be looked at rather than used.

"Be careful of the chair. There's a set of the fucking things, but we've already broken half of them. Sir Cork Tip says they're worth a fortune."

"Sir Cork Tip?"

"That's what they call Larry in one of the papers here, because he did a cigarette commercial. It suits him." She affected a prissy, superior expression and voice. " 'Let's try it *one* little time more, shall we, Marilyn darling?' "

"It's been as bad as that?"

She shivered. "Worse. The pits, David honey."

"I saw that photograph of you downstairs, the one on Arthur's table. You look happy enough in that. It's quite something."

"Yeah." She nodded and then gave me a sweet little smile. "I fucked the guy who took it, you know. I guess that's why it's such a good picture."

It certainly explained her expression in it. I felt a sense of dismay —she and Miller had only just been married, after all.

163

"That sounds terrible, doesn't it, David?"

"It's none of my business, Marilyn—but yes, it doesn't sound good. Was it worth it?"

She shrugged. "Oh, David, I *know* it was a lousy thing to do, don't worry. But you can't imagine how lonely I am without Jack, or what it's like here with Old Grumpy. . . ."

"Old Grumpy?"

"That's what Paula calls Arthur." She lowered her voice. "He's got writer's block, he says. He blames me for it. On top of that, he's always taking Sir Cork Tip's side. All I hear is Larry this and Larry that, and from my own husband!"

"So you paid him back. Does he know?"

"You don't understand a thing about it, David," she said without anger—merely as a statement of fact.

"I wasn't criticizing you."

"The hell you weren't. You, by the way, are not the one who's married to Mr. Big Writer of the Century, who never wants to go anywhere, or see anyone, or have any fun."

"And who's downstairs pasting your clippings in a book?"

"I didn't ask him to. I thought he was going to write great plays, and we'd read them together and talk about them, and instead, he just sits around the house looking gloomy and telling me I'm wrong and Larry is right." She dabbed at her eyes with a Kleenex, then kneaded it into a hard ball in her fingers.

I leaned over and took her hand. "I'm sorry," I said.

"Thanks." Her hand was cold, though it was warm in the room. She sighed and shook her head. "Wrong man," she said sadly. "Wrong picture. Wrong country. How come I make so many mistakes?"

"They may not all be mistakes. You're just down today. Buddy Adler told me your rushes are terrific."

That brightened her up a bit. "No kidding? Sir Cork Tip isn't thrilled by them, but I bet that's because I'm upstaging him." She giggled.

"How's life been here otherwise?"

"What otherwise? My marriage is going to pieces, and I'm working with a guy who hates me. We're stuck in this big house and treated like freaks. We went bicycling together the first couple of days, and that was okay, but then the press started to follow us and we had to give it up. I didn't think Arthur was having much fun anyway, you know?"

I tried to imagine Marilyn and Miller bicycling through the English countryside, and failed.

I glanced around the big, untidy room. There were cardboard boxes full of her belongings all over the floor. The one nearest to me contained books. I noticed that Jack Kennedy's *Profiles in Courage* had joined Carl Sandburg's biography of Lincoln in her traveling library. "Why don't you get away from this house?" I suggested. "Take a couple of days off. Fly over to Paris for the weekend."

"Stop playing the marriage counselor, David. It doesn't suit you." She got up, poured two glasses of champagne, and gave me one. It was eleven in the morning. "Have you seen Jack?" she asked.

I could tell by the gleam of interest in her eyes how much it meant to her to be able to talk to someone about him. "He's never been better," I said.

"I miss him."

I nodded sympathetically. Since his second back operation, Jack's life had suddenly emerged from the doldrums. *Profiles in Courage* made the *New York Times* best-seller list and was already being touted, with my help, for a Pulitzer Prize. With Bobby's help—and against the Ambassador's advice—he had taken on his enemies in Massachusetts and emerged victorious from a bitter battle, with the entire state Democratic apparatus and—more important—its delegation to the national convention securely in his hands at last. He had even been picked by Dore Schary to narrate the film—*The Pursuit of Happiness*—that would open the 1956 convention, a decision that was destined to make him seem more glamorous and powerful to the delegates than poor Adlai Stevenson, the candidate himself. Dore was a friend of mine, and I had been very largely responsible for getting Jack this particular plum, despite his initial misgivings. And as if all this weren't enough, Jackie was pregnant.

I relayed all this to Marilyn briefly. "I talked to Jack a couple of days ago," I said. "He's in great shape, but walking on eggshells, if you know what I mean."

She shook her head. "I *don't* know what you mean."

"Well, Jackie's pregnancy, for one thing. You know how much that means to him. And it's been always touch and go for her. . . ."

Marilyn nodded, her expression hard to read. I hastened to move to a less emotion-filled subject. "Then there's the convention," I said. "There are a lot of people going to Chicago who think Jack would be a better choice for Stevenson's running mate than Estes Kefauver."

She brightened up and smiled. "Well, *sure* Jack would be a better choice! Does anybody disagree with that?"

"Yes. Jack. And his father, even more strongly. Adlai's going to go down in flames again, and if Jack goes down with him, everybody will say Adlai lost because Jack's a Catholic. If Jack accepts the vice presidential nomination, it's a kamikaze run—sheer political suicide."

"So what's the problem? He'll say no."

"The problem is that things could get out of hand. What we *don't* want is a last-minute Kennedy boom. Have you seen Dore's film?"

She drained her champagne glass and giggled like a naughty little girl. "I saw it," she said. "Jack screened it for me before I left for England. I'm going to tell you a secret. When he told me he was going to do it, he made it sound like it wasn't any big deal, but I could tell he was worried, so I asked Paula to coach him. Paula was so impressed she told Jack any time he wanted to give up politics, he could take up acting and join the Studio! I helped too."

It is not often that I am dumbfounded, but what Marilyn had just told me took my breath away, if only because it explained something that had puzzled me—and Dore Schary, too. Up until then, Jack's speeches were long on charm and deft historical quotation, but short on any real passion or feeling. He always won over the women in an audience instantly simply by being himself, but he came across a little shallow and younger than in fact he was. In Dore's film, Jack suddenly seemed *mature*—older, tougher, and touched by genuine passion, a startling transformation that I had attributed to his two terrible operations or perhaps his political victory in Massachusetts.

"How on *earth* did you manage to persuade him?" I asked. I had been after Jack for years to take speech lessons to improve his delivery and he had stubbornly resisted, afraid, I suspect, of losing whatever it was that worked with the voters of Massachusetts.

"I can be pretty persuasive," she said with a wink. There wasn't any doubt in my mind about that, or about the kind of persuasion that would work best with Jack.

"How did you do it?"

"Well, Paula put together a lot of film clips, so he could see what works and what doesn't. He wanted to be natural on film, but I explained to him there's no such thing. Coming across naturally on film is the hardest work of all, I told him."

"How did he take that?"

"He doesn't like being lectured, but I told him this is *my* profession—*I'm* the expert, just like some guy who knows all about banks, or Russia, or whatever. What I *really* had to get him to work on was breathing."

"Breathing?"

"Oh, honey, it's the key to everything. Jack didn't know when to stop for breath, which is the first thing an actor has to learn. He'd just talk on and on, and run out of breath just when he needed it. . . . Paula and I got some guy from CBS to bring up a lot of clips of Winston Churchill, so Jack could see that it isn't just a trick actors learn. Churchill knew how to breathe just as well as Larry Olivier, I can tell you. Well, of course that made it okay, because Jack's a real sucker for *anything* Churchill did. See, you have to take a really deep breath and hold it down here. . . ."

She demonstrated, breathing deep and patting her diaphragm. The thin fabric of her blouse stretched taut over her breasts as she did so, and I was unable to take my eyes off them. I cleared my throat—no matter how often one saw Marilyn, her figure remained an object of awe, like the best kind of art.

"Well, he owes you one," I said. "It's a new Jack. Of course, that's the problem. We're going to the convention saying, 'He's a winner, the best thing that's happened to the party since FDR made the nominating speech for Al Smith, *but for God's sake, don't give him the vice presidency!*' The last thing his father told Jack before he went off to Antibes for the summer was, 'Mind you don't let it go to your head, Jack, just keep saying no!'—as if Jack were a virgin on her way to her first dance."

She laughed. "Does Jack always do what his dad wants him to?"

"Mostly. Anyway, whatever happens, he's been busier than I've ever seen him. Bobby too."

"I wish I could be there," she said wistfully. "I've never been to a convention."

"Well, you've missed a big slice of American life."

"Anything would be more fun than this damned movie, David, believe me. Larry goes out of his way to humiliate me. He tried to fire Paula, you know?"

"I heard."

"I told him, she goes, *I* go! So she stayed. Then he told me he wants me to play the part just the way Vivien did! So I told him, I'm not Vivien, buster. I'm *Marilyn!* And in case you've forgotten, you're working for me."

She wiped her eyes again with a Kleenex and refilled her glass. I wondered if she was supposed to be working today. She bit her lip, then sighed. "That's when I discovered Milton had given Larry final cut! I mean, I'm paying for this movie, and I don't even get approval! I could just *kill* Milton!"

She looked as if she could, in fact, and maybe would. "He probably couldn't get Olivier any other way, Marilyn."

"I *know* that! But he should have *told* me, goddamn it, David! I can't trust anyone, that's the truth of it."

"I promise you can trust *me*," I said, I don't know why. At that moment I really believed it—it wasn't just a question of telling her what she wanted to hear.

"I know," she said, giving me a steady look that I found somewhat unnerving. I was still under the illusion that I could mediate between Marilyn and the rest of the world—a task that would have made acting as the link between Jack Kennedy and the mob an easy one!

We sat silently for a few moments. "I'm sorry the picture is such a pain," I said. "You and Larry Olivier! It sounded like a marriage made in heaven."

She laughed bitterly. "Oh, honey, if only! There's no such thing, not for me—*that* I know."

"Any chance of my visiting the set—just in case I can be of any help with Larry?"

"Sure, why not?"

"Forgive my asking, but aren't you supposed to be working today?"

She refilled her champagne glass defiantly. "I *was*," she said. "But frankly, I was so pissed off with Larry that I called him this morning and told him I couldn't make it to the studio because I was having this monster period. Talk about *embarrassed!* I guess Vivien never said anything like that to him, huh?"

It occurred to me that she was probably right. Then again, on second thought, knowing Vivien, I wasn't so sure. In her day, she had done everything she could to embarrass Larry, and by all accounts she was still doing a pretty good job.

I decided the sooner I got to the studio and saw what was going on with my own eyes, the better.

"You picked a hell of a day to visit us! Marilyn won't come out of her bloody dressing room, dear boy! On the other hand, perhaps it's a stroke of luck. You may be able to talk to her. I give up."

Olivier was clearly unstrung, almost hysterical. He had been shooting around Marilyn—a procedure recommended to him by Logan and Cukor, both of whom had learned to ignore the schedule and shoot the scenes in which Marilyn didn't appear, whenever she was having problems.

He was partly in costume, white buckskin breeches and glossy thigh-high cavalry boots with gold spurs. With a monocle and his neck shaved, he looked like Erich von Stroheim.

I asked what happened.

"I haven't a bloody clue. Usually she's just late, doesn't know her lines, blows a few dozen takes, and spends the whole bloody day sitting in a corner while the Strasberg woman whispers to her and feeds her pills. Today she arrived in tears, God knows why. She pulled herself together and we did a couple of takes of a perfectly simple scene. Then she started to cry, flounced back to her dressing room, and slammed the door. She hasn't come out since."

"Has Milton talked to her?" I noticed he was nowhere in sight. Neither was Arthur Miller.

"She won't talk to Milton," he said. "Thinks we're in cahoots."

"I'll go see her."

He sat down and pulled his boots off with a sigh. "I'll be grateful for anything you can do to get her back to work again. I curse the day I let myself be talked into this. I must have been mad."

I know misery when I see it, and his went beyond theatrics. "I saw Buddy Adler at the Connaught," I said, to cheer him up. "He said the rushes are terrific."

He flung his head back and let out a cry. "Oh God! Of *course* they are! Take after bloody take, scores of them, and with each take she gets better while the rest of us—myself included—lose whatever we had in the beginning. On the first take, I'm good and Marilyn's hopeless—doesn't have a *clue*—and on the last one, when she's finally got it right, she's wonderful and I'm bloody *awful*. Has anybody else ever had the same experience, I wonder?"

"Just Groucho Marx, Louis Calhern, George Sanders, Paul Douglas, Robert Mitchum, and Cary Grant. This is not exactly a new complaint, Larry."

"I see. Be a good chap, go talk to her, David. Tell her it's in *her* best interest to get this film finished, not just mine. *She's* the one who's going to lose money if we fuck it up, not me. I'm just a hired hand."

I turned to go.

"David," Larry called out. "Tell her that she's doing wonderful work. Tell her I said so."

He meant it, I could tell. I made my way past the set and down a long corridor of cinder block, painted a glossy off-white, with a scuffed green linoleum floor—standard for British film studios, which have none of the flashy decor of the big Hollywood studios.

I had no difficulty finding Marilyn. At the end of the corridor, a small group of people were gathered as if they were waiting outside a hospital room for bad news. Miller sat, deep in thought perhaps, on a small, battered sofa. Milton leaned against the wall, eyes closed; his face was puffy and he looked as if he had aged years since the last time I'd seen him, in Marilyn's suite at the St. Regis.

We greeted each other warily. "I'm just going to say hello to Marilyn," I said.

"Be my guest," Milton said. He sounded exhausted. Miller said nothing.

I knocked on the door.

"Go away!" Marilyn called.

"Marilyn, it's me—David."

There was a muffled conversation on the other side, between Marilyn and Paula; then the lock clicked and I let myself in. The little group waiting outside did not seem to envy me.

The curtains were drawn, so the room was dark and stuffy, full of the kind of shabby old furniture the English like. Marilyn was sunk deep in an armchair, still in costume, while Paula, dressed as always in voluminous black, sat next to her, arms around Marilyn's shoulders as if to shield her from me.

I sat down without waiting to be asked. "Larry told me how terrific you are in the rushes," I said, trying to sound cheerful. "He told me to say that you're doing wonderful work. Those were his exact words."

Paula sniffed. "Of *course* her work is wonderful—no thanks to him. We don't need Sir Cork Tip to tell us that!"

That struck me as ungracious. "Look, perhaps the chemistry isn't right, Paula," I said rather curtly. "That happens."

Marilyn's face was hidden by the yards and yards of Paula's dress —it was odd how a woman as small as Paula could take up so much space, and odder still that although Paula had always been rather elegant, since she'd met Marilyn, she had taken to wearing a kind of black schmatte, as if she were costumed for a Greek tragedy.

Marilyn looked up and stared at me over Paula's embrace, her eyes red-rimmed and brimming with tears. I thought I had her attention. I said: "Larry can't be tougher to work with than Billy Wilder, from what you've told me, Marilyn."

Marilyn's eyes, now that I looked at them more closely, were wide open, the pupils dilated, as if she were staring right through me. There were enough pill bottles for a pharmacy on her dressing table, I noticed. She made a sad little noise, as if she had cried so much she had lost her voice. "David, tell me what you do when a person betrays you?" she asked in a hoarse whisper.

"Well, I don't know," I stammered. It was a tribute to Marilyn's power to spread guilt and a sense of failed responsibility among those around her that I thought she was accusing *me* of something, and tried to imagine what it was. I could think of nothing.

"He's disappointed in me," she sobbed.

"No, no, he just told me he *isn't*," I said.

"Not Larry," Marilyn howled. "*Arthur!*"

I stared at her. "Arthur?" It was beginning to dawn on me why her husband was sitting outside her door in misery, and why the entourage looked like a funeral cortege in disarray. "What happened?"

"I read his notebook," she whispered.

"On his desk," Paula added helpfully.

It's always a mistake to read other people's letters, diaries, or notebooks, and all the more so when the writer is an artist—it's the marital equivalent of a child playing with a loaded gun. "The notebook on his table?" I asked. "Next to the photograph?" I remembered exactly where I had seen it.

"It was open," Marilyn said. "I was looking for my script."

I believed her. Marilyn had no great talent for lying, as it happened, least of all about things that mattered to her. I wondered how —or rather, *why*—a man as intelligent as Miller would have left his notebook where she could find it, let alone left it open. Carelessness? A Freudian slip? Or a writer's way of letting her know what he hadn't the strength to say to her?

"What did he write?" I asked.

"He thought I was some kind of an angel, but now he guesses he was wrong," Marilyn said. It was hard to understand her through her sobs and moans.

"He wrote that Olivier thinks she's 'a troublesome bitch' and 'he no longer has a decent answer to that one.'" Paula spat out the words with such venom, her face so contorted with fury and outrage, that I involuntarily moved my chair back. The veins were standing out on her forehead, and her lips were trembling.

"He compared me to his first wife," Marilyn said, snuffling.

"Wrote that he'd made the same mistake twice," Paula added, as if they were reciting in harmony.

"Oh God, I wish I were dead," Marilyn sobbed.

"Now, now, honey."

I sat there while the two women keened and wailed together, arms around each other. I had a notion that the only sensible thing to do was go outside and tell Miller to save himself a lot of agony and take the next plane back to New York, but I couldn't bring myself to do it. "Maybe it was a work in progress," I suggested wildly. "A play?"

Both women stared at me as if *I* were suddenly the enemy. "Of course, even if it is," I added hastily, "it's a terrible shock. Did you ask him about it?"

Marilyn shook her head.

"She isn't talking to him," Paula snapped. "Why should she?"

It was on the tip of my tongue to say because he was her husband, and that none of it was Paula Strasberg's business.

"Paula honey," Marilyn said, "I have to talk to David a moment. Could you just leave us for a couple of minutes?"

Paula shot me a look of pure hatred, but she gathered up her big handbag and made her way into the next room—of course, there was no way she would go out into the corridor and stand with Milton Greene and Arthur Miller, the traitors! My heart went out to both of them.

Marilyn wiped her eyes. "I feel like shit," she said, a little more calmly. "I look like shit, I bet."

I shook my head. "You look fine."

She tried a small smile. "Oh, David, you're a real pal. You really think those were notes for a play?"

I shrugged. "I've no idea. It's a possibility, isn't it? With a writer, the line between the real and the imaginary is sometimes hard to find. It's worth asking Arthur, if you want to stay married. If you don't, then it doesn't matter, of course. What's the name of the woman you were seeing in New York?"

"Marianne! Dr. Kris! Oh, if *only* I could talk to her, for real I mean, not on the phone. Explain what happened, ask her what to do. . . ."

"Well, why don't you? Olivier is shooting around you, anyway. Take a couple of days, fly to New York, see Dr. Kris. Take Arthur with you."

She shook her head violently, fear darkening her eyes. "I can't deal with him until I've talked to Marianne." She was beginning to recover herself, now that she had a plan to cling to and a guru to run to for wisdom. A little color had returned to her cheeks. "David," she said, grasping my hand—her fingers were ice-cold, her nails digging into my flesh—"can you get me to New York, what's it called, incognita?"

I thought about it. I knew people at the airlines who could do that. I'd arranged it before, for reclusive clients. The best way, I decided, in Marilyn's case was to have her dress up as a stewardess returning home off duty, in a uniform and a dark wig—just another pretty girl catching up on her sleep before working her next flight. I'd need to do some fancy footwork with the immigration people at either end, but they were usually happy enough to do favors for celebrities like Marilyn if they were approached the right way.

"I can do it, yes," I said firmly. Juan Trippe, the founder of Pan American, was a neighbor and an old friend. "Give me twenty-four hours and your dress size, and have somebody bring your passport to the Connaught for me."

She flung her arms around me. "Oh, David, you're *terrific!* How about one other favor?"

I beamed happily. Marilyn, when she wanted to, could make you feel you were the cleverest, most powerful man in the world. "Name it," I said. I should have known better.

"I want to go to Chicago."

"Chicago?"

"For the convention, silly. I want to see Jack, even if he *isn't* going to get the vice presidency." She laughed. "I'll be his consolation prize!"

There were about a million reasons why this was the worst and most dangerous idea in the world, but God help me, here was Marilyn, clinging to me, her eyes close to mine, lips pressed hard on my lips, and suddenly happy again! I felt like a doctor who has just cured somebody who was mortally ill. I could perform miracles! "Why not?" I heard myself ask. Then, more cautiously: "But, what will Jack say?"

"Let's not ask him," she said.

———

In the end, of course, I *did* ask him, though not before it was too late to cancel Marilyn's trip home. In view of the marital crisis that was paralyzing her, Olivier and Greene were happy enough to let her go for a few days. She was certainly no good to them in the state she was in, and Miller was probably just as relieved to be rid of her as they were.

As I had predicted, getting Marilyn out of England and back into the hands of Dr. Kris was easy enough. I flew back with her, and she attracted no more attention than any other pretty stewardess in uniform deadheading home. Just to be on the safe side, I sat beside her so she wouldn't have to talk to strangers.

Marilyn had a genius for disguise, and she didn't need Paula or Lee to tell her how to play the role. Oddly enough, in her trim Pan American uniform and her dark wig, she did not radiate the sexuality that had made her famous. It wasn't that she switched it off; it simply wasn't there, an amazing act of will, or sleight of hand, or whatever it was that turned her into one more pretty girl—though not necessarily any prettier than one or two of the other first-class flight attendants, all of whom had been briefed to pay no attention to Marilyn, incidentally, since there was no way to keep the deception from the crew.

Once safely back in New York, Marilyn holed up in the half-furnished Sutton Place apartment she had bought when she first decided to move east, emerging only for her sessions with Marianne Kris—who, like all Marilyn's therapists, might as well have had only one patient. Dr. Kris and Marilyn were on the telephone to each other for hours every day, and very soon Marilyn was able to inform me that when she went back to London, Dr. Kris would accompany her.

Poor Miller, I thought. Marilyn was bringing up the heavy Freudian artillery—*his* goose was cooked! So was Olivier's, for he would now have to contend not only with Paula Strasberg telling him how to make his picture but with Dr. Kris as well.

I put off calling Jack, on the theory that once Marilyn had poured out her side of her marital problems to Dr. Kris, the good doctor, a shrewd and lively Hungarian, would surely discourage her plan. But if Dr. Kris had any objections, she kept them to herself—or perhaps Marilyn simply didn't bother to bring the matter up, as it occurred to me much too late.

I was finally obliged to call Jack, who was in Boston overseeing the political mopping up that followed his successful coup. When I reached him in his apartment on Bowdoin Street, he was undisputed leader at last of his party in Massachusetts. He sounded irritable and tired, and when he heard the subject of my call, he exploded. "Jay-

zus!" he said—in Boston, Jack cultivated an Irish persona, right
down to the accent, and was not even above standing on a bar
counter arm in arm with Bobby to sing "Heart of My Heart" for his
admirers—"What the hell do you *mean,* Marilyn is coming to the
convention?"

"She'd be incognita, Jack, to use her favorite new word."

"Holy Mary, Mother of God, David! Have you gone out of your
fucking mind? Incognita, my ass!"

"Look, Jack, this isn't my idea. Marilyn is doing this for you. The
point I'm trying to get across is that in her present state of mind she's
quite capable of flying to Chicago by herself and turning up at your
hotel—"

"Christ!"

"Averell Harriman has asked me to go as an observer with the
New York delegation, so I can bring Marilyn with me and keep her
under control. If she goes on her own, you've got a big problem,
Jack, but make no mistake about it, she's going, one way or the
other."

"I've got a bigger problem than you think," he said grimly. "Jackie
is coming."

"Jackie? But she's pregnant! And she never comes to this kind of
thing."

"Well, she's decided to come to *this* one, David." He sighed. "It
doesn't make any sense to me either. She figures that since nothing
much is going to be happening for me at the convention, we'll have
some time together."

"Jack, if anybody's going to tell Marilyn not to come, it's not
going to be me. You have no *idea* what things were like in London
—she's a basket case. The marriage is a disaster, and so is the picture,
and for some reason she seems to think you're the one person who
can make her feel right about herself."

"You're turning soft on me, David."

"No. There are just certain things I won't do, that's all. *You* call
her and tell her not to go to Chicago. She'll take it from you. Blame
it on Jackie—Marilyn's a pushover on the subject of pregnancy. Tell
her about the political problems—she's a smarter lady than maybe
you know. . . ."

"Don't lecture me, David." In the background I could hear Frank
Sinatra singing, and a tinkle of ice cubes. It occurred to me that Jack
was almost certainly not alone. There was a long pause. "All right,"
he said. "Do whatever you think best." He sounded more cheerful,

now that he didn't have to face the task of saying no to Marilyn. "Hell, it might even be fun! A challenge anyway. Otherwise, frankly, it's going to be a hell of a dull convention for me."

"Where are you staying?" I was already thinking about the logistics.

"Jackie and I are staying with Eunice and Sarge at their apartment. I've got a suite at the Conrad Hilton, too, just for political meetings and so on, of course. . . ."

Well, of course, I thought. Jackie might be coming to the convention with Jack—her sister, Lee, had always advised her to stick close to him and give him what he wanted instead of letting him go off alone on the campaign trail into the arms of other women. But pregnant wife or not, there was always a suite, or even several, for Jack's pleasures and a staff of retainers to make sure the girlfriends didn't bump into the wife or each other. Whether this well-oiled system would work with Marilyn remained to be seen, of course. Given her extraterrestrial attitude toward time and her vagueness when it came to any plan, I wasn't optimistic.

"I'm at the Conrad Hilton too," I said. "I'll get her a suite there. It'll all be easier under one roof."

"Can you do that?" Jack asked, astonishment in his voice. Hotel rooms in Chicago had been booked months, even years, in advance for the convention.

"Trust me, I can do it." Conrad Hilton was an old friend. Like all hotel magnates, he always kept a couple of suites, just to do favors for people who mattered to him; I had no doubt that I could ask Conrad for anything I wanted and get it, no questions asked.

"Jesus!" Jack said, dropping his Irish vote-getting accent. "Talk about an embarrassment of riches! What do you think the chances are of my getting away with this?"

"Better than fifty-fifty, but not much."

"Same odds we had when PT-109 went down!" he said jubilantly.

PART TWO

STRAWHEAD

15

There was so much energy flowing in Chicago that she hardly even noticed how hot it was. It wasn't until she and David had finally reached the hotel that she realized she was soaked in sweat, her stewardess's uniform clinging to her clammily.

It had taken nearly two hours to get in from the airport—the streets of Chicago were blocked by people waving banners and chanting, a surprising number of them wearing the green and carrying posters with Jack's picture on them.

She let David fuss around the suite for a few minutes, schmearing the help, checking the air-conditioning, opening her ritual bottle of champagne; then she pleaded a headache to get rid of him. She could tell he didn't want to leave, partly because he was falling in love with her—if he hadn't already, poor guy—partly because he saw it as his duty to hand her over to Jack like a postman delivering certified mail.

He left her with a laminated pass made out in the name of Alberta "Birdy" Welles, Town Clerk and Librarian of Milan, New York, and local Democratic heavyweight. Miss Welles had apparently tripped over her cat and broken a leg on the eve of the convention, and David had somehow secured her credentials.

He also left her with strict instructions: She was not to go anywhere without him. She was not to talk to anyone. Once she was on the floor with him, under no circumstances was she to shout, "Jack Kennedy for vice president!" or even *think* it. A lot of the New York delegates, he explained—oh, how David loved explaining!—thought Kefauver was a hick. They were committed to Mayor Robert Wagner as New York's "favorite son" candidate, but it wouldn't take a lot to stampede them into supporting Jack Kennedy. . . .

She heard a noise behind her and turned around to see Jack grinning broadly. Giving a squeal of surprise, she ran across the room to kiss him. "What's a favorite son?" she asked.

"You're looking at someone who *isn't* one. A delegation picks a favorite son so they can sit through enough ballots to get a decent price for switching their votes to a serious candidate at the last minute. It's an art form, among politicians."

"Where did you *come* from?" she asked.

"The suite next door. At the moment it's filled with politicians trying to make a mountain out of a molehill, and it smells like a cigar factory." He looked around admiringly. "Say, this is a much nicer suite than mine."

She could smell the aroma of cigars in his hair. He led her over to the bar in the corner and poured himself a drink. Then he lay down on the sofa and with a sigh put his feet up on Conrad Hilton's most expensive upholstery. There was a dish of peanuts on the coffee table in front of him. He tossed them into the air one by one and caught them in his mouth.

She sat down beside him, stroking his hair as if to assure herself that he was really there. This was what she had always dreamed of having with her husbands—a moment of quiet intimacy, however brief—but never had with any of them. "What's going on in there?" she asked, glancing toward the door that joined her suite to his.

"The fellows who don't like Estes Kefauver—big-city bosses like Mayor Daley here in Chicago, Dave Lawrence in Pennsylvania, Mike Di Salle from Ohio—they've been trying to persuade Adlai he needs me on the ticket. I've been trying to persuade *them* to lay off."

He yawned. "Dad's right. Getting the vice presidential nomination could lose me any chance at the presidential nomination in '60, maybe even in '64."

She ran her fingertips over his face gently, bending so close to him that her hair brushed against his cheeks. "Why do you want to be president?" she asked.

He didn't laugh. On the contrary, his expression was suddenly serious, even somber, as if it was something he'd asked himself many times. "It's the only thing I can do," he said quietly, none of his usual jaunty bravado in evidence for once.

"The only thing you can do?"

"Well, it's what I've been trained for—raised for, really, since Joe's death."

"Isn't it something *you* want?"

"I didn't use to. But lately it's been growing on me. When I look around me and see the assholes who want to run. . . . I mean, Jesus, there's Adlai, who can't even make his mind up about what he wants to eat for breakfast, and Lyndon Johnson, who only got where he is by kissing Sam Rayburn's ass, or Hubert Humphrey, who's just Eleanor Roosevelt's eunuch. . . . I can do better than any of *them,* that much I know. Somebody has to be president. It may as well be me."

"I wasn't challenging you, Jack. I was just curious."

"I used to wonder how I could get out of it. . . . Funny, I never told anybody that before, except Bobby."

"Not Jackie?"

"No. Jackie wants to be First Lady. She figures she's owed it by now, and maybe she's right."

"Is that the problem between you two?"

"No," he said, "that's not the problem."

Something in his voice warned her to back off.

"I always thought you were ambitious," she said jokingly. "I thought that was one of the things we really had in common, ambition."

"Oh, I'm ambitious enough, I guess. It's just that I can't think of anything less than the presidency to be ambitious *about.* It's the only job worth reaching for, you see. I mean, look at Averell Harriman— all the money in the world, ambassador to Moscow in the war, when that was a big deal, friend and adviser to FDR and Truman, governor of New York, but he never got to the White House!"

"Maybe he never wanted to."

Jack laughed. "Oh, Averell wanted it so bad he could taste it. Still does, probably. But he never fought hard enough for it, so he'll always be a footnote to history—a long footnote maybe, but that's it. It's better to go out with a blaze and rate a whole chapter."

Go out with a blaze and rate a whole chapter! That was her own life story right there, the belief that had guided her all the way to stardom. That was what made them improbably alike—they both took risks that would have stopped most people cold. Other people might doubt that Jack Kennedy could be president—he was too young, he was Catholic, his father was hated, his private life made him vulnerable—but she had the same absolute faith in his star as she did in her own.

"How much time do you have?" she asked.

He smiled. "Ten minutes. The natives are restless. A whole bunch of heavy hitters from the big cities are in there listening to Bobby tell them that they have to take Kefauver if Adlai wants him, like it or not. We're getting full marks for loyalty, but it's not the message they came to hear."

"I guess ten minutes will have to do." She pulled off her uniform jacket and blouse, tossing them to the floor, then stood up and stepped out of the skirt. It occurred to her briefly that she hadn't locked the door or put up the Do Not Disturb sign, but she didn't give a damn.

She stood for a moment, while Jack, still fully clothed and lying on the sofa, looked at her. "Jesus!" he whispered softly.

"This won't take but a minute, Senator," she said, smiling and unbuttoning his trousers. She placed her hands on either side of his head to steady herself; then, straddling him, she leaned forward and kissed him. Absurdly excited by the contrast between her nakedness and his respectable dark suit, she moved faster and faster, in control of both their bodies, pushing herself down until she could feel him deep, deep inside her.

She felt her own breath coming in quick, ragged gasps, faster and faster, until she gave a great, shuddering cry, and collapsed on top of him. It occurred to her that she was probably messing up his suit, but then she decided she didn't give a shit. "How was *that*, Senator?" she asked huskily.

"Not bad. With a little practice you could get pretty, ah, *good* at this."

She gave him a long kiss. "I wish you were mine," she said.

"Well, at the moment, I *am*."

"I don't mean right now."

"I know you don't."

She put another ice cube in his drink, brought it over to him, and poured herself a glass of champagne. "What do you think they'd all say in there," she asked, "if they knew you'd been in here fucking Marilyn Monroe?"

"They'd probably ask me to take Adlai's place on the ticket. There wouldn't be a man in the country who wouldn't vote for me if it was known."

She gave him a big, wet kiss. "That's what I think too, my darling," she said. "Maybe you ought to use it. Will I see you tonight?"

He was on his feet now, in the bathroom, already concentrating on what he had to do next. "Tonight?" he asked. "I don't know. I'll try." He did not sound as if he would try very hard. "Are you going to be on the floor for the movie?"

"David's taking me. I wouldn't miss it."

"I'll try and get word to you." He gave her an unmistakable look of warning. "For God's sake, be careful, Marilyn."

She was still naked. Well, it wasn't anything he hadn't seen before. "I'll be careful, Jack, don't worry," she said.

She tried not to resent the warning. She was not some inexperienced housewife having her first affair. She had dated Howard Hughes for several weeks way back in her fledgling starlet days, and there was nothing she hadn't learned then about secrecy and disguises, for Howard was already beginning to show the first signs of paranoid craziness and insisted on meeting her in secret rendezvous in the middle of the night, as if they were spies.

He washed his face, combed his hair with his fingers, straightened his tie, fixed his PT-109 tie clip in place. He dabbed at a few stains on his suit with a piece of Kleenex, then brushed himself off. He looked every inch the senator again.

"Knock 'em dead, tiger," she added softly as he went to the door.

He gave her a jaunty thumbs-up, and opened it. A wisp of cigar smoke drifted out. She heard a deep voice say, "Where the fuck *is* Jack? How the hell long does it take him to have a crap?"

He turned and gave her a wink. Just before the door closed behind him, she heard him reply: "Sorry about that, gentlemen, but I had a piece of business that required my, ah, *full* attention. . . ."

She put on a robe and called David on the phone. She hated eating alone—the fate, as she well knew, of every mistress of a busy man.

————

She had never seen so many people in one place except for her visit to Korea to entertain the troops. The convention hall was packed with people, thousands of them, waving placards, wearing funny hats, chanting and singing, while in the background a band played "Happy Days Are Here Again," over and over, through loudspeakers turned up so high her ears ached. The air-conditioning was working full tilt, but no amount of cold air could cope with the body heat of several thousand people, and she was instantly drenched in sweat.

Holding his credentials in front of him, David pushed his way toward the New York delegation, many of whom held signs with Robert Wagner's name on them. None of them looked particularly enthusiastic.

In the distance, on the flag-draped podium below giant portraits of FDR, Harry Truman, and Adlai Stevenson, somebody was shouting into the microphone, his bellow incomprehensible above the music and the background noise. Nobody was paying attention—people chatted, gathered in clumps to discuss politics, greeted one another boisterously, while the speaker, whoever he was, droned on.

She wasn't all that interested either in hearing what the speaker had to say, but she supposed it would be polite to listen. David was busy shaking the hands of flushed, sweating strangers, greeting people by their first names as if *he* were running for office, even smiling when they slapped him on the back or gave him a bear hug. From time to time he introduced her as Miss Welles, but in the echoing din of the hall, she never caught the name of anyone he introduced to her. Everybody deferred to him, she noticed. Clearly, he was an important figure in the Democratic party.

Nobody paid much attention to her. She wore a dark wig, no makeup, and a pleated linen skirt, a little on the long side, with a modestly cut matching jacket and flat-heeled shoes. When she looked at herself in the mirror, the word that came to her mind was "mousy," but just to be on the safe side, she had added a pair of horn-rimmed glasses with clear lenses, with a cord around her neck, and a large, plain shoulder bag. Someone who was paying attention would surely notice the body underneath the drab clothes, but certainly no one would guess she was Marilyn Monroe—and apparently, the excitement of politics was such that very few of the men even gave her a second glance!

David pushed her in the direction of a tall, patrician-looking gentleman who had been complaining loudly about the sound system. At the sight of David he leaned over close, one hand cupped to his ear to hear her name above the noise. "Averell," David shouted, "this is Miss Birdy Welles. Miss Welles, Governor Harriman."

Harriman smiled, but there was a puzzled look on his face. Uh-oh, she thought, we've been here ten minutes and already we're in trouble! "Not from Milan?" Harriman asked, squinting as he tried to read the credentials pinned to her bosom. He rubbed his craggy jaw for a moment, then gave David a fishy stare. It was clear to her that he had the professional politician's memory for names and faces. "I seem to remember meeting a lady of that name in Albany," Harriman said, his accent as sharp as a knife. "A much older lady, I think. Not as attractive, to be quite frank. Not *nearly.*"

"My aunt!" she said brightly. "She had an accident, you see, so she sent me in her place."

"Isn't that a little—irregular?" the governor asked, raising an eyebrow—something he did with the skill of Cary Grant, except that with him it wasn't acting.

David's face, she noticed, was crimson, but luck was on her side, or Jack's, for at that moment the lights dimmed, the loudspeaker gave a final squawk, the crowd fell silent out of habit as the huge movie screen lit up, and Governor Harriman was pulled away by unseen hands.

There were no empty seats. In fact, there were more people standing than sitting, and most people with seats had to rise to their feet to see anything. Below the screen she could just make out a row of figures lining up on stage: she recognized Adlai Stevenson—until recently her hero; Governor Harriman, still arguing furiously, presumably about the sound system; a squat, bullet-headed man with a knowing smile whom she took to be Mayor Daley; and Mrs. Roosevelt herself, whom she, like most American children of the Depression and the war, regarded as a kind of secular saint.

She clapped and cheered and shouted for Mrs. Roosevelt. Then Jack Kennedy's voice rang crisp and clear throughout the huge hall. His face appeared in front of an American flag, looking incredibly young, handsome, and self-confident, eyes flashing, hair tousled by the wind. In a single moment, his image on the screen made everybody on the stage seem old, withered, and lifeless. Adlai Stevenson, with his rumpled suit, his bald head, and the deep pouches under his eyes, looked like a tired old hound dog, and the rest of them looked worse. She could tell that the delegates saw it too. They stared at the screen in dead silence, the way Marlon told her the audience had listened when he made his Broadway debut in *Streetcar*.

In a way, she thought, this was Jack's debut, and it was a smash hit. Nobody here really expected Stevenson to beat Ike; up to this moment, despite the noise, it had been a convention ready to acknowledge defeat before the campaign even began, prepared to cheer Adlai because he seemed like a decent man and a good loser, but conscious that he was a loser all the same. Jack, narrating the film, somehow managed to remind them that there was such a thing as a winner.

She and Paula had done well by him; he spoke firmly, paused at the right moments, radiated sincerity, looked the camera straight in the eye. As she glanced around the convention hall, she could see that women of all ages were staring at the screen as if Jack were a movie star.

It was working too, and not just with women. As Jack brought his filmed narration to a conclusion, the applause started before he had even finished, the delegates shouting, louder and louder, "Ken-ne-dy, *Ken-ne-dy!*" over and over again, clapping, stamping their feet,

185

until the whole hall seemed to shake. The band took up, presumably because of its regional associations, "Yankee Doodle Dandy" and then, lest anyone forget PT-109, "Anchors Aweigh." The people on the platform looked annoyed, particularly Mrs. Roosevelt, while the chairman banged away helplessly with his gavel, trying to restore order.

All over the arena, people began to hold up pictures of Jack with the caption "Our Choice"; banners were raised with pictures of Jack and PT-109; volunteers, most of them pretty young girls, spread through the crowd passing out more banners, Kennedy balloons, even Kennedy buttons, one of which she pinned to her jacket. The noise seemed likely to go on forever, punctuated by the banging of the gavel magnified until it sounded like a jackhammer. She grabbed David's hand. "What's *happening?*" she shouted.

He had to put his lips against her ear to make himself heard. "Jack's friends just fucked him," he said, grinning. "They're trying to stampede him into making a run. Just look at Adlai's face up there! He must be kicking himself for letting Jack narrate the movie!"

She glanced at the platform, where Stevenson was deep in what seemed to be angry conversation with Mrs. Roosevelt.

"Is that Mayor Daley up there? The bruiser who looks like an Irish cop?" She pointed at a heavyset man grinning from ear to ear, apparently having the time of his life, while Stevenson and Mrs. Roosevelt, firmly seated, glared at him disapprovingly from time to time, without effect.

David nodded. "That's him."

"Did he set this up?"

"The demonstration for Jack? I expect so. I guess Daley took care of the sound system, too. After all, Chicago is his town. I think you could safely assume that anyone with something to say that His Honor doesn't want to hear is going to have problems with the sound system."

It hadn't occurred to her that the problems with the system might not be an accident, simple bad luck. She had a lot to learn about politics, it seemed.

The demonstrations all around them went on and on, ebbing only to start again louder than ever. She had been carried away by the noise and excitement, but now she was beginning to wish it would stop. Then, quite suddenly, like an explosion, the crowd went wild.

She stood on tiptoe and saw that Jack was on the platform in person now, a shy smile on his face. He handled himself with the grace of a born actor, she thought. He did not exactly *ignore* the demonstration seething in front of him, but he managed to suggest by his detached manner that it might be for somebody else. As he leaned over to shake hands with Stevenson and Mrs. Roosevelt, his expression implied that he was as embarrassed by all the fuss on his behalf as they were.

Mrs. Roosevelt's face was a study in granite disapproval as Jack talked to her—here, at last, was a woman who was impervious to his charm! He straightened up, gave Mayor Daley and his cohorts a wink, and went over to the side of the platform to stand modestly with the party faithful, leaving the limelight to the candidate, whom the crowd was ignoring completely.

She was being pushed forward by the pro-Kennedy faction of the New York delegation, which was apparently determined to follow the Massachusetts delegates to the speaker's platform, where the television cameras would have a better view of them.

At first she found the experience exhilarating, but the thrill soon gave way to growing fear as she was swept on by the noisy crowd chanting, clapping, pushing, and shoving, carrying her along as if she were a piece of flotsam in the surf.

She lost David—couldn't even turn around to find him anymore. She was terrified of falling, or being tripped, pressed in on all sides by sweating, noisy strangers. She was used to the press of crowds, but when she was in them, there were always people on hand to whisk her away to safety if necessary.

The band was playing "When Irish Eyes Are Smiling" now, and the Massachusetts delegates were eddying against the podium, being pushed to either side by the crowds behind them. She felt someone pinch her ass hard and kicked out. She had the satisfaction of feeling her toe make sharp contact with somebody's shin and heard a man cry out in pain.

She kicked and fought her way forward, finding herself suddenly part of what seemed to be a rough conga line dancing toward the podium arm in arm. She felt her wig slip to one side; her clothes were drenched in her own sweat as she held on to the people on either side of her for dear life.

Ahead of her she saw the red-white-and-blue bunting of the platform sticking up above the crowd. Then she felt her heel break, plunging her forward. She landed against the rough, flag-draped lumber of the platform and clung to it as people bumped into her, pressing against her until she was sure she would be crushed. Her stockings were torn, one of her bra straps was broken, and she was gasping for breath. Suddenly a hand reached down from above her and grasped her wrist firmly. *"Jump!"* she heard a familiar voice shout over the noise.

She gave a leap and found a place to put her foot on the scaffolding as he pulled her by the arm; then she was clear of the crowd. From over the railing above her head, Jack was looking down at her, grinning. "Good fishing today!" he said cheerfully, hauling her up a little higher. "Nice catch."

She managed to get one hand on the railing, then swung herself over it onto the platform, tumbling into his arms. She could see the flashbulbs popping as news photographers recorded her rescue. "What's your name, honey?" a reporter shouted.

She panicked—she couldn't remember what it was supposed to be, but Jack made a show of glancing closely at her bosom to read her credentials. "Miss Birdy Welles, of Milan, New York," he called out. "What do you do, Miss Welles?"

That, she could remember. "I'm a librarian," she said.

"You sure don't *look* like a librarian," Mayor Daley growled, in what she took to be the spirit of gallantry. "If our librarians here in Chicago looked like you, I'da read more books when I was in school."

"I'm town clerk, too," she said, remembering suddenly.

"Tell the truth, you don't look like no town clerk neither."

"I'm glad to have been of service," Jack said. "It looked like a real mob scene down there. Are you okay, Miss, ah, *Welles?*" He gave her a wink.

"I broke a heel," she told him sweetly, raising her leg so he could look at her shoe—and her ankle.

"Ah, yes, I see. Well, I guess it could have been worse." He winked again. "I'll get someone to see you back to your hotel, Miss Welles, so you can change shoes." He waved off stage, and Boom-Boom appeared at a run, raising one massive eyebrow at the sight of her.

Jack was grinning from ear to ear.

"Somebody pinched my ass down there so hard I bet I'm bruised," she whispered to him.

"Nobody ever said politics wasn't a dangerous business," he whispered back. "I look forward to getting a close look at your battle scars later on."

"Promises, promises, Senator. When?"

"I can't say. Things seem to be getting out of control. . . . Order up some food—a couple of club sandwiches maybe—and I'll join you when I can."

"What about Jackie?"

"Jackie's back at the apartment, watching this on television. Let's hope she can't read lips. Let's hope *nobody* who's watching can!"

"I wish I could give you a kiss."

She said it in such a low voice that no one but Jack could have heard her, but still, he blushed. Then she heard the unmistakable voice of Mrs. Roosevelt saying: "Birdy Welles! My Lord, I knew I heard that name before, and now it comes back to me, of course. She's a neighbor."

Mrs. Roosevelt was beginning to turn, her vision partly obscured by the press of people around Jack and by her flowered hat. For a moment Marilyn was paralyzed by the fear that she was about to have a face-to-face confrontation with Eleanor Roosevelt in front of the television cameras, but Jack took her by the arm and pushed her toward Boom-Boom, who practically tore her off the platform without letting her feet touch the ground.

"Miss Welles just left," she heard Jack say to Mrs. Roosevelt. Then she was back in the world Boom-Boom seemed to know best, that of back corridors, secret stairways, and service elevators.

It suddenly occurred to her that David must be sweating bullets at having lost her. She smiled, a little guiltily, at the thought.

———

She took pity on David and left a message to let him know that she was safely back in her suite. She ordered sandwiches to be brought up, a couple of bottles of Dom Perignon, and a bottle of Jack's favorite Ballantine scotch. On second thought, she called back to ask room service to put a couple of cartons of vanilla ice cream in the refrigerator, along with a bowl of chocolate fudge sauce—for Jack's sweet tooth—then settled down on the sofa in her dressing gown to read Carl Sandburg. She picked the book up each time with the best of intentions—she *wanted* to read more about Mr. Lincoln—but after three years of reading, he was still in Illinois, a country lawyer.

She put the book down and tried Harold Robbins's *79 Park Avenue* instead, which certainly moved along faster.

People often made fun of her pretensions when it came to reading, but in fact she read a lot, although without any consistent plan, as Arthur was forever tiresomely pointing out. She enjoyed reading at her own pace, and if she wanted to switch from Carl Sandburg to Harold Robbins and back again, whose business was it but her own? " 'It's just that she's not for you,' " she read. " 'She's been brought up without love and has no understanding of it.' "

She put her finger on page 23 to mark her place and closed the book. Perhaps the reason why she was such a slow reader (though that had never bothered anyone before Arthur) was that she was always finding phrases that made her stop and think. Surely that was the whole *point* of reading, she had once told Arthur, arguing back for a change, but she suspected that, like many intellectuals, he read chiefly to reinforce ideas he already had, or for new arguments to support them.

She lay back and thought about the evening. At some point she had come to the realization that Jack Kennedy was going to be the president one day. Out there on the floor of the convention, she had *felt* it in the voices of the demonstrators, seen it in the eyes of Stevenson and his supporters on the platform.

It was hard to imagine Jack as president—presidents to her were mostly old men, their faces craggy, weary, lined: Ike, Truman, FDR, and Mr. Lincoln. Jack had a kind of college boy charm, and it was easy to forget that he was not only a serious politician but a very rich man. In the movie he had narrated—to such stunning effect—he had talked about the poor, the workers, the blacks, the small farmers, ordinary people, the meat-and-potato voters who were the backbone of the Democratic party. But how much did he really *know* about people like her mother, who had earned her living processing movie film at Consolidated Film Labs before she went over the edge into madness and state care? *She* knew what it was like to be working class, it was her own, and there was some core of her in which she wasn't sure she could trust the sincerity of Jack Kennedy's commitment to the kind of people she had been raised among. Oh God! she thought. Who am I to be looking for a white knight at this stage of my life?

She was so absorbed that she didn't hear the door open at two a.m. A sixth sense told her that someone else was in the room, and she rose to find herself looking at an embarrassed Bobby Kennedy. Jack was already at the bar, pouring himself a Ballantine. David followed Bobby and closed the door behind him.

Jack took a deep drink, then came over and kissed her, running one hand down her back and leaving it there. Bobby, she noticed, looked as rumpled as if he had been standing under a shower in his suit. Only David looked cool and elegant, in a dove-gray summer-weight suit, with his trademark white vest and a flower in his button-hole, as if the convention was a vacation for him—which, since he was a successful businessman and this was his hobby, she supposed it was.

Jack took off his jacket, dropped it on the floor, sat down on the sofa, and patted it to indicate that she should sit beside him. He stretched out, feet on the coffee table, looking so exhausted that she almost forgave him for keeping her waiting for hours.

"I'm really sorry, Marilyn," he said. "Things have been a little tense in there."

David took a brandy snifter and poured himself a large cognac. Bobby, his face an angry mask, didn't go near the bar. He leaned against the connecting door, silently massaging his face and combing the hair out of his eyes with his fingers. "You have to go, Jack, that's all there is to it," David said. "You can't cancel breakfast this late. Go and listen to what Adlai has to say—that's my advice."

"I don't need advice. I need somebody who can get things back under control."

"What happened?" she asked.

Jack sipped at his drink. He placed one hand on her thigh. She felt for a moment as if they were an old married couple; then he moved his hand a little higher, and she was reminded that they weren't. "The telephone lines have been going crazy," he said. "People calling in about the film."

David cradled his drink. He was clearly enjoying himself. "It was broadcast on national television tonight," he explained to her. "People have been calling the networks until their switchboards were tied up. And calling the delegates here to say how much they liked Jack. By the thousands."

"Old ladies mostly," Jack said with a laugh. " 'Sure and he looks like such a nice boy!' "

"They aren't *all* old ladies," David said. "But the majority of the calls were from women, yes."

"I'm not surprised," she said. She gave Jack a kiss. "You looked pretty sexy out there, Jack."

Bobby Kennedy's voice was a snarl, the voice of conscience and duty, and it made her shiver. "The question is, do you go for it or not, Jack?"

"Everybody in there thinks we've got a shot," Jack said. He didn't say what *he* thought, she noticed.

"A shot!" Bobby snapped contemptuously. "You don't want to get into this to take a goddamn *shot* at it," he said, his eyes flashing. "If you go for the vice presidency, Jack, you go to *win!*"

She caught a tone in Bobby's voice—a mixture of passion, rage, fierce determination, and reckless courage—that was like nothing she had ever heard before. His expression was stubborn, almost mulish, his eyes fixed on Jack's, challenging him. She looked at Jack, and what she saw there was just as chilling. His mouth and jaw were set as if in anger, and he suddenly seemed much older and infinitely tougher. He stared back at Bobby, and she was struck by the thought that she had never seen two colder pairs of eyes.

He's going to go for it, she thought. Then Jack took a deep swallow, his face still looking as if it were carved in granite, and said, "Tell them to start counting our delegates."

"They're already doing that. What are you going to tell Adlai at breakfast?"

Jack gave a grim smile. "To get ready for a fight."

Bobby nodded somberly—no hint of a smile.

"Who gets to tell the Ambassador?" David said.

There was a long silence while the brothers looked at each other with stony faces. Then they both turned their attention to David, who shook his head. "No," he said firmly.

She was impressed by the force with which he said it. So were Jack and Bobby, she thought. Jack did not try to persuade him. "One of us is going to have to bite the goddamn bullet," he said glumly. He closed his eyes for a moment. "It's about nine in the morning in France. He'll be having breakfast. Go call him, Bobby."

Bobby's expression was mutinous. "Why me?" he asked.

"Because you're my younger brother."

Bobby's jaw muscles clenched, but he slouched off, head down, hands in his pockets, into her bedroom—without asking her permission.

"Better him than me," David said. Jack nodded.

From the bedroom she could hear Bobby presenting his best case to his father, his voice low; then he was silent for a very long time. He stood up and paced around the room, the telephone receiver jammed between his ear and his shoulder. At one point he stopped in the doorway and held the receiver up toward them. Even from across the room she could hear the anger in Joe Kennedy's voice, rasping like an electrical storm being broadcast from the South of France.

Bobby put his hand over the mouthpiece. "Dad says we're god-damn fools."

"He could be right. Tell him we didn't want to get into this fight, but now that we're in it, we have to bet the farm."

"He says don't tell him what he already knows." Bobby held the receiver out. "He has some choice words for you."

Jack groaned, rose from the couch, took the telephone from Bobby, went into the bedroom, and closed the door. Bobby poured himself a soda. Sweat was running down his face. He rubbed his eyes —she didn't think she had ever seen anybody so haggard.

"What else did he say?" David asked.

Bobby drank his soda slowly, as if he were afraid he wouldn't be offered another for a while. "Dad says we should nail down Jim Farley right away, if we can. Joe junior did Farley a favor in the 1940 convention. He'd like you to try."

David nodded. "He's right. Your brother refused to switch his vote to FDR even when it was obvious that Farley was out of the running. There was terrific pressure on young Joe to make it unanimous for FDR, but he wouldn't budge. He didn't even like Farley all that much, but he was loyal."

"Dad thinks Farley will try to weasel out of supporting Jack. He says he's a lily-livered, ungrateful son of a bitch."

"He said the same thing in 1940, as a matter of fact. I'll give it a shot. Farley used to like me."

Bobby nodded quickly, dismissing the problem from his mind now that somebody had been assigned to deal with it. There was a kind of brisk efficiency to him that she found attractive. His gestures were emphatic but economical, his clothes not so much careless as simple and basic—wash-and-wear suits, button-down shirts, loafers, his hair long because he had no time to waste on barbers. He seemed to have no vices or luxuries, she thought, unless you counted getting Ethel pregnant once a year.

His attention suddenly fixed on her, as if he had only just noticed her presence. She felt a tiny shiver; there was so much going on in that face, or *behind* it! When he was talking to David, Bobby's face had been craggy, the lines in it harshly accentuated, the nose as sharp and cutting as an eagle's beak. As he looked at her now, his features softened, and he seemed years younger. "I'm sorry I used your bed-room," he said.

"Why? I wasn't in there or anything." He was blushing. She had thrown her clothes on the bed, she remembered, but surely the sight of a bra or a pair of stockings shouldn't embarrass a man who had so many children.

"I should have asked first."

"That's okay."

He cleared his throat. She noticed his shirt was frayed at the collar and cuffs. "The fact is, I didn't know you were here. Jack didn't tell me until he was just about to open the door. Frankly, I don't think it's such a hot idea."

"My being here?"

"It's a big risk for Jack to take. Now that he's going for the vice presidential nomination, it's a bigger one."

"It's a risk for me, too."

"Not the same kind."

There was no denying that. She didn't need Bobby to tell her that a Catholic politician with a pregnant wife who was discovered having an affair with a movie star could kiss the presidency good-bye, and probably the vice presidency as well.

She caught the gleam of accusation in his eyes, and it stiffened her backbone immediately. "He's a grown-up," she said defiantly. "He knows what he's doing."

"We're all grown-ups." He spoke sadly. "Maybe that ought to stop us from doing dumb things, but it never does. Just try to keep a low profile, okay?"

"Will he get it? The vice presidency, I mean?"

"It's going to be damned close. I don't know if he'll get the *vice* presidency, but I can guarantee you he's going to be president, because I'm going to help him get it."

Impulsively she leaned over and gave him a kiss. "I want us to be friends," she said.

She was afraid that he'd be angry, but he gave her a big smile—his smile was even bigger than Jack's. "We'll be friends," he said. "Don't worry." There was a smudge of lipstick on his cheek. She took a Kleenex and rubbed it off, feeling oddly motherly as she did so.

"Okay then." She took his hand in hers, moving his fingers until she had him in the secret handshake of her days in Van Nuys High School, thumbs crossed, fingers interlaced. "It's a promise?"

The handshake was unfamiliar to him, but the idea of it was familiar enough, whether at Van Nuys or the more rarefied boarding schools of the East Coast that he had attended. "It's a promise," he said with a laugh, but his eyes made it very clear that he meant it. Promises, she guessed, were something Bobby took seriously.

Jack came out of the bedroom and caught David's eye. "He wants to talk to you now, David," he said. "Be prepared. He's not a happy man." He looked at her and Bobby holding hands and raised an eyebrow. "I'm glad to see the two of *you* are getting along so, ah, well together. God knows what Ethel would say."

Bobby's face flushed; he held himself back from replying. She watched with interest. It seemed to her that Bobby, tough-minded and independent as he was, would always defer to Jack—as if the relationship between them had been settled forever in childhood, during a thousand touch football games, arm-wrestling matches, and fights: Jack was older, bigger, and that was that. She searched Bobby's face for a hint of real resentment, but it wasn't there. He loved his brother fiercely, which, she thought, was very likely the only way he knew how to love. "Well?" he asked.

"It's a good thing I wasn't expecting a paternal blessing," Jack said with a rueful smile. "I told Dad I'd call him back after I've talked with Adlai." He winked at Bobby. "He told me not to let you drag me into a fight. 'Bobby's the goddamn hothead,' he said."

"The hell I am!"

"Listen, don't feel bad. He told *me* not to let other people do my thinking for me. It's going to be real fun taking his calls when I'm in the White House!"

Jack loosened his collar and tore off his tie. "Bobby, go next door and tell them I want to know how many votes we can count on before I have breakfast with Adlai. And no bullshit, okay? I don't want a wish list. I want to know who we can goddamn *count* on, not maybes, or should bes, or guesses."

Bobby nodded. What had to be done he would do; it was that simple. David, who had relinquished the phone at last, seemed to have found a new lease on life too. She understood, belatedly, why a man as wealthy and powerful as David Leman deferred to Jack Kennedy and gave so much of his time to his affairs. It wasn't wholly, or even primarily, friendship—David, she realized, craved the excitement, the sense of being a mover and shaker in politics. He *needed* to be an insider, to be playing, as Frank liked to put it, at the big table, one of the high rollers.

"Your father says Adlai might try to mousetrap you by floating out the name of another Catholic candidate, just to show he's not prejudiced," David said. "I think he's right."

"I guess that just *could* occur to Adlai," Jack said grimly. "That means we have to get pledges of support from Mike Di Salle and Dave Lawrence right away. Bobby, you go see them first thing in the morning, even if you have to get them out of bed. *Nail them down,* Bobby!"

He stretched, yawned, and rubbed his hands down his back, wincing in pain. "I'm going to get some rest myself. You too, David. Tomorrow's going to be a ball-breaker. How about it, Marilyn?"

Jack steered her firmly into the bedroom, leaving Bobby and David standing in the living room. He sat down on the bed wearily and pulled off his shoes. "I'm sorry," he said. "I didn't expect this."

"It's the breaks, honey." She was not as displeased as he supposed her to be. She liked action for its own sake as much as David appeared to. Maybe things would have been different with Joe, she thought, if he had still been playing instead of sitting around watching sports on TV. Maybe, too, she had underestimated the sheer tedium of a writer's life before marrying Arthur Miller.

She helped Jack off with his clothes, unfastened her dressing gown, and got into bed beside him, enjoying the feel of his beard against her lips, the taste of his sweat on her tongue. "Fuck me, my darling," she whispered in his ear, and with a sigh of contentment—the profound feeling that right now, at this very moment, she was *wanted,* deeply, passionately—she put her arms around his hard, muscular body, inhaled that lovely aroma of sweat and after-shave lotion and whatever else it was that made men smell miraculously different, and buried herself in him.

————

She slept dreamlessly, without pills for once—not from choice, she had simply forgotten to take them—her body so close to his that she couldn't tell where his began and her own left off, the bed sweetly sticky from their juices, the light in the bathroom still burning, the air conditioner roaring and changing speed like a Saturday night drag racer pulling away from a light on Ventura Boulevard, but still failing to cope with the heat and humidity of Chicago in August.

As she woke to the first light of dawn—they had forgotten to pull the blinds and curtains completely closed—she felt strangely restored. Every muscle ached pleasantly as she yawned and stretched —really, she thought, Jackie was a lucky lady, but then marriage being what it was, perhaps not.

Jack was sleeping on his back. He was built like the college athlete he had once been: long limbs, a flat, slender waist, strong shoulders, no hips. There was a mass of pale scar tissue down his spine from his wound and the three operations he had undergone. She wondered if Jackie had been expecting him home last night, or at least expecting a call. If *she* had been sitting across the city, eight months pregnant, waiting for her husband to call, she would have been mad as hell, but perhaps Jackie was made of sterner stuff, or no longer cared —and in any case, it was none of her business. It was Jack's job to worry about Jackie, not hers.

She got on her hands and knees and straddled him, her hair brushing his face, her breasts touching the matted red hair on his chest. She gave him a kiss—a butterfly kiss, as they used to call it in Van Nuys High School when the girls talked among themselves about all the subtleties of the art of kissing. She licked her lips, then touched them against his so gently that it was almost as if no more than their breaths were touching. She licked his lips softly with the tip of her tongue until he began to stir in his sleep. He opened his eyes. The lids were still half closed, the lashes—long enough that any girl would be proud of them—sticky from sleep. "Oh my God!" he muttered thickly. "What time is it?"

"Six-thirty, honey. I wanted to be the one to wake you."

"Did you now? I figured you for a late sleeper."

"I am. But it just so happens that I like kissing a guy awake."

"It beats an alarm clock any day, let me tell you."

"Doesn't it just? Can you imagine how many guys there are in the world who dream about having Marilyn Monroe wake them up like this?"

He took his watch out from under the pillow and glanced at it. There was something transparent and touching about the gesture— he was trying to calculate if he had time for a quickie.

He slipped the watch back under the pillow, put his arms around her, and pulled her down on him. "Let 'em dream," he said.

————

Jack came out of the bathroom in a cloud of steam, a towel wrapped around his thin hips, his hair wet and standing up. She poured him a cup of coffee—one sugar and cream, as she had learned—and a glass of orange juice, which he downed at a gulp. He padded through the suite to the connecting door, opened it, and said, "My God, it smells like the club car after an all-night poker game in here."

She heard Bobby's voice, raw with fatigue. "We figure we can count on at least two hundred sure votes on the first ballot."

"Not good enough."

"We can double that in two days if we work our butts off."

"Maybe."

"Did you get any rest?"

"I've never slept better in my life. Give me a moment to get dressed, and we'll go over the names before I go down to Adlai's suite. Then you'd better go shower and change, Bobby. It's going to be a long day. I don't want you fading out on me."

"Fuck you."

"I wish I had your gift for repartee."

"Very funny. Maybe you should look at the papers this morning, Senator. You may have to do some explaining to Jackie when she sees the front pages."

She grabbed the papers off the breakfast table before Jack could get back to the bedroom, and spread them on the bed. Nothing much caught her eye except headlines about the Kennedy boom. Jack came up behind her and peered over her shoulder, his face troubled. They both looked at the *Examiner,* but there was nothing there. She pushed it on the floor and unfolded the *Chicago Tribune.* There, on the front page, was a photograph of the "spontaneous" demonstration for Kennedy, taken at just the moment when the crowd had forced its way to the podium. In the very center of the picture, a woman was climbing up the side of the platform, legs showing right to her tush, as the Senator pulled her to safety over the flag-draped railing. He had his hands around her, and the angle of the photograph made it look almost as if they were kissing. The caption read: "Kennedy Saves a Supporter!" Below that, she was identified as "Birdy Wales, a librarian, of Milan, New York, and a lifelong Democrat."

They both stared at the photograph silently for a few moments. If you looked closely enough, she thought, you could almost make out her ass. On the other hand, her face was obscured, and the dark wig made it unlikely that anybody would guess who she was.

She giggled. "They got my name wrong." She noticed that he wasn't amused. "How bad is it?" she asked.

He rubbed his cheeks. "Well, politically speaking, it's no big deal. I pulled a pretty girl to safety. No harm in that. It might even win me a few votes, I suppose. Jackie may take a more, ah, *judgmental* view of the incident. Particularly since I didn't go home last night."

"Or phone."

"Or phone, right." A look she knew well—husband in distress—crossed his face.

"I don't see how she can make much out of this photo," she said hopefully.

"No. I think the sooner I call Jackie, the better, all the same." He gathered up his clothes. "You tell David to be careful. I don't know if it's a good idea for you to be on the convention floor at all. . . ."

She gave him a hard look. "I'm not going to stay locked up in this goddamn suite, Jack, if that's what you're thinking."

A look of anger crossed his face. "Don't give any interviews then. I mean it. There's a lot at stake."

"I'm not a dummy, Jack. I *know* that."

"Well then." He walked to the connecting door, restless to be dressed and on his way. "Wake up David," he snapped. "He's always talking about how good he used to be at damage control, back in the old days in Hollywood. Tell him to get to it."

"Tell him yourself." She stared him down and was delighted to see him blush.

Jack stood there for a moment, his dignity sharply diminished by the fact that he was holding a small towel around his waist. He looked mildly hurt. "Well, I didn't mean it that way," he said.

"Yes you did, but I forgive you. Just don't do it again."

Having made her point, she walked over, gave him a kiss, and slipped her hands under his towel. "Just remember, lover, with me it's like baseball: three strikes and you're out. That was strike one."

She felt him stiffen. Really, she thought, it was *remarkable* how much energy he had! "Later," she said, giving him a final squeeze and a push toward the door.

He gave a reluctant glance at his watch. "I don't know when," he said.

She knew that the right thing to say was something like, "I'll be waiting," but instead, she said: "If you want me bad enough, you'll find me somehow."

He was still puzzling that one out as he opened the door and went back into his own suite, where Bobby and the Irish Mafia who had helped him win control of the Massachusetts Democratic party were waiting for him.

She went back into the bedroom, took her nail scissors, and clipped out the picture on the front page of the *Tribune*.

It was the only time, so far, that they had ever been photographed together.

For all she knew, it might be the last.

16

Special Agent Jack Kirkpatrick was not much given to introspection. As far as he was concerned, his job was getting the information —it was up to somebody else to decide what to do with it, or how it fit into what the Director liked to call the big picture.

Dressed in the overalls of a hotel maintenance man and furnished with a set of blueprints of the hotel and a telephone wiring plan, he had placed a tap on each of the phones in the Kennedy suite and a mike in the baseboard of each room twenty-four hours before the convention. Kirkpatrick had learned the art of wiretapping from Bernie Spindel himself, in the days when Spindel was still operating, at least partially, on the right side of the law. Neatness and attention to detail were Spindel's watchwords. He was a master at the cosmetic concealment of his devices—no job was complete, he taught his pupils, until the paint had been perfectly retouched, every mark removed, the smallest traces of plaster dust vacuumed away. Kirkpatrick carried in his toolbox a set of camel's hair artist's brushes, tiny tubes of paint, a Swiss-made miniature vacuum cleaner, a can of English furniture polish. By the time he was through with a job, he liked to say to trainees, you could get down on your hands and knees with a magnifying glass to look for his handiwork, and never find it.

Kirkpatrick had broken into the suite to place his devices there, only to discover, from his informant behind the desk of the Conrad Hilton, that David Leman had booked the two suites next to Jack Kennedy's. A lesser man might have ignored the news—the FBI did not encourage initiative so much as blind obedience. But Spindel had taught him well: "You can never be sure where something is going to happen," he had always said, and it was true. People held business meetings in their bedrooms, or made love in their offices, or plotted murder in their cars—you never knew where the right spot was for a mike, so you tried to cover all the bases.

Kirkpatrick had thought it over for less than a minute before going back upstairs and slipping in to do a job on the adjoining suites, just in case. Luckily, all the wiring was routed into a utilities cupboard on the floor. He had used his skeleton key to open it, spent a few minutes sorting through the maze of wires, then connected his leads to the right terminals, checked them out, and marked them with a piece of tape, so he could come back and remove them later, leaving no traces.

Now he sat in a Chicago Bell Telephone Company truck outside the hotel, where three agents, changed every four hours, listened to everything being said in the three wired suites, recording it in duplicate. Normally they recorded only conversations that had a direct bearing on the subject of an investigation, but since in this case they weren't sure what they were looking for, they taped it all.

Other teams were spread out all over Chicago, and it was his job to oversee them. There was going to be an awful lot of tape to go through before this convention was over, Kirkpatrick thought. He hoped it was worth it. Each bank of recorders bore a label: the one for the Kennedy suite was marked "JFK"; David A. Leman's, "DAL"; and the big one in between them—Conrad Hilton's own, when he was in Chicago—was simply marked "?"

The agent surveilling David Leman's suite swung around in his chair for a chat—Leman was sleeping soundly, apparently. "The Director and Tolson are walking on the beach in Florida," he said. "Have you heard this one?"

Kirkpatrick shook his head. There were hundreds of stories about Hoover, and almost every FBI agent had a favorite. He himself never told Hoover stories, but he was always willing to listen. Privately, he thought that agents who told funny stories about the Director were goddamn fools—the saying "Even the walls have ears" might have been coined for the FBI.

"They keep on walking until they come to a part of the beach that's deserted. Nobody in sight. So Tolson looks right, he looks left, and he says to Hoover, 'It's all clear, Edgar. You can walk on the water now.' "

Kirkpatrick laughed. He had heard the story before, of course. He made a mental note of the agent's name—you never knew when a man's loyalty to the Director might be questioned. The agent listening in on the middle suite flipped a switch and started his recorder. He scribbled a few notes and signaled to Kirkpatrick. "Same broad as last night," he said. "We got some pretty intimate stuff on tape. Here, listen in."

Kirkpatrick took the earphones and pressed his ear against one of the rubber pads. Years of experience had reduced his prurient interest to zero. He would have traded all the groans and moans and pillow talk in the world for one good, solid indictable statement, so he could break down the door, read the perpetrator his rights, and go home to bed. He heard the soft rustle of sheets, then a familiar, breathy voice. *Can you imagine how many guys there are in the world who dream about having Marilyn Monroe wake them up like this?*

He couldn't believe his ears. You had to admire Kennedy's balls, he thought—bringing Marilyn Monroe to Chicago when his wife was across town in the Shrivers' apartment, near which a similar truck was discreetly parked. . . .

Let 'em dream, he heard Jack Kennedy say; then there were all the usual sounds of lovemaking: the wet kisses, the sighs, the soft suck of flesh opening for flesh. He had heard it all before—it didn't differ from one couple to another. A senator and a movie star didn't sound any different from a mobster and a call girl, or anyone else, come to that. He wondered if her cries were genuine or faked, but that, he decided, probably didn't matter either.

Kirkpatrick handed the earphones back.

He'd heard as much as he wanted to hear.

————

We were sitting in the coffee shop of the Conrad Hilton, Marilyn and I. She was reading about herself in *Life* and nibbling on a cheeseburger. There was a spot of ketchup on her chin. She picked up a french fry, dipped it in ketchup, and popped it into her mouth, managing to turn it into a sexy gesture—like everything else she did.

I had spent the morning with Jim Farley, who had proved Joe Kennedy right again by refusing to back Jack for the vice presidential nomination. Farley, I thought, was certainly going to be on the short list of people whose tax returns would be audited by the IRS the moment Jack got to the White House.

"Isn't it wonderful news about Jack being asked to make the big speech?" Marilyn asked, starry-eyed.

I didn't bother to ask how she had heard the news already—Jack was clearly keeping in touch with her if not with Jackie. "It is and it isn't," I said cautiously, unwilling to spoil her enthusiasm.

"I mean, it's great, isn't it? Stevenson asking Jack to nominate him? It's like the starring role of the whole convention!"

"The supporting role is more like it, really. Adlai's the star of this picture. But the truth is, Adlai mousetrapped Jack at breakfast. Sure, it's a big honor to be asked to make the speech nominating the candidate—it's the high point of the convention, no question about it. But—and it's a big but—it just happens to be a tradition of American politics that the person who nominates the presidential candidate isn't supposed to be a vice presidential contender."

I told her that Jack was still kicking himself—and Bobby—for having failed to foresee Adlai's move in time to spare himself an embarrassing moment, which they both attributed to Eleanor Roosevelt's meddling. Despite their later reputation for ruthlessness, at this stage of their careers Jack and Bobby were still occasionally capable of being surprised by the duplicity and cunning of older, more traditional politicians.

Marilyn's eyes were wide-open, clear blue pools of admiration for my political wisdom, or so I fancied, for nobody was better than she was at playing up to the self-importance of a man.

As it happened, her own political judgment was shrewder than mine (or Jack's, for that matter): when I told her that Jack had been persuaded to pay a courtesy call on Eleanor Roosevelt, much against his will, she rightly predicted it wouldn't do him any good. "You only had to look at Mrs. Roosevelt's face last night, when she was up there on the platform," she said. "That's a woman who doesn't forget or forgive easily. Believe me, I *know* just how she feels!"

I smiled. "It's hard to think of you and Eleanor having anything in common."

Marilyn gave me a steely stare. "She's a woman," she said. "So am I."

I turned that over in my mind. Frankly, nobody had thought of Eleanor Roosevelt as a *woman* for years—decades—not even FDR. For most of her later life she had been thought of as his ambassador to the poor and the minorities, a kind of national monument, ugly but treasured. Of course, Marilyn was right. One of the reasons Adlai got along so well with her, it occurred to me suddenly, was that in a very mild and respectful way he flirted with her—something he did rather well, since he was almost as much of a ladies' man as Jack.

Marilyn wiped her mouth daintily—every so often, traces of her genteel upbringing at the hands of foster parents shone through. She licked her lips, always a sign she was nerving herself to ask a difficult question—not necessarily difficult for her but difficult for *someone*. "David," she said, "there's one thing I don't get. Where's Jackie in all this?"

"You're already suffering from the Other Woman syndrome," I said.

"What's that?"

"An unhealthy interest in the wife."

"I was just curious. She doesn't seem to be a part of all this. How come?"

I glanced around the coffee shop, which was jammed with delegates, many of them wearing funny hats. They were packed in at the entrance like sardines, waiting for tables or a seat at the counter, men and women alike dressed in wash-and-wear, drip-dry synthetics. I couldn't imagine Jackie being any part of it. She was an unapologetic elitist, and her disdain for the sweaty, seamy side of the political process bordered on contempt. To his sisters' fury, Jack had to bargain for every public appearance Jackie made when he was campaigning, with his father or Bobby often acting as the broker.

"Well, she's pregnant," I said. "Having a baby is very important to them both. And Jackie's pretty independent—she's not exactly the kind of political wife who tags along after her husband with a smile on her face. Anyway, she's mad at Jack."

"Why?"

"They were supposed to be spending some time together here— mending fences, if you want to know the truth. Jackie assumed he'd have plenty of time on his hands and they'd spend it together— instead of which he's hardly been back to the apartment since he arrived, so she's sitting there alone watching the convention on TV and steaming, when she could have been at Hyannis Port or her mother's place at Newport."

"Mending fences?"

"There's been some kind of problem between them for months. I know it looks as if Jack can do anything he wants so far as Jackie is concerned, but there *are* certain rules, and I suspect he broke one of them."

"Such as?"

I shrugged. I had no idea what the rules might be, in fact. Keeping out of the gossip columns was certainly one of them. Not fucking friends of Jackie's was probably another, but to my knowledge, Jack had broken that one a long time ago. "I don't know," I said. "They're complicated people. It's a complicated marriage. Jack can do what he wants, but only so long as Jackie gets what *she* wants."

"Which is?"

"Prestige, respect, the right to spend a lot of Jack's money without hearing any complaints about it from him, his undivided attention when she wants it. Something like that."

"That sounds pretty cold. Does she love him?"

"Oh, she loves him, all right. And he loves her too. They're a challenge for each other. She's married a man—forgive me, Marilyn—who can't be faithful for twenty-four hours. He's married the one woman who can cut him down to size like *that*." I snapped my fingers.

"Cut him down to size?"

"When Jackie's not happy, she knows just how to drive Jack crazy." That, I thought, was putting it mildly.

"It doesn't sound like much of a marriage to me," Marilyn said. Perhaps she caught my expression, because she blushed slightly and added: "Well, I guess mine haven't been so hot either."

"Actually, I don't think it's a bad marriage, as marriages go. They're a good match for each other; they enjoy each other's company at least *some* of the time. Jack's proud of her taste, she's proud of his career, and neither of them tells the other what to do. . . . They could do a lot worse."

"But are they *happy,* do you think?"

I sighed. "No, I don't suppose so. Perhaps that doesn't matter in marriage as much as you might think."

As soon as the words were out of my mouth, I realized that I was talking about myself, but Marilyn didn't notice. "It does to *me!*" she said fiercely.

The thought of Marilyn desperately trying to extract happiness from her marriage to Miller, or DiMaggio—and perhaps never quite sure how to recognize it if she found it—saddened me immensely. It came as a relief when a bellboy pushed through the crowd to give me a message that Senator Kennedy wanted to see me upstairs urgently.

He didn't have to say there was a crisis. I could guess.

———

Jack was in a rage, pacing back and forth in Marilyn's suite—which he now treated like an annex to his own—his complexion a mottled red. He was eating a tuna sandwich, taking huge mouthfuls of it like a shark attacking its prey. Bobby's eyes were fixed soulfully on the sandwich, or so it seemed. She was tempted to ask why he didn't order one of his own, but it hardly seemed the right moment.

"She *sandbagged* me, the old bitch!" Jack said. "I thought we were going to meet alone, just the two of us. Instead, I come into a room full of people and she gives me a lecture on how I should have stood up to McCarthy, as if I were a fucking *schoolboy!* With Hubert Humphrey simpering away on the sofa like the teacher's pet." He glared at Bobby, who was stony-faced. "Somebody should have warned me."

"Adlai's behaved like a real prick," Bobby agreed.

"Jesus! I know *that,* Bobby!" Jack stopped pacing and stared at David. "What do *you* say, David?" he asked. He seemed not to have noticed her until this moment. He shrugged, as if to say, *I'm sorry about all this, but I can't help it.*

Now that the chips were down, David seemed to have grown in stature. It wasn't that he was older than they were by ten years or so —neither Jack nor Bobby was a respecter of age. It had more to do with the fact that he was connected in their minds with their father —and that he was a self-made success in his own high-powered world. Having caught his second wind, David had reverted to his usual cool, perfectly dressed self, a man who seemed to thrive on crises, like a Hollywood producer appearing on a set when everybody else is dropping from exhaustion, to insist on one more take. As if to reinforce the impression, he selected a cigar from an elegant crocodile case in his pocket, trimmed it with a small gold knife, and lit it calmly. "Adlai didn't happen to give you a speech, did he?" he asked between contented puffs.

Jack looked surprised. "How did you know?"

"I didn't. I guessed. I know Adlai. I know Eleanor, too. I can see her hand in this. It's just what she'd advise him to do."

"Damn that woman." Jack glumly took a few folded sheets of paper out of his pocket and handed them to David, who scanned them briefly.

"Who wrote it?" David asked, holding it with distaste, as if it were dirty.

"Arthur Schlesinger. A bleeding-heart college professor. Just right for Adlai."

David handed the speech back. "There's not a word in it you should say, Jack, in my opinion. If I were you," he said firmly, "I'd throw it away and spend the next twenty-four hours writing the speech of a lifetime."

There was a long silence. Jack frowned. Then he grinned, rolled the speech Stevenson had given him into a ball, and tossed it neatly into a wastepaper basket on the far side of the room. "Fuck him," he said. "Fuck Schlesinger. Let's do it. Bobby—get Sorensen up here on the double, and tell him to start drafting something."

He rattled off the names of people whose ideas he wanted, journalists who should be consulted, his anger and irritation giving way rapidly to ebullience.

He came over and gave her a hug and kiss, shot a string of rapid-fire instructions at Bobby, sent David off to see what the party elders were up to. Jack hadn't sought the task of making the nominating speech for Adlai Stevenson, but now that he had it, he was determined to make it a speech nobody would forget.

Once they were alone, he kicked off his shoes and made for the bedroom. "Hey!" she said. "You might at least *ask* me first!"

He turned in the doorway, pulling off his tie, an ironic smile on his face. "It's two o'clock," he said. "Though you may not know it, it's my custom to take a short nap every afternoon. When I was a very young man, in London, Winston Churchill himself told me it was the secret of his long and productive life. I figured if it worked for him, why not for me?"

"I guess." It hadn't occurred to her that a grown-up, active male might take a nap.

"Of course, there's no law against you joining me," he said.

She laughed. "Is that a fact?"

"You might even make sure I wake up—the way you did this morning."

"I'll think about it."

There was a knock on the door, and she remembered she hadn't put the Do Not Disturb sign up. "I'll be in in a moment, darling," she called. She opened the door a crack and saw a plump, balding man, with dark, furtive eyes, a nervous smile, and a thick mustache. He was wearing a white shirt with the logo of the telephone company embroidered on the front, as well as the name "Bernie," in script. He carried a toolbox, and several thick strands of wire were looped over one shoulder. His pockets bulged with what she presumed were the tools of his trade—a flashlight, a telephone handset, screwdrivers.

"Is this the suite with telephone trouble, ma'am?" He had a soft voice, with an unmistakable New York accent. She went over to the nearest telephone, picked it up, heard the dial tone, and came back.

"We haven't had any trouble," she said.

He nodded. "Well, they probably gave me the wrong room number," he said. "It happens all the time."

There was something faintly disturbing about the intensity of his look, but not enough to make her think twice. Men looked at her intently all the time, even when she was in disguise. All the same, it wasn't really the look of a man admiring her tits—it was the kind of look that would have told her "vice cop" back in the old days when she was hanging around the Ambassador Hotel with her lifeguard boyfriends. For a moment she even thought of calling down to the front desk to see if there really *was* a telephone repairman at work on the floor, but she decided she was being silly.

"I guess so," she said. "Thanks." She hung the Do Not Disturb sign on the knob, closed the door sharply, then double-locked it and fastened the security chain, though she couldn't have said why.

She decided that it was just her imagination, poured herself a glass of champagne, and went into the bedroom to join Jack.

17

When I told Marilyn that Jackie was mad at Jack, I was putting it mildly. I had been over to the Shriver apartment to pay my respects and found Jackie parked mutinously in front of the television set with Jack's sister Eunice beside her. Even in a maternity dress, Jackie managed to look cool and elegant.

"Thank God *somebody* remembers I'm here," she said when I leaned over to give her a kiss. Eunice looked uncomfortable. Jack's sisters would never accept criticism of him from anyone, even Jackie.

"Jack's got his hands full," Eunice said, as if I might not have noticed what was happening at the convention.

Jackie's face was a picture of angry contempt. "How *nice* for him!" she snapped.

There was a long silence while iced tea was served by the Shrivers' maid. "Wasn't that something last night?" Eunice asked breathlessly —she had a full measure of the family's enthusiasm, and of all the Kennedy women she had always seemed to me the one who most took after her mother, a quality that would hardly endear her to Jackie.

I nodded. "The demonstration for Jack? It was incredible, yes."

Jackie gave me one of her most ambiguous looks. "And wasn't it *amusing* when Jack reached down and rescued that girl? What was her name?"

"Welles?" I said. "Something like that."

"A librarian. Isn't it *just* Jack's luck to meet the only librarian in New York State with great legs?"

"I heard she's an old friend of Eleanor Roosevelt's," Eunice said.

"Oh, *really!*" Jackie dropped the dark glasses that she wore on top of her head down over her eyes and stared at the television screen. It was a habit she shared with my wife Maria, who had the same abrupt way of dismissing people who had overstayed their welcome or tried her patience. I finished my iced tea, made my excuses, and got up to leave.

"Did you get a chance to meet Miss Welles, David?" Jackie asked. I shook my head. "Not at all. I only saw her from a distance."

"*What* a shame! She reminded me of someone—I'm not sure who, but it will come back to me."

She inclined her head slightly, for me to give her a good-bye kiss on the cheek, which I did. "You're a bad liar, David," she whispered.

"Perhaps so," I said. "That's why I seldom lie, you see."

She gave me a smile—Jackie and I really liked and understood each other. "You're getting a lot better at it," she said sadly. "That's what comes of hanging around with politicians. Good-bye. Give my best to Maria, please."

⸻

They were together in her suite when I returned. Marilyn was lying on the sofa wearing a robe, a towel wrapped around her hair, filing her nails while Jack, in shirtsleeves, paced up and down reading aloud from a few sheets of lined yellow legal paper. "Look at this," he said.

It was a good speech, head and shoulders above the one that Adlai had handed him. "Not bad," I said.

"Not bad isn't good enough." He took it back, went to the far side of the room, and began to declaim. He made his way through the first page—gestures, pauses, and all—while Marilyn, still working on her nails, looked at him with veiled intensity.

"You've *got* to get the breaths right, honey," she said. "If you get ahead of your breathing, you end up taking a big gasp in the wrong place or just dribbling off. . . ."

Jack had the grim look on his face that all the Kennedys got when they were determined to master something difficult or new, but more surprising to me was his willingness to take criticism from a woman.

He backed up, started again, and got it right this time—an even delivery, tremendous sincerity, long, impressive pauses at just the right moments.

"The speech still sucks," he said. I noticed there was a trail of discarded paper forming a rough oval track all around the room, and wondered how many drafts he had already gone through. He crumpled up the first page, went to the door between the two suites, opened it and tossed the paper in, aiming it high.

Through the door I caught a glimpse of some of the Kennedy team hard at work: Bobby stretched out on a sofa with a telephone receiver pressed between his ear and his shoulder; Ted Sorensen hunched over a coffee table, scribbling furiously; half a dozen old and new hands working away at index cards, or manning the many telephones that had been hastily set up in the suite. Politics has a way of destroying hotel rooms, as I had noticed over the years, and this one was no exception—it looked as if an occupying army had camped out in it, and it smelled of cigarette smoke, stale coffee, and sweat. "It's not tough enough," Jack said.

"You don't want to attack Eisenhower," Sorensen said, looking up from his labors.

Jack thought about this. He *did* want to attack Ike, for whom he had a certain degree of contempt, but he knew as well as Sorensen did that it was a dangerous thing to do, given Ike's popularity.

Marilyn looked up from her nails, a serious expression on her face, which had the paradoxical effect of making her appear much younger, almost like a schoolgirl having problems with her homework. "Arthur—my husband—always says Nixon does Ike's dirty work for him," she whispered, I suppose so Sorensen wouldn't hear her. "That way Ike can take the high road, he says."

She smiled and went back to her nails, while Jack and I stared at each other. Normally Miller's left-wing views would not have interested him, but he looked thoughtful.

"I don't *have* to attack him, goddamn it," he shouted at Sorensen. "Everybody knows he takes the high road as a candidate while Nixon takes the low road. I can say that."

"It's risky."

"Put it in," Jack snapped. There was always an edge to Jack's relationship with Ted Sorensen. Sorensen had been drafted to "help" Jack write *Profiles in Courage* and Jack was so determined to put down rumors that Sorensen had really written the Pulitzer Prize-winning book instead of him that he kept a page of the first draft in his own handwriting in his desk drawer to show to doubters. What he felt about Marilyn giving him one of his best lines, I don't know.

We chatted for a few moments, until Marilyn, who moved to her own rhythm, got up, stretched, exposing most of her bosom, and went off to bathe and dress.

Jack and I both stared at her, failing to conceal our admiration from each other; then we sat down on the sofa she had vacated. Close up, I could see how tired he was, the skin drawn tight over the bones of his face, deep circles under his eyes; he had the slightly unfocused and punch-drunk look that comes from a couple of days of high stress and only a few hours of sleep. Jack was tough—nobody was a better campaigner, not even Bobby, when his turn came—but there were limits to his endurance. He was still at the age when he could ignore the limits, but only just. "How was Jackie?" he asked.

I made a wavy motion with my hand.

He sighed. "Not too happy?"

"Not happy at all."

"I hadn't counted on this happening." He didn't make it clear whether he meant Marilyn or getting into the vice presidential race. Perhaps it didn't matter.

"It mightn't hurt to go over there. She's feeling pretty lonely."

"Yes? I guess so." He did not seem concerned.

"Jack, it's none of my business, I know, but she's angry about something too—*really* angry. I noticed it when I was at Hickory Hill for lunch last time. It was the same kind of anger I could feel today, over at the apartment—a cold, hard anger, not the kind that's about something that's only just happened. . . . Am I out of line? Or full of shit?"

"You're not full of shit, David," he said glumly, raising an eyebrow, since, as he well knew, I use words like that only when I feel there's no other way to get my point across.

"Does Jackie know about Marilyn?"

He shrugged. "Oh, probably. Not that she's in Chicago. But in general, yes."

"Is that the problem?"

"No, not really. You know Jackie and I have"—he paused, looking for the right word, or perhaps simply regretting that he had allowed the conversation to take this turn—"an *agreement?*"

I nodded. The "agreement" between Jack and Jackie was one of the deeper Kennedy mysteries, even to me. Her cool, ironic acceptance of her husband's constant—indeed, institutionalized—infidelities puzzled almost everyone, even then. Later on, when Jackie was in the White House, the stories about her wit and self-control became part of the Kennedy legend, the seamy underside of Camelot, as it were—her contemptuous dismissal of Jack's two obliging young blond staff secretaries, "Fiddle" and "Faddle," as the "White House dogs," her handing Jack a pair of black panties she had found under the pillow of their bed and telling him to see that they were returned to their owner because they weren't her size.

"So Marilyn isn't the issue?" I asked. "I thought at lunch, when Jackie brought her name up . . ."

Jack waved his hand impatiently. "It doesn't make that much difference to Jackie whether it's Marilyn or anyone else. I may have gone too far, that's all." He gave a deep sigh. "I was hoping to get a chance to talk things over with Jackie here, away from Hickory Hill," he said. "If I'd known it was going to be a three-ring circus . . ."

"Is it serious?"

"Serious enough. I'm hoping the baby will solve a lot of the problems between us. Hell, we'll see." He did not seem hopeful. If he had not been a Catholic and a politician, I would have said he sounded like a man who has already come to terms with the end of his marriage.

"I'm sorry to hear that," I said. "Surely it wouldn't hurt to go across town and see her? Having a fuss made over them is the one thing wives always want."

"Marilyn told me the same thing."

"Well, she has a lot of common sense."

"Yes." He didn't sound happy about it. "I guess there's no way to prevent Marilyn from going to the arena to hear my speech tonight, is there?"

"None that I can think of."

"Just keep her off the front page of the *Chicago Tribune* this time, David, will you?"

"I'll do my best." The truth was, I hadn't the foggiest notion how I was going to keep Marilyn—even in her librarian disguise—hidden and unnoticed.

He stood up. His eyes had the faraway expression of a man whose big roll of the dice is fast approaching. I didn't know how I would have dealt with that kind of pressure; Jack, I suspected, would deal with it by going to bed with Marilyn.

As if to confirm my guess, he made for the bedroom, taking off his tie, looking amazingly cool and calm; then he was gone, and the door closed behind him and Marilyn.

———

All around her the arena hummed with sound; the floor underfoot was thick with discarded paper cups, candy wrappers, trampled streamers and confetti. She didn't mind being out of the limelight for a change. Here, dumb as it was, she felt free—free from the problems of being Marilyn Monroe, free from having to worry about Arthur Miller's unhappiness, free from the threats of 20th Century–Fox, from the snide contempt of Sir Cork Tip and his fading wife, from the guilt of having to see Milton every day when they both knew their partnership was doomed. . . .

David sat beside her, clearly determined not to let her out of his sight. From time to time party bigwigs came over to pay him homage. He did not attempt to introduce her, which was okay with her, since she wasn't sure she was up to doing the Birdy Welles number again. The music blared on, competing against the drone of a voice from the platform going through some sort of procedural point.

"What this thing needs is a good director," she said.

"Another few minutes," David said, glancing at his watch.

She leaned close to him, obliged to shout into his ear to make herself heard over the din. "Is Jackie here tonight?" she asked.

David shook his head. "If Jack gets the nomination, she'll be here to stand beside him. She doesn't waste herself on small events."

"If I were married to Jack, I'd never let him out of my sight. She *really* doesn't mind that he fucks other women?"

"I suppose she *does,* at some level, yes. But she's got it under control. That's the interesting thing about Jackie, you see—she's got *everything* under control."

"You're saying she's cold."

"No. I don't think she's cold at all. I would have said that Jackie's a very passionate woman, myself. I don't think Jack would marry a woman who *wasn't* passionate—but more important, you only have to see the way she looks at him. . . . No, no, there's real fire there, believe me."

"Have you seen her since we've been here?" she asked. She was delighted to see David hesitate, like a married man whose wife has just asked after his girlfriend. David was loyal, you had to give him that.

"Yes," he said reluctantly. "I had tea with her."

Of course! *Tea with her!* What else would you have with Jackie Kennedy? "How was she?"

"Fine. She looked pretty good. Considering."

"I bet she has the *nicest* maternity clothes," she said, not even bothering to disguise the envy in her voice.

David nodded. "Well, you know what Jackie's like about clothes.

Or perhaps you don't. . . . I will say that for a woman who's about to give birth, she looked very chic."

Chic! Nobody had ever described *her* as chic! "Did she mention me?" she asked.

He looked wary. "Mention you? No." He hesitated. "Not really."

"Not really? What does *that* mean?"

"She did say that Birdy Welles reminded her of someone."

"Oh God!" She felt the familiar stab of fear at being "found out." Then she reminded herself that it was Jack's problem, not hers.

"Well, it was only an impression," David said consolingly. "She couldn't help noticing you last night when Jack was hauling you out of the crowd." He stared toward the podium as if the spectacle fascinated him, though nothing much was going on there. "I think she'd been looking at the photographs in the papers very closely too. I noticed there was a magnifying glass on top of her copy of this morning's *Tribune.*"

"I thought you said she didn't care?"

"She cares about *you,* apparently."

Her throat tightened. "About me? What makes you think that?"

"She mentioned you once before. When I was having lunch at Hickory Hill, oh, quite some time ago. She was furious with Jack."

"Why?"

"I don't know. She asked if I could introduce Jack to you next time he was in California. But it was the *way* she asked, you understand. Even *Jack* was embarrassed—which is unusual for him. It was as if she knew about something"—he paused—"something that broke whatever the rules are between them."

She felt a cold shiver. "Hickory Hill," she murmured. "That's the house in Virginia, isn't it?"

He nodded. "It's funny. It's always been *Jack* who wanted to get rid of it and move to Georgetown, and Jackie who insisted on keeping it. . . . But now it's Jackie who's after him to sell." He shrugged. "Something happened there, I don't know what, but something went wrong. . . . It's sad. Such a beautiful place."

"Yes," she said distantly, thinking back to that day in Washington with him, and the afternoon they had spent in bed together at the house, and the long line of wooded hills glowing in the late-afternoon sun when she finally rose from bed, leaving him sleeping there like a child, to slip into the dressing room and go through Jackie's drawers. . . .

"I remember the view—" she said. Then she was suddenly conscious that David was staring at her. He shook his head slowly, as if he had been stunned.

A cold chill ran through her. She had given away one of the guiltiest of her guilty secrets, and he would know now just how foolish and careless Jack had been, and perhaps guess how hard she had pushed him. She wanted David to like and respect her, and she couldn't help feeling that in one moment she had forfeited all that, which made her sad. She grabbed his hand. "Be my friend, David!" she whispered. "Please. Always. Whatever I've done? Whatever I do?"

He let out a long breath. Then, almost regretfully, like a man taking on a burden he wasn't sure he could carry, he nodded.

"Promise?" She didn't know why it mattered so much, but it did. Perhaps because she had so few friends. Husbands, lovers, lawyers, agents, business associates, doctors, and therapists—all of those, sure, but *friends?*

"I promise," he said softly, and she kissed him, tears welling up. They sat together for a few moments, hand in hand, sharing unspoken thoughts, and she was strangely comforted, as she could surely never have been by a lover.

There was a sudden hush in the arena. She had been so busy worrying about what David thought that she'd almost missed Jack's arrival. All around her she could feel a kind of tingling, electric excitement. She squeezed David's hand so tight he cried out, and leapt to her feet shouting and jumping up and down like a high school cheerleader as Jack walked onto the platform grinning and made his way slowly toward the flag-draped podium as if in a triumphal procession.

She instantly recognized "star quality" when she saw it. In an arena full of pallid, tired, sweaty people—thousands of them—he seemed like a visitor from another, more glamorous world, his skin deeply tanned, the way only movie stars and the very rich look, the big grin displaying glistening white teeth, the unruly hair proclaiming his youth, his broad athlete's shoulders hunching as he braced himself against the podium.

He made a small ceremony of getting his speech neatly placed, just as she had told him to, performing a piece of business the way an actor would, milking it for maximum suspense while the crowd cheered and chanted, *"Kennedy, Kennedy, Kennedy!"* and the band played "Anchors Aweigh" over and over again.

Jack let the celebration run its course, grinned through the release

of the red-white-and-blue balloons, the waving of banners and photographs of himself. The Texas delegation made a rush for the podium, throwing novelty Stetson hats into the air while the band
played "Yellow Rose of Texas." "Jack and Lyndon must be striking
a deal," she heard David whisper to her. Then the Massachusetts
delegation, led by a red-faced old-time Irish pol in a wide-brimmed
Borsalino hat, came pushing down the aisles, cheering themselves
hoarse, and the band switched to "The Bells of St. Mary's"—a
choice that seemed to puzzle Jack. The noise was deafening, and
seemed likely to go on forever, despite Rayburn's gavel and Stevenson's frown. Then Jack raised his arms, and as if by magic, the arena
fell silent.

She shut her eyes. She knew the speech by heart—an amazing feat,
she thought, for somebody who could never remember her own
lines! She repeated every word to herself a beat before him, as if they
were in a duet. His delivery was flawless, his pauses eloquent, the
applause thunderous at just the right moments. It was not young
Jack Kennedy, playboy senator, old Joe Kennedy's spoiled son,
speaking but a whole new man of depth, maturity, vision, who was
articulating just what everybody wanted America to be. He spoke
the obligatory praise for Adlai Stevenson—after all, he was here to
nominate him—but nobody could mistake the fact that this speech
was for himself and for the country, not for Stevenson, who everybody knew was going to lose to Ike again in November.

Tears were running down her cheeks by the time he brought his
speech to a climax. She opened her eyes and saw him turning to
Adlai Stevenson, as if offering him a present. And even Adlai seemed
caught up in the emotion of the moment as the crowd went wild,
not for him, as he must have realized, but for young Jack Kennedy,
for the future. She yearned to rush to the podium, climb up to hug
him as hard as she could. . . .

Then, in the shadows at the back of the platform, she saw a small
figure in a pink maternity dress edging forward, Bobby Kennedy at
her side. Even in the stupendous heat, Jackie looked poised, cool,
every hair in place.

Jack and Adlai exchanged stiff hugs, with the embarrassment of
men who neither liked nor respected each other—and who didn't
like being touched by other men. Then Jack moved quickly to take
Jackie by the hand and lead her forward.

Somebody had given Jackie a bouquet of red roses, which she held
across her swelling belly. If she was nervous, it didn't show. Jackie

waved gracefully—like a queen, really, as if this whole convention were in *her* honor—and gazed adoringly up at Jack.

"I want to go home," she told David, crying even harder now. She put on her sunglasses.

He turned in surprise. "Jesus, Marilyn," he said. "The best is still to come! After that speech, Jack might just win it."

"I know. I want to go anyway."

"Back to the hotel?"

She shook her head. "Back to New York. Back to London. Back to work."

He took her hand in his. You couldn't fault David for insensitivity. She knew that he wanted to stay, to see his friend begin his run for the vice presidency, but he didn't hesitate.

"Let's go then, Marilyn," he said gently.

18

Bernie Spindel sat in Hoffa's office in Detroit, holding his battered, bulky old leather briefcase in his lap with both hands.

He had driven from Chicago in a car rented under an assumed name from a cut-rate company that was happy to take cash and not ask too many questions. Spindel didn't like flying. Airports were full of cops and Feds, and who knew what they were looking for, or when one of them might look up and recognize a familiar face? Besides, you had to give the airlines a name, and Spindel hated doing that. He felt safer cruising down the highways along with millions of other people, in a rusted old car with faded paint and acned chrome, which would attract no attention. He never drove above the speed limit, and always made sure all the lights were in good order before he started out, so there was no chance of being stopped by a trooper.

He stopped only once, for a quick piss—carrying his briefcase with him—a tank of gas, a cheeseburger and a Coke, arriving at the Teamster building exactly one minute ahead of schedule. Spindel was a man who believed in precision. He liked to boast to his students that they could set their watches by him, and he expected them to.

Hoffa sat behind his desk, trying to pretend he wasn't curious, his small eyes as black and dead as a shark's. Spindel didn't care. He didn't have to like Hoffa. He hadn't liked Hoover either. What he liked was the *work,* the knowledge that he was the best.

"So whatcha got?" Hoffa finally asked, cracking his knuckles so loudly that anybody but Spindel would have jumped out of his skin.

Spindel smiled. He wanted to be seduced, to hold back a little, like a broad who knows she's going to fuck the guy but still wants to be talked into it. Hoover had understood that better than Hoffa, but Spindel and Hoover had never really gotten along, and in the end, Spindel found he was more comfortable with the bad guys, and better paid, too.

"He damn near got it, Jimmy," he said. "I was almost rooting for him myself, at the end."

"Fuck you were. That fucking papa's boy with his five-hundred-dollar suits? Don't shit me, Bernie."

"Well, you know what I mean. . . . It was like a horse race. He was thirty-three and a half votes short on the second ballot, and if Tennessee and Pennsylvania hadn't switched to Kefauver on the next one . . . I never seen nothing like it, Jimmy."

"I read it in the fucking papers, Bernie. Anyway, it don't matter. Ike and Nixon are going to walk all over Stevenson."

"It'll be Kennedy in '60, you want my opinion, Jimmy."

Hoffa laughed harshly. "Over my dead body." He cracked his knuckles again. "Or his." He sat silently for a moment. "So, you got anything, or not?"

"I got." Spindel put the heavy briefcase on the big, polished desk, took out a reel-to-reel tape recorder, plugged it in, removed a reel from its unlabeled cardboard box, and threaded the tape, his fingers moving with the precision of a surgeon's. "Funny thing," he said. "When I put the taps in the phone box, in the hotel, somebody had been there before me."

Hoffa frowned. "Who?"

"FBI!" Spindel grinned. "I recognized the technique right away, see. I taught them how to do it! So I had to get back and remove my taps before he did, you know, so he didn't know mine were there too, right on top of his."

Hoffa smiled grimly. "So Hoover is building up a file on Jack too? Now *that* is interesting, Bernie. You done good. That gets you a bonus, my friend."

"You wait till you hear this, Jimmy."

Spindel pushed the button. The tape hissed, and there was a background noise that sounded like the rustling of sheets, the clink of ice cubes, perhaps the soft, liquid sound of skin moving against skin. Spindel knew his job, all right—you couldn't ever complain about the quality of his work. *This won't take but a minute, Senator,* a woman said, and even to somebody who was no movie fan, like Hoffa, Spindel knew, there was no mistaking the voice of Marilyn Monroe—that familiar high, breathless little voice, at once a little girl's and a sexy woman's, with the slight hesitation between words that was almost a stutter but not quite. Spindel could almost see her, all white and pink, with her bold mascaraed eyes and her bright straw-colored hair, just as she had been when she opened the door of her suite in the Conrad Hilton, and spoke to him. . . .

Hoffa reached across the desk and shook his hand solemnly. Then he sprang to his feet and went into a boxer's crouch, feinting and shadow-punching his way around the floor, his big shoulders working as if he were still the twenty-year-old tough guy he had once been, making his way up from the ranks of loading-dock day laborers with his fists, against men twice his size.

Spindel winced as Hoffa smacked a big fist against the palm of his other hand, with a sound so loud and sharp it might have been a gunshot. *"Bingo!"* Hoffa shouted joyfully. "Bull's-eye!"

———

I returned Marilyn to New York and deposited her into the care of the good Dr. Kris. Shortly afterward, she returned to England to resume work on *The Prince and the Showgirl,* taking Dr. Kris along for moral support.

I was not surprised to read in the gossip columns of the rumors of tension between Marilyn and her husband, as well as a nasty scene between her and Olivier when he tried to ban Paula Strasberg from the set again and she made him back down.

Marilyn's troubles in London were overshadowed by another item, in Drew Pearson's column—that Jack and Jackie were "estranged" and discussing separation, after the birth of a stillborn child.

I had known about the stillbirth, of course, which had taken place only a couple of weeks after the convention, though it was kept as quiet as possible. Jackie had been at her mother's, Hammersmith Farm, the Auchincloss place at Newport, so I'd called her there to commiserate. Jack was not there yet, which I found puzzling at the time, but I assumed he was hurrying back from the South of France, where he had been visiting his father and planning to take a sailing trip to unwind from the convention and prepare himself for two months of brutal nationwide campaigning for Stevenson.

A call from Joe Kennedy's secretary, asking if I could join him for dinner, was enough to put me on the alert, since I had assumed he was still enjoying himself in the luxurious villa he rented every summer at Biot, a short drive from Cap d'Antibes. I knew only a family emergency of the most monumental proportions could have brought him back to New York early, so I prepared myself for trouble.

We met at La Caravelle. Henri Soulé's Le Pavillon had been the Ambassador's favorite restaurant in New York, until the day Soulé forgot to prepare a chocolate cake for a Kennedy family celebration. Not only did Joe never go back, he even went to the trouble of financing Soulé's chef and maître d'hôtel to leave and open a rival restaurant, which was, of course, why we were dining at La Caravelle.

He was waiting for me at his usual banquette table, looking as tanned and energetic as ever. Bergson might have intended the phrase *"élan vital"* to describe Joe—"life force" was what he was all about.

We exchanged small talk while Joe waited impatiently for me to finish my drink so he could get on with the business of ordering his meal. For an Irishman, he was the least convivial of drinkers. I explained that I was a temporary summer bachelor, Maria having left for the South of France ahead of me.

He glared at the menu. "You read the news?"

"Drew Pearson's story? Yes. Is it true?"

"That slimy fucking Pearson! I'd like to break his neck for him."

I took this to be an admission that Pearson's story was correct.

"Where's Jack?" I asked.

The Ambassador sipped his drink. "He's up at Newport, with Jackie," he said tightly. "Where he belongs."

His expression was grim. I did not press him. He would tell me what he wanted me to know in his own time—or what he wanted me to do, more likely. We chatted about his "vacation" in the South of France while we ordered.

"How was your summer?" I asked. "Apart from all this."

"Apart from the fact that you and Bobby dragged Jack into a fight he couldn't win, there in Chicago—it's been dandy. Did you know they made Rose a papal countess?" He did not say who "they" were. Joe and Rose maintained what amounted to a "separate but equal" relationship with the hierarchy of the Catholic Church, hers motivated by piety and a certain degree of snobbery, his by the simple need to exert his power everywhere he could. Rose liked to spend her summers traveling from one religious shrine to another, culminating in a visit to the Vatican for an audience with His Holiness. Her pilgrimages suited both of them nicely—she was spared the direct knowledge that Joe was sleeping with his mistresses under her

222

own roof, while he was free to do what he wanted without going to a lot of trouble to conceal it.

"A countess?" I said. "I'm impressed."

Joe grimaced. "It cost me a fortune."

"Well spent, I'd say."

He gave a small sigh of contentment, tasted his pea soup, frowned, and demanded more croutons—he believed in keeping people on their toes. "This story about Jack," he began hesitantly, between spoonfuls of soup. "How far do you think it's going to spread?"

"Is it true?" I asked again.

"Not anymore."

"What happened?"

Joe finished his soup, wiped his mouth, and glared at me. Then he took off his spectacles and wiped them. His eyes, I saw, were sunken and tired, lacking their usual flinty sparkle. "Jack came to see me at Biot. He was going off on a sailing trip with George Smathers."

I didn't need to be told what a sailing trip with Smathers would be like. Smathers and Jack had been freshmen congressmen and bachelors-around-town together. They had acquired such a reputation for fast living that the Ambassador was finally obliged to arrange for Eunice to move to Washington and take a job there so she could keep an eye on her brother. "While Jackie was at home, in the last weeks of a difficult pregnancy?" I asked, raising an eyebrow.

"There was a girl on the boat with Jack—twenty-something, blond, unbelievable figure. . . ." He chuckled. "A real beauty," he said. "I wouldn't have minded a crack at her myself." He may have caught the expression on my face, because he added rather defensively, "Hell, I thought Jack deserved a good time after Chicago."

"He'd been having a good time, so far as I know. He should have been with Jackie."

He took a sip of ice water and gave me an angry stare. I stared right back at him. That seemed to calm him down. "Jack said there'd been a lot of tension between him and Jackie," he continued. "That he needed a little time away from her. It didn't sound like such a bad idea to me."

I'll bet it didn't, I told myself. Joe had been absent at almost every moment that might have mattered in his own marriage, despite his reputation as a family man.

"When Jackie miscarried, Jack was at sea, with this girl. I radioed the news to him, but he decided to go on with the trip anyway."

"He went *on* with the trip?" Even I was surprised.

"Jack said it wasn't worth going home, since the baby was born dead," he finally said, unhappily.

I stared at my plate. "That might be thought selfish and callous," I suggested. "By some."

"Yes. Jackie's mother gave me an earful on the subject, collect on the phone from Newport to Biot. Even Bobby was . . ." He groped for the right word.

"Dismayed?"

"Yeah. Anyway, word leaked out, and Pearson heard about it. I put in an emergency radio call to Jack on the fucking yacht and told him if he didn't get back to port pronto, he could kiss his political career good-bye."

It was an unedifying story, but Jack was, above all, his father's son, and it would therefore never have occurred to him not to put his own pleasures first.

"I take it you came back to make peace?" I asked.

He nodded.

"Not an easy task, I would think."

"Not easy, no." His eyes, and the deep lines on his tanned face, made clear how hard it had been. "Not cheap either."

I could imagine. Still, there were things I didn't want to know, and that was one of them. "You were lucky the story broke in Drew Pearson's column," I said. "Even his colleagues don't trust him. If it had been Winchell, say—"

"I talked to Winchell."

"I'd talk to Jack again, if I were you." I thought hard. This kind of thing was how I made my living, after all. "What you need is a storm," I said.

"A storm?"

"A storm at sea. You radioed the yacht; they had to fight their way back against heavy seas and gales to make the nearest port. Jack was distraught, anxious, urging everybody on to put on more sail, or whatever it is they do. . . . It's got a nice resonance to it too, because it's going to remind people of PT-109. But Jack can't spread the story himself—somebody else has to make him a hero."

The Ambassador stared into the middle distance thoughtfully. How many times, over the years, had we sat together searching for some line to give the press that would present things in the rosiest possible light? "I like it," he said at last. "I like it fine."

"You need to get Jack and his pals on board fast."

"No problem there."

"How about the girls?"

"What girls?"

"The ones on the yacht."

"Their—ah—goodwill has already been secured."

A couple of pretty American girls, I guessed, were going to get a chance to travel around Europe for a while in luxury, keeping clear of the press. The Ambassador hadn't wasted any time.

"And Jackie?"

"What about her?"

"You don't want her telling people there wasn't a storm."

"She wasn't there. If Jack says there was a storm, who's to argue? The Mediterranean is funny that way. You can have great weather, a flat sea—then suddenly, out of nowhere, you get a squall . . . A dangerous place. Every sailor knows that."

He signaled for the dessert tray, already looking happier as he caught sight of a chocolate mousse cake. He pointed at it imperiously. "It wouldn't be a bad idea to have a few pictures in *Life,* would it now? Jack and Jackie—tragedy strikes the glamorous young couple of American politics, that kind of thing."

"No, it wouldn't be a bad idea. Will she stand for it, do you think?"

Joe dug into his piece of cake with a fierce thrust of his fork. "You see if you can sell it to *Life,*" he said. "I'll deal with the rest."

But in the end, the story never ran, probably because Jackie put her foot down. The legend of Jack's return to port through the raging seas to rejoin Jackie caught on well enough, however, and from time to time they even joked about it, though the subject always made Jack look a little nervous.

Early in the new year, after Jack had worked his guts out on the road for Adlai, and had the satisfaction of seeing him buried in the landslide for Ike, I would hear from Joe that Jackie was pregnant again, so the reconciliation was complete, timed perfectly for Jack's emergence as the one bright, shining hope for the Democrats as they looked ahead to 1960.

19

I dropped in to visit Jack in his Senate office on one of those misleading early spring days when the grass is turning green again, crocuses are appearing and the cherry trees beginning to blossom, and winter seems over at last—the kind of day that usually precedes a cold snap or a late blizzard. He looked relaxed as we drank our coffee, from big stoneware mugs with the Senate seal on them—a gift from Jackie, he told me. Nearly six months had passed since their crisis, and they seemed to have been reconciled.

"So things are going better between you two?" I asked.

He nodded, not quite sure how much I knew. "We've decided to move to Georgetown," he said warily. "No more commuting, thank God," he added, though it was news to me that he cared. "Bobby and Ethel bought Hickory Hill."

"I guess they plan to fill it."

He laughed—a bit hollowly, I thought. "I guess they will too," he said. Then, as if eager to change the subject from Ethel's phenomenal fertility: "Jackie found a nice little house on N Street in Georgetown. A red-brick Federal."

I nodded. I knew the house. Jackie's taste, as usual, was flawless and expensive.

"Have you heard from Marilyn?" he asked me.

"She's back from England," I told him. "I hear the picture is okay —*she's* terrific, Olivier's not, which is going to surprise the critics. . . . Not that it matters at the moment. She and Miller have gone into a kind of retreat, at his house in Connecticut. She's trying to be what she calls a good wife. She bakes pies, she vacuums, she makes him coffee. She's having a baby. After all, she dragged him off to England, where he suffered from writer's block while she worked, so she feels she owes him some time to get another play under his belt. Or a screenplay."

"That's very decent of her."

"Marilyn's a very decent person."

"Do you see a lot of her?"

"A lot? No. She comes into town every once in a while to see her psychiatrist. Sometimes we have coffee, or a sandwich."

"Is she happy?"

"She puts on a pretty good show. To hear her talk, all she's ever wanted to be is a housewife. On the other hand, since she also told me she's discovered that barbiturates work faster if you prick the capsule with a pin before swallowing it, I'm not so sure. I would guess Marilyn's got a few reservations about doing Miller's laundry while he writes his play, or whatever."

"Is that true, about the capsules?"

"Probably. It's not the sort of thing she'd make up. I suspect she's pretty unhappy. I think she knows the marriage has failed—that she's just going through the motions."

He nodded glumly. It clearly wasn't a subject he wanted to pursue. "Speaking of Bobby," he said (though we hadn't been), "it looks as if he's struck pay dirt at last. He's got enough on Beck to put him away for life. Mob connections, strong-arm tactics, tax evasion, theft of union funds, you name it. Can you imagine? Beck built himself a luxurious mansion with Teamster money, then sold it back to the union at a profit and continued living in it. He used union funds to build a hundred-and-eighty-five-thousand-dollar house for his son!" He shook his head. "Some of the things going on around Beck would curl your hair, David. It's going to be a big, big story."

"With Bobby at the center?"

"With Bobby and *me* at the center, yes. My guess is, it's going to require some landmark legislation to combat these abuses, once we've got them out in the open."

Investigating Dave Beck and his cronies would make the Kennedy name familiar to voters all across the country, and a piece of major labor legislation, emerging from the hearings and bearing Jack's name, would firmly establish him as a "serious" senator, once and for all. Since I had played a role in putting together this dramatic exposé of the forces of darkness, I felt a certain satisfaction at the neat way in which the pieces were now falling into place.

Red Dorfman and I had seen each other several times in the past few months—without striking up a closer friendship, I might add. From time to time, on my business trips to the West Coast, Jack Ruby left his Dallas strip joints to hand-deliver packages of information on Dave Beck and the Teamsters to me. Ruby didn't know what was in them, of course, which galled him almost as much as having to leave "his girls" unsupervised. We usually met in dark parking lots and got our business over as quickly as possible, but not so quickly that I didn't hear from him about all the difficulties of running a string of hookers in Dallas and, with considerable pride on his part, about how good his relationship was with the cops there. I did not look upon Ruby's sweaty presence as a pleasure, but frankly, I found him less objectionable than his boss, at any rate less threatening.

Every now and then, I asked myself what I was doing with these unlikely new playmates. I can understand now that I was simply bored with my life. I already had all the money I could ever spend, my marriage held no excitement for me (or for Maria, to be fair), I had become an "elder statesman" in my own company, and it was clear, even to me, that Marilyn and I were never fated to be anything more than friends. Playing Jack Kennedy's messenger to the forces of evil gave me the kind of thrill that a love affair might have done. Looking back, a love affair would have been a better idea.

On a couple of occasions, when it was absolutely necessary, I also met with some of Hoffa's own people, in conditions of strict secrecy. Somewhat against my better judgment, I had set up a meeting between Bobby and Hoffa which was to precede the hearing—a way for each man to get a feel for the other, as well as a kind of rehearsal for Hoffa before he submitted to being questioned in public.

I was more worried about the way Bobby would behave at the hearing than I was about Hoffa—Bobby knew perfectly well that this particular horse race was fixed, but he didn't like the idea a bit, and I was afraid that he might try and win it anyway, once he was out of the starting gate. Jack, as usual, assumed things would go his way smoothly.

"When is the great event scheduled for, actually?" I asked.

"Midsummer. August of all the goddamn months! Just when I want to be on the Cape. . . . You ought to come down and watch, since you had such a lot to do with it."

Washington is not my idea of a good place to be in August, but I was tempted. I had an idea—"premonition" is perhaps too strong a word—that history was going to be made, Kennedy family history anyway.

As matters turned out, the confrontation between Jimmy Hoffa and Bobby was to take second place in the headlines to a much bigger event in most people's eyes—a new tragedy in the life of Marilyn Monroe.

———

"I knew something bad was going to happen, right there on the beach at Amagansett, when we saw the fish."

Marilyn and I were sitting at a back table in the Hole in the Wall Delicatessen, a tiny place on First Avenue around the corner from her apartment at 555 East Fifty-seventh Street, where she went unrecognized by Stanley, the owner; his wife behind the cash register; and the waitress. Or perhaps they were simply used to incognito celebrities, since Garbo also lived around the corner and often ate breakfast there. Marilyn's face was thin and drawn, which made her eyes look huge, like those in a Day Kean painting. Only a week or two before, she had been rushed to a hospital in New York from Amagansett, in agony. She had been diagnosed as suffering from a tubal pregnancy and operated on immediately, since she was, as the tabloids proclaimed the next day, "in mortal danger."

"The fish?"

"They were on the beach." Her eyes opened wide, as if the scene were being reenacted on First Avenue. "See, the fishermen pull up their nets on the beach to empty them, and the fish they can't sell, they just toss out. Sea robins? Like that?"

I nodded, though I wasn't sure exactly what a sea robin was. Marilyn bit her lip sharply. "They just lie there helplessly, flapping, opening their mouths and gills, until they die," she said.

She managed to invest the scene with such emotion that I was almost tempted to cry myself at the death of the sea robins—Tippy all over again, I reflected.

"Arthur gave me this long, serious explanation of market forces, and how commercial fishermen make their living and so on, and all the time, I was dying, right along with the fish. So I started to pick them up, one after the other, and toss them back into the sea, even though I hate touching fish."

She shuddered. "He stood there for a while, looking grim, watching me save the fish; then he walked up beside me and started to help, and we both threw the fish back in until they were all gone. . . .

I was touched, you know? Because it wasn't something he believed in, or really wanted to do. That night we made love, and I knew I was going to have his baby." She glared at me briefly. "Don't ask me how, David. Women know these things, believe me."

"I believe you."

"No you don't, but you're wrong." She took a sip of water. Outside on the street, in the muggy heat, a woman went by wearily pushing a baby carriage. Marilyn stared at her until she was out of sight, then sighed. "I knew I was going to be pregnant," she said. "I knew I wasn't going to have the baby too. The fish were like a sign, do you know what I mean?"

I didn't, because I don't believe in such things, but I nodded.

"It wasn't meant to be," she explained, in case I'd missed the point.

"It's rotten luck—"

"It hasn't got anything to do with luck!" She reached under the table and clenched my hand tightly. Her palm was wet and clammy. "I don't love him enough, you see." I must have looked puzzled, because she added: "I don't love Arthur enough to have a baby with him, so the baby died."

I felt suddenly chilled, but I couldn't think of anything helpful to say. "It isn't your fault about the baby."

"Yes it *is*."

We sat silently, holding hands, while the waitress refilled our coffee cups. Marilyn had a scarf over her head—a cheap one, the kind you might buy at Lamston's. She wasn't wearing any makeup or her false eyelashes, and she had let her eyebrows go unplucked. Her skin was the color of mother-of-pearl, very pale, with a hint of blue, as if she were bruised. I couldn't help thinking that this was what she would have looked like if she'd remained Norma Jean.

"How's Arthur taking it?" I asked.

"He's being very sweet about it, which makes me feel even worse. He's given up his play, you know? He's writing a screenplay for me instead."

"That's nice of him."

She shrugged. "Yes. I don't know, though. From what I've read of it so far, he's made the heroine me. Or what he thinks about me."

"That might be uncomfortable. I can see that."

"Try painful."

"Is it any good?"

"That's the worst thing, David. It's the best work Arthur's done in years." She sighed. "You were right," she said. "Those notes, in England? They were for this screenplay, they weren't about me. He told me."

From the way she said it, I knew she didn't believe it. I didn't either. I guessed it was something she had to convince herself of in order to make a fresh start with the marriage. "Are you going to do it?" I asked.

"I think so," she said without enthusiasm. "Eventually. There's a part for Gable in it, as a cowboy. I've always wanted to work with Gable." She sighed again. "Anyway, I'm going to do another picture first, otherwise I'll go crazy."

"I thought you were happy being the housewife?"

She gave me an impatient look. "I'm not planning to spend the rest of my life washing dishes, David, if that's what you mean," she said sharply. "Billy Wilder's supposed to be sending me a treatment about a girl who's running away from the mob with two guys in drag. . . . Arthur thinks a comedy might be good for me."

"I thought you hated Wilder."

"I do. But he knows how to direct me, and after Sir Cork Tip, I haven't got time for amateur directors." She seemed a little more cheerful now that she was talking about her career. "What are you doing with yourself?" she asked.

"All work, no play, basically," I said. "But I'm going to Washington tomorrow."

"I wish I could go with you."

"Well, that wouldn't be easy. I'm going down to watch Hoffa's appearance before the Senate Subcommittee. Bobby's big moment."

"Oh? I haven't been following it."

I filled her in briefly on events to date: on Dave Beck's sweaty collapse as Bobby pummeled him with questions, on the reams of testimony and evidence, much of it provided by me, that condemned Beck and his cronies.

"This whole business gives me the willies," she said.

"Hoffa? The Teamsters? It's just politics. Some people go to prison, some get reelected—that's the way the game is played."

"It's dangerous. I told Jack that."

"He knows what he's doing, Marilyn."

She shook her head irritably. "No he doesn't. Tell him to be careful, please. Real careful!"

"I will."

She did not look as if she believed me. "Tell him how much I'd love to have his baby."

I swallowed hard. "I don't think he'd appreciate that message coming from me, Marilyn."

"Maybe you're right. Tell him to call me, then."

"Okay."

"We'd have a beautiful baby, Jack and me. I can feel it, right here." She put her other hand flat against her stomach. Her nails were chipped and dirty at the edges. "I love *him* enough for the baby to be born, David, I know it." She was trying to hold back her tears now, but not very successfully. "I'd love the baby, too."

"I'm sure you would," I said.

"Jack would be the father, but he wouldn't have to *be* the father, do you see what I mean? He wouldn't have to leave Jackie, or acknowledge the baby, or anything. He'd know and I'd know, and that would be enough. I've thought it all out."

"You certainly have," I said, with as much enthusiasm as I could manage.

———

Washington was even hotter than New York. It was a relief to get into the committee room where the Senate Government Investigations Subcommittee, better known as the McClellan committee, after its somewhat unenthusiastic chairman, was in session. Bobby was seated at a small desk, surrounded by documents, a pair of reading glasses perched on his head. His brother sat on the dais behind him, along with the other members of the subcommittee, most of them fully occupied with the task of trying to look like serious statesmen for the media.

It was a packed house—to use the theatrical term, which was appropriate under the circumstances—for Hoffa's appearance. Hoffa was not yet the famous figure that the hearings were about to make him, but his name had come up so often in previous testimony that everybody was curious to see what he looked like.

He entered like a prizefighter surrounded by his trainers—in this case, lawyers—a small, powerful fireplug of a man, cocky and intense. He waved at Bobby, who glared back at him.

The dinner meeting between the two of them had not gone well, Jack had told me. Bobby had turned down Hoffa's invitation to armwrestle and, instead, asked some embarrassing questions about the paper locals in New York City, by means of which Hoffa and the mob were trying to gain control of the New York Joint Council of Teamsters.

Hoffa had left the meeting asking Bobby to tell his wife that he wasn't as bad as everyone thought he was, but Bobby told Ethel later that he thought Hoffa was worse. As for Hoffa, he came away from the dinner with the impression that Bobby was "a damn spoiled jerk."

This wasn't a happy augury, nor had matters been improved when Hoffa was shortly afterward arrested in the lobby of the Dupont Plaza Hotel by the FBI, charged with trying to bribe a witness with two thousand dollars in cash. Intermediaries had been working overtime to settle this little last-minute problem. I knew because I had seen my old friend Ike Lublin, a heavyweight lawyer in LA, who was reputed to have "mob connections," having breakfast in the Hay-Adams, and he had told me some of it—as much as he wanted me to know, no doubt.

Bobby started slowly now, guiding Hoffa through a series of cream puff questions. It was not exciting stuff, and both the press and the subcommittee members looked disappointed. Beck had been a sweaty villain, and his coconspirators a collection of earthy figures straight out of the pages of Damon Runyon, with colorful pasts that included extortion, murder, and racketeering. Hoffa, by contrast, was on his best choirboy behavior, and answered the questions in a careful, prissy style that may have been his way of making fun of Bobby. Certainly Bobby took it as such, and I could see his face turning red, his eyes that icy blue that meant trouble. He was working hard to give Hoffa an opportunity to make the brief *mea culpa* that was required of him, but Hoffa wasn't giving it to him. Hoffa's expression was richly contemptuous, as if to say that Bobby could go fuck himself.

"Some of these practices are just plain wrong, aren't they?" Bobby said at last, after what seemed like hours of futile shadowboxing.

"What do you mean by wrong?" Hoffa asked, with a sneer that he may have intended as a smile.

"Criminal," Bobby snapped. "Contrary to the best interest of your members. Does that explain it?"

"I know of no such practices," Hoffa said, frowning as if he were trying hard to think of some.

"You have made no mistakes?"

"None I can think of, Bobby."

Bobby's eyes flashed at the familiarity. "Not many men can say that, Mr. Hoffa," he said, shaking his head.

Hoffa smiled. "I can."

Bobby tried again. "Surely there's something you can remember, Mr. Hoffa, that you wish you hadn't done."

Hoffa suppressed a laugh. "I wish I'd been born a rich kid, like you, Bobby," he said, while his entourage, beefy men in polyester suits, with diamond rings on pinkies the size of German sausages, laughed and clapped. "But stuff I shouldn't have done? Zip."

He was making a mistake, of course. I could see Ike Lublin among the spectators, scribbling a note to send up to Hoffa. Jack, I noticed, was alert, as if he could sense that the whole perfectly planned scenario was about to get out of control, with God only knew what unforeseen consequences. I remembered Red Dorfman's warnings and shivered.

Bobby flipped through the papers in front of him. He had given Hoffa ample time to eat a little humble pie before the subcommittee. Now he took his time as he chose his next question. He glanced at the piece of paper he had been searching for, then looked up at Hoffa. "Do you know Joe Holtzman?" he asked.

There was a flurry of activity around Hoffa, while the lawyers on either side of him whispered in his ears. He shook his head angrily. His big jaw jutted out, his nostrils flared, his eyes were dark pools of anger—a man betrayed, I thought. "I knew Joe Holtzman."

I had no idea who Holtzman was, but it was clear it was a name Hoffa hadn't expected to hear here. "Then was he a close friend of yours?" Bobby asked.

"I knew Joe Holtzman."

"Was he a close friend of yours?"

Hoffa's face was the color of marble, rough-hewn. "Now listen here!" he shouted, his voice echoing loudly in a room where most people had to be urged to speak up. "I knew Joe Holtzman! But he wasn't any particular friend of mine."

Bobby ignored Hoffa's raised voice. Looking him right in the eye, he said, "I'll ask you again until I get a proper answer. Do you know Joe Holtzman?"

"I knew Joe Holtzman."

"Was he a close friend of yours, Mr. Hoffa?"

There was a long silence. Jimmy Hoffa had a pencil in his meaty hands, and he broke it in two with a snap that made everybody in the room start.

Ike signaled me and I slipped out of the room. "This isn't good," he said. "Your man is asking tough questions."

"*Your* man is behaving like a smart-ass. He's supposed to be contrite."

Ike sighed. "We got a problem," he said.

I thought so too, but I couldn't think of anything to be done about it. I scrawled a quick note to Jack, begging him to talk to Bobby as soon as there was a recess, gave it to a guard to pass up to him, and stepped inside again.

In my brief absence, things had apparently gone from bad to worse. Despite the ornate trappings of the room and the presence of the television cameras, it had the feeling of a bullring, a place of combat and death—and indeed, there was something that reminded me of a bull in Hoffa's stubborn, relentless refusal to give way before Bobby's thrusts.

"We have here an expense voucher for twenty-three Minifons," Bobby was saying, his clear Boston accent cutting through the quiet room. "Mini-phones," he explained. "Small German tape recorders purchased by the Teamsters . . . for you, Mr. Hoffa. Could you tell this committee now what they were used for?"

Hoffa smiled—a shit-eating grin is how I'd describe it. "What did I do with them?" he asked. "What did I do with them?" He paused, turning to wink at his supporters. "Well, what *did* I do with them?"

"Yes. What did you do with them?" Bobby's voice was flat.

"I am trying to recall."

"You could remember that."

"When were they delivered, do you know? That must have been quite a while ago. . . ."

"You know what you did with the Minifons. And don't ask me!"

"Well, well. . . ." Hoffa feigned honest ignorance. "Let me see— what did I do with them?"

Bobby's voice was harsh now, the disgust evident on his face. "What did you do with them, Mr. Hoffa?" he repeated angrily, Hoffa's name delivered as sharp as a slap.

Hoffa looked contrite, or tried to. He was sticking to his guns out of some deep hatred for everything Bobby stood for—wealth, privilege, education, idealism—that went far beyond his self-interest, which was to make Bobby look good for the media. "Mr. Kennedy," he said, "I bought some Minifons. And there is no question about it. But I cannot recall what became of them."

Ike leaned over, from the row behind me now. "*Oy,*" he said.

"What's with the Minifons?" I whispered.

"Jimmy and his guys wore them to entrap other guys who were loyal to Beck. Stuff like that."

"That's a federal crime, isn't it?"

Ike nodded darkly. "That's why he can't answer the question."

Of *course* Hoffa couldn't answer the question. He would be incriminating himself. And he was reluctant to plead the Fifth Amendment because George Meany had now instructed all *his* people not to. Since the Kefauver hearings on organized crime, taking the Fifth had become the last refuge of gangsters, in most people's eyes sure proof of guilt.

"Yes? It must be difficult to remember with such a selective memory," Bobby said.

Jack, I could see, was reading my note. He caught my eye and shrugged, as if to say, *I will, I will, but you know Bobby. . . .*

"Well," Hoffa went on, "I will have to stand on the answers that I have made in regards to my recollection, and I cannot answer different, unless you give me some other recollection other than I have already answered."

This piece of nonsense set off a roar of laughter from Hoffa's supporters, which Senator McClellan, seeming to come to life for the first time, tried to gavel down. When the noise died, Hoffa sat smirking at Bobby, as if challenging him to do his worst.

"Mr. Hoffa, did you ever wear a Minifon yourself? In order to record a fellow Teamster?"

Hoffa cocked his head sideways. His expression was a little warier now. Bobby obviously had more information than Hoffa supposed. He had underrated Bobby's passion for doing his homework. "You say 'wear,' " Hoffa said. "What do you mean by wear?"

Bobby rolled his eyes. For over an hour he had tried to get Hoffa to make a clear reply to any question, and to offer the ritual apology that Bobby had been promised.

He brought up next the subject of two Teamster officials whom Hoffa had continued to employ and pay while they were in prison for taking kickbacks from employers. Hoffa's face registered surprise, even alarm, as Bobby concluded, "You continued paying them while they were in prison! What were you afraid of?"

There couldn't have been a question more guaranteed to make Hoffa lose his temper. Hoffa, like Bobby himself, was absolutely fearless. He had spent his life in an industry in which tire irons, guns, baseball bats, dynamite, and meat hooks were used every day against people who got out of line, and he boasted often that he had never backed down from a fight. His face turned white and he rose halfway out of his seat, as if he were going to attack Bobby, while his lawyers tried to pull him down. "I was not charged with any crime connected with them!" he shouted, the veins bulging in his forehead. ". . . I was not afraid they were going to expose me, because they have nothing to expose!"

". . . How can you possibly explain being so solicitous of them? Unless you received some of the money yourself? Can you explain that?"

But Hoffa's rage had overcome him. He couldn't explain, or wouldn't. He shook his head. "I think I made my statement," he muttered hoarsely, his fists clenched.

Bobby was about to pursue the matter further, but Senator McClellan—prodded, I couldn't help noticing, by Jack—banged his gavel and called a recess for lunch.

I made my way toward Bobby, who was still sitting at his desk, just as Hoffa, who had broken loose from his lawyers, stormed up to him, shoulders hunched, eyes blazing. Bobby didn't move or even blink.

I was close enough to hear Hoffa's rasping voice as he stuck his face close to Bobby's and said: "You *fucked* me, you little college boy prick! You're not going to make your brother president over Hoffa's dead body!" Then, quickly, before his lawyers and the guards could drag him away: "You're dead meat, Bobby, you go on with this." His voice had dropped to a searing hiss, like steam escaping from a vent. "You and your fucking brother both."

Bobby's expression was glacial, his lips tightly compressed. He answered in a quiet, conversational tone, without a trace of emotion: "Mr. Hoffa, I'm going to put you in prison if it's the last thing I do. And please stop calling me Bobby."

Hoffa pushed the guards and lawyers away and stood his ground, smiling at Bobby. "Hey, Bobby," he called out mockingly, "I'll promise you one thing. It's *gonna* be the last thing you do. You got Hoffa's word on that."

———

Ike Lublin and I had dinner together that night, both of us a little subdued. I had known Ike since he moved out to LA from Cleveland as his mobster clients expanded their interests westward. Many of the biggest stars were his clients too, and he was respected as a dealmaker, a divorce lawyer, and, above all, the man you went to see when you were in real trouble. Ike frightened most people with his aggressive tactics, but he didn't frighten me. I happened to know that he was devoted to his wife, who had become a hopeless alcoholic after the death of their only child during a polio epidemic. There was a soft side to Ike, though he preferred to hide it.

"Bobby fucked Jimmy," he said, wolfing down his shrimp cocktail. "The deal is off."

"Come on! Hoffa didn't come through with his end, Ike. You know that."

"He delivered that putz Beck."

"He was supposed to make like a good guy for the subcommittee. Instead, he came off as a hard-ass." I'd decided it would save time to use Ike's own language.

Ike shrugged. "Why does seafood always taste better in the East?" he asked—he had ordered Maryland crab cakes for his main course.

"Maybe it's just that people back east still remember how to cook. What happens now?"

"How would I know? Ask Red. You wanna guess? Jimmy's gonna fight back. Hard. Dirty. Somebody's gonna get hurt."

"It has to be stopped."

The waiter served Ike his crab cakes, and he ate silently for a few moments; then he sighed and put his fork down. "Your salmon okay?"

I nodded.

"It can't be stopped, not unless Bobby lays off. Is he gonna lay off?"

"I'll talk to Jack, but I doubt it. Not unless Hoffa pays some respect to the subcommittee. And Bobby."

"Then it can't be stopped. Jimmy hates him now."

He ate for a while, thinking about what he'd said. "I don't mean he dislikes Bobby, unnerstan', David? He's not a reasonable man, Jimmy Hoffa, like you and me. Hear what I'm saying: *He hates Bobby!*"

"I understand."

"I don't think you do. Somebody's gotta warn Bobby that Jimmy's *dangerous*. Somebody's gotta tell him that there are areas he can't go into, or there's gonna be real trouble."

"What areas?"

Ike finished his crab cakes and wiped his mouth. He leaned close to me in the booth, so close that I could smell his after-shave. "Stuff that involves Moe and Red, and the boys in Chicago. Stuff about the casinos and the Central States Teamsters Pension Fund. Stuff like that is very sensitive, David, very serious. People could get hurt. Where's the sense in that?"

"I understand, Ike." I did too. And I agreed.

"Personal stuff too. Listen, I *know* Jimmy, David. Money don't interest Jimmy. What the hell, you see the way he dresses! But that don't mean he's a saint. Jimmy likes to pretend he's the family man, but he's got a mistress, did you know? Some broad whose husband's in the laundry business. She's the one who introduced Jimmy to Moe in the first place. They had a kid together, Jimmy and this broad. Jimmy really cares for the kid too. . . . What I'm trying to tell you is that if Bobby gets into that side of Jimmy's life, all bets are off."

"Why are you telling me this?"

He shrugged. He took his cigar case out of his pocket, and we each lit an Upmann English Market with our brandy and coffee. Ike was picking up the check. He would charge the meal to one of his clients; still, it was a nice gesture. "I don't like trouble," he said. "I profit by it, sure, but my job is to prevent it. Preventative maintenance, David, that's the best service I can offer my clients. Jimmy Hoffa, now, I don't give a fuck about him—Bobby Kennedy sends him to Atlanta to get his ass reamed out in the showers by a lot of niggers, I'm not gonna lose any sleep, personally. But if Jimmy gets into deep trouble with the Feds, it's gonna make problems for my clients, guys like Red or Moe, maybe even Momo, God forbid. Then people start getting killed and what not, and business suffers. . . . It's not worth it, David, that's all I'm saying."

"I don't disagree."

"Of course not. You're a sensible man. Everybody knows that. I told Red and Moe that myself. I said, 'It ain't David's fault. Don't blame this on him.' "

"I'm grateful, Ike."

He nodded. "You oughta be, David," he said gravely. "I got you off the hook, frankly. If you can't get Bobby to slack off on Jimmy, just make sure he don't push too hard on Moe or Red, okay? You'd be doing me a favor." He smiled broadly. "Hell, you'd be doing *yourself* a favor."

I knew a warning when I heard one. I didn't even need to look at Ike Lublin's eyes through the wreaths of cigar smoke to take it seriously.

Jack and I had breakfast the next day in his rented house in George-town. There were newspapers spread out all over the dining room table. Jack had been devouring the stories about Hoffa's appearance before the subcommittee and was so pleased with himself that I almost hesitated to bring up the fact that he and Bobby had made an enemy of Hoffa.

When I did, he looked surprised. "Hoffa pissed Bobby off. He wasn't supposed to do that. *He's* the one who broke the deal."

"Well, yes, but that's not the way Hoffa sees it, Jack. The Minifon stuff—that wasn't in the script."

"Whose side are you on, anyway?"

"Yours. But you shouldn't have let it get out of control. And you've got to stop it from going farther."

Jack ate his eggs neatly. He broke his toast up into small pieces, then carefully placed a tiny fragment of toast, a piece of egg, and a piece of bacon on his fork. "David, this story is playing well. Better than what we had in mind."

He wasn't wrong. Every major newspaper and political columnist in the country, right and left, Republican and Democrat, even those who were notoriously hostile to the Kennedy family, had come out in praise of Bobby's courage in confronting Hoffa, and Jack's states-manlike position. Hoffa came across, in editorials, cartoons, and the news stories, as a dangerous thug—Bobby might as well have been Saint George slaying the dragon.

"When you come right down to it," Jack went on, "it was a piece of good luck that Bobby and Hoffa hated each other on sight."

"Yes and no."

He raised an eyebrow, a little impatiently. From his perspective, a defiant Hoffa was a more interesting figure than an apologetic Hoffa. The general impression the average voter—unless he was a Teamster —would take away from the newspaper reports was that this was a fight between the Kennedys and the forces of darkness. Jack liked the look of it all, and I couldn't blame him. But he was dead wrong.

"You're not considering how dangerous this is, Jack," I told him. "I had dinner with Ike Lublin last night. A lot of the mob people who do business with Hoffa are upset, he says. They thought Hoffa had a deal. Now they're worried. Frankly, I got the impression from Ike that there was some talk about punishing me."

Jack laughed. "I wouldn't take that kind of thing seriously, David."

I did not join in his laughter. Jack's feelings about danger were not the same as mine. "I do," I said. "And I'm not the only one who should be worrying, Jack, if Lublin is telling the truth."

"He's probably exaggerating."

"I wouldn't bet on it."

"If you're going to go, you're going to go, David. I never worry. And if it's going to happen, a bullet is the best way. It's so quick you don't even know it's happened. . . ."

"I'm hoping to die of old age," I said.

Jack didn't crack a smile. "I can't imagine dying of old age," he said firmly.

I changed the subject. "Be that as it may, Jack, Bobby let things get out of hand. You had a deal with Hoffa—"

Jack held up his hand. "What deal? Hoffa agreed to cooperate in an investigation, as I understand it. I'm not familiar with the details, but his attitude before the subcommittee wasn't what I would call cooperative."

"I see." I saw, all right. Plan A, which involved Jack and Hoffa helping each other at Dave Beck's expense, had been shelved, due to what divorce lawyers refer to as "personality differences." Plan B was now in effect, in which Jack made himself a national reputation at Hoffa's expense. In the meantime, he was putting as much distance as he could between himself and Hoffa. He was not his father's son for nothing, I reflected. Then I thought about Red Dorfman, and his reputation for having people who displeased him hung from meat hooks, and realized that Jack was playing with *my* life as well as his own. "For Christ's *sake*, Jack," I said, my voice rising, "you're going to get us *killed!*"

He gave me a look of sheer astonishment. "Take it easy," he said.

"Take it *easy?* Do you have any idea who you're dealing with? I told you right back at the beginning of this that these are dangerous people. They're not politicians! They expect promises to be kept."

There was a look of hard, cold anger in Jack's eyes now. "I didn't make your friends any promises," he said.

That did it! I'm not normally a man who loses his temper, but Jack's ruthlessness enraged me.

"*My* friends?" I shouted. "Since when are they *my* friends, Jack? *You* asked me to get in touch with them for you. They're *your* friends now, Jack, like it or not. I made a deal with them on your behalf, and don't you forget it! I'm not going to get blown up in my car or drowned in my own swimming pool just because you can't control Bobby!"

Jack stared at me, his anger gone even though I had been shouting at him. "David," he said quietly. "Calm down."

"Calm down? When you're talking as if you had nothing to do with all this? Don't tell *me* you're not familiar with the details, Jack. Save that kind of thing for your press conferences when you get to the White House. If you live long enough to get there."

He held up his hands in mock surrender. "All right," he said with a rueful smile, "all right. Maybe you've got a point."

"You don't *really* want these guys putting a sniper on some rooftop across the street from you, do you? Because believe me, Jack, they're quite capable of it."

"I'm not afraid of that," he said, and I knew he meant it—Jack's courage was never in doubt, not even by his enemies. "On the other hand," he went on, "I guess there's no point to pissing them off any more than we have to."

I was almost as relieved that he had stopped calling the mobsters *my* friends as I was that he was seeing reason at last.

"I don't know how much I can do for Hoffa," he said. "He hung himself, right there on national television. And he threatened Bobby personally. A big mistake."

"No argument."

"I can't stop Bobby from going after him. Not after what Hoffa said to *him*."

"Just because Bobby's going after Hoffa doesn't mean he has to catch up with him, does it?" I suggested.

Jack thought this over, frowning. You never had to spell out the details with Jack. He was *born* with a mind that would have pleased Machiavelli. He chuckled. "I'd hate to think of Bobby like one of those greyhounds in the dog races, always chasing the rabbit without ever catching it."

"So would I, Jack, but it beats being killed by the mob. Does Bobby have to know?"

"No. Not yet anyway. Once I'm elected, it's another story." I noticed he did not say "if." He poured us each a cup of coffee from a silver Thermos jug. He was still in his shirtsleeves, smelling briskly of scented soap and after-shave. "Of course, if Hoffa does something dumb again, like that bribery thing . . ."

"He says he was set up."

"Of course he'd say that. . . . Look, Hoffa's got to stay on the reservation from now on. I can't be expected to save his ass if he goes around committing major felonies in broad daylight."

"I think his associates might understand that, if it was put to them the right way."

"Can you do that for me?"

I hesitated. "I don't know if I really want to keep on doing this, Jack. It's getting a bit too dangerous for my taste."

"I know it isn't the kind of thing you like doing, David, but I can trust you. And you *do* seem to have built up a certain amount of, ah, *trust* with these fellows. . . ." It was basically the same message Dorfman had given me, more eloquently put. He looked me square in the eye. "I don't want to have to plead for your help, David, but if I have to, I will."

I sighed and gave in, as I always did. Jack had the gift of getting people to do what they didn't want to do, or think they *could* do— perhaps the most important quality for a president. Besides, I thought I could handle the problem better than anyone else—another illusion. "I'll do it," I said. "Just this once."

"Good. What do you need?"

"Well, there's a case that Hoffa has coming up in Tennessee. I'm not up on the details, but it involves a trucking company he may have bought in his wife's name. Ike thinks it would be a good idea if the subcommittee steered clear of that and left it to the courts."

Jack nodded. "He'd like it to drag its way to trial as slowly as possible, without too much publicity, so there's plenty of time for him to get to the jurors, or the judge?"

"Something like that."

"I'll see what I can do." He did not look happy about it.

"The other thing is, Hoffa has a mistress and an illegitimate son—"

"Jesus!" Jack said, his interest always aroused by sexual gossip. "And all this time we thought he was a choirboy in that area!"

"Apparently not. Ike says to stay clear of that side of things. Hoffa's sensitive on the subject. Maybe even irrational."

"Hell, his private life's his own business, just like anyone else's. I don't see why Bobby has to go into that."

"His investigators aren't going to miss it. People talk. Ike's no dummy, and what he says is: *Don't push that button!*"

"I'll talk to Bobby." He leaned forward, his voice dropping confidentially. "Is she pretty?"

"Ike didn't say. But she was Moe Dalitz's mistress for a while, and Moe has pretty good taste."

"These guys swap mistresses?"

"Well, it's a small world, you know. The kind of people we're talking about have to be sure a girl isn't going to gossip about what she's heard."

"That makes sense." Jack was always curious to know how other more or less public figures arranged their sex lives. Up to now he'd had it easy. Nobody cared all that much about the private life of a United States senator. If he really did succeed in becoming president of the United States, his private life would be much more difficult to maintain. Between the Secret Service and the White House press corps, the president hardly has a moment when he's not being watched. President Harding was obliged to make love to his mistress in a downstairs coat closet, standing among the galoshes and umbrellas. Jack, I felt sure, would do better.

"Hoffa!" he said with a laugh. "I knew he was going to do us some good, but if he goes on butting his head against Bobby's, the son of a bitch is going to take us all the way to the White House!"

Jack had a point, of course. Hoffa was to play the role of villain in the drama that would turn Jack and Bobby into heroes in the eyes of the public—a drama scripted, in part, by me. But Hoffa was right and royally screwed, and it was a fatal error to underestimate his rage or his capacity for revenge.

I should have known better, and should have made Jack listen, but like everyone else, I was lulled by Jack's self-confidence, as well as by the fact that we were sitting there comfortably in the seat of government, surrounded by power—the Senate, the FBI, the Justice Department, the Secret Service, all of which seemed like a mighty fortress that could hardly be threatened by the likes of one crooked, loudmouthed labor leader and his thug pals.

"Hoffa's Catholic, isn't he?" Jack asked.

"I have no idea. Why?"

"Bobby doesn't approve of Catholics having sex out of marriage." He smiled broadly. "Of course, he does make exceptions."

"Try to make sure this is one of them, Jack. For your own sake. And mine."

"Sure. Christ, I'm the last person who'd want a guy's sex life used against him politically. . . . What else?"

"Don't let Bobby go after people like Red Dorfman, or Moe Dalitz, or Sam Giancana. These guys have plenty of problems with the law as it is, so why tie your name into some kind of campaign against them? From their point of view, remember, they did you a favor."

He didn't say anything, so I continued. "You got Beck. The sub-committee got a good look at Hoffa. It's a good score—headlines, great press, a chance to write some major legislation. You don't need to bring these guys into it as well."

"One or two of them will have to appear before the subcommittee," he said cautiously. "There's no way I can stop that. It's too late."

"Okay, that's understood, but don't make them walk the plank, Jack, that's all I'm saying. No contempt citations, nobody goes to jail, okay?"

"Will they settle for that?"

"Probably. I hope so."

"I'll do my best," he said, and I could see that was all I was going to get.

Jack stretched, grimacing with pain. He used a wooden rocking chair at home instead of a regular dining chair, but sitting for any length of time still hurt him. "Do you know a Dr. Burton Wasserman in New York?" he asked.

"I know of him. Marilyn mentioned him."

"No kidding? I saw him last time I was there. A couple of people recommended him. Wasserman's the man to see for pain. He gave me an injection—B vitamins and so on—and it was like a miracle! I didn't have any pain at all for the next twenty-four hours—haven't felt so good for years!"

"Wasserman's a celebrity doctor. I know a lot of his patients. They all say he's a miracle worker. The injections work, no question about it, but the problem is, you have to keep going back to him for more. Bill Paley went to him after that skiing injury he had, and eventually he was going every day."

"Well, I don't mind going once or twice a week, if it gets rid of the pain." He grinned. "I can find plenty to do in New York, as a matter of fact."

He rose—he was moving less stiffly, I noticed—and we shook hands.

I was willing to bet that Marilyn would soon be spending more time in the city, instead of playing housewife for Arthur Miller in Connecticut.

20

It was dark in the bedroom. She moved a little closer to the man beside her and rubbed her foot against his. "You can't be ready for more," he said. "Not yet."

"I'm not. I'm pooped. Fucked out, if you want to know the truth. I just want you to hold me."

He put his arms around her and pressed her close to him. She could feel the hair on his chest and belly against her skin, a delicate prickling sensation that she loved. She put her fingers on his penis and held it gently, loving the feel of its warmth and the slight, throbbing pulsebeat of arousal, however tired he was. She was sore, wet, sweaty, the sea-salt taste of his sperm still in her mouth—*sodden* with sex, she told herself happily.

"I was sorry to hear about the baby," he said.

There hadn't been any time to catch up when she entered the suite. He had put his arms around her and kissed her hard. She'd surrendered instantly to his impatience, tearing off her clothes as he pulled her toward the bedroom, laughing and sobbing as she fell face forward on the bed, half in her clothes, half out, while he stood behind her, driving himself deep into her with fierce, urgent thrusts. She had come twice before they even got the rest of their clothes off, turned down the bed, and slipped between the cool sheets to make love again, this time slowly, inventively, athletically.

"Your back must be better," she said now. She didn't want to talk about the baby.

"You noticed."

"I'll say! It's a change from you lying on your back with me on top."

"You didn't like that?"

"I liked it fine," she said. "I just meant I liked this better."

"We aim to please. I've been seeing that doctor everybody's talking about. Wasserman. I had one of his vitamin shots today. It's like magic. My back doesn't hurt a bit. Christ, I could go through every position in the *Kama Sutra*." He ran his hand down her back slowly, letting it come to rest on her ass, his fingers gently playing with her pubic hair.

She shivered. She could have stayed here like this forever, safe from the world. She might even be able to sleep in his arms. "Be my guest," she said. "I'm glad Dr. Wasserman performed such a miracle for you."

"David told me you went to him too."

"Mm," she murmured noncommittally.

"You don't sound enthusiastic."

"Well . . . I thought he was creepy, frankly. Did you know they call him 'Dr. Feelgood'? I mean, those injections—I don't think they're just vitamins, if you know what I mean. . . ."

"They work for me. Didn't they work for you?"

"Well, they did and they didn't. I felt good for a while, then I had these terrible downers. . . . Besides, I hate injections—they really scare me. I guess the real problem I had with Dr. Wasserman was that he wouldn't give me any prescriptions. I had to come to his office. And he used to make me undress just to give me a shot, so I decided he was just a dirty old man."

He laughed. "I'd do the same if I was a doctor."

"You're a dirty old man too."

"Not yet, but I hope to be someday. It's always been my ambition."

"It's an ambition, I guess," she said, licking the dried sweat off his chest like a cat, with long strokes of her tongue. "I always wanted one. For a while I thought 'Living well is the best revenge' might do it." She had seen that on a needlepoint pillow in Amy Greene's bedroom, and it had made instant sense to her.

"It won't do for me," Jack said. "I've always lived well."

"How about for Jackie?"

He looked thoughtful. "Yes," he said. "That might do fine for Jackie."

"How are things going now with Jackie?"

"What do you mean?"

"I read the newspapers, you know. Besides, David fills me in on all the gossip."

"He talks too much."

"He's a lot nicer to me than you are. Anyway, you may as well tell me. I'll worm it out of you sooner or later."

He sighed. "We had a breakup, it's true. After she lost the baby. Now we're back together. And Jackie's pregnant again."

"How nice," she said, unable to disguise her sadness. "What was the breakup about?"

"No one thing, you know. . . . It happens."

"*Tell* me about it. Since she's pregnant, I guess you've got things sorted out."

"Basically."

"It's a pity. Otherwise, you could have married me."

He gave a nervous laugh.

"I mean it!"

"I know you do," he said, keeping well clear of expressing any enthusiasm of his own for the idea.

"We'd be so happy," she said. "We'd have the most wonderful baby!"

She could feel him stiffen in alarm. "I was just dreaming out loud," she whispered, putting her arms around him to prevent him from getting up. "It's such a lovely dream."

He was eager to change the subject. "What are you doing next?"

"I'm going back to LA for a while, to do a picture with Billy." She reminded herself that Jack wasn't in the industry. "Wilder," she added.

He nodded vaguely.

"He directed me in *The Seven Year Itch,*" she explained.

"That's great. I liked it. What's the picture going to be?"

"I've only read the outline. I'm going to play Sugar Kane, a singer and ukelele player who gets mixed up with a couple of guys who dress up as women to escape from the mob. Tony Curtis and Jack Lemmon are going to be in it with me. . . ."

"Jack Lemmon is great."

"Mm," she said. The fact was, she was terrified of working with Lemmon, who was a real pro, a "comedian's comedian," as Arthur said. Worse still was the prospect of working with Curtis, who had a reputation for being brash, tough, and highly competitive.

She longed to get back to work in Hollywood, where her stardom was uncontested, but already she was afraid of facing the camera again, of the endless takes, the pressure from the studio, the demands of the director. . . . And this time she would have to go through all that without Milton, for she had ended her partnership with him once and for all in a rage over the personal expenses she thought he had charged to *The Prince and the Showgirl,* thus breaking a friendship that had been one of the most important of her whole life. Afterward, she discovered it wasn't true, but by then it was too late.

"What's, ah, Sugar Kane like?" Jack asked, making conversation.

"A dumb blonde."

"I thought you didn't want to play dumb blondes anymore."

"I don't. But it's what I do. Like you running for president. Anyway, once I've done this picture, and maybe one more, I'm going to make the one Arthur is writing for me—*The Misfits.* I play *me* in that one. That's going to be a *lot* harder."

"I would have thought it was easier."

"Oh, honey, never. Being yourself is the hardest. I'd rather play somebody else any day."

"I'm going to be out there on the West Coast a lot, later in the year."

"Mm, good," she whispered, feeling him become hard again. Her body took over, her mind drifted in neutral, she could forget about her marriage and the next picture.

But even as she moaned with pleasure, in some corner of her mind she was still wondering how she was going to manage to play Roslyn in *The Misfits,* the tormented, neurotic, unfaithful heroine Arthur had treacherously written for her. . . .

———

Special Agent Kirkpatrick was shown without delay into the Director's office by his motherly secretary.

Hoover was sitting behind his desk impassively, as if he were carved out of soapstone. As always, Tolson sat by his side.

"Good work, Kirkpatrick," Tolson said.

Hoover nodded agreement, his jowls wobbling slightly.

"I've got more," Kirkpatrick said, patting his briefcase. "We taped a conversation between Strawhead and Lancer a couple of nights ago, at the Carlyle Hotel in New York." As the volume of tape mounted up, Kirkpatrick had deemed it advisable to give code names to each of the major figures for security purposes, as well as to put a Top Secret classification on the whole project. He had no idea where it was going, but he knew enough about politics to smell a nasty scandal if any of this leaked out to the press.

"I know where the Carlyle Hotel is," Hoover growled, as if his familiarity with New York had been questioned.

"They say it's very nice," Tolson said.

"The Waldorf Towers is good enough for me," Hoover said. "The Kennedys keep an apartment at the Carlyle," he explained to Tolson. "The Ambassador uses it, as well as Senator Kennedy. You can imagine what for."

"Oh, I can imagine, Director," Tolson said. "It's a real shame that people like the Kennedys, with all their money, can't set a higher moral tone."

Hoover blinked, resembling for a moment a giant bullfrog. "All too often it's the rich and privileged who betray their country," he said. "Look at Alger Hiss. That's why I won't have a man from any Ivy League college in the Bureau. Hotbeds of immorality, Agent Kirkpatrick. *And* treason."

Kirkpatrick nodded. He couldn't imagine anybody from an Ivy League school like Yale or Harvard trying to join the FBI, with its miserable pay scale and slow promotion.

"It's strange," Hoover said. "You take a young man like Jack Kennedy, a war hero, wealthy, a good-looking boy. He has everything going for him, yet there's something missing, something wrong. . . ." He paused, staring at his hands, folded in front of him on the spotless, empty desk, a thick gold signet ring glittering on one pudgy finger. "I've given it a lot of thought," he went on. "His weakness is a fatal fascination with celebrities. Movie stars, gangsters, leftist authors—it doesn't matter who they are, he always falls for glamour." He let this sink in. "It's one of the reasons why he wouldn't make a good president."

As Kirkpatrick watched Clyde Tolson beam his approval, it struck him that the same could be said of Hoover, who was notoriously eager to kiss the ass of anybody famous—athletes, stars, Hollywood studio heads and columnists, particularly. But wisely, he nodded as if awestruck by Hoover's wisdom.

"You've done a splendid job, Kirkpatrick," the Director said.

"Thank you, sir. I'm sorry we slipped up on Hoffa." Kirkpatrick had been part of the team hastily assembled the previous summer to observe Hoffa passing a manila envelope full of hundred-dollar bills to a government witness. It had been a setup, of course, like most successful operations of the kind, instigated by Bobby Kennedy, who was looking for a way to trip Hoffa up. To Bobby's fury—he had promised to jump off the roof of the Capitol if Hoffa wasn't found guilty—but not to Kirkpatrick's surprise, the jury had acquitted Hoffa, who sent Bobby a parachute as a joke.

At the trial, it had seemed to him that the prosecution was less than enthusiastic, and that some of the evidence was tainted or poorly presented. He had attributed that to inefficiency in the Justice Department, but the way Hoover and Tolson were looking at each other now made him wonder if there hadn't been a conspiracy at the very highest level of the Bureau to let Hoffa off. To humiliate the Kennedys? Very likely, he thought. Because Hoffa and the Bureau had some connection? It was possible, he decided—Hoffa, for his own purposes, might even be a secret informant. One never knew. In the FBI, only Hoover—and perhaps Tolson—had the "big picture."

"Don't worry about it," Hoover said expansively. "You did your best. No man could do more."

So far as Kirkpatrick was concerned, that clinched it. If Hoover, whose only standard for his agents was success, was willing to praise a failure, it must be because he had *intended* the case against Hoffa to fail.

"That will teach young Bobby to jump the gun," Tolson said as Hoover nodded ponderously.

Kirkpatrick cleared his throat nervously. "About the tapes, sir. I have them in my briefcase, in case you'd like to hear them."

Hoover stared into the middle distance. "I suppose I ought to, Mr. Tolson, don't you think?"

Tolson nodded.

"I don't *enjoy* listening to this kind of smut, Mr. Kirkpatrick. I have to force myself. For the good of the country."

"Yes, sir." Kirkpatrick opened his briefcase, took out the tapes, and handed them to Tolson. "I took the liberty, sir," he said, "to make a short tape of the, ah"—he hesitated for a second—"most, ah, *significant* moments." It had been on the tip of his tongue to say *"dirtiest* moments," but he was happy he'd thought better of it.

Hoover took the small reel of tape from Tolson and put it in his desk drawer. "That was a thoughtful thing to do, Mr. Kirkpatrick," he said. "It will come in very handy. The Vice President will enjoy listening to *this,* won't he, Mr. Tolson?"

"I should say so, Director," Tolson said.

"Keep it coming, Kirkpatrick," the Director said, getting up from his desk to shake hands, for the second time in Kirkpatrick's career.

Nixon! Kirkpatrick thought, beginning to see at least an outline of what was going on. He wondered if the Kennedys knew of the lineup of the forces against them, from the Teamsters and the mob to Nixon and the Bureau. He wondered if they would *care.*

251

Still, he wasn't paid to worry about the Kennedys, he told himself as he went back to his office.

––––––

Anybody who knew me well would have been surprised to see me enter the lobby of a motel in New Jersey, just across the George Washington Bridge, at ten in the evening.

At times like this I asked myself what a Phi Beta Kappa and graduate of Columbia University was doing dealing with people like Red Dorfman—but of course, a love of mystery and the thrill of dealing with low-life types (what the French call *nostalgie de la boue*) is a natural weakness of the educated and safe, and nowhere more than among Americans, with our fascination for gangsters. It was Maria's opinion that I was going through "a midlife crisis," and I suppose she was right, though it wasn't, perhaps, the kind of crisis she had in mind.

I had called Jack Ruby in Dallas twenty-four hours after my breakfast with Jack to tell him I needed to speak to Dorfman face-to-face, and Ruby, who usually whined and protested about everything, must have caught the tone of anxiety in my voice, because he called back almost instantly with the time and place of the meeting.

I always found it difficult to understand why Dorfman placed any trust in Ruby. He was certainly loyal to Dorfman, in the manner of some large, ugly mongrel dog, but beyond blind loyalty he had no redeeming virtues that I could see. "I'd kill for Red Dorfman," he once told me breathlessly, in the front seat of a rented car in the parking lot behind the Hollywood Brown Derby, but I figured that was just the exaggeration of a born loser who wanted people to think he was a tough guy.

The few seats in the dingy lobby of the Hideaway Motel were occupied by women who were very clearly hookers, and the people waiting to sign in at the reservations desk had the furtive look of adulterous couples nerving themselves up to pretend they were man and wife. I made my way to the elevator and, sharing it with a couple locked in passionate embrace, went up to the top floor.

I found the room number I had been given, and knocked on the door. A familiar gravelly voice said, "Come in."

Dorfman had installed himself in what must have been the Hideaway's only suite. He was standing in the middle of the room glowering at me threateningly, a little bit like Mussolini greeting a visitor to his office at the height of his power. I refused to be intimidated, not from any special degree of courage but because I knew it would be fatal to let Dorfman know I was afraid of him. He was like one of those animals that don't become dangerous until they scent fear—wolves perhaps, or one of the more savage breeds of guard dogs. I walked over and shook his hand briskly, which disconcerted him, possibly because he had expected some kind of preliminary groveling on my part, or maybe because he wanted to be the one to offer his hand before there was any shaking.

"So what's the fucking problem?" he asked by way of a greeting.

I looked around. It was the living room of a perfectly ordinary motel suite—no special features except for enough fruit, liquor, and cocktail snacks for a hospitality suite. The door to the bedroom was ajar, and I could tell there was somebody in there—a woman, I presumed.

"It's not bugged," Dorfman said, misinterpreting my glance. "We own the joint."

"I see. Why are we meeting in New Jersey?" Dorfman was a thug, but I didn't see him as the kind of guy whose natural habitat was a cheap motel, at this stage of his career.

A look of embarrassment crossed his face. "There's a kind of"—he sought for the *mot juste*—"tradition," he tried. "You don't go into another guy's town without asking permission."

I raised an eyebrow.

"If Vito Genovese wanted to go to Chicago for some reason," he explained, taking the head of one of the five New York families as an example, "he would have to ask the permission of Momo Giancana, and vice versa. You don't go to Miami without asking for the okay from Meyer Lansky, or to Havana without getting the okay from Santo Trafficante, see? It's a question of good manners, that's all. We wanted to keep this thing secret, so we didn't get an okay from anybody in New York. That's why this place. We're on the other side of the bridge."

The "we" puzzled me, but I let it ride. Dorfman had already answered one question, and I didn't want to provoke him by asking another, even more indelicate. I took it that "good manners" was Dorfman's way of describing a jurisdictional dispute that was enforceable by death. One likes to imagine (I did, anyway) that one of the advantages of being a big-time criminal is that you can do what you please and break all the laws, but it turns out to be untrue—they are no freer than law-abiding citizens, and their rules are much more strictly enforced.

Dorfman might be able to have people killed, but at least I could cross the George Washington Bridge back into Manhattan without asking anybody's permission. That thought cheered me up, until it occurred to me that he could have me killed right there and buried in some New Jersey junkyard or the Pine Barrens without anyone being the wiser.

"Why don't we sit down?" I suggested. "I'll have a scotch on the rocks." Dorfman ground his teeth together. I had the distinct impression that he wanted to get this over with as quickly as possible, and I therefore took a certain pleasure in prolonging it.

"Help yourself," he said gruffly.

I made myself a drink from the well-stocked bar. Dorfman poured himself a cup of coffee—he had the look of a man who had once been a big drinker and had given it up—and we sat down together on the sofa. I noticed that from time to time he glanced at the door to the bedroom. His expression as he did so was not so much one of longing as of fear, as if the lady waiting for him was very impatient indeed.

"So what's the big fucking deal that Ruby made me come all the way out to Jersey for?"

"Ike Lublin gave me a little warning, over dinner in Washington. He told me your people are unhappy about what happened to Hoffa. He threatened me. He threatened Senator Kennedy."

Dorfman blew on his coffee noisily. "He didn't threaten nobody. He's only a fucking lawyer."

"Very well. He passed on a threat. Is that better?"

"Sure. You don't wanna go round accusing a lawyer of making threats. A lawyer could be disbarred for doing something like that."

A lawyer could also plausibly deny almost anything he said, I thought. "Anyway," I said, "threats *were* made."

"Hotheads," Dorfman said, shaking his head sadly. "Listen, didn't I tell you Hoffa had a short fuse, back there in Vegas? I told you."

"It's not just Hoffa we're worried about."

"I were you, I'd worry about Hoffa a lot. Jack and Bobby fucked him, the way he sees it."

"How do *you* see it, Red?"

"I don't work for Hoffa. I think he acted like an asshole, there in front of the subcommittee. So they're a bunch of schmucks, the senators, so what? There's a time when you gotta show respect, even for guys who don't deserve it, right? You piss on the cops, they break your balls. Senators too. Hoffa shoulda played nice."

"That's the view Jack takes."

"Yeah? On the other hand, Bobby's a real prick, David, you want my opinion. He provoked Hoffa, on purpose. And the bribery thing, that was a setup. Bobby had no call to do that."

"Maybe." I agreed with Dorfman, as a matter of fact. I hadn't the slightest doubt that Bobby had tried to frame Hoffa. He played by the rules of Kennedy family touch football: Anything goes so long as you get away with it. It occurred to me that Hoffa probably played by similar rules, except that the loser got killed.

"The fact is," I said, "Jack isn't any happier with the way things turned out than you are."

Dorfman laughed harshly, like a truck with a starting problem. "Who says we're unhappy?" he asked.

"I assumed from what Ike said . . ."

"Ike don't know the whole story. I got nothing against him, but he's not on the inside, you get what I mean. . . . The fact is, David, Jack and Bobby did us a favor. They got rid of Beck for us. Now we got Hoffa in his place, which is what we wanted." He smiled at me. "We didn't have to clip Beck, right? Jack and Bobby put him away for us."

"Hoffa seems to think he got a raw deal."

"Fuck him. He's president of the International. What more does he want? Between you and me, David, nobody on my side wants to see Hoffa get too big for his britches, unnerstan'? That's why Beck had to go. We don't wanna see Hoffa go to the slammer—we got a major investment in him, and anyway, he might talk—but his troubles are not necessarily our troubles, okay?"

"Okay." This was news to me. I had assumed that Hoffa and the mob were one and the same, but I was beginning to understand that while Hoffa had used the mob to get what he wanted—Dave Beck's chair in Washington—the mob intended to use Hoffa to get what *they* wanted. Neither party to this arrangement liked or trusted the other, which would have come as news to the Justice Department.

"So long as you're all happy . . ." I said.

Dorfman gave me the snarl that passed, in his range of facial expressions, for a smile. "Who says we're happy? It's time for you guys to back off Hoffa some. Enough's enough, right? We gotta live with the guy. You too."

"That may be hard to do."

"So find a way. Also, what about all these fucking subpoenas?

People like Momo can't do business if they're in hiding, ducking subpoenas. It's not right."

"Their names came up in testimony. Believe me, Jack doesn't like the idea any better than you do, but they have to appear."

"They're not gonna like it."

"Tell them not to worry. Jack will make sure that nobody gets indicted. Bobby will ask them some tough questions—there's nothing we can do about that—but that's not such a big price to pay for putting Hoffa in Beck's place, is it?"

He grimaced. "You have Jack's word?"

I nodded.

Dorfman glanced at the bedroom door again. There was a faint aroma of Havana cigar emanating from the doorway. Neither Dorfman nor I was smoking. The person in the bedroom, I reflected, was surely not a woman, unless the mistresses of big-league mobsters smoked Upmanns. I guessed it was somebody higher than Dorfman in the Chicago mob, which probably meant that Giancana himself was listening to our conversation. Whoever was inside coughed once. It was a deep, guttural cough, like a lion clearing its throat. Definitely not a woman's.

Dorfman's eyes flickered back in my direction. "I guess that's okay," he said. Whether or not it was Giancana on the other side of the door, there was no doubt who was the boss here, and it wasn't Dorfman. "You tell Jack they'll testify like good citizens. These are men of respect in their world, you unnerstan'? They're not gonna shove it to the senators, the way Hoffa did. They may take the Fifth, but they'll show respect."

"Respect will be fine. I'll tell Jack. He'll be grateful."

"Yeah." Dorfman's expression said it all on the subject of gratitude from politicians.

I was rapidly coming to the conclusion that the sooner Jack moved from labor reform to the high ground of foreign policy, the better for all concerned. A man could get elected without having a domestic policy—Ike had proved that in '56. I nodded, anxious to be on my way, now that it was clear it was Hoffa who was really after our blood, not the Chicago mob.

For some reason, I was relieved.

21

There was something about Peter Lawford that always made her nervous, an indefinable air of charm gone to seed, of hidden, secret corruption. On the surface, he was a wisecracking Englishman, but her experience in England with Olivier had made her realize that Lawford was a fake, just a kid who had been brought up English in Los Angeles to play English roles at MGM. Everything English about Lawford was phony, from his accent to the kind of clothes he wore. It was only in Hollywood, where there was no real line dividing the fake from the real, that he could pass for the Englishman he wanted people to think he was.

Lawford had no great talent as an actor, in her opinion, but he made up for it by a desperate desire to please. He sucked up to the studio heads, to bigger stars like Sinatra, to the Kennedy family, particularly Jack, and to her. Under the circumstances, it was hardly surprising that Lawford was willing to put his Malibu beach house at Jack's disposal whenever he wanted it, or that he was happy to act as Jack's beard whenever Jack was on the West Coast.

Since she had returned to Los Angeles to make *Some Like It Hot*, she'd met Jack twice at Lawford's place in Malibu—once when he came to California to make a speech, once when he appeared at a gala Democratic fund-raiser, both times without Jackie. It was easier for him to find time to get away than for her, since she was in the studio all day.

She hated the picture, now that she was actually working on it. Even with the help of Paula Strasberg, she couldn't make any sense of her role, or see any way to avoid being completely upstaged by the comic antics of Jack Lemmon and Tony Curtis in drag.

Camped out with Arthur in a bungalow at the Beverly Hills Hotel working six days a week on the picture, she found it almost impossible to escape his scrutiny. His own work on *The Misfits* was going badly—Gable, without whom it couldn't be made, seemed unable to imagine himself in the role of Gay Langland, which had been written for him—and Arthur spent his days on the set, suffering in silence while she consulted Paula instead of him. She chafed at his constant presence.

The first time, she managed to get away by pleading that she needed a day off. She and Jack spent a magical, life-restoring day in bed or lazing by the Lawford pool naked, he in the sun, she in the shade—for she remained the one California girl who didn't tan herself brown. The second time, she told her husband she had to pay a hospital visit to a friend. That too had been a magic day. Jack smoked some of Lawford's grass—there were drugs everywhere in Lawford's house, concealed in the most unlikely places, so that you took your life in your hands by putting sugar in your coffee—and she took him to the nude beach where she used to go in the old days with Jimmy Dean. She and Jack had sat there naked, unrecognized, having the time of their lives, she in a dark wig, he in nothing more than one of Peter Lawford's hats. . . .

She dozed comfortably in one of the big reclining chairs in Frank's private plane, on the way to Tahoe with Lawford. Jack had called her to say he was going to be in Palm Springs for a couple of days, and asked if she could meet him there. Palm Springs had proved to be impossible because of her schedule, but she had agreed to meet him in Tahoe instead. For Arthur she had concocted a story about needing a rest and having been offered the use of Frank's own bungalow at the Cal-Neva Lodge, where he was scheduled to open; she knew that Arthur didn't like Sinatra and the people around him, and so would be happy to stay in LA sweet-talking Clark Gable. The fact that Peter Lawford was taking her there in Sinatra's plane added a certain degree of believability to the story, for Arthur, improbably, liked Lawford, recognizing that so far as she was concerned, he was completely harmless.

She reached over and shook Lawford's shoulder. He opened his eyes, with the deeply puzzled and unfocused look of a man waking from a drugged sleep—he had been stoned when he picked her up from the Beverly Hills Hotel in Frank's limo, had poured himself one scotch in the car and ordered another as soon as they were on the plane. "Whazza matter?" he mumbled.

"We're landing," she said. She fastened his seat belt for him.

"Good-o!" He closed his eyes. Despite years of hard living, Lawford had the bright eyes and clear skin that, as she knew, drug addicts always had until they finally went to pieces. Whatever else cocaine, heroin, and marijuana did, they gave people beautiful complexions.

The plane landed smoothly and taxied to one side of the field, where a limo was waiting with a couple of Frank's gorillas beside it, to handle the luggage and what he always liked to call "personal security." She thanked the pilot and walked down the folding steps into the warm sunshine, followed by Lawford, trailing her like a zombie.

Once they were in the limo, he poured himself a scotch from the bar, washed down a couple of pills with it, and lit a joint. The combined effect of alcohol, uppers, and grass brought him back to life again as rapidly as if a switch had been turned on, as chatty and bright as ever. When he was "up," Lawford was so chatty and bright in his brittle and bitchy English way that had she not known better, she would have thought he was a faggot. In fact, she knew, he liked girls, the younger and the more of them, the better. Group sex was his thing, he told her at every opportunity—not with poor Pat, of course—but as it happened, group sex was the one thing *she* didn't much like, since half the pleasure of sex for her was having the sole, undivided attention of a man.

"God," Lawford said. "I have to keep reminding myself I may be the president's brother-in-law one day." He shook his head, took a deep drag on his joint, and offered it to her, but she declined. "He's going to do it, you know. Joe Kennedy always gets what he wants, and what he wants most of all is the White House for Jack. Dear God, what a family!"

"You're part of it, Peter."

"Don't I know it, darling! Not the most *welcome* part of it either. The old man positively gnashes his teeth at the sight of me, and my mother-in-law can't ever seem to remember my name—or *pretends* not to be able to anyway, the old bitch. Do you know she pins reminders to herself to the front of her dress, and walks around the house with Scotch tape on her forehead to prevent wrinkles? She's a monster, darling, worse than the Ambassador, as everybody insists on calling Joe Kennedy. When Jack's sister Kathleen wanted to marry Peter Fitzwilliam—and she was madly in love with him, the real thing, you know, red-hot passion—Rose told her that if she

259

married a divorced Protestant, she'd disown her—never see her again, ever!"

He paused for breath. "Everybody behaves as if the Kennedys were patricians! Not a bit of it. They're just a bunch of brawling bloody *Micks!* Oh, Jack has some class, I grant you, but he's the only one. At least he's a skeptic, like his father. Bobby's a religious fanatic, and the girls believe every bloody word the priests and nuns have put in their heads since they were tiny kids. I'm sorry, I don't mean to offend you, if I have. . . . You're not a Roman Catholic, are you?"

"No. I guess I'm a Christian Scientist, if anything."

"A perfectly sensible religion. At least they're not against birth control and divorce. Do you know what Rose gave me as a wedding present? A rosary, blessed by the Pope! I ask you!"

The car pulled up in front of a small white cottage, surrounded by fir trees, with a view of the lake. Jack Kennedy stood at the front door in white trousers, loafers, and a cable-stitch sweater—looking like a college boy, she thought, with a big grin on his face.

She got out, ran up the steps, and threw her arms around him. Lawford followed. "Hi, Jack," he called out. "Mission accomplished."

Jack gave a mock salute. "See you at dinner, Peter." He dismissed him without shaking his hand.

Lawford made his way unsteadily to an adjoining bungalow, stumbling badly as he tried to climb the steps. "He needs help," she said.

Jack shrugged. "He'll make it. Don't worry about him."

She felt a small chill at the coldness of his reaction. She did not like Lawford much but she felt pity for him, as well as a certain camaraderie of the spirit, for she recognized in him a lost soul, desperately looking for help but never finding it.

She pressed herself against Jack's sweater for warmth.

————

She woke to the sound of a voice in the next room, slipped on Jack's robe, and tiptoed to the door. She felt a little weak at the knees from so much sex after several weeks of abstinence. Her dress—a white summer frock, cut low at the neck—lay crumpled on the floor beside one of her white, high-heeled Delman pumps. Her bra, improbably, was draped over the lamp on the bed table.

"Jesus, Bobby!" she heard Jack say. "I know you have a hard-on for Hoffa, but go easy. . . . Well, yeah, but I'm not so sure we *want* him in jail, Bobby. . . . Sure he belongs there, but that's not the point. . . . I *told* you: Keep those guys' names out of it as much as you can. Talk to David about it, he'll explain. . . .

"Oh shit, who leaked *that?* Look, call Bradlee and ask him—no, fucking *beg* him, if you have to—not to run the story about Hoffa's mistress. . . .

"I *know* you're not scared, Bobby, and neither am I, but that's no reason to *ask* for a bullet in the head, is it? Right. And one thing more: Find out who it is on the staff that's leaking and cut his fucking nuts off, okay?" He caught a glimpse of her in the doorway and waved. "You have a good time too, little brother," he said, and slammed down the receiver hard.

"Problems?" she asked.

"Always."

"With Bobby?"

"With his staff. Some of them are eager beavers. They want to kick Hoffa in the balls, make an example of him, you know. . . . Bobby's a little inclined that way himself, but I'm against it personally."

"So am I. As you know."

"I know." He stood up and took the linen cover off a room service trolley, happy to change the subject. "I ordered lunch," he said. "You were out like a light, but I thought you'd probably be hungry when you woke up."

He passed her a club sandwich, and popped the cork off a bottle of champagne.

She realized she was hungry. She picked the bacon out of her sandwich and ate the rest of it in ravenous bites.

"You don't like bacon?" he asked, lifting an eyebrow at the stains on his expensive robe.

"I like it all right, but it's all salt. Salt bloats me. I've got problems enough getting into my costumes for this stinking picture as it is."

He eyed her breasts, bulging against the thin silk. "You don't look bloated to me," he said.

"You don't have to squeeze and shimmy your way into a skintight dress at the studio every day. Or put Band-Aids on your nipples so they don't show through if, God forbid, they get hard from the heat from the lights."

Jack was wearing a shirt—one of those silly-looking golf shirts with a little alligator on the chest—and Bermuda shorts, eating his sandwich in neat bites, a napkin on his lap.

She got up, unfastened the robe, removed his napkin, and sat down on his lap, holding her plate and continuing to eat. She turned her head and kissed him, plunging her tongue into his mouth, tasting him and the food at the same time.

He looked a little taken aback, not quite sure he liked it. She licked his lips clean, in tiny, catlike licks, and kissed him again.

She picked a few pieces of turkey and cheese out of his sandwich and popped them one by one into his mouth. Some of them fell on his shirt. At first he resisted mildly, but then he relaxed. She could feel him growing hard beneath her as she sat on his lap, and slowly turned around until she was facing him, opening her legs to let him enter her.

"Christ," she heard him say, his mouth still full, "I'm glad I packed a lot of clothes!"

———

Dressing for dinner, always a long process for her, was all the more so now, since she wasn't used to having a man around while she was doing it. She always had her own bathroom and dressing room, and at least a maid to help her, very often a makeup man and a hairdresser as well. She had finally been obliged to eject Jack from the bathroom to the small powder room. "Listen," he had said, "I'm a married man. I'm used to this kind of thing. Jackie takes hours to get ready."

"Honey, if you think Jackie takes hours, you ain't seen nothing yet," she said.

The truth was that this was at once her greatest pleasure and her greatest everyday fear. When she looked in the mirror, what she saw there, before she went to work, was Norma Jean, and it was her job to turn that plump-cheeked girl with the funny bump on the end of her pert little nose and the slightly-too-prominent chin and the naturally mousy, frizzy hair into Marilyn Monroe.

Makeup was the art she understood best. She herself had concocted the exact mixture of Vaseline and wax that she applied after putting on her lipstick, to give her lips a high gloss as well as the moist look of someone who has just been kissed. She herself had made the decision, years ago, not to cover up the mole on her left cheek but to accentuate it with an eyebrow pencil, as if it were a beauty spot.

She stood in front of the full-length mirror and turned around. She wore another simple white dress, with a pleated skirt and a neckline that bared her shoulders and much of her back. Given a choice, she always wore white. White made her feel clean.

She picked up a long white scarf to wrap around her shoulders in case the air-conditioning was too cold, walked into the living room, and did a quick pirouette for Jack's benefit.

He was lounging in an easy chair, dressed in a blue blazer, gray slacks, and a shirt and tie, talking intently on the telephone, but he looked up and grinned his approval.

"Jesus, Ben," he said on the phone, "this isn't news, it's gossip. Hoffa has a mistress. Big deal! I thought you were a serious journalist."

His tone was light and bantering, but his face betrayed real concern. "Well, then how about as a favor to me?" It was a nicely voiced plea, one gentleman to another, but the hard glint in his eyes and the grim downturn of his mouth made it clear enough that it wasn't working.

"Well, okay," he said at last, "if your answer is, 'Let the chips fall where they may,' to quote you, so be it. I guess the chips won't be falling on *your* head, will they? . . . No, I'm not being overdramatic. I think I'm being realistic. Sure, Jackie's fine. My best to Toni too. Thanks."

He slammed down the receiver with a crash. "That fucking *bastard,* with his holier-than-thou First Amendment bullshit! We're supposed to be friends, it's Toni this and Jackie that, but when I ask him for a favor, I get a lecture on the ethics of journalism, which is all a load of crap to begin with—"

She came over and gave him a kiss on the forehead to calm him down, though it didn't seem to have much effect. "Is it the Hoffa story again?"

"The guy has a mistress. She and Hoffa had a kid together. Hoffa's fond of the kid—practically adopted him. David thinks Hoffa might take it personally."

"I wouldn't be surprised. Hoffa may be thinking of the woman, you know? And the child. Is it a boy or a girl?"

"I don't remember. A boy, I think."

"It's a terrible thing to find out that you're illegitimate. I should know. Hoffa may want to spare the boy that. Why *wouldn't* Hoffa take it personally, if it hurts people he loves?"

"Hoffa's a crook, Marilyn. Don't waste tears on him."

"Even crooks have feelings, Jack." She was growing heated, she realized. "People ought to be nicer to each other," she added lamely, conscious that she had already lost the argument.

"Hoffa's not a nice man. But as it happens, I don't think a man's private life should be used against him." He gave her a rueful smile.

263

"I mean, look at *us*. If I could stop the story, I would, but I can't. The only thing now is to hang tough, that's what I told Bobby. . . . If we apologize for the leak, we'll look guilty *and* incompetent." He sighed. "It'll probably blow over."

"And if it doesn't?"

He grinned. "Then I'll buy myself a bulletproof vest. And one for Bobby, too, I guess."

She didn't laugh—she didn't think it was funny at all. "We'd better go, if we're going to eat before we hear Frank sing," she said.

He opened the door and they strolled arm in arm toward the main building of the lodge, past other secluded rustic cabins. There was nobody in sight on the paths, which had been designed so that people could go back and forth to the lodge with the minimum chance of seeing other guests on the way. Walking arm in arm with Jack gave her a cozy domestic feeling.

As they approached the entrance to the lodge, a room service waiter appeared, pushing a trolley table. He stopped and made way for them, with a deferential bow of his head.

It was not until she was past him that it occurred to her his face was familiar. Where, she asked herself, had she seen that plump, swarthy face with the black mustache, the balding head, the tinted glasses that failed to hide a penetrating stare?

Then it dawned on her that he looked like the man she had seen in Chicago, at the door of her suite, who asked her if her telephones were working. She turned around to look at him again, but all she saw was a broad back in a white waiter's jacket, vanishing past the shrubbery that lined the winding path. The more she thought about his face, the less sure she was, and by the time they were in the lodge, where Peter Lawford was waiting for them in the bar, a young woman on either side of him, his trembling fingers clutching what was surely not his first martini of the evening, she had put the whole thing out of her mind, dismissed as a coincidence.

———

The table had been set for eight people, and she had assumed that Frank was planning to join them before the show, but instead, just as they were finishing their coffee, the headwaiter appeared and said that one of the owners of the lodge, a friend of Frank's, wanted to come over and say hello to his distinguished guests.

She nodded, and almost immediately, as if they had been waiting for the headwaiter's sign, there appeared a thin gentleman in his late fifties, heavily tanned, with the profile of one of the more degenerate Roman emperors, accompanied by an attractive dark-haired young woman with beautiful pale skin, wearing a pale green low-cut evening dress that matched the color of her eyes—not a great beauty perhaps, but with the unmistakable professional sexual buzz that only the highest-priced call girls know how to project.

The man, dressed in a well-cut white dinner jacket, his eyes hidden by wraparound sunglasses, gave a courtly bow, pulled out a chair for the young woman, and sat down next to Marilyn. "It's an honor to have you as a guest, Miss Monroe," he said.

He reached across the table and shook hands with Jack and Peter Lawford. "A pleasure, Senator," he said. "Any friend of Frank's is a friend of mine."

He had a low voice, warm, husky, and sexy, though there was nothing warm about his deeply lined face, with its powerful nose, prominent cheekbones, and strong jaw. His thinning hair was so black and shiny that she suspected he used Grecian Formula; he wore it combed carefully over the top of his head to hide a bald spot.

"Giancana," he said, introducing himself with an ironic smile, as if his name were a challenge. "Sam. My friends call me Momo." He placed a hairy, well-manicured hand on the young woman's bare shoulder in a gesture that was more possessive than affectionate. "This is Miss Campbell. Judy."

Miss Campbell smiled, displaying less than perfect teeth. Giancana's grasp on her shoulder had been strong enough to leave small, pale, moon-shaped indentations, which would soon turn into bruises.

Giancana's name did not ring a bell with her, but it clearly did with Jack, who was looking at his host with fascination. She couldn't help noticing that he'd taken a pretty sharp look at the Campbell woman, too.

"Are you comfortable? Is everything okay?" Giancana was busy passing himself off as a friendly innkeeper looking after his guests, but it seemed false to her. Hotel owners were invariably outgoing personalities, but Giancana's face was veiled and secretive.

She'd supposed—because it was usually the case—that this Giancana guy, whoever he was, had pushed his way to the table with his bimbo to meet *her*, but it was immediately obvious that it was Jack who interested him. Giancana asked a few perfunctory questions about what she was doing, told her which of her movies were his favorites—she had the impression, from the wooden way he recited the titles, that somebody else had selected them for him, perhaps the sultry Miss Campbell—then focused his attention on Jack, leaving her and Miss Campbell to exchange pleasantries about how much they liked Frank.

Giancana snapped his fingers the moment he sat down—a signal for the maître d' to appear with a magnum of Dom Pérignon on ice, which had obviously been kept waiting in the wings. He made a small production of clicking his glass against hers and Jack's. "*Salud!*" he croaked hoarsely—he had a real chain-smoker's voice. He did not bother to click glasses with Miss Campbell, Lawford, or Lawford's sulky girls.

"I have a great admiration for you, Senator," he said. "Even if we're on opposite sides."

"Which sides would those be, Mr. Giancana?"

"Momo, Senator, please. I meant only that I'm a Republican. No disrespect, but I like Ike."

"I thought you might be referring to other things."

Giancana smiled. He had big white teeth, like a Sicilian peasant. "Some people make the laws, some people break them," he said with disarming frankness.

Jack laughed. "That's putting it nicely, Mr. Giancana."

"I must give credit where it's due, Senator. I didn't invent that."

"Who did?"

"Al Capone, may he rest in peace. He was referring to the IRS, by the way, not himself. He felt the government had used the IRS to frame him."

"It happens. Even today." There was just a faint hint of warning in Jack's voice.

"You're frank. A man after my own heart. I'm a great admirer of your father, by the way. He too is a man of great frankness. He lets the chips fall where they may, as the saying goes."

Was it just a coincidence—surely it *must* be—that it was the exact phrase Jack had used on the phone only a couple of hours ago? Marilyn wondered. Jack didn't seem to notice; he was too busy steering the conversation away from the subject of his father.

"Ah, you *do* know, Mr. Giancana, that I'm a member of the Senate Government Investigations Subcommittee? I only mention it to spare us both a certain—embarrassment...."

Giancana flashed another of his thousand-watt smiles. "Of course," he said softly, "that's understood. That has nothing to do with personal feelings, Senator. That's just politics—and business."

"What business *are* you in, Mr. Giancana?" she asked.

"This and that, Miss Monroe. I own a piece of this hotel. I own a piece of a lot of things. I used to be in the liquor business in a big way, like the Senator's father."

Jack frowned. He hated it when people brought up the way his father had made his fortune. "Mr. Giancana, Marilyn, is one of the leaders of the Chicago mob," he said coldly.

Giancana shook his head, smiling ruefully. "The things people say, Senator! Hoover's been bad-mouthing me for years with all this mob talk. I don't suppose he tells the truth about you either. I'm just a simple businessman, Miss Monroe. It's the same with me as it is with Frank—just because you're of Italian origins, as soon as you've made it, everybody whispers mob, *capiche?*"

"Mr. Giancana has been arrested more than seventy times, Marilyn," Jack said, his voice steely.

"And convicted twice," Giancana said with a shrug. "And both of those times were misdemeanors." He cleared his throat. "Real bullshit items." He smiled at her. "You should excuse the expression."

She nodded to indicate that it was nothing she hadn't heard before. Giancana did not exert the same kind of fascination on her as he did on Jack. She had known a good many mobsters in her time. Giancana was more courtly and presentable than most, but he was still the kind of guy who probably wouldn't hesitate to have acid thrown in a girl's face if she displeased him, which perhaps explained the nervous flicker in Miss Campbell's eyes.

"This subcommittee," Giancana said, leaning over to get closer to Jack. "I hear from a source close to you that I'm going to be called?"

Jack looked embarrassed and annoyed. "That's Bobby's decision, Mr. Giancana," he said. "But probably, yes."

"I haven't done anything to interest the United States Senate."

"I seem to remember reading something about Teamster Local three-twenty in Miami. The man who set it up worked for you, didn't he? Fellow called Yaras?"

"The name doesn't ring a bell."

"The way I read it, he was a, ah, hit man for you, back in Chicago. The FBI recorded a tape of him describing how he tortured a government informer to death with a cattle prod, a meat hook, and a blowtorch."

Giancana's smile didn't waver a bit. "I may have met this Yaras once or twice," he said. "I meet a lot of people. I don't know what a hit man is. I recall him as being in the import-export business in Havana."

"And head of Local three-twenty."

"That could be. There's no law against being a labor leader that I know of."

"No. Though I believe Mr. Yaras was arrested fourteen times, once for the murder of a Mr. Ragen, in Chicago, with an ice pick."

"Jim Ragen, rest in peace." Giancana sighed. "You've done your homework, Senator."

"To be honest, my brother Bobby did the homework. I just happen to have a good memory."

"It's a valuable asset. Forgetting is even better." Giancana let this sink in. "He's a tough guy, your brother, Senator. That's what they tell me."

"Tough enough, Mr. Giancana."

"Don't get me wrong. That's good. And it's good he's working with you. A brother, you can trust. I'm a great believer in keeping things in the family, myself. How about you, Miss Monroe?"

"I'm an orphan."

"*Madonna!* That's a shame." He placed a hand on hers before she could move it. His palm was dry—it felt the way she would have expected a snake to feel to the touch. For a small man, he had remarkable strength: he exerted enough pressure so that she couldn't move her hand out from under his. "You ever need help, Miss Monroe," he said, putting his face close to hers, "you call me. Think of me as family."

"Thank you," she said reluctantly, then wriggled her hand until he got the message and let her go.

"Senator," he said, turning his attention to Jack, his voice pitched to extreme sincerity. "It's been a real pleasure meeting you. You're doing great work for the country. I want you to know I'm on your side. Even if I do get subpoenaed. I have the greatest respect for you and your brother."

He placed his right hand briefly over his heart, as if he were pledging allegiance to the flag. "If I can help out in any way, count on me —I mean it. Information, advice, anything I can help you with— without losing honor and respect among my colleagues, of course— just let me know."

He reached into his pocket and took out a flat leather notepad and a gold pencil, scrawled a number on it, and handed the paper to Jack. "This will get me, anytime, day or night. We don't have to meet, you understand, Senator? I'll get somebody to act as a messenger, a—what's it called?—go-between, right?" His eyes flickered briefly toward Miss Campbell, then back to Jack. "Somebody we can both trust."

He put his arm around the young woman's bare shoulders. "Somebody nobody would be surprised you wanted to see anyway. That's the kind of go-between I'm thinking of."

He let his fingers rest lightly on Miss Campbell's right breast and smiled gently at her. "I'll think of somebody—you can be sure of that," he said, and gave Jack a wink, man to man.

Giancana pulled his date to her feet just as the lights began to dim and Frank stepped out onto the stage. The orchestra struck up the first bars; then Frank, as if offering a greeting in honor of somebody in the audience, began to sing, "Chi-cago, Chi-cago . . ."

She looked around and saw that Giancana and his companion had returned to their own table, where they were surrounded by large beefy men with blond-beehived wives or girlfriends. A spotlight was turned on their table, and Giancana beamed as Frank crooned his tribute to Chicago.

Giancana laughed, raising a glass to toast the famous singer, but even from a distance, the sight of him affected her like a bad omen.

She turned to look at the stage, took Jack's hand, and guided it under the table to her thigh, for comfort.

———

"What was *that* all about?" she asked as she was taking off her makeup, Frank's music still running through her head. He had come over to the table after the show and been at his most charming, flirting with her and trading dirty stories with Jack. Jack behaved in Sinatra's presence a little like a college freshman being interviewed for membership in a fraternity.

"Giancana, you mean?"

She nodded. It was strange, she thought, how spending the night together in a hotel produced instant domesticity. Here she was, removing her makeup in front of the bathroom mirror like any wife after a dinner party, wearing her old terry-cloth robe and her slippers, while at the sink next to her, Jack, a towel wrapped loosely around his waist, brushed his teeth with the care of somebody who had had dental hygiene drummed into him as a child. He gargled forcefully and spat.

"What did you think of him?" he asked.

"Mr. Momo? He's a gangster. Smoother than most, sure, but so what, sweetheart? Guys like him are bad news."

Jack bared his teeth and examined them closely in the mirror. He had that slightly blank expression that comes over a husband's face when his wife has just said something he doesn't agree with but isn't in the mood to argue over because he wants to get laid. Boy, did she know that expression! She tossed a wadded-up ball of Kleenex at him. "Hey, knock it off!" she said, with a smile to show she wasn't angry (though she was, a little). "We're not married, Jack."

He tried hard not to look annoyed. "Well, of course we're not. . . ."

"Then stop acting like a husband. This is a love affair, not a marriage. If you want to tell the little lady to mind her own fucking business, go home and do it to Jackie."

Just in case she had gone too far, she moved closer to him, opened her robe and let it drop to the floor. She squeezed between him and the sink, so that her ass was pressed tightly against his crotch, and carried on with washing her face.

"Okay," he said. "You're right. I'm sorry."

"Forget it," she said. She loved him too much to hold a grudge—besides, she didn't want to spoil the night ahead.

She reached over, flicked out the lights, unwound his towel, and pushed him backward into the big stall shower. She turned on the water—the hell with her hair, she would worry about that tomorrow!—and raised herself up on tiptoe to kiss him as the hot water poured onto them from every direction. He had left his gold watch on and it didn't look waterproof, but she wasn't about to stop for that. She soaped him all over, then let him soap her, laughing as the suds cascaded down until they were ankle-deep in bubbles. She opened her legs and let him wash her ass, her cunt; then, when she could tell from his expression that he couldn't wait another second, she guided him deep into her and let him lift her up, his arms under her thighs, moving her back and forth until he came, in the hot spray and mist.

They dried each other with the same towel and lay down side by side on the bed. He had poured a nightcap for himself and a glass of champagne for her to take her pills with. "Jesus," he said. "That was something."

"Mm." She hadn't come herself—as it happened, she didn't get off on fucking in the bath or shower, preferred, on the whole, to spend a lot of time alone there, dreaming happily in the warmth as if the rest of the world didn't exist. She had simply guessed it was the most unwifely gesture she could make on the spur of the moment.

"So what does Giancana want?" she asked, cuddled naked next to Jack.

"He wants to avoid being indicted. I think he was also reinforcing personally the message from the boys in Chicago. It goes something like this: Do what you have to do with Hoffa, but keep us out of it as much as possible, and please don't push him too far. In return, if you ever need any help from us, just whistle and it's yours, Senator."

"*Help?* From the Chicago mob? They're murderers!"

"Mm. Well, you never know. There are times when it might not be such a bad idea to know people who can carry out a murder. I can think of lots of people I'd love to have murdered." He laughed.

"These guys are criminals, Jack. Scum."

"Oh hell, Marilyn, let me tell you a story: One of the old-time Boston pols, when some crooks offered to make a contribution to his campaign fund, took the money and said, 'Well, Christ never turned away sinners, so who am I to turn them away?' "

"Who said that?"

"My grandfather."

She laughed, but she felt uneasy. Still, who the hell was *she*, she told herself, to preach to a third-generation politician—who was clearly on his way to the presidency? "What did you think of Miss Campbell?" she asked.

"Oh," he said, "I didn't pay much attention to her."

"Liar," she whispered. She reached over and tickled him until he was helpless, rolling back and forth on the bed and pleading with her to stop. She upended her glass and poured the rest of her champagne on his chest and belly.

"Hey, that's *cold,* goddamn it!" he shouted.

She turned out the light on the bed table and moved down under the covers to take him in her mouth. "I'll warm you up."

This one, she told herself, was for *her* pleasure, and she was going to make him do it exactly the way she liked it, and for as long as she wanted.

After all, she was a star, not some hooker like the Campbell woman!

"God," she whispered as she drew herself back up in bed to kiss him, "I could spend the rest of my life in bed with you."

———

I could spend the rest of my life in bed with you.

Bernie Spindel adjusted the headphones so they were more comfortable, and checked to make sure the tape was running smoothly, though that was not really necessary. He used nothing but the finest equipment—the Uher 5000, German-made, the same recorder as the networks—and always ran two units simultaneously so there was a backup in the unlikely event of a mechanical failure.

He listened to the soft, sweet sounds of lovemaking, perspiration running down his face, as he bent over the recorders he had installed in a utility closet in the main lodge.

It was ironic, he thought, that people—even intelligent people like Senator Kennedy—never managed to catch up with technology. They still believed in the sanctity of their own privacy, closed the door, pulled down the blinds, talked in whispers, before making an illegal deal, or spilling their guts out to a girlfriend, or fucking somebody else's wife—as if Spindel could be stopped by doors or drawn blinds or whispering! He used the same ceramic bugs as the CIA, marvels of electronic technology that could pick up a whisper from anywhere in a room and transmit it, crystal-clear and amplified, to recorders concealed hundreds of feet away. There wasn't a telephone in the world that was safe from him—he had even tapped the White House phones for Hoover, back in his FBI days! He had all the latest Japanese devices, things even the CIA and the NSA didn't know about yet.

The notion that privacy still existed would have made Spindel laugh had he been the laughing type, which he wasn't—for the price of eavesdropping as a profession was that his view of human nature was deeply pessimistic. Like a priest in the confessional booth, he never heard good news. His tapes recorded nothing but lies, cheating, and corruption.

Oh, Jack, JACK! Ja-aack! he heard her cry, her voice rising to a shriek, then descending to a low, animal moan. That made three times, by his count, that they had made it since she'd arrived twelve hours ago.

He tried to remember if he had ever fucked a woman three times in twelve hours, and concluded that he'd never even come close.

22

For once, she was arriving for work on time, to her own surprise—and to the utter astonishment of Billy Wilder. The moment she was in her dressing room, she took off her clothes and put on an old, cosmetic-stained silk kimono while her makeup man Whitey Snyder and the hairdresser and his assistants began the endless process of turning her into Sugar Kane.

As part of her long-term scheme of self-improvement, she had brought a copy of Thomas Paine's *The Rights of Man* with her, since Jack had mentioned it in one of his speeches, and she made her way through it doggedly, concentrating fiercely, while her hair was styled. It was even harder going than Carl Sandburg's life of Lincoln, and she put it down gratefully while Whitey did her face. Whitey glanced at the book. *"The Rights of Man,* huh?" he asked. "What about the rights of women?"

"He hasn't mentioned any so far, Whitey, this guy Paine."

"That figures." Whitey had a blue-collar contempt for intellectuals, in which category he placed all writers, including Arthur.

He leaned down, close to her shoulder. Together they peered at her brightly lit image in the mirror as if it were a work of art in the making. Whitey shook his head. "Nobody ever had prettier skin, doll," he said. "You were born for Technicolor. I can't believe Billy is making this picture in black and white!"

"Well, you *know* why, Whitey. He showed me the tests of Jack and Tony made up as girls. Their faces looked like they'd been embalmed at Forest Lawn. It was *creepy* instead of funny. Like a horror movie, you know? So Billy had to do the picture in black and white."

"I know that, doll, but I'm thinking about *you*. What the audience cares about is how *you* look, not those two guys—particularly, you should excuse the expression, that snotty shithead Curtis."

Curtis had been so angered by her delays—not to mention the endless retakes in which she got better and better while he lost the edge of his performance—that he did everything he could to screw her up. When somebody asked him what it was like to play a love scene with her, he had replied, in a screening room full of Fox executives, "It was like kissing Hitler!"

Of course, she heard about it, as he intended her to, and it upset her so badly that she burst into tears on the spot. She had so desperately wanted Curtis to *like* her, just the way she had wanted Joan Crawford, and Robert Mitchum, and Larry and Vivien to like her, and instead, he had said terrible things about her, and even done savage impersonations of her at dinner parties all over town!

Thinking about it was enough to bring tears to her eyes again, or would have been had Whitey not already done her makeup. She stood up and slipped out of her robe, naked except for her bra. She had done a peroxide job on her bush a week ago—without burning herself for once, thank God!—so at least she didn't have *that* to worry about for another couple of weeks. The wardrobe people came in now, carrying the bits and pieces of her costume, which would have to be sewn together on her while she stood still.

She sighed. It wasn't easy to stand absolutely still for an hour or so, even though she knew that the slightest movement might get her pricked with a needle or a pin. Whitey cut a big circular collar out of brown wrapping paper and placed it on her shoulders to make sure the seamstresses didn't accidentally smudge her makeup. "Home stretch, doll," he said cheerfully.

Home stretch, indeed! she thought. She put on a white garter belt, slipped on her stockings, fastened them to the suspenders, taking care not to damage a fingernail, put on white high-heeled pumps, then stood still, arms outstretched. The head seamstress from Wardrobe held each piece of the dress against her body while the assistants, on their knees at either side of her, carefully sewed the dress together; she felt like one of the vestal virgins being prepared for a ceremony—a scene she remembered from some picture set in ancient Rome. Of course, the moment they started to sew, she inevitably wanted to go to the bathroom—she wondered if the vestal virgins had felt the same back then. . . .

With an effort she brought her mind back to the job at hand. The dress was finished. She turned carefully in front of the mirrors as her various helpers examined her closely, the way the designers of a new airplane might look at it before its first test flight. Even Whitey, an old hand, looked somber and serious, his brow knit in concentration, one hand rubbing his chin. Then he nodded and gave a thin smile. "Okay, doll," he said. "Showtime."

She stood—as her retinue put the finishing touches on their work —flipping over one of Whitey's newspapers, and suddenly saw a photograph of Jack and Jackie, standing arm in arm on the stoop of their new Georgetown house. "Kennedys expecting as they move into new house," the caption began. She felt suddenly sick, her head aching as if she had been struck down by a migraine.

There was a muffled knock on the door, and a young man stuck his head in. "Excuse me, Miss Monroe," he said diffidently, "but Mr. Wilder wanted me to tell you he's ready—"

Without a moment's hesitation, as if she were responding to an electric shock, she turned on him and screamed, *"Fuck off!"* He blushed and shut the door.

She could feel the curtain of disapproval descend around her, even from Whitey. It was a rule of the profession: A star didn't shout at underlings who were just doing their jobs. You could tell the director, or the producer, or a fellow star to fuck off, but never, *never* the working stiffs. "Christ," she said, her head throbbing, "I'm sorry."

Everybody nodded, but their mood was mournful, like the retinue of a bullfighter who has just revealed a streak of cowardice. "I'm *really* sorry," she said, eyes wide open and humid in distress.

"It's okay, doll," Whitey said, patting her shoulder, but she knew it wasn't.

Worse still, she was ashamed of herself, even though she knew it was the shock of seeing the picture of Jack with the pregnant Jackie that did it.

At moments like this she was always tempted to go home, lock the door, and hide herself away, but she knew it was out of the question. She opened one of the dozens of bottles scattered on her dressing table, pricked a couple of capsules with a pin, and swallowed them dry so as not to smear her lipstick by taking a drink of water.

She waited to feel the hit, a kind of dull, fizzy reaction in her stomach, followed by a warmth that spread from deep in her guts to her toes and fingertips, bringing with it a kind of false peace. Before she lost the feeling—for she knew it was evanescent—she opened the door and walked out.

Wilder was sitting beside the camera, looking reproachful. "They tell me you're reading Tom Paine's *The Rights of Man,*" he said—there were no secrets on a set. "That's good, but you know, the boy has his rights too."

"I know, Billy. I'm sorry."

"So." The German accent was strong—the word came out as "Zoh." He shook his head. "Respect for people who are just doing their job, that's important, yes? Respect for colleagues—say, by not being two hours late—this is important too, no?"

"Don't push it, Billy."

Wilder gave her the charming smile of a man who had once made his living, improbably, as a gigolo. "Not another word," he said. "Now let's get to work."

"Vord." "Vork." Oh, how she *hated* all that softly accented Central European bullshit, which was the lifeblood of Hollywood creativity! Half the people who mattered in the industry were German, or Austrian, or Hungarian, or something, and spoke in riddles, with accents like Bela Lugosi's.

"To repeat what you already know then," he said, speaking slowly, as to an idiot, "you knock on the door, and as you open it to come into the room, you say, 'Hi, it's Sugar.' Tony says, 'Hi, Sugar!' That's it. One take will do it, I bet. You'll see."

She had never done anything in one take in her life, and he knew it. Besides, whenever people—especially directors—told her something was simple, she immediately became suspicious. She couldn't help it—she needed to have everything explained to her exactly and in detail.

"So let's get it done, darling?" Wilder said hopefully.

But she wasn't ready. She walked across the set, past Tony Curtis, who was glowering at her, rocking back and forth on his high heels, and Jack Lemmon, who looked weary and dyspeptic, like a man who has been waiting so long for his wife that he no longer wants to see her. They didn't look like women to her—they *stood* all wrong, for one thing—and she had difficulty relating to them, as she did to all forms of transvestism.

Paula was waiting, sitting implacably, wearing the black schmatte that had so infuriated Sir Cork Tip. She sat down beside Paula. "I'm supposed to be sharing my happiness with my girlfriends," she said, as if it were a hopeless task.

Paula glared malevolently at Wilder through her dark glasses. "What does *he* know?" she asked.

"He wants me to make it light and funny. I don't see how."

"Of course you don't, poor darling," Paula murmured soothingly.

"I don't see what I'm supposed to be so fucking *happy* about either. What's my reaction when I open the door and see the two of them? Why won't he tell me?"

Paula put an arm around her shoulder, her face as close as a lover's. "Don't think about him, darling," she said. "What do you care? He doesn't understand the depths of an actor's soul. He's just a good mechanical director. And he's intimidated by working with a talent like yours."

"Yes? But how do I play the scene?"

"It's Christmas Eve. There are presents under the tree. You want to share the news with your friends." Paula stroked her hand. "You're a Popsicle, darling."

She thought about it. It made sense, if you understood Paula's language. Once, when Olivier had talked himself hoarse trying to get her to act dejected and unhappy in *The Prince and the Showgirl*, Paula had simply whispered, "You're a wet soda cracker, Marilyn," and she'd gotten it right on the next take.

"A Popsicle!" she laughed. It made sense to her, in a way that no director could. She got up and walked into the bright lights toward her mark. She stared at the bare wood of the door—unfinished on this side of the set because it wouldn't show—as if it were the door to hell. She heard the sharp clack of the clapper board, reached for the door, and opened it, momentarily blinded by the lights. "Hi, Sugar, it's me," she said, and it wasn't until she heard Wilder call out, "Cut!" and Tony Curtis sigh that she realized she'd blown it.

While they fussed over her hair and makeup to get her ready again, she tried to work out why she had screwed up over something so simple when she had been determined to get it right.

She waited for the clapper, boldly grasped the door handle, and said, "Sugar, hi, it's me."

On the next take she got it right, but she didn't say it until after she'd opened the door, which was no good.

Wilder was too smart to become abusive like Preminger, but she could see he was getting upset. There followed a dozen takes, in each of which she got the sequence slightly wrong or fluffed her line.

Finally Wilder, drained and exhausted himself, rose and came over to her, an expression of desperation in his eyes. For a moment she thought he was going to hit her, and flinched, but instead, in his gentlest voice, he said, "We'll get it right. Don't worry, Marilyn, really."

Instinctively she opened her eyes wide, becoming in real life just the dumb blonde that she hesitated to give him on screen, and replied with perfect innocence: "Worry about what?"

The look in his eyes showed her that she had made her point. He wouldn't condescend to her again.

She got the scene right on the very next take—got it so perfect that Curtis, who was tired and angry, might as well not have been in it at all! It was hers, one hundred percent, a triumph.

She was the only person who left the set that night as fresh as a daisy.

———

I had seen a rough cut of *Some Like It Hot,* and I thought it was the best thing Marilyn had ever done. It was as if she had hit her stride at last.

Whatever Marilyn thought of it, I don't believe any picture she made captured her beauty better—especially the transparent, luminous quality of her skin, or all that extravagantly luscious flesh, so soft it looked like fresh whipped cream.

As it happened, there was a reason why she looked so good—at some point during the making of *Some Like It Hot* she had become pregnant again, as she told me shortly after she returned to New York.

Since she didn't tell me that the baby was Jack's, I assumed—correctly—that it wasn't, which was something of a relief. I had visions of poor Jack dealing with *two* pregnant women in his life at the same time! Besides, I knew it had been some time since she had seen Jack, or even spoken to him. *Some Like It Hot,* like every picture she made, consumed her totally.

Marilyn and I were sitting in her apartment on Fifty-seventh Street, where I had stopped for a drink on my way home. Miller was out—he had recently taken a suite at the Chelsea Hotel, his old stomping grounds, in order to have a quiet place to work on the script of *The Misfits.*

There was nothing in the apartment to suggest it was home, to him or to Marilyn. The walls were white, the few pictures still leaning against them, stacked on the floor, the bare parquet floors scuffed and unwaxed, the windows without curtains or blinds. There was not enough furniture, and what there was might have been bought on sale at Macy's—graceless, bulky chairs and sofas, upholstered in nubbly off-white fabrics that looked worn and dusty even though they were new. Here and there was evidence of Marilyn's stardom:

a professional hair dryer, stationed above a towel-draped dining chair, a chrome-and-glass manicurist's table, tangled electric cables and transformers on the floor for a photography session that had just ended.

The sequined dress Marilyn had been photographed in was draped carelessly over a chair. She was wearing a short robe now, sitting opposite me on the sofa, her bare legs tucked under her. We were drinking dry vermouth, her supply of champagne having run out for once. She glanced at the coffee table, and a look of shame crossed her face. "Gee whiz," she said, "no snacks." Marilyn had the instincts of a middle-class homemaker and avid reader of the *Ladies' Home Journal*.

She uncurled her legs and rose to her feet. I caught an opalescent flash of inner thigh and tried to hide my stare—unsuccessfully, because Marilyn laughed, that wonderful, full-throated, sexy laugh of hers.

"Dream on," she said huskily. "Are you hungry?"

I shook my head. "I had a late lunch," I said. "With Steve Smith."

Marilyn raised an eyebrow. Stephen Smith was Jack's brother-in-law, the man his father had hand-picked to look after the Kennedy fortune so his boys wouldn't have to bother. Anything to do with the Kennedy family interested Marilyn, but hunger was her first concern, so she got up and went off to the kitchen, returning a moment later with a box of Girl Scout cookies.

"How did you come by the Girl Scout cookies?" I asked, intrigued.

She laughed. "In the country. A little girl came to the door—her daddy had brought her in his car—and asked if I wanted to buy any Girl Scout cookies. She was so sweet! So I said sure, but I didn't have any change, so I gave her a fifty-dollar bill. Well, she and her daddy didn't have change of a fifty, so now I've got *cartons* of these cookies. I bet she got a badge or something for the biggest cookie order in Girl Scout history! . . . I never got to be a Girl Scout or anything like that," she added sadly. "We were too poor."

I nodded sympathetically, but perhaps not sufficiently so. "You don't believe me," she said. I told her I did.

"No you don't. But it's true. You had to buy the uniform. It didn't cost much, but my foster parents didn't have anything to spare—not for me anyway. . . ."

She set her jaw, as she often did when her childhood came to mind. She was not about to forgive anyone who had been associated with it. "Tell me about Steve Smith," she said.

"Steve? He's a tough nut—exactly the man Joe wanted at least one of his daughters to marry. Not glamorous but one hundred percent reliable. And useful. I don't think Steve could ever make a fortune himself, but he's perfect for looking after one."

"Does he know about me?"

"Probably, but he's too discreet to mention you to me."

"His wife knows."

"Jean? What makes you think so?"

"Jack told her. She'd heard about it from Pat Lawford and wanted to know if it was true, and Jack told her it was."

"He did?" I wasn't as surprised as I may have sounded. Joe Kennedy's children may have had secrets from their spouses, but seldom from each other. Jack's sisters adored him, and all of them were star-struck—even Pat, who, being married to Lawford, might have known better—so they'd be thrilled about his having an affair with Marilyn.

"Absolutely. They want me to meet his father one day."

I sighed inwardly. I guessed this was Joe's idea rather than his daughters'. "Be that as it may," I said, "I suspect that's exactly the kind of thing Jean *doesn't* talk to Steve about. He did tell me that he couldn't believe how quickly Jack had taken to fatherhood."

It was a thoughtless remark and I regretted it instantly, but to my relief, Marilyn merely smiled. "I know," she said. "All he wants to talk about when he calls me is Caroline. It's cute." She sighed. "I can hardly *wait* to be a mother so I can tell *him* about it. Just think, if I have a boy, maybe he and Jack's little girl can date one day. . . ."

"Do you want a boy?"

She nodded dreamily. "Mm. Girls have to go through such a lot of terrible things, growing up. . . . I just *feel* it's a boy too. . . . I told Jack he'd better get up here and see me *soon*. I mean, my body is doing the most *wonderful* things. . . ."

"Is Arthur happy about it?"

"Mm. I guess." She closed off this avenue of discussion firmly. "I think it's *great* Jack is such a good father, don't you?"

"Well, I don't think he's actually changing Caroline's diapers or burping her at night. But yes, I *do* think it's nice that he likes having a child, now that he and Jackie have one at last. Plenty of people don't."

"Tell me about it!" She helped herself to another cookie. "So you liked *Some Like It Hot?*"

"I think it's the best thing you've ever done. It's going to be a big hit," I said. "Count on it."

She shrugged. "Maybe. I'd rather die before I made another movie with that shit Billy, I'll tell you *that*."

"What's next?"

"The baby. Then I'm supposed to do a picture for Fox. It's about a zillionaire who falls in love with an off-Broadway actress. Older man, younger woman, you know? Jerry Wald is going to produce it. Last I heard, George Cukor's going to direct. I'm going back to California in a couple of weeks for it. . . ."

She seemed alarmingly indifferent about what sounded like yet another of 20th Century–Fox's inept attempts to showcase their most successful star. Despite Milton's efforts, Marilyn had never really succeeded in breaking away from the studio completely. Like a rebellious daughter, she was always coming home to be forgiven. "I thought you were going to do Arthur's script next," I said.

"He's still working on it. And we don't have Gable yet. Or John Huston. Anyway, I have to do another picture for Fox. It's all in the fucking contract Milton drew up for me, back in '55. Poor Milton. He should have stuck to photography."

I must have shown that I thought this was unfair, because she added quickly, "Oh, I don't mean it. I miss Milton more than anyone, really I do, but I could still wring his neck every time I think about that contract."

I didn't think the contract was Milton's fault—not entirely anyway. Over the years, Marilyn's contract with 20th Century–Fox had been amended and extended and modified and renegotiated until it defied interpretation. It governed her life, from the number of pictures she could make to the directors the studio could offer her and even the amount of time she could spend on the East Coast. Although by now most of it had been rewritten on her behalf by countless lawyers, she was still in constant rebellion against it.

Marilyn settled herself comfortably back on the sofa, legs tucked up again, the box of cookies in her lap. "Is Jack going to be president?" she asked, her expression suddenly serious.

"I think so. Doesn't he talk to you about it?"

"Well, I think it embarrasses him to talk about it. With *me* anyway. . . ."

I could imagine that easily. Women were Jack's recreation, his way of escaping from the growing pressures of fulfilling his destiny. The last thing he would have wanted to discuss with Marilyn was the presidency.

"Things are looking good," I said. "Jack probably doesn't want to put a jinx on them by saying so, that's all."

"Oh, I'm the same way," she said. "I always say '*If* I get the part,' or whatever, never 'when.' "

"There are no sure things in politics," I said cautiously, "but Jack's doing better than anyone had hoped. Between what Jack's been doing on the Labor subcommittee and what he's been saying on the Senate Foreign Relations Committee, he's the only Democrat anybody's really talking about. Jack is beginning to *stand* for something in people's minds—a certain kind of cool, smart toughness, together with a lot of style. All he has to do is stay out of trouble and look more presidential than Lyndon Johnson or Hubert Humphrey. That shouldn't be impossible."

She giggled. "Staying out of trouble might be."

"Well, sure. But most of the press is on his side—even the reporters and columnists who don't agree with Jack *like* him. I don't think they're going to print anything about his love life."

She glanced at the watch on her wrist, frowned, and held it up to her ear to see if it was ticking. Marilyn seldom wore a watch, and even when she did, it never did much good. She simply had no sense of time, a problem that had manifested itself long before she became a star. It was entirely appropriate that, like the White Rabbit, she wore a watch that didn't work.

"What time is it?" she asked.

"A little after seven."

"Oh my gosh!" Her eyes opened wide. "I'm supposed to meet Arthur."

"What time?"

She bit her lip. "Six-thirty?"

"Where?"

"Downey's. We're going to the theater."

"You're going to have to hurry."

"Mm." She gave no sign of hurrying. Her expression suggested that the task of getting ready for the theater was beyond her. "Lena!" she shouted to her maid. "I'm late."

Lena appeared, looking flustered—Marilyn's inability to deal with time was catching, so that those who worked for her soon found themselves moving, by fits and starts, to her own uncertain rhythm. She carried a white dress on a hanger. "I'll run your bath," she said.

"Forget it. I don't have time. Besides, I like the way I smell." Marilyn glanced at the dress and shook her head, rejecting it as well as the bath.

"I'll go," I said. "I'm keeping you."

She nodded. She was on her feet now, frowning as she began to think about what she was going to wear. She had her reputation to think of: Marilyn Monroe was often late, but never a disappointment.

"Lena," she called, "get the red one, the one I wore for *Look?*" She gave me a wink. "It's cut down to here," she said, laughing, indicating a sweeping cleavage with one hand and a bare back down to her ass with the other. "What the hell, if you've got it, flaunt it, right?"

"Right." I gave her a kiss on the cheek.

"You're a real friend," she said, kissing me on the lips. I could taste her fresh, warm breath as her moist lips pressed briefly against mine, her eyes half closed as they were in the darkest and most shameful of my erotic fantasies about her. "Gotta go, honey," she whispered. Then she stopped, took both my hands in hers, and said, "I can't *wait* to be a mommy, David! I just know I'm going to be so *good* at it!"

"Of course you are," I said, but I didn't believe it. Nobody with Marilyn's problems could have been a good mother, and I suspect Marilyn—and certainly Arthur—must have known it.

As I was to learn, she turned up so late at Downey's that she never had time to eat anything, but her red dress caused a sensation, both at the restaurant and at the theater—particularly when she and Arthur went backstage after the performance to congratulate the star.

It was an evening of French songs, a one-man show by Yves Montand, who had starred in the French production of Miller's *The Crucible* in Paris, and whom Marilyn was to meet, fatefully, that night for the first time.

23

Timmy Hahn sheltered under the awning of Marilyn Monroe's building on East Fifty-seventh Street, hands deep in the pockets of his worn navy surplus pea jacket. He had skipped school again to keep his lonely vigil as the most faithful of her fans.

Timmy could hardly remember a time when he hadn't been a fan of Marilyn Monroe's. Even as a little kid, he followed her comings and goings in the press, waited for hours outside restaurants and hotels for a glimpse of her. By the time he was thirteen, he knew more about her life than any gossip columnist, and was the acknowledged leader of a small pack of youths of both sexes for whom being Marilyn Monroe fans was their whole life.

Most of these kids, in Timmy's opinion, were amateurs. He followed Marilyn's life in New York with the skill of a detective, and once managed to wave to her as she got into a cab on East Fifty-seventh Street, only to appear before she did at the door of the Actors Studio, waiting for her to arrive! When Marilyn stayed out late, he followed her faithfully, often guessing where she was going, since he knew her routines. His mother had long since given up complaining —he came and went as he pleased, sometimes spending the entire night on the street in pursuit of Marilyn, or, when he missed her, watching her old movies in all-night theaters.

By now he was something of a mascot to Marilyn. When she arrived at movie premieres or parties, she looked around for him, and if she couldn't see him in the crowd, she asked, "Where's Timmy?" and had the security guards find a place for him up front.

Through rain, snow, summer heat, and darkest night, Timmy had done his best to become Marilyn's shadow, but even he would have found it hard to explain why. Being a fan was something you couldn't explain to other people, Timmy thought. It was as if there were a bond, almost an electric current, between him and Marilyn. He knew about her unhappy childhood, and sometimes wondered if she saw in him some reflection of her own lonely years in foster homes and the orphanage. On *his* side, simply seeing her made him feel happy, that and the feeling that he was somehow serving her loyally by being there wherever she went.

It was almost like having a big sister, for he saw her not only when she was all done up, breathtakingly beautiful for some big event, but also when she was sneaking out to go shopping, her hair hidden under a scarf, without makeup or false eyelashes, wearing jeans and an old sweater. He knew which doctors she went to, the name and address of her dentist, where she shopped for groceries when she was in a domestic mood, the pharmacy where she got her prescriptions filled and bought hundreds of dollars' worth of cosmetics at a time.

He even left flowers with the doorman on her birthday, and was once rewarded with a brief note, written with what appeared to be an eyebrow pencil on a cocktail napkin monogrammed "MM," in a hand that was as unformed and childish as his own: "Dear Timmy, Thanx, you're a pal, Marilyn—P.S. Don't you ever go to school?"

The note was Timmy's greatest treasure—along with the school exercise book in which he laboriously recorded Marilyn's daily comings and goings with meticulous attention to time, place, and detail, for he thought of this as his life work.

Timmy sometimes wondered if Marilyn tried to fool him, but if that was the case, she wasn't very good at it.

It didn't take him long to find out about her visits to the Carlyle, and he was soon rewarded by the sight of Marilyn leaving the hotel disguised in a raincoat, with a scarf thrown over her hair. He did not show himself—he was adult enough to guess that she was seeing a man, and respected her privacy enough not to embarrass her by his presence, nor would he have dreamed of telling a soul. Still, he was curious to know whom she was visiting.

As a fourteen-year-old kid, he could hardly expect to get into the lobby of a hotel like the Carlyle, let alone question the desk clerk, but as luck would have it—and Timmy was a great believer in luck—he found the solution to the problem by accident, when he saw her come out of a side entrance with a man he recognized as Senator John F. Kennedy.

Politics did not interest Timmy; the fact that Marilyn was having an affair with Senator Kennedy did not impress him. He wrote it all down in his notebook, and kept as careful a log as he could of her visits to the Carlyle, but it didn't excite him the way seeing her together with another star did, like the unforgettable day when he had caught her having tea at Rumpelmayer's on Central Park South with Montgomery Clift.

He hoped she was happy. Her husband, Arthur Miller, always looked sort of grim when he was with Marilyn. Timmy, more than anything else, prayed for her happiness.

He couldn't help noticing that in recent weeks he wasn't the only person watching Marilyn. In addition to himself and the rest of the little band of loyal fans (none as loyal as *him*, of course!), there were other, more shadowy watchers, grown-ups, unsmiling men in dark suits, white shirts, and plain ties, with the highly polished, thick-soled shoes that said "cops" to Timmy (he had an uncle in the Bronx who was a detective), or even "FBI."

Night after night he stood under the streetlight, straining his eyes, and wrote it all down in his notebook in a firm schoolboy hand, while the agents watched.

He wondered why they were interested in Marilyn; then it occurred to him that perhaps it was Senator Kennedy they were interested in, not her. From time to time he said hello to them, as if they were colleagues on a stakeout, but they never said anything back, or even cracked a smile.

FBI, he concluded. Definitely.

He noted down David Leman's departure—by now he knew everybody who visited Marilyn—then settled down to wait for her to leave for dinner or the theater.

He didn't mind waiting, however long it took.

24

When I got home from Marilyn's, I found a note waiting for me —a simple, typed message, on plain paper, inviting me to dinner the next day—from Paul Palermo.

Maria was skiing in Gstaad, where I was to join her in a few days, and I had no plans, so I called his service and accepted. Paul didn't frighten me; in fact, I rather liked him.

The fact that Paul even *had* a service indicates how different he was from his colleagues, most of whom still did their business from pay phones, carrying bags of dimes. Paul was the new breed. He owned nightclubs, restaurants, a couple of off-Broadway theaters; he even invested in plays from time to time, which is how I first made his acquaintance. He was also a member of what law enforcement agencies always referred to as "the Bonanno Crime Family," as well as, more important, a nephew by marriage of Joseph Bonanno himself.

Bonanno was the leader of one of New York City's five families and, as such, among the most powerful—and respected—figures in organized crime. More than this, he was a don, a "man of honor" of the old school. Not only did he have five hundred soldiers working for him in the streets of Brooklyn, running numbers games, loansharking, hijacking, and carrying out a rich and profitable trade in extortion, he was also the respected leader of his community, a kind of lawgiver and supreme fixer for his fellow Sicilians—and, later, the model for Mario Puzo's "Godfather."

Although he had already moved west to semiretirement in Tucson, leaving his son to look after the family's interests in New York, his

287

word was still law in most of Brooklyn, as well as respected by his fellow dons on the Commission, where he had until recently reigned as *capo di tutti capi,* or "Boss of Bosses," being one of the few to give up that honor alive.

Paul had great respect for his uncle by marriage—he would have been foolhardy not to—but he was himself a very different kind of man, at least on the surface: a graduate of Fordham who ordered his suits custom-made at Morty Sills's and had a handsomely appointed office in the Paramount Building. Once when somebody asked him if he ever carried a gun, he replied, "Sure, when I was officer of the day at Camp Pendleton." Paul had not only been a Marine, he was a member of the Knights of Columbus, the New York Veteran Police Association, and the Mayor's Task Force on Juvenile Crime.

I met him the next evening at eight, at Rao's, on 114th Street and Pleasant Avenue in East Harlem. In those days, it was still a straight-forward mob restaurant. Once, just before the Fourth of July, some kids set off firecrackers in the street outside, and at the sound of the explosions everybody in the restaurant dove for cover and drew a piece. Rao's was that kind of place, and also served good, honest Sicilian food, the best in town, before celebrities like Woody Allen and Pete Hamill made it fashionable.

Palermo was waiting for me in booth 1, the nearest to the kitchen. I ordered a dry martini—the bartender at Rao's looked like an ex-prizefighter, but his skill would not have been out of place at the Ritz Bar in Paris. Paul drank wine while Annie, Vinnie Rao's wife, who helped him in the kitchen, told us what we were going to eat. There was a menu at Rao's, which never changed, but it was under-stood that you ate what Annie thought you should eat and what Vinnie wanted to cook, and you were better off that way. *"Bene,"* Paul said with satisfaction, as if he had chosen our meal himself. "It's good to see you, David."

I lifted my glass. Paul and I had, as they say, "a history." He usually came to me when there was trouble in store for one of my clients—a famous television comedian who ran up more debts than he could handle with a bookie; a radio talk show host in Miami who was way behind on paying his weekly "vig" to a loan shark, despite having been held upside down by his ankles off the balcony of his penthouse suite at the Roney Plaza; a singer who had so far forgotten his roots that he turned down a request to top the bill at a Las Vegas casino. . . . In each case, Paul had gently pointed out to me, over dinner, the importance of making my clients do "the right thing," before, as he liked to put it, "things got out of hand" or "the wrong people" got involved.

Do not think that I wasn't grateful for such advice. Anything that kept my clients from being killed or jailed was all right with me. What Paul wanted in return were comparatively minor favors, mostly getting some of the bigger talent to appear in his clubs from time to time, and occasional help with PR.

We chatted about the theater while we ate our seafood salad—the best in the city, by far. It wasn't until we'd finished our veal chops with sweet and sour peppers that Palermo got down to business over the espresso and Sambuca. "You know," he said, "your friends the Kennedys might want to let up on Hoffa. It's just a friendly suggestion."

I raised an eyebrow. Hoffa's friends were in Chicago and Vegas. The New York families, so far as I knew, had other fish to fry. "Hoffa wasn't a cooperative witness," I said. "It's nobody's fault but his own. I had the impression everybody understood that."

Paul shrugged. His dark, doelike eyes were infinitely sad. "They understand. But it's a worry, you know? It was a lousy thing the papers got hold of that story about how he has a girlfriend and they have a kid together."

"I agree. So does Jack. It wasn't anybody's fault. Some hotshot young lawyer from the Justice Department leaked it. These things happen."

"Well, sure. But Hoffa's a madman on the subject, which is hard to figure because his wife knew all about the other broad anyway. She and Sylvia were friends. They all lived together for a while in one house, believe it or not—Hoffa, the wife, the mistress, and the kid. . . ." He sighed. "I should be so lucky. My wife would kill me. My mistress too, probably."

Paul shook his head. "Frankly, Hoffa is making a lot of wild threats, David. Talking about taking out a contract on Bobby Kennedy, even on the Senator." He leaned close to me across the table. I could smell the garlic on his breath. "I got a call from Tucson," he whispered, in the same tone of awe that a bishop might use to describe a call from His Holiness in Rome.

"Tucson?"

"From Mr. B." Paul always referred to the retired Boss of Bosses as Mr. B.

"I'm surprised he's interested. Isn't this a little out of his, ah, jurisdiction?"

Paul looked pained. "Just because he's in Tucson doesn't mean Mr. B. doesn't take an interest. He hears things, David. What he hears lately, he doesn't like."

He accepted a cigar and went about the business of lighting it. "Mr. B.," he went on between puffs, "thinks of himself as an elder statesman, you know what I mean? He's not going to tell the members of the Commission what to do, but he offers them his advice, the wisdom of his experience, whenever he feels there's a problem."

"And what exactly is upsetting him out there in Tucson?" I asked.

"To tell you the truth, David," he said, "we have *big* problems, which is one reason why we don't need all this Hoffa shit on top of everything else." His expression made it clear that we had come at last to the reason for this dinner. "I mean, you tell *me* how the United States government let this bearded Commie punk Castro take over in Cuba! It's like we're a second-class power! Mr. B. told me if Harry Truman was still president, this would never have happened, and he's got a point. We'd have sent in the fucking Marines. If Batista couldn't hack it, we'd have put some guy who could in his place, am I right?"

I nodded. Castro's recent seizure of power in Cuba was on everybody's mind, including Jack's, who still hoped that Castro might turn out to be a liberal reformer, sympathetic to the United States. I suspected that Mr. B. and his friends were probably correct, since they knew more about Cuba than anyone else, and had predicted just these events.

"How bad is it?" I asked.

"Bad. The casinos alone are worth billions, and they're gone, just like that." He lit a match and blew it out. "A fucking catastrophe. Ike should have dropped an A-bomb on this cocksucker Castro when he was still in the Sierra Maestra."

Paul shook his head again, presumably at the weakness of politicians and generals. The fact that Batista's fall was a financial disaster for the mob was something that nobody had as yet considered. Their investment in Havana was huge—casinos, hotels, beach resorts, prostitution, and narcotics earned them millions, far more than Las Vegas. Castro's first act had been to send them packing, even going so far as to jail Santo Trafficante, which, so far as the mob was concerned, was the equivalent of locking up the American ambassador.

"Frankly," he went on, "the worst of the whole thing is that it makes Vegas more important than it was. Before, we had casinos in

Havana and in Vegas. Now there's only Vegas—and that makes Hoffa more important." He stared at me questioningly. "Why?"

"Because construction of the Vegas casinos was financed by the Teamster pension fund?" Moe had explained this to me years ago.

He nodded approvingly. "I always said you were smart. I told Mr. B. so the other day."

I wasn't exactly pleased to have been a subject of conversation between Paul and Mr. B.

"I don't know that there's too much I can do," I said. "I'm not sure there's all that much Jack can do, come to that. Anyway, he's got to get elected first."

"Well, we know that, David. But let's say he *gets* elected, a tough policy on Cuba—*really* tough, I mean getting rid of Castro—is something that would win him a lot of friends. Powerful friends." He paused to give me a significant look. *"Grateful* friends."

"I see."

"Another thing. The people I'm talking about, they *know* Cuba—*really* know it, David, not like these fucking Ivy League amateurs in the CIA. My people can get things done over there in Cuba that nobody else can do, if somebody says the word. Nobody in this administration wants to listen to us, which is crazy. You tell the Senator that if he's gonna get tough with Castro, we're with him, all the way. He helps us, we can help him, okay?"

"I'll pass the word on, Paul."

"Good." Paul called for the check, his mission, I thought, accomplished. He leaned even closer instead. "On the Hoffa thing, all anybody asks is don't send him to the slammer. It's the one thing that really scares the shit out of him. He's afraid of getting fucked in the ass." He laughed. "We need the son of a bitch, so his worry is our worry. Besides, if he goes to the slammer, all hell is going to break loose. I mean, the Senator has to do what he has to do, sure, but tell him not to let Bobby push Hoffa too far. It's like this thing with Hoffa's mistress. I mean, how would the Senator like it if everybody knew about his girls?"

I stared at him, hoping that I looked outraged and unbelieving. "What girls?"

Paul paid the bill from a thick bankroll. "Come on, David, you know what's going on, we know what's going on. It's no big deal. What you have to remember is, *Hoffa* probably knows what's going on too. That, the Senator *should* worry about."

We stood up. Paul made his rounds, shaking hands, embracing his friends, giving a kiss on the cheek to more senior *mafiosi* of the old school. We said our lengthy good-byes to the Raos, squeezed together in the hot little kitchen, then stepped out into the street, taking a deep breath of fresh air, the salt smell of the East River bearing away the garlic odor and the cigar smoke. "Hoffa's a mad dog," Palermo said. "I've seen them before. With mad dogs, it's kill 'em or leave 'em be."

"I'll tell the Senator what you said."

Paul's car was approaching, a Cadillac with blacked-out windows. Mine was waiting across the street.

"Tell him it's what Mr. B. says, not me. Mr. B. looks at the big picture. Hoffa doesn't matter that much in the big picture. Still, something's got to be done; otherwise, someone's going to get hit in the long run."

Paul stepped into his car. "Good night, David," he called as the door closed. "Sweet dreams."

————

If I had expected Jack to be shocked by Palermo's offer to assassinate Fidel Castro for him, I would have been disappointed. He was too much the realist to be shocked by anything except incompetence. I could tell by the gleam in his eye that he was interested, and I instantly regretted having told him.

He was lying in bed at the Carlyle, a breakfast tray across his lap. He had come through New York at the tail end of a series of speaking engagements—since the convention, he was the one Democrat people wanted to hear from, and a whole staff of people had been engaged to schedule his appearances, as well as a new brain trust, fortified by liberal intellectuals and academics who had deserted the Stevenson camp to join him.

Relations with the eggheads, as Jack called them, were testy at first, since they had attacked him and his father bitterly during the fight for the vice presidential nomination, but the association soon paid off in the form of better, crisper speeches, numerous articles in *The New York Times* under Jack's name, and a generally enhanced intellectual atmosphere. Needless to say, the members of what Bobby called, with undisguised contempt, "the faculty club" were kept well away from the Ambassador and out of any meetings involving strategy, for fear of contaminating their innocence. There was no need for Jack's new brain trust to know that their candidate was in communication with Mafia leaders, or to hear about the deals his father was making with Democratic political bosses all over the country.

I couldn't help noticing that the sheets of Jack's bed were rumpled beyond what even the most restless sleeper could achieve, and there were lipstick stains on the pillows. There was a familiar scent of Chanel No. 5 in the room, from which I concluded that Marilyn had been there.

I helped myself to a cup of coffee from his tray while he filled me in on his plans. Bobby was coming on board to take charge of the campaign, which stood badly in need of his energy, ruthless dedication to winning, and total devotion to Jack. The Ambassador, meanwhile, was dropping—somewhat unwillingly—out of sight, on the grounds that the less the public saw of him, the better.

Jack's travels around the country, in the new family plane, *Caroline*—another useful contribution from the Ambassador—had, if nothing else, hardened his attitude toward Fidel Castro. He was beginning to discover that the opinions of the average American voter on foreign policy are diametrically opposed to those of the academics and intellectuals. Since he was determined to appeal to both groups, he had his work cut out for him.

"Your guinea friends have got the right idea about Castro," he told me. "I'll say that for them. Ike has gone weak at the knees. He's an old man—too old to be president."

"You won't be saying that when you're his age, Jack."

"Christ, I'm never going to reach his age. You say they're still worrying about Hoffa?"

"They don't like him any better than you do, but they have a major investment in him to protect. All they want is to make sure he doesn't have to go to jail."

"I can't promise that. Jail is exactly where Bobby wants him."

"You said you'd ask Bobby to stall."

He looked annoyed. I guessed Bobby hadn't been easy to win over, or that Jack hadn't even tried. "It's not in his nature to stall," Jack said. "Still, as Bobby takes over the campaign, he'll be busy. I can make sure he doesn't have the time to think about Hoffa. In the meantime, something may happen. . . . We'll see."

I thought Jack's attitude was a little too casual, as usual, on this subject. "Jack," I said, "I'm telling you: *Take this seriously.*"

Something in my voice must have convinced him. "I understand," he said impatiently. "I'll take care of it, David. I promise."

Of course, looking back on it, I can see that this was the time to tell Jack I was off the case, especially since a certain shifty look in his eyes warned me that he hadn't any real intention of laying down the law to Bobby, but like Jack himself, I was suffering from presidential fever, vicariously in my case. In the big picture, the complaints of Jimmy Hoffa and the mob seemed like a minor problem, one of the countless small difficulties that could be smoothed over once Jack was in the White House.

"What else did they have to say?" he asked.

"A thinly veiled warning that they know about what Paul Palermo called your 'girls,' " I told him.

Jack threw back his head and laughed. "Jesus!" he said. "You've got to be kidding!"

I shook my head. "Paul said they knew all about them. He hinted that Hoffa may know about them too."

"Christ, *everybody* knows about them! There's hardly a journalist in New York and Washington who *doesn't* know about my private life, but you and I both know nobody's ever going to print anything."

"Well, I'm not so sure. About most of it, sure, but a story that involved Marilyn might be too juicy not to print."

"You've got Marilyn on the brain, David. Sometimes I wonder why. . . . Anyway, nobody really knows about me and Marilyn, except people who won't talk to the press, like you and Peter."

"I didn't like what Paul had to say—or rather, the way he said it, Jack. It sounded to me as if he knew a lot more than he was saying, frankly."

"Did he mention her by name?"

"No."

"There you are. How the hell would he know anything? We've been pretty goddamn discreet."

It was on the tip of my tongue to point out that bringing Marilyn to the Cal-Neva Lodge in Tahoe wasn't my idea of discretion, but I didn't. "I'll tell you what went through my mind when he was talking to me," I said. "What if somebody was bugging you?"

"Bugging?"

"Microphones. Telephone taps. That sort of thing."

He shook his head wearily. "You've been reading too many spy novels. It's not possible, anyway."

"Why?"

"Because Dad's old pal J. Edgar Hoover has somebody check that out at regular intervals—here, at home, in my Senate office—as a favor to Dad. Hoover's been taking care of that for years."

Jack, I noticed, talked about Hoover as if he were a family re-
tainer. Knowing the old fox as I did, I didn't share that view. It was
Hoover's listening devices I was afraid of—I had a professional
sweep my office and apartment regularly—but I knew Jack had an
exaggerated faith in Hoover and, of course, absolute faith in his
father.

"Well, if you think there's nothing to worry about..." I said,
unconvinced.

"Who's worried?"

"I am."

"It's not worth it, David. Worrying does no good." He stretched
his arms, grimacing from the pain in his back.

"Did Marilyn talk to you about her having a baby?" I asked.

"Christ, yes! She gave me an earful on the subject! It's hard to
imagine her as a mother, somehow. . . . Although she seems pretty
happy about it."

"Too happy, I thought."

Jack raised an eyebrow. "After all," I went on, "having the child
means affirming the marriage. And I'm not sure she *wants* the marriage. Or the father."

"He seems like a nice enough guy," Jack said with a shrug, "according to Marilyn." He chuckled. "And easygoing," he added. "For
a writer."

I was not sure either of those descriptions suited Arthur Miller—
though certainly they represented ideal qualities in Marilyn's husband from Jack's point of view.

"Have you ever heard of a woman who was happy with a nice
enough guy as a husband? In the long run?"

He thought about this for a moment, grinning hugely. "No, I guess
not," he said. "Though most of the married women I've slept with
always start out by saying how much they love their husbands. Even
Marilyn. Arthur is noble. Arthur is a genius. Arthur deserves a better
wife than she's been. She doesn't want to hurt Arthur. She wants
Arthur's happiness more than anything. Arthur would die if he knew
what she was doing. All this, you understand, while she's fucking
me." He sighed. "Do you suppose anybody understands women?"

"You seem to do pretty well," I said. I didn't recall hearing Marilyn say any of this to *me* about Miller. She must save it all for Jack,
I thought. I glanced at my watch, anxious to leave rather than sit
here listening to Jack share Marilyn's pillow talk with me.

He glanced at his own watch on the bedside table. "Christ, I've
got to get going myself," he said, swinging out of bed. He slipped

into his robe. "The reason I do pretty well, David"—he flashed me that famous Kennedy grin—"is that I don't even *try* to understand women. It's a waste of time, in my opinion. I leave the understanding to their husbands."

25

From the moment she was back in California and read the script for *Let's Make Love,* she despised it. Once she was comfortably installed in her bungalow at the Beverly Hills Hotel and read it again, she despised it even more. It was typical 20th Century–Fox schlock —exactly the kind of thing that she had outgrown.

Her doubts about the script were reinforced when it became impossible to find a leading man, but Fox pushed on, determined to get a new Marilyn Monroe picture in distribution as soon as possible to capitalize on the success of *Some Like It Hot.* She had contractual approval of her leading man, but it was Arthur who finally suggested Montand.

The suggestion was an odd one, and at first nobody took it seriously, least of all her. Montand was a French singer, unknown to the average American moviegoer, although he had a certain reputation among intellectuals for his performance in *The Wages of Fear* and because he was widely known to hold left-wing views.

When she met Montand backstage in New York, she had been impressed by his compact, rough-hewn good looks and his Gallic charm, but she was more impressed by his wife, Simone Signoret, whose electrifying performance in *Room at the Top* had made her suddenly famous.

Even the presence of Mme. Montand had not prevented Montand from flirting with her, but she assumed that that was normal for a Frenchman, and attached no importance to it. Even Simone had joked about it: "Look at him!" she growled affectionately, in a low, rasping, chain-smoker's voice that managed to be sexy and tough at the same time. "He can't take his eyes off you."

297

The two couples became friendly in New York, often dining together after the theater, and for the first time in ages, Arthur seemed to be enjoying himself. Arthur and Yves (as she was soon calling him) shared not only a political outlook but all sorts of cultural references, as Arthur did with Simone. Simone treated Arthur with the special respect the French reserve for great writers, sometimes, only half jokingly, calling him *Maître*—the equivalent of calling him a genius if you were American, Simone explained to her.

The friendship with the Montands was the one bright spot in Arthur's life. She had lost the baby, and with it, any desire to try again, while he was still grimly rewriting *The Misfits* in an attempt to make Gay Langland into someone Gable could see himself playing. In some mysterious way Yves and Simone became vital to her marriage.

When it became obvious at last that none of the male stars who were acceptable to her wanted the part of the multimillionaire in *Let's Make Love,* and that she would not accept any of the studio's countersuggestions, Montand was brought up again and instantly accepted by the studio. Within twenty-four hours he was flown to Los Angeles, tested for the part, and offered more money than he had ever made before.

The truth was, as she knew perfectly well—but Yves didn't—that the studio would have accepted anyone she was willing to work with. Fox was a sinking ship. Her old nemesis Darryl Zanuck, embittered and feeble, had been driven into exile in Europe, leaving the studio in the uncertain hands of desperate, frightened men, awash in a sea of red ink. Her contract was their major asset. Her name was their only hope.

Nobody was more pleased at the news that Yves would be working with her than poor Arthur, reduced now to a minor supporting role as her husband, with nothing much to do in a town where the only thing anybody cares about is what you are doing. He arranged to have the Montands moved into bungalow 20 at the Beverly Hills Hotel, next door to them with a connecting door.

In bungalow 19, below their adjoining suites, lived Howard Hughes (who had once tried to hire her after seeing her photograph on the cover of *Laff* magazine in 1945) and his wife Jean Peters, who had played in *Niagara* with her in 1953. The idea of living in the same bungalow as Howard Hughes was fascinating to Simone, who spent many hours a day waiting in vain for a glimpse of the reclusive billionaire.

Relations with the Montands were easygoing and neighborly, as if they were sharing a summer cottage. In Hollywood, they were strangers in the world she had grown up in, happy to have her advice and companionship. She and Simone went shopping together, exchanged gossip, even cooked meals together sometimes in one of their tiny kitchenettes.

As for Yves, he stuck as close to her as a faithful dog at the studio. He had never worked in a Hollywood studio, and was acutely conscious of his own lack of status as a foreign singer whose only big movie played in "art houses." Lonely, slightly bewildered, afraid of failing now that his big break was at hand, Yves spent the time between takes in her dressing room, traveled back and forth in the same studio limousine with her, rehearsed his lines with her, asked her advice about everyone he met.

She found his presence strangely comforting. He was a good listener, unfailingly sympathetic, interested in everything she did. For the first time in years, she *enjoyed* going to the studio, and with his gentle, supportive coaxing even managed to turn up on time, or very nearly so, and remember her lines. It was, she thought, as if she were his teacher when it came to the ins and outs of Hollywood and studio politics, while he became her teacher in preparing herself for her role. Not that he was a great actor, but he approached his work with the robust calm of a competent workman, without doubts or drama, and some of his calm rubbed off on her. Of course, Paula was jealous, but for once she could live without Paula's mothering and yentalike advice. In some curious way, hating the picture, hating being back in Hollywood again, knowing her marriage to Arthur was on the skids, she was happy playing Yves's studio tour guide. . . .

———

When she was young, she had always wanted to be "a good girl," had but never quite succeeded. Even at twelve or thirteen, her body was so startlingly mature that nobody ever gave her the benefit of the doubt.

There was still a part of her that yearned for virtue—the good girl within, truthful, obedient, and chaste. She yearned to be true to *someone,* but being true to a man who was married, had lots of girls, and was a candidate for the Democratic presidential nomination was hard to do. She'd *told* Jack he'd better visit her soon, and he hadn't listened. Or rather, he had listened and treated it as a joke.

It wasn't anything as simple as wanting to teach Jack a lesson—

she wanted him to be here, and he couldn't be, so in a spirit of resentment she told her troubles to Yves, who proved a willing if baffled listener.

Maybe it was part of Yves's charm, maybe it was because he was French, but he could listen for *hours,* fascinated by every detail, not afraid to ask the most intimate questions, quick to laugh or touch her hand in a gesture of sympathy.

It was like confessing to the world's sexiest priest—one who had made no vows of celibacy—and she felt herself offering up to him her innermost fears and secrets.

She felt bad about even the *idea* of fucking Yves, not only because of Jack but because she liked and admired Simone and thought of her as a friend. But when Simone was nominated for Best Actress by the Academy and she wasn't, she felt such rage and jealousy (which she was obliged to conceal under a nauseating mask of gracious congratulations) that she might have hopped into bed with Yves then and there out of sheer revenge. She had appeared in twenty-seven movies, in at least eleven of which she had a starring role, and had never been nominated even once, while Simone, a foreigner, had copped a nomination for Best Actress first time out, despite the fact that she was practically a Communist, according to Louella Parsons! It wasn't fair, she told herself over and over, especially since *Some Like It Hot* was the best shot she'd had at an Oscar in years.

It *still* might not have happened if Simone hadn't actually *won* the fucking Oscar, becoming, overnight, a sensation in Hollywood. For Simone's Oscar was a popular choice, proof that Hollywood could reward quality and recognize talent in a low-budget foreign movie with foreign stars; proof, too, that the dark days of the McCarthy era were over, that despite Louella Parsons, and Hedda Hopper, and Ronnie Reagan, and all the right-wing witch hunters who ran the studios, a woman who stood up for left-wing causes and was associated with the French Communist party could still win. Simone made Hollywood feel proud of itself, and it showed in the way people greeted her in the street when she went shopping, or stood up and applauded her when she entered a restaurant or the lobby of the Beverly Hills Hotel—while at the same time, nobody had a good word for *her* performance in *Let's Make Love,* which everybody in town was already dismissing as just another piece of mindless, lackluster vulgarity. . . .

She could tell that Yves wanted her, even though he liked Arthur and felt a great bond with him. Even in France, it seemed, fucking your best friend's wife was frowned upon by good guys, and Yves was a French version of a good guy.

So she and Yves managed somehow to stay on their best behavior, while she and Simone went shopping, or had their hair done together, or tried on each other's clothes, wandering back and forth from one suite to the other in their negligees (or, in Marilyn's case, undressed) as if they were all one big happy family.

If she had cried when Simone won the Oscar, she cried even harder when Jack called to cancel his LA trip for the *third* time. Oh, she understood his reason—California was in the bag, he thought, it was the East he was worried about—but she took it as a rejection, and took it harder than he knew. Still, she did her best to hold herself back.

What did it, finally, was the fact that Simone was obliged to go back to Paris to start a new picture, while Arthur, with a blindness few husbands could have matched, decided to fly to Ireland to make the final revisions on the script of *The Misfits* with John Huston, leaving her, as he put it, "in Yves's hands."

It was almost, she thought, as if Arthur *wanted* her to have an affair with Yves—or perhaps it was just that he was by now so separated from her feelings that he no longer noticed them, and therefore ignored the obvious attraction between them. Yet even when they were finally alone, she and Yves didn't go to bed together until the night they appeared at a supper party at the David Selznicks', hand in hand, causing everyone present to lift an eyebrow in surprise—except for Byron Holtzer, one of Hollywood's most famous bachelor men-about-town and toughest superlawyers, and for many reasons no friend of hers, whom she happened to overhear telling somebody that Joe Schenck was dying, had already slipped into a coma.

She felt a stabbing pain as guilt shot through her. She had known that Joe was gravely ill, but she had a thousand reasons for not going to visit him, beginning with her intense fear of death and sickness, and ending with the fact that she hadn't any desire to relive her days as Joe's mistress. All the same, Joe had been good to her—better than anyone else in those days. Once she became famous, she had neglected the old man, and was ashamed of it now.

"He *can't* be in a coma," she cried. "Someone would have told me!"

The moment the words were out of her mouth, she knew it was a mistake. Plenty of people had told her. Holtzer was a close friend of

Schenck's, and a formidable opponent in court and out, who had no reason to spare her feelings. *"Bullshit!"* he growled fiercely, his powerful voice bringing the entire room to instant silence. "Save your fucking tears for somebody who doesn't know you, Marilyn."

Now that she was engaged in a contest with him, she couldn't back off. The Selznicks were Hollywood royalty—Mrs. Selznick was Jennifer Jones, David Selznick had produced *Gone With the Wind*. Almost everybody who mattered in the industry was gathered, their attention now fixed on her, Holtzer, and a puzzled Yves Montand, who didn't know who Joe Schenck was, or Holtzer for that matter.

"I've got to see Joe," she said. "Now. He needs me."

Holtzer scented blood. *"Needs* you? He's unconscious. He was naive enough to hope you'd come to say good-bye, but you didn't give a shit, did you? Now it's too late."

Even the waiters stood, trays in hand, transfixed by the scene. Her skills as an actress failed her completely. "Hold on a minute!" she stammered angrily, tears running down her cheeks, while Yves held her arm, trying to pull her away, muttering, "We have to go, *chérie,* we have to go."

She shook her arm loose and confronted Holtzer. "Joe would understand," she said.

"He understood, all right. He understood you didn't give a shit about him. It broke his fucking heart."

"If you're not going, I am," Yves said, horrified at being at the center of this storm. "I can't take this."

She hardly even heard him—or rather, she heard the words but missed their significance entirely. It wasn't until Doris Vidor and Edie Goetz had pulled her away from Holtzer, tears still streaming down her face, her hands trembling, that she realized Yves had gone, at which point, deserted and alone, knowing that everyone would surely take Holtzer's side against hers since he was one of the old guard, she pushed aside the two women and ran into the driveway screaming, "Wait for me, wait for me!"

She ran as fast as she could, stumbling on her stiletto heels, her hair coming apart, her clutch bag opening to spill keys, Kleenex, her compact, and a couple of just-in-case Tampaxes onto the Selznicks' Spanish-tiled driveway. Ahead of her she saw the taillights of Yves's rented car gleaming, but she knew she could never catch up with him. She was screaming at the top of her lungs now; then she saw the brake lights come on, and knew he had stopped, and felt her whole body inside turn liquid.

She flung open the door, grabbed him in her arms, so roughly that she tore his shirt, kissed him fiercely, driving her tongue deep into his mouth, moaning, keening in a high-pitched voice as if she were in the grips of pain too terrible to bear.

"Not here," he whispered. "Not like this." He put the car in gear, comforting her in French in a low voice.

She closed her eyes. The drive seemed endless, though it was only a few minutes from the Selznicks' to the Beverly Hills Hotel. He parked the car in the street illegally, close to the bungalow, and half carried, half dragged her inside, dropping her on the bed. Then he undressed her, slowly, carefully, as if now that he knew they were going to make love at last, he wanted to savor it fully. . . .

26

She hadn't anticipated the size and impact of the scandal. Her affair with Jack was a secret, partly because secrecy mattered to him; partly, she had begun to realize, because the Kennedys had friends and power everywhere in the media, but Yves enjoyed no such protection. He was merely an actor and a singer, married to a movie star who had just won Best Actress—fair game for the press.

Besides, unlike Jack, Yves shrewdly sensed that the affair with her was his ticket to fame. He was intensely ambitious for Hollywood stardom. After all, Maurice Chevalier had proved years ago that a Frenchman could become a major Hollywood star, and as soon as the news about himself and Marilyn broke, people stopped asking, "Who's Yves Montand?"

As for her, she had what she had so far never had with Jack—a kind of make-believe marriage, with all the burrs and rough edges of marriage removed. Not only could she *talk* to Yves, they spent their nights together, ate together, went to work together.

She even enjoyed being told what to do by Yves, she who never did a thing her husbands wanted her to do! He played the role—which came naturally enough to him—of a European husband who puts up with no nonsense from his wife, while she played the dutiful little woman who does what he says, including turning up for work on time! She even cooked for him, in the tiny kitchen of the Miller suite, while he praised her efforts extravagantly. She felt renewed, as if she had finally succeeded in turning over a new leaf.

Her headaches stopped, her period was practically painless, she slept like a log with only a minimum maintenance dose of sleeping pills and woke up early every morning with a clear head. The only thing that made her anxious was that they never talked about the future.

Of course, not wanting to spoil things, she didn't press him—she had already guessed it wasn't something he was going to bring up himself. Yves, she knew, received letters and telephone calls daily from Simone, while Arthur, sounding tired and withdrawn over the transatlantic phone line, called her regularly, reporting on his work with Huston. At some point, she knew, he would return; at some point they would have to start work on *The Misfits;* at some point it would be necessary to discuss what had happened—but in the meantime, it was easier to forget all that in Yves's arms.

Cukor took advantage of her good mood to press on with *Let's Make Love,* with a speed never seen before on a Marilyn Monroe picture, and that made her happy too, except for the nagging thought that the sooner the picture was over, the sooner she and Yves would have to face reality.

She did not really notice how public the affair had become until it was too late. She and Yves had better things to do than read the gossip columns or the international gutter press, after all. It was as if a glass wall separated them from the rest of the world—people could see them, but nobody could reach them.

Only Cukor breached the wall to warn her gently that they were playing with fire.

She told him not to worry. She could handle it. . . .

———

As fate would have it, I flew to California with Arthur on his return from Ireland. I switched seats to sit next to him—I didn't want him to think I was avoiding him—but we didn't speak much. He seemed preoccupied and withdrawn, which wasn't like him really, because he was usually pretty outgoing for a serious writer.

There were a number of French film people on the airplane, traveling to Los Angeles on some deal, and I remember being embarrassed on Arthur's behalf that they were all passing around a copy of *Paris-Match* with a photograph on the cover of Marilyn and Montand kissing—clearly a passionate, private kiss captured by a hidden photographer. The French movie people talked about "*Yves et Marilyn*" all the way from New York to Los Angeles, while Arthur, hunched over in his seat, did his best to conceal his misery and, for all I knew, anger.

We talked about Ireland, about Huston, about *The Misfits,* which I thought he was clinging to fiercely. Perhaps by now he had invested so much of himself and his time in the script that he couldn't bear to let it go unmade—as if it were the only thing he could salvage from the ruins of his love for Marilyn.

At some point in the journey, after the meal, I dozed off. When I woke up, Arthur was staring out the window at the bright blue sky, his hands clenched so tightly in his lap that the knuckles showed white, his dinner tray still untouched before him. There were tears on his cheek, reflecting the harsh, stratospheric light so they shimmered and shone on his sallow skin.

Coward that I am, I closed my eyes and feigned sleep rather than confront his misery. I consoled myself that he probably wanted to be left alone.

After we arrived and I claimed my bags, I found him waiting outside with his luggage, obviously looking for a driver.

"It looks as if nobody's been sent to pick me up," he said.

I offered him a lift, and we rode together to the Beverly Hills Hotel. "It's not a town I'm fond of," he mused glumly, looking out at Sepulveda Boulevard. "It's a town for beginnings, not endings."

There didn't seem anything to say to that, so we sat in silence until we arrived beneath the hotel's famous pink porte cochere. "Good luck," I said, but he merely nodded, his mind on the coming scene.

———

I ran into Marilyn in the coffee shop the next morning. Her eyes were puffy and she looked as if she hadn't slept all night. It was as if all her glamour had gone, along with her brief happiness. "How did it go?" I asked her. "With Arthur?"

She looked at me over the rim of her coffee cup and shrugged. "Not great," she said.

"We flew in together, you know."

"He told me. He was grateful for the lift. I was supposed to order a car for him, and I forgot."

"Well, he's a gentleman. Have the two of you decided what you're going to do?"

"Stay married, I guess," she said, in a tone of utter dejection. "What are you doing here?"

"Well, the convention's going to be in Los Angeles, you know. . . ."

She looked puzzled for a moment. At this moment of her life

nothing was real to her except her own problems. "Oh," she said at last, "the *convention*. Sure." Then she brightened a little. "How's Jack?"

"Good. Going twenty-four hours a day. You know Jackie's pregnant again?"

"Uh-huh." Marilyn's pupils narrowed, and she quickly changed the subject. "Is Jack going to win the nomination?" she asked, moving to safer ground.

"I think it's likely." I knocked wood on the countertop. "Have you been following things?"

"Not as closely as I'd like, frankly." That, I guessed, was putting it mildly, given what had been going on between her and Montand.

I made myself comfortable and proceeded to fill her in. In the beginning of the year, I told her, Bobby had dropped the first shoe by announcing that Jack was entering the New Hampshire primary, which, as a native New Englander, he won easily. The other shoe dropped with a loud thud when the news leaked out that the Kennedy brothers had outmaneuvered their opponents by persuading the reluctant governor of Ohio to endorse Jack's candidacy, which meant Jack would be free to put all his resources into confronting Hubert Humphrey in the Wisconsin primary.

Jack had to beat Humphrey convincingly on Humphrey's own turf, and knock him out of the race early on so he could arrive in Los Angeles the favored candidate. A long, bitter struggle against Humphrey would divide the party and leave the nomination open to Symington, who had the support of Harry Truman and the older party regulars, or Johnson, who was campaigning hard in the Senate cloakroom.

Already the tide of dirty politics was washing up at Jack's feet—there were rumors that he had been secretly married before his marriage to Jackie, that his health or his religion would prevent him from being elected, that he took his orders from the Vatican. Harry Truman remarked, "It isn't the pope I'm afraid of, it's the pop"—a shaft at his old enemy Joe Kennedy. In Wisconsin, people were passing around quarters on which the bust of George Washington was altered with red nail polish to resemble Pope John XXIII, as a warning of what would happen to America if Jack Kennedy were president. The Kennedy campaign was being run, by no accident, in the spirit of the PT boat that was the campaign symbol—full speed ahead all the way because at the slightest sign of slowing down, the whole thing was likely to capsize and sink.

I explained all this to Marilyn, who sighed and said: "It's hard to imagine Jack as president, isn't it? Like Lincoln?"

It wasn't for me—though Lincoln seemed an odd choice to compare Jack to, despite Marilyn's fascination with him. "He'll still be Jack," I said. "The office doesn't change the man—it just brings out the best or the worst of what was already there."

"President John F. Kennedy," she mused in a whisper. "It's great billing."

We both laughed.

"What's *your* billing going to be, David?" she asked. "If he wins."

I shrugged. "There's nothing I want, really," I said, but the look in Marilyn's eyes clearly read: *Don't give me that crap!* so I told her the truth. "Ambassador to the Court of St. James's," I said.

She looked puzzled.

"Ambassador to Great Britain," I explained. "It's called that."

"Oh. Everything there is called something else. I couldn't understand half of what people said to me. *Englishmen!*" she said cryptically. "Oh boy!" She must have been thinking of Olivier because she crinkled her nose and asked: "Why do you want to live *there*?"

"I love England. And it would please Maria. Besides, I've always thought it was the one job I was cut out for. I'd look good in knee breeches and silk stockings, I think."

Marilyn laughed. "Well, I hope you get it if it's what you want." Her expression turned wistful. "I just wish I could find a way of helping Jack," she said.

I raised an eyebrow. So far the one rumor that *hadn't* raised its ugly head against Jack was his affair with Marilyn. If there was anything the campaign didn't need, it was Marilyn endorsing him, if that was what she had in mind, or worse yet, cheering him on in person through the primaries.

"When is Jack coming out here?" she asked. She must be conscious that others had surely taken her place in Jack's bed while she was making eyes at Montand, I thought. She had to be conscious too of the fact that Jack's star was now rising while hers was descending sharply. He was famous now, on his way to the Democratic nomination, while her affair with Yves was giving her a bad press for the first time in her life, and the word about her new picture was awful.

"It may not be for a while," I said. I explained that all the big excitement was going on back east, not out here. Jack already had California pretty much sewn up, thanks to the deal Bobby and I had made with Governor Pat Brown on his behalf. In a sense, Marilyn had missed the boat—written herself out of the big story because she was busy fucking Montand while Jack was making history without her. I wanted to tell her to go back to Miller and try to save whatever she could of her marriage, warn her that there was no place for her in Jack's future—or perhaps only a place that would destroy her in the end—but to my shame, I didn't.

She took my hand and squeezed it. "Does Jack miss me at all?" she asked.

"Missing people isn't something Jack does a lot of," I said. "He lives in the present. But he talks about you a lot when the two of us are together."

She closed her eyes for a moment. The lids were pale blue, almost translucent. She seemed to me to have lost weight—more than was good for her, I thought. "That must be tough on you," she said.

I was surprised and touched, both by her perception and by the gentle, caring way she expressed it—for she was right, of course. Jack in his hearty, man-to-man way shared many of his feelings about Marilyn with me, without ever noticing how strong—and painful—my own were, or how deep my envy ran. "It is tough," I admitted. "Sometimes."

"How are things at home?" she asked. Marilyn seldom inquired about Maria, who she seemed to feel instinctively (and correctly) was not her friend.

"Not bad," I said. It was true enough. Things between Maria and me *weren't* "bad"; they just weren't *good*.

"Poor David," Marilyn sighed. She took my hand in hers. "I want to ask a favor," she said.

"Anything."

"It's not going to make you happy."

"Is that a concern?"

She nodded. "Yes," she said. "I wish I *could* make you happy, David, I really do. But I can't. I know how you feel about me."

"And I'm wasting my time?"

"Probably. I don't know. Listen, David, the truth is, I'd only make you *un*happy. You're better off, believe me."

"Forgive me if I don't agree with you. What's the favor?"

I felt her fingers dig deep into my palm. "I want to see Jack," she said. "I have to explain what happened. Between me and Yves."

I was plunged into sudden misery by her need to explain herself to Jack, who didn't care, when I was sitting right here beside her. Still,

I swallowed my pain and resentment, as I always did—which was perhaps a sign of just how much I loved Marilyn—to give her a gentle warning about Jack's position now that he was the front-runner. "You're going to have to be careful—more careful than before. It's serious now."

"I *know* it's serious, David, really I do—the White House and all. But tell him I need to talk to him."

I nodded. We sat silently in the tiny coffee shop downstairs, where, this being Beverly Hills, everybody pretended Marilyn was just an ordinary customer. For the first time since I had met her, way back in '54 at Charlie Feldman's, she seemed to me fragile. She had always been robust, fleshy, indecently healthy, a big girl straining the seams of her clothes, but this morning she seemed almost ghostlike.

She must have sensed what I thought or caught my expression, because she said, "I look like shit, I know."

"I wasn't thinking that."

"Yes you were. Christ, people are always saying I'm too fat." She laughed bitterly. "Well, they can't say that now, can they?"

"You look good to me."

"David, I'd look good to you if I was dead." She gave me a quick kiss on the cheek.

I saw her through the lobby into the waiting studio car. She walked unsteadily, leaning heavily on my arm. She looked into the car as the door was opened for her. "Yves was always in the car waiting for me," she said sadly. "This is the first time he hasn't been."

She slipped into the darkness of the limousine, with its tinted windows. She closed the door, lowered the window, stuck her head out and kissed me.

"You're a real pal, David. I hope you get to be ambassador to the Court of whatever it is." She laughed. "Toodle-oo," she said; then the window went up and the car pulled away.

———

Later that same day, I called Jack, who was in Oshkosh, Wisconsin, catching him in his motel room. He sounded exhausted. "California!" he croaked. "I wish to Christ I were there. It was fifteen fucking degrees below zero this morning. Dave Powers got me up at five-thirty to stand outside a meat-packing plant and shake hands with the workers."

"You sound played out."

"No shit? I'm sitting here with my hand in a bowl of warm water and antiseptic, courtesy of room service. You try taking off your glove and shaking fifteen hundred hands at fifteen below! My right hand is so bruised and scratched I can't even pick up a fork with it."

"How many votes did you pick up? As your father would ask."

"Some. It's hard to tell. People don't smile much around here— it's too cold, I guess. Jackie's out here with me, believe it or not. She's a better draw than me."

"I believe it. It sounds rough."

"Well, you know how it is. . . . One funny thing—the only one. A guy comes up to me in Ashland, where it's so cold you can't take a piss without freezing your dick off, and asks, 'Is it true you were born with a silver spoon in your mouth, that your dad's a million-aire, and you've never had to do a day's work in your life?'

"Well, it's too cold to argue, so I say, 'Yes.' So *he* holds out his hand and says, 'I'd like to shake your hand, Senator. Let me tell you —you haven't missed a fucking thing!' "

We both laughed. Telling the joke seemed to raise Jack's spirits: he was one of those very rare public men who enjoy it when the joke is on them.

"It would be great to get away to Palm Beach for a few days," he said. "Just to thaw out."

"Can you?"

"Only if I lose. Otherwise, not yet. And I'm not going to lose. How's California?"

"Brown is behind you one hundred percent. Unless you start los-ing primaries, of course. . . ."

"Of course." He sighed.

"I saw Marilyn this morning, Jack."

"Yes? Jesus, I wish she were here right now. She'd warm me up a lot quicker than long johns."

"That's where she'd like to be too, as a matter of fact. In Wiscon-sin, with you."

"How is she?"

"Going through a difficult time."

"Aren't we all?"

"She's in a bad way, Jack. I mean it."

There was a long pause, while the seriousness of my tone worked its way through his fatigue. "What happened?" he asked cautiously.

"Have you heard that she had an affair with Yves Montand? The French singer?"

"Jackie made sure I heard all about it, of course," he said.

"It hasn't done a lot for her marriage. As you can imagine."

"I can imagine," he said grimly—nobody, I thought, would know better.

"She's worried that you're angry. That you won't forgive her."

"Oh Christ, Marilyn isn't somebody who's going to sit home and do needlepoint, or cook for her husband. If you want her, you've got to take time for her, and I haven't. I guess Miller didn't either, poor guy. . . . Tell her she's forgiven. No, better yet, tell her there's nothing to forgive."

"I think she'd prefer to hear it from you."

There was another pause. "That's a little complicated," he said. "Jackie's campaigning with me. You happened to catch me while she's taking a bath, but I don't want Marilyn to start calling at all hours of the day or night. Which she will."

"So call her. She's desperate, Jack."

"I'd forgotten your sentimental side, David. It's what prevents you from being a real politician." His tone was snappish, very much his father's, and he must have realized it, because he apologized immediately. "I'm sorry," he said. "It's been a long, hard day. You'd have to be here to understand."

"I understand. And it's okay. Listen, Jack, you're going to win. That's what matters. But call her."

"Tell her I'll call her at noon tomorrow, her time, okay?" he said quickly. There was a faint noise in the background. "Here's Jackie," Jack said cheerfully. "She sends you her best, David."

"Give her mine. Tell her it's balmy here in LA. Seventy degrees."

"David says it's seventy degrees in LA, Jackie." His tone was jovial—a little too much so to sound sincere to any intelligent woman, I thought, but then Jackie was surely used to that.

I couldn't hear what she said in reply, but Jack's voice sounded strained and I wondered if she had walked in from the bathroom when he was still talking about Marilyn. "As I was saying, David," he went on, "I want a really good committee of stars out there in Hollywood." He sounded more like his old self again, as if talking about politics was all it took to revive him. "Frank can help a lot there, getting the really big names."

"I've talked to him."

"Good." Another pause. Then, with a snap of authority that once again reminded me of his father: "Just don't let him become chairman or anything like that, David. Be tactful but firm. I *like* Frank, you understand, he's a buddy, but he's got some bad friends. . . ."

"Ah, don't we all, Jack?"

He laughed—that laughter which nobody could ever resist, least of all me. "Sure, David, and you ought to have been born Irish," he said.

It was the greatest compliment he could pay. I said good night, left him to Jackie's care, and called the studio to let Marilyn know that she was forgiven.

In Wisconsin at least.

———

Jack's victory in Wisconsin, to his fury, was not the triumph he had hoped for. He carried six of ten congressional districts and picked up the majority of the electoral votes, in a state where Humphrey was practically regarded as a native son, but his votes had come mostly from Catholic areas, and he had lost to Humphrey in the traditionally Protestant ones. So the whole battle had to be fought all over again in West Virginia, starting the next day.

I was dragged away from my business by Jack's father to help out in what was clearly the crucial moment of the campaign. A loss in West Virginia, a rural, backwoods Protestant state, would send the signal to every politician that a Catholic couldn't carry the country in 1960 any more than Governor Alfred E. Smith had been able to carry it in 1928—a point that the Ambassador made to me forcibly and at length on the telephone from Palm Beach, where he was keeping out of sight. "Round up every big-name Protestant you can get to come out for Jack," he barked. "Who's the big man in New York?"

"The Episcopal archbishop."

"That's right. And the dean of the Harvard School of Divinity. And that fellow, what's his name, Niebuhr, and all the rest of the Protestant theologians. 'Protestants for Kennedy'—that's what we need, in a hurry."

" 'Jews for Kennedy' would be easier."

"What's the matter with you, David, for Christ's sake? Jack's already *got* the fucking Jews!"

So I got on the telephone, swept away by the atmosphere of crisis, and succeeded in persuading the eminent Protestant divines that freedom of religion was at stake in West Virginia. In his television debate with Humphrey—and more important, with the reluctant Protestant ministers of West Virginia—Jack's position as the leading Democratic candidate was guaranteed, and Humphrey was buried once and for all, along with Lyndon Johnson and Stu Symington, neither of whom had had the guts to take Jack on in the early primaries.

Yves Montand returned to France a national hero, for it was ob-

vious to his compatriots that if Marilyn was the world's acknowledged sex goddess, her lover ought naturally to be a Frenchman.

Luckily for Marilyn, she was about to start work on *The Misfits*
—luckily because working with Clark Gable would at least take her
mind off the end of her affair with Montand, luckily too because it
was her real chance to be a *serious* actress, and that still mattered to
her.

Not so lucky was the fact that she would have to spend weeks on
location in Nevada with the husband she had betrayed, and on
whom she had now focused all her guilt, anger, and resentment.

27

I was in Key Biscayne with Maria about a week later, trying to get a few days' rest, when I got a call from Joe Kennedy in Palm Beach. He sounded hysterical, and for a moment I wondered if he'd had what the French call *un coup de vieux,* a sudden collapse into senility. "You've got to get her out of sight," he said. "Back to New York."

"Who?"

"Who the hell do you think? Marilyn Monroe!"

"Marilyn? What are you talking about?"

"She came down here, checked into The Breakers, and called Jack. He's over there now."

I tried to make sense of the news, and couldn't. "She didn't check into The Breakers under her own name?" I asked, praying she hadn't.

"No. But there must be plenty of people who could recognize her. There are reporters all over the goddamn place. This could destroy Jack's chances, you know that, don't you?"

He seemed to feel I was to blame, but I knew that was just the way he was—whoever he talked to first got the full blast of his wrath.

"Where's Jackie?"

"In Washington, thank God, resting. Doctor's orders. Jack just flew down here for a couple of days of sun, between stops. Is this woman *crazy?*"

There was no quick or easy answer to that question. "She's impulsive," I replied.

"Impulsive, my ass! Jack should know how to control his women. I told him so, in no uncertain terms."

It did not seem the right moment to remind Joe Kennedy that Gloria Swanson had led *him* around like a bull with a ring in his nose. Like most people, he was a lot tougher with other people's emotional problems than he was with his own.

"Well," I said, "Jack is probably the only one who can defuse the problem. He's the one Marilyn wants to see, after all."

"No. She wants to see me, too, apparently. You'd better get over here right away. We've got a full-scale crisis on our hands."

I thought so too. I made my apologies to Maria, who was dressing for lunch with her friends, at the Everglades Club, and told her I wouldn't be going with her.

"Really, David!" she said. "If one didn't know better, one would think you had a mistress."

"It was Joe Kennedy," I explained. "With a problem."

"Of course it was, darling. The D'Souzas will be heartbroken to miss you, but never mind. Be an angel and fasten these hooks for me before you go."

I stood behind her and fastened the tiny hooks and eyes that can only be found on the handiwork of major French couturiers, of whom Maria was a favorite *cliente,* because of both her money and her figure. D'Souza was a Brazilian millionaire whose hobbies were women and polo. I was not sorry to be missing his lunch. It was more Maria's kind of thing than mine.

"Is Jack here?" she asked.

I nodded.

"Tell him not to be a stranger," she said as I finished closing the last fastener. "Somebody told me he's carrying on with Marilyn Monroe? Is it true?"

"Not to my knowledge."

"It's a good thing you *don't* have a mistress, David darling. You're a rotten liar."

I found the Ambassador just where I had expected to—in his "bullpen," a fenced-off sunbathing area in which he could sit nude, wearing only a straw hat to shade his face, while he read the papers and made his calls. Joe Kennedy had a horror of pale, untanned skin, as well as something of a fetish for physical fitness, and was a firm believer in nude sunbathing as a way of warding off all sorts of ills. Nobody was allowed to intrude on his privacy, not even his own children, but he always tried to persuade young women—friends of his girls or his boys—to visit him in his hideaway by the pool, and over the years, many did. The number of upper-class young women whose early sexual experience included slathering suntan lotion on the naked body of Ambassador Joseph P. Kennedy was unknown but significant, and his boys often joked about it, albeit with a certain degree of envy.

To my dismay, Joe, Jack, and Marilyn were in animated conversation by the pool. Joe, to my relief, had his swimming trunks on. Jack, looking thin and tired, was dressed in a pair of white duck trousers and a blue tennis shirt. Marilyn was wearing a white, bare-shouldered sundress, with a scarf over her hair and dark glasses—her usual disguise. The three of them were laughing uproariously. Joe had obviously calmed down.

"Hello, David," Marilyn said cheerfully as I kissed her cheek and took a seat. "I've never seen you without a suit before. You look nice in sports clothes."

Joe was putting himself out to be charming, as he always did with beautiful women. I had interrupted him in the telling of a story about his own days as the owner of a movie studio, with which he had succeeded in reducing Marilyn to giggles. For his part, the Ambassador could hardly take his eyes off her breasts, a good part of them revealed by the low scoop neck of her dress.

"I've been telling Marilyn about the old days, David," he said.

"Oh, it's been *such* fun, Ambassador!" Marilyn cried in her most bubbly, breathless voice—the voice of Sugar Kane in *Some Like It Hot.*

"Joe, please," he corrected her, leaning forward to pat her knee.

"*Joe,*" she said with another giggle. Jack, I noticed, looked relaxed —not at all like a man who might be on the verge of kissing the Democratic nomination good-bye because of a sex scandal with a married movie star. He had one arm resting lightly over Marilyn's shoulders, his fingers just touching the bare skin of one breast, in a manner that could only be described as proprietary. I guessed that whatever he had intended to tell her when he went to The Breakers, she had changed his mind pretty rapidly. Any thought of putting Marilyn on the next flight back to New York—or safer yet, shuttling her aboard the *Caroline*—had clearly been forgotten, even by Joe, whose sense of political reality was as strong as anyone's.

"Have we solved our public relations problem?" I inquired, a little put out.

"Jack got Marilyn out of the hotel with no trouble," Joe said.

"Nobody there seems to have recognized her. You might have a word with the owner, David, but they're pretty discreet over there."

Nobody would know that better than Joe, I thought. He must have had countless opportunities over the years to test the discretion of The Breakers.

"I'm just staying another day," Marilyn said. "Jack is giving me a lift back to New York on the family plane." She giggled again. "It's so nice to be with a family with its own plane." I noticed that the Ambassador's inflexible rule about not serving alcohol before sundown did not apply to Marilyn. There was a bottle of champagne in a cooler beside her, and she had a glass in her hand. I got up and poured myself a glass—Dom Pérignon, I observed; the Ambassador wasn't stinting his famous guest.

"I'll deal with The Breakers," I said to Jack. "My advice is stay clear of the pool area and the restaurants. That's where the journalists are. Put out an announcement that you have a cold and you're resting up. Once they've been told nothing's going to happen, they'll relax and go to the beach. They must have been just as cold as you were, up there in Wisconsin and West Virginia, so they'll all be glad to take a break in the sun."

Jack gave me the kind of look that means, *Why the hell aren't you working for me, since you're so smart?* and went off to give the necessary orders. I knew perfectly well that the entire press corps attached to him would shortly be stretched out on the beach or at poolside, tropical rum drinks in their hands, and that the chances of Jack and Marilyn being observed, provided she kept her hair covered, would be minimal.

Joe was preening himself under Marilyn's admiring stare. Of course, she had a knack for flirting with older men, I recalled, remembering Joe Schenck.

"I'm glad to see you looking well," I said to her. "Last time we met, you were way down in the dumps."

"Don't I know it, David honey."

"It's Jack who's cheered her up," his father said proudly. "Isn't it, dear?"

"Mm." Marilyn nodded. I couldn't see her eyes behind the dark glasses, but I would have been willing to bet that her pupils were dilated. Jack may have cheered her up, but I guessed that she'd been popping pills—uppers, I presumed—all the way from New York.

As if to confirm this, she opened her purse, took out a gaily striped capsule—there seemed to be a quantity of them rolling around loose at the bottom of the purse—and swallowed it with a gulp of champagne. "It's for my hay fever," she explained cheerfully, giving me a wink.

"I expect it's all these goddamn flowers," Joe said indulgently. The Kennedy pool, while not grand by Hollywood standards, was surrounded by flowering shrubs, which grew a little out of control, since the Ambassador disliked the presence of gardeners when he was sitting by his pool.

"I've never been in Florida before," she said.

"You ought to come here more often." Joe gave her one of his most ferocious smiles.

"I'd love to, every once in a while."

Joe laughed. "You see, David, I'm getting old. A few years ago, she'd have said she'd love to be here every day!" He put his hand on her knee again and simply left it there, the blunt fingers, deeply tanned by the sun, dimpling her pale, soft flesh. For some reason, I found the sight nauseating, but Marilyn didn't seem to mind—or to notice. She was floating on some sparkling high, induced partly by chemicals, I had no doubt, but also by the sense of sheer adventure. She had managed to leave LA (and her husband) and get to Palm Beach on the spur of the moment.

It was as if she was playing girlish pranks in the middle of a presidential campaign, which seemed to be dangerous behavior from Jack's point of view. But Jack loved this kind of game: secret meetings, middle-of-the-night romantic assignations, always appealed to him.

Jack returned from his task looking relaxed. "No sweat," he said. "I have a cold, officially. The ladies and gentlemen of the press are on their way back to their hotels for a little well-earned R and R. Thanks, David. You've done it again. Let's go, Marilyn."

She pouted prettily—an expression that nobody ever did better or more alluringly. "I was just beginning to have fun," she said, winking at the Ambassador.

Whatever happened, I thought, she was going to have an ally in the Kennedy family from now on—perhaps still the most important one. "You don't waste a day like this on an old man," he said with mock gallantry.

Marilyn rose to her feet—very unsteadily—bent over, and kissed him on the forehead. "I never knew my father. I'm going to think of you as my father from now on," she said sweetly.

"Come again," he said. "And take care of Jack. He needs to rest and put some flesh on his bones."

This was a familiar message. When Jack was campaigning, he

often forgot to eat, and the Ambassador had charged several of the veteran members of his son's staff—Dave Powers, Joe Gargan, and Boom-Boom Reardon, specifically—with making sure he was fed, a practice going all the way back to Jack's first congressional campaign.

Marilyn put her arms around Jack protectively, teetering slightly on her high heels. "He's in good hands," she said with a giggle, in case he missed the double entendre.

"Yes," the Ambassador said, grinning. "I can *see* that."

Marilyn came over and kissed me good-bye, blushing slightly, I was pleased to notice.

When they had left, the Ambassador and I sat silently for a few moments, while I lit a cigar.

"Jack's a lucky boy," he said at last.

"No argument. He's playing with fire, though."

"Yes."

"You're not worried anymore?"

"Of course I am. I was worried when he joined the Navy and volunteered for the goddamn PT boats, but I didn't stop him, did I? He needs to take risks, and that's all there is to it. Anyway, you came up with the solution, as usual, David, so let him have his fun."

"At the risk of losing the presidency?"

"Oh, cut the crap, David! If Jack loses—and he's not going to—it won't be because he spent an afternoon fucking Marilyn Monroe, lucky fellow. It'll be because Nixon is stronger and smarter than I personally think he is." He leaned forward, smiling—always a dangerous sign. "You know what your trouble is?" he asked.

"I know you're going to tell me."

"Don't play the smart-ass with me, David. We've known each other too long. Your trouble is, you want to fuck her, don't you? I could see it on your face a mile away—from the way you look at her."

"Well, it's not an uncommon desire. Maybe one hundred million other American men share it."

"Yeah, but the difference is, there's something *between* you and Marilyn. I can tell that from the way she looks at you, David. It's the kind of look that women give men who almost fucked them but didn't. Is that what happened?"

"Nothing happened, Joe," I said uncomfortably. "Marilyn and I are friends, that's all."

"Bullshit, David!" He lay back and closed his eyes, the sun full on his face. "You're a fool," he said in a tone that was strangely kind. "You *should* have fucked her, David, if you had the chance. There's more problems caused by *not* fucking a woman you want to fuck than by fucking one, in my experience.... Jack wouldn't have minded. She'd respect you more. You'd feel better about yourself. And you wouldn't be holding any bitter feelings toward Jack."

"I don't have any bitter feelings toward Jack. You're wrong about that."

He did not open his eyes. "No I'm not," he said quietly. "But I know you won't do anything about them, so I'm not worried." He paused. "All the same, keep it in mind. We're old friends, so I can tell you this frankly: Don't ever do anything to hurt Jack just because he fucked Marilyn and you didn't. That wouldn't be fair to him, David."

"I promise you I won't."

He held out his hand to mine and we shook. His was covered in suntan lotion, and I had to wipe mine on a cocktail napkin. "That's good enough for me," he said. "Are you going to work for Jack once he's elected?" he asked after a long silence.

"I haven't given it a lot of thought."

He gave me a hard look. "Don't bullshit me, David," he said.

I was never able to hide anything from Joe—not many people could. Besides, he was clearly sounding me out. "An ambassadorship would be nice," I said casually.

He snorted. "You'll be sorry," he said. "It costs a fortune to do it in style. I should know. The goddamn government doesn't pay for anything—you have to pick up the tab for a pisspotful of freeloaders.... The job is all responsibility and no power. The president and the State Department call the shots. Which one do you want?"

"The Court of St. James's."

Joe's expression was inscrutable. "That's the big one," he agreed casually. "That, and Paris maybe. And of course, Moscow now, but Moscow is usually for professional diplomats.... Anyway, who wants to spend two or three years in Moscow?"

"Not me."

"There you are."

I wondered if that had been an attempt on Joe's part to see if I would accept a lesser embassy, and wondered too if it had been smart to let him know what I wanted. Sooner or later, I told myself, I had to make a move, and telling Joe was the same as telling Jack. Besides, Joe's feelings would have been bitterly hurt had I asked Jack for his old job without telling him first. No, I had done the right thing, I decided, and left it at that.

We sat companionably for a few minutes, the Ambassador taking the sun, I sheltered by my Panama hat.

"She phoned him here, you know," he said, breaking the silence.

"Marilyn? She called *here*?"

"How do you suppose she got the number?"

I thought about it. The Kennedy family's telephone numbers were not only unlisted and secret, for obvious reasons, but changed regularly. Nobody knew better than Joe how much trouble a telephone call could cause, particularly from a woman to a man's home. "I'd have to conclude that either she found it on Jack's desk or he gave it to her. Nobody else would."

"Mm." He opened one bright ice-blue eye and stared at me. "Do Marilyn and Jack talk a lot? Phone calls, I mean."

"A good bit. More from her. She's a compulsive late-night caller. When she can't sleep, she makes calls. Some of them to Jack, I guess."

He thought this over. "I'd hate to think that her phones might be tapped."

"The idea has occurred to me, but Jack isn't worried."

Joe looked thoughtful. "I was halfway tempted to get Hoover to have his boys check out her lines, just to make sure they're clear, but then I said to myself, why give the old bastard a piece of knowledge he doesn't have?"

"What makes you so sure he doesn't have it?"

He laughed. "You could be right. What the hell, even if he does, what's he going to do with it? Jack's girls, for Christ's sake! If the FBI's keeping a file on all of them, we should buy shares in the company that sells them filing cabinets!"

He looked at his watch and rolled over onto his stomach—his schedule for tanning was as precisely regulated as everything else in his life. "You'll stay for lunch?"

I said I would.

"You might have a word with Marilyn, though, since the two of you are such pals. Just to tell her careless lips sink ships, okay? And we'll keep Hoover out of it, shall we?"

"With pleasure," I said. The last thing we wanted was Hoover involved in Jack's love life.

"This is a big honor for you, Agent Kirkpatrick," Tolson said, showing him down the stairs. "Something to tell your children."

Kirkpatrick had no children, but decided not to correct Tolson—it *was* a great honor, undoubtedly, to be invited to the Director's home, though a bit of a disappointment, for he had expected something grander than this small, shabby house, decorated with framed photographs of J. Edgar Hoover with celebrities of every world from sports to politics.

He wondered why he was being escorted to the basement, but the mystery was cleared up when Tolson opened the door at the bottom of the stairs and ushered him into a small, dimly lit den or game room, with a small stand-up bar and four barstools at one end of the room, and a fake fireplace with a gas log at the facing end. The furniture was heavy and almost aggressively masculine: a couple of chairs made out of wine barrels, a big leather couch, a coffee table with a top taken from a green-baize gaming table.

The walls were what caught Kirkpatrick's eye, as they were surely meant to: from floor to ceiling they were covered with "cheesecake" photographs and drawings taken from magazines like *Esquire* and *Playboy*—Vargas girls, Petty girls, and Playmates of the Month exposing their breasts and buttocks or raising improbably perfect legs, ending in spike-heeled "Fuck me!" pumps, as far as the eye could see. Somebody had carefully cut them out by the hundreds, pasted them to the walls, then varnished over them.

More astounding to Kirkpatrick than the mural was the sight of the Director, standing behind the bar, while a mirror in back of him depicted a generously proportioned female nude doing something unmentionable with a swan. To one side of him was what appeared to Kirkpatrick to be the world's biggest collection of sheriff's badges, to the other a wooden board carved in folk art style with the message "Hogtown Drinking & Pistol Club—Drink all night, piss 'til dawn!" Glasses, mugs, and tankards hung in rows above Hoover's head. It was what Kirkpatrick had always imagined the bar at an Elks Club lodge might look like, though as a middle-class Catholic from Danbury, Connecticut, who had come to the FBI via Fordham Law School, he had never been in one.

"Welcome," Hoover said ponderously.

Kirkpatrick sat at the bar, uneasy in these strange domestic surroundings. There was a lever for drawing draft beer in front of him, the handle of which was a girl's legs, and coasters with *Playboy* cartoons on the polished mahogany surface of the bar. "What's your pleasure?" Hoover asked, trying hard for an expression of geniality without altogether succeeding.

Kirkpatrick was not a drinking man. "Scotch and water?" It seemed like the simplest thing to ask for here. Hoover made the drink, then busied himself mixing two elaborate drinks for himself and Tolson, slicing fruit and sticking maraschino cherries on plastic toothpicks with surprising dexterity.

Immediately above Kirkpatrick's head was a row of boxing gloves, each signed by a World's Champion Heavyweight. Softly in the background he could hear Frank Sinatra singing. It struck him as mildly ironic that the Director enjoyed Sinatra records—Kirkpatrick had been tapping the singer's telephone lines for years at Hoover's orders, as well as Phyllis McGuire's, Peter Lawford's, and those of a whole host of other show business celebrities whose private life, politics, or organized crime connections were of interest to the FBI.

Kirkpatrick had made himself, more or less by accident, the Bureau's "show biz" expert, and even read the "trades" daily to check on the whereabouts and career moves of his targets. He had been astonished to find out how many famous names in Hollywood were under surveillance for one reason or another, and even more astonished at the number of equally famous people who had been active FBI informants for years, including well-known stars like Ronald Reagan and John Wayne, large numbers of studio executives, and producers such as Cecil B. DeMille. Agents informed on their clients, stars on their costars (and often on their spouses or ex-spouses), studio bosses on their employees, and writers on everyone.

It wasn't Kirkpatrick's idea of law enforcement, or what he had dreamed of when he joined the Bureau. He would have given a lot to get a crack at making an arrest with a tommy gun in his hands, but in the meantime, his career was soaring, so he wasn't about to complain.

"Do you follow politics?" Hoover asked.

Kirkpatrick wondered if this was a trick question.

"Keep up with *The Washington Post, The New York Times,* that sort of thing?" Tolson chimed in, before he could reply. As it happened, in his present assignment, Kirkpatrick was more likely to read the *Hollywood Reporter* or *Variety,* but he nodded cautiously— within the FBI, the *Post* and the *Times* were viewed as not very different from *Pravda.*

"Good!" Hoover said. "It's important to keep well informed."

"And to know how to read between the lines," Tolson added. "You have to separate hard news from Commie propaganda."

Hoover nodded. "Indeed. Words of wisdom, Mr. Tolson." He turned to Kirkpatrick. "Since you follow these things, it won't have escaped your attention that Senator Kennedy is the Democratic front-runner?"

"No, sir."

"It's unfortunate," Hoover said darkly, "that a brash young man of low moral habits like Senator Kennedy may end up as our president. . . . It's almost enough to make one lose faith in the democratic process."

"You think he'll win the nomination, sir?"

"No question about it," the Director said. "Kennedy will win, you mark my words. Poor Humphrey is just the kind of namby-pamby liberal do-gooder—if not an outright Marxist—who was bound to lose against Kennedy. Symington didn't put up a fight. Johnson seems to be under the mistaken impression that presidents are elected by a Senate vote." He sighed.

"And the election, sir?"

"Ah," Hoover said. "That's another story. Vice President Nixon is a bare-knuckle fighter, a formidable opponent. Of course, Nixon has his own problems, doesn't he, Mr. Tolson?"

Tolson smirked. "He certainly *does*, Director."

"To be sure, not the same *kind* of problems as Senator Kennedy's, Agent Kirkpatrick, you understand."

Kirkpatrick nodded. He hadn't thought it likely there were any sex scandals in the Director's files on the Vice President. Nixon didn't look the type, though that could be deceptive, as he well knew. . . .

Still, the thing that interested him most was that the Director was as knowledgeable about Nixon, whom Hoover liked, as he was about Kennedy, whom he *disliked*. Clearly, Nixon's phones were tapped and his home and hotel rooms routinely bugged, just like Kennedy's. He wondered whether the Bureau's microphones and wires extended into the Oval Office itself.

"Young Kennedy's success poses a dilemma for us, Kirkpatrick," Hoover went on. "Confidentially"—he glanced around the room with dark, furtive eyes—"there has been great pressure on me to make available some of the, ah, *fruits* of your labors. Senator Johnson is anxious to know whether we have compromising tapes on Senator Kennedy, and if so, what's on them. Vice President Nixon is even more anxious to know. I have to keep the best interests of the country in mind, of course. In the short run, there might be advantages to be gained from letting Nixon or Johnson hear certain sections of the tapes, even though I'm against involving the Bureau in politics. . . ." Hoover's expression was that of a martyr to patriotic duty. "But I must ask myself," he went on, "what happens if Senator Kennedy *wins* the election?"

He gave Kirkpatrick a steely glare—a warning, Kirkpatrick took it, that he was about to be initiated into the Director's darkest secrets.

"*If* Kennedy wins," Hoover went on, "your tapes will be the best way of keeping the President in line. The only way perhaps. It will be my responsibility to control the worst excesses—and impulses—of the President."

The Director's gaze focused in the middle distance, at some point beyond Kirkpatrick's Adam's apple. "One might even say that the very future and well-being of our nation may rest on these tapes, eh, Mr. Tolson?"

"And in your hands, Director."

Hoover inclined his head modestly. "So you see, Mr. Kirkpatrick, we must expand our efforts in the interests of national security. And tighten our own secrecy."

"We're already covering the Senator pretty well, sir."

"Cover his brother, Kirkpatrick. Cover Miss Monroe. She may be talking to her friends about Kennedy. He may be telling her things we should know. Spare no effort, no expense."

Kirkpatrick was enough of a bureaucrat to realize that he was being given a blank check to expand his turf. "I could use some more men," he said tentatively.

"You shall have them. Give Mr. Tolson your needs."

"And a field office of my own in LA. It isn't secure enough, working out of the Bureau field office."

"Very well."

"And better equipment. Bernie Spindel has more up-to-date stuff than we do."

Hoover frowned. "I don't want to hear that man's name again. He was disloyal to me. I can't forgive that, Kirkpatrick—not for my own sake but for the Bureau's."

"I understand, sir."

"However, you shall have what you need. Draw up a list. We'll get it from the CIA or the military, if we have to."

"Thank you, sir."

"Continue to report to myself or Mr. Tolson personally. You'll be given a cover story—put on some kind of top-secret investigation, of organized crime perhaps. You'll take care of the details, Mr. Tolson?"

"You can rely on me, Director."

Hoover smiled, displaying teeth that were so small, even, and perfect that Kirkpatrick concluded they must be false. "I know I can," he snapped.

"What happens if Senator Kennedy *doesn't* win, sir?"

"Why, then we'll just play the Nixon card," Hoover whispered.

28

She hated Nevada from the day she arrived.

She had been in Vegas once or twice, of course, as Frank's guest, but Reno, where she was now, had none of Las Vegas's phony, electric glamour. Reno was basically just a small town, so she could never escape from the rest of the crew—or from her husband. All the exteriors were going to be shot on the ragged, sandy wasteland around Reno—an arid, dusty, Martian landscape, so hot she felt her brains were frying, with nothing to look at but stunted shrubs, the occasional ghost town, and the low, lumpy mountains on the horizon, which seemed to grow farther away as you drove toward them on the ruler-straight roads. It was a dead landscape, and all it reminded her of was death.

Everything conspired to depress her. Monty Clift, her old friend whom she had counted on for support, was in as bad a way as she was, apparently, and spent most of his time locked in his hotel suite with his own little entourage, while Eli Wallach, as a big-time New York actor, gravitated rather ostentatiously toward Arthur, sucking up to him, she thought, for a bigger role and better lines for himself.

Monty *could* have cheered her up if anybody could. He was witty, bitchy, unexpectedly kind, and his troubles were as bad as hers, or almost, which gave the two of them a very special kind of friendship —strong enough even to survive the fact that he was also "best friends" with Liz Taylor.

She saw him briefly in the lobby the first day, and hid her feelings at the sight of his ruined face, as she always had to do. It was painful to remember how beautiful he had been before the drunken car accident that gave him a permanent scowl. It made her nervous to look at him, since it reminded her of just how fragile beauty was, and how easy it was to lose it in a fraction of a second. There were those who believed that the accident had made Monty a better actor, but she didn't buy it, not for a moment. So far as she could tell, it had merely made him more difficult, more morose, more introspective than ever. It was as if he now wanted to hide from the world, trusting nobody but his makeup man and longtime lover.

He took her to a dark corner of the bar. His eyes seemed to stare at her angrily, but she knew it was just a result of his unfinished plastic surgery, which had made the whites of his eyes look much too large and paralyzed the left side of his face. He dabbed at his broken nose with a bandanna handkerchief—the accident had also left him with a permanent sinus condition, accompanied by massive headaches.

"You're looking good," he said. "Is it the Frenchman?"

She shook her head. "That's over. It was fun while it lasted, but he's going back to Simone." Her voice turned husky. Monty preferred to keep things bright and smart and heartless—with problems like his, he liked to say, the last thing he wanted around him was self-pity—so she fought back her tears, but of course, he noticed.

"I'm sorry," she said. "I'm still down in the dumps over him, I guess."

"I know the feeling, honey. Welcome to the club. I was once in love with a Frenchman myself. . . . This place ain't gonna help a *bit*, by the way. It's the dumps. 'The Misfits, Dumps, Nevada'—that ought to be our mailing address." He laughed, an uncertain quavering laugh. "Oh, *fuck* it, Marilyn honey," he said quietly. "Happy endings are only for the goddamn movies."

"I guess."

"Oh, bullshit, Marilyn. You and I are both such suckers for happy endings." He took her hand and squeezed it in his thin, dry fingers with a kind of desperation. "My Frenchman went back to his wife too, by the way."

Monty released her hand and lit a cigarette with trembling fingers, keeping the match lit until it must have started to burn them. The accident, she knew, had left him with odd areas in which the nerves were insensitive. He was always scalding himself in the shower, or burning his lips trying to drink coffee that was too hot. He winced, and dropped the match onto the floor, grinding it out on the carpet under his heel. "Anyway, you're looking good, honey, which is more than I can say of myself. . . . No, don't contradict me, I *know* what I look like. . . . Since I assume it isn't the marriage that's making your skin bloom, does that mean that things are looking up with the Senator?"

She put her finger to her lips. "Shh!" she whispered, giggling. "I don't know what you're talking about, baby."

"This is Uncle Monty you're talking to, honey. It's the worst-kept secret in town. Even your husband must know by now."

"He does *not!* Anyway, there's nothing to know."

"God, you look pretty when you lie. Marilyn, people *know.*"

"They only *think* they know."

Clift shrugged, giving her a crooked, enigmatic smile. "If you say so, honey. . . . Oh, Marilyn. You and I—Christ, we're alike. Born without armor, you know? The Kennedys, sweetheart, they're born in full armor, you can't reach *their* soft parts."

She giggled again. "I sure reached Jack's."

Despite himself, Monty laughed. She could see a ghost of his former self beneath the ruins of that angelic beauty.

He closed his eyes for a moment, his whole body trembling now, as if the effort of laughter were too much for him. He tried to light another cigarette and dropped it, his fingers twitching as if he were spastic. She picked it up and lit it for him.

"Don't *do* that!" he snapped sharply, his face contorted in what seemed for a moment like genuine rage, but he allowed her to put the cigarette to his lips anyway. He held it precariously between his thumb and forefinger in the European style, as she had come to recognize from watching Yves, though in Monty's case it was because he was afraid of dropping it and setting his pants on fire. "Oh Christ, Marilyn, I'm a fucking *mess,* aren't I?"

Watching him was like seeing her own worst fears about herself. "You're going to be okay, Monty," she said, but she didn't believe it for a second.

"The hell I am," he said. He leaned close to her. "You know what? Before I signed up for this goddamn picture, I went to the doctor. I'd been having dizzy spells, fuzzy vision, memory loss. . . . It turns out that I've got cataracts and thyroid deficiency. It's like being an old man, dear, and I'm only thirty-nine! The one thing I can't do is drink, and of course, it's the one thing I can't stop doing."

He sat for a moment without speaking, as if telling her about his condition had exhausted him. She felt an irrational fear that his condition might be catching, that it might destroy the picture, or worse yet, *her*.

"Don't, for Christ's sake, tell anyone, pussy," he whispered. "That sadistic motherfucker Huston doesn't know what kind of shape I'm in, or the studio would never have agreed to let him give me the part."

"I promise."

The truth was that Huston knew the whole story, as Arthur had told her, and had concealed it from the studio so that he could have Monty for the part of Perce Howland. He had also concealed Gable's heart condition and downplayed *her* problems.

Huston was a gambler, never happy unless the odds were against him and he was walking on the brink, and *The Misfits* was his biggest gamble so far. Still, she wasn't about to destroy Monty's illusion that he had put one over on Huston.

"Are you taking anything?" she asked.

He laughed, a harsh, croaking laughter. "Just the usual, pussy. Nembutal. Doriden. Luminal. Seconal. Phenobarbs. Vitamins. Calcium. And booze."

"Gosh!"

"Don't give *me* that innocent shit. I know what *you* take." He gave her a leer, in which she managed to read such a wealth of shared pain that she put her head close to his and kissed him softly, feeling the lifeless scar tissue against her lips. "How's the insomnia?" he asked her.

"The same as yours, I guess."

"Ain't life a bitch?"

"You must have brought quite a supply out with you?" she said, trying to make it sound casual.

"Do I take it that you're running low?"

She nodded. "The doctor I had in New York was getting to be a real pain in the ass about prescriptions, you know? So I went to another doctor, only he didn't like making the prescriptions refillable, so I had to go back and see him every time I ran out—"

"Stop, Marilyn, *please!* I know the song, every last fucking word of the lyrics. What *are* you taking, just out of curiosity?"

"About the same as you, I guess, except for booze. Uppers for the day, downers at night. Benzedrine and Nembutal, mostly."

"Do they help?"

"Life's pretty terrible with them, but I don't want to think about how it would be without them."

"What do you take at night?" he asked, as if they were a couple of cooks comparing recipes.

"Four or five Nembutals. I break them open and lick the powder right out of my hand. It's quicker that way, you know?"

He lifted one scarred eyebrow, impressed. "Does it work?"

"Sometimes. A massage helps." She was lying, of course. She had a masseur who worked on her from midnight to two in the morning, but even so, her drowsy and drugged state seldom led her into real sleep until dawn, if at all. She had slept the night through, at first, in Yves's arms, and on the rare occasions when she and Jack spent the night together, she slept like a baby, once or twice even without the help of pills. "Mostly it's shitty," she admitted quietly.

"Amen. I make long-distance telephone calls, myself. Hell, if I can't sleep, why should my friends? How are you fixed for Nembutals?"

"Okay for a while. They work better with chloral hydrate, but I couldn't get any of my doctors in New York to prescribe it."

He gave a grim smile. With trembling fingers he removed a pen from the pocket of his stained and creased linen jacket and wrote a name and telephone number on a cocktail napkin. "He's a local doctor," he said, putting the pen back in his pocket with difficulty. He had failed to retract the point, which left a bright blue ink stain on his coat. "Tell him I sent you. He's a celebrity-fucker. Play him the right way and he'll write you out a prescription for anything you want."

"Thank you," she said.

"Don't thank me, dear. It's nothing to be thankful for."

He sighed, and stood up unsteadily. One of his entourage, who had been waiting just out of hearing in the shadows of the dimly lit cocktail lounge, came forward and took him by the arm. "Beddy-bye time, Monty," he said. "Time for your nap."

Monty nodded wearily, the light going out of his eyes as if someone had turned it off. "You see how it is," he said.

She saw.

29

Historians write as if Jack's nomination was a sure thing, but he didn't treat it as such, and he was right. His primary victories had given him the votes, but he knew, as we all did, that if he didn't win on the first ballot, erosion would set in and the tide might turn toward Symington or Johnson, either one of whom would have been more palatable to the old guard of the Democratic party.

Jack sent a small family army out to Los Angeles ahead of him—his father, who rented the estate of his old friend Marion Davies, Hearst's mistress; Bobby, who was at the Biltmore, along with Jack's staff; brother Teddy, who had been thrown into the fray with the responsibility of keeping the western states in line; and most of his sisters, who were spread around town. I had flown out earlier, at the Ambassador's request, to help prevent Governor Brown from backsliding. The only person missing was Jackie, whose delicate pregnancy required her to stay put at Hyannis Port, or so the story went.

Jack had sent Dave Powers out a week before everybody else with instructions to find him a secret "hideaway" in Los Angeles. On my advice, Dave rented a furnished, three-room penthouse apartment in a building owned by Jack Haley, the comedian—close to the Los Angeles Sports Arena, where the convention was being held—with a hidden entrance and a private elevator. Dave also managed to obtain a model home on display at the Sports Arena as the Kennedy "communications center"—which presented Jack with a secluded, fully furnished private hideaway at the Arena as well.

That, and the fact that he had left Jackie at home, seemed to me enough to make Jack happy, but when he arrived, he was in a foul mood, the black Irish temper having overwhelmed the Irish charm.

It was Lyndon Johnson who was responsible for Jack's anger. Johnson, it emerged, had been spreading rumors about Jack—that he was suffering from Addison's disease and wouldn't survive a term in office, that he planned to make Bobby secretary of labor (a rumor certain to cause panic among labor leaders), and, most damaging of all, that there were secrets in Jack's private life that would prevent him from being elected. Adding to Jack's anger was the fact that he had heard about all this from friendly reporters rather than from his staff.

I happened to enter his suite at the Biltmore just as he was winding up a stinging criticism of his staff, who were standing around the seated candidate with hangdog expressions, even Bobby and young Teddy, who was getting his first direct exposure to the Kennedy family business.

"You heard about what's happening?" Jack asked me. He was sitting bolt upright, an extra pillow behind his back—a sure sign that he was in pain, as was often the case after a long plane trip. All the same, he looked healthy and relaxed, in sharp contrast to Bobby, who was so thin, drawn, and exhausted that he looked every bit as terminal as Johnson claimed Jack was.

Jack sent Teddy off to work the delegates, and dismissed everybody except Bobby and me. He grimaced, then gestured for us both to sit down. "I've never liked Lyndon, and I know damned well he doesn't like *me*, but I didn't realize he *hated* me."

The relationship between the two men had always been prickly. Johnson patronized Jack, while Jack thought Johnson was a hick and a liar.

"He's an ungrateful, two-faced son of a bitch," Bobby snarled. "He told reporters you were 'just a scrawny little fellow with rickets.' He called Dad 'the man who held Chamberlain's umbrella'!"

Jack stared gloomily into space. "Yes," he said. "I heard. Actually that's a pretty good line, the one about Dad. Lyndon's got some smart people writing his stuff for him. He wouldn't have come up with that one himself. What do you think we should do, David?"

"None of it is going to hurt you much. I'd say Lyndon is just blowing smoke. . . . Except for the stuff about secrets in your private life. I don't like the sound of that."

"What does Lyndon know that everybody in the press doesn't?" Jack asked. "Anyway, he's not going to tell the world about my private life, is he?"

"We can nail *him*," Bobby said. "Dad helped him out of a financial crisis a couple of years ago. He knows stuff about Lyndon's business affairs nobody else does, even in Texas."

I glanced at Jack and shook my head. What Bobby said was true enough, but what he left out was that this help had been Johnson's payoff for giving Jack a coveted seat on the Senate Foreign Relations Committee, which had served as a perfect platform for moving him away from the narrow field of labor relations into the broader, more "presidential" uplands of foreign policy. "I think you might lose more than you'd gain," I warned.

Bobby glared at me. He was dying to be let loose at Johnson. He believed in punching back as fast and as hard as he could, never forgetting or forgiving an insult. So did Jack, as a matter of fact, but he concealed it with cool wit, and liked the world to imagine he was holding Bobby back.

"We can let the world know about Lyndon's love life," Bobby said. "I know for a fact that he's been fucking one of his secretaries for years. He's so cheap he doesn't even rent a hotel room. They do it on his desk in the Senate."

Jack smiled. "You know the first thing Lyndon said to me when I took my seat in the Senate? He said, 'I hear you're a man who likes pussy too.'" He laughed, while Bobby continued to scowl. "I can't see we'd gain anything by passing the word around that Lyndon likes pussy. He'd probably pick up a few votes, that's all. Why are you looking so glum, David?"

"I'm just wondering if somebody out there could be feeding Johnson information. Something more specific."

"Like what?"

"Well, you and Marilyn, for example."

"Who would do that?"

"The FBI? Hoffa?"

"You've got Marilyn on the brain, David, I've told you that before."

"Hoover would never do that," Bobby said. "And Lyndon wouldn't have the guts to get involved with Hoffa."

"I don't trust Hoover," I said to Jack. "And I don't trust Johnson either. I think you should be careful."

"Careful about what?"

"About being seen with Marilyn."

"Don't worry about it, David. I'm here to work, not to play," Jack said, but I noticed a gleam in his eye.

"So we let Lyndon get away with it?" Bobby asked.

Jack looked thoughtful. "Any ideas, David?"

"Spread the rumor that he hasn't recovered from his heart attack yet," I suggested. "It will make him mad as hell, but it's not too far below the belt. And Lyndon's no fool. He'll take it as a warning that if he doesn't knock it off, you'll follow it up with really bad stuff. All you have to do is show him you're ready to fight back. He's a coward and a bully. He'll back off."

"Sounds like good advice to me," Jack said, visibly relaxing. He turned to Bobby. "Do it," he ordered. "Not yourself. Get somebody else to do it, somebody who isn't connected to us."

He was learning fast, I told myself. So was Bobby. He nodded, and went off without a word of protest, and by the end of the day the rumor about Johnson's heart condition was all over town. That evening Jack even called Lyndon to commiserate with him and say how shocked he was to hear about such an irresponsible rumor. Lyndon got the message, of course, and no more was heard about Jack's secret love life, or his ill health.

All the same, I was nervous, and a call from Marilyn to my Sunset Boulevard office the next morning made me even more so. She had talked her way out of Reno, it appeared, so as not to miss the convention.

"I'm so excited," she said. She was bubbling with nervous energy —just on the edge of hysteria, I thought. "Did you hear that Lyndon Johnson had a heart attack?"

"I don't think so. . . ."

"It's all over town. Good, is what I say! He's a big, ugly, mean-minded, white-trash Texan, and I hate that kind of man."

Of course, she was right about Johnson. He was just about the most mean-spirited man I ever met in politics, and I've met quite a few, and his hatred of Jack was pure envy.

"How's *The Misfits* going?" I asked.

"Awful. Maybe I can do the picture and get divorced at the same time." She laughed uneasily. Reno's reputation as a divorce mill was such that most people only went there for that purpose—ironically, Roslyn, the character she was playing in *The Misfits,* was waiting out her divorce in Reno.

"Are things that bad, Marilyn?"

"Oh, honey. Don't ask."

"Jack's here," I said. "He arrived yesterday."

She giggled. "I know." Her voice dropped to a conspiratorial level. "Listen, honey," she said. "That's one of the reasons I called. I'm supposed to be at Jack's this morning—he called me last night—and I lost the address."

"He's at the Biltmore. Suite nine-three-three-three."

"Not that," she said irritably. "The *other* place."

"The one on North Rossmore? Jack Haley's place?"

"Right!"

"Five twenty-two is the number," I said. "The apartment right above William Gargan—"

"The guy who plays the detective on TV? Thanks a million, lover," she cried. "I've gotta run."

As it happened, I had an appointment with Jack for that afternoon, to report on my luncheon meeting with Sinatra and Lawford, who were orchestrating the appearance of the "Stars for Kennedy" both at the convention and, hopefully, at the Los Angeles Coliseum for his acceptance speech—a meeting at which the question of whether Marilyn was "under control" was raised several times.

When I turned up at the hideaway on North Rossmore Avenue, Jack himself opened the door for me, wearing a dressing gown. He was grinning, but the grin had a sharp edge to it. "If I'm elected," he said, "I'm going to nominate you for CIA director."

I stared at him, not getting the joke. "I was hoping for something better."

"No. CIA would be perfect for a guy who can keep a secret the way you can."

"What secret?" I asked. Clearly, I had slipped up on something, though I was relieved to see that he wasn't so much angry as determined to enjoy a joke at my expense.

"Marilyn's asleep in the bedroom, believe it or not. It was really great of you to give her my address here—particularly since you were the one who told me yesterday I should be careful about seeing her! You're not working for Lyndon by any chance, are you, David?"

I stared at him, blushing. "She said she'd spoken to you."

"Yes. And that she lost the address. That didn't sound a little implausible to a man of your great worldly experience?"

Now that I realized what Marilyn had done, of course it sounded wildly improbable. Marilyn was always threatening to join Jack on the campaign trail whenever we talked, and as a rule I didn't take her seriously. I recognized, with a certain degree of guilt, that I had underestimated her again. "Well, all I can say is that she sounded to me as if she was telling the truth. . . ."

"David, if Marilyn told you black was white, you'd believe her."

It was true, which made it worse. "I could wring her neck," I said.

He laughed. "Yes, I guess so, but I don't suppose you *will*. You'll forgive her." He poured us both coffee from a silver Thermos. The apartment was nicely furnished and comfortable, though there were cables all over the floor for the extra telephones that had been installed, including a direct "red phone" linking the apartment to the Kennedy "communications shack" at the Arena.

"I'm really sorry, Jack," I said.

"No harm done. Actually, I was relieved. I was thinking about what you said, you know. . . . Should I call her, should I not? And all of a sudden the doorbell rang, and there she was, carrying a bottle of champagne, at eleven in the morning. She's sleeping like a baby now."

"You're a lucky man."

"Yes," he said simply.

A door opened and Marilyn appeared, dressed only in one of Jack's shirts. "I heard noises?" she said. "I didn't know where I was." Even from across the room I could see that her pupils were alarmingly small, tiny black pinpoints. She thought for a moment— a long moment—then said in a tiny voice: "Where am I?"

She was holding a glass of champagne in one hand and a lot of brightly colored capsules in the other. She tossed the capsules into her mouth, knocked back some champagne, and smiled, a little vaguely, I thought. "Hi, David," she said. She walked across the room as if the floor were a tightrope requiring her full concentration, and gave me a kiss. Her skin smelled as sweet and fresh as a baby's, and she gave off the warmth of someone who has been sound asleep, despite the icy air-conditioning in the apartment. She leaned against me, her face close to mine. "I'm really sorry for what I did to you," she said. Tears welled up in her eyes. "It was a shitty thing to do to a friend."

Jack was right, of course. I forgave her instantly—I couldn't help it. Kicking a cocker spaniel would have been easier.

"You're my *best* friend, David." She put both arms around my neck, giving me an ample view of her bosom. "I mean it."

"I know." There was even a certain amount of truth to it, I reflected sadly.

"I *would* have told you the truth, but I thought you might not give me Jack's address."

"I probably wouldn't have."

"So you see? I was right!" She sounded satisfied with her logic. She turned to Jack. "Did I fall asleep, or didn't I?"

"You did."

"Oh, baby, I haven't slept like that in so long. . . . I have to have some more champagne, honey."

Jack looked at his watch. "I'm not sure that's such a smart idea," he said.

Her jawline hardened, and all of a sudden she didn't look soft and helpless anymore. "I said I want some more fucking champagne, Jack," she snapped.

Jack stared at her for a moment, his face flushed; then—wisely, I thought—he decided to treat it as a joke. "You've got Irish blood in you," he said, and taking the glass, he went into the tiny kitchen and filled it for her.

She gave him a hug, then a long, sexy kiss. "Oh, lover," she moaned, "I'm sorry. I'm always cranky before my period. I didn't mean to shout at you, of all people." She went over to the sofa, rummaged through her handbag, picked out another capsule and washed it down with champagne.

"Are you sure that's wise?" I asked. "Taking all those pills on top of alcohol?"

"Oh, David, they're just for my allergies. And vitamins. Anyway, champagne isn't *alcohol?* It's, like, wine?"

Jack was grinning—having a good time. He *enjoyed* this kind of scene—it was his way of relaxing from the pressures that were building up ten minutes away in the Sports Arena, where his ambition— or his father's—was being fulfilled at last.

A telephone rang, then another. Jack picked up the nearest one and said, "I was taking a nap." He listened intently, his face turning somber. "You tell that son of a bitch his fucking *delegates* are for me. I got the biggest write-in vote in the history of Pennsylvania, and my name wasn't even on the ballot. . . . No, come to think of it, I'll tell him myself! I worked my ass off for years for this nomination, and I'm not going to have the goddamn governor of Pennsylvania fuck it up."

He banged down the telephone and picked up the other, dismissing us both with a wave of the hand. Clearly he had no more time for Marilyn, and more important things on his mind than Stars for Kennedy.

I have to say for Marilyn that when it was *absolutely* necessary, she could get herself pulled together in record time, no doubt from having spent so much of her early life in other people's bedrooms. Whatever she was taking, it apparently gave her instant energy, but at some cost. She walked unsteadily and managed to bump into several pieces of furniture on her short trip across the living room.

"Good-bye, lover," she said, giving Jack a kiss that left a smudge of lipstick on his cheek, which I hoped he would notice before he sat down to deal with Governor Lawrence of Pennsylvania.

"Do you have a car?" he asked.

"I came in my own," she said. She searched through her purse, held up a set of car keys, and dropped them on the floor.

Jack and I exchanged glances. The same thought crossed our minds simultaneously—Marilyn was in no condition to drive—and it also occurred to me that her car would be recognized by any reporter who was familiar with Hollywood. She still drove the same Cadillac convertible she had received as a gift before her marriage to DiMaggio. To those in the know, she might as well have left a sign outside 522 North Rossmore Avenue reading "Marilyn Monroe is visiting here."

"I'll drive you home," I said.

Jack nodded. "Good idea!"

Marilyn didn't object. She didn't seem to be able to pick her car keys up off the floor, so I did. I put my arm in hers and walked her to the door, leaving Jack to get on with his nomination.

Marilyn's car was parked at an angle in front of a fire hydrant, with a parking ticket on the windshield. I put her in the front seat and walked over to my car, to tell the driver to meet me at the Beverly Hills Hotel.

As I slipped behind the steering wheel, I glanced over at her. She was sitting back gracefully, one arm resting on the top of her door, the other stretched across the top of the white leather seat so that her fingers just touched the back of my neck. Her skirt had risen, and I could see a considerable portion of thigh, bisected by a lacy white garter strap. I was about to live out the most deep-seated fantasy of every American male—driving a convertible, top down, on a sunny day in Southern California, with the most beautiful blonde in the world beside me, her head back, her eyes half closed, her lips parted as if ready for a kiss.

Marilyn stroked the back of my neck as I drove, and turned the radio on—Sinatra, singing "Our Love Is Here to Stay." Marilyn sang softly along with Sinatra, as if it were a duet. She had a good voice, with a kind of breathy, sexy delivery that made men, myself included, dream. "Oh *God,* I love Frank!" she moaned. "He is *so* sexy."

"Mm."

"Don't be jealous, lover."

I sighed. "It would be nice to hear that *I'm* sexy for a change."

She moved closer and gave me a kiss. My eyes were on the road, but I felt her lips, wet and astonishingly warm, almost hot, on my cheek. "You're sexy," she whispered. "There. And I'm sorry for what I did, really."

She ran her hand down the front of my trousers, stroking my crotch gently with her fingertips, eyes closed, as if she were thinking about something else. She giggled. "This is *fun,*" she said. "Let's go to Malibu."

I was due at the Ambassador's in a few minutes, and had appointments stacked up one after the other until late in the evening. Still, I asked myself, could I live with myself for the rest of my life if I turned down what was clearly—if I played my cards even halfway right—the opportunity to sleep with Marilyn? I knew that if I went to Malibu with Marilyn, I would end up betraying Jack—and Maria, of course—and I didn't care. I made a U-turn, and speeded up.

"We don't have swimsuits," I said.

"Mm. We'll go to the nude beach, lover. Then we'll drink some margaritas. I *love* margaritas. Then maybe we'll go dancing. . . ."

"Anything you say."

"You're a different person when you're having fun, David, you know?" She giggled again. "Maybe you should slow down, though," she said. "You just went through a stop sign."

"No I didn't."

"Believe me, sugar."

I caught a sudden flash of red lights in the rearview mirror, then heard the siren. A black-and-white police car appeared.

"Oh, shit," I said. "Better get the registration and insurance out of the glove compartment."

Marilyn looked blank. "Registration? Insurance?"

My heart sank. I pulled over, straightened my tie, and wondered whether a twenty-dollar bill slipped into my license would help matters. I thought not—the LAPD had a reputation for honesty, combined with storm trooper hostility toward traffic offenders. Then it occurred to me that my New York State driver's license was at home —I had a chauffeur in LA, so I never bothered carrying it.

The policeman was everything I had expected—tall, lean, wearing silver reflecting sunglasses, and as remote as a Martian. I explained my predicament and handed him my business card, which he held as if it were contaminated.

"Is it your car, sir?"

"No," I said, "it's this lady's." Marilyn had been staring straight ahead, still humming along with Sinatra.

"Honey," I said gently, "would you just hand me over the papers for the car?"

She opened the glove compartment, releasing an incredible avalanche of junk: stockings, an old bra, pill bottles—not to speak of loose pills—Tampax, makeup, used and unused Kleenex. Marilyn sifted through the debris deliberately, and shook her head. There were no papers for the car.

The policeman's eyes were on the pills—not a good sign. "Let me get this straight," he said to me. "You went through a stop sign. It isn't your car. You don't have a driver's license. There's no registration or proof of insurance."

"That's about the size of it. Look, I understand this is a serious matter, officer, but I have an office here, you can check up on who I am. Chief Parker knows me. I'm involved with the Democratic convention at the moment, and if there's any way of dealing with this quickly . . ." I took a shot at what mattered: "And privately," I suggested. "With the minimum of fuss and publicity."

There was no reaction. "I'm a Republican myself," he said. "Is this your car, miss?"

Marilyn stopped humming for a moment and nodded. "Yes," she whispered, her voice barely audible. "I think so."

"You *think* so?"

"I mean yes, it is. It was given to me. I don't know if it came with any papers, though?"

The policeman shook his head and took out his notebook. "If I could just explain . . ." I began, but he cut me off.

"Listen," he said, "*you*, my friend, are looking at some jail time." He turned to Marilyn, who still hadn't looked in his direction. "What's your name, miss?"

There was a long silence. "Marilyn Monroe," she said in a tiny voice.

The policeman wrote it down, then stared at it. "Don't you screw around with me, lady!" he snapped angrily, losing his cool for the first time. Then, as if she had been waiting for the moment, Marilyn took off her sunglasses and turned to face him, smiling sweetly.

"But I'm *not* screwing around, officer," she said, in that inimitable voice. "Honest."

"*Jesus!*" he said, awe in his voice. "You weren't kidding."

"I'm sorry I don't have the papers for the car," she said. "My husband probably kept them."

"Mr. Miller?" Like any Los Angeles cop, this one was well read on the home life of the stars.

"No. The husband before. Mr. DiMaggio."

"He was my hero when I was a kid."

She looked wistful. "Mine too," she said.

The officer took off his sunglasses. Without them he looked less frightening—just another third-generation California Okie from Bakersfield. "You mean you've been driving this car for what—four or five years?—without a registration slip?"

"I guess so."

"May I make a suggestion?" I interrupted, thinking quickly. "My lawyer is Ike Lublin. Couldn't he come down to headquarters and sort all this out for us?"

The name had a visible impact on the police officer. Ike was one of the best-known attorneys in Los Angeles. Although he often defended major organized-crime figures, he kept on the good side of the cops, giving generously to police charities and appearing at police banquets, where he always took a whole table.

"You still have to come downtown," he said to me. "You were driving. You committed a moving violation. Miss Monroe too."

"Call me Marilyn," she said. "What Mr. Leman is trying to say is that I'd be really *embarrassed* if there was a story about this in the papers. My husband would be just *furious* with me. And the studio would be upset too." Her eyes teared up on cue. She picked up a Kleenex from the floor and dabbed at them prettily.

His Adam's apple bobbed. "Yes ma'am." He took off his hat and rubbed his head for a moment. "I tell you what I *can* do," he said. "You follow me. I'll take you into the police garage. You can call Mr. Lublin from there. That way police reporters won't even know you're there."

I could tell it was the best deal we were going to get, so we took it. We followed the black-and-white cruiser at a steady thirty-five miles an hour, while Marilyn, obeying my orders for once, dumped every pill bottle and pill out into the street.

Good as his word, our policeman whispered quickly to his sergeant—the names Marilyn Monroe and Ike Lublin did the trick—

and we were placed in a small office next door to the holding pens in the basement, inhaling the smell of rank sweat, urine, and stale tobacco. Some of Marilyn's good spirits evaporated; she was brooding over the fact that I had made her throw away her pills. "Now is when I *need* them," she complained.

"No. If you think the cops will buy the allergy line, you're wrong. They may be your fans, but they live to bust people like you. Look what happened to Robert Mitchum."

She giggled. "The marijuana arrest? That was practically before I was *born!* I played opposite him in *River of No Return.* He wanted to fuck me, but he was so nasty about it I said no."

Marilyn's stories of her love life could be divided into two separate categories: people you were surprised to learn she'd fucked, and people you were surprised to learn she'd *refused* to fuck. It didn't seem the time or place to hear about it, however.

She was sitting behind a green metal desk, shielded by her dark glasses, her skin pale under the bright overhead fluorescent lights. "I hate this place," she said.

"Nobody likes police stations," I said soothingly, holding her hand. From the other side of the door came the zoolike noises of the holding cells: screams of anger, the sounds of vomiting, the noise of toilets being flushed, the crash and clank of locks and steel doors, a long, mournful, keening wail from some tormented soul.

She shivered. "It's the lights," she said. "It reminds me of the morgue."

"Come on, Marilyn. You've never been in a morgue."

"No. But I dream about it sometimes. And the lights in the dream are always like this."

"You dream about visiting the morgue?"

She shook her head. "I dream about lying there."

I recognized the signs that the effect of Marilyn's pills was wearing off. "Would coffee help?" I asked.

She shrugged. I went out, found a coffee machine, and returned with a couple of cups. Marilyn seemed to have cheered up a bit, perhaps because she had discovered one of her "allergy" pills wedged in a corner of her handbag—I noticed her palming it as she drank her coffee.

"How long are we going to be here?" she asked.

"Not much longer." Her hand was trembling. "We were about to have a great afternoon," I said to her gently. I don't think I have ever felt such a sense of loss, defeat, and failure—certainly I would feel nothing like it again until Marilyn's death, then Jack's, and Bobby's —and for a moment I was close to tears.

"Poor David," was all she said, for at that moment the door opened and Ike Lublin bustled in. He was smoking a big cigar, as was the sergeant, who came in behind him. It was clear from their expressions that the fix was in.

Within minutes, Marilyn had been smuggled into the back seat of Ike's limo and whisked off to the Beverly Hills Hotel, while Ike paid a fine for failure to register and insure a vehicle, plus over one thousand dollars in unpaid parking tickets dating back to 1954. I pleaded guilty to a moving violation and was fined fifty dollars.

Marilyn's part in the incident never surfaced, a tribute to Ike's influence in the LAPD, but my own involvement, in a much modified version, leaked rapidly outward and upward, so that when I finally got to see Jack early the next morning, his attitude was admiring.

"I never thought of you as a wild man," he said. "I guess I'd better not make you my CIA director after all."

"I don't know what you're talking about."

He laughed. "When I heard about it, I said, 'That sounds more like my little brother Teddy than my old friend David.' I couldn't believe my ears when somebody told me you'd been arrested for drunken driving. And a hooker in the car with you! It's a whole new side to your character, David. Is it a permanent change, do you think, or just a midlife crisis?"

"It's all nonsense, Jack. A wild rumor."

"Sure." He grinned. His respect for me had obviously increased, which was ironic, I told myself with some satisfaction, considering how close I had come to fucking his girl.

I spread my papers out on the coffee table, and he began to concentrate on them. Then, all of a sudden, Jack looked up at me and grinned hugely. "Just tell me this," he said. "Was she worth what she cost?"

30

She was watching the convention on television when Jack's call came. She had hoped to watch the nominating speeches and the roll call with him, but the two days before the presidential nominations on July 13 had turned out to be unexpectedly confusing and difficult. She had seen Jack only twice, briefly—both times for a "quickie" in the hideaway on North Rossmore, with the phones ringing in the next room, and a couple of his aides waiting impatiently in the living room to take him to another state caucus or a visit to some divided delegation.

"I think we've got it," he said to her on the phone. She knocked on wood. *He* might not be superstitious, but she was. "We picked up four votes from South Dakota that had been pledged to Humphrey this morning, and thirteen and a half from Colorado. New Jersey is still a big problem. That prick Governor Meyner is still holding his delegation to vote for him as a favorite son on the first ballot, the bastard. Christ, are we going to get *that* son of a bitch when we get to Washington!"

"Where are you, lover?" she asked.

"At Marion Davies's house, with my father and mother. I'm going to have dinner here with them, then go back to the apartment and watch the balloting."

On television, Sam Rayburn was nominating Lyndon Johnson, while the Texas delegation, in white Stetsons, demonstrated. They did not look particularly excited to her. "Can I come over later?" she asked.

His voice was cautious. "The apartment isn't safe anymore. When

346

I left, I had to climb down the fire escape at the back of the building and over a fence. It's surrounded by press and TV, and tonight will be worse. Besides, it's going to be two in the morning before I get to bed. . . ."

"Lover," she whispered, "say the word and I'll be there to help you celebrate. Even if it's at *four* in the morning. I don't care."

She could feel his resolution weakening. "I'll send a car for you," he said briskly. "There'll be someone in the garden with a flashlight to get you over the fence and up the fire escape steps. It may be one-thirty, two a.m., I can't be sure, so you'll have to stick close to the phone."

She made a soft kissing sound. "I'll be waiting. However long it takes. I'm going to give you a *presidential* kiss, sweetheart. It's a promise."

She heard voices in the background, one of them the Ambassador's. "I've got to go," Jack said. "We're going to eat."

"I'm not going to eat a thing until I get there, sugar. I'm saving my appetite for you." She giggled.

"Thank you for your—ah—support," he said: clearly, his parents were in the same room now. "I'll—ah—hold you to that promise."

"Knock 'em dead, tiger!" she said; then he hung up.

She put the receiver down, dialed room service, and ordered a fresh bottle of Dom Pérignon and a hamburger. She picked up her address book and got on with the tedious business of replacing the pills she had thrown away—she could *kill* David, she thought, for making her do it.

Keeping herself in pills took up a lot of her time. She got prescriptions from her New York internist, from Dr. Kris, and from her gynecologist in New York, but these were never enough, and the three doctors often talked to each other to make sure she wasn't getting too much medication, or the wrong kind. Luckily, she had a gynecologist and an internist in Los Angeles, too, who would write out prescriptions, but they still weren't enough to supply her needs, so although she was no hypochondriac, she went from specialist to specialist for more or less imaginary ailments ranging from back pains to allergies, and always finished by complaining of sleeplessness, or low energy, or the need to diet for a part. Very few doctors would refuse to write her out a prescription as she left the office, and if she was lucky, they sometimes made them refillable. By now nobody, not even Dr. Kris, had any idea of her total intake of barbiturates.

On the screen, Eugene McCarthy was nominating Stevenson. He had the delegates in tears as he cried out: "Do not reject this man who has made us all proud to be Democrats! Do not leave this prophet without honor in his own party!"

She cried herself, between bites of hamburger—she liked Eugene McCarthy, whom she had met in New York a couple of times, and Stevenson was the man she admired most after Clark Gable.

McCarthy's speech was followed by a tumultuous demonstration that seemed to go on forever, which would have made her worry about Jack's chances, except that he had warned her this was exactly what was going to happen. "Adlai has everything except the votes," he had said contemptuously.

The TV camera caught a fuss in the stands and zoomed in on Mrs. Kennedy, Jack's mother, taking her seat. Jack's father, she knew, was watching from the Marion Davies house because it had been decided at a tense family conference that his appearance at the Arena might frighten the delegates. It amused her that she and the Ambassador had something in common—they were both kept out of sight!

The chairman of the convention banged his gavel and called on Alabama, which cast twenty votes for Johnson and only three and a half for Jack. She cursed the southerners, racists and bigots one and all, and big, ugly Lyndon Johnson, with his mean eyes and Texas swagger.

She had sat through countless Academy Award ceremonies, but she had never felt such tension before as she wrote down the delegates for Jack in a long column, under the number 761—the votes he needed to win.

She lost track of the time, until the roll call finally reached Wyoming, with Jack still eleven votes short. Then she caught sight of his brother Teddy in the middle of the Wyoming delegation, a big, toothy grin on a face that was a coarser, plumper version of Jack's own, and she knew Jack had won, even before she heard all of Wyoming's fifteen votes go to Kennedy. . . .

————

At a quarter to, a car picked her up. Boom-Boom Reardon, looming hugely in the front seat, was driving. He gave her a doubtful look as she got in. "You ain't gonna be climbing over a backyard fence in that, I'm thinking," he said in his surly way, which she had learned not to take personally.

"*What* fence? I thought I had to climb a fire escape. I can do that!"

She had dressed to please Jack, not for climbing obstacles. "Isn't it great about Jack?"

"Sure. But I never doubted it."

It was true, she reflected—none of the people around Jack ever seemed to doubt that he would get exactly what he wanted every time, whether it was her or the presidency. "How is he?" she asked.

"Pretty good. We had a little party for him at the apartment— sang 'When Irish Eyes Are Smiling,' while the Senator drank a beer."

"That must have been nice." She wished she had been there— wished that *she* had people around her who were devoted and loyal like Jack's. "I guess you'll be going to the White House with him if he wins."

"He'll win." She had forgotten that nobody around Jack ever said "*if* he wins."

She scrunched up in the back of the car as they passed the army of press and TV people in front of the house—even her own appearances in public produced nothing to equal *this,* she thought. They pulled to a stop in a dark alley, where two policemen and a couple of men in dark suits waited. There *was* a fence, she was dismayed to see as one of the cops turned on his flashlight, and there was no way she could imagine climbing over it in her tight dress.

"I'll never make it," she whispered—for everybody was glancing nervously toward the end of the alley, as if the TV news crews might appear at any moment.

"You can't stand around here too long," one of the security men said nervously. "You should have worn blue jeans."

"Save your advice on clothes for your wife," she snapped at him.

There was a moment of silence; then the cops exchanged glances. One of them nodded, climbed over the fence, and dropped down the other side. The first one bent over and held out his hands to form a step. She took off her shoes, tossed them over the fence, and with a giggle placed her foot in the cop's hands. She grabbed the top of the fence as he straightened up, then closed her eyes and took a blind leap over it, landing in the arms of the other cop, who swung her to the ground just in time, for the activity in the alleyway had attracted the attention of a few reporters, who had drifted down to see what was going on.

She picked up her shoes and with the policeman's help reached the bottom rung of the fire escape—he had to pick her up until she was sitting on his shoulders, shoes dangling from her hand. "Thanks," she whispered. "My ex-husband's an LAPD cop."

"I know," he said. "Jim Dougherty. I'll tell him we met."

"Don't tell him you had your head between my legs, will you?"

He laughed. "Anytime, lady. My pleasure."

Then she was on her own, climbing the steps in the dark in her stocking feet, being careful not to look down, until she reached an open window, from which Jack Kennedy, Democratic nominee for president of the United States, leaned out, a broad grin on his face.

———

Hoffa glared at the television screen in his office as if he could stare it into submission. Kennedy was squinting uncomfortably. The setting sun was in his eyes as he made his acceptance speech in the Los Angeles Coliseum—a rare piece of bad planning.

In Detroit, it was already late in the evening, and Hoffa had delayed taking his visitor to dinner to hear the speech. "What is all this 'new frontier' shit?" he asked petulantly.

Paul Palermo shrugged. He admired Kennedy's sense of style, which he associated with his own, and thought Hoffa was a slob with his white athletic socks and his greased-back hair, furrowed like a plowed field by the tracks of his comb.

"It's like Roosevelt's New Deal," Palermo said. "It's a good slogan. It sounds important, but it doesn't mean anything."

"Fuck him. Nixon's gonna win, you'll see. My money's on him."

Palermo reflected that this was true, literally as well as figuratively, for Hoffa was already strong-arming every Teamster local into making a contribution to Nixon's campaign fund. But Palermo wasn't so sure that Nixon would win. There was a whole world out there Hoffa knew nothing about, people one generation removed from union membership, who had college degrees, lived in the suburbs, never got their hands dirty, and aspired to some vision of glamour and style that Jack—and just as important, Jackie—now represented.

The more Palermo thought about it, the more certain he was that Kennedy was going to win. The fact that Kennedy had had the balls to defy the party elders by choosing Johnson for the vice presidential slot merely confirmed his opinion.

It wasn't really Palermo's job to tell Hoffa he was backing the wrong horse, but there *were* things he was supposed to make Hoffa understand, and he wasn't finding it easy. He stared at Kennedy on the screen, impressed by his grace and vigor. He listened to his acceptance speech with admiration marred only by Hoffa's interruptions, which he did his best to ignore.

Every so often, the TV camera panned to the audience for a reaction shot. Sitting among them were a lot of recognizable Hollywood celebrities, whom the camera lingered on—another smart move of the Kennedys, Palermo thought. He saw Frank Sinatra, Peter Lawford, Sammy Davis, Jr., Shelley Winters, Angie Dickinson, even Marilyn Monroe, staring transfixed toward the podium, tears rolling down her cheeks, hands clenched to her bosom like a Madonna, as Kennedy reached the climax of his speech. If *that* didn't win Kennedy votes, Palermo thought, nothing would!

"Ain't that Marilyn Monroe?" Hoffa asked, leaning forward for a closer look at the screen.

Palermo nodded. He had a drink, but he wanted his dinner. He knew food didn't interest Hoffa, who often skipped meals, or ate from a vending machine.

Hoffa lowered his voice conspiratorially. "She's been fucking him, every night, during the convention. Did you know that?"

Palermo knew, and it only increased his admiration for Kennedy. He stared at the screen. There was no point in letting Hoffa find out what he knew and what he didn't.

"I got it all on tape," Hoffa said. "I even got a photo of her climbing the fire escape to his bedroom. Guy took it with infrared film and a telephoto lens, clear as day. What do you think of that?"

Palermo pretended to be impressed. The more he heard of Jack Kennedy, the less he believed blackmail would work with him. Mr. B., who had been informed of Bernie Spindel's efforts on behalf of Hoffa, had not been impressed either. "So Kennedy sleeps with movie stars?" Mr. B. had said, in the safety of the Tucson basement, for the FBI not only had microphones in the rest of the house but filmed the old man night and day through the windows with high-speed telephoto cameras so that lip-readers could transcribe his conversations. "So what? Let him sleep with who he wants if he gets rid of Castro and we get our casinos back." That was Mr. B.'s view of it, and it made good sense to Palermo.

"All that's fine, Jimmy," he said to Hoffa, "the tapes, the photo, and all that, but if he's elected . . ."

Hoffa stared malevolently at the figure on the screen. "It'll never happen."

" '*If*,' I said—"

"If it does, which it won't, he and his brother are dead men, they don't lay off the Teamsters. I can tell you *that* right now."

"That kind of talk is a mistake, Jimmy. If he wins, we want him to help us get our action back in Havana."

Hoffa shrugged. The vast audience in the Los Angeles Coliseum was going wild. Kennedy stood there, in front of what looked like an endless sea of people applauding, shouting, pressing forward toward the rostrum—so many people, so much enthusiasm, that even Kennedy himself seemed overwhelmed. "Fuck Havana," Hoffa growled. "I got no interest there."

The camera caught Marilyn Monroe jumping up and down in the crowd like a cheerleader, an embarrassed David Leman by her side. The image flashed on the screen so quickly that Palermo wasn't sure he'd actually seen it. "I thought we were on the same side, Jimmy," he said mildly.

"We are."

"Then our troubles are your troubles. We worry about Havana, *you* worry about Havana, right?"

Hoffa glowered at him. "You guys got Vegas—thanks to me. What do you want Havana for?"

"Vegas is way out west, Jimmy. It's a long flight. Havana is ninety miles from Key West. Half an hour by plane from Miami, three hours from New York. Do you want me to draw you a map?"

"Don't get fucking smart with me. I get the picture."

Palermo smiled with his perfect teeth, though at the back of his mind was the hope that he'd be around to watch Hoffa getting whacked when it finally happened—as he was pretty sure it would, eventually.

Palermo hated rudeness and despised Hoffa, but Mr. B.'s instructions had been crystal-clear, as always. Promise Hoffa anything, he had said. As long as the East Coast families were cut off from the lucrative Cuban gambling revenues that had made them rich, they had to go begging hat in hand to the Chicago mob for a piece of the action in Las Vegas, and that meant building more casinos, and building more casinos meant borrowing more money from the Teamster Central States Pension Fund, which meant, of course, that Hoffa was in the catbird seat.

It was really very simple—though nobody in law enforcement seemed able to grasp the dynamics of the thing: The families couldn't borrow money from banks, or float an underwriting on Wall Street, or build casinos with hundreds of millions of dollars in used bills of small denominations! Convicted felons couldn't be directors or company officials, or sign for loans, or issue stock. So they needed a front and a source of unlimited, no-questions-asked loans, and Hoffa could provide both, in return for which they supported his control over the union.

So far as Palermo was concerned, the sooner the New Jersey legislature legalized casino gambling, the better. Once Atlantic City was off and running, the East Coast families could dispense with Hoffa and take their long-awaited revenge against Momo Giancana and the Chicago mob. Unless, of course, Castro was to fall, in which case all these good things would happen sooner.

Palermo thought about the possibility pleasurably—he pictured Hoffa in the back seat of a car, a garrote around his thick neck, the beady little eyes popping as he struggled for breath, the thin-lipped mouth open like that of a gaffed fish. . . . He dismissed the image. For the moment, Hoffa was needed.

He made a small, placating gesture with his hands. "I know you get the picture, Jimmy. You're a smart guy. That's just what I'm saying."

"Try telling me something I don't know. Like why I'm up to my ass in subpoenas while your guys are sitting pretty."

Palermo knew there was some truth to Hoffa's complaint, though much of it was Hoffa's own fault. He was a loudmouth, so he drew a lot of heat down on himself. "Jimmy," he said soothingly, "if it's the grand jury thing in Tennessee you're talking about, what can I tell you? . . . Grand jury tampering is a no-no, you know that."

"It's done alla time, Chrissake."

"Sure, but not getting *caught!*"

"I'll beat the fucking rap, no thanks to your guys. If they think they can hang Jimmy Hoffa out to dry, they're wrong."

"They don't think that, Jimmy. They have great respect for you."

"I don't give a shit about their respect. When I'm in trouble, I want their help. You tell your guys, I go down, *they* go down. I want someone whacked, they *whack* him, whoever the fuck he is, even if it's J. Edgar Hoover. That was the deal."

"They understand that." They did too, and it scared the shit out of them, even Mr. B., who felt that Giancana himself should have been whacked for giving his word to Hoffa on behalf of the Commission. Now, of course, they were stuck with it—as men of honor, it could hardly be otherwise.

"They *better* understand." Hoffa glanced at his watch. "Let's go eat," he said.

He got up, walked over to the television, and snapped the set off, turning the knob so hard with his blunt fingers that he broke it off. He tossed it across the room into the wastepaper basket beside his desk. "Fuck Jack Kennedy," he growled. "Him and his brother both. They want to get tough with Jimmy Hoffa, I'll show them what tough is."

He opened the door—there were no bodyguards outside, as if Hoffa wanted to prove that he wasn't afraid of anything.

That was typical of Hoffa, Palermo thought, and stupid. A man should know when to be afraid. A man who didn't feel fear was dangerous to himself—and other people.

31

No sooner was she back in Reno from the convention than *The Misfits* turned into a kind of freak show.

People came from both coasts to visit the production, mostly to see for themselves whether it was true that her marriage was breaking up, but also to catch a glimpse of Monty Clift in action. If that wasn't enough to inspire curiosity, there was Gable, struggling to keep his temper in a company of people he tended to regard as undisciplined upstarts. Journalists and photographers were everywhere—it was the most photographed picture she had ever been in—as well as people like Frank Sinatra, Clifford Odets, Marietta Tree, David Leman, and Aaron Diamond, all of them drawn by the rumor that something very special was happening here.

The tone of the production was set at the very beginning, when a group photograph was taken of herself, Gable, Monty, Eli Wallach, Huston, and her husband, all of them posing together to mark the first day of shooting. She was seated in the center foreground on a broken old swivel chair, sweating in the hundred-degree heat, wearing the revealing white dress with big red cherries (a joke nobody but Monty recognized) that she herself had chosen for Roslyn, with everybody else gathered around her. Both Gable and Wallach were pissed off, when they saw it, at being pushed to the side of the photograph, though she couldn't see what they had to complain about—poor Monty, perched beside her on the desk chair with just the corner of his ass, looked so wizened and scrunched over that he might have been a dwarf.

There were many unspoken realities hovering around the company of *The Misfits* in Reno that summer. One of them was that she and Arthur were sleeping in separate bedrooms and scarcely speaking, kept together only by mutual recriminations and the need to get this picture in the can. Another was that Gable, for all his rugged appearance of manly strength, was ailing—the slightest effort turned his face ashen gray beneath the outdoorsman's tan, and when he thought nobody was looking, he popped nitroglycerin tablets, for angina.

And Huston hated Monty. Like most successful directors, Huston enjoyed playing God, and because he was so cunning, he made a dangerous game of it. He let Gable know that he didn't think he still had the guts to do his own stunts; he taunted Monty, as well as playing him off against Eli Wallach; he treated her with barely concealed contempt, as if she were a basket case.

Of course, it didn't help a bit that her character, Roslyn, was so unmistakably her husband's idea of *her*—flirtatious, destructive, impulsive, a nervous bundle of nameless, unidentifiable fears and anxieties, a basket case, in fact.

Arthur knew her as only a husband could, and knew just how to angle the blade for a thrust to the heart! Roslyn was one of those beautiful women whose only real talent is for attracting men, and whose ego is so weak that she can only survive by proving over and over again that she can seduce them, even when she doesn't want them. . . . The worst of it was, he had hit the bull's-eye—Roslyn *was* her. She didn't need to agonize over what Roslyn would do in this scene or that scene, she only had to be herself.

For her, any picture was a battlefield, but never before had she been gripped by such fierce and conflicting emotions—rage against Arthur, with whom she was obliged to share a suite, if not a bed; fear of Huston, who was like some kind of devilish magician, able to see directly into her soul and torture her with what he found there; her hopeless schoolgirl infatuation for Gable, her ideal man; and a terrible, sinking feeling of companionship with Monty, whose troubles seemed to echo, if not to dwarf, her own.

———

As the weeks went by, Monty got more and more remote, almost glassy-eyed, hanging by his fingernails to what remained of his sanity, while Huston continued to make savage fun of him. Her spirits went down with Monty's, as if she were in free-fall. . . .

All around her—except for Gable himself—hatred flourished: Eli

Wallach and her husband rewrote the script to turn her into a hooker and make Eli the hero instead of Gable; Huston, like Olivier before him, tried to get rid of Paula Strasberg. . . . Finally she went over the edge, took so many pills that she couldn't focus her eyes, let alone say her lines, and had to be sent back to Los Angeles and placed in the hands of a new psychiatrist, Dr. Ralph Greenson.

She really didn't have a choice. So far as the studio was concerned, it was that or close down the picture, and she had too much at stake to let it be closed down. Dr. Greenson, whom she liked immediately, put her into a nursing home, where her dependence on Nembutal was gradually reduced to a more tolerable level, and persuaded the studio to put the production on hold.

Unlike Dr. Kris, Dr. Greenson was part of the industry, one of those "reliable," "realistic" doctors whom producers called whenever a star had a serious problem that threatened the shooting schedule. Like an army surgeon's, Greenson's job was to patch up the wounded and get them back into the trenches as soon as possible. Within ten days he had her back in Reno again, ready for work.

She staggered through it, sustained now by Greenson, by Dr. Kris —long-distance daily from New York—and by Paula. She was determined to make it to the end, when to nobody's surprise, she would bring the marriage to an end as well.

At the beginning of November, she played her final scene, on the Paramount lot, with Gable, sitting in the front seat of Gay Langland's old car. Gable leaned close to her, in the artificial moonlight, and said, "Just head for that big star straight on. The highway's under it. Take us right home."

He did it in one take, professional to the end. The next day Arthur moved out of the bungalow at the Beverly Hills Hotel where she and Yves had so recently carried on their affair, and she watched alone as John F. Kennedy was elected president of the United States.

PART THREE

LANCER

32

Jack listened to the returns at Hyannis Port surrounded by his family. He and Jackie were the only ones who looked relaxed. His sisters and his sister-in-law Ethel had the nervous look of women who had been slaving for days to prepare a big party and, now that the night was upon them, weren't sure it was going to be a success. The Ambassador, Bobby, and Teddy spent the evening on the phone, dealing with the most important men on election night: the county sheriffs who guard the ballot boxes—and can make them disappear.

I had been invited, just in case there was any high-level problem with the press or the networks, but since there wasn't, I spent the evening penciling electoral votes on a list prepared by Ethel on the back of a piece of shirt cardboard, while Maria, much to Jackie's annoyance, flirted mildly with Jack.

Jack watched television off and on all evening without saying much, except when he saw Nixon, his family beside him, as he walked past his supporters to his hotel. "The guy has no class at all," he said then. "Maybe it's just as well I'm going to be president instead of him."

About midnight, Bobby, who had been intently engaged for what seemed like hours in a conversation with Mayor Daley of Chicago about the ballot boxes in Cook County, came over and stared at my list, grim with tension. "It's close," he said, "but I think we're winning. Why doesn't that son of a bitch Nixon concede?"

Jack shook his head at Bobby. "Why should he?" he said. "I wouldn't."

He finished his bottle of beer and stood up. "I'm going to bed," he said, and left the room. He slept, as he told us later, "like a baby," and didn't discover he was the next president of the United States until he woke up in the morning.

The atmosphere the next day was curiously muted. The only person who was unabashedly elated was the Ambassador, who was already drawing up his own "enemies list" of people who had not shared his vision or had opposed it over the years.

Jackie, I thought, seemed guardedly pleased, as if Jack had finally done something she approved of, but Jack himself was, if anything, a little withdrawn. I suspect that as the Secret Service took up their posts around what was soon to be called "the Kennedy compound," the reality was finally sinking in—he was the President-elect. Perhaps he was a little awed by it all, despite himself. "What do we do now?" I had heard him ask Bobby when they saw each other before breakfast.

Since for once Bobby didn't have a ready answer, Jack went for a walk along the beach, and seemed to have recovered some of his good spirits by the time his usual breakfast was served—two eggs fried in butter, three rashers of bacon, and toast.

"I still can't believe it's over," he said to me.

"Oh, it's over, all right. You should see the telegrams. Hundreds of them already, Mr. President." It was the first time I called him that. I supposed it would get easier with time.

He grinned. "That's music to my ears!" He leaned back in his chair and lit a cigar—a sure sign he was in a good mood. Jackie and the rest of the family had come down to breakfast, so we were no longer alone. "Have you looked through them?" he asked me.

"A few." I pointed to the floor. I had brought them in a wastepaper basket that was already overflowing. Before the end of the day a full secretarial staff would arrive to take care of such things. I picked one out at random. "Congratulations from Cardinal Spellman," I said. "He's praying for you."

Jack laughed. "He supported Nixon, but he's praying for me? He should pray for Nixon."

I picked up another. "Governor Meyner. He says New Jersey is part of the New Frontier."

"He's right at the top of Dad's enemies list. Mine too, if I had one."

I had leafed through dozens of telegrams from celebrities, politicians, big businessmen, ordinary citizens, world leaders, when one caught my eye. "DEAR MR. PRESIDENT," it read, "ALL THE STARS ARE

TWINKLING AT YOUR VICTORY, BUT THIS LITTLE STAR IS SHINING JUST
FOR YOU. CONGRATULATIONS AND LOVE, MARILYN."

I must have held the telegram in my hand long enough to make
everybody curious, for Jackie asked, "Who's that one from?"

I gulped. "Some nuns at a parochial school in Los Angeles," I
extemporized wildly. Jack grabbed the telegram out of my hand
before I could stop him.

"Oh, how sweet! Read what it says, Jack," Jackie said.

Jack glared at me for having put him on the spot. He frowned, as
if he found it hard to read without his glasses, then said: "Dear Mr.
President: All the faculty and children of Immaculate Conception are
rooting for you, and praying for you and Mrs. Kennedy. Sisters
Roseanna, Mary Beth, Dolores, and Gilda."

He folded the paper up and slipped it in his pocket. "I'll have to
answer this one personally," he said solemnly.

"Sister *Gilda?*" Ethel asked.

"That's Los Angeles for you," Jack said lightly. He stood up and
stretched. "Come with me," he said to me.

We stepped outside and walked down the beach. A brisk breeze
was blowing off the sea. The President-elect was dressed in chinos, a
sweater, and Top-Siders, while I was shivering in gray flannels, a
blazer, and city shoes. On the dunes, silhouetted against the gray
sky, we could see Secret Service agents slipping into place as we
progressed along the beach.

"I'm not going to find it easy to get used to them," Jack said.

"They come with the territory. Besides, you may find them useful
eventually. They caddy for Ike."

He shook his head. "I don't intend to give up my freedom just
because I'm the president."

I knew that for Jack "freedom" meant women. If anything,
I thought, the Secret Service would be helpful—no government
agents were more susceptible to presidential glamour, or more eager
to be seduced. Jack would have them eating out of his hand before the inauguration. They would do everything short of pimp for
him.

"They've given me my code name," he said. " 'Lancer.' Everyone
and everything gets a code name, apparently. Bobby is 'Legend.' The
White House is 'Castle.' In case you're wondering, you're 'Blazer.' "

"Blazer?"

"I guess they were struck by the way you dress."

I wondered if the Secret Service had a list of code names for Jack's girls as well. Later I was to discover that Marilyn's was "Straw-head"; someone there had a sense of humor.

We trudged on. "How is Marilyn?" he asked. For nearly four months he had been campaigning night and day. There had been no time for him to stay in touch with Marilyn and her troubles.

"From what I hear, the picture was a nightmare. Pills, problems, stress. . . . Huston had to interrupt shooting so she could go back to Los Angeles and spend a week or so in some kind of psychiatric nursing home. . . . The marriage is over, you know. Kaput."

I didn't tell him that adding to Marilyn's woes was the fact that Clark Gable had suffered a heart attack on Election Day, only twenty-four hours after playing the final scene of *The Misfits* with Marilyn.

"I'd better have a word with her," he said thoughtfully, "about that telegram. She's a great girl, but she's sometimes a little too—ah —enthusiastic." He glanced at me. "We don't want her trying to reach me at home all the time, do we?"

I thought the "we" was a nice touch, but I merely nodded. I wasn't about to volunteer for the task of telling Marilyn to be more careful, nor, as it turned out, was Jack willing to do it himself. The Secret Service, ever obliging, solved the problem by giving her a special number to call at the White House so there was no risk of her getting through to the private quarters upstairs, where Jackie might pick up the phone.

Much as he might have liked to talk about Marilyn, as president-elect he had other things on his mind. "Do you want a job in the administration?" he asked suddenly.

"Well, I've been giving it some thought. . . ."

He did not look particularly pleased or receptive. It occurred to me, to my dismay, that he might have been hoping I would say no. "What did you have in mind?" he asked briskly.

"Well, I was hoping—"

Before I could finish, he interrupted me. "USIA?" he suggested. "That's a possibility, I guess. I'd like to see the agency upgraded. Hell, part of our problem with the Third World is that we don't get our story out to them. We've got more to offer them than the Russians, but you'd never know it."

"I don't see myself handing out copies of *The Federalist* to the natives, Jack, if that's what you're thinking," I said to him rather stiffly. He knew damned well I wasn't interested in becoming a Washington bureaucrat, and that director of the United States Information Agency was a dogsbody job, carrying with it no access to the president and endless aggravation from right-wing congressmen who wanted copies of *Huckleberry Finn* or *The Grapes of Wrath* removed from USIA libraries all over the world.

"You can do better than that," I snapped, not bothering to hide my anger a bit.

He flushed. "Like what?"

I was pretty sure his father had passed on my desire for the London embassy to Jack. There were few secrets between the two of them where politics was concerned. "I had in mind London, frankly."

"Ambassador to the Court of St. James's?" he asked, shaking his head. We walked on in silence for a few hundred feet while he thought about it—or pretended to. "I don't know, David," he said at last. "I'm not sure the London embassy is, ah, right for you. . . ."

He was tactful enough not to say that *I* wasn't right for *it*, but all the same, I was furious. I had earned the right to ask for what I wanted, and *get* it, I thought. "I think I'd do a good job," I said sharply. "And I think I've earned it."

"I guess. I mean, sure, David, no question about *that.* . . . Let me think about it, okay?"

"Certainly." I wasn't about to plead my case further with Jack. I had too much pride for that.

Still, I was deeply hurt by his ingratitude, and angered, of course —but worst of all, I felt *foolish.* Luckily, I had shared my ambition with nobody except Joe and Marilyn—thank God I had never discussed it with Maria!—but I felt cheated, as if Jack had closed me out of his inner circle, while at the same time I despised myself for still wanting to be there.

He must have caught my expression, because he put his hand on my shoulder and said, "I'm going to need you close by me, David. Closer than London. You know how much I value your advice."

"Thank you."

"And help. I wouldn't have won the nomination without you, I know that." He could see I wasn't warming to this flattery. "I'll think about the ambassadorship, David. I really will. We'll talk about it soon."

We walked on for a while, but the mood between us was broken. Jack, I told myself, would probably end up offering me the ambassadorship after consulting with his father, and I would almost surely end up accepting it, but it wouldn't be the same as if it had been offered with enthusiasm when I asked for it, and we both knew it.

He noticed I was shivering in my blazer. "You're cold," he said.

"Let's walk back." He sighed as we turned around, the wind at our backs now. "This whole business of jobs is a real pain in the ass," he went on, drawing me into it, no doubt to smooth my ruffled feathers. "I've already had three calls recommending Adlai for secretary of state. . . . Over my dead body!"

Reluctantly, I *was* drawn back into Jack's plans in the role of adviser, which was clearly where he wanted me. "What about Bobby?" I asked.

"What *about* Bobby? I'd love to have *him* at State, and he'd be damned good there, but it's out of the question. I've been thinking of putting him in Defense, but the fallout would be bad from that, too. . . ."

"What does *he* want?"

"Bobby? He doesn't know. One day he wants a major Cabinet post, the next he wants to leave Washington and teach. . . . What would you think if I made him attorney general?"

I whistled, impressed despite my anger. "Talk about controversial! With his reputation for being ruthless. . . ."

He laughed. "Bobby's no more ruthless than I am. He's just shy, that's all, but it comes across on camera as ruthlessness. It's an idea, though, isn't it? Attorney general? It would make a lot of people sit up and take notice."

"J. Edgar Hoover would be one of them."

"Ah?" A veiled expression crossed his face—that of a man about to reveal a secret. "To tell you the truth, David, I've been thinking it might be time for Hoover to go."

We were back at the house—thank God! My fingernails were purple with cold. "Are you sure that's such a good idea?" I asked.

Jack looked at me, and for the first time it struck home to me that he *was* really the president-elect. His eyes had a determination I hadn't seen there before, his mouth was set with the firmness of granite. "Yes," he snapped, "I'm completely sure."

He opened the door, and I could feel the warmth of an open fire beckoning me, and hear the Kennedy women's boisterous laughter.

"It's time for a change," he said.

_____

She awoke, confused and aching, in a strange room, lying naked on the cold floor. The last thing she remembered was shouting, "You can't do this, I'm Marilyn Monroe!" as the door was slammed and locked.

The room was small, furnished with a simple hospital cot, the legs bolted to the floor, and an equally immovable bedside table. The window was opaque, covered with wire mesh so you couldn't throw yourself out of it or break the glass. The tiny bathroom had no door, and the mirror was made of some kind of unbreakable plastic, firmly screwed to the tiled wall. It was a cell, really, if you wanted to face facts, which she didn't.

She lay there thinking about the events that had brought her here to Payne Whitney. Her collapse had begun with her return to New York after the completion of *The Misfits*. Arthur had moved out of the apartment on East Fifty-seventh Street, leaving behind the portrait of herself that she had given him in London, which made her feel even worse.

A week later, she drove up to Roxbury to collect her belongings from what was now his house, and say a tearful good-bye to Hugo, the dog they had bought when the marriage still seemed to have a chance. She had cried all the way home in the rented car, driving with the windows down, despite the cold, because she was afraid she was suffocating.

A few days after that, she got the news of Joe Schenck's death, followed by that of Arthur's mother, of whom she had been fond. She felt death was pressing in on her—she stayed at home, surrounded by the untouched cartons she had brought back from Roxbury, trying not to think about the future.

She heard about Gable's death when a reporter called her at two in the morning for a comment, and she became hysterical with grief and sorrow, as if Gable really *had* been her father. She knew it would provoke comment if she didn't attend his funeral in California, but she didn't feel strong enough to go, afraid she would collapse in public as she had at Johnny Hyde's, so she stayed in New York, miserable and guilty. She watched the funeral on television alone in her apartment and heard many of the mourners, as they were interviewed, wonder why she hadn't even bothered to turn up.

Other events too seemed to be happening without her, as if she were receding from life. She watched Jack's inauguration on television in the VIP lounge at the Dallas airport on her way to Juárez with her lawyer, to get her divorce from Arthur.

Her isolation from the world—and its increasing hostility toward her—made her feel like a prisoner in her apartment, but she hadn't had the strength to leave. All the people she might have called upon for help were away—Jack immersed in the crucial first hundred days of his presidency, David in Europe with his wife, Paula ill herself. . . . She had nobody to turn to, and things seemed to have reached rock bottom for her—so much so that she could hardly imagine how they could get worse.

But soon they had. A reporter called her in the middle of the night again, this time for her comment on a story that Kay Gable had blamed *her* for Gable's death. It was the final blow, the one that brought her here to this bare room in New York's most prestigious psychiatric hospital, where she had allowed Dr. Kris to commit her only because it was understood that she was going to get a chance to rest and recuperate away from the press, and where, instead, she had been treated like a dangerous lunatic in an insane asylum.

She remembered now why she was naked. She had objected to being placed in a room with a peephole in the door so the attendants could spy on her, and having lost that one, fought against being put in a short hospital gown as if she were sick. She had torn it off and ripped it to shreds in a fit of anger. The attendants, tough-looking women who reminded her more of female wrestlers than nurses, had made an attempt to get her into a fresh gown, but she fought them off, kicking, biting, and scratching.

"Squat bare-ass naked as long as you like, you crazy bitch!" the senior of them said, when they finally gave up, and that was exactly what she was doing, unable to think of anything better. Screams, shouts, threats, pleas, and begging had failed. Her nightmare—the worst one of all—had come true: she was locked up like a crazy person, locked up like her mother and her grandmother too.

She *knew* this wasn't what Dr. Kris had intended, but she had no way to reach her—or anyone else, for that matter. She was learning, the hard way, what Monty had once told her: The saner you are, the harder it is to prove it.

When the door opened, she let out a scream. The man standing there was tall, thin, balding, with the face of a Jewish intellectual and horn-rimmed glasses—the spitting image of Arthur, who she had supposed it *was* for a moment, despite the white coat.

He looked puzzled. "Mrs. Miller?" he asked. "Are you okay?"

"No!" she shouted. "Of *course* I'm not! Do I *look* okay? And I'm not Mrs. Miller anymore either. I'm Marilyn Monroe."

"Yes, I know. The only thing is, you're registered as Mrs. Faith Miller, you see. To keep the press guessing, I suppose." He peered at her hesitantly. "Ah, would you like to put a gown on?"

"I would not! I want to get out of here."

"Sitting around naked isn't going to do it, I'm afraid."

"Call Dr. Kris, *please*. She'll tell you I don't belong here. It's a mistake."

"Yes? Of course, *everybody* here says it's a mistake."

He sat down on the bed and made himself comfortable. Out of the corner of his eye he caught her glancing at the door to her room. "It's not locked," he said pleasantly. "You could probably make it through the door before I caught you. But there's an attendant outside, one of the ones who tried to put a fresh gown on you; then there's a locked door at the end of the hall, and after that, a guard at the elevator. And if you got past all that, you'd just end up in the lobby stark naked, and it's full of reporters who seem to have worked out that 'Mrs. Miller' is you."

He sighed. "We'd have to put you in a straitjacket, which is no fun at all, so why bother?"

"I'm not looking my best," she said irrelevantly.

"Is that a fact? You look pretty damned good to me. Listen, you were talking about mistakes a moment ago. Tell me: Do you think it was a mistake to open the living room window and try to throw yourself out onto Fifth-seventh Street?" He asked her earnestly, as if he wanted the answer to a reasonable question.

"I didn't do that."

"It says here you did."

"I opened the window and started to climb out on the ledge."

"But you *were* planning to take a swan dive out the window? From the fourteenth floor? Otherwise, why go out on the ledge?"

She was a little surprised by his breezy informality. "I guess," she admitted.

"Why didn't you jump?"

"I looked down and saw someone I knew walking along Fifty-seventh Street. A kid named Timmy—a fan. I couldn't do it in front of him. I should have just kept my eyes shut and jumped."

"Yes, that's the way to do it, all right."

"They say your mind blanks out when you fall—you don't know a thing about it."

"Oh, I don't think so. I've had patients who jumped and survived, more or less. They all saw the ground coming up at them, and felt it when they hit. They didn't like it a bit."

He took his glasses off and polished them with the end of his tie. He had nice eyes, gentle and shrewd. "What made you do it?"

"I was tired of life. And unhappy."

"Well, aren't we all? No, what I want to know is what *specific* thing? Did you forget to buy toothpaste, for instance?"

She stared at him in astonishment, wondering if he was making fun of her. "Toothpaste? I don't get it."

"I had a patient—an attractive, wealthy lady—who came back from shopping, realized she hadn't remembered to buy toothpaste, opened the window, and jumped out onto Park Avenue. She landed on a canopy, so she survived."

He put his glasses back on and smiled at her, as if he were seeing her clearly at last. "Forgetting the toothpaste brought home the inconsequentiality of her life, her growing inability to deal with details, the fact that a trip to the drugstore or D'Agostino's had become the high point of her day. . . . Her husband had left her for a younger woman, by the way. I suppose a strict Freudian might decide that the missing tube of toothpaste was a phallic symbol—the husband's penis, you see—but I don't think it's necessary to go symbol hunting. She knew why she tried to kill herself, and so do you."

She wrapped her arms around herself as if she were cold, though it was warm in the room. "It was the stories about Gable's death that did it," she said softly.

"Forgive me, I don't follow these things closely. He died of a heart attack, didn't he—oh, several months ago or more? So why do it now?"

"Kay—his wife—said I killed him." She had not thought she could say it.

He raised an eyebrow. She tried to explain. "It was in every newspaper, in every goddamn, stinking, fucking gossip column. Kay said it was *my* fault he had a heart attack, because of the strain of dealing with my lateness and my moods."

He did not look shocked. "And do you think that was true?"

"Everybody thinks so. Millions of people think he died because of me now."

He nodded. "Possibly, but that's not what I asked. I don't care what Mrs. Gable or the great American moviegoing public think. I want to know what *you* think."

She took her time before she answered. If anybody was responsible for Gable's death, it was John Huston, who had taunted him into a totally unnecessary display of courage and strength just to get a sharper performance out of him. She *did* feel guilty, of course, for having put Gable through so much professional misery, but he had always behaved toward her like the gentleman he was.

When she heard about Kay's accusation, she had gone numb with horror. Her grief had been silent—she had simply walked to the window and stepped out onto the ledge, and if she hadn't seen Timmy Hahn down there, in his familiar windbreaker, she would have thrown herself to a silent death. Timmy, really, had saved her life—Timmy and Dr. Kris, who had come over the moment she was called. . . .

She wanted to answer the doctor's question honestly. "I *feel* guilty," she said hesitantly, "but I don't think I *am* guilty."

He gave a satisfied smile, as if she'd passed a test. "That's very good," he said. "May I call you Marilyn?"

"Sure," she said. She was beginning to like him.

"I think it's a sign of real progress, Marilyn."

"You don't think I'm nuts?"

"Everybody here is nuts. Some a little, some a lot."

"I guess so."

"The doctors most of all," he said with a laugh. He rubbed his nose between his thumb and forefinger, just like Dr. Greenson—apparently it was something all analysts did. Along with the gesture, his expression turned suddenly serious. "To answer your question properly, Marilyn, I would say you're not any more nuts than most people in here. Or outside, for that matter. You feel things too deeply, that's all."

"Then I don't belong here?"

"Who does?" He looked through her chart again. "What kind of physical shape are you in?" he asked. "Any problems?"

She found that a little puzzling. "Why?" she asked.

"*Mens sana in corpore sano.* A healthy mind in a healthy body. People—even doctors—separate mental problems from physical ones. That's a mistake. The mind and the body are one."

"That's what I was brought up to believe, sort of!" she cried excitedly. "We were Christian Science."

He winked at her. "Don't tell anyone I said so, Marilyn, but Mary Baker Eddy was no dummy. I'll tell you what—stand up and do a few deep knee bends."

"Knee bends?"

"I want to see what kind of shape you're in, that's all."

She got up—it was a pleasure not to be squatting on the floor like an autistic child—and did a few knee bends.

"Thank you. Now touch your toes a few times."

She was one of those lucky women who kept in pretty good shape without doing much about it, except for dancing practice, where her roles called for her to dance. She touched her toes easily without bending her knees.

"Run in place for a while."

She ran in place, stomach pulled in tight, working up a pleasant, gentle sweat, as her breasts jiggled in time to her steps.

"*Very* nice, Marilyn," he said. "No problems so far as I can see." He rose and put his ear against her chest, then placed his hand on her left breast, about where the heart was, his palm warm and slightly damp. "Good breathing, good heartbeat. Why don't you slip that gown on now, like a good girl?"

She picked up one of the gowns the nurse had tried to get on her, and sat down on the bed. "How do I get out of here? Will you call Dr. Kris?"

"Certainly. I can see no reason to keep you here at all." He gave her a bright, reassuring smile. "Good luck, Marilyn," he said, lingering in the doorway for a moment. Then he was gone and the door clicked shut behind him.

She could feel a small but growing sense of calm coming over her. Dr. Kris would soon have her out of here. She wasn't suicidal, after all—she had merely been overcome by the accumulation of bad luck: the divorce, Gable's death, then the press furor over Kay Gable's comments. . . . Anybody would break under such a load, she told herself.

She was beginning to feel hungry at last, and wished she hadn't refused to eat the last meal she'd been served. There was a knock on the door. "Come in," she called out, hoping it was lunch.

Should she apologize to the nurses? she wondered. She supposed so. They had just been doing their jobs. . . .

But it wasn't lunch. It was another doctor, a heavyset, elderly man with an impatient expression, who frowned at her over his half-moon glasses. "I see you've decided to put your gown on," he said curtly. She disliked him on sight—he had the fussy look of an unsuccessful producer.

"When do I get out of here? Have you talked to Dr. Kris yet?"

He puffed out his cheeks. He had sideburns and the florid complexion of a man with a touchy temper. "I have *not* talked to Dr. Kris, no," he said. "I have no reason to. You are in my care at the moment, not hers. As for when you get out of here, that will depend on my evaluation of your case. Judging from your behavior so far, it will not be soon."

That was not the kind of tone she was willing to accept, now that she was beginning to feel like a star again. "Fuck *you!*" she said. "Do you know who you're talking to? Marilyn Monroe, that's who."

"I'm talking to a patient suffering from clinical depression, severe neuroses, and a variety of addictions, who attempted to take her own life, *that's* who I'm talking to, young lady."

"I don't *belong* here."

He raised an eyebrow—an ineffectual gesture, she thought. Sir Cork Tip could have shown him exactly how to do it. "Why do you think that? I would say that this is exactly where you *do* belong."

"That's not what the other doctor said. Why don't you two guys get your act together?"

"What other doctor?"

"The one who was here a few minutes ago. Younger than you, better-looking, and a lot nicer. *He* said I was fine. He told me he'd have me out of here in no time too."

A look of deep suspicion had crossed his face, as if he thought she might be suffering from delusions, but now it was replaced by an unmistakable, sweaty concern, like that of a speeding driver who sees the flashing lights of a police car in his rearview mirror. "Ah, what did this doctor say his name was?"

She looked at the small nameplate pinned to his lab coat. It identified him as "Bernard Metzger, MD." She gave him a steely look—or as steely as she could manage in the circumstances. "He didn't say, Dr. Metzger, any more than you have. Is it okay if I call you Bernie?"

Metzger blushed. "Ah, certainly, of course. . . . What did he look like?"

"Tallish, thin, nice body. He looked a lot like my ex-husband. Arthur Miller," she added helpfully. "Only the doctor was younger and not as gloomy."

"Oh God!" Dr. Metzger said. His face had gone from red to an unhealthy white.

"What's the problem? He seemed okay to me—a lot more helpful than *you* are, Bernie. He examined me. . . ."

"*Physically?*" There was a look of horror on his face. "Not physically, surely?"

"Well, sure? He's a doctor, after all. What's wrong with that?"

Metzger sat down on the bed. "That's the problem. He's not a doctor."

"He's *not?*"

"No. He's a patient. When he gets loose, he steals a lab coat and poses as a doctor. He's supposed to be firmly locked up. Did he give you an, ah—*intimate*—examination?"

She saw a window of opportunity. If the hospital was in the wrong, she was sure the authorities would be happy to let her go rather than be exposed to the possibility of a lawsuit—or of publicity that would make them look ridiculous. "Very intimate," she said. "I thought he was a gynecologist. He had a gentle touch too."

Metzger banged his fist against his open palm. "This is terrible," he said.

She nodded. "It sure is. I'm going to have to tell Aaron Frosch, my lawyer, for a start."

"Aaron Frosch!"

"He's a *killer,* Aaron is. And that's not even *thinking* about the publicity. I mean, wait until I call a press conference. . . ."

Metzger seemed to be mumbling in a monotonous undertone. "Ruined," she heard him say.

She put a hand on his shoulder. "Bernie," she said, "I wonder if we could talk about sneaking me out of here without any publicity —not through the lobby, if you see what I mean?—to someplace quiet where I can have a phone and get some rest."

"Why, yes," Metzger said in a strangled voice. "I'm sure we could."

"Marilyn. Call me Marilyn, Bernie."

"Marilyn."

And so, two days after being locked up in Payne Whitney, she was moved to a lovely suite in the Neurological Institute at Columbia Presbyterian Hospital, without the press being any the wiser, with round-the-clock nursing by *real* nurses, not disguised female prison guards, and without bars on the windows.

She even had a telephone.

The first number she called was the White House.

33

Hoover wasn't used to being kept waiting, not even by presidents—*especially* by presidents, he told himself.

Presidents were ordinary men, after all—he had served them for decades, since 1924, "the year before the present attorney general was born," as he had arranged for tour guides to tell visitors to the Justice Department.

He had known all about FDR's affair, not to speak of Mrs. Roosevelt's odd "friendships"—had even recorded the embarrassing and indiscreet night she had spent with Joe Lash in a New York hotel room, and played it for the bemused President. He had had the goods on the financial shenanigans of Harry Truman's Kansas City friends in the Pendergast machine. He had intercepted all the letters to Eisenhower from his former mistress, Kay Summersby, reminding the President that he had promised to leave Mamie and marry her. . . .

Oh, he had known them, all right! Known the dirty little secrets of their sex lives, the buried political skeletons, the incautious friendships at school or college with young men who had turned to the left, or become homosexuals, or both, the flirtations with Moscow or married women, or Wall Street financiers. . . .

He did not flatter himself—he was a realist. They may not have liked him, they may not have trusted him, they may not have invited him to dinner in the White House private quarters upstairs—*but none of them had ever kept him waiting!*

The new president's appointments secretary and his chief of staff stood by the door as if they were guarding it, having exhausted their small talk. He could tell by their faces how much they disliked him.

Well, let them, he told himself. Had not some Roman emperor said, "Let them hate me, so long as they fear me"? He had only to look in his files to get his sweet revenge—the forgotten subscription to some leftist magazine, the girlfriend for whom an illegal abortion had to be procured, the college "discussion group" that was, in fact, a party cell. *I've got you, you insolent young puppies!* he thought, but then, to his horror, he realized it wasn't fear he saw in their eyes, it was pity.

Pity! That could only mean he was going to be asked to resign! He felt his temples throb, his throat turn dry, his hands holding the briefcase on his knees tremble.

Retirement! What would he *do*? What would become of him and Clyde, two old men living somewhere on the Florida Gold Coast, taking sedate walks on the beach, shopping for groceries together, spending their evenings going over his scrapbooks?

"The President will see you now, Director."

Blindly he rose and walked on unsteady legs into the Oval Office. The President stood up briefly, then sat down again behind his big desk, gesturing for Hoover to sit down in front of him.

This was not what he was used to. Presidents had always left their desks for him, to sit beside him on the sofa—except for FDR, who would place him in an armchair in front of the fire, then wheel himself so close their knees almost touched.

Discourtesy! he thought wildly, frightened by the speed at which his heart was pounding. He should have realized by the way the President's young lout of a brother had treated him what was in store. Bobby—he hated to even *think* of him as the attorney general —had removed the private line that linked the director of the FBI to the attorney general, so he had to go through a secretary like any-body else! Bobby had appeared in Hoover's office unannounced and in shirtsleeves, had summoned Hoover to his office and kept him standing while he played darts, occasionally missing, so they struck the paneling, a clear desecration of government property, and— worst of all—had encouraged FBI agents to report directly to him.

He cleared his throat, willing himself not to think about these insults to the dignity of his office. "You wanted to see me, Mr. President?" he asked.

The President looked like a schoolboy, he thought. It was strange —many of the new agents seemed to him so young that he had asked whether the minimum age had been changed, and was surprised to learn that it hadn't.

The President seemed nervous. "Ah, yes," he said curtly.

There was a silence. Hoover knew more about the use of power than almost anyone in Washington. From the way he had been kept waiting, the place where he had been seated, and the President's reluctance to begin the conversation, he now knew for certain what was to come. If he was lucky, the President might agree to keep him on till his seventieth birthday, but it was unlikely—these were ruthless young men, Hoover reminded himself, their father's sons.

"I was thinking about the future," the President began.

"Fraught with danger, Mr. President," Hoover said, desperate to put off the inevitable sentence he saw in the President's eyes. "The Communist conspiracy flourishes abroad—and at home, more strongly than ever. . . ."

"Maybe. That's not what I was thinking of, Edgar. I was thinking about the future of the FBI."

"So am I, Mr. President, night and day."

A look of annoyance crossed the President's handsome young face. "At every level of government, I'm committed to new ideas, young blood, change."

Hoover was drenched in sweat, but smiling grimly. "Experience is worth something too, Mr. President," he said in a strangled voice.

Any moment now, he thought, he's going to ask for my resignation, and I'll have to give it. Not even the director of the FBI could refuse a direct request from the President.

"So is change," Kennedy said with a little smile.

Damn him! Hoover thought, he's beginning to *enjoy* this! He opened the briefcase—now or never, he told himself. "I'm all for change," he said, staring right into his executioner's eyes. "Take technology, for example. Under my stewardship, the FBI has achieved a level of sophistication in surveillance techniques unmatched by any other security service in the world, including the Soviet KGB."

Kennedy raised an eyebrow, interested—and wary. "That's very gratifying, but—"

"I have here, for example, a transcript of a conversation between a known Soviet spy and a member of your administration, recorded from a distance of over one hundred yards, in Rock Creek Park. . . ." He took a piece of paper stamped "Top Secret" out of the briefcase.

The President's face hardened. "Put it back," he said harshly. "I'm not afraid of that kind of shit, real or faked. I don't believe there's an Alger Hiss in my administration, and I'm not going to have you inventing one, but if there *is*, I'll bust his ass into a federal penitentiary before you can even pick up the phone to Westbrook Pegler." He stared at Hoover, unblinking. "Nothing is forever. Not even you."

Before the President could say another word, Hoover took a second piece of paper out of his briefcase and slipped it faceup on the desk. Sweat was pouring down his face, but he willed himself not to take out his neatly pointed breast pocket handkerchief and wipe it. "I think this conversation may interest you more, sir," he said softly.

The President picked up the piece of paper with distaste and scanned it quickly, then he read the page over a second time, very slowly indeed.

"Who is, ah, Strawhead?" he asked, but Hoover could tell he was stalling for time.

"Miss Marilyn Monroe, sir," he said, savoring every syllable.

"I see." Kennedy read it again. His face was flushed. "Where did this piece of shit come from?" he asked.

"A source."

"Don't play games with me, Mr. Hoover. Have you been taping me?" The fury in his voice would have terrified most men, but Hoover merely feigned righteous indignation.

"Certainly *not*, Mr. President," he snapped. "We believe this conversation was recorded by a so-called 'surveillance expert' who works for Hoffa and a certain mob figure. . . ."

"Am I to understand that Mr. Hoffa has been bugging my apartment at the Carlyle?"

Hoover stared at him without blinking. "It appears so, yes."

"For how long? How much of this is there?"

"Quite a lot, Mr. President. It is not, ah—limited to Miss Monroe."

"I see. And you allowed this to happen?"

"By *no* means. As soon as I discovered what was happening, I sent one of our best men, Special Agent Kirkpatrick, to check on your residences. The eavesdropping devices have been removed, Mr. President. You can breathe easy. The secret is just between you and me."

"And Mr. Hoffa."

"Well, yes. But I anticipate that Hoffa can be dealt with." He coughed, covering his mouth politely with his hand. The President's expression was one of sheer, unadulterated hatred, and Hoover, sensing victory, reveled in it. "We have things on Hoffa that you wouldn't believe, Mr. President," he whispered. "An example—"

"I don't want to know," Kennedy said.

"As you please." Hoover affected an expression of injured dignity. "Is there anything else?"

"There are, ah—photographs. . . ."

"I meant, was there any other matter you wished to discuss?" The President had control of himself again. His expression was cold, hard, remote.

Hoover had only to look at him to know that if he ever made one slip, even the smallest, slightest one, the Kennedys would have his ass—that finding a good reason to get rid of him would be priority number one for them.

He didn't care. He felt twenty years younger—better yet, as if he were back at the peak of his career, tommy gun in hand, when he had burst upon the national consciousness with the death of Dillinger.

He would *never* give them a chance to get rid of him, he told himself triumphantly.

He would outlive them both!

———

"So the doctor was a phony?" Jack was still laughing at her story.

"You bet!"

"And now you're out. Cured."

"Who said cured? I'm still nuts. I've got this delusion that I'm in the Carlyle Hotel and I just fucked the president of the United States. If that doesn't prove I'm crazy, what does?"

"How was he? The President?"

"*Comme ci, comme ça,*" she said, waving one hand from side to side.

He reached over and tickled her. "Hey, knock that off!" she gasped, between fits of giggles. She took a deep breath. "Oh God," she said, "I can't *stand* being tickled."

"Mm. How about this? How does *that* feel?"

She gave a low, throaty moan. "I *like* that."

"I thought so."

"Don't stop, Mr. President."

He didn't. She lay back and let the pleasure flow through her body, erasing all the agony of the past few weeks. There was nothing like sex for taking your mind off things, she thought—unlike pills, it never failed, and there was no limit to how much you could take. . . .

She had wondered, at first, if it was going to be different being in bed with him now that he was president, and of course, it was and it wasn't. On the one hand, he was the same old Jack, but on the other, there was an undeniable kick from fucking the president of the United States. She supposed it was the same thing that men felt about fucking *her*—that because it was *Marilyn Monroe* they were fucking, it had to be special, so, in their minds, they made it so.

"Is it different?" he asked. "Now that I'm president?"

She giggled. "I like the Secret Service better than your old guys. They're better-looking."

He laughed. "They're really ballsy guys, the best in the world. I'd hate to be the guy who tries to kill *me*!"

His eyes shone—his enthusiasm for elite units was part of his romanticism. He had regaled her with stories about his discoveries in Washington. Bobby had just found out about the Green Berets; Jack was in love with the hard core of the CIA, men who used words like "infiltration" and calmly discussed the merits of poisoned darts versus silenced pistols. The secret agents, with their long tradition, their code words, their dark glasses and advanced technology, fitted into this category of special warriors, a small private army of James Bonds at the president's beck and call.

They held hands under the tangled sheets. "What's it like, now you've got it?" she asked.

"What?"

"The White House. The presidency."

He was silent for a moment. "It's like a wonderful machine that nobody's used in years," he said. "Whatever you want done, there's somebody in government who can do it. The trick is finding him."

He stared at the ceiling. "Some of it grabs you by the nuts," he went on. "There's an Air Force guy close to me twenty-four hours a day with 'the Football'—a briefcase with all the codes for starting a nuclear war. That makes you think, at first. Then you get used to it, like hearing 'Hail to the Chief,' or going through a door first even when you're with a woman."

He moved closer to her, his long, hard body against hers. "When I went up to Hyde Park to pay my respects to Eleanor Roosevelt," he said, "I stood aside to let her go through the door first, and she said to me, 'No, no, Mr. President—*you* always go first from now on.'"

He laughed, but she could tell he had been impressed. "That really got to me somehow, coming from Eleanor. . . ."

"Where is he now?"

"Who?"

"The guy with the codes."

"Sitting in a room down the hall, next to a secure phone."

"I'll bet he wishes he were in here."

"I'll bet he *does*. Well, fuck him. I'm the commander in chief, and he's only an Air Force warrant officer, so that's the way it is. Whoever said life is fair?"

"I don't know. Not me, for sure."

"That's my girl," he said. A telephone rang beside the bed. It was red, without a dial, and for a moment she felt her stomach turn cold. By some lunatic coincidence, was this going to be the moment when Jack would actually have to call for the Air Force warrant officer down the hall?

He picked it up and listened. "This *is* a secure line," he said with some annoyance.

He straightened up with a grunt of pain, while she slipped a couple of pillows behind his back. "Leave it to me, I'll talk to Bobby," he said. "Of course he isn't going to like it, he's got a hair up his ass over these guys, but they can't do the job in Cuba if they're in prison."

He listened impatiently. "I *said* I'd talk to my brother," he snapped, his voice cold and harsh. "I don't want to hear how difficult it is to find Castro . . . I don't *care* if he never sleeps in the same place two nights running. . . . It's your job to find out where he is, understood?"

He slammed down the receiver. "Goddamn Castro!" he said. "He's all I hear about. You'd think this administration is going to succeed or fail according to whether or not we get rid of Castro."

"I sort of *like* him," she said. "He's sexy."

His annoyance turned to interest. "You know, it's funny," he mused. "Jackie says the same thing. . . . I guess he *is* sexy too, if the CIA is right about his love life. . . ." He shook his head. "Castro's got star quality, all right, I'll give the son of a bitch *that*. Why is it that the people on *our* side seem so dull?"

"They aren't sexy."

"It's a problem for the free world."

"The free world has you, lover. That's sexy enough."

"If you say so."

"I say so. I'd swear it in court."

"God forbid!" he said, knocking wood on the top of the night table.

"I bet you'd *like* Castro, if you met him," she said.

"You think so?"

She nodded.

"Maybe you're right," he said thoughtfully. "He's young. He's smart. He's got a younger brother who's tougher than he is. He likes pretty women and he smokes cigars." He laughed. "I ought to have made *you* secretary of state."

He shook his head. "It's not the way it's going to be, though. Maybe Ike could get away with a Communist Cuba ninety miles from Key West, but I can't. Castro has to go. It's us or him."

"My money's on you," she said, giving him a kiss.

"Good," he said.

Then, with more doubt than she had ever heard in his voice before: "I hope to Christ you're right."

34

The first I heard about the Bay of Pigs was Adlai Stevenson's indignant denial in the UN that the United States was involved in the invasion of Cuba. The next was a call from Bobby, who said, "Come on down here right away. We just broke our cherry."

That was enough to tell me that poor Adlai had been hung out to dry in full view of the world by Jack and Bobby, and that we were in it, as their father was fond of saying, "up to our ass."

The Ambassador called as I was heading out the door on my way to La Guardia. "Those fucking bastards in the CIA," he growled. "I *warned* Jack I wouldn't give a day's pay for the whole lot of them. Now look what they've done to my boy!"

He was so angry that he was almost inarticulate. His voice was odd and I wondered if he had a cold; then I realized that he was crying. *"They've ruined my son's presidency,"* he howled, and his pain made me realize just how bad things must be.

If it hadn't been for the atmosphere of crisis, the whiff of defeat tarnishing Jack's presidency almost before it had begun, I would never have plunged in to help so quickly. I was still smarting over Jack's cavalier treatment of me the day after his election. Maria and I had been his guests at the inauguration, but though she was pleased to be at the center of attention, it didn't make up for his refusal to promise me the ambassadorship I coveted. Nothing, of course, could dim *her* admiration for our new president.

In the end, if Jack (and my country) needed me, I would go. Who, after all, can resist an appeal from the President of the United States? Particularly if you've known him since he was a schoolboy.

Besides, I was feeling restless and bored after my exertions in the campaigns for the nomination and the presidency. I not only missed the political action, I even missed my role as Jack's liaison with the mob—for now that he was in the White House, he had other matters on his mind, and so, it appeared, did they. Once he was elected, Jack's interest in Hoffa diminished to zero, and Bobby, who had sworn to put Hoffa in prison, found himself with more pressing matters on his hands as attorney general—civil rights being the first, containing J. Edgar Hoover the second. The war against Hoffa was relegated to the back burner, much to the relief of the boys in Chicago, and I was spared more of Jack Ruby's messages and further meetings with Red Dorfman.

I was ushered in to see the President without delay. Jack was pale, his face puffy, his eyes sunken and glazed with fatigue. "Well, David," he said, shaking my hand, "thanks for coming down. The shit has really hit the fan this time."

"What can I do for you, Mr. President?" I asked.

"Get on the phone right away and call in your markers, David. Damage control! Talk to Harry Luce, Punch Sulzberger, Bill Paley. . . . Do what you can. If you think my talking to any of them will help, I will, but I don't want to let myself in for any high-minded lectures on foreign policy or truth-in-government. Understand?"

"You've got it," I said. His expression was tight, all emotion banished, a stone mask. I wondered what was going on behind it. One thing about Jack I knew. He did not blame others when things went wrong; he blamed himself. "How bad is it?" I asked. "Bottom line."

He let out a long sigh. He was sitting tilted back in his chair behind his desk, his feet on the gleaming surface. "They stuck it to me good," he said.

"The Cubans?"

"The CIA."

"Strangely enough, that's what your father told me this morning."

"He's right. As usual."

There was a certain bitterness in Jack's voice. Close as he was to his father, the President of the United States was no more pleased to hear "I told you so" from him than was any other son.

"How are things going on the beachhead?"

"It's a slaughterhouse."

"Are we going to go in and help them?"

"No." His voice was remote, emotionless. "I've decided against any air strikes or naval bombardment. There's no point in reinforcing failure."

"Are we going to be able to get the men off the beaches?"

He stared out at the gray sky, his mouth set in a hard line. "Probably not," he said grimly.

"I see." In other words, it was a highly public failure, accompanied by every possible evidence of bad faith, incompetence, and subterfuge. Jack's worst enemies could not have produced a more devastating—or humiliating—scenario. He had played chicken with Castro and lost. "Where's Bobby?" I asked.

Jack shook his head. "He's been a rock," he answered, speaking slowly and softly. "I've learned a lesson, David. Bobby's the only person I can trust down here."

He picked up a paper clip and twisted it until it broke in his fingers. "The rest of them aren't worth *shit*," he said. "When we took over, Bissell told us all the wonderful things the CIA could do. 'I'm your man-eating shark, Mr. President,' he told me. Some shark! A minnow is more like it! The moment the shit hit the fan, Bissell was fielding the ball to the Joint Chiefs, and they were fielding it right back. The only thing they all agree on is that I'm responsible."

He swung back and forth in his chair. The Oval Office was absolutely silent, as if there were no crisis. Clearly, he had left instructions not to be disturbed.

"I thought sitting behind this desk made you powerful," he said. "You gave orders, things happened. But the president is the most vulnerable man on earth, out on a limb twenty-four hours a day, taking the blame while the bureaucracy calls the shots."

He seemed to have aged a decade since I had last seen him, only a few weeks ago. He would recover, of course—he was too young and vigorous not to—but after the Bay of Pigs disaster, I never thought of him as a young man again. He had grown into the presidency the hard way, I decided.

"By God," he said, "we're going to play hardball from now on—no more half-assed amateur operations. Maybe I'll go down in history as the president who failed to get Cuba back—though I'm not finished with Castro yet!—but I'm not going down in history as the president who lost Laos or Vietnam."

"It's an ambitious agenda." A dangerous one, too, I thought.

"I haven't even begun." He sighed and stood up stiffly. "I can't stand these meetings, but I have to go back. They're like autopsies—a bunch of doctors standing around a corpse trying to decide what went wrong. . . . Those poor bastards on the beach."

"The survivors, if there are any, may present a few problems too, Mr. President."

He nodded. "Who can blame them? We'll take care of them somehow."

"A few of them will be mad as hell."

"They won't be the only ones. Some of your old friends were backing the landings pretty heavily."

"*My* friends?"

"You know who I mean."

I knew whom he meant, and I didn't like it. "I didn't know *our* friends were involved, Mr. President."

"You didn't hear it from me. You didn't hear it at all. But the CIA had a separate plan. It was going to be a pincer attack, you see. The mob was supposed to take care of Castro just before the landing."

"Take care of?"

"Ah, neutralize."

"Neutralize?"

"*Terminate!*" he snapped impatiently. "You know what I mean."

I was appalled at the sheer stupidity of it all. "Jesus, Jack," I cried, forgetting to address him properly for the first time. "I'm the one who passed the offer on to you in the first place, but I never thought you'd *do* it. . . . It's *dumb!*"

"Well, yes. That's what everybody says, now that it's failed. . . . The mob doesn't turn out to be any more efficient than the CIA."

"I could have told you that. I *know* these people!" I glanced at him. "I should have been consulted."

I must have shown my resentment at being left out now that Jack was in the White House, because he looked embarrassed—as well he might. "It was all on a 'need-to-know' basis, David, as they say. . . ." He had picked up the jargon. "Anyway, you were better off *not* knowing, frankly." He paused. "I'm sorry," he said. "Really."

"These people have a *relationship* with me, for better or worse, let me remind you. I don't want them blaming me for something I had no knowledge of."

"I don't think you have anything to fear, David. They blame the CIA. They blame me."

I wasn't convinced. "Who communicated with them? And with whom, on their side?"

Jack's expression grew wary. "Giancana was their point man," he said. "He was the fellow the CIA dealt with."

He coughed. "A lot of people did the communicating, as a matter of fact," he added offhandedly. "I even had a, ah, *contact* myself." There was a guilty look in his eyes.

I was amazed. "A contact with Giancana? How *could* you take that risk? You should have used someone else. You should have used *me*."

"Yes," Jack said vaguely, nodding his head. He seemed embarrassed. "Yes, that would have been a good idea. In retrospect. But it just wasn't practical in this case, David. This was a case for a close, ah, *personal* contact. . . ."

He glanced at his watch, and I took the hint and went off to see what I could do with the press. Clearly, I was needed here, and he knew it.

———

Despite my efforts, the stories over the next few weeks were horrendous, even in papers that were normally sympathetic to Jack. The only ray of sunshine, so far as I was concerned, was that the mob connection never came up in any of them. I breathed a sigh of relief —prematurely, as it happened, for I eventually received a telephone call from Bobby, his voice more sharp-edged and impatient than usual, to inform me, in guarded terms, that "the natives were getting restless."

The natives in question, I guessed, were Giancana's people. I told him I didn't want anything more to do with them.

"Do it, please," Bobby said when I flew down to Washington to see him at his father's urging. Bobby had learned to mistrust the phones, a situation I found ironic for the attorney general of the United States! "For Jack's sake," he added, knowing that would clinch it.

"I don't know Giancana."

"So what? You know people who do."

"Jack—ah, the President—gave me to understand there's a direct connection to him, at a much higher level."

Bobby glared at me. "Forget you ever heard that!" he barked.

He was sitting behind his huge desk in the attorney general's dark, paneled office at Justice, with his dog, a surly Newfoundland, at his feet. It was considered a badge of honor in the New Frontier to have been bitten by Brumus, but it was not one I aspired to. I stared at the dog fiercely, and he stared back.

"My goddamn brother," Bobby said softly. "If only he could keep his pants zipped. . . ." He sighed. "Well, never mind. Whatever you heard, she's over and done with."

It was my first inkling that Jack's "contact" was a woman. I wondered how that had happened, then decided I didn't want to know.

"I still don't think going directly to Giancana was a good idea," I said. "However it was done."

"It was a lousy idea. Let's not make the same mistake twice. If you want to use a go-between, that's fine. Use your own judgment. Do whatever you have to, just so long as the message gets home."

"What message?"

"That they'd better keep their goddamn mouths shut."

"You think they won't?"

"I think they're already leaking, hoping the press will treat them like heroes. I want it stopped."

I didn't argue with Bobby—he was in no mood for an argument. Jack had made him his "prime minister" and chief hatchet man, giving him the power to wander into the most secret and sensitive parts of the government to root out those who had failed the test of toughness or, more important, loyalty to Jack. Bobby was fast becoming the second-most important man in government, and the most feared, and it showed on his face. It was Bobby who fired people who failed Jack, turned the IRS loose on Jack's opponents, found ways to send Jack's enemies to prison.

I was happy enough to leave him, in his present mood, and flew back to New York on the next plane. As luck would have it, I was no sooner home than I got a telephone call from Marilyn, who wanted to know if I could come over and have dinner with her. I had been dreaming of a hot bath and dinner on a tray in front of the television set, since Maria was out at a theater benefit, but from the sound of Marilyn's voice, she needed company badly, so I put my coat back on and walked over there.

Dinner, I saw, was to be Chinese food from take-out cartons—not at all what I had in mind. Marilyn did not look her best. Her face was puffy, her skin blotchy; her nails were badly chipped, the roots of her hair dark. Clearly, life as a divorcée did not suit her. I moved old newspapers, magazines, and record album covers off a chair so that I could sit down, while Marilyn poured champagne into two not-very-clean Baccarat flutes.

"It's just *terrible*, all this news about Cuba," she said. "Jack must be going crazy?"

"I saw Bobby today in Washington. He was very down."

"I called Jack. He sounded awful. He said if there was any truth to reincarnation, he wanted to come back as a movie producer instead of a politician, next time. 'Oh, no you don't!' I told him."

"How are *you* doing?" I asked.

"Oh, honey! You wouldn't believe! I'm practically *unemployable*."

"You?"

"Me. I was going to do *Rain* for NBC. You know? By W. Somerset Maugham?"

Marilyn always assumed that everybody's hold on culture was as tenuous as her own. "What happened?" I asked.

"They got cold feet when they heard about my problems," she said. She drained her champagne. "That's the breaks."

I was surprised that any network would pass up a chance to have Marilyn Monroe on prime time. Her stock must have fallen very low indeed, I thought, if even the TV people refused to buy.

She cracked open a fortune cookie. " 'Tell your best friend what's on your mind,' " she read.

"Not bad advice."

"You can't beat fortune cookies. They make more sense than analysts every time."

We ate quietly for a while, to the accompaniment of a stack of Sinatra records Marilyn had put on the turntable. When we were both sated to the point of nausea, Marilyn poured us each another glass of champagne and leaned back against a pile of cushions with her eyes shut. "David," she said. "The message from the fortune cookie? I made it up. Can I ask you about a couple of things that have been worrying me?"

"Of course. It sounded a little pat, frankly."

"Listen, if I told most people about this, they'd say I was crazy, you know? I've got a friend, a kid named Timmy Hahn. He's one of my fans—he follows me wherever I go in New York. You've probably seen him."

"About sixteen years old? Windbreaker and jeans? Sad face, like a little old man?"

"That's Timmy. I think he's kind of cute myself. He's devoted to me, anyway. He'll wait for me outside on the street when I go somewhere, sometimes until one or two in the morning. I call his mother sometimes, you know, and promise to look after him, but he doesn't know that. . . ."

"That's some fan, Marilyn."

"He worships me. I'm not exaggerating. He *literally* worships me, Timmy does. I've had dogs who looked at me more objectively." She sipped her champagne. "But he's smart, you know? He doesn't make things up. Anyway, I stopped to talk to Timmy this morning, on my way to the studio, and he told me he's been burglarized? He was really upset, poor kid."

"Well, sure. His house?"

"His room."

I raised an eyebrow. I couldn't imagine what this had to do with me, or why Marilyn seemed upset by it. Or why anybody would burglarize a sixteen-year-old kid's room.

"He keeps a diary, Timmy does," she explained. "That's what was stolen."

"Why would anybody take a kid's diary?"

"Well, it's not really a *diary*. It's more, like, he writes down everywhere I go—dates, times, places, and so on. . . ."

"Everything?"

"Everything," she said miserably, eyes downcast. "He's a pretty observant kid, Timmy. Persistent too. He doesn't miss much."

"I see." I saw, all right, and I was horrified.

"Timmy was really upset."

"Timmy isn't going to be the only one."

"He went to the police—his uncle's a cop—but they didn't take him seriously."

"No, I can understand that."

"Though Timmy said they were surprised. Apparently it was a really professional job, you know?"

It would be, of course, I thought.

"I wondered, should I tell him to call the FBI?"

It seemed to me the consequences of that might be appalling. "I don't think telling the FBI is a good idea, Marilyn," I said carefully. "Oh?"

"What I mean is, it may not be what Jack would want you to do."

She absorbed this. "Is it going to be a big problem for him?" she asked.

I didn't know. There was no shortage of compromising material in circulation about Jack's private life, but on the other hand, it sometimes takes only one small spark to create an explosion. Besides, rumors are one thing, written documents quite another. Anything in writing has a life—and a permanence—of its own, which, I suppose, is why Jack never wrote love letters.

"It's probably not a *big* problem," I said hopefully. "But I think Jack should be warned."

"I can tell him in Florida."

"You're going to Florida with him?"

"Not exactly. I thought I might go see Jack's father—and Jack, if he's there."

I remembered Jack *had* mentioned that he was playing with the idea of spending a couple of days in Palm Beach, "if the dates worked out." He had not said which dates—or whose—he was thinking of.

"Didn't I read you were going back to California?" I asked, annoyed with myself for sounding as if I were Marilyn's husband or father. She had no obligation—I reminded myself—to keep me informed of her movements. Still, I felt left out, even cheated.

"First I'm going down to visit my ex," she said.

DiMaggio had reentered Marilyn's life after the Payne Whitney episode, out of genuine concern for her welfare, I believe, since he was a thoroughly decent man. It is possible that he may also have had hopes of getting together with her again, which, knowing Marilyn, I suspect she may have encouraged, but he continued to feel—as he would to the end—a responsibility toward her. She was convinced that he was the one person who would always come to her rescue if she was in real trouble, and she was probably right.

"I promised I'd cheer up Jack's dad," she went on. "He's been sick, you know."

I was so startled that I swallowed down the wrong tube and started to choke. Marilyn rushed over and got behind me, pounding away at my back until I caught my breath at last. She was amazingly strong for a woman of her size. "Are you okay?" she asked.

I nodded. My surprise had been caused by the fact that Joe Kennedy's increasingly poor health was the deepest of family secrets. Even in the family it wasn't discussed—or perhaps *noticed,* for Joe's children were so used to his robust vitality and unfailing good health that they were emotionally incapable of seeing that he was becoming old and frail. The razor-sharp tongue and hair-trigger mind were still there, but he who had always been so proud of his physique was now painfully thin, almost emaciated, his heavily veined hands trembled, and he was beginning to walk with an old man's cautious shuffle. Being who he was, he refused to acknowledge this himself. As for Rose, she had schooled herself over the decades not to see anything that could cause her pain.

Jack *had* noticed, probably because Bobby, who was so much closer to the old man, pointed it out to him—and had discussed it with me cautiously, as if he was bewildered by the phenomenon. He had proclaimed at his inauguration that the torch was being passed to a new generation of Americans—an expression of his annoyance at the way Ike had lectured him as if he were a junior officer during the transition, when he was president-elect—but he was not yet prepared for the torch to be handed over to him in the Kennedy family. Nor was his father, who was busy running a one-man campaign to put Teddy into Jack's old seat in the Senate—a project that failed to stir any enthusiasm on the part of Jack and Bobby.

"Sorry about the coughing fit," I said. "I didn't realize Jack had told you that his father isn't well."

She gave a moue, intended, I guess, to show her mild annoyance at my underrating the confidence Jack placed in her. "Baby, Jack *talks* to me. He doesn't have any secrets from *me*. . . . Well, I don't mean he tells me about the missile gap or anything. But personal stuff, you know, like his family, he tells me a lot. . . . I mean, it isn't just *sex* between us, you know? Jack can unwind with me. He talks to me a lot more than any of my husbands ever did. It's funny," she went on dreamily. "It's like having a family of my own, at last. I get these nice notes from Jack's father, even from his *sisters*. The Ambassador sent me a smoked salmon the other day. I put it in the freezer."

She had picked up the family habit of referring to Jack's father as "the Ambassador," a post he had not held for twenty years. As for the salmon, this was one of the Ambassador's small acts of institutional generosity. He had an interest in some company that imported Irish smoked salmon, and was determined to prove to the world that the Irish variety was superior to that of Scotland. Jackie had even been persuaded to serve it at the White House, until the Pacific salmon smokers got wind of it and insisted on her serving American smoked salmon instead.

The idea of Marilyn settling down to a kind of cozy illicit membership in what was rapidly becoming America's First Family was strange to contemplate.

"I *like* Jack's father," she said. "He's feisty."

"You could say that, yes."

"He was really upset about this Cuba thing, though."

"He's got cause to be."

"He told me not to worry—that Jack's going to get Castro yet. 'His days are numbered,' he said."

"He told you *that*?"

"Mm."

I leaned over and took her hand. "Marilyn," I said, "do yourself a favor, please. Don't ever breathe a word of that to *anybody*."

She giggled, and gave me a good-night kiss. She had been taking pills throughout the evening with her champagne, and while she was not yet sleepy, her words and movements were beginning to slow down, like a movie in slow motion. "Don't worry about it," she said, articulating very carefully. "My lips are sealed."

———

"I'm not interested in all this gossip, Edgar, nor is my brother," Bobby Kennedy said stiffly. "It's all lies. I mean, if the President and I were going to keep a bunch of call girls on tap, do you suppose we'd put them on the twelfth floor of the LaSalle Hotel and have the Secret Service close the floor off two or three times a week for us? We might as well do it in the lobby of *The Washington Post*."

Hoover nodded majestically. "I did not take this rumor seriously, General. But I feel it incumbent upon me to pass on any rumors relating to the President or his family."

"It's a waste of time. Whoever is digging up all this nonsense ought to be working on putting the bad guys behind bars. Who was the source for this crap, anyway?"

"A chambermaid at the LaSalle Hotel."

"Oh, *great!* Is that all?"

Hoover kept smiling, sustained by his all-consuming hatred of the Attorney General. "No," he said, "it's not all."

"If it's another rumor about a paternity suit, like last week. . . . If your people can't come up with anything better than rumors, I'm going to have to start questioning the FBI's efficiency—and common sense."

Hoover placed on the Attorney General's cluttered desk, right next to an ashtray that seemed to have been made in a kindergarten crafts class, what looked like a school notebook, with a red cover and a label on which somebody had carefully lettered, in different-colored inks, the single word "MARILYN," with the dot above the *i* lovingly rendered as a heart. Below, in less ornate letters, was the name "Timmy Hahn."

"What's this?" Kennedy said.

"It's a diary. Perhaps you should look at the pages I've had paper-clipped."

There was a long silence while Bobby Kennedy turned the pages.

His expression gave nothing away—he was not about to give Hoover that satisfaction. When he had finished, he put the notebook back on his desk and sighed. "Where did this come from?" he asked.

"I'm satisfied it's genuine."

"That's not what I asked."

"We obtained it," Hoover said. "To protect the President."

"I see. Did you have a search warrant?"

"It would have been incautious to bring this matter before a federal magistrate, don't you think?"

"Mm." The Attorney General was not about to excuse a felony out loud, even in his private office.

"I think it's important that this is brought to the President's attention."

"Why?"

"First of all, to urge greater caution on him. Secondly, to show him that the FBI is working night and day to protect his interests— and privacy."

Kennedy nodded glumly. "I'll make sure he hears about it."

"Good. And we'll keep up the good work, you may be sure."

"I'm sure." Kennedy did not stand up. He merely reached across the desk to shake Hoover's hand. "By the way," he asked casually, "is there a copy of this?"

Hoover stood, feet firmly planted, chin thrust out, the living image of bulldog tenacity. "Only for my files," he said. He smiled grimly. "It's safe there."

———

I decided that the mission Bobby had given me to pass a message on to Giancana was best carried out by having breakfast with Paul Palermo.

We met in the Oak Room at the St. Regis, across the street from my office. Paul had several more or less legitimate business interests that could explain my meeting with him, and if anybody in law enforcement happened to notice us together, the Oak Room would at least seem like an improbable place for the commission of a felony.

"We got problems," Paul said, as soon as the waiter was out of earshot.

"I know. That's why I wanted to see you. My people"—I was not about to mention the name Kennedy here—"were disappointed by what happened. Or, to be more precise, by what *didn't* happen."

"Hey, that's too bad, but it's not our fault." Paul leaned forward, his voice a whisper. "Our people did what they were supposed to. The material they were provided was defective."

I had the wit not to ask what material he meant. I simply raised an eyebrow as I ate my eggs.

"Look," Paul went on, holding his hands out to indicate that he was being honest with me, "no workman is better than his tools, right?"

I nodded, as if I knew what "tools" he was talking about.

"These guys were supposed to poison the man's cigars, right? They risked their lives to put the poison in the cigars, and what happens? Zip, that's what happens! The man lights up one cigar after another and doesn't turn a hair. That's not our fault. Then there's the stuff we're supposed to sprinkle in his fatigues that will poison him when he starts to sweat? Our guys got some broad to do the job while he's asleep after fucking her, some German girl, which she *does;* then he gets dressed and goes out and gives a four-hour speech in the sun, sweating like a fucking pig, and *nada!* Defective materials were supplied."

I was more than a little shaken by these revelations, but I tried not to show it. "The people you're dealing with pay only for success, Paul. I don't think they're going to buy the 'defective materials' argument, frankly."

"They're gonna *have* to, David. My people did what they said they would. It isn't their fault it didn't work out. They took risks. They had certain expenses. They have a right to what they were promised."

"I'm not aware that promises were made."

"All right, maybe not promises, but strong hints. Instead of which, look what's happened! Momo gets held for hours by the Feds on his way to Mexico, which is very embarrassing because he's traveling with his girlfriend. Carlos Marcello—you know who he is?"

I nodded glumly.

"Carlos gets deported to Guatemala over some bullshit citizenship thing. Put on a plane, flown out of the country, and dumped in the middle of nowhere. Look, you have to understand what's at stake here. Momo went to Johnny Roselli with this Cuba thing, and Roselli went to Meyer Lansky, laid it all out for him beside the pool of the Deauville Hotel in Miami; then Lansky brought in Carlos Marcello and Santo Trafficante because they're the ones who know Cuba inside out. . . . Momo made certain promises all the way down the line, and now he's embarrassed, he's lost respect. . . . In his line of work, that's *dangerous,* David. He's got Hoffa on his back too. He's not a happy man."

"My people aren't happy either, Paul."

"Well, but they have the big guns, David, your people. *My* people aren't in the White House. Not yet, anyway." He laughed. "Meantime, they're mad as hell."

"The chief concern at the moment on our side is whether they will keep their mouths shut."

Paul looked pained. "David, these are stand-up guys. They won't talk. That's not the problem. The problem is, you have to do the right thing by them. They don't think the right thing was kicking Carlos Marcello out of a car in the middle of the fucking jungle in his five-hundred-dollar alligator loafers and telling him to start walking."

I could see that. I had met Marcello once, on a visit to Havana in the old days, and he hadn't struck me as a man who did much walking.

"They just want what's right," Paul emphasized, finishing his eggs and wiping his mouth fastidiously. His diamond pinkie ring gleamed, even in the subdued lighting—the one sign that he didn't belong here. "Just so there aren't any misunderstandings."

"I'll pass it on."

"Please do. I mean, it's already *been* passed on, right to the top, they tell me, by a certain lady who shall be nameless, right?"

"Right," I said, wondering who the lady was.

He laughed. "Maybe she was too busy doing something else to make the point."

"It's possible," I said, a little stiffly.

Paul rose, and we shook hands. "Always a pleasure," he said. "The next one is on me."

———

Bobby and I met the next day at lunchtime at Hickory Hill.

The house had none of its former elegance. Neither Bobby nor Ethel cared about that kind of thing—their houses were designed around children and dogs. There were so many of both in the house that it was impossible to speak, so Bobby took me outside, where we paced back and forth, surrounded by a pack of large dogs, some of them Bobby's, some of them visitors from neighboring estates. He was wearing a leather flying jacket with the insignia of the squadron that had presented it to him, and his hair, longer than usual, was blowing in his eyes; he had to brush it back with his hand from time to time. His eyes, I thought, were sadder and more remote than ever, as if his new role as the President's troubleshooter was exposing him to secrets he would have been happier not knowing.

I told him about my breakfast with Palermo, and he listened silently. "I don't believe they did a thing," he said when I'd finished. "I think they fed the CIA a whole pack of promises and lies, and extorted money and weapons from them for nothing. The whole thing was a con game from the beginning, and the CIA guys were too goddamn stupid to realize they were being taken."

"It sounded convincing to me."

"Of course it did. These guys are pros. The German girl, the poisoned cigars, the powder in Castro's fatigues—that's exactly what the CIA wanted to hear."

"Did they provide the mob with all that stuff—the poisons and so on?"

"Yes. They've been developing things in their labs you wouldn't believe. Shellfish toxins that can't be detected in an autopsy, silent poison-dart guns, transmitting devices a woman can insert in her vagina. . . ." His expression was one of disgust.

He picked up a stick and threw it, sending the dogs off in noisy pursuit. "Of course, they were dying for a chance to try out all this crap, so when these fellows Marcello and Trafficante promised to use it against Castro, they fell all over each other at Langley to give them everything they asked for. . . . Money, speedboats, radio transmitters, guns, you name it. The hoods must damn near have died laughing."

"You think it was a hoax?"

"Absolutely. And now they're back, asking for pardons! Over my dead body!"

"They think Jack promised them that—or something like it."

"Well, he didn't. He didn't promise them a goddamn thing. And I keep telling you, they didn't *do* anything either, unless you count cheating the CIA out of hundreds of thousands of dollars and all sorts of weaponry nobody should have put in their hands in the first place."

"Bobby, do you know it for a fact?"

"There are no facts here. The guys at the CIA wouldn't recognize a fact if it bit them. As for the mob guys, they have never told anyone the truth in their lives."

"How about the German girl?"

"I think they put that part in to interest Jack. That was the first question he asked—was she good-looking?"

"And?"

"Of course she was. They wouldn't have produced a photo of an *ugly* blond girl, would they?"

"Speaking of girls, Palermo mentioned there's one who's the link between Jack and Giancana. He didn't mention any names."

"It's true," Bobby said grimly.

"Wasn't that a little dangerous?"

His eyes bored hard into me—his way of warning me to get off this subject. I stared right back—I hadn't worked for the Ambassador for so many years for nothing. "Yes, it's a problem," he said through clenched teeth. "Some things have to change, I know it, but it can't be done in a hurry. Jack is Jack—he's not about to take up a life of celibacy just because he's the president. Or give up the Sinatra connection right away either, though he knows what I think about it. So forget about Giancana's girl, this Campbell woman." He sighed. "I had to deal with one the other day who turned out to be an East German agent, and get Hoover to deport her quietly. . . ."

He paused. "There are people, particularly out on the West Coast, who have been taking advantage of Jack's good nature," he said. "When the time comes, I'm going to make sure they get what they deserve."

"Bobby," I said, "are you sure you know what you're doing?"

His eyes were ice-cold as he turned to me. "Completely sure, David," he said sharply.

I was about to argue the point, when a horde of children came pouring noisily out of the house and surrounded us. Bobby, like the Pied Piper, led them off into a rough-and-tumble game of touch football.

I went back inside, said good-bye to Ethel, and told my driver to take me to National Airport.

I tried to convince myself that Bobby was right, but I didn't believe it for a moment.

35

The first thing she noticed was how much the Ambassador had aged. Quite suddenly, in the bright Florida sun, she was looking at an old man.

"I get these goddamn shooting pains in my arm," he complained. "And headaches. I don't know what the hell's the matter with me."

She got an empty feeling in the pit of her stomach. Gable had made the same complaints during the last weeks of shooting *The Misfits*. They had been the warning signals of a heart attack.

"You should see a doctor," she said.

"I don't believe they know a goddamn thing, Marilyn. I had a bad cold, that's all, and I'm at the age when you don't bounce back. Hell, I play golf every afternoon and I'm fit as a fiddle." He gave her a roguish wink, though the effort was anything but cheerful: his lined, emaciated face was made somehow more skull-like by the big, square Kennedy teeth.

"What are you going to do with yourself now?" he asked, apparently anxious to get away from the subject of his health.

"I'm going back to LA."

"Good! New York is no damned good. The Jews have taken over the media and Wall Street, and before you know it, the niggers are going to be moving downtown from Harlem and you won't be able to walk in the streets, mark my word. I liquidated all my property there, got out while the going was good. I hope you're going back to work?"

"If anybody will have me."

"They'll have you. You're a star." He talked about her career the

399

way he talked about his boys', she thought—as if all he had to do was will them to succeed. Maybe he was right. She hoped so. The few properties 20th Century–Fox had shown her so far were awful, remakes of remakes, or second-rate song-and-dance pictures. The studio was a different place now, since the board had finally worked up the courage to throw her old nemesis Zanuck out, and nobody seemed to have the foggiest notion what use to make of her.

"Maybe," she said. "They're not in any hurry, I can tell you."

"Wait the bastards out. And don't rent when you get out there. Renting is a mug's game. Buy a nice little house for yourself. If you have any problem raising the money, tell me and I'll help you out. You've got to *own* things, Marilyn, that's what I always told Gloria. You won't be young and beautiful forever."

She nodded like a good little girl, and thanked him for his advice.

He eyed her suspiciously. "You look just like Jack when I give *him* financial advice. He nods and forgets about it. Nobody in this family would have a pot to piss in if I hadn't made a fortune for them. How does Jack strike you?"

"He's in terrific shape."

"He's coming into his own," the Ambassador said, adjusting his rakish straw hat. "This Cuba thing did him a lot of damage, but people have short memories. He's going to be the best president of the century. There's no doubt at all in my mind on that score."

"Me too." It was true, she thought. It was scary how much faith she had in Jack, she who had never really trusted any man. She would do anything in the world for him except say good-bye, and she couldn't imagine that he would ever want her to do that.

A car door slammed, and a couple of Secret Service agents stationed themselves behind the flowering hedge, at the far side of the pool. The moment they were in place, Jack appeared through the small gate into his father's private domain, grinning cheerfully. "This is the life," he said. "They don't live this way at the Kremlin, I'll bet."

"No," his father said, "but they pay attention to business, those guys. It might not be a bad idea to follow their example."

At first she hadn't understood that the insult, the jab to the ego, was the family style, that nothing personal was involved, but she had come to understand that the Kennedy family was like a pride of lions who played, and showed affection for each other, by fighting. Their claws were retracted just far enough to leave nothing worse than a scratch, and though they might draw blood, they never bit to the bone.

"If Khrushchev could see the way we live, he'd convert to capitalism," Jack said. He came over and gave her a kiss, resting his hand on her lower back, then letting it drop an inch or two lower.

The gate opened and David Leman came over. She offered him her cheek. "You're sexier in Florida than you were in New York," he said.

"Flatterer." The truth was, she *did* look better here. She was a California girl. Sunshine usually cheered her up.

"David and I have been talking strategy," Jack said. He did not elaborate on what *kind* of strategy, but she noticed that there was a trace of anger and resentment behind the relaxed, good-natured facade—enough to make her wonder what David had come all the way down to Florida to tell Jack.

"Did you boys get your business settled?" the Ambassador asked. She suppressed a giggle. Only Joe Kennedy would describe the President of the United States and David Leman as "boys."

Jack nodded. He had slipped his sunglasses on, which made his expression hard to read. He said nothing.

"Bobby's right," the Ambassador persisted. "I *know* these guys. I've dealt with them. They're just scum. You don't want to let them push you around."

"I'm not *planning* to let them push me around."

"Well then. Tell them to go to hell. Take my word for it, they'll back off like mongrel dogs, isn't that right, David?"

David's face was a study in polite confusion. Whatever was under discussion, it was clear that he didn't agree with Joe Kennedy's rosy view of it, but also clear that he wasn't anxious to get in an argument with the old man. "Probably," he said cautiously. "But it doesn't pay to squeeze them too hard, in my opinion. Give them an out. Let them save face. That's my point."

"You're soft," Joe snapped. "Soft for a bunch of fucking guineas. Let Bobby deal with them."

"Bobby's *going* to deal with them," Jack said flatly, ending the discussion. He took her by the hand. "Let's go for a, ah, *drive,* shall we?"

She went over and gave the Ambassador a big kiss on his dry skin. He clutched her with a clawlike hand and said, "God, but I wish I were twenty years younger!" His fingers dug deep into her flesh, as if her youth and vitality might keep him going for another day.

She gave David a quick kiss while Jack said good-bye to his father; then he guided her through the gate, down a small flight of stone steps, and out through a door in a thick flowering hedge into a kind

401

of alleyway, where an ordinary gray sedan with blacked-out windows waited, with a couple of "backup" cars behind it. There were perhaps a dozen Secret Service agents standing around, who sprang into action at the sight of the President. She was half led, half pushed into the car, which moved off before the agents standing beside it had even finished slamming the doors shut. "Lancer and Strawhead on board," the agent at the wheel said into his microphone.

As they turned into the street, a white sedan pulled out ahead of them. There was another somewhere behind them. "Isn't all this kind of obvious?" she asked. "Everybody in Palm Beach must know who you are and where you're going."

Jack grinned. "Not at all. About five minutes ago, the presidential limousine pulled away from the front door of the house with flags flying and police cars in front and behind flashing their lights. The presidential press corps is off in full pursuit, and when they get to the Everglades Club—a long drive, by the way—they're going to see my old friend Lem Billings get out."

She laughed. "They'll know you gave them the slip."

"So what? It's the old cat-and-mouse game, with me as the mouse. I figure I'm entitled to my privacy. Though it took me a while to convince the Secret Service." Both agents in the front seat laughed. They obviously enjoyed playing the game as much as Jack did.

The car pulled into a driveway screened by high hedges, a garage door rose in front of them, and they stopped inside, remaining in the car until it closed behind them. One of the agents opened a door and led them up a flight of stairs into the famous hideaway she had visited before, which the Ambassador had prudently bought years ago so his pleasures wouldn't be interrupted by the presence in Palm Beach of his wife.

Jack popped open a bottle of champagne for her. She kicked off her shoes and flopped down on the big white sofa beside him.

Jack, now that he was indoors and at rest, looked more tired and disgruntled than she had thought. He let out a sigh, slipped off his loafers, and put his legs up on the sofa. She snuggled up beside him, unbuttoning his shirt. "Is the job getting to you, Mr. President?" she asked, rubbing her hands down his back.

"You could say that."

"It's what you wanted."

"It's not what I want right now."

"I'm all for everybody having what they want," she whispered, giving his ear a gentle bite.

She let him unzip the back of her dress, then lay down on top of him, listening to the faint, antiseptic hum of the air-conditioning system. At first she thought she wasn't going to get aroused, despite her feelings at the pool when he touched her, but there was something about the scene itself that suddenly got to her—the fact that he was fully dressed while she had on only her bra; the fact that they were in a secret hideaway surrounded by armed agents, their radios crackling as they patrolled the perimeter, that he was Lancer, the president of the United States, and she was Strawhead, the country's number-one blonde; the fact, above all, that this was just about the only thing in her life that still made any sense, for the moment the only thing she could still *feel*, except panic. She had never felt more intensely how much she loved him, and it excited and frightened her at the same time.

They both came rapidly, and she lay on top of him for what seemed like a long time, her lips against his, matching her breathing to his, wondering if he was asleep and wishing that the air-conditioning weren't set quite so high, for she was beginning to get goose bumps.

"That's the best thing that's happened to me today," he said.

"Me too. I'm going back to California, you know."

"I'll be coming out there. Often."

"Good, darling. I've got to get back to work. Sitting around New York on my ass isn't right for me."

"It's quite an ass." He glanced at his watch—the one she had given him, long ago. "Christ!" he said. "I've got to be going." He swung himself to his feet—wincing in pain as he stood up—zipped up his pants, and slipped his feet into his loafers, ready to go, whereas she was still sprawled on the sofa, bare-assed, her hair like a bird's nest and her makeup a disaster area. "You'll have to give me a few minutes," she said.

"Sure," he said. She went into the nearest bathroom, which some thoughtful soul, knowing how the house was used, had filled with every possible cosmetic and perfume, and set about repairing her face. Jack came in, restless as always after sex, and sat down on the bidet. He had a bottle of soda in his hand. "Are you going to be okay in LA?" he asked.

"I guess so, lover. I've been there before. Why?"

"It's going to be tough going back. Where are you staying?"

She shrugged. "The Beverly Hills Hotel, at first. Then, I don't know. Rent some place maybe, until I can buy a house."

"If you need anything, I can call Frank or Peter."

"I'll be fine." She wasn't sure it was true. Living in New York, she had seen more of Jack than ever before—seen enough of him, in fact, to grow used to it, for, as poor Timmy Hahn's diary no doubt recorded, the President spent the night at the Carlyle Hotel more often than anybody supposed.

It wouldn't be the same—*couldn't* be—once she moved back to LA, and she was dreading that part of it. It had been five years since she left California at Milton Greene's urging, she thought for good, to start a new life in New York as a serious actress and the wife of America's most admired playwright—as somebody who was a *person*, not the ultimate Hollywood "Blond Bombshell." Now she was returning, divorced, unemployable, and still saddled with the same contract she had been trying to break when she first met Milton, a lifetime ago.

She looked at her face in the mirror, then turned, tears forming in the corners of her eyes, and cried, "Oh, Jack, I'm so fucking *scared*."

He got up, put his soda down, and embraced her, holding her tightly against him. He held her for as long as she needed to be held, then said, in a quiet, gentle, serious voice: "Don't *ever* be scared of anything."

36

But fear set in by the time she was on the plane to LA.

Five years, she told herself, was a long time. In the eyes of the world she was still the reigning blonde, but her name on a picture was no longer box office magic, and the stories about her lateness and personal problems frightened directors and producers off. Maybe she could overcome that, but what she *couldn't* overcome was her sense that she was returning to the town of her birth a failure.

She felt it so strongly in her bungalow at the Beverly Hills Hotel, the same one in which she had begun her affair with Yves and ended her marriage to Arthur, that she moved out after a week to Frank Sinatra's house—he was out of town—while she looked for an apartment, only to find that her old one, at Doheny and Cynthia Streets, was vacant.

She moved in with her suitcase, hardly even bothering to unpack. She slipped into a round of regular appointments with her analyst, Dr. Ralph Greenson; her internist, Dr. Hyman Engelberg; and several other doctors she neglected to tell Greenson about.

Gradually she began once again the endless round of acquiring what she needed in the way of prescriptions, spending her days in doctors' offices and her evenings tracking down neon-lit, all-night pharmacies where she wasn't known, for, to her terror, she required ever larger quantities of pills to have the slightest effect on her system —quantities that would have set off alarm bells in the minds of Dr. Greenson and Dr. Kris.

She was soon swept up into "the Rat Pack" as a kind of camp follower, following in their hard-drinking wake, "best friends" with

Frank, with Peter Lawford, Sammy Davis, Jr., and Dean Martin, picking out the girls for them, knocking back the drinks with them, sharing their dirty jokes, noisy fun, and rebellion against all the rules of stardom and the studios.

Oh, she loved them all—thought of them as "her boys": Dino, Sammy, Frankie, Peter—and they all respected her, since they were in on the secret of her relationship with "the Prez," as she now referred to Jack, but her nights were still spent wakeful and alone in her bed, in the same rented apartment from which she had set out to conquer the world.

Frank sent her a little dog to keep her company, since after a few drinks, she would always complain tearfully about poor Hugo, the dog she had left behind in Connecticut with Arthur. The dog was small, fluffy, white, a real Miami hooker's dog, and immediately became hopelessly devoted to her. She named it Mafia, as an in-joke between herself and Frank, and quickly shortened it to "Maf," though everyone pronounced it "Mof," to rhyme with "mop," which the dog sort of resembled.

She called Jack at least once a day on the private number he had given her. She didn't always reach him, but that was understandable —she didn't expect to every time. When she did, he was sometimes able to talk for only a moment, though at other times he seemed to have time to spare.

There were times when they talked for hours, and others when he took a call from her during a meeting and spoke in a hushed whisper, pretending that she was someone in the Pentagon, and even one unfortunate slipup when Jackie picked up the telephone and hung up immediately.

All the same, the calls to the Prez kept her going, and on days when she had talked to him, she slept a little better, and needed fewer pills. Sometimes when she spoke to him late at night, she would masturbate, lost in a lazy, sensual state of half dreaming, half waking, her senses glowing with the sound of his voice, the pills, and the wine.

It was not missing Jack that depressed her the most—though that was bad enough—it was the fact that the studio really had nothing to offer their biggest star. Much as she had hated Zanuck, at least he would have put her in a picture or even two pictures by now. The new management were cost-cutting, accountant types, in the process of letting the whole studio drift into bankruptcy, yet they treated *her* as if she were Typhoid Mary!

"How've you been, kiddo?" Aaron Diamond, the superagent, shouted at her one night when they ran into each other at a party at Frank's house.

"Great, Aaron," she said, leaning over to kiss his bald head as if it were a good-luck statue, a polished Buddha.

"Then how come you look like shit?"

She wasn't offended. Diamond was tough as nails, but deeply sentimental—a combination peculiar to the movie industry.

"I thought I looked pretty good, Aaron," she said.

"Nah. You can't look *bad*, kiddo, it ain't in you, but you don't look happy. How's the love life?"

"The love life is *comme ci, comme ça.*" She waved her hand.

"How's the career?"

"More *comme ci* than *comme ça*, I guess."

"Those schmucks in your own studio are talking you down, you know that, don't you? They'd rather go down the toilet with *Cleopatra* than put you to work."

"They've shown me some things. . . . Nothing I've liked."

"*Bubkis,* right? They're hoping you'll turn everything down, then they can sue you for breach. Listen, I got a property, a remake of an old Irene Dunne/Cary Grant picture, *My Favorite Wife*, I think, which Dino wants to do. It's called *Something's Got to Give* now. The script is terrific—a really smart comedy, just your kind of thing. Let me talk to them."

"Mm." She was tempted by the idea of working with someone she *liked*, like Dean Martin. Dino, she felt sure, would back her against the studio, if and when there were problems. "I'll read the script, Aaron," she said. "Send it round."

"Done. First thing tomorrow." Diamond patted her bottom and vanished into the crowd as if he had never existed, but the script turned up at her apartment the next morning.

The moment she read it, she could tell it *might* work for her. It was about a woman who has been missing for seven years and comes back to find that her husband has remarried since her presumed death. The dialogue was good, with just the kind of brittle wit that appealed to her, and there were some nice comic touches she could do something with.

Everything seemed hunky-dory, at last.

Then she fell apart.

When I heard that Marilyn was in a hospital in New York, I rushed over there immediately. For once, she had managed to get herself admitted with a minimum of publicity, and I found her resting comfortably, though looking as thin as Audrey Hepburn.

Apparently, she had been overtaken by a series of physical disasters. First her doctors in LA had rushed her to Cedars of Lebanon for a pancreas operation; then she had flown to New York, I guess to see Jack, where she suffered a gallbladder attack and required another emergency operation.

I hadn't realized how delicate her bone structure was until I saw her in the hospital. "How are you feeling?" I asked, giving her a kiss.

"Okay. Really. The doctor was sweet. He promised to keep the incision really tiny, and he did."

"No pain?"

"Not much. The Ambassador's old friend Marion Davies was in Cedars. Dying of cancer. She called me and said, 'Us blondes seem to be falling apart.' I guess it's true."

"You don't look as if you're falling apart."

"Oh, you'd say anything to make me happy," she said, and I could tell she didn't mean it as a compliment.

"I hear the studio is in a panic."

"Fuck the studio," she said, in her sweetest little-girl voice. "I can't help it if my pancreas and my gallbladder gave out."

"It's tough luck."

She shrugged. "The worst of it was that I was on my way to see the Prez. I mean, how do you like that? Canceling a date with the President of the United States! He's been sweet, though. He sent me a sheepskin to put under my back in bed, the one he used after his back operation. It made a big difference, he said. I told him it was a pretty lucky sheep to have had Jack Kennedy sleeping on it!"

She laughed. She seemed in pretty good spirits for a woman who had just undergone serious surgery twice in less than a month.

I didn't tell her, because I didn't want to upset her, that she had been the target of a strange series of anonymous hate letters that were being sent to the heads of the major studios, threatening to reveal that she was Jack Kennedy's mistress and promising other, sinister revelations that would bring down the Kennedys and put an end to the career of "his harlot." One of the studio heads had shown me the letters, and I thought it very likely that the threat of a major scandal explained some of her own studio's reluctance to use her.

The FBI was busy investigating the source of these letters, which were specific enough to briefly unite Hoover and Bobby in a common cause, but from the sound of them, they came from some major Hollywood "insider," somebody who hated the Kennedys and Marilyn and hoped to destroy them both. I had the sense that the shadows were somehow drawing in over Marilyn—some presentiment of disaster—and made up my mind to keep an eye on her.

I said good-bye to her, and as I was standing in the corridor, putting on my coat, I heard her make a telephone call and say, in a voice loud enough to be heard through the door, "Jack, it's me, Marilyn."

As I moved on, I couldn't help wondering how long Jack would encourage Marilyn to be a daily caller, and what she would do if he ever put a stop to it.

———

She flew back to Los Angeles in a daze. She had nearly succumbed under anesthesia during the second operation because she hadn't told the anesthetist what she had already taken, and even now, a few weeks later, she still felt light-headed and butter-fingered, and had trouble with such simple things as buttoning her own clothes. Physical pain, she hardly felt at all, not that it worried her all that much, but even *emotional* pain filtered through to her in a diffused and distant way, like the tinkling of a far-off piano on a quiet day.

She had seen Dr. Kris in New York, and even through the fog of medication had noticed the expression of alarm on her face, particularly when she started to tell her about all the men she had slept with during the past few months, and about her total inability to feel any kind of pleasure with them.

The only person she wanted was Jack, but since he was seldom available, she tried to console herself with an endless succession of substitutes. Anything, she told Dr. Kris, was better than spending a night alone, but Dr. Kris looked doubtful—with good reason, for the more men her patient slept with, the more depressed and worthless she felt.

Dr. Kris agreed to call Dr. Greenson in LA, to convey her unease, but Dr. Greenson let it be known that he thought his New York colleague was being something of an alarmist. He managed to calm Dr. Kris, who still felt that Marilyn was *her* patient, and to wave aside all Dr. Kris's objections to her return to Los Angeles. Dr. Greenson would look after her like a mother hen, he promised—there wasn't a thing to worry about.

She was *longing* to place herself in Dr. Greenson's hands and let him run every detail of her life (except her intake of pills). She was simply too tired to do it herself anymore, and the decisions Dr. Kris wanted her to make were exactly the ones she couldn't face. She wasn't up to making hard choices, she told herself, and Dr. Greenson was the last person who would want her to. The only thing that disturbed her on the flight back to LA was the fact that the stewardesses all seemed to be younger than she was.

She stopped off at Schwab's drugstore—where she had once hung out with all the other young hopefuls—to fill a prescription. While she was waiting, she looked through the greeting cards. She picked one that showed a mournful bunny holding a bunch of flowers, borrowed a pen from the lady at the cash register, and wrote in large capitals:

> DEAR MR. PREZ:
> ROSES ARE RED, BUT GOSH I'M BLUE,
> THIS LITTLE BUNNY'S STILL HOT FOR YOU!
> MISS YOU BADLY. LOVE,
> MARILYN

She kissed the bottom of the card, just below her name, leaving a clear imprint in lipstick of her lips, then sealed it, addressed it to Jack in the White House, and scrawled "SWAK" on the flap.

It had become a habit, sending small gifts and messages to Jack. She had sent him a pair of cashmere socks in emerald green, with a note that said they were to keep him warm when she wasn't in bed with him, and a red flannel nightshirt with a variation of the same message, as well as a gift subscription to *Playboy* and innumerable small reminders of herself of a more or less intimate nature.

It did sometimes occur to her that what had begun as an occasional joke was becoming an obsession—that perhaps at the receiving end it might not seem as funny as it did to her—but she couldn't help herself. After the breakup with Arthur, her feelings about Jack had changed. She had always loved him, but it had been the kind of love she could keep in a corner of her life—part of the background, as it were, not the foreground—the icing on the cake. Then, in some way that was beyond her control, her feelings started to intensify, as if the relationship with Jack was filling her emotional life at just the point where Jack himself was becoming more remote, leaving her, she began to fear, behind. . . .

She went home, back to the apartment on Doheny, greeted Maf, the only living creature who seemed to have missed her and to be happy she was back, then called Dr. Greenson to ask if he could see her, which, of course, he could.

Her temporary secretary had placed her mail neatly on the dining table, not that there was much of it, and her temporary housekeeper had managed to keep the place reasonably clean, despite Maf's occasional "accidents," for nobody had time to train the poor dog properly.

She glanced around the apartment, bewildered, as if it were somebody else's. She had done nothing to make a real home of it, but because she had lived here before she made her break with Fox and married Arthur, it sometimes seemed to her that her whole life since then was a hallucination, that she had never left here at all. . . .

She took off her clothes, popped open a bottle of champagne, and took some of the pills she had bought at Schwab's. Every once in a while, she caught sight of her naked body in a mirror as she wandered around the apartment, and it looked to her as if she were a ghost, except for the angry red surgical scar. She called her answering service, but there were no messages, which made her feel even more ghostlike—Hollywood's biggest, sexiest star with no messages!—but then she remembered that she had told her secretary to change the unlisted number at regular intervals, since she was getting crank calls—the people she *gave* the number to gave it to others, until it inevitably fell into the hands of crazies. . . . That meant that a lot of people couldn't reach her, and very often she couldn't even remember the number herself. . . .

She went into the bedroom. She had put a couple of Jack's election posters above the bed so that he was looking down at her, with his firm, manly, vote-gathering expression. She blew him a kiss—she was feeling light-headed from jet lag, champagne, the pills, and the fact that she hadn't eaten anything for hours—then dressed in a pair of Jax slacks and a sweater. She needed a bath, but she couldn't be bothered, so she simply made up her face and put a scarf over her hair, then took her car keys, went to the garage, and backed her Cadillac out onto Doheny.

Dr. Greenson's office had a back entrance, to allow the more famous of his patients to slip in unseen. He wasn't the kind of

411

stickler for Freudian etiquette who insisted on his patients lying down on the couch, but basically she liked lying down during her sessions, since she was able to talk more freely that way. All her best conversations came in the form of pillow talk.

Dr. Greenson pulled the blinds closed so his tastefully furnished office was dim, and sat back in his leather swivel chair, an expression of soulful ecstasy on his handsome face, as if he were in a postcoital mood. "So how are we?" he asked.

"Okay."

"Really?"

"Well, not so hot, actually."

"The postoperative period is never easy. You had a serious operation. Two, in fact. Don't expect miracles from yourself."

"Actually, I feel okay. About the operation and all, I mean."

"And the career?"

"That's pretty depressing. I guess I'll do this picture with Dean Martin, if Fox ever gets around to scheduling it. George Cukor is supposed to direct it."

"I heard. I read the script. I think it's a good part for you. I wrote some suggestions in the margins—a few little things about dialogue and so on."

Dr. Greenson, like everybody in Hollywood, fancied himself a scriptwriter.

"I feel kind of lost," she said. "Drifting."

"From man to man?"

"That's part of it. I mean, I can't see an *end* to all this. . . . Another guy. Another movie. Another pill. What for?"

"You have to learn to enjoy life for its own sake. You need a project, a goal, apart from the picture. I've been thinking that you should be looking for a house, perhaps. . . . That's a positive step, very life-reinforcing. . . . I know a good realtor. I'll have him call you. And I have somebody who would be a terrific housekeeper too. Just the woman you need, you'll adore her. . . . And the affectional life? Any news on that front?"

She hated the phrase "affectional life," but she let it go. When Dr. Greenson meant sex, he said "affectional moment," or so she had thought until he explained that an "affectional moment" didn't have to involve sex, which came as news to her, and would have come as even more surprising news to most of the men she had known.

"Well, with the operation and all, it's been pretty dry. . . . I still have these dreams. . . ."

He leaned forward, eyes glittering. Dreams were what he wanted to hear about most of all.

"I keep dreaming that I'm going to marry Jack Kennedy," she said.

He nodded, as if that were a normal dream.

"It's not even just a *dream.*"

"No?"

"I mean, it's like, in some part of my mind, I really think it's going to *happen?*"

"There's nothing *wrong* with fantasy," Dr. Greenson said. "Fantasy is the safety valve of the unconscious." He smiled, as if he had just coined a phrase that he would use again.

"Yes?" she said. Then, after a pause: "But you see, the problem is, I'm not sure it's just a fantasy...."

———

She was sitting next to Peter Lawford at Chasen's, in her best black spaghetti-strap dress, feeling no pain, with Frank at the head of the table, and Sammy on the other side of her, and Dino, and a lot of other Rat Packers.

They had all been at a party at Frank's, where they had, she thought, behaved pretty badly—though, mercifully, she couldn't remember the details. Then they had come here because Dino said he wanted to eat, and afterward they were going on to see some show in Hollywood that Sammy said they shouldn't miss, then probably back to Frank's, for poker and more drinks, or maybe out to Peter's place at Malibu....

Peter's face seemed to be going in and out of focus, which was odd, and she wondered if the pills he had given her, "to cure her blues," might have something to do with it. They'd shared a couple of joints, too, on the sly, because their host, despite his reputation for wild self-indulgence, didn't approve of that sort of thing in his home, and with all the champagne she had been drinking on an empty stomach too, she was beginning to feel as if she were floating in the air, like one of the blimps you occasionally saw patrolling the Pacific, just beyond the beach....

Lawford had been throwing bread rolls at everybody except Frank, who didn't react well to that kind of thing, but he had calmed down now, or perhaps just run out of rolls, and was leaning against her, exchanging obscene insults with Sammy while she giggled between them.

"Fuck you, man," Sammy said unrancorously. "You know who you're talking to?"

"A jig," Lawford said amiably. "A blind-in-one-eye nigger who fucks white girls."

Sammy Davis, Jr., shook his head slowly and with dignity. "No, man," he said. "You are talking to a *Jew*! I converted, remember? I expect to be treated with respect as one of the Chosen People."

"Funny, but you don't *look* Jewish."

"Luckily for you, Limey motherfucker, looks ain't everything. . . . Last time I saw Jack"—he lifted his glass in a toast—"your esteemed brother-in-law the President, I told him if he wanted a new ambassador to Israel, I was ready to serve."

"What did Jack say?"

"He said he would consider it. He asked if I'd been circumcised and if it hurt."

"I'm going to marry Jack," she said firmly, in a louder voice than usual.

Lawford's eyes snapped wide open. "I beg your pardon?"

She thought he hadn't heard her above the noise. "I'M GOING TO MARRY JACK KENNEDY!" she shouted. "I'm going to be First Lady, instead of Jackie."

"Are you sure, honey?" Sammy asked. "Are you okay?"

"Of course I am. Jack asked me."

"I'm not sure it's a good idea to be saying this in public," Lawford said, fear on his face. He was part of the Kennedy family, by no means completely accepted but still acutely aware of what the limits were. Marilyn, his expression seemed to be saying, had just exceeded them, and he looked anxious to disassociate himself from her.

But it was too late. Dino, or somebody else from the far end of the table, shouted out raucously: "What did you say, Marilyn?" and in the silence that followed she shouted back, as if somebody else were in charge of her voice: "DRINK UP, EVERYBODY! JACK KENNEDY IS GOING TO DIVORCE JACKIE AND MARRY ME!"

A hush fell over the restaurant. The waiters even stopped serving.

She heard somebody growl, "Get her the fuck out of here!" but she didn't care.

If none of them could take a joke, that was *their* problem.

37

By the summer of 1961, Jack's presidency seemed to be sailing on an even keel, to use one of his favorite metaphors.

The Bay of Pigs fiasco had damaged him seriously, but he recovered, mostly because his image remained youthful and "upbeat."

Although the ambassadorship remained a sore point between us —one that we did not discuss—Jack kept me busy with important commissions, and made sure I had "access," the most coveted privilege a president can offer. I performed some tricky unofficial diplomacy for him in Israel, where I had many close friends in government, and in Miami, among the angry Cuban exiles. Hoffa's name, I was happy to note, had receded from the front pages, and apparently from Jack's mind.

What I *didn't* know was that Hoffa was still on Bobby's mind as much as ever. In his new role as Jack's "prime minister," Bobby at last had the authority and the power to get Hoffa—nor was Jack, with bigger problems on his mind, about to restrain his brother, if he even knew what he was doing.

Lulled by this false sense of security, I was taken by surprise when I received a call from Stuart Warshavsky—one of the few old-time New York labor leaders who maintained a truce, however uneasy, with the Teamsters—begging me for a meeting with the President on urgent business. I could tell from Stuart's voice that he had a serious problem—too serious to talk about over the phone—and I knew enough about labor politics to guess Jack would probably want to accommodate him.

I'd known Stuart for years, and had gone to a lot of trouble to gain his support for Jack. When his fellow New York Jewish Liberals (with a capital *L*) reacted in horror to Jack's choice of Lyndon Johnson as a running mate, it had been Stuart who reminded them that the alternative to Kennedy/Johnson was Nixon/Lodge.

Jack was grateful to Stuart, all the more so because New York politics was something of a mystery to him. At first he had assumed it was sufficient to promise more arms for Israel and invoke Franklin D. Roosevelt's name as often as possible. Stuart, at my urging, had been one of those who taught him otherwise.

Since Stuart had never asked for anything on this scale before, I passed his request on with a strong personal recommendation, for what that was worth. It was worth a good deal, it seemed, for word came back shortly that Stuart had been invited to a White House dinner that Maria and I were attending.

Jack had apparently concluded that the invitation would stroke Stuart's ego. As it happened, this was a misreading of his character. His father, a Menshevik, had shared a room with Trotsky, on the Lower East Side. As a Socialist, a Zionist, and a labor leader, Stuart had never owned a dinner jacket and wasn't about to buy one. He was as puzzled by the invitation as I was, but once I had obtained special dispensation for him to wear a dark suit instead of "black tie," he accepted gracefully enough.

When he presented himself to the President and the First Lady in the receiving line, Jack shook his hand warmly, introduced him to Jackie—who was staring at his rather rumpled blue suit and badly knotted tie with a certain amount of exasperation—and whispered that he hoped to have a few words with Stuart after dinner. Somebody had the good sense to seat him next to the wife of the Israeli ambassador to the United Nations, and Stuart seemed to me to be enjoying himself, despite the elegant surroundings and the fancy food. Maria was seated between Jack and Prince Radziwill, Jackie's brother-in-law, so she was even happier, since they were the two best-looking men in the room.

Jackie had introduced classical entertainment to the White House dinners (the Eisenhowers liked to get their guests out of the White House by ten o'clock at the latest), and it was Jack's habit to sneak away for a few minutes between coffee and the beginning of whatever entertainment was scheduled, sometimes with a lady who had attracted his attention, sometimes for a bit of politics.

A White House aide discreetly ushered Stuart and me to a small sitting room, and we sat down together and lit our cigars. Jack was in an expansive mood—Jackie loved entertaining and was terrific at it, and the Kennedys as a couple never seemed happier with each other than when they were on display. As the furor over the Bay of Pigs receded, Jackie was busily improving her French for their forthcoming state visit to France, and Jack was flexing his muscles for the Vienna summit meeting with Khrushchev. Both of them were beginning to enjoy being in the White House.

"It's good of you to see me, Mr. President," Stuart said.

"You carried the ball when I picked Lyndon as a running mate, Stuart. That took guts. I owe you one."

"I know," Stuart said. As a New York politician, he could measure favors received and repaid as precisely as a Toledo scale. "That's why I'm here. I've got a problem."

Jack's face wasn't exactly stony, but like the politician *he* was, he knew just when to convey total blankness.

Stuart leaned forward confidentially. "Look, my people know all about bad unions. Believe me, paper locals, goon squads, sweetheart contracts, mobsters, you name it—this kind of stuff, we know, and we're against."

"Good," Jack said. "So am I."

Stuart shrugged away the interruption. "But at the same time, we're against union busting. We're against persecuting labor leaders, even the ones nobody likes or invites to the White House for dinner."

"Which ones have you in mind?"

"Hoffa, Mr. President."

"He's a criminal. He's sold his own people out to the mob."

"Maybe. To a lot of working people, he's a hero. What I'm saying, Mr. President, is, enough is enough. It's always Hoffa this and Hoffa that, send the son of a bitch to jail, but we don't hear about the Justice Department setting up a special task force to prosecute a banker, or the CEO of a Fortune Five Hundred company."

It was my first hint that Hoffa was a live issue. It may have been Jack's, too, for he looked surprised. "George Meany wants to see Hoffa in jail as much as Bobby does," he said.

"Mr. President, forgive me, but there are those of us who think George Meany is a fink."

Jack looked at Stuart shrewdly. "What's up, Stuart?" he said. "You don't like Hoffa. You don't want mobsters controlling unions any more than we do."

"Sometimes you have to work with mobsters, Mr. President. I'll make a deal with anybody who'll help me organize sweatshops— and I *have*, I'm not ashamed to admit. . . ."

Stuart leaned farther forward, hands on his knees, eyes fixed on the President's, his rugged face, with the big, broken nose and the bushy eyebrows that were his trademark, set in a serious expression. "We have to live with the Teamsters, Mr. President. Okay, you don't, your brother doesn't, but if the Teamsters don't ship materials in and finished goods out, my people are out of work. You understand, Mr. President, that means they don't *eat*. Maybe I don't like Hoffa and his friends in the mob, but I got to do business with him and with them."

"You wouldn't be carrying a message from Hoffa, would you, Stuart?" Jack asked quickly.

Stuart nodded. "A guy came to see me, Mr. President, fellow you never heard of called Big Gus McKay, one of Hoffa's 'inner circle,' you might say. Nice enough guy, size of King Kong, but very soft-spoken, sort of an old Eugene Debs Wobbly type gone wrong, like a lot of the Teamster leadership. . . . He asked me to tell you that Hoffa wants to make a deal."

"He should call the Attorney General for that, Stuart."

"He doesn't trust Bobby, frankly. And it isn't that kind of deal."

"What kind is it? Just out of curiosity."

"McKay mentioned that Hoffa would keep his mouth shut about how Dave Beck got put in jail."

Jack's eyes caught mine and I shrugged. I wasn't, after all, responsible for Hoffa's behavior.

"I don't know anything about that," he said to Stuart, his face impassive. "It sounds like old stuff."

"McKay also hinted that Hoffa knows what he called 'a lot of national security stuff' involving Cuba."

"Garbage, Stuart. I can't believe you came down here with this crap." Jack was angry now, and Stuart was beginning to sweat, but I guessed that there were probably worse things in store for Stuart than Jack Kennedy's anger if he didn't deliver his full message.

Stuart wiped his face with his handkerchief. "There's one more thing, McKay told me," he said. "But it's sort of embarrassing, and, ah, *personal*. . . ."

Jack glared at him coldly.

"It's, ah, about Marilyn Monroe, Mr. President," Stuart blurted out. "Apparently, she's going around telling people you're going to divorce Mrs. Kennedy and marry her. Hoffa's got proof of it somehow. McKay says if he doesn't get a deal, he's going to take it to the papers." Stuart looked contrite. "Mr. President, I'm sorry. But I thought you ought to know."

Jack's face was ashen, but he was too good a politician to lose his temper with Stuart. He simply rose, shook his hand abruptly, and thanked him for coming.

Just as he was leaving the room, he turned, gave Stuart a look of startling intensity, and said, in a low voice, for there was an aide and a Marine guard waiting for him: "Stuart, pass this message back, will you? The President says Hoffa can go fuck himself."

Then he turned back and walked briskly out into the corridor, from the end of which we could hear, Stuart and I, the sound of a cello being tuned.

As I was leaving the White House after the concert, Jack gave me a hard look and whispered, "Don't you ever do that to me again!"

———

I saw Jack again in the Oval Office the next day. He was still angry about Stuart's messages. Maria had commented on the fact that he had seemed rather cold to me when we made our good-byes after the White House dinner, and he hadn't warmed up much since then.

I wasn't about to point out to him that Hoffa's attempt at blackmail had come about because Bobby, against my advice, was still trying to put him behind bars. Hoffa was Bobby's obsession, something that Jack could neither explain nor control.

Jack gave me an impatient look and said: "I've been thinking things over, David."

"What things?" I asked.

"The London embassy. I said I'd think it over, remember?"

Jack had delayed appointing an ambassador, and from time to time I had wondered if his purpose was to keep the carrot dangling in front of me. I still *wanted* it, of course—but nothing like as much as I once had. Had it been offered to me willingly when I asked for it, that would have been one thing, but I sensed that if it was going to happen now, it would be grudging, and probably hedged in with unacceptable conditions.

All the same, I felt a faint but perceptible thrill. Jack had been in office a few months, gained confidence, learned the ropes—he was in a better position to make the appointment now, I reasoned, leaning forward expectantly in my chair.

He frowned. "I can't do it," he said, with the brisk authority of a man biting the bullet.

I was momentarily taken aback. "Can't *do* it?" I asked. "Why not?" It occurred to me that Jack might be getting his revenge for my having exposed him to Stuart's visit.

"I'm not going to give you a lot of crap about your qualifications,

David. We both know you're qualified. But I want a man there who has the confidence of the establishment."

"Theirs?" I was about to point out that the prewar British establishment had been outraged by his father's appointment, which didn't stop FDR, but before I could, he snapped back: *"Ours."*

He swung his chair around and stared out the window at the garden, avoiding my eyes. "The Brits are important," he said. "They're really the only allies we have in Europe we can *trust* not to make a separate deal with the Russians. . . . I need someone in London who has the confidence of our foreign policy establishment, David—the Council on Foreign Policy crowd, the people who write pieces for *Foreign Affairs,* and so on."

"They're mostly Republicans," I said. "Spiritual followers of Nelson Rockefeller. No friends of yours."

"Yes," he said distantly. "Those are exactly the people I want on my side. I'm going to send David Bruce's name to the Senate. I wanted you to hear it from me first."

I understood what was on his mind. He wanted to insure himself against criticism from the right, to co-opt the foreign policy establishment so it couldn't turn against him again, as it had over Cuba, maybe even to steal Nelson Rockefeller's "brain trust" away from him, in case Nelson won the Republican nomination in '64. . . .

It was good politics, but I still felt a deep sense of disappointment for having waited so patiently. I was angry, too. I knew Bruce, and although he was an affable enough fellow, he wasn't in my league. But you can't argue with the President of the United States. *"Thank you,"* I said, not bothering to conceal my rage.

I was briefly tempted to get up and walk out, but something held me back—my friendship with Joe perhaps, or the simple fact that I could never bring myself to dislike Jack.

I would have preferred that he had simply never brought the subject of my ambassadorship up again, that somehow we had been able to let it lie, and I'm sure he did too, but of course, he was the president, so he couldn't.

Politics, I told myself, was a game for grown-ups. There was no room for hurt feelings. I should have known that better than anyone.

For a moment poor Marilyn flashed in my mind, and I wished there were some way to explain to her how dangerous it was to have a president for a friend—still worse, to love him.

"You're upset," Jack said. "I understand that. But it has to be, David. If there's anything else you want . . . I don't suppose Mexico would interest you?"

I shook my head, momentarily speechless. Mexico! What did he take me for?

"Look, you'll think of something, David. Or I will, okay? I owe you. You know that."

"I know that, Mr. President."

There was a knock on the door and his secretary appeared, summoned, I had no doubt, by a hidden button under Jack's desk.

"Duty calls," Jack said, and we rose and shook hands formally, farther apart than we had ever been before.

———

Once I was back in the Hay-Adams—and in control of my feelings —I called the Ambassador, in Palm Beach. I was put through to him right away, but for a moment I didn't even realize it was he. It was the voice of an old man, high-pitched, querulous, hesitant. I was shocked—ashamed too, for, caught up in the excitement of Jack's problems in the White House, I had been neglecting Joe.

"Jack gave you the news, did he?" he asked.

I suddenly wondered if Joe had been on my side. I assumed he would have been, but you could never tell with Joe, particularly where "his" ambassadorship was concerned, for he viewed it in a proprietorial way, and was always angry whenever a president appointed a new ambassador to the Court of St. James's without consulting him.

"He gave me the bad news," I said. "I'm disappointed, of course."

There was a long silence. "Yes," he said softly. "You would be." He sighed. "It's not my doing, David. I'll tell you that. Oh, don't get me wrong—I don't suppose the goddamn Brits would like a sheeny PR man any more than they liked a Mick Wall Street speculator, but I thought you'd earned the right to it. . . ."

I thought I'd earned it too, several times over in fact. What I wanted to tell Joe was that if I wasn't good enough to be Jack's ambassador to the United Kingdom, I didn't see why I should continue doing any of his dirty work with the mob, or helping to cover up the administration's more flagrant mistakes, but there was something in his voice that made me hold back. I wish I hadn't, now. If ever there was a time to make a clean break of it, this was the moment, but I listened to Joe Kennedy instead.

I had to listen hard too, to make out what he was saying, his voice was so frail. It wasn't like him to apologize, or to let slip even the smallest difference of opinion between himself and Jack. "I'm not always consulted the way I used to be," he said. There was a longish pause. "What are we talking about?" he asked. He sounded confused.

"The ambassadorship."

Another long pause. "We're old friends, David," the Ambassador said, "aren't we?"

"We are that," I agreed, wondering where this was leading.

"So I can ask you for a favor?"

"You know that."

"Don't hold this against Jack, David. He's our president now. He's not the old Jack anymore, not for you, not even for me. He has his own place in history to look out for. I wish he'd chosen you—maybe he does too. But he has to make up his own mind, and when he has, we have to back him."

"I understand," I said. I understood more than had been said. Jack was no longer consulting his father. He was his own man at last. It must have been painful for Joe, but stoic as always, he had accepted the reality of the situation. He was even determined to make sure that I accepted it—that Jack wasn't making an enemy of me.

"When are you going to come down here and see me, David?" he asked. It was a plea.

I was astonished—the Joe Kennedy I had known for thirty years, fiercely unsentimental and demanding, would never have asked such a question. I realized then that I was talking to a man who had, finally, come face-to-face with the fact of dying, and was deeply afraid of it. Joe had none of his sons' fatalism—nor his wife's, for that matter. If anybody had ever thought he was going to live forever, it was Joe Kennedy. Something had clearly taught him otherwise.

"I'll be down in a couple of weeks," I said. "I'll make a point of it."

"Fine." He tried to sound hearty, and failed. "We'll talk more about it then."

I felt even then, as I hung up the phone, a certain chill, like the drawing down of the shades on a winter afternoon—a feeling, irrational and not at all like me, of impending tragedy.

As things turned out, two weeks was leaving it too long.

38

"I thought I told you I didn't want to hear any more of this crap," Robert Kennedy said impatiently.

Hoover leaned forward. "I think you ought to hear *this*," he said in an urgent voice. "Believe me, I've got your brother's best interests at heart."

Kennedy sighed. The week before, he had discovered that the New York office of the FBI was compiling its intelligence on organized crime by clipping stories from the *New York Post* and the *New York Daily News,* and he assumed that Hoover's visit was in the nature of a counterattack, to prove that he and his people were on the ball *somewhere* at least.

"This is Special Agent Kirkpatrick," Hoover said. "He is our leading expert on electronic surveillance."

The Attorney General glared at Kirkpatrick, recognizing another tough and ambitious Mick when he saw him. Kirkpatrick stared right back, a good sign. Kennedy respected men who weren't afraid of him.

Kennedy nodded glumly. Kirkpatrick placed a reel-to-reel portable tape recorder on the polished desk, plugged it in, and pushed a button. There was a faint hum, perhaps the sound of air-conditioning, then a familiar whispery voice, like a little girl's but with undertones of grown-up sexiness, spoke: *. . . I still have these dreams. . . .*

A man's voice, patient, deep, clearly a doctor's, replied. *Tell me about them.*

I keep dreaming that I'm going to marry Jack Kennedy. There was a pause. *It's not even just a dream.*

423

No?

I mean, it's like, in some part of my mind, I really think it's going to happen?

Yes?

. . . I'm going to marry Jack Kennedy.

There's nothing wrong with fantasy. . . . Fantasy is the safety valve of the unconscious. . . .

Yes? But you see, the problem is, I'm not sure it's just a fantasy. . . . There was a long pause, with muted sounds of traffic in the background; then Marilyn Monroe spoke very clearly: *He means it, Doctor, you see—he really means it!*

Robert Kennedy's eyes were shut, as if he was in pain. He waved his hand, to have Kirkpatrick turn the machine off.

"Thank you, Edgar," he said wearily. "I'll take it from here."

———

It was a hot Indian summer day, though no longer the humid heat that made people want to stay indoors with the air-conditioning on full blast.

It was the kind of weather that made Jack and Bobby Kennedy think of Hyannis Port, of sailing and clambakes on the beach—itchy to get away, as if the sea were bred in their bones. But for the present they were stuck here. As much for the need to be outdoors as for security, Jack led Bobby out into the White House Rose Garden, where they strolled, hands behind their backs, heads close together, two brothers who were now running not only the country but a large part of the world.

"Jack," Bobby said, "I *know* how you feel, but this is serious."

"You don't know how I feel."

"I've had my—adventures. I'm not exactly a goddamn virgin."

Jack laughed. "Adventures? Is that what they're called? And here all this time I thought you were a Boy Scout."

"You know better than that. But this isn't a joke like the old paternity suit Hoover keeps telling me about."

"What paternity suit?"

"Hoover claimed there was evidence you settled out of court with some girl for sixty thousand dollars. I sent someone to track her down and interview her, and she just laughed and said you still owed her the two dollars you borrowed for your taxi fare."

Jack looked interested. "What was her name?"

"Giselle something. Hubert? Hulme?"

"Giselle Holmes," Jack said, grinning. "Autumn of 1950, the year I was running for a second term in Congress, waiting for Paul Dever to make up his mind whether he was going to take a second shot at the governorship or run against Lodge for the Senate. . . ."

"You're lucky he decided to go for a second term. You'd have made a terrible governor."

"You see? That's the difference between us. I wasn't thinking about politics. I was thinking about women. I met Giselle while I was campaigning, went to her apartment, spent the night. I can remember it to this day. I think she probably gave the best head in Massachusetts at the time. Anyway, in the morning I discovered I didn't have any money on me, so I borrowed two bucks off her to get back to Bowdoin Street. I guess I never paid her back. Where's she living now?"

"Springfield, Illinois. She's married to an oral surgeon."

"That figures."

"I'm not trying to cramp your style," Bobby said. "But you're playing with fire."

"I'd appreciate it if you wouldn't throw clichés at me. You *are* trying to cramp my style, and I'm not going to have it."

"We don't all have your gift for rhetoric."

"Stop it, Bobby. You and I are too close for this kind of shit to come between us. I *like* taking risks, it's part of what makes life worth living for me. And I like chasing women, as many of them as I can, because—and listen to me carefully—each and every one of them is completely different from all the others, and on the other hand, they're all the same. If that isn't a phenomenon interesting enough to spend your life exploring, I don't know what is."

"Look, I didn't come here for a sex lecture—"

"It doesn't appear you and Ethel *need* one, frankly. You seem to have got the rudiments of the thing doped out."

Bobby pushed on stubbornly. "It's political dynamite, Johnny," he said. When he addressed his brother as "Johnny," it was always serious. "Here's Marilyn Monroe, the most visible woman in the world, going around telling people the two of you are having an affair, and that you're going to *marry* her. It's a weapon in the hands of Hoover. You should *hear* the tape he's got of Marilyn talking to her analyst. She told him you'd asked her to marry you—that you'd promised to divorce Jackie."

"I know." Jack shook his head. "It seems everybody's talking about it, even our pal Hoffa. He sent word he'll make a deal—with me, not you. Immunity, for all the usual stuff, *plus*—are you ready for this?—he won't reveal to the press that Marilyn and I are getting married!"

Bobby's face turned dark. "That *bastard!*"

"Don't worry about it. Even if he tries, I don't think anybody will print it."

"It's just what I was warning you about, Johnny, all the same." Bobby brushed the hair out of his eyes. "This thing with Marilyn, Johnny, it's going to blow up on you. I feel it in my bones."

"I'm not giving Marilyn up. I'm telling you that right now. The Leader of the Free World is entitled to some privileges, Bobby, and Marilyn happens to be one of them."

"Then tell her to shut up." Bobby paused. "Has it occurred to you she might be crazy?"

"All women are crazy."

"I'm serious!"

Jack's expression turned sadder, almost solemn. He suddenly seemed a lot older than Bobby. "Yes," he said softly, "as a matter of fact, it has."

"She could hurt you, Johnny. I hate to say it, but she could cost you your second term. Not to speak of what Jackie would say."

Jack nodded. At the mention of a second term he seemed to drift into silence, as if Bobby had finally driven the reality of it home to him. He always knew, in the end, when to listen to Bobby. Somewhere deep inside him, in that secret part of his mind where he had always hidden his real feelings and emotions, he knew that it was Bobby who was the serious one, the one who cherished responsibilities, the one who wasn't scared of the tough decisions—the one, truly, who should be president.

"I'll *think* about it," he agreed. "If I decide it's getting out of hand, I'll put an end to it, I promise. I hope to God I don't have to, though. It's funny. I really love Marilyn, you know. . . ."

He stopped and stared back at the armored glass windows of the Oval Office. "Sometimes it's not so great, being president," he said.

"I understand."

"No, you don't. But I guess you might find out yourself one day."

"There's one other thing, Johnny. . . . There's this girl you're seeing who's connected to Giancana. That's a worry too. . . ."

"Oh, come on, Bobby!" Jack said impatiently. "Judy's a whole different thing. I mean, there's nothing *personal* there. So she knows Giancana? So what? She knows a lot of guys."

"She doesn't just *know* Giancana, Jack. She's his mistress."

" 'Mistress' is a big word. Let me reassure you. I don't tell her state secrets while we're fucking, and my guess is that Giancana doesn't talk to her about his business either. She has certain valuable talents, but being Mata Hari isn't one of them. Do I make myself clear?"

"It's still a dumb risk," Bobby said stubbornly. "If it ever comes out, it's going to look terrible. I mean, how much would it cost you, frankly, to give her up? There are plenty of other girls around."

"And I hope to fuck every one of them. But I'll tell you what: I'll decide who I want to fuck, okay?"

"Okay."

The two brothers turned back toward the glass door opening out onto the garden, where a Secret Service agent stood watching them.

"Giselle Holmes," the President said with a fond smile. "Great legs. Not too much on top."

39

"Of course, it's important to be able to distinguish fantasy from fact," Dr. Greenson said.

"My whole life I've been part of other people's fantasies. I'm entitled to my own for a change."

"Other people's fantasies?"

"Sure. Ever since my tits started to grow. All my life I've known what men think when they see me—know that when they go home to fuck their wives or jerk off, it's me they're fucking in their minds, my tits they're licking, my cunt they're coming in. . . .

"It's a weird feeling, you know? It's like I don't belong to myself at all, I belong to *them*, all those guys who fuck me in their minds. I could be dead, it wouldn't matter, they'd still be jerking off over photos of me. I'm not real, see? I'm just the girl your wife or girlfriend could never be, the one who's always ready for it, never has a headache, doesn't care if you come before she does. . . .

"Even the guys who have *married* me always had some kind of fantasy in mind, not me. It's like they were marrying Marilyn, not Norma Jean. But I'm Norma Jean, really. It's hard work being Marilyn. I don't feel like doing it every day."

"I understand that."

"That's why I love Jack. It's hard work for him, too—being Jack, I mean. Jack's in everybody's fantasies too. Women dream he's fucking them instead of their husbands, men dream of being rich and handsome like him, or of being the president, or being a war hero, or maybe being married to Jackie. . . . But once you get to know him, you realize he's as much of a fraud as I am. He's still the puny

428

little kid with a tough big brother and an even tougher father. He desperately wants to be loved, but he's afraid to show it, and he's not too sure how to ask for it because he's been taught to despise weakness. . . . But there he is, everybody's hero. We're a pair, we are. We'll make a terrific couple."

"*Will* make?"

"I believe it, just the way I once believed I was going to marry America's greatest playwright, even though he hardly knew me, and was married with two kids, and lived twenty-five hundred miles away. . . . And that *happened*, didn't it? And when I was just a kid, picking up dates in Hollywood bars, hoping they'd buy me a hamburger before they dropped me home, *if* they dropped me home, I had this fantasy that I was going to marry America's biggest sports hero, who looked to me like the sexiest man in the world. . . . And *that* happened too, didn't it? So why shouldn't *this* happen? Tell me that? If I can go from being an orphan of LA County, with one pair of shoes, to the biggest star ever, why shouldn't I marry Jack Kennedy?"

"Mm."

"The only problem is, why do I feel like I'm not even *living*—like this is all just some kind of waiting room before they take me to the mortuary?"

"You have to learn to accept life. That's what we have to work on here."

"Oh, I *accept* it, all right. . . . I just don't *like* it much, is all."

———

She sat by the pool of Peter Lawford's Malibu house looking out over the picket fence that had been erected to give Jack privacy when he visited, staring at the starry sky and listening to the surf. Lawford sat beside her, smoking a joint, a glass of scotch in his hand, humming from time to time in a tuneless way. They had both taken refuge out here from a dinner party.

"Jack would be a lot happier with me," she said.

"Mm."

"You know he would."

"What on earth does that matter, darling? Marriage isn't about happiness. Least of all Jack's."

"Then what *is* it about?"

"Oh, I don't know. It's just something one *does*, isn't it? A protective screen behind which people can get on with their real lives?

There's something of that in Jack's marriage. Do you know what's going to happen to you, by the way, if you keep telling people Jack is going to marry you?"

She took the joint and inhaled. "No. What?"

"Something bad, I expect. Just because Jack's a sweet chap doesn't mean he can't look after himself, if you push him hard enough. Not to speak of my dear brother-in-law Bobby. Or, God forbid, my father-in-law. Jack was in love with a Danish girl during the war. *She* told people she was going to divorce her husband to marry Jack. I heard the old man had her deported as a spy. Shot, for all I know. These are not, frankly, people to fuck with, Marilyn dear."

They sat without speaking for a few minutes. "Pat likes me," she said. "I can tell that. All Jack's sisters do."

"Yes, very likely. . . . Marilyn, you have to understand the way they've been brought up. What I'm telling you is that while the Kennedy girls are strict Catholics, no meat on Friday and all that sort of thing, they don't have any hang-ups about mistresses at all. As Jack's mistress, they may very *well* like you, but that doesn't mean they want you taking Jackie's place."

"Jack is the only thing in my life that makes any sense, Peter," she said, handing him back the joint.

His voice came to her quietly, like a ghost's, muffled by the sound of the surf and the conversation from the dinner party inside. "If Jack is the only thing in your life that makes sense, Marilyn," he said, "you're in even worse trouble than I am."

———

Early in the fall, she flew back to New York, since principal photography on *Something's Got to Give* was delayed until early in 1962.

It was the usual story—half a dozen different script rewrites by half a dozen different screenwriters, at a cost of several hundred thousand dollars, intended to satisfy the objections of the studio, Dino, George Cukor, and herself, had produced a script that satisfied nobody, so yet another rewrite was taking place.

She couldn't wait around in California—she knew she was going to pieces there. In New York, at least she had Dr. Kris to fall back on, as well as the Strasbergs and all her old actor friends from the Studio. Besides, New York was so big and busy that she could pass unnoticed there—she was even able to date the Slugger without anybody in the press noticing or commenting on it. She did not tell him that she planned to marry Jack Kennedy. Joe might not understand, she thought.

She spent a few days at the beach, staying in a borrowed house, and even posed for some photographs, on the condition that her surgical scar be airbrushed out. In some of the photographs seaweed and kelp clung to her, giving her the appearance of a drowning victim, in others she was covered in patches of wet sand. She liked them all.

Studying the proofs with a magnifier, she felt pretty good about the way she looked. Her tits were still resisting gravity, she still had the famous hourglass waist, her ass was as firm as ever, or almost, though she had let her hair go a little dark.

She hadn't been in town a week before she got a call asking her to the Carlyle.

———

Jack was the same, she thought, but different. He seemed to have filled out somehow. She knew he was taking cortisone, which explained the puffy cheeks—and the suggestion of breasts, which he hated so much that he kept his shirt or dressing gown on until the lights were off. . . .

What the hell—what with her surgical scars and bruises, she was just as happy herself to fuck in the dark. Maybe they were both approaching the age when it paid not to look too closely, she thought. . . .

But it wasn't so much that he had filled out *physically*—he had filled out *psychically*, as if the role of president had taken him over. The man lying beside her in the bed was first and foremost the president of the United States now—it was as if his specific gravity had changed, making him heavier, more solid, bigger than life.

She had once dreamed, in a dopey way, of making love with Lincoln, her old hero, and now, somehow, Jack had *become* Lincoln in her mind. She could sense his greatness, a certain remoteness, as if there was a part of him that could never belong to her, or any other woman, not even Jackie. Not that he was pompous about it, no, but *he* knew it had happened too. He had confronted Khrushchev in Vienna, holding his own against him, had been greeted as an equal by De Gaulle and Macmillan. He wasn't the old Jack.

She could sense, too, in him what she was sure she would have sensed in Lincoln: the loneliness of power. Civil rights protesters, the "captive nations" of Eastern Europe, people all over the world who yearned for freedom and a better life—everyone looked to this man beside her for hope and help, and everywhere from Laos to Cuba men were fighting and dying at his orders.

He stirred in bed. She thought he had been napping, though he might have been lying there thinking about who could say what world problem. But to her surprise, he had been thinking about her. "How have you been?" he asked. "Really."

" 'Really'? Would I lie to you, lover?"

"About yourself? Probably. Word has reached me that you've been feeling a little—down?"

"I missed you."

"I'm flattered. But you shouldn't, you know."

"I can't help what I feel."

"Sure you can. That's what matters most—controlling our feelings."

"You're better at it than I am. I guess that's why you're president."

"There *may* be other reasons. Look, having feelings about me is one thing. Going around feeling blue because of them, that's another. It's not part of our deal. Neither is talking about them."

"I didn't know we had a deal, Jack."

"Not in so many words, no. But there *is* one, and it goes something like this: I'm married, and have a public career I have to protect; you *used* to be married, and have a public image *you* have to protect. So we don't make waves for each other or challenge the status quo."

"Status quo?"

"The way things are."

"I'm not challenging the whatever—the way things are. I've got a right to dream things were different, though, don't I?"

"I don't think so. Dreams are dangerous. It's not a good idea to dream about things that can't happen. You start by dreaming, then you begin wanting them to happen, and pretty soon you begin to believe they're *going* to happen. . . ."

"Things like wanting to marry you?"

"Like wanting to marry me, yes. Exactly. That's definitely not part of the deal, is it?"

"I just wish—"

"Shush." He put his hand gently over her mouth. "Don't *say* it to me. Don't even *think* it!"

"I understand," she said. "It's going to be hard. I'm not sure I can do it."

"You can do it."

"But I love you."

He sighed. "I know," he said. "That's why you'll do it. For me."

She went down in the private elevator, accompanied by a Secret Service agent she hadn't seen before.

"We've got a car waiting for you on the side street," he said, without calling her "Miss Monroe." He gave her a wink. "That way you won't have to go through the lobby." His voice made it clear that he wasn't doing *her* any favors—he was simply protecting his boss.

She paused. "Why shouldn't I go through the lobby?"

"Because my orders are that you don't, lady."

"Well, fuck *you*," she said defiantly, and pushed the button marked "Lobby" before he could stop her.

"You can't do that!" he shouted, grabbing her arm.

"The hell I can't, asshole," she cried as the door opened. "I can do any fucking thing I *want*! I'm a free citizen! And a star!"

He tried to pull her back into the elevator, but with the quick reflexes of a trained dancer she gave him a kick in the groin—not hard, but fast enough to make him double over in self-protection—at the same time slapping him twice, back and forth, zip-zap, the way she'd learned from Robert Mitchum while making *River of No Return*. Then she was out of the elevator and in the lobby, where a dozen people, some of them in evening clothes, were staring at her.

"I'm Marilyn Monroe!" she screamed at the Secret Service agent, who was coming after her now, his cheeks flushed with embarrassment and, she hoped, pain.

He reached out for her. "I don't care *who* you are," he said. "Back in the elevator!"

She waited until he was in reach, then raised her hand and raked her fingernails hard across his face.

She hardly even heard his scream. She was out of control, her vision obscured by a film of red, as if her own eyes were full of blood. She could see the well-dressed little group—the men holding their keys, the women clutching their handbags—backing away from her, wide-eyed, wealthy people from the suburbs who had come into the city for a night out. They looked horror-struck, but she didn't care. She stood there, staring down an armed Secret Service agent in her white dress with the bolero jacket, swinging her handbag at him as if it were a dangerous weapon, the look of battle shining in her eyes.

"You touch me again and I'll *kill* you, you motherfucker!" she cried, tears of anger streaming down her face. "You hear me?"

Her voice filled the handsome lobby, with its black-and-white marble floors and working fireplaces, and brought the doorman running in from outside.

"You'd better treat me with respect," she heard herself cry, hardly recognizing the voice or the words as her own. "I'M MARILYN MONROE! I'VE BEEN FUCKING THE PRESIDENT!"

She pushed past the startled doorman, ran through the revolving doors, shielding her face against the flashguns of the inevitable paparazzi, sprinted down Madison Avenue blindly, not even sure which direction she was going in. A hand grabbed her arm, and she swung her handbag wildly again, rage and fear still controlling her, until she heard a schoolboy voice say, "Miss Monroe, please, it's Timmy—everything's going to be okay."

She was suddenly exhausted and helpless, unable to move on her own, hardly even aware of where she was.

She let Timmy Hahn, her teenage fan and follower, get her into a taxi and take her home.

——

The next day she felt no better. She had sent Timmy home with money for the taxi ride back to Queens—though she was pretty sure he'd save the bill rather than use it—and spent the night trying to reach Jack to explain or apologize, she wasn't sure which, but she couldn't get through, and in the morning, he was gone.

She was seized by a kind of insane restlessness despite the sleepless night, a false energy that had to be tapped, the way she sometimes felt a sudden sexual need that was almost painful in its intensity.

She called everyone she knew in New York before she realized it was a Saturday. Dr. Kris was not in her office, and everyone else was away for the weekend—for it was one of those perfect late September days, still warm, but with a crispness that promised autumn, the kind of day people in California had in mind when they talked about missing the changing seasons.

She couldn't stand being alone in the apartment, so she slipped into a pair of slacks, a blouse, and a loose jacket, pulled on a man's old felt hat—one that Milton had used as a prop in photographing her—and went shopping. The idea of plunging into the crowds appealed to her. It was a way of hiding, or pretending that she was an ordinary person, like everyone else.

Bloomingdale's was packed, which was just what she wanted. She wandered through the store, wide-eyed as a hick, for she was so seldom in stores that they always struck her as wonderful, magic places, even though there was very little in them she wanted to buy.

Some slacks caught her eye—not that she really *needed* any, but she felt obliged to buy *something*. She managed, with some difficulty, to attract the attention of the saleslady, though with a sinking heart. She *hated* New York salesladies, she remembered too late, dragon ladies, with tinted sequined glasses, blue-rinsed hair, and relentless voices, who treated you like a piece of shit, even if you were a star. She always did her little-girlish best to charm them, which never worked, and doing it filled her with self-disgust and anger at her own weakness.

This one was clearly no exception, a prim mouth set in disapproval, eyes gleaming with impatience to get the sale made and move on to the next customer—hopefully, one who was better groomed and dressed, the woman's expression seemed to suggest. By the time she was in the dressing room, she already regretted the whole thing —didn't want the slacks, but didn't have the courage to tell the saleslady that she'd changed her mind.

She felt a mind-numbing claustrophobia come over her in the dressing room, and opened the curtain a little to make it go away. She slipped out of her own slacks, wondering what in God's name she was *doing* here alone, and was about to put on the pair she had chosen, when the saleslady thrust herself through the gap in the curtain holding another pair on a hanger.

"You might wanna try these, dear, they're a size larger—" Her eyes opened wide in shock and disgust. "You got no panties on!" she cried.

"I never wear any. Please get out."

But the saleslady pushed her way into the tiny cubicle and made a grab for the first pair of slacks. "You can't try on clothes naked, dear," the woman said. "It's *disgusting!*"

She was wedged against the back of the dressing room, naked from the waist down, without enough space to get into the slacks, which were, as the saleslady had correctly guessed, a size too small for her. "Get *out!*" she cried.

"Don't you shout at *me!*" The saleslady too seemed paralyzed by the sheer embarrassment of the situation, or perhaps by her own anger, unable to retreat. She gave a sniff of distaste. "You're not only naked, dear, you *smell*. How dare you come in like that to try on clothes?"

She didn't smell—it was a monstrous accusation, unfair, unkind, untrue. She had bathed in the morning, soaked in the tub for ages while she sipped her coffee. Any smell was her *own,* her natural juices, the personal aroma that was distinctly hers, a combination of sex and Chanel No. 5 that men adored, and that she herself could sniff for hours with pleasure.

She pushed the saleslady—not hard, just a gentle shove, more out of panic than anything else.

"Help! Help! *Help!"* The saleslady was screaming, the veins standing out on her forehead, her eyes popping—apparently riveted to the spot.

She gave her a hard shove this time, determined to get the woman out of her way. This time the saleslady was sent flying, screaming now at the top of her lungs.

She pulled the slacks up, squeezing her hips into them, and ran, in sheer terror at the sound of the woman's screams, which seemed to fill her head. She caught a glimpse of herself in a mirror—a crazy-looking woman in a funny hat, a pair of tight slacks, half unzipped, with the price tags still flapping on them, running desperately' through the store, while people stared at her in horror or jumped out of her way.

Before she reached the escalator, a burly man in a blazer stepped in front of her and caught her in his arms. She lashed out furiously, as terrified of being held as a wild animal, hearing her own screams now. He held her harder, with the strength of the beat cop he had no doubt once been. She fought, struggled, kicked, bit, and swore, until a couple more security guards rushed up panting and she was pinioned roughly, her hands twisted behind her back.

"Assault and shoplifting," the man in the blazer said, dabbing at his scratches with a handkerchief.

"I wasn't shoplifting, you son of a bitch. Tell these guys to let me go or you'll be sorry."

"Those are the store's pants, lady, not yours. You haven't paid for them. That's called shoplifting. You assaulted a saleslady, and you assaulted me. We're going down to my office quietly; then I'm going to hand you over to the cops."

"She insulted me. She pushed me."

"Sure. Tell it to the judge, lady. I'm just doing my job."

"Do you know who the hell I *am,* you fucking idiot?"

He looked at her. "No," he said. "And I don't care. If it was up to me, I'd teach you not to use language like that to me or anybody else. Just because you're a woman wouldn't stop me, okay? So don't try my patience no more."

The two guards moved her to a door, away from the crowd of curious onlookers, the ex-cop unlocked it, and she was carried, helpless, into an elevator and down a long corridor at the end of which was a small, windowless office. They dumped her in a chair, while the security man sat down at the desk.

"What's your name, lady?" he asked, uncapping his pen.

"Marilyn Monroe."

He gave her a hard, humorless stare. "Sure. And I'm Fred Astaire." He reached across and grabbed her jaw in his pudgy fingers, the big Police Academy ring gouging her flesh. "A word of advice, toots. Don't get smart with me. You a pross? I don't know what I got to do to teach you girls to stay the fuck out of the store."

Rage overcame her, welled up from deep inside her, as if she were choking on her own vomit. She couldn't move, because he had her held, but she spat into his face, and a moment later, she felt the sudden, sharp pain as he brought the flat of his meaty hand against her cheek. The blow was strong enough to make her fear for her teeth—strong enough, too, to bring her to her senses.

"Open my handbag," she said.

He nodded, perhaps aware that he, too, had crossed a line beyond correct behavior, spread out her few credit cards, unfolded her California driver's license (out of date, as usual), and in a low, awed whisper said, "Holy Mary Mother of God."

It took less than an hour for a young lawyer to arrive—everybody more senior was away for the weekend—but once he was there, she was out of the store through the freight entrance in ten minutes, and into the waiting limousine, clutching her handbag, still dressed in the slacks that were too tight for her.

She went back to the apartment, tore off the slacks, and took a few pills to calm her nerves; then she decided she needed to sleep, so she opened another bottle, spilling a few capsules on the floor, which she got down on her knees to pick up; then she couldn't stand up— she was kneeling bare-assed on the white shag rug of the bathroom —and decided she might as well curl up on it and take a nap. . . .

———

I don't know what would have happened if I hadn't made a date to take Marilyn to a screening late that afternoon, to be followed by a steak at Gallagher's, one of her favorite places. Maria had gone to Paris for a week of shopping and was staying there with the D'Souzas, so it seemed like a perfect opportunity to catch up on what was new in Marilyn's life.

I spent one of those New York Saturdays that I love—a stroll along Madison Avenue, looking in at all the art galleries, a stop at Judd and Judd, to look at the latest books, a bone-dry martini and a chef's salad at the Carlyle Hotel, then a brisk walk home, pausing to pick out a couple of shirts at Sulka.

To say I was in a good mood when I arrived at Marilyn's would be understating it, and I was therefore irritated when she didn't answer the doorman's call.

"She's expecting me," I said.

"Yes, Mr. Leman. She mentioned it to the day man. I know she's in."

He called again. There was no reply. "Do you want to go up and try?" he asked.

I took the elevator up to her apartment, and asked the elevator man to wait. I rang several times, then banged on the metal door, but there was no sound from inside, which I thought was odd, because Marilyn always had music on—usually a stack of Sinatra records.

I knew she left a spare door key under her mat—she was always losing the one in her purse—so I dismissed the elevator man, reached under the mat, found the key, and opened the door.

"Marilyn?" I called out. There was a strange kind of silence—a heavy, unnatural silence, not that of an empty apartment but, in some way, the silence of sleep or death. I knew she was there, not just because the doorman had told me but because I could feel her presence, smell her perfume, sense that I wasn't alone.

I think I already guessed what I would find—it was one's first thought, with Marilyn. I just wasn't sure where I would find her. The bedroom was empty, although her handbag on the tangled sheets confirmed that she was home. The bathroom door was ajar, so I knocked on it, then pushed it open, realizing, to my shame, that it was the first time I had seen Marilyn naked, or almost so, for she still had on her bra and her unbuttoned blouse, as well as her white, spike-heeled shoes. She was lying on her side, eyes closed and mouth open. Her pubic hair was darker than I had expected it to be. Her skin had a bluish tone, almost violet in places, and my first thought was that she was dead.

Then she breathed, thank God—not deeply, just a gentle sigh that brought a few bubbles of saliva to her lips and made her breasts lift slightly.

I went to the bedroom, called a private ambulance service and my own doctor, then a special number at police headquarters, which would bring the police in a hurry *without* any reporters. Finally I called the doorman on the house phone to warn him of what was coming, and pledge him to silence.

After that, I went back to the bathroom, soaked a washcloth in cold water, and held it to Marilyn's face, resting her head against my knee. She didn't seem to be choking, and her breathing, though faint, was regular. Her eyelids fluttered at the touch of the cold washcloth. Her lips moved and I thought she said, "Water!" so I filled a glass from the sink tap and held it to her lips. She swallowed a couple of times, then, without any warning, threw up all over my new shirt and tie.

Perhaps that saved her life. I don't know. They pumped her stomach at Doctors Hospital anyway, and the incident never made the papers—nor did I ever ask her what the immediate cause had been.

When I went back to her apartment the next morning to pick up a few things for her, since she was being kept "under observation," there was a messengered package from Bloomingdale's.

I opened it, and found an old pair of pants from Jax, the kind Marilyn wore all the time, and her Bloomingdale's credit card, neatly cut in half.

———

She went back to California the day after she was released from Doctors Hospital, as if the only thing that mattered now was fleeing the city. She phoned Sulka and had them send a half-dozen silk shirts to David, but she couldn't bring herself to speak to him, besides which her throat still ached and her voice was still hoarse from the stomach pump.

Dr. Greenson himself picked her up at the airport, alerted by Dr. Kris to the seriousness of her case. Suicide attempts brought psychoanalysts to action stations, for they meant failure.

Of course, Greenson pretended that it was an overdose of prescription drugs, an "accident," but his eyes told a different story. He knew exactly what had happened, and he made plans to prevent its happening again on *his* watch, as he liked to say. First he proposed that she stay with him and his family, which she didn't want to do; then he switched to a second idea, which was to buy a house close to his—he had just the house in mind. He already had a "housekeeper" on tap, somebody she could trust, somebody *he* could trust:

Eunice Murray, a lady who had a lot of experience "looking after people," as he put it.

By the end of the week, she had met Mrs. Murray—who turned out to be gently soft-spoken, but with a thrusting jaw and, behind glistening spectacles, steely eyes that promised an iron will—and hired her. Mrs. Murray's duties were elastic—she did not cook or keep house, really, but she drove the car, answered the phone, and, most important of all, kept vigil on behalf of Dr. Greenson.

It was all a great relief. She had placed herself, finally, in Greenson's hands completely: Mrs. Murray watched her at home and drove her to her sessions, Greenson's buddy Henry Weinstein was now going to produce her new picture, if it ever got off the ground, while Greenson's realtor went house-hunting for her, with instructions that the house be as close as possible to Dr. Greenson's own, and resemble it if possible. . . . As if all that weren't enough, Mrs. Murray had a daughter named Marilyn!

She felt protected at last. The house they found for her on Helena Drive in Brentwood was like a miniature version of Dr. Greenson's —really *tiny,* which was exactly what she wanted, and dark as a cave because of the encroaching tropical garden outside, which suited her present mood perfectly.

She exulted in the idea of owning it. She and Jim had rented what amounted to a shack, she and the Slugger had never bought a house of their own, the house in Roxbury was really Miller's, not hers. This one, small as it was, cramped as its rooms were, overgrown and untended as its garden might be, was *hers.*

She asked Mrs. Murray to redo the kitchen so that it would look exactly like Dr. Greenson's, with bright colors and lots of Mexican tiles, and moved in as soon as she could with her meager store of belongings, most of them still in cardboard boxes, and put her Kennedy for President poster on the bedroom wall.

She had her own pool, too, at last—not that she swam in it. Indeed, its only role in the household was as a hazard to little Maf, for she was terrified that the dog would fall in and drown. Still, she ordered pool furniture, and Mrs. Murray arranged with a service to send a man around to clean it three times a week.

Of course, there were a lot of things missing, things that nobody had thought of in the rush to move in. There were practically no cooking utensils, the heating system worked spasmodically, the phone jacks were left unchanged, which meant that her private telephone—the unlisted one, without an extension—had to be placed in the living room, and carried upstairs at the end of a long cord when she wanted to use it in her bedroom at night. . . . She didn't mind. It was home.

She was in it, dressed in her terry-cloth robe with a towel wrapped around her hair, when she heard on the radio that Ambassador Joseph P. Kennedy had suffered a massive stroke after a game of golf in Palm Beach.

———

The President stood in the hospital corridor, with Secret Service agents at either end. He was still wearing a winter-weight suit. He had flown down from Washington as soon as he could disengage himself, but Robert Kennedy had arrived before him.

"Christ, it's an awful thing," Jack said. "He always said this was the one thing he was afraid of, that he'd rather be dead than helpless."

"He'll get better," Bobby said fiercely. "There's therapy, rehabilitation exercises. . . . He's got the guts to come back." There were tears in his eyes.

Jack Kennedy put his arm around his brother's shoulder, and they walked the length of the corridor. "You've seen him," he said. "It was a *massive* stroke. They don't think he'll walk again. They aren't even sure he'll ever recover his speech. It's best to face facts."

"I won't face those."

"You may have to." They moved away from the window, at a gesture from the nearest agent. Already there were agents and police sharpshooters deployed against snipers on the nearby rooftops. The President grimaced and made a mental note to put a stop to this kind of display, which smacked of a police state and made him feel like a Latin American dictator. "God, I hope this doesn't happen to me," he said. "A gunshot, something quick, that's the way to go."

Bobby shook his head. "Don't talk like that," he said. His expression turned, if anything, a shade grimmer. "Did you know Marilyn sent a long telegram to Mother, telling her how sorry she was, and how much she loved Dad? She wrote that she felt as if she was a member of the family, and offered to fly out and look after him. . . ."

"Oh God."

"There's worse. She gave a press conference at Twentieth Century–Fox to say how sad she was, and how close she felt to the family."

"Shit. Is Mother upset?"

"Puzzled. But it's a real problem. David is working hard to contain the story. Still . . ."

A doctor was approaching, with the look that always spells more bad news. Jack turned toward him. "You win, Bobby," he said. "She's getting out of hand."

"This on top of what happened in New York with the Secret Service . . ."

"I know, I know. I *said* you win, so don't rub it in. It's got to be done. I understand." His voice was weary.

He held up a hand, stopping the doctor in his tracks for a moment. His eyes were full of regret, but there was also the hint of something else—relief perhaps at having finally made the tough, inevitable decision, a look Bobby had seen before when Jack called off the air strikes at the Bay of Pigs. "Go to California," he said. "See if you can get her off my back."

"Why me?"

"Because you're better at that kind of thing than I am."

Bobby nodded, his expression dark, as if he was acknowledging, without pride, that it was true.

"Do it as nicely as you can," Jack said, waving the doctor forward, already moving on to the next problem. He shook the doctor's hand, his face stern, his eyes concerned, every inch the president.

"But be firm, Bobby," he added.

PART FOUR

LEGEND

40

She sat between Peter Lawford and Bobby Kennedy at dinner, having the time of her life.

She knew Bobby, of course, but she didn't really *know* him. He had always seemed to her remote, sometimes even unfriendly, so it had come as something of a surprise when Peter told her Bobby wanted to see her. Peter was planning a dinner party for Bobby, he said, a "Welcome to LA" sort of thing, and he hoped she could make it.

Since she had nothing much to do but sit at home with Mrs. Murray, she had been only too happy to oblige. She had always wanted an opportunity to have a heart-to-heart with Bobby, and had come to the dinner with a carefully prepared list of questions. As he was a Kennedy, however, she had also prepared for the occasion by having her hair bleached white and set in a soft curl and by getting the studio makeup man to come over to the house to do her face. She had chosen a silver lamé dress with a daring V-shaped neckline that left her shoulders and her back bare, exposed her breasts almost to the nipples, and plunged down to her navel—a dress that very few women would have risked wearing, and about which even she had had doubts—not that she couldn't get away with it, but it might embarrass Bobby.

She had made a big effort to arrive on time—for her—which was to say that everybody had already had a couple of drinks and looked at their watches a few times, while Pat had gone into the kitchen once or twice to calm the cook. She timed her entrance just at the precise moment when people had begun to think she wasn't coming.

445

She knew her business—she simply *appeared* at the top of the steps leading down into the big sunken living room and stood there, the lights reflecting off her dress, until someone looked up and said, "Marilyn!" followed by complete silence as everybody stared at her in awe, even those who knew her well.

She stood there in the silence, then flashed her smile as the room exploded into applause, cheers, and wolf whistles. This was what her life was *about,* what she knew how to do better than anyone. *Nobody* could do this to a roomful of movie people, except maybe Elizabeth Taylor, and even Liz couldn't have matched the blinding silver and platinum blaze that flashed and glittered off the world's most famous blonde, plunging everyone else in the room into the shadow.

Except Robert Kennedy. For she noticed that Bobby, slight as he was, and wearing what looked like an off-the-rack wash-and-wear summer-weight suit from Sears, his hair sticking up like a rebellious teenager's, had the *look,* the look of his brother but in spades—that mysterious star quality that made him stand out as if he were as spotlit as she was—the bright blue eyes, the compact, wiry body that exuded almost visible waves of energy.

She walked slowly down the steps, to receive a careful peck on the cheek from Lawford, who as an actor, however lousy, knew better than to smear a star's makeup. "Marilyn, *darling!*" he shouted, already a bit drunk. "You were worth waiting for!"

"Who's waiting?" she asked. "I thought I was early?"

Lawford giggled appreciatively. "You've met the Attorney General, I think," he said, doing his unsteady best to play the gracious host.

"Oh my, yes," she whispered. "Welcome to Los Angeles, Mr. Attorney General." She wasn't sure it was the right way to greet him, but it sounded respectful.

Bobby shook her hand, blushing. "Bobby, please."

She held on to his hand. "Bobby, then," she said, and she continued to hold on to him as they went in to dinner.

She had him to herself at the dinner table. At first she had an uphill struggle against what seemed to be a mulish obstinacy on his part not to be charmed by her, but by the time the soup had been served and removed, he was warming up to her. "Why can't Jack do more to help the Freedom Riders?" she asked him boldly.

"He's doing what he can."

"I think it's disgusting that the Klan and all those bigots are allowed to throw rocks and shoot people."

446

"It's a free country."

"Not for Negroes, apparently."

There was a flash of anger in his eyes; then he nodded. "I'm with *you*," he said. "It turns my stomach. But Jack was elected by a paper-thin majority. He can't win in '64 without the South, and that means he can't move as fast as he'd like to. He signed an order desegregating federal housing, you know, and the shit really hit the fan below the Mason-Dixon line."

"He promised to do that when he was campaigning in 1960," she said firmly.

His eyes opened wide. He was impressed. "You remember *that?*"

"Just because I'm a blonde doesn't mean I'm a dumb bunny." Her confidence was high tonight, for the first time in many months. She was pilled up, tranquillized and energized to take her beyond her normal fears, but something about Bobby—his directness, his quick grin, some hint of sadness in the depths of those bright eyes—made it possible for her to shine.

"He had to wait for the moment," he said.

"A *year?* And how about the fact that African diplomats can't stop for a meal or use a rest room when they're driving through Maryland to and from New York?"

He looked surprised. "We're looking into that."

"I heard that Jack—the President—told Angie Biddle Duke he ought to ask them to take the shuttle instead."

"That's not true. Well, okay, maybe it *is* true," he corrected himself, looking at her eyes, "but he was joking."

"But it isn't *funny*. Doesn't he *care* about these things?"

"Of course he does, you know that, but he's a practical politician. . . . Things take time. Listen, we've spent nine months getting Castro to release the Bay of Pigs prisoners, and that's something the President cared about a *lot*."

"What's the point of releasing the Cuban prisoners if Negroes can't even use a rest room in their own country?"

"We'll deal with that, too, in time."

"Does that mean you're a practical politician too, Bobby?"

He paused, his expression troubled, as if the question had somehow touched some deep, hidden part of him. "I don't know," he said at last. "In some ways, yes, I am. The problem is that I don't really *want* to be. It comes naturally to my brother, but it's harder for me."

He was silent for a moment. "So much for the ruthlessness, I guess."

She reached out and touched his hand under the table. "You never looked ruthless to me," she said.

"You could be wrong about that," he answered gruffly, an expression of infinite sadness on his face.

By the time dinner was over, she felt she knew Bobby, and liked him better than she had expected to, although there was still something about him she didn't understand, almost as if he were *afraid* of her.

Coffee was served; people were starting to drink more seriously. Bobby led her to a dark corner of the room. "I need to talk to you," he said. "In private."

For some reason, she shivered. "This is pretty private," she said.

He shook his head. "Let's go outside."

They walked out onto a terrace. "Are you up for a walk on the beach?" he asked.

She was about to point out that she was wearing a silver lamé evening gown and open-toed stiletto pumps, but something in his face made her change her mind, so she took off her shoes and left them on the terrace, then, stepping into the shadow of the doorway, she leaned over, unfastened her stockings, slipped them off, and stuffed them into her purse. "Let's go," she said, and together they walked out onto the sand and down to the shoreline, where the sea curled in phosphorescent wavelets in the moonlight. She loved the feel of sand between her toes, though her dress was so tight it made walking difficult.

"Are you cold?" Bobby asked. He touched her hand briefly, almost as if it was an accident, but she was pretty sure it wasn't. His face in the moonlight was serious, almost grim. Then he took a deep breath, like a man about to dive into cold water. "I was sent out here to talk to you, you know," he said gently, like a doctor breaking bad news.

"What about?"

"About Jack."

"What about him?"

"He's—ah—got to put some distance between himself and you, Marilyn."

She walked on, suddenly numb. She knew exactly what he had come for now, and in a way she had been expecting it, waiting for the ax to fall without daring to look at it. Well, it was falling now— one look at Bobby Kennedy's face was enough to make that obvious.

"Are you saying it's over?" she asked, trying to sound calm.

"I'm saying it's over."

"Why?"

"He's the president, Marilyn. He's got enemies. That, ah, scene in the Carlyle lobby. The letter to Mother. Talking to the press about Dad's stroke. Telling people he's going to leave Jackie and marry you. . . . That kind of thing is dangerous. I know you love him, but if you *really* love him, you'll give him up."

"And if I don't?"

"You will." His voice was harsh, and she realized it was a sentence without appeal.

"Why couldn't he tell me this himself? He owes me that." She could feel the quick rush of anger, warming her like a fire, and understood instantly why he had wanted her outside.

He stared out to sea. "Jack wanted to tell you himself. I told him not to."

"Why?"

"He's the president, Marilyn. It's my job to save him from himself, if needs be."

"What happens if I call him?"

"I don't know. I *do* know this: if you call him on the special number, you won't get him. I had it cut off today."

"He wouldn't let you!"

"He doesn't know yet." He stared at her, shaking his head. "Marilyn, Marilyn," he said softly. "In the last three weeks you called him thirty-six times. You must have known it couldn't go on."

"You superior little *prick!*" she shouted. "What the fuck do you know about it? He *loves* me."

"Yes," he said quietly, his head slightly bowed. "I believe he does." He shrugged his shoulders. "But that doesn't change anything."

"It does, it *does!*" she cried, and charged at him, splashing wet sand against the hem of her dress, fists raised to hit out at him. He dodged her easily enough, but she turned and came at him again, teeth bared, eyes blazing, and this time they collided. He grabbed her with both arms, holding her as tightly as he could, his head back, so she could only flail away impotently with her fists. She brought her head forward sharply and bit his ear, exulting in his sudden howl of pain, but he held on to her, despite her struggles, until she went limp, suddenly exhausted by her own rage.

"You carried it too far, don't you see?" he said, as softly as ever. His earlobe was bleeding, a line of blood, black in the moonlight, running down his neck and staining his collar.

"I broke the rules, you mean?"

"You broke the rules, right."

"Is he angry?" she asked.

Bobby shook his head, his hair falling over his forehead like a kid's. "No, he's not angry," he said. "He doesn't blame you. You're not to blame. He's not to blame." He kicked at the sand with his shoes. "There are people who know about this affair," he said. "People who would use it against him. I can't let that happen."

"What people?"

"People. The less you know, the better."

She shivered. Bobby took off his coat and draped it over her shoulders. "It was the best thing in my life," she said. "The thing that made the most sense. Loving Jack, I mean."

"It meant a lot to him, too."

"It wasn't just the sex. We were—I don't know—right for each other. I helped his back. He made me laugh, and sleep without pills. Our bodies fit together, you know? Like the right pieces in a jigsaw puzzle?"

"Yes?" He seemed to be turning the image over in his mind.

"I'd have done anything for him. Anything he asked. I've never felt like that about anybody before."

"He knows that. This is what he's asking you to do. Break it off."

She was shaking now, although she didn't really feel cold. She didn't feel anything much, in fact. He put his arm around her shoulder. "Are you going to be okay?" he asked.

"I don't know. I'm not going to drown myself, if that's what you mean."

"That wasn't what I meant."

She walked into the shallow, curling surf, the waves breaking over her feet, the bottom of her silver skirt soaking wet, and for a few minutes they splashed together along the beach, the spray around them gleaming in the moonlight, the shining drops of salt water clinging to the tiny golden hairs on her arms.

"It wasn't just an illusion, was it?" she asked. "I need to know that. Jack did love me, didn't he?"

"He did. He does. If he weren't the president, it might be different, but he *is*."

She had always dreaded this moment, but now that it had come, she found, to her surprise, that she wasn't hysterical. She was calm, in control of herself—Dr. Kris and Dr. Greenson would be proud of her! She guessed that it was because she had known for a long time it would happen. Still, she felt a deep, almost bottomless sadness inside her, so big that she wasn't sure how she could live with it, or even if she *wanted* to.

They turned, in unspoken accord, and walked back toward the Lawford house.

"It's important," Bobby said, "that none of this ever happened."

"I wasn't planning to write a book."

"I didn't mean that. If there are letters, souvenirs—that kind of thing. . . . Lock them away in a bank vault, if you have to keep them."

"There isn't much. Jack never wrote."

Bobby nodded.

They were nearing the house. She wondered briefly what people must be thinking, but she didn't care.

"Dreaming that Jack and I were going to be together someday—that's been what's kept me alive, for a long time."

"It's hard. I know."

"I'm not sure you do." They were almost at the door now, the bright light from the windows blinding after the walk in the dark. She was beginning to cry—not hysterically, just a gentle, slow fall of tears. "I can't go inside," she said. "My dress is ruined. Not to mention my face and my hair."

"Do you have a car?"

She did, of course, but she shook her head. She took his hand in hers and squeezed it hard. "Take me home," she said. "Please. I don't want to be alone yet. I'll be all right once I'm home."

There was a look of hesitation on his face—or was it something else? She couldn't be sure. "Well," he said, "I don't know. . . ."

"I've been good, haven't I?" she asked fiercely. "I haven't screamed, or shouted, or made a scene?"

He nodded, his eyes hooded in the bright light like a hawk's. It was a more complicated face than his brother's, she thought, more secretive, in some ways harsher, in others more vulnerable, the planes and angles of it more sharply cut. "You'd better get your things, then," he said.

She picked up her purse and her shoes, and followed him, barefoot, around the house and into the alleyway where a black sedan was parked. A man was sitting in it—probably a Secret Service agent. She waited in the shadows, Bobby's coat still draped over her shoulders, while he whispered something to the man in the car, who got out and handed Bobby the keys. The bottoms of Bobby's trousers were wet, and his shoes leaked puddles of water on the asphalt. He waited until the agent had vanished around the corner of the house, then waved to her.

"You'll have to show me the way," he said, opening the car door for her, then got in after she had slid across the bench seat.

Now that she was in the car, she felt the cold, and with it the first tremors of emotional shock. She was trembling uncontrollably, teeth chattering as if she had just been pulled from the coldest water after some accident.

"My Lord," Bobby said. "We'd better get you warm."

He started the car and turned the heater on, but she was still shaking, so he put his arms around her, holding her tight. She could see her face reflected in the mirror, the eyes hauntingly large, the lips parted, showing tiny, perfect teeth. Her shoulder straps had slipped, so it was almost as if she were naked, except for her bra, under his jacket.

"Oh God," she moaned. "Hold me, hold me, hold me tight."

"Okay, okay, you're going to be okay," he muttered thickly, trying to calm her. "It's going to be okay. . . ."

Okay, okay, okay. . . . She heard him say it over and over again, but his voice was muffled now, for her lips were pressed hard against his, her hands grasped his head, pulling him hard toward her, her body pressed against his too. "Hold me, *hold* me, *hold* me," she whispered, over and over again.

She had no idea how long their embrace lasted. She was trembling now, but warmer, sweat running down her torso. "Don't let me go," she pleaded. "I need to be held."

It was dark in the car, the only light coming from a street lamp a hundred feet away. She could feel his body, so much like Jack's but somehow different, slighter, more tightly muscular. There wasn't much room in the front seat of the car, but she managed to slip down, lying flat, so that he could lie between her legs, her skirt, completely ruined now, hiked up around her waist. She had one knee jammed against the dashboard, the other against the back of the seat. Her head was pillowed uncomfortably on some kind of thick vinyl notebook. The sharp edge of it cut into her neck, but she didn't care, because his face was against hers, his breath mixing with her own, his weight pressing her down. She could taste the sea salt on his lips and cheeks, smell his astringent after-shave, a different brand from Jack's, hear his breathing, heavy and deep like that of an athlete recovering from a winning effort, feel his hair, coarse like Jack's but longer. Then, with a long, gentle moan of submission, she let go of his head and lowered her hands in the dark, unzipping his trousers and closing her eyes, tried to picture Jack in her mind . . .

It was only when it was over, and they were lying in each other's arms, sweating from sexual exertion and the warmth of the car's heater, limbs messily intertwined, unable to move because his legs were trapped under the steering wheel, that she realized it hadn't worked the way she thought it would.

She had tried to picture Jack, but his image had faded as Bobby was fucking her. It had been Bobby's name on her lips as she came, and suddenly she realized that it didn't matter how it had happened, or *why* it happened, or whether it was right or wrong—whatever was meant to be, would be. . . .

Improbably, she felt at peace.

———

He was awake early in the morning, looking around the small, bare bedroom with curiosity.

"What *time* is it, lover?" she asked.

"Six-thirty."

"So early?"

"So late, I was thinking. The Secret Service agents must be going crazy by now."

"Fuck them, if they're anything like the one I slapped."

"What time does your housekeeper get in?"

"Not for a while. Come here and kiss me, then I'll make you coffee. I make pretty good coffee, believe it or not."

She took his hand and smiled. She could see herself in the mirror, and now glimpsed the catlike, self-satisfied smile of a woman who has captured another woman's husband. Bobby, she thought, would have some explaining to do, and not just to the Secret Service. There were the Lawfords and their guests, who must have guessed what had happened, and Ethel, whom he telephoned religiously every night when he was traveling, as all the stories about him pointed out, and Jack, she supposed. . . . She would have some explaining to do herself, not least to Dr. Greenson, who was unlikely to find her behavior evidence of sound emotional judgment. Ah well, she thought, fuck 'em. I'm alive again.

"Coffee? I believe it," he said. "You seem to do everything else pretty well."

He slipped back into bed again. He had the body of a high school athlete, neat, trim, not a scrap of superfluous fat on him. The sight of it, oddly, made her feel old, as if she had seduced a sixteen-year-old football player who had just delivered the groceries—a fantasy that made her giggle.

"What's so funny?"

"Oh, I don't know. Last night I thought my life was over, this morning I want it to go on forever. That's pretty funny, don't you think?"

"I guess so. What's not so funny is what I'm going to tell Jack."

"Because you fucked his girl?"

"No. Because I fucked up." He sighed.

She squeezed herself against him, pulled him close, her lips pressed so hard against his that he couldn't speak. From outside, she could hear the sprinklers starting up as they made love on the tangled sheets, half the pillows on the floor, the others at the wrong end of the bed, her ruined dress on the shag rug, with poor little Maf asleep on it. . . .

When they were done, he rolled over and looked into her eyes. If he felt guilt, he didn't show it. He had it under control, she decided, which was just as well, because she couldn't have handled a lot of breast-beating. But of course, she should have known better—he was a Kennedy: he didn't waste time on guilt or regret.

He held her in his arms, his lips against her ear, and in a whisper that she hardly even heard, said, "Tell me, was I as good as my brother?"

———

I was drafted to make sure nobody reported on Marilyn's ill-advised declaration of concern about Joe Kennedy's stroke to the press, and at the same time to minimize the seriousness of Joe's condition. We were cranking out bulletins about the Ambassador's recovery when in fact the poor man was lying paralyzed in a hospital bed, drooling from lips he could no longer control, his hands curled up like a bird's claws, the only words he could form a scary "No, no, no, no, no, no . . ." murmured over and over again, as if trying to repudiate what had happened to him, refusing to admit it even to himself.

Jack seemed better able to make contact with Joe than anyone else. He sat beside him for hours, talking to him as if his father could reply. It was as if Jack understood that their roles had been suddenly reversed.

Myself, I could not see Joe without breaking down and crying. Oh, he was not an easy man to like, but we had been friends a long time. Besides, like his sons, I had thought him invulnerable, and now I, like them, was suddenly face-to-face with the frailty of life, the irony of fate, which had brought Joseph P. Kennedy everything he wanted, then laid him low with the one thing that he feared most.

At the time, I didn't have the leisure to brood about what had happened, since my hands were full keeping Marilyn's name out of the papers—as well as dealing with my own feelings when I heard that Jack had made a break of sorts with her, at Bobby's urging.

I called her instantly and was surprised to find that she sounded pretty cheerful. I was prepared to hold her hand and console her, so it was a little disappointing to find that she didn't seem to need consolation.

I decided to go out to California anyway, since I had business there, but before I did, Jack called and asked me to join him in Washington for breakfast.

——

Jack came back from visiting his father to find the world ablaze—or so it seemed to him. There were rumors that the Diem government was about to fall in Saigon, where Buddhist monks were setting themselves on fire in time to make the evening news on American television; in the South, Negro protests had awakened the old hatreds—there were shootings, bombings, riots, threats of southern defection from the Democratic party in '64; in Europe, it looked as if the Soviets might try to grab Berlin and set off World War III. Jack looked drawn and grim as we ate. "It's gotten so I can't stand reading the papers," he said.

"Maybe you shouldn't. Ike never did. He only read the comics."

"I might give that a try."

"The good news is, the story about Marilyn isn't going to run."

"Well, that's something, at least."

"I had to give up a few markers."

"Yours or mine?"

"Yours. You're going to have to give a couple of exclusive interviews, stand still for some picture sessions, and invite one or two newspaper publishers to lunch. . . ."

Jack nodded. Nobody knew better than he did how news was managed. "Speaking of Marilyn," he said, "it turns out she wasn't inconsolable." He didn't sound any too pleased about it.

"Odd you should say that. I had the same impression. She sounded quite cheerful, for her."

The President seemed to be wrestling with deeper feelings. "Here I was worrying about how she'd take it," he said, "imagining suicide attempts and all that—and guess what?"

I shook my head.

"She's fucking Bobby now."

I stared at him in amazement, unable to believe my ears.

He shrugged. "Amazing, isn't it? Who can ever understand women? I ask you. I thought there'd be at least a big scene, maybe worse, but nothing of the kind. . . . They went for a moonlight walk. Then—are you ready for *this?*—they actually fucked in the front seat of a Secret Service car, parked in the alley behind Peter's house, like a couple of teenage kids."

"I can't believe that!"

"It's true. Bobby told me the whole thing. He felt he owed me the truth. The Secret Service told me about it, too. They were embarrassed as hell."

"She must be out of her mind!"

For a moment I thought Jack was going to agree with me. I could tell that for once in his life he was shocked, probably even hurt, but of course, being who he was, he was determined to put up a good front. It wasn't in him to be angry with Bobby for long, and certainly he couldn't very well be angry at Marilyn, since he had broken off with her, so I suppose he was angry with himself. All the same, he clearly needed to talk to someone about it, and he had chosen me. I was at once appalled and flattered.

"Out of her mind?" he mused. "I don't know about that, David. I think maybe I'm the one who's crazy, not Marilyn. Do you want to know the truth of it? I miss her already."

I wondered whether Jack had ever had this kind of experience before. With the exception of Jackie, his love life had always run on rails—certainly he was never the one to end up feeling blue—so this kind of pain was new to him. I could see he didn't like it a bit.

"All the same, it was the right decision," I said, hoping to make him feel better—though I don't know why, since I was still smarting over the ambassadorship.

"I guess so," he said without conviction. "I sure don't feel good about it, I'll tell you that."

"I can imagine."

"What really surprises *me,*" he went on, "is that Bobby had the guts to do that to Ethel. . . . You look a little green around the gills, David. Are you okay?"

I wasn't okay, not really. I had never thought I could steal Marilyn away from Jack, but once he had broken with her, I felt, obscurely, that it was my turn.... Now that had been taken away from me too, along with the ambassadorship, and for the first time I felt a sense of regret, of *waste*, as if all my years of friendship with the Kennedy family had led me nowhere, won me nothing. It was no longer Jack who needed my protection now; it was Marilyn.

I waved away his concern. "I'm fine," I said.

He looked at me shrewdly. "You're pissed off about it, aren't you?"

"It's not my business."

"The hell it's not. You've been in love with Marilyn since the day you set eyes on her, six, no—Christ!—*seven* years ago."

"What you say may be true, Mr. President—"

"Don't pull that 'Mr. President' crap on me when we're having a personal conversation. Is it me you're mad at or Bobby?"

"You."

"Because I dumped her? Let me tell you, very few things in my personal life have caused me as much pain. I should have done it a long time ago, and you know it. I put it off and put it off. . . ."

It was true, and I couldn't deny it. I didn't.

The President looked out the window, as if he longed to be anywhere but here in the White House. "The presidency seemed like fun for a while," he said. "I mean, I worked hard enough to win it, so I didn't see why I shouldn't enjoy it. But now that I've settled into it, I realize winning it is nothing. What matters is how you *leave* it."

"The itch for greatness," I said. "Seizing one's 'place in history.' " I smiled. "It comes over most people who occupy this house, sooner or later."

"It does that to you," Jack agreed.

"Perhaps it should. Perhaps that's why it's worth preserving, this old house. I'm impressed. Did your father know?"

"I talked to him about it. Before the stroke, thank God. He said it was what he'd been waiting to hear."

"Yes, I can imagine." I sipped my coffee. "Of course, I hadn't realized that chastity was a requirement of presidential greatness."

"Chastity? What do you mean?"

"Actually, that's the wrong word. Monogamy? Fidelity? Are you really turning over a new leaf?"

He laughed. "No. Not yet. But I will be a little more discreet. I don't think the president's girlfriends should be giving press conferences about their relationship with him, do you?"

"Marilyn was being foolish, I agree, but she must have been terribly upset. She's fond of your father. . . ."

"I appreciate all that, but that's the kind of risk I can't afford." He sighed. "You know, Jackie's settling into *her* role too. She hates being called 'First Lady'—she says it sounds like a saddle horse—but she's a damned *good* First Lady, in fact. I think we're even getting along better. . . . Maybe Marilyn became a luxury I couldn't afford? I think that's part of it."

"And Bobby?"

"He's a grown-up. He can make up his own mind what to do. It's a little strange that he preaches caution to me, then goes and fucks Marilyn in the Lawford driveway with half of Hollywood giggling about it in the living room, but at least it proves he's just as human as the rest of us."

"Is human weakness a good thing in an attorney general?"

"No, but it's okay in my brother."

We shook hands and said good-bye, standing outside the Oval Office. "When the history of this administration is written, I want it to be about great events and great decisions," he said. "Not about pillow talk and gossip."

"Well," I said, "you've got seven more years. Time enough."

"Oh, yes," he said, laughing. "All the time in the world."

41

As luck would have it, one of the members of the 20th Century–Fox board, an old friend and client, begged me to look into things at the studio, the next time I was in California. "It's chaos," he said. "Amateur hour. It makes me almost wish Zanuck was still there, and you know how I feel about Zanuck. They're hemorrhaging money, between Liz Taylor's illness and Marilyn Monroe's lateness. . . ."

Five minutes into lunch at the studio commissary (where the menu still featured "Fresh Sea-Food Salad à la Darryl F. Zanuck"), it was apparent to me that my client's estimate of the way things were going at Fox was, if anything, insanely optimistic. *Cleopatra* had careened totally out of control—too much money had been spent to make it feasible to stop production, but there was no end in sight. Elizabeth Taylor had recovered from her illness only to plunge into the most scandalous and public adulterous love affair of the century with Richard Burton, while nobody in the studio seemed to have the foggiest idea of what was happening with the picture.

As for *Something's Got to Give,* Marilyn's picture, principal photography had begun with a script that pleased nobody. George Cukor was writing it at night with a "friend" brought in to help him, so Marilyn, who found it difficult enough to memorize her lines in the first place, arrived on the set every morning only to find that the lines she had struggled to learn were no longer there. It took very little of that for Marilyn to decide that Cukor, despite his legendary reputation as a "woman's director," was the enemy.

Since Marilyn disliked open confrontation, she fell back on her time-honored methods of showing displeasure—illness and lateness. Sometimes she turned up on the set hours late, sometimes not at all, sending occasional health bulletins by way of intermediaries like Dr. Greenson or Mrs. Murray. When she *did* turn up, she seemed to be in a state of panic barely kept in check by medication, so that even the simplest thing took hours for her to do. Animal scenes are notoriously difficult to shoot, but in one scene where she was supposed to fondle a dog, the dog got it right on the first take while Marilyn blew *her* line twenty-three times.

All I heard at lunch were horror stories about Marilyn—this in the studio whose biggest and most profitable star she had been for ten years! Marilyn didn't even *look* like Marilyn, I was told—she had lost fifteen pounds, so that her whole wardrobe had to be re-made, and she now photographed more like Audrey Hepburn than herself. She had hired writers of her own to rewrite Cukor's rewrites, she hated the kids who were playing her children in the picture, and was having trouble with the notion of Marilyn Monroe playing a mother in the first place, and so on, and so on. . . .

I decided I had better go see her as soon as possible. I found her at home, looking healthy enough for somebody who had been pleading illness for weeks.

Her new house, which she showed me proudly, was dark and cramped, the decor mysteriously Mexican (I did not know that Marilyn was attempting to duplicate her analyst's house). There were Mexican tiles everywhere, the ones around the front door with a coat of arms and the motto *"Cursum Perficio,"* which, according to my schoolboy Latin, meant "I am finishing my journey"—a message that ought to have set off alarm bells in my mind.

She opened a fresh bottle of champagne—it was noon—and we sat down in the tiny living room, although it was a beautiful day outside. "Isn't the house *great?*" she asked.

Actually, it looked as if it had been furnished out of a Mexican junk shop—primitive paintings of the kind that tourists buy on the streets of Mexico City, cheap tin-framed mirrors and sconces, "Indian" horse-blanket rugs, and heavy stained-oak furniture of vaguely Spanish design.

"I made a special trip to Mexico City, to buy all this," she said, though I would have thought there wasn't much in the house she couldn't have found in any cheap furniture warehouse in Los Angeles. "Boy, did I have fun!"

She giggled. "I met this Mexican screenwriter who showed me all the sights. . . ."

She took a couple of pills and knocked back her champagne. "The only thing is, he thinks he's going to marry me, which he's not." She showed me the pill bottle. "One thing he *does* do is send me these—Mandrax." She giggled again. " 'Randy-Mandys,' they call them. You take them with a little alcohol and you feel really warm and sexy and *relaxed,* for hours. You can buy them in Mexico without a prescription."

Now that I looked at her more closely, I could see that her eyes were unnaturally bright, the pupils dilated. She seemed to have trouble focusing on one spot, as if she were nearsighted. "I hope you're not overdoing it," I said.

She laughed. "Same old David! Always a stick-in-the-mud when everybody else is having fun."

I was hurt, and probably showed it. "I may be a stick-in-the-mud," I said, "but at least I'm *concerned* about you."

With no warning, she burst into tears. "Oh, I know," she wailed. "I'm sorry."

I took her hand, which was cold as ice, although it was a warm day. She dabbed at her eyes with Kleenex from a box on the table, dropping the used ones on the floor, which bore the stains that Maf, still imperfectly housebroken, had put there. She seemed to me to be overreacting, and I said so.

She gave a sniffle. "I know you care," she said. "I shouldn't have said you were whatever."

I waved "stick-in-the-mud" away. "That's all right. But *are* you okay? I mean *really* okay."

She shrugged. "I guess. You know Jack ditched me?"

"I know. I saw him a couple of days ago. We talked about it."

"How *is* he? What did he say?"

"He's sad about it, Marilyn. It wasn't an easy decision for Jack. I've never known him to be as—frank—about himself. Or as presidential, somehow. He already misses you."

"I know," she said sadly. "We were good together, Jack and I, you know, all those years. Good for each other."

"Yes. I always thought so."

She looked forlorn. "You know about Bobby and me?" she asked. I nodded. She must have guessed how I felt.

"Poor David," she said.

"How's it going with Bobby?" I asked, anxious to avoid a discussion of my own feelings.

"Oh, well, you know, it's kind of a long-distance love affair. . . . I can't go east so long as I'm stuck here making this lousy picture, and

I guess the attorney general can only find so many reasons to come to LA. . . . Of course, it's only been going on a couple of weeks, but I don't know when we're going to see each other again. . . ."

She sighed. "In a lot of ways, Bobby's nicer than Jack. More— sensitive."

Bobby's dark, brooding, Celtic sensitivity was a well-known attraction, and many a heart had been broken by it on the campaign trail. That Marilyn would be bowled over was perfectly predictable: he was concerned, he loved children, he was a good father—perhaps the best and the most patient I've ever met—and he cared about everything she cared about, from blacks to orphans, the poor, and stray dogs. It was a marriage made in heaven, except that she was crazy and barely functioning, while he was married and the attorney general of the United States. As a kind of love token he had given her, she told me proudly, his private number at the Justice Department, which she had taped to her refrigerator.

"Yes," I said, "Bobby's sensitive. I'd be careful about making the same mistake twice, though."

"What mistake would that be?"

"Talking about it."

She laughed—a little unsteadily. "I *know* that," she said. "I've learned my lesson! I'm not telling a soul. Just my analyst."

I had my doubts. In my experience, people who tell their secrets to analysts have usually already divulged them to their friends. Still, there was very little I could do about it, except to warn her. She would have to learn for herself, I thought, that Bobby's view of human weakness—his own included—was harsher than Jack's.

The telephone rang. Marilyn picked it up, said, "Hello," then shook the receiver, as if something was wrong with it. She hung up, a look of mild annoyance on her face. "Ever since I moved in, I've had phone trouble," she complained. "Weird noises on the lines, or the phone rings and nobody's there. . . . It's a real *pain.*"

She turned her attention back to me. "Don't look so sour," she said. "I'm happy. Really, I am. When Bobby told me about Jack, I thought, Well, this is it, I'm going to kill myself, this time I'm really going to do it. But it didn't work out that way at all. Maybe my luck's changing, David," she said. "What do you think?"

"I hope so, Marilyn."

"So do I, honey," she whispered. "God, so do I!"

But her luck didn't change. The next day, I heard, she went to the studio—late, as usual—and flubbed so many takes that even the technicians on the set—gaffers, grips, prop men, electricians, guys who got paid by the hour plus overtime so they didn't care how long it took to shoot a scene—let out a collective groan, together with a few hisses, when she stumbled over the same simple line for what might have been the twentieth or thirtieth time.

By the end of the day, the studio executives, normally invisible, were lined up behind the camera in their dark suits sweating nervously, which made everything even more difficult for her. "Don't be afraid, darling," Cukor called out encouragingly, but fear wasn't it—her problem was *panic.*

Going before the camera had become like walking the high wire without a net. Even the presence of Dr. Greenson on the set didn't help. The camera, which had made her famous, was her enemy now.

————

"The camera may be a phallic symbol?" Dr. Greenson suggested. He did not sound convinced.

"I'm not afraid of cocks. I've seen enough of them, God knows."

"Admittedly. The subconscious may be, however. ..."

She lay back, eyes closed, listening. She found Dr. Greenson's voice soothing, rather like having a massage, even if he wasn't about to pull a psychiatric rabbit out of his hat.

The camera wasn't a phallus, though—she knew that perfectly well. It represented power of a different kind. All her adult life she had fought and sweated to please the studio, singing, dancing, smiling, shouting out silently with every gesture and glance, *Love me, choose me, I'm the prettiest girl of them all!* while at the same time hating and fearing their power simply to ignore her, or to push her back into the ranks of all the failed pretty blondes who waited on tables all over Los Angeles. Her stardom was a kind of slavery, and the camera was the symbol and magic totem of the slave masters.

She had explained all this to Dr. Greenson, but behind his sympathetic eyes she could sense a certain reserve, for he was, after all, part of the Hollywood establishment and found it difficult to accept the studio itself, or the picture business, as the cause of her illness.

"I always did what everyone wanted me to," she said. "I got pushed around, and bullied, and exploited, but I figured, Okay, I can take this, because I'm going to be *a star.* I thought, When I'm a star, I'll have power, then I'll show them! Only it turns out that the only power I have is the power to fuck things up for them, by being late, by being sick, by saying no to what they want me to do. . . . It's like being a wife. The only real power you have is to say no to your husband, right?"

"Mm."

"That's my relationship to the studio, you see? It's like a husband. I can't fight the studio—it's bigger than I am and stronger—but I can say no. I can have headaches. I can be late. I can make sure the studio doesn't get laid when it wants to get laid. Am I making any sense?"

"Yes," he said. "But in that case, my original idea remains correct. The camera *is* a phallus—the studio's phallus—and you're afraid of it."

"I'm *not* afraid of it. I just don't want to give it what it wants."

"That, my dear, is called fear." He made a little steeple of his hands. "How is the rest of your life going?"

"I miss Bobby," she said. "I guess that's one reason why I don't care about this picture. I want to be with him."

"That would surely be difficult?"

"New York is a lot closer to Washington than LA. I think we're getting a lot closer, you know? We have a real intimacy."

"That's good. Intimacy is what you need."

"I call him all the time—three or four times a day. We talk every night when he's working late at the Justice Department, sometimes for hours. He's interested in everything I do—and he tells me all about his day, and what he's doing, and about his family. . . ."

"About his family?" Greenson asked doubtfully.

"Oh, yes. I told him what to buy Ethel for her birthday. And one of his sisters even wrote to me." She pulled a couple of pages of expensive writing paper out of her handbag, as if to prove it. "She told me how pleased the whole family is that Bobby and I are a thing."

A look of alarm came over Greenson's face. "I would be careful not to show that to anyone."

"Well, of course I wouldn't. I'm just trying to show you that this is a *good* relationship—positive, just the kind you're in favor of. Bobby's coming out here soon. I can hardly *wait.*"

Greenson's expression was troubled, as if he were trying to work out what was positive about a clandestine affair between his most famous patient and the equally famous, married Attorney General of the United States, but he held his tongue. His job, as he saw it, was to patch his patient up, not to discourage her.

"Yes. Well, he's got business to do as well," she went on. "He told me he's determined to nail Jimmy Hoffa—he's really *scary* on the subject. He's even scarier about Giancana, who I *met* once, did I tell you? I'd hate to be in *his* shoes, the way Bobby talks about him. . . .

"Anyway, apparently Hoffa is involved in some land swindle called the Sun Valley Retirement Community—he got the members of his own union to invest their savings in land that was worthless —and Bobby's coming out to talk to a former Teamster official who's willing to testify against him. 'Knuckles' Boyle his name is, believe it or not! I mean, if you used it in a movie, nobody would believe you. . . . Anyway, we'll spend some time together."

"Be careful," Dr. Greenson said.

"Always," she said. "Believe me, I know *that!*"

Hoffa and Giancana did not often get together. Both of them preferred to deal through intermediaries—they were the targets of so much law enforcement surveillance that any meeting was fraught with danger and difficulties.

When Hoffa demanded a sit-down, Giancana balked at first, but since Hoffa had never insisted on one before, Giancana eventually gave in—though with many complaints because it involved a long and tedious journey, changing cars at many points and zigzagging miles out of the way in order to ensure that he wasn't being followed by the FBI.

By the time Giancana arrived at Hoffa's "lodge," a small log cabin deep in the Michigan woods, he was chilled and irritable. The dark pine forest, dripping wet, depressed him, and the cabin itself didn't help, with its cheap varnished knotty pine furniture and its stone fireplace. There was a gun rack on the wall, containing a .30/30 Winchester lever action, a bolt-action rifle with a telescopic sight, and a 12-gauge Winchester pump-action shotgun. Apart from that, the only decoration was a mounted deer's head, an eight-pointer, and some color prints of fish jumping. At least, the fire was lit. He accepted a cup of coffee with a dash of brandy in it, and warmed himself for a few minutes.

Hoffa was dressed for the surroundings in a red-and-black-checked wool lumberman's shirt and old corduroy pants stuffed into laced-up boots, in contrast to Giancana's silver-gray mohair suit and custom-made shirt and tie.

"See that .270?" Hoffa asked. "That son of a bitch is the most accurate fucking rifle I've ever owned. One of these days, he don't back off, I'm gonna get that greedy little Ivy League cocksucker Bobby in the crosshairs and let him have it."

Giancana shrugged. He disliked people who made threats, and talk of violence dismayed him. Violence was very often necessary, but you never talked about it—you gave a whispered order, and that was that. Hoffa, he thought, was a dangerous guy, a loudmouth. Not for the first time, he wished he'd never involved his people with the Teamsters.

They sat down in front of the fire, facing each other, no love lost between them. Giancana's bodyguards were in the car outside, as was Hoffa's driver. The two men met alone, as was only proper, out of respect for each other.

"The reason I mention the rifle," Hoffa said, "is—never mind how I know—Bobby is coming after you."

"He's already after me."

"Yeah, but the Cuban thing, that girl of yours who was going with Jack, all that don't mean shit no more. All bets are off. Jack's listening to that little prick brother of his. No more deals. They're out for your blood. And mine."

"They wouldn't risk it. Not with what I can tell about them."

"Don't bet on it. Jack's made up his mind not to run scared anymore, that's the word I get. He probably figures if you tell the world about the whole CIA-Cuba thing, he'll deny it, maybe fire some people at the CIA, and send you to the slammer, where with any luck somebody will stick a blade in your heart. He's gonna run for a second term over our dead bodies, that's what he plans to do."

"Where does all this come from, Jimmy?"

"Here. There. I got a bug in a certain lady's house, is one place, and in her analyst's office, is another. Do you know this lady—who was fucking the President—is now fucking Bobby, that little hypocrite, who's supposed to be such a family man?"

Giancana controlled his expression carefully. He *had* heard about Marilyn and Bobby from his singer girlfriend, who was a pal of Peter Lawford's and knew all the Hollywood gossip, but he wasn't about to tell Hoffa.

"The real stroke of genius was putting a bug in the shrink's office," Hoffa said. "Plus she and Bobby are phone pals, they talk for hours, can you believe it? That Sun Valley thing, you know? That piece of shit they been trying to indict me on for years? Bobby actually *told* her the name of his new informant, the one he was going out to see in LA!"

"That's a piece of good luck," Giancana said, smiling though he thought Hoffa was a walking time bomb who couldn't shut up. "What did you do?" he asked.

Hoffa smirked. "Just what you and I are gonna do to Jack and Bobby," he snarled, leaning closer. "I'm gonna have the fucking snitch whacked, whaddya think? Jack gets a second term, we're all gonna be looking at life from behind bars."

Giancana said nothing. He knew what he knew, and he didn't need Hoffa to tell him. Still, Hoffa had a point, he had to admit. There were bad times ahead if Jack Kennedy won a second term.

But murder, he thought, was always a risk, even when it involved small fry. Things went wrong, however carefully you planned. The murder of a president was unthinkably risky, so risky that he felt himself break into a sweat at the mere thought that he was sitting here listening to Hoffa talk about it. Didn't Hoffa realize that if he could bug the Kennedys, they could bug him? That if Bernie Spindel could tape Marilyn Monroe's shrink, somebody else could tape Hoffa's cabin?

He thought about the weather outside, and the mud, then thought with regret about his custom-made five-hundred-dollar shoes. "Let's go outside for a walk," he said. "A breath of fresh air."

42

It was just the kind of weekend she had hoped for—dinner at the Lawfords', the two of them pretending to be "just friends," the star and the Attorney General. The need to keep up appearances for several hours in front of other people heightened their desire for each other, so that by the time they reached her house in Brentwood— Bobby had offered to "drop her off" on the way back to the Beverly Wilshire, with a fairly convincing display of indifference, except to those in the know—they didn't even wait to get to the bedroom before they pulled off each other's clothes. They fucked right there in the living room, on the big sofa she had ordered in Mexico City, tossing the cushions to the far ends of the room to give themselves space.

Bobby spent the night, going downstairs once to call Ethel, she presumed, on the house line, because he returned looking embarrassed. She congratulated herself for not sneaking out after him to listen in.

Her bed was small and narrow—like the house itself, it had been designed with the needs of only one person in mind—but that made it better in a way, for they were pressed against each other as tightly as if they were sharing a Pullman berth, reminding her inescapably of *Some Like It Hot*.

They talked late into the night—unlike Jack, Bobby was one of those rare men who *didn't* close their eyes and fall asleep the minute they'd had sex. She told him about Tippy and the orphanage, and listened while he talked about his childhood, which seemed to contain all the things she'd never had: a mother, a father, brothers and sisters, grandparents, money. . . .

"I always wanted children," she told him.

"They're the best thing life has to offer, believe me. Why didn't you have any?"

"Bad luck," she said. "There's still time." She didn't feel like telling him that she'd terminated so many pregnancies over the years that there was almost no chance of a successful one now. . . .

"I wish we could have a baby together," she whispered. "Just one. After all, Ethel's got dozens."

He laughed nervously. Sensitive he might be, but he didn't take her seriously about this. "Not dozens," he said. "Not even a dozen."

"Lots, anyway. I only want one—a boy."

"A boy? Why a boy?"

"Because boys have it made. I wouldn't want a girl. I *know* what girls have to go through, lover."

"It might not be the same."

"It's always the same."

They made love again, in the cool dawn. Before she finally fell asleep, she said, "How do you feel about middle-aged women with strong jaws and glasses?"

"They're not really my type. Why?"

"Because if you don't get dressed, you're going to meet Eunice Murray in the kitchen. It's okay with me—I don't have too many secrets from Mrs. Murray—but you might not want her to see you here."

He nodded and gave her a kiss, then she fell asleep. When she woke, he was gone, and she could hear Mrs. Murray padding about downstairs, straightening things. From the way her clothes were scattered around the living room, Mrs. Murray would certainly have guessed what had happened, though not with whom. But she was pretty unshockable, and never commented on what went on in the house or the occasional man she found there in the morning. Far from disapproving, she seemed to enjoy Marilyn's confidences, giggling and blushing like a schoolgirl. It was like having a big sister in the house, or maybe a broad-minded sorority mother, even if part of her job *was* to report on everything to Dr. Greenson, and to deal with "emergencies" if they arose.

During the day, she asked Mrs. Murray to drive her over to the market in Brentwood—given the amount of "medication" she was taking, she could no longer drive herself—and spent nearly fifty dollars on "goodies"—not that Bobby was a big eater or much of a gourmet, but she felt ashamed of the fact that her refrigerator contained nothing but a few bottles of champagne, a carton of orange juice, a box of powerful sedative suppositories bought in Mexico City, and a small carton of half-and-half for Mrs. Murray's coffee. The cupboards contained nothing but Maf's dog food.

She bought olives, crackers, several different kinds of cheese, cold cuts, nuts, potato chips, filling her cart in a kind of orgy of domesticity, imagining that she was an ordinary housewife shopping for her man—as she might have been, for in her white Capri pants and blouse, without makeup and with a scarf knotted over her hair, she could have passed for an eager young bride stocking up on delicacies to greet her husband with when he returned home from work.

This vision kept her going through the afternoon, as she and Eunice tidied up the house, dusted and vacuumed, laid out plates of hors d'oeuvres and bowls of nuts. At six, breathless with excitement, she said good-bye to Eunice, bathed herself in Chanel No. 5, changed into a filmy black negligee—giggling at the sight of herself, the quintessential seductress—and settled down to wait for Bobby.

But when he arrived—two hours late—it took only one look to know that there was a problem. His face was flushed, his eyes as cold as granite, his mouth an angry down-turned slash. He flung off his coat, with an excess of force that made it clear how furious he was.

"What's the matter?" she asked, terrified by his obvious anger. Why did a man's anger always make her feel guilty?

He unfastened his wrinkled, sweat-stained button-down shirt—none of Jack's made-to-measure, French-cuff shirts for Bobby!—and tore off his tie, as if he were trying to break his neck with it. "Hoffa. The scum he's in with. There's this fellow, Knuckles Boyle, basically a decent guy who could have put Hoffa away for years. No reason why you'd have ever heard of him. He was just an ordinary working slob. . . ."

In fact, she *had* heard all about Knuckles earlier, from Bobby himself, but the look on his face made her decide there was something to be said for playing dumb. Knuckles, she seemed to remember, had only become a "working slob" after coming to blows with Hoffa as a Teamster official.

"*Was?*" she asked.

She slipped a hand behind him and rubbed his neck, which was stiff with tension.

"Was," he said flatly. "Somebody ran over him with a forklift at the warehouse where he worked. Not more than an hour before he was supposed to meet me."

He closed his eyes. "Somehow, there was a leak, somewhere. . . . He was going to testify against Hoffa and the mob, on the Sun Valley thing. We had him ready to go the whole fucking nine yards, and now he's dead, before he could give us a thing! The worst of it is that we killed him somehow. I don't see how it happened. Hardly anybody knew. I *promised* Boyle complete confidentiality, and I betrayed him."

"It wasn't *your* fault, Bobby," she said soothingly, feeling a slight edge of panic, for he had told *her* about Boyle in detail and with great pride, and while she didn't think she had told anybody, she couldn't be sure.

"Yes it was. I gave Boyle my word, and now he's dead." He stared into the middle distance, his face a mask of hard, unforgiving Irish anger. "When I find out who's responsible for the leak, I'm going to have his balls."

She had a growing memory of having mentioned Knuckles Boyle to somebody, but she couldn't remember who. "What about the people who killed him?" she asked.

"I'll get them," he said. "I'm going to get them *all*, sooner or later. Not just Hoffa and Giancana either. I want the guys who do their dirty work, too, like this fellow Santo Trafficante in Miami, or Carlos Marcello in New Orleans, or this Johnny Roselli here, who's an out-and-out killer, probably the one who took care of poor Knuckles for Hoffa. . . . People you've probably never heard of. . . ."

She *had* heard of Johnny Roselli. As it happened, Roselli had been a pal of sorts in the old days when she was with Joe Schenck. She did not think it was a good idea to inform the Attorney General of the United States of her knowledge.

She snuggled close to him, until, finally, he started to relax. Since he didn't drink, she was obliged to loosen him up in other ways, but it didn't take her more than half an hour to get him into bed. She took a bottle of champagne into the bedroom with her—he might not need a drink, but *she* did—and put it on her night table, next to all her pills.

It was strange, she thought, that Bobby never seemed to notice her pills or her drinking. It wasn't that he deliberately ignored it, the way some men did—it was almost as if he didn't *understand* it, perhaps *couldn't* understand that anybody could be so dependent on pills or booze, and therefore simply didn't see the evidence. . . .

It wasn't, of course, that she needed booze or pills to get rid of her inhibitions, since she had none; it was just that without them she felt unable to face even the simplest of demands. Lately, it seemed to her, it had been getting worse—she was occasionally aware of stumbling when she walked, of her speech being slurred, of moments of memory loss. There were even times when she wasn't sure whether she was in bed with Bobby or with Jack.

Bobby dozed in her arms, his head cradled on her breast, breathing gently, his own particular demons temporarily at bay. She stroked his forehead with her fingertips, rejoicing in the fact that he was, for this tiny moment, *hers*—not Ethel's, or Jack's, or the people of the United States—content with her happiness.

43

"That's Nixon's place."

"I know that, Chrissake."

The big powerboat cut through the mild swell off Key Biscayne, offering those on board a view of the island's most lavish homes, all of which were hidden from the road behind high hedges and walls, but whose broad lawns sloped down to the sea, revealing gardens, pools, statuary, and private docks at which multimillion-dollar yachts were moored.

None of the yachts was bigger than *Aces Wild,* which flew the Panamanian flag from her stern and was registered to a Grand Caymans corporation. Seated around a teak-and-brass table in the stern were three gentlemen in leisure clothes, yachting caps, and sunglasses, their fishing rods locked into sockets, the lines trolling unattended behind the boat. Incongruous amidst all the nautical paraphernalia, a portable tape recorder sat on the table.

Santo Trafficante—who had pointed out Nixon's place—was the host. His guests were Carlos Marcello, head of the New Orleans crime family, and Johnny Roselli.

Trafficante, de facto chief of organized crime in Miami, and Marcello had been partners in Havana—running the casinos and other interests on behalf of the five families of New York and their East Coast associates—until Castro threw them out.

Roselli operated mostly out of LA and Vegas, and had a reputation as a very heavy hitter, even among heavy hitters. The three of them did not constitute a fan club for Sam Giancana—whom, for different reasons, they all hated.

If Giancana had known the three of them were together, he would have sweated blood. For that matter, if the Feds had caught sight of them together, there would have been hell to pay; they were all convicted felons, forbidden to associate with one another. In addition, Marcello was still fighting Bobby Kennedy's attempt to have him deported again.

Here, at any rate, they were sure they weren't being bugged, either by Giancana or the FBI. The only person in earshot was the helmsman, a made man in Trafficante's family.

"You guys heard the fucking tape the same as I did," Roselli said, his voice rising above the expensive burble of the big twin V-8s like a piece of heavy earth-moving machinery working hard. "I played it the minute it arrived from Hoffa. You wanna know do I take it seriously? You bet I do! You think it's just pillow talk? I don't. Neither does Hoffa. That little cocksucker Bobby Kennedy is going to put us all away for life, his brother gets elected again." Roselli, despite his styled silver hair and Hollywood playboy tan, still talked like a professional murderer and a thug, which he was.

Trafficante shrugged, his eyes hidden by thick dark glasses. "Men speak a certain way to women, Johnny. They talk big, they boast. Not everything they say in bed is true. It's human nature." He puffed at his cigar, watching the smoke drift astern. "I'm not speaking personally, of course," he added. "Still, that's the way it is." Trafficante, though Sicilian, had acquired through his years in Havana a measure of Spanish courtesy and polish, along with a taste for fine cigars.

Marcello exchanged glances with Roselli. Both of them thought that Trafficante was a bit too much the diplomat-philosopher for his job. In the old days, he had been as quick to order a man's death as anybody else, and years ago, before his rise to don, he had done his share of killing, but lately he seemed to yearn for the respectability of elder statesman status, like Joe Bonanno.

"With respect, I think Bobby means what he says, Santo," Marcello said. "Even if he does say it in bed, to Marilyn Monroe." Somewhere along the way, Marcello had developed a deep southern accent, perhaps because he thought it was appropriate to the crime boss of New Orleans.

"It's *vendetta*, Chrissake," Roselli growled.

The three men sat silently, considering the most powerful word in their vocabulary. If Roselli was right and Bobby Kennedy had sworn *vendetta* against them, then there was only one response, and they all knew it.

"*Vendetta?*" Trafficante repeated, with cautious respect, for it was not a word to be spoken lightly. "He's Irish, not Sicilian."

Roselli snorted. "Who gives a fuck, Santo? You think the fucking harps don't unnerstan' *vendetta?* Let me tell you something. They unnerstan' *vendetta* just like us. Look at the fucking IRA. Look at the cops. Don't give me he's Irish, not Sicilian. I'm telling you it's him or us. You don't believe me, listen to the tape again."

Trafficante held up his hand, and Roselli fell silent, for Trafficante had the ear of Meyer Lansky, and Lansky was listened to with respect by the heads of each of the five families. Anyone who fucked with Santo Trafficante as good as fucked with Lansky, and anyone who fucked with Lansky was dead. "What do *you* think, Carlos?" Trafficante asked.

Marcello's face was as expressionless as an Easter Island statue's. "When a man swears *vendetta* against you," he said quietly, "what do you do?" He crossed himself quickly, for this was a serious business. "You kill him first," he said, answering his own question.

They sat in dead silence as the boat churned through the offshore swell, gently rolling at trolling speed. There was a sudden sharp crack that made them all start; then the helmsman called out, "Fish! We got a bite." He cut the throttles and pointed to one of the lines, which had snapped clear of the outrigger. He eased off the line, and shaded his eyes as the fish jumped a few hundred feet away, to seaward. "Tuna," he said.

"Fuck the tuna!" Roselli said. "I wanna tuna, I'll buy it in a fucking can."

Trafficante frowned. "Play the fish, Johnny," he said, in a voice that made it clear he was giving an order. "Somebody's watching from the shore, it wouldn't hurt we were fishing."

Roselli grunted. He moved into one of the two white vinyl-and-chrome fighting chairs, and with the help of the captain brought in a good-sized albacore. He watched as the captain gaffed it, the blood staining the surface of the sea a brief, dark red. "May Bobby Kennedy go like that," he said.

Trafficante frowned again. He didn't like that kind of talk. Business was business—there shouldn't be anything personal about it. "Let's say Johnny's right," he murmured. "I'm not saying he is or isn't, you understand, but if he *is*, maybe it's not Bobby we should go for."

The other two men looked at him. Trafficante might no longer be the man he once was, but nobody ever denied he was smart.

"Carlos is correct," he went on slowly, thinking it through. "A man swears *vendetta* against you, you kill him, of course. But you forgot something, Carlos—you also got to kill his family, even his children, because otherwise they grow up to kill you. We kill Bobby, his brother is going to come after us with everything he's got, and his brother is president of the United States."

He looked out at the horizon, as if it held some object of surpassing interest. "On the other hand, my friends, you kill Jack Kennedy, Bobby's got no more power. You want to kill a snake, you cut off the head, not the tail, right?"

"Kill the President?" Marcello whispered. "That's a heavy number."

Roselli laughed. "What the fuck! He's just another guy, like you or me. He's not even that hard to get to, believe me."

Marcello nodded. He came from Louisiana, a state in which assassination was virtually a normal part of the political process. "Let's say we do it," he said. "Then what?"

"Then Lyndon Johnson is president," Trafficante said. "A man we can do business with, I think. No friend of Bobby's either. Not such a bad deal all around, I would say. *If* we do it."

"I say we go for it," Marcello said. "I got better things to do with my life than spend the rest of it fighting off Bobby Kennedy." Marcello was a small man, almost gnomish, but he never seemed small to people when he looked them in the eye. He was not a man to forget that Bobby Kennedy had deported him to Guatemala, where he had been left to fend for himself in the stinking jungle.

"How would you do such a thing, Carlos?" Trafficante asked. "Just out of curiosity."

"I would not use any of our people."

Trafficante and Roselli listened intently. Marcello had a reputation as a good planner, a strategist, not a hothead. He had turned New Orleans from a honky-tonk town of pimps and whores into the center of a billion-dollar-a-year narcotics empire.

"I would look for a nut," he said. "Somebody who wants to kill the President anyway, for his own crazy reasons. Somebody with military training maybe, who can handle a rifle. . . . I wouldn't pay him or let him know he's working for us. He might want to believe he's working for the Russians, or the CIA, or just for himself, who knows? Whatever he wants to believe is what we tell him. You find the right guy, you just have to get him a gun and point him in the right direction. Hell, you don't even need to get him the fucking gun, he'll buy his own."

"Where would one find such a man, Carlos? If one wanted to?"

"There are plenty of them around, Santo—guys with some kind of a grudge. There are a couple of them in New Orleans. Probably dozens of them in Dallas or Houston. It wouldn't hurt to have a whole list of shooters so we cover most of the cities the President is going to visit, sooner or later. . . . If we had access to the Secret Service files that list people in every city who are suspected of being a threat to the President, we could pick and choose until we found the right ones. I think that would be the way to start."

Trafficante nodded. "That could be done," he said cautiously. "I have friends in the Miami United States Attorney's Office. If we decide to go ahead with this thing, that is."

The waves slapped against the hull as the boat changed course. Nobody seemed willing to be the first to talk. Then Roselli cleared his throat and said, "With all respect, we got no choice."

The other two men said nothing. Trafficante signaled to the helmsman to turn and head for home. "It's an idea," he said. "It's worth thinking about. It wouldn't hurt to start looking for the right man. Just in case."

He raised one hand in what appeared to be a papal blessing, the ring glittering in the sun.

"Let's keep in touch," he said.

———

J. Edgar Hoover sat alone in his office, reading a single-spaced report marked for his eyes only. It was the end of a long day, but his cuffs were as white and stiff as they had been at the beginning of it.

His desk was clear, not even a trace of dust on it. He held the papers—an original and a carbon copy—firmly in both hands. It was late. The building was silent, almost empty. Somewhere nearby, Clyde Tolson waited—impatiently, no doubt—for the Director to buzz him so they could go home and have a well-deserved drink, then dinner, served in front of the television set on the folding trays by George, the Director's faithful Negro butler—the *right* kind of Negro, Hoover thought, unlike this fellow King. . . . He was content, however, to be alone at present. The memorandum in his hands was something he couldn't share with anyone. He read it again, slowly, concentrating on every word.

It was from an FBI field agent in Miami, reporting on a regular conversation with one of his informants, a soldier in the Santo Trafficante crime family who served as the captain of a charter yacht when he wasn't smuggling narcotics into the country, or running a numbers game, or shipping truckloads of cigarettes to the North without tax stamps. This informant had overheard a conversation between Santo Trafficante himself, Carlos Marcello, and Johnny Roselli, during what was ostensibly a day's fishing off Key Biscayne.

Hoover stared at the paper. If it was to be believed, the three mobsters intended to assassinate the President of the United States to revenge themselves on Bobby Kennedy! He did not find the idea incredible. Who knew better than he how headstrong and arrogant the President and his brother could be?

Hoover had no respect for mobsters, though he preferred them to left-wingers by a wide margin. Over the years, he had kept his men from investigating "organized crime," and had even denied before a Senate committee that the so-called "Mafia" existed, but that was because he didn't want FBI agents exposed to the inevitable corruption of mob money, which might bring them down to the same level as big-city police departments, where everybody was on the take. There was no corruption in the FBI; by concentrating his men on the threat from subversives and Communists, he had made sure there would be none.

Still, he himself knew a lot about the mob—after all, it was he who had brought down Capone! If men like Trafficante, Marcello, and Roselli were discussing the murder of the President, then it would happen, sooner or later—certainly before Kennedy's second term. He did not think Marcello's plan was a bad one either—it had a good chance of working. As for the Miami United States Attorney's Office, it was, as Hoover was well aware, a sink of corruption, which was why he had moved his Miami field office as far away from it as possible. If Trafficante thought he could get the Secret Service list of presidential threats from there, he was probably right. . . .

It was his job to pass all reports of a threat to the President's life on to the Secret Service and the Attorney General, and if he deemed it necessary, to bring it to the attention of the President himself.

He sat as if in prayer for a few moments, then made up his mind. He carefully initialed the original and the copy and made a mental note to transfer the FBI agent who had sent them to Alaska or New Mexico to deal with felonies on Indian reservations. Then he got up from behind his desk, walked into his secretary's office, and ran both copies through the shredder.

He picked up the telephone and rang Tolson's extension. "Time to go home, Clyde," he said.

44

It was just a question of time, and she knew it, before the brass at the studio moved from concern to alarm and from alarm to sheer panic.

She had caught a cold, and seemed unable to get rid of it; then she gave her cold to Dean Martin, so he couldn't work for days.

Of course, that was only part of the story. She *hated* the script— simply couldn't believe in the character she was playing, or accept that any man would prefer Cyd Charisse to *her*. Her simmering dislike of George Cukor had turned into raging hatred, for she had heard, from one of the crew who was loyal to *her*, that Cukor actually told somebody she was "crazy, just like her mother and her grandmother."

This had precipitated a major crisis. She would not speak to Cukor, would not even *look* at him, and stayed home for days at a time nursing her cold, sending health bulletins via Mrs. Murray to assure the studio she was too sick to work—for Dr. Greenson was on vacation in Europe, with his long-suffering wife.

The picture was already a million dollars over budget, and Cukor had shot around her to the point where he could shoot no more. Of course, things had been just as bad on *The Misfits*, but she had *respected* everybody on that picture, Huston, Gable, Monty, even Eli Wallach—they had been *pros*, and they had respected and supported *her*, recognizing that without her they wouldn't have a picture. To Cukor she was just a pain in the ass, and she had already heard rumors that he had suggested replacing her with "another blonde," Kim Novak perhaps, or Lee Remick. Everybody in the cast except

Dino hated her, even the dog and the children—she could feel it whenever she appeared on the set, which was increasingly rarely.

Every night, she told her problems to Bobby Kennedy on his private line at the Justice Department, almost as if she were one of his "causes," like Negroes in the South, or the urban poor.

She kept hoping he would fly out to visit her, so it surprised her when he suggested instead, as if it were the most natural thing in the world, that she should come to New York to join in the celebration of the President's birthday.

"Jack would love it," he said.

"Where is it being held?"

"Madison Square Garden. It's to raise money for Jack's reelection campaign. A kickoff for '64."

"Won't Jackie be there?"

There was a long pause.

"Ah, no. Jackie has a—ah—conflict that day."

"A conflict?"

"She's going to a horse show." He let that sink in.

"Look," he went on, "what we had in mind"—he did not say who "we" were—"is that you sing 'Happy Birthday,' that's all. Maybe with some special lyrics. You'd fly in with Peter, spend the afternoon rehearsing, do your number, and then—"

"And then what?"

"Then maybe we can spend the night together."

She giggled. Bobby had none of his big brother's persuasive charm. He said it stiffly, with a certain amount of embarrassment, but she found that charming. "It's the best offer I've had in a long time," she said.

He was silent.

"The only trouble is, I'm still a working girl. The studio will never let me go."

"For the President's birthday? Of course they will. They'll love it. It's great publicity."

"They won't see it that way."

"I'll bet you they do," he said confidently. "You'll see."

———

She should have made the bet with him, because she turned out to be right.

The studio didn't give a damn about publicity at this point—they wanted the picture in the can. The notion that she was well enough to fly to New York to sing "Happy Birthday" to President Kennedy, but not well enough to take a twenty-minute limo drive to the lot, confirmed their worst fears and suspicions. Peter Levathes, the head of Fox, passed the word down to her that he would not allow her to go to New York.

The next day he found out that she had already gone.

———

I had been opposed to the President's "birthday bash," as Lawford called it, from the first. A black tie evening in Madison Square Garden for several thousand people, most of them fat cats who had paid through the nose for the privilege of being there, did not seem to me the right spirit in which to reconsecrate the New Frontier. Blacks were being shot and beaten throughout the South, the Soviets were pouring arms into Cuba and making threatening noises in Berlin, Southeast Asia was mired in revolution and war, and our response was to fly in Marilyn Monroe to sing "Happy Birthday" for the President.

I was even more doubtful about the wisdom of having Marilyn sing "Happy Birthday." Enough people were in on the secret—or had heard rumors of it—to make her appearance seem tasteless, particularly in Jackie's absence.

What I hadn't guessed was that Marilyn wouldn't be in any better shape to sing before a live audience than she was for George Cukor. Five minutes after I reached her suite at the St. Regis Hotel, I knew we were in bad trouble.

"She keeps asking for you," the show's producer said. He was on his way out the door, clutching his briefcase as if he were holding fast to a life vest. "Is she always like this?"

"Like what?"

He seemed a pleasant enough man, but a career of producing celebrity specials had not prepared him for dealing with Marilyn Monroe's particular brand of stage nerves. "She can't remember the words of 'Happy Birthday.' "

"The special lyrics?" I couldn't remember them myself.

He shook his head. "No," he said, "the ordinary ones. 'Happy birthday to you,' and so forth."

Since he seemed about to continue, I held up my hand to indicate that I, at least, was familiar with them. "I'll have a word with her," I said, with more confidence than I had a right to feel.

"Be my guest."

481

The living room was the usual chaos: a hairdresser was setting up her things, Marilyn's makeup man was unpacking his kit, while a manicurist packed up hers. The furniture had been moved to make space for a cottage industry devoted to Marilyn Monroe.

I found the center of all this activity in the bedroom, stretched out on the bed in a dressing gown with a damp washcloth over her face. "God," she said, "why did I agree to do this?"

I raised the edge of the washcloth, gave her a kiss, and sat down. "Because you're a good sport?"

"The hell I am." She groaned. "I have a major-league hangover," she said. "I flew in from LA with Peter, and we were drinking champagne spiked with Russian vodka all the way. . . . Oh boy!" She took my hand. Her own was trembling, and hot, as if she were shaking from a fever.

"Are you sure you're okay?" I asked.

She took the washcloth off. Her eyes were vague and unfocused, or rather focused on something only she could see, the pupils like pinpoints. "I feel really *yucky*," she said wearily. "What time is it?"

"Four o'clock. You've got three or four hours to pull yourself together. Is that enough?"

She bit her lower lip. "It's going to *have* to be." With great effort she managed to swing her legs off the bed. Her robe parted, revealing her nakedness. The scars from her two operations were still raw. Her skin was pale—almost pasty—and there were mottled bruises on her thighs.

She put an arm around my shoulder and I helped her to stand. For a moment I had the feeling that if I let her go, she would fall, but gradually she managed to gain control of her feet, so that she was merely leaning on me for support.

"How about a bath?" I asked encouragingly, thinking it might bring her back to life.

"No time."

She tied up her robe and walked rather unsteadily into the living room of the suite, where her retainers instantly took her in hand like grooms around a valuable racehorse.

She sat down on a stool, while the hairdresser—I recognized him as Mr. Kenneth himself—busied himself with her hair. Now that she was back at work again, the fog seemed to have lifted from her brain. It occurred to me that this was the reality she understood best, not the performance but the preparation for it.

"I was really looking *forward* to this, you know? Even though it's the first time I've played before a live audience this size since I was in Korea. I had Jean-Louis make me a special dress—it's like this transparent nude fabric, stitched with tiny beads, skintight, so I have to be sewn into it. . . ."

"How about your lines?" I asked. "Comfortable with them?"

"Lines?"

"Well, there's 'Happy Birthday.' "

She shut her eyes. " 'Happy birthday to you, happy birthday to you.' " She opened them again, wide, with that expression of perfect innocence that nobody else could manage or imitate. " 'Happy birthday, dear Mr. President, happy birthday to you.' . . . See?"

She hadn't tried to sing. She simply recited, in a tiny voice that seemed to be coming from deep under water. Still, she *had* remembered the lines.

"Very good," I said. "How about the special lyrics?"

She gave me a wicked smile and a finger. "Don't push it, David," she said. "They're dopey, but I'll remember them."

"Well," I said, "you're in good hands. I'll order you some coffee and be on my way."

"You do that. And tell Jack not to worry."

————

Of course, Jack wasn't worried.

The grapevine had already alerted him to Marilyn's problems, but all Jack had said was, "She'll do fine."

I thought she would probably do fine too. When I called later in the afternoon and spoke to Marilyn, she sounded in good spirits. I had no idea she hadn't touched the coffee—that she'd been drinking champagne and popping pills as they worked on her face and her hair.

I had enough on my plate that evening that I didn't get around to worrying about Marilyn again until she was already in her dressing room at the Garden. I don't think I have ever seen more press anywhere, not even at a national convention—the combination of Jack Kennedy and Marilyn Monroe was the most potent "draw," to use a favorite picture-business word, in history since Anthony and Cleopatra, even to those not in the know.

I had arranged for the President's birthday gala to be televised, and there were camera crews, lights, and cables everywhere, the atmosphere somewhere between that of a national convention and a circus. Unlike the circus, however, there was a pervasive spirit of amateurism about the entertainment. The people around the President had a brilliant sense of how to stage a political event, and in Jack they had a natural star performer, but they had no real knowledge of show business, and assumed that the stars would simply appear one after the other and keep the audience amused.

I made my way through the crowds of television people, photographers, and security people to her dressing room, knocked on the door, and slipped in. She was standing in front of a full-length mirror, with a team of stylists fussing over her. She could not have sat down in Jean-Louis's dress if she had wanted to—it looked as if it had been painted onto her. Her back was completely bare, right down to her buttocks, and the gossamer-thin, flesh-colored fabric was tightly molded over her breasts and stomach, so that at first glance she seemed to be nude, except for the ruffle of beaded material around her ankles, where the dress belled out as if, like Venus, she were emerging naked from the waves.

That was my first impression. My second was that Marilyn looked as if she were somehow imitating herself, dwarfed by a gleaming mass of platinum-white hair that was so stiff and bouffant it resembled cotton candy. The body was that of America's sex goddess; the face, in the harsh light, could have been that of a million women in their mid-thirties, wondering where their youth had gone and how they had gotten into their present fix.

I placed my hand on her bare shoulder and brushed my lips against her cheek, taking care not to smudge her makeup.

"You look great," I said.

"I feel like death. I think I'm coming down with a cold."

Marilyn must have noticed my expression, because she said, "Don't worry, I'm going on." She giggled and threw a salute. "*Semper fidelis,* Mr. President," she said. "Isn't that what the Marines say?"

"It's their motto, yes." When she smiled, her face lit up—she no longer looked drawn and weary. It was a remarkable transformation, but paper-thin. "It means 'Always faithful.' "

"Oh dear," she said. "I guess it won't do for me."

I glanced at my watch. "I've got to go. It's feeding time at the zoo."

"It's funny you should say that. I thought it *smelled* like a zoo in here."

"It's the circus."

"Oh," she said. "That figures. It explains why I feel like one of the freaks tonight." She picked up her purse and shook a few pills from it, borrowed a pin from the seamstress to stick holes in them, popped them in her mouth, screwed up her face at the taste, and washed them down with a gulp of champagne from a Madison Square Garden coffee mug. "Toodle-oo, as they say in England," she said. "Give the Prez a kiss from me." Swallowing the pills seemed to have cheered her up a bit.

"I think he'd prefer if you delivered that yourself."

"I'll *bet* he would. Where's Bobby?"

"Out front, with Jack."

"Tell him to come and see me right afterwards, David. *Please.*"

She said it with terrifying intensity, her momentary good spirits vanishing as quickly as they had appeared. "Tell him I've *got* to see him."

"I will."

"I *mean* it."

Her expression was at once demanding and pleading, a combination that is probably only possible for a movie star.

"It's a promise," I said.

———

She gave herself a last, careful look in the mirror, professional to the last, keeping in mind that her profession consisted of looking her best. Emmeline Snively, the head of the Blue Book Model Agency, who had given her her first break, always said just that to her, in exactly those words. It was Emmeline who had sent her to Frank and Joseph's Hair Salon, on Hollywood Boulevard, in 1945, to be transformed into a bleached blonde. The other thing that Emmeline always told "her girls" was not to get pregnant. . . .

Well, here she was, seventeen years later, she told herself, blonder than ever, and pregnant again! She took a last sip of champagne, just to clear her throat, really, and giggled. *Pregnant!* "Knocked up," as they used to say back in the days when she was hanging around with the lifeguards at the Ambassador Hotel pool, before Mr. Big Deal Ted "Me and My fucking Shadow" Lewis became the first man to knock her up, as well as the first to hand her a wad of bills and the name of a doctor on Melrose who "took care" of problems like this.

Oh, she knew the score all right, when it came to getting rid of the problem. *Thirteen* abortions at last count, she had confessed to Amy Greene, in LA, in Tijuana, in New York. . . . She could have written a book on the subject. Gynecologists shook their heads in dismay and indignation every time they examined her, as if she were some kind of object lesson on what *not* to do with the female reproductive system.

But this time things were going to be different! She was going to *have* this baby! He would grow up—she was sure it was a boy—to be as handsome and as smart as his father, maybe handsomer, for he would have some of her looks as well. She closed her eyes and tried to imagine what he would look like—the love child of Marilyn Monroe and Robert Francis Kennedy. . . .

There was a knock on the door. "Time to go, Miss Monroe," a page called out.

Not even she could be late for the President of the United States. She took one last look at herself in the mirror while Mr. Kenneth, the seamstress, and the makeup man gave her the thumbs-up sign and a patter of applause; then she stepped out into the corridor, a dimly lit shaft of painted cinder block.

She turned a corner, then another, before realizing that her page was nowhere in sight. Somewhere ahead of her she could hear the noise of a vast audience, and the familiar voice of Peter Lawford warming them up for her.

She decided not to turn back—she was obviously going in the right direction. She continued down the corridor, which seemed to zig and zag more than she would have liked, and smelled as if it had recently stabled horses, or worse, until she finally reached a big metal door marked "STAGE." She pulled at the handle, but it was firmly locked.

She began to feel panic.

"*Mr. President,*" she heard Lawford say, his voice booming from a hundred loudspeakers, "*on this occasion of your birthday, this lady is not only pulchritudinous but punctual. . . . Mr. President—MARILYN MONROE!*"

The audience cheered, whistled, and stamped their feet, while the orchestra burst into her big song from *Some Like It Hot.* She ran down the corridor, trying door after door, all of which were locked, panic grasping her by the throat now. She turned a corner, expecting to find her dressing room door, but she had obviously taken a wrong turn again in the maze of corridors underneath the Garden.

"*A woman of whom it may truly be said, she needs no introduction!*" There was a roll of drums, followed by more applause, a little more hesitant now. She ran ahead as fast as her spike heels could carry her.

She could hear laughter now, as Lawford milked the situation—but of course, what *else* could he do, standing out there on stage in the spotlight in front of seventeen thousand people, left hanging high and dry?

At the end of the corridor, she found a metal staircase and clambered up it. There was a door with a red light over it, and she shoved it open, stumbling into the dark of what was clearly the backstage. She pushed through the crowd to the light, where Peter Lawford's PR man saw her and, grabbing her by the arm without ceremony, said, "Jesus Christ! Get the fuck *on!*" He pushed her toward the wing of the stage, from where she could see Lawford, sweat dripping down his face, grasping the microphone as if he were hanging on for dear life, a look of desperation on his face.

Out of the corner of his eye he must have seen her hair glittering in the spill of his spot, for he turned, shaking his head with exasperation; then, facing the audience, he grinned and shouted out: "*Mr. President, because in the history of show business, perhaps there has been no one female who has meant so much, or who has*"—he paused and winked broadly—"*has DONE more for her country and her president . . .*" The audience tittered, and as those in the know caught on, began to guffaw. Lawford joined in; then he reached out his hand toward where she waited, head throbbing, tears in her eyes, her cheeks and the back of her neck burning. "*Mr. President!*" he cried out, above the noise, bringing the audience to silence. "*Here she is—the LATE Marilyn Monroe!*"

The double entendre took her breath away. She stood there, unable to move, while the audience howled and roared. Then she was given a hefty shove, which almost knocked her flat on her face and boobs on the stage, and catching her balance, she stepped out into the bright, intense circle of the spot, smiling so hard she was afraid her jaw would break.

She blew Lawford a kiss, daggers in her eyes, and walked to the podium, blinded by the glare. She waited for a moment while her eyes adjusted to the light. She looked up and saw Jack Kennedy, in the presidential box, feet up on the rail, smoking a cigar. Bobby, hunched over beside him, was staring at her.

What would happen, she wondered, if she announced that she had fucked both of them, that even now she was carrying Bobby's child? She didn't feel any friendliness emanating from the huge arena. Her dress had caused a storm of wolf whistles and not a few gasps of shock. She sensed that the audience was getting restless now, so she pulled herself together, and clutching the sides of the podium, she sang:

> "Happy birthday to you,
> Happy birthday to you,
> Happy birthday, Mr. President,
> Happy birthday to you."

She sang slowly in a tiny voice, hesitating between each syllable, so that even with amplification, it wasn't until the third verse that the audience, a little embarrassed, started to join in.

She paused, gathering strength now, and sang the special lyrics Richard Adler had written for her, stumbling over the words as she struggled to remember them:

> "Thanks, Mr. President,
> For all the things you've done,
> The battles you've won,
> The way you deal with U.S. Steel,
> And our problems by the ton,
> We thank you—so much."

Then she held her trembling arms up, the audience rose to their feet, and she led them in another ragged chorus of "Happy Birthday."

———

I was sitting behind Jack and Bobby when Marilyn finally appeared on stage. Jack's relief when she finally *did* appear was short-lived. He could see, as well as I could, that her dress was a mistake, that she had crossed the line, had ceased being everybody's favorite blonde and was now an object of blatant sexuality. She simply did not represent the image the President was anxious to display to the nation on his birthday.

Marilyn, breasts as visible as if she were stark naked in Jean-Louis's flesh-colored masterpiece, was a challenge to each and every wife in the audience, the home wrecker personified. Nor was there any denying, when she started to sing in that high-pitched, breathless, little-girl-lost voice of hers, that she seemed to be drunk or drugged. Her movements not only were slow but seemed to have

488

nothing to do with the music, and there were long pauses—*very* long pauses—between words, and even syllables.

It was like watching a film of an accident played back in slow motion, a piteous public exposure of poor Marilyn's nervous eagerness to please.

To say that Jack noticed all this would be to put it mildly. He smiled—he was no mean actor himself—but he whispered out of the corner of his mouth, "What the fuck's the matter with her, David?"

"She may have a cold," Bobby said protectively, before I could answer.

"A cold? She's fucking *stoned*, that's what she is."

He was not a leader for nothing. Before Marilyn had quite finished —and before she fell flat on her face, or did anything else embarrassing—he rose.

The spotlights turned on him instantly. "Thank you," he said, grabbing a microphone. "I can now retire from politics after having had, ah, 'Happy Birthday' sung to me in such a sweet"—he paused for a moment and grinned—"*wholesome* way!"

The audience roared with laughter, the other performers came on stage, surrounding Marilyn and Peter Lawford, and Jack, with his usual deftness and perfect timing, brought his own gala to a conclusion.

"Remind me never to do this again," he said as we made our way out of his box past the cops and the Secret Service. "I'd rather be shot."

45

She didn't need Paula Strasberg or Natasha Lytess to tell her she had fucked up—she could see it in everybody's eyes, even David's.

Still, the big advantage of being a star was that nobody had the guts to tell her to her face. The President stood on one side of her, Bobby on the other, both of them beaming as they were surrounded by well-wishers and those of the press tame enough to be allowed close. Adlai Stevenson came over to congratulate her, and Governor Harriman, and what seemed like hundreds of other, lesser mortals, and all the while, Bobby guarded her as if she were his own personal property. The President gave him a warning look a couple of times, as if to tell him to make it a little less obvious that he was having an affair with her, but Bobby, being Bobby, stuck to his guns.

She drank champagne, trying to get rid of the feeling that she had disappointed the President. He didn't *look* disappointed, but she knew him better than most people and could see the telltale signs of displeasure, which had the effect of making her drink more. It was a relief when he finally said good night, pleading fatigue, and left for the Carlyle, looking not in the least tired.

She knew somebody was waiting for him there, the way she had done in the old days from time to time, probably already snuggled up in the presidential bed. She wondered who it was, but it wasn't really any of her business. There were rumors about a certain long-legged television star who had taken her place, but she wasn't the only one. . . .

She leaned close to Bobby. "I need you," she said. "I have to be with you tonight."

He nodded, giving her a warning glance to keep her voice down.

490

"I want to go now," she said.

"I can't."

"Then I'm going."

She could see he was torn between the desire to go and his duty to stay, but the latter, to her disappointment, won out. "Then go," he said.

"You'll come over later?" she asked, trying not to sound as if she was pleading.

He nodded. "An hour," he said. "Two at most." Then, seeing the expression on her face: "As soon as I can."

Back at the hotel, she undressed, flinging Jean-Louis's five-thousand-dollar dress on the floor, furious that she had turned herself into a freak, as if all she had to show for twelve years of hard work and stardom was her tits and her ass. She popped open a bottle of champagne, and took a couple of pills, pacing furiously around the suite, feeling her anger come to a boil. It wasn't just that somebody else was in the President's bed at the Carlyle right now; it was that so much of her life had been spent like this, preparing for days for some event, turning up—always late—to wag her tail and show her tits for the studio, or, in this case, the President, then home in the limo alone, to remove her makeup and her borrowed finery, take her pills and wait for sleep, if it came. . . . How many times, in Hollywood, had she gone straight from the spotlight and the flashbulbs of the press to the studio to hand back her evening gown, as if Marilyn Monroe were a prop, as much a studio invention as Minnie Mouse or Lassie?

She glanced at her watch. She had lost track of the time, and the number of pills she had taken—she was no longer even sure what she was taking them for. She felt drowsy, which was something of a miracle, but of course, she didn't *want* to be drowsy for Bobby's arrival, so she took a couple of pep pills to wake her up, and a Randy-Mandy to get her juices flowing, and, on reflection, a couple of tranks to mellow out her feelings, washing them down with champagne.

She had left her makeup on, and was walking around in her bra and her high heels, occasionally bumping into the furniture—some idiot seemed to have moved it so it was in her way—leaving a trail of spilled champagne behind her, as if to mark her path, and that was the way Bobby Kennedy found her when he finally arrived—on her back on the floor, one shoe on, one shoe off, a big bruise on her thigh and her eyes shut. He thought she was dead.

She could hear his voice, but faintly, and feel his hands as he sought for a pulse or a sign of life with a layman's clumsiness. ". . . get you to a hospital," she heard.

She shook her head feebly. No hospitals, no emergency room— she didn't want that, not here in New York where the press would know it before her stomach was pumped. She was pretty sure he wouldn't want it either, since there wasn't much chance of keeping *his* name out of it.

She managed to whisper David Leman's name. She wasn't sure Bobby had heard her—she couldn't tell whether her voice was working or not—but he must have, because he went off to telephone, then came back with some ice from the champagne bucket wrapped in a hotel napkin, and held it to her head.

She *felt* the cold, which was a sign of life, but it didn't revive her. Bobby went to the bedroom and got a blanket, which he put over her. She blinked to show her gratitude, though in fact she wished he would simply leave her alone.

He sat there on the floor beside her until David's doctor arrived with his hypodermic needle and his stomach pump, to bring her back to life.

―――――

"You scared me stiff," Bobby said. He was sitting by the bed, his face haggard and exhausted. He had been up half the night while the doctor worked on her.

"I scared myself." Her throat hurt from the tube the doctor had pushed down it, and her voice was hardly more than a hoarse whisper, which sounded to her like a croak.

"Why did you do it?" His expression was puzzled, as if there was no way he could understand the notion of suicide, no way he could accept it.

Of course, she wasn't sure suicide had been on her mind at all— she never was, after one of these "episodes," as Dr. Greenson liked to call them. There was simply a point at which she not only lost control but lost interest in living, in the future, in herself. It wasn't so much that she was intent on killing herself—it was that dying didn't scare her as much as living. Sometimes she simply couldn't take the pain a moment longer.

Twice during her marriage to Arthur she had tried to kill herself, and both times he had brought her back from the brink. By the end of their marriage, he was like a psychiatric nurse, counting her pills and watching over her like a hawk—he even had the locks removed from the bathroom doors. Johnny Hyde had rescued her a couple of times too—anybody who got close to her sooner or later assumed responsibility for her life, as Bobby, with whatever reluctance, was doing now.

"I didn't do anything," she said. "It just happened, that's all."

"I don't believe that. Is it something I did?"

She shook her head. Why did men always think that? Johnny and Arthur both asked the same question. Did they suppose the only reason a girl could have for taking too many pills was a man? She wanted to tell him it had nothing to do with him, but she was too tired, and besides, that wasn't completely true. If he hadn't kept her waiting, if he'd left the party *with* her, none of it would have happened, or so she told herself.

"Stay with me," she whispered. "For the night. What's left of it." She would sleep in his arms, unafraid, and in the morning, over breakfast, when she felt a little stronger, she would tell him about the baby—*their* baby—and things would be better, the pain would finally recede. . . .

But he shook his head. "Sleep," he said. "I've got to go soon."

When she woke up, he was gone.

She left that evening for Los Angeles, bundled in the back of a limousine on the way to Idlewild Airport, staring out through the tinted glass as if she was never going to see New York again.

46

She was back at work on Monday, to everybody's surprise, and for a week afterward she was on her good behavior, grateful that the studio hadn't put her on suspension for going to New York.

As was so often the case after she had escaped death, she felt stronger and better now, full of new energy, though she knew it was an illusion. She had missed another period, and she could not put off telling Bobby about the baby much longer. She sensed that despite his concern for her, her "episode" with the pills in New York had made him wary of just how high the cost of his affair with her might be, in terms of scandal and bad publicity.

A week after her return to work, she had to shoot a scene in which she swam naked in her husband's pool at night, then started to climb out when he called to her from a window. She was supposed to wear a flesh-colored body stocking so the camera wouldn't actually catch her naked, but once she was in the water, she wriggled out of the suit, which was uncomfortable and silly, and on the spur of the moment, enjoying herself in front of the camera for the first time in years, she swam into movie history—for nobody had ever been filmed naked before in a mainstream Hollywood movie.

Cukor was too surprised to stop her. He called out for more lights and ordered the cameraman to start shooting as she swam back and forth, laughing at her own daring, doing a dog paddle to keep her breasts and her ass just below water. Along the edge of the pool, three still photographers, including Larry Schiller, on assignment from *Paris-Match,* kept their motorized Nikons clicking. She didn't care. She was still 37, 22, 36, even though she was about to turn thirty-six—and pregnant!—and she wanted the world to see her.

The stage was silent except for the click of the cameras, her own splashing, and a lot of heavy breathing; then she began to feel chilled. She cried out, "Here I come, ready or not," and hauled herself out as her wardrobe man rushed forward to drape her blue robe over her. For one second the photographers saw it all—Marilyn Monroe naked, from the front, blond bush and all—then she wrapped the robe tightly around her and waved good-bye.

The next week was her thirty-sixth birthday. The crew threw her a party on the sound stage, but their hearts weren't in it, and neither was hers, and she left early to go to Dodger Stadium to throw out the first ball at a benefit game for the Muscular Dystrophy Association; though she felt depressed and tired, it was a commitment she had made long before.

When she got home, she dialed Bobby on his private line at the Justice Department, where he was working late.

"Happy birthday," he said. He had sent her flowers—unlike the President, who was never a sentimentalist about that kind of thing.

"I missed you," she said.

"I wish I could have been there."

"When can you get out here?"

A pause. A slight hesitation. "It's hard to say."

"I have to see you."

"Well, I know. . . . I've been worried about you. Are you all right?"

"Bobby," she said, "I love you."

"Yes," he said, his voice sad. "I know." She knew how much he disliked being told that she loved him, and understood that it was because he was reluctant to say "I love you" back.

"You don't have to say anything, Bobby," she told him. "Really you don't. I'm not asking for that. I just want to be able to say it to you myself—that I *love* you. You don't even have to say thanks."

"I understand." His voice showed how anxious he was to get off the subject.

She took a deep breath. "Bobby, I have to tell you something very difficult."

"Yes?" His voice was cautious now, a lawyer's voice.

"It's about me." She paused. "About us."

"Look, I'll find a way to get out to LA. It's a promise."

"No, it's not that . . . I mean, that's great, I want to see you. But what I'm trying to tell you is: I'm pregnant."

"Pregnant?"

"You know, going to have a baby?"

"I know what pregnancy means," he said dryly. "How the hell did that happen?"

"Well, the usual way. . . ."

"I see."

Say you're happy about it, she begged him silently, but there was simply a long pause at the other end of the line.

"Jesus," he said at last. Then, after another pause: "You're sure?"

"Sure I'm pregnant, or sure it's yours?" she asked.

"Both."

"Yes."

He let out a long whistle of breath.

"Look," she said, "it's my problem, not yours." She did not really believe that, but she felt obliged to let him off the hook.

"What are you going to do?" he asked, without any suggestion that he might be involved in the decision.

"I think I want to have the baby," she said firmly.

"*Have* the baby?" There was shock in his voice, perhaps even the faintest trace of fear.

"I think so. It's my thirty-sixth birthday. This may be my last chance."

"I never noticed you had the maternal instinct."

"There are a lot of things about women men never notice."

"I'm just not sure it's the smartest move, Marilyn. . . ."

"You're a Catholic. I thought Catholics were against abortion."

"They are. *We* are. I am. But I'm also a politician, a married man, the father of seven children, and the brother of the President of the United States. And you're the most famous woman in the world."

"I'd give that up like a shot. Tomorrow. Tonight. Ethel doesn't love you the way I do. We could have a life together."

"That's just not possible—"

"It *is!*" she cried out fiercely. "It is if you want it to be! And even if it isn't, you could at least say you wish it was! For God's sake, give me some *hope,* at least," she pleaded, crying now, despite her determination not to. "Tell me that you love me, that you want me, that you'll love the baby, that there's a life ahead for us somehow, that you'll be with me! Tomorrow you can tell me you didn't mean any of it, but tonight I *need* to hear it."

"Take it easy—" he began.

"No!" she shouted. "You've *got* to help me, Bobby! You've got to tell me that it's going to be all right! I swear to God, if you don't,

I'm going to take care of it the way I tried to in New York, only this time you won't be around to bring me back."

"Don't even talk about it. . . ."

"You've got no right to tell me what to do!"

"I'm trying to *help* you."

"I know all about that kind of help. That's the kind of help my father gave my mother. He gave her a hundred bucks and told her to get rid of the problem, then walked out and never came back."

"Be sensible, Marilyn. . . ."

Be sensible! How many times had she heard *that*, from men who were only thinking about themselves.

"Good night," she said abruptly, and hung up.

———

The next day she felt too ill to go to the studio. Dr. Greenson had been told to get over to her house right away, in case of trouble, the message having been passed from Bobby Kennedy to Peter Lawford, and from Lawford to Greenson, accumulating added urgency with repetition.

Greenson had been surprised to find her wearing a black sleep mask and an old black nightgown, lying on her back, with Maf at her feet. He had clearly expected to find her dead or dying. "Everybody was worried about Nembutals," he said. "I told them I'd stopped prescribing them for you a long time ago.

"The studio is going to be upset," he went on. "I wonder, is it wise not to go in?" He pulled his chair up closer. "I hear on the grapevine," he said—she knew every grape on *that* vine!—"that Levathes is going around saying he's had it up to here." He placed the edge of his hand at his throat.

"If he doesn't have me, he doesn't have a movie."

"Maybe he doesn't care anymore. He's taking a lot of heat from New York. There are a few guys on the board who'd like to make an example out of you. Why give them the chance?"

She paid no attention. The stupid movie was the last thing on her mind at the moment. "What do you think of a fella who runs away from the woman who loves him when she gets pregnant?"

"A bad situation."

"I mean, even if the guy is really *important* he shouldn't do that, right?"

Dr. Greenson's expression was wary. "That would depend," he said.

"I mean, even if he's the attorney general of the United States, he ought to stick by her, don't you think? If he really loves her?"

"Perhaps." Greenson was sweating now. "It depends on the circumstances."

"He's a nice guy, actually," she said dreamily. "Bobby, I mean. And I really love him. But he shouldn't make a girl feel that way about him if he doesn't want her. He shouldn't tell a girl he's going to leave his wife if he doesn't mean it, should he?"

"*Did* he tell you that? I find it hard to believe."

"Well, not in so many words, I guess. . . . But I know that's what he *felt*."

Dr. Greenson sighed. "Feelings," he murmured, playing for time. "Feelings are important. You're sure you're in love with him?"

"I love him, all right."

"And how did your conversation with him go? Was he angry?"

"No." Bobby hadn't raised his voice. He had sounded, if anything, sad, and a little rattled, of course, which was natural under the circumstances.

"Did he tell you to get rid of the baby?"

"Not really, no," she said, for now that she thought about it, Bobby hadn't told her to do anything of the kind. He had merely asked her if she was going to have the baby—he hadn't told her *not* to. "He said he wouldn't leave Ethel and the children for me."

"One would *expect* him to say that, frankly. Besides, any man in his position—particularly a public figure—is going to be surprised and shocked by this kind of announcement."

"I asked him to play along with me, to tell me he was going to leave Ethel, that I needed to hear it, just to make it through the night, but he wouldn't. . . ."

"Possibly that was a manifestation of responsibility, of *caring*. You asked him to lie to you, and he wouldn't. It seems to me that the stand he took is admirable, if uncomforting. I'm not sure you should have hung up on him, by the way."

"You think I should call him back?" she asked hopefully.

Greenson nodded, forming his fingers into a judicial steeple before his lips. Marilyn Monroe on the telephone talking to Robert Kennedy was a better prospect for survival, he might have been thinking, than Marilyn Monroe alone in her bedroom brooding on his rejection of her.

"It couldn't hurt," he said.

———

Washington KL 5-8210, Washington KL 5-8210, Washington KL 5-8210—again and again she gave the number to the operator, placing a dozen or more calls in an hour, sometimes only a couple of minutes apart, desperate to reach him, desperate to hold him on the phone when she was put through.

He did not avoid her—sometimes he was unavailable, in conference, or out of the building, but his secretary, Angie Novello, was invariably polite and helpful, and when he could, Bobby always picked up the phone and talked to her, sometimes at length, though never about the subject that concerned her the most.

Dr. Greenson had been right—once the initial shock of the news of her pregnancy had worn off, Bobby was his usual caring self, listening to her troubles, telling her he would make plans to come out to California. . . . She should take care of herself and not worry. When he got there, they would talk about it. . . .

When? she asked. In a couple of weeks, tops, he told her. Things, he assumed, could wait until then? The thing that concerned her could certainly wait that long—though not much longer, as she pointed out.

She scribbled a few lines in her notebook. She had bought it years ago, with the intention of writing a diary, but she had neither the time nor the discipline to keep one. Sometimes she wrote down her thoughts—"In life death seems like an illusion; perhaps in death life seems like an illusion," she had written early on, along with poems that had caught her fancy, like the ancient Indian love poem that ended:

> For this is the Wisdom; to love, to live,
> To take what fate, or the Gods, may give,
> To ask no question, to make no prayer,
> To kiss the lips and caress the hair,
> Speed passion's ebb as you greet its flow—
> To have—to hold—and—in—time—let go!

She flipped through the notebook—there were whole periods of her life, years sometimes, when she had written nothing in it at all, others when she filled pages. Not many, she reflected ruefully, saddened by the thought that you could compress all the wisdom and the poetry of a lifetime into half the pages of a diary.

"Bobby," she wrote, and underlined it twice, then enclosed it in a heart. Then:

"When I'm in his arms
I feel safe!
When I'm in his arms
I can sleep!
When I'm in his arms
I dream of life,
Not death!!!!"

She read it over and underlined the word "death" several times. She liked it more than the Indian poem, she decided.

Late in the afternoon, she took a couple of the cold pills that Mrs. Murray had bought for her at the Brentwood Pharmacy, and drifted off into the kind of uncomfortable doze that a bad cold produces. She woke to the sound of the telephone ringing beside her.

She picked up the receiver groggily and shoved it between her shoulder and her ear. "Hi, Bobby," she said in a sexy, sleepy voice.

There was a moment of silence at the other end, and then a voice that wasn't Bobby's said: "Ah, this is Peter Denby, Miss Monroe. Of the *Los Angeles Times*."

She came to with a start. It occurred to her, too late, that it had been some time since she had bothered to change her private number. She knew Denby, who reported on movie industry news. Denby was a Brit, and had been one of those who grilled her so relentlessly when she arrived in England to make *The Prince and the Showgirl* —she remembered a florid face above a polka-dot bow tie.

"I wondered," he went on, in his plummy English voice, "if you had any comment on tonight's news."

"What news?"

"Surely you've *heard*? Twentieth Century–Fox has fired you. You're off the picture."

"*Fired*? I don't believe it." She was wide awake now.

"I have it from an impeccable source. One of the Fox executives said, 'It's time to draw the line—the inmates are taking over the asylum.' Any comment on *that*?"

She couldn't think of anything to say. Was the studio saying she was *crazy*? She couldn't imagine it—there was no crueler remark anyone could have made about her. She felt . . . She wasn't sure *what* she felt—one emotion kept bubbling up on top of another in quick succession, like lava from a volcano: anger, pain, shame, fear. She could hardly even hold the telephone, she was so shaken.

"You must have seen it coming a mile away, surely?" Denby went on cheerfully. "They're weeks behind schedule." He pronounced it "shed-you-ell" to her temporary bewilderment. "At least a million dollars over budget. They screened your footage last night, all of it, and Levathes said it wasn't a performance—there was hardly anything they could use. They're going to sue you, I hear. . . . Hello?"

"Sue me?"

"Oh my, yes. Sure to, I should think. May I say that you were 'shocked and bewildered'?"

"I don't have anything to say."

" 'Shocked and bewildered, Marilyn refused to comment.' Right-o."

"No, wait!" She couldn't let him go without saying something, couldn't let the studio blacken *her* reputation without any reply from her. "You can write I said it's time some of the studio heads realized what they're doing. If there's anything wrong with Hollywood, it starts at the top. And something else. It seems to me it's time they stopped knocking their assets around."

He read her quote back to her. "Any plans for the future?" he asked.

"As soon as I'm well enough, I'm going back to work and finish this picture," she said. "This is all just bullshit."

"I can't use that," he said briskly, and hung up.

The telephone rang again instantly. She wondered why Mrs. Murray didn't pick it up. Then she remembered that Mrs. Murray had gone out to see a movie. She got up, took the phone into the living room, went back to her bedroom, and closed the door. Hundreds of journalists and columnists were surely trying to reach her, and she couldn't talk to all of them. She lay in bed listening to the constant ringing of both telephones, feeling worse and worse. To be rejected by the studio! After sixteen years of working at Fox! The studio had given her her *name*, for God's sake!

She went back into the bathroom, took a handful of pills, lay down in bed again, and covered her ears with the pillows.

———

The next day Peter Levathes gave a press conference, calling her "unreliable," and threatening to sue her for half a million or a million dollars because her chronic and disruptive lateness had made it impossible to complete the picture. There were even rumors that her costumes were being altered for Lee Remick so she could take her place and shooting could resume.

Bitter and hurt, she stayed at home, relying on Eunice Murray to drive her to her daily session with Dr. Greenson. Her telephone numbers had been swiftly changed, so at least she was able to call out—though the downside was that none of her friends now knew her number, and she didn't have the energy to give it to them, so the house was often as still as a tomb, just herself and Maf, with Mrs. Murray brooding silently in the kitchen.

She had hoped for some demonstration of affection and support, but there was nothing, or next to nothing—no flowers, no telegrams, no offers from other studios. True, Dino let it be known that he had signed on to do a Marilyn Monroe picture and wouldn't work with Lee Remick, which was nice, but that meant the picture had to be shelved, and in the movie industry that was as bad as things could get.

Since Bobby, happily, wasn't in show business, he had no idea of the extent of her disgrace in Hollywood. For him, it was just a labor dispute in an industry he didn't understand or take seriously. She was a star, so it would all work out, he told her every time she called.

The subject of her baby (*their* baby, she reminded herself), he avoided. He had other problems, and she was happy enough to listen to them. He was bored and restless, sorry he had ever agreed to take the job of attorney general. Everywhere he looked, he told her, he saw failure: he had been unable to get past Hoover to reform the FBI; Hoffa was still free, as were his gangster friends; the administration was dragging its feet on civil rights, so that southern blacks were beginning to talk about demonstrating against the Kennedys instead of the racists. . . .

"It's the winter of our discontent," he said sadly—he had been reading a lot of Shakespeare lately, as part of his perpetual self-improvement scheme—even though it was in fact summer.

He was to address a convention of federal prison wardens in Boulder, Colorado, toward the end of the month, he told her, and might detour to Los Angeles on his way back.

It was the only thing that kept her going in those bleak days after she was fired—the thought that Bobby was going to make things come out right for her. . . .

———

I was in London when I learned that Marilyn had been fired by Fox. I wasn't surprised. She had never disguised her dislike of the picture from the very beginning, and the chemistry between herself and

Cukor was all wrong. I'm not sure Peter Levathes and the Fox board were to blame either—at that moment in her life it's possible that nobody could have coaxed a picture out of Marilyn. I called her immediately, but I was unable to get through.

I called again from New York, with no better luck. Much as I disliked him, I called Lawford, who told me that while Marilyn was "upset," she was basically okay, an opinion with which my friend Ike Lublin agreed. "It could be the best thing for her," Lublin said, with the built-in optimism of a show business lawyer. "That picture was a piece of shit anyhow."

I might not have taken Marilyn's problems so much to heart if I hadn't had a call from an old friend of mine in LA, one of the many liberal academics mauled by Joe McCarthy and his witch hunters, who had fled to become the host of a late-night radio call-in show. Folksy, unshockable, and intelligent, Alan Burke had become a minor cult figure in Los Angeles, at any rate among insomniacs, to his own surprise. He didn't waste words with me—once upon a time, we had known each other too well for that. "You know Marilyn Monroe, don't you?" he asked. I said I did. "You'd recognize her voice?" I said I would.

"Well, listen to this." I heard the click of a tape recorder, then that unmistakable soft, breathless little voice. *I'm going to marry a very important man in government. He's going to leave his wife for me.*

Alan spoke next. *What's your name, dear?*

Marilyn.

Like Marilyn Monroe?

A low giggle. *That's right.*

And what do you do?

I'm an actress. Or I was. Another giggle. *I just got fired.*

And who's the 'important man in government'? Can you tell me?

A pause. I could hear Marilyn's breathing on the tape. *Bobby Kennedy. . . . Whoops! I guess I shouldn't have said that.* There was a click as she hung up.

"Jesus!" I said.

"It's her, isn't it?"

"It *sounds* like her. Is this the only call?"

"No. She calls every night, sometimes a couple of times a night. She says she's pregnant and that Bobby is the father. Listen, there's more. She asked if she could *meet* me. I sounded so sympathetic on the air she *had* to see me face-to-face. . . . Well, you know, I don't like doing that at all. A lot of the people out there are cranks and loonies, so you never know who you're going to meet. . . . Still, she sounded so desperate that I said okay. Besides, I figured what the hell, it might turn out to be Marilyn. . . ."

"And did it?"

"No question. She met me in the bar of the Hollywood Brown Derby, round the corner from the studio. It was Marilyn, all right."

"What did she say?"

"We talked for a couple of hours. She told me a lot about Bobby Kennedy and the President, really intimate stuff, and it sounded to me as if she knew what she was talking about. I remember her saying, 'I've had fame, all I ever needed and more. What I want now is happiness, and I'm going to find it or die.' "

"Was she drunk, do you think?"

"No, I don't think she was drunk. She had a glass of white wine with me, that's all. She sounded like somebody who'd just landed on earth from some other planet, but not drunk, no."

"What have you done with these tapes?"

"Nothing. Listen, forget about the tapes, David. I've got an audience of half a million people out there every night, listening to her saying Bobby Kennedy is the father of her child, and that he's planning to leave Ethel for her. Sooner or later somebody's going to notice."

"Could you stop taking her calls?"

"No," he snapped with a trace of anger. "That would be unprofessional, David. Besides, I'm not sure it isn't the calls that are keeping her *alive,* frankly. This is a very crazy, very lonely lady. She needs help. That's why I'm calling. I don't want to be responsible for her killing herself, thank you."

"I wasn't suggesting that, Alan. . . ."

"Yes you were," he said without rancor. "I know who you work for. Don't forget—Bobby's not a hero to me. He's just another of the vicious little shits who drove me out of my job because I wouldn't name names to the Committee. There isn't a bit of difference between him and Roy Cohn, and Jack was just as gutless as the rest of the Senate when it came to McCarthy. If you want to worship the Kennedys, David, be my guest, but don't expect me to. I know too many people whose lives were ruined. My own among them."

"I understand."

"Then understand that I'm not going to keep Marilyn off the air to protect Bobby's reputation as a faithful husband. I'm on *her* side."

"So am I."

"In what way?"

"I don't want her to get hurt."

There was a pause as Alan digested this. "Yes," he said. "They're just the people to hurt her too, I should think. Can you stop it?"

"I don't know. I'll try."

"I won't stop taking her calls, but I'll try to steer her off the subject as much as I can."

"I'm grateful, Alan. For *her* sake. I'll be in Los Angeles tomorrow, at the Beverly Hills Hotel, if you need me."

"I thought you just got in from London."

"I did," I said grimly, at the thought of another long flight.

———

I tried to call Bobby, but he was in the air on the way to Hyannis. I *did* reach the President, who was already there, and testy about being disturbed with a telephone call. "I'm about to go sailing," he said. "This had better be good."

"It's not good, Mr. President. It's about Marilyn."

"I heard they fired her at the studio. That's a shame. How is she taking it?"

"It's hard to say. I thought I'd go out there and find out. Has Bobby talked to you about her?" I asked.

"He showed me a strange telegram she sent him. She was invited to a dinner Bobby and Ethel gave for Peter and Pat at Hickory Hill —which seems like a pretty dumb idea to begin with, in the circumstances—and she sent her regrets. . . . Wait a minute, Bobby gave me a copy. . . . Here it is."

There was a pause, I guessed while he put his reading glasses on. " 'Dear Attorney General and Mrs. Robert Kennedy: I would have been delighted to have accepted your invitation honoring Pat and Peter Lawford. Unfortunately I am involved in a freedom ride protesting the loss of the minority rights belonging to the few remaining earthbound stars. After all, all we demanded was our right to twinkle. Marilyn Monroe.' "

He cleared his throat nervously. "What do you make of that?"

"It may have to do with her being fired. Fox took away her right to twinkle? That would fit."

"That's what I thought."

"There's another possibility. It might have to do with Bobby."

"What's that?"

I explained to him about the calls she had been making to Alan's late-night call-in show.

"Christ!" he said. "She's gone nuts."

"It's a possibility."

"You don't think it's *true,* do you?"

"About her being pregnant? It could be, sure."

He was silent for a moment. "Just because she's having an affair with Bobby doesn't mean he's the father. We've all been through that kind of thing."

All too often, I thought, in Jack's case, remembering many scrapes with fatherhood from which his father had extricated him. "It's possible," I said. "Either way, it's not a story you want in print."

"God no!" There was another pause.

"Will you talk to Bobby about it? He's playing with fire."

I heard Jackie's voice in the background, and then the President said, "I'll take it under advisement and discuss the matter with the Attorney General." His voice was clipped and formal, the chief executive at work. "In the meantime, keep me advised of any, ah, developments."

"I guess it's not the moment to give Jackie my best."

"Thank you for your concern," Jack said crisply, and hung up.

I should have guessed—and was later to discover—that since my old friend Alan had once been associated with left-wing causes and briefly married to the daughter of what used to be called "a card-carrying" member of the Communist party, his broadcasts were regularly taped by the FBI, just in case he uttered some subversive statement on the air.

Thus Marilyn's late-night calls came to the attention of J. Edgar Hoover, who took the trouble to order a quick search of her gynecologist's files.

He was soon able to inform the President that, in this particular case at any rate, the lady wasn't lying—pregnant she definitely was, whoever the father might be.

47

Of course, I didn't know that the FBI was already aware of Marilyn's pregnancy—and of the presumed father—when I arrived in Los Angeles, on a day of blistering heat. I called her as soon as I was settled into my suite. When she came on the phone, she sounded astonishingly cheerful. I invited her out to dinner, and from her reaction, you would have thought nobody had asked her out for years.

Assuming that Marilyn probably wanted to stay out of the public eye, I suggested a couple of discreet little restaurants I knew she was fond of, but they turned out not to be what she had in mind at all. "Oh, come *on*, David!" she said. "You can do better than that!"

"I just thought . . ."

"I *know* what you thought. I'm tired of hiding away. Let's go out and have a little fun!"

"How about Chasen's?"

"That's your idea of fun? It's full of has-been actors having dinner with their wives. Let's eat someplace glamorous, then go dancing or something—make a *night* of it, you know?"

"Romanoff's?"

"Better—for a start, baby." She gave me a noisy kiss over the telephone. "We'll paint the town!"

Her voice was loud—alarmingly so, considering how small and soft it normally was. Most of the time when Marilyn was on the phone, I felt as if I needed a hearing aid.

"Eight?" I said.

A giggle. "Nine." She hung up.

It should not have surprised me that at nine forty-five I was still chatting with Mike Romanoff and sipping my second dry martini. "Who's joining you?" he asked.

"Marilyn Monroe."

He whistled. "Maybe you should order a shrimp cocktail, or something. Punctual, she's not."

"I know."

I buttered another breadstick and tried not to check my watch again. I had ample time to look around the restaurant—one of the last establishments in Beverly Hills where people still dressed for the evening as if they were in New York.

It didn't seem like Marilyn's kind of place—Romanoff's was a restaurant for the "old guard." Sinatra and his pals, or Brando and *his*, wouldn't have been caught dead here. But then, I reflected, Marilyn had never wanted to be an outsider—*her* struggle was for acceptance by the Hollywood old guard. For her, Romanoff's represented some part of that world to which she had craved acceptance all her life, ever since the days when she had stared out the windows of the Los Angeles orphanage at the RKO lot next door.

There was a collective gasp from around the room, and I looked up just as Marilyn was making her entrance. Her hair was bleached a pale platinum, with hardly a trace of blond in it; her face was made up as if for filming. She was wearing a short evening dress of glittering black sequins, suspended precariously from her shoulders by the narrowest of spaghetti straps.

I stood up and gave her a kiss, unable to stop myself from thinking that I was the envy of every man in the room. "You look good enough to eat," I said.

"That was the idea." She sat down next to me on the banquette, ignoring all the people who were smiling or waving to her. This wasn't rudeness, by the way—Marilyn was shy and nearsighted, a combination that made table-hopping, or even table-waving, difficult for her. Mike popped open a bottle of Dom Pérignon for her, beaming when she tasted it as if he had trodden the grapes for it himself. She nodded at him—has there ever been such a thing, I wondered, as a *bad* bottle of Dom Pérignon, and would Marilyn have known the difference? "Do you know who first brought me here?" she asked.

I shook my head.

"Johnny Hyde. Poor little Johnny. He took me out and bought me new clothes, specially for the occasion. 'I'm gonna show you off, kid,' he told me. Did I have stage fright!" She laughed. "Johnny had *class*, you know, so he wanted *me* to have class."

She drained her champagne. There was an edge of bitterness in her voice—certainly not sentimentality or nostalgia. The captain came over, and I started to shoo him away, but she said she was hungry. She ordered a shrimp cocktail, a rare filet mignon, baked potato, and a Caesar salad—Vegas food.

"Did you have a good time?" I asked. "When Johnny took you here for the first time?"

Her eyes were sad, and strangely opaque, as if she were looking inward, still hurt and bewildered by what she saw there. "It was awful," she said, shaking her head. "Johnny had taken me to I. Magnin's, and bought me a dress, bare-shouldered, with this big wide skirt and a kind of matching wrap, and shoes the same color, sort of the Dior look, I guess, the kind of thing his wife would have bought, and I felt like a little girl dressed up in her mother's clothes. . . . And everybody in the restaurant stared at me, you know? I could almost hear them whispering, 'So *that's* the girl Johnny left his wife for!' Johnny liked to table-hop, you know—he was an agent, after all—but *nobody* came over to the table that night, and I could tell it bothered Johnny. I mean, people could accept that he had a girlfriend—what guy in his position didn't?—but here he was, bringing *me*, the girlfriend, to Romanoff's, and that wasn't *done*. Romanoff's was where you took your *wife*, see, not your girlfriend."

I thought she might be about to cry, but then her shrimp cocktail was served, and she ate it hungrily, picking up each jumbo shrimp by the tail between her long, bright red fingernails and dipping it in Russian dressing. She ate quickly, still at heart the girl from the wrong side of the tracks out on a lucky date with a big spender, afraid she might be asked to leave before she'd finished her meal.

"All the guys in my life have wanted to teach me things," she said sadly. "And I'm still the same dumb blonde I always was."

"You're not a dumb blonde."

"Not as dumb as people think, no. But I always ask myself—if men love me as much as they say they do, why is it that the first thing they want to do is change me? I'll say one thing for Jack—he never tried to teach me a thing."

"And Bobby?"

"Let's not talk about Bobby, okay? I will say this for him: unlike Jack, Bobby's the reforming type. He figures it's his responsibility to save me."

"From what?"

She looked at me with a certain amount of pity. "From myself, sugar," she answered. "What else?"

The next course was served, and she cut her steak with quick, sharp slashes—nothing delicate in her approach to it. "You're a nice guy, David," she said between bites. "I can *talk* to you."

She resumed her reminiscence. "I cried in the ladies' room that night. Sobbed my twenty-two-year-old heart out, sitting in a toilet stall in my sapphire-blue grown-up Dior look-alike. It was supposed to be my big night, and I could tell everybody was whispering that I was just some no-talent *bimbo* who was fucking Johnny Hyde."

She finished the steak except for a few scraps, which she asked the waiter to wrap up for her. I told him to give it to my chauffeur. Marilyn might not mind walking out of a restaurant with a doggie bag of leftovers, but I did.

I ordered another bottle of champagne, and since Marilyn had signified her intention to eat what she called "a killer dessert," I asked the captain to prepare crepes suzette.

She clapped her hands together and squealed with pleasure. "You're a *mind* reader!" she cried. "I've got to go to the ladies' room." Her walk was so sexy that the entire room fell silent, but I noticed a certain unsteadiness to it.

By the time she returned, the captain was setting up his chafing dish. Marilyn's walk had become steadier—so much so that she almost seemed to float across the room, though it seemed to me that she had a little trouble navigating around obstacles.

She dropped herself onto the banquette seat so hard that she bounced. "Whoosh!" she said, just as the captain, who had been waiting for her return, put a match to the crepes, sending a burst of flames high into the air.

It caught her by surprise and she let out a blood-curdling scream that brought all conversation to an instant halt. She threw her arms around me and pressed her face against my shoulder. I could feel her breasts, only barely restrained by the thin fabric, against my chest, the nipples, perhaps from the shock, noticeably hard. Glancing down, I couldn't help noticing that her skirt had ridden up, exposing her soft, pale thighs and her stocking tops, fastened to the thin, white suspender straps of her garter belt.

I held her tightly. She looked up at me and opened one eye. "Oh, Jesus!" she wailed. "I've made a fool of myself again."

Actually, I thought her behavior was charming. I reflected that poor Johnny Hyde had been wasting his time on the Pygmalion and Galatea act so far as Marilyn was concerned.

"I do that every time," she said. She straightened up, but remained close to me, her thigh pressed against mine, an out-of-place wisp of hair across her face. She brushed it back, oohed and aahed at her crepes, and wolfed them down as if she hadn't eaten for ages.

We were most of the way through the second bottle of champagne before I brought up the question of the calls she was making. She looked at me blankly. "What calls?" she asked, eyes wide open.

The possibility that she might be genuinely crazy flashed through my mind. I dismissed it.

I mentioned Alan's name, and reminded her that she had gone to meet him. "I've never heard of him," she said.

"He said you've been calling the show every night."

"Me?" She stuck her fork in my crepes and raised an eyebrow.

I nodded. She finished the sauce off my plate with a spoon, then emptied her champagne glass, and mine.

I was about to press her further on the subject, but she leaned her head against my shoulder and said, "Let's go dancing, darling."

It was not an offer I could easily refuse. In her head Marilyn seemed to be dancing already. Her eyes closed, her arm around my waist, I could feel her body moving to a rhythm only she could hear; her lips puckered in a silent whistle, as if she were following the tune. She was unbuttoning my white vest in an absentminded way, as if not even aware that her hand was busy. I didn't move, caught between the hope that she would get to work on the buttons of my fly and the fear of her doing it in front of everyone at Romanoff's. "Loosen up," she said dreamily. "I don't know why you wear so many clothes. What's the point of a vest, anyway?"

I couldn't think of an immediate answer to that one. "It holds the stomach in, I suppose," I said. I sucked in my gut sharply, but of course, it wasn't going to stay sucked in for long.

"I think a little belly in a man is *cute*," Marilyn said, mercifully removing her fingers.

"Where does one go dancing these days?" I asked.

She laughed. " 'One'? That sounds so—British. Where do *you* like to go?"

I hadn't gone dancing in Los Angeles for many years. I had a vague memory of the Ambassador—I remembered dancing there one evening with Grace Kelly, then an unknown young actress, to the music of Freddy Martin's band, and meeting his singer afterward, a fresh-faced kid called Merv Griffin. "The last place I remember going to was the Ambassador," I admitted.

"Oh, God," she said. "The Ambassador!" She laughed, a trifle unsteadily—a high-pitched, brittle sound, not very loud, like a crystal glass breaking on a carpeted floor. "Does it still exist?"

"I don't know. Probably. But not the way it was."

"Let's go," she said. "I'll pick the place."

She was silent for a long time on the drive down Sunset Boulevard to Malibu—where she had told the driver to go—holding my hand in hers in the back of the limousine. The doggie bag for Maf was on the floor by her feet, as well as a bottle of champagne in an ice bucket, which I had asked the restaurant to place in the car. She sipped it as if refueling her spirits, which had sagged at the mention of the Ambassador Hotel. "Do you think people change?" she asked suddenly, as if she had been thinking about the question ever since we left Romanoff's.

"No. Not in my experience. Not in any way that matters."

I thought she was referring to Jack or Bobby, or some other man in her life, past or present, but I was wrong. It was herself she was thinking about. "You don't think you can just stop being whatever you were, and become something else?"

"Turn over a new leaf? I suppose. People try. But most change is on the surface, I think. In the end, we're always the same person, in a new suit, a new marriage, a new job."

"God, I hope you're wrong!" she said.

The car pulled off the Pacific Coast Highway. We stopped at a kind of Hawaiian beach hut with a fake palm-frond roof and a carved totem pole on either side of the front door, like those that guarded the entrance to Trader Vic's. A neon sign gave the name of the place: "The Tahiti Club."

I had never heard of it, but Marilyn was obviously at home here. She swept out of the car, carrying the bottle of champagne, as I followed behind her. A grinning doorman, dressed in a faded beachcomber's outfit and a frayed straw hat, opened the door for us, releasing a blast of loud music and hot, smoky air into the cool, damp California night. Marilyn plunged into the noisy semidarkness, holding up the champagne bottle, and shouted, "Another one of these!"

We were led through the gloom to a small booth. As my eyes adjusted, I could see the place was decorated with the usual Polynesian artifacts: I had a dim impression of palm fronds, fishing nets, stuffed fish, and carved masks. From the rafters a war canoe was hung—or a papier-mâché studio prop version of one, anyway. There were half a dozen couples on the small dance floor and a live orchestra packed onto a tiny stage disguised as a beachcomber's hut. Most of the action was at the bar, which was jammed three deep.

Marilyn went off to the ladies' room, while I sat down. The place was so dark that her journey across the room hardly caused a ripple, although on the way back, as some of the lights caught her, there were a few whistles. She sat down opposite me, looking more cheerful, I thought, her eyes glittering again—though the pupils were mere pinpoints.

The captain, a swarthy fellow who looked like a hood, snapped his fingers and an ice bucket appeared, with a bottle of Dom Pérignon. "Johnny's compliments, Miss Monroe," he said.

"Who's Johnny?" I asked her as he popped it open with his thumbs.

"Johnny Roselli."

I stared at her through the hazy gloom. "Johnny Roselli? The gangster? You *know* him?"

She looked defensive. "He isn't such a bad guy."

I let that pass. Roselli was a very bad guy, even by the standards of bad guys—generally supposed to be the point man for the Chicago mob's penetration of the West Coast. Like all mobsters, he had built up a small empire of his own, which allegedly centered around narcotics and illegal gambling. "How on earth did you meet Roselli?" I asked.

Marilyn was swaying to the music, eyes half closed, drinking champagne. "I've known him for years."

"From where?" Marilyn's breadth of acquaintances fascinated me.

She frowned. "He was a friend of Joe Schenck's." She looked at me and giggled. "Well, maybe not exactly a *friend*, you know? Joe was paying off Willie Bioff—so much a month and Bioff made sure there weren't any strikes at Fox. Everybody did it. Joe just got caught, that's all."

"What did Roselli have to do with it?"

"Johnny was the bagman. He picked up the money for Bioff. Then Joe got worried that the Feds might be watching him, so he used to send me around to Johnny with the payoffs. That's how Johnny and I became friends. I used to go around to his house a couple of times a month, with a big paper bag full of money in a canvas tote."

I was speechless. From the way she was smiling, that secretive smile, eyes half closed, I could guess that she had almost certainly fucked Roselli while she was delivering Joe Schenck's money to him.

The thought of the young Marilyn in the arms of such a thug dismayed me.

She grabbed my hand and pulled me onto the dance floor, then put her arms around my neck and closed her eyes. It was sexy enough—she was pressed hard against me—but I couldn't help thinking that if she didn't hold on, she would slump to the floor.

I wondered if she had taken anything while she was in the ladies' room. It also occurred to me, belatedly, that there might be something stronger than booze for sale in any nightclub owned by Johnny Roselli—that the dim lighting was probably only one of the attractions of the Tahiti Club.

"Do you come here often?" I asked.

Marilyn had a little trouble focusing on the question, but she did her best. "Used to," she said, her words slightly slurred. "Peter Lawford's house is just down the road. Came here with Jack all the time."

"Jack? Here? While he was a senator, I guess. . . ."

She giggled, and slowly drew a fingertip down my nose to my lips. "He's been here since he was elected president," she said. "The Secret Service went bananas, but he insisted. He liked to come here at night, to dance. Lunchtime, he likes it across the street, at the Sip-N-Surf Bar, where all the surfer girls hang out."

The notion of Jack dancing in a nightclub—a roadhouse, really—owned by Johnny Roselli was chilling.

We were dancing slowly now, Marilyn's head on my shoulder, her feet moving to the rhythm as if they were on automatic pilot. "Marilyn," I whispered, "talking about Jack . . . and Bobby. . . . How are things going?"

"What things?" Her voice was muffled, since her mouth was pressed against my neck.

"Well, you and Bobby. . . . This story that you're pregnant?"

"Where did you hear that?"

"On the radio."

"It's supposed to be a secret."

"So it's true?" I asked.

"Mm."

"And it *is* Bobby's?"

"Nobody else's, lamb chop. Cross my heart. I can tell."

"How?"

"It's just something I can feel happening when it happens. I felt it with Bobby and I knew we'd just made a baby."

"What does Bobby think?"

"He's thrilled."

"He is?"

"You bet. *You* don't sound too thrilled, though." There was a sharp edge to her voice.

"No, no," I said quickly, "I *am,* really! I just wondered what you plan to do."

"He's going to leave Ethel and marry me."

I held her a little more tightly as we danced, or rather swayed together, in the darkness. "Are you sure?" I asked gently. "He'd be destroying his career, you know."

"He'll do it for me," she said dreamily.

"If he *doesn't,* you know, you can always count on me."

"Mm. I know that, baby."

"I mean *really,* Marilyn. Now. Always. You know how I feel about you. . . ."

She raised her head and looked at me, a trace of suspicion in her gray-blue eyes. "David," she said, "are you putting the make on me?"

I felt myself blush. "I guess I am."

"I thought you were my friend."

"I *am* your friend."

"No. You just want to fuck me, that's all. That's why you're telling me that Bobby isn't going to leave Ethel. That's a shitty thing to do."

It took me a moment to master my emotions. Marilyn was right —I did want to fuck her—but I also cared for her enough to want her to know the truth. I tried to get her to see reason—or what I took for reason, anyway.

"He isn't going to leave Ethel, Marilyn. You know that as well as I do."

"He *is* too!" She pulled away from my embrace, so that we were standing in the center of the dance floor, facing each other. "You're jealous," she said. "That's all. You know what your problem is? You've wanted to fuck me ever since the night we met, at Charlie Feldman's party. And the joke is, you missed your chance when you had it."

I looked at her, puzzled. "*What* chance?" I asked.

"I would have fucked you in the library, that night at Josh Logan's party, when the president of Indo whatever the fuck it was tried to make me, but you didn't even *notice*! You missed your chance,

David. You should have taken it when it was going, lover." She spoke the word "lover" with contempt.

She laughed—a loud, hurtful laugh, not the breathy, musical little laugh that I always found so sexy.

I tried to cast my mind back to that evening, so long ago, and for the life of me I couldn't remember having had even a clue that Marilyn was attracted to me. I could remember every detail of the room, I could remember exactly what she was wearing when she entered it, surprising me while I was admiring Bill Goetz's collection of bronzes—but I had no memory at all of the moment when, if Marilyn was to be believed, she had been willing to fuck me.

I was speechless with anger, at myself for having missed the one opportunity she had offered me over the years—worse, for not even having *noticed* it—at her for never giving me another chance. Over the years, I thought—how many? Six? Seven?—how often she must have laughed at me, the schmuck who had missed his chance and didn't even know it! Had she told Jack, too? Had they laughed at me together? "I don't believe you," I said furiously.

"Oh, you'd *better* believe it, David!" She glared at me. She looked demented, I thought. "You could have *had* me, right there on the sofa, I'm telling you. You've been sniffing around me all these years, and you didn't even know how close you were." She laughed hysterically.

I have a horror of scenes in public places, and in an instinctive effort to get Marilyn off the dance floor, where she was very conspicuous indeed, I grabbed her wrist. It was a mistake. Eyes blazing, she took a step back and slapped me.

I rubbed my flaming cheek, while she continued to glare at me, arms crossed in front of her chest, eyes now black as obsidian in the purple light above the dance floor.

"Bobby isn't going to leave Ethel for you," I said—sorry I'd said it even as the words came out of my mouth. "You have to know that."

"You should have fucked me, David," she said, more calmly now. "I still might not have loved you, but you'd have liked me a whole lot better than you do."

She shook her head. "I'll find my own way home," she said, and turning on her heel, she walked off into the gloom, leaving me alone on the dance floor.

They gave me a bill for the bottle of Dom Pérignon. I guess it was only a gift from the management if Marilyn stayed with me for the evening.

I slipped the money into the leather folder the bill had been presented in. "Give my best to Johnny Roselli," I said. "And see that Miss Monroe gets home safely."

The maître d's expression was carved in stone as he pocketed the folded-up bill I slipped him. "Johnny who?" he asked.

I wrote "I'm sorry" on the doggie bag from Romanoff's and asked the driver to leave it outside Marilyn's front door in Brentwood after he left me at my hotel, but she didn't call me the next day, and Mrs. Murray wouldn't put me through to her.

I flew back to New York, and tried to put the whole scene out of my mind.

48

"What's the mandatory federal retirement age?" Jack Kennedy asked crisply.

"Sixty-five."

The two brothers were sitting by the pool in the family compound at Hyannis Port, in swimming trunks. The President had a towel around his shoulders and a gob of sun cream on his nose. His chair was surrounded by discarded newspapers and news magazines. There was a briefcase at his feet.

"On the button," Jack said without a smile. He raised his sunglasses and rummaged briefly among the documents in his case. He held up a piece of paper. "This," he said, "is a handwritten letter from me exempting a certain federal employee from the mandatory retirement age. Can you guess who it is?"

Bobby stared glumly at the piece of paper, his Adam's apple bobbing. "I can guess," he said.

"Good for you. And can you guess *why* your president—the Leader of the Free World, who has bigger things to worry about—had to write J. Edgar Hoover a personal letter assuring him that he can remain on as director of the F-fucking-B-fucking-I until he drops?"

"Yes."

"Yes? Would that be because Hoover's men dug up the story that Marilyn is pregnant, with *your* child? That she's telling everybody you're going to leave Ethel for her?"

Bobby nodded wearily.

"It isn't just Hoover either, though that's bad enough. I had David on the phone telling me about some late-night radio show in LA she's been telling her troubles to. And she turned up at Peter's house in Malibu last night, to tell *him* her story. Pat saw her in the morning, and said she seemed 'confused.' To use Pat's exact word."

"It's all horseshit."

"Is it? She *is* pregnant. Hoover's guys, with their usual care for the constitutional niceties, broke into her gynecologist's office and photographed her file—to protect *you*, of course." He laughed mirthlessly. "*Is* it yours?"

"I don't know. I guess it might be."

"Wonderful." Jack looked across the pool at his father, who was taking the sun in his wheelchair, a Panama hat on his head, his hands grasping the arms of the chair like a bird's claws on its perch.

Jack waved to him with a big grin, but all his father could do was grimace in return. He sighed. "I don't know what *he'd* tell you to do, Bobby, but what *I'm* going to tell you is to get rid of this problem, *fast*. Tell Marilyn it's over. Be as tough as you have to, but make sure she understands it."

"And the baby?"

"And the baby? What's the *matter* with you? Christ, I always thought 'fucking your brains out' was just a *phrase*. Are you planning to stand up and acknowledge the kid, like a proud father? Are you going to ditch Ethel?"

"You know goddamn well I'm not." Bobby's face was scarlet with anger—and perhaps shame.

"Then don't sit there pissing and moaning about Marilyn's kid. Tell her to get rid of it. Tell her it isn't yours. Tell her whatever you like, *but get her to shut up!* Do I make myself clear?"

"Yes."

"Then do it." The President leaned back in the sun. In the distance there were the shouts of children playing noisily, and the sound of the waves breaking against the beach. He looked relaxed and content, but his voice when he spoke again had an edge to it. "I know it's tough," he said. "Nobody knows that better than me! You really loved her, didn't you?" He put it in the past tense with a precision that made it clear it was deliberate and not a slip of the tongue.

"Yes, I do."

Jack ignored his brother's defiance. "So did I," he continued softly. "And it's going to make you feel really *shitty*, breaking it off. All that guilt is going to hurt, believe me."

Bobby nodded. The noise of the children was coming closer, and he shaded his eyes against the sun to look for them.

"Well, that's okay," his brother said. "You *should* feel shitty. It's appropriate, and good for the soul. Look, she's a terrific girl, one of the best. Maybe *the* best. . . . It's like having an ice cream sundae—you were *entitled* to it. . . . You want my opinion, she was probably even *good* for you after all those years of doing your duty with Ethel. The problem was, you let it go too far, that's all. Everything you did was okay, except for two things. You didn't figure out she was crazy, that's number one. And you fell in love with her, that's number two."

"There's a part of me that wishes I could drop everything—everyone—and be with her." Bobby's voice was stubborn, as if this was something he had to say.

"Sure there is. But you're not going to. Maybe you'll always feel that way. Maybe I will. Maybe you'll wake up in the middle of the night every once in a while, for the rest of your life, with Ethel lying there in the bed beside you and think, Christ, why didn't I have the guts to do it? Welcome to the club, Bobby, welcome to the club."

The children appeared, running toward the pool from the beach, carrying sand pails, shovels, inflatable toys, screaming like wild Indians. The younger ones still behaved toward their grandfather as if he were perfectly healthy, perhaps unable to tell the difference. Their presence made him a little more animated, though in a manner that was painful to watch, for his facial expressions were grotesque, and the older children kept their distance.

Jack rose to his feet. "It's a tough world, Bobby," he said. "Just remember that this is what matters, and you'll be fine." He grabbed a couple of the smaller kids and tossed them in the pool. "A clean break," he shouted over his shoulder. "It's always the best. And the kindest."

He paused before diving in after them. "If that matters," he added.

———

It seemed to her that her whole life was on hold. Her days were full enough, but the fullness was contrived and artificial: after Mrs. Murray drove her to Dr. Greenson's for her session, her masseur would come over, and then her press agent; then she would spend the afternoon on the telephone, trying to put together some sort of plan for the evening, until the day was over.

Often enough, the evenings weren't much different. She would eat take-out food or have a cookout on the lawn with the people who had been with her during the day, then retire to her room with the phone and a pile of magazines to spend the night calling friends.

Though she had expected to be deluged with offers of work and scripts, there were still none. The only people who wanted to see her were photographers and interviewers, so she sat for as many interviews and photographic sessions as she could, if only to have something to do. Besides, she was anxious to show the world that even if Marilyn Monroe had lost her job, she hadn't lost her looks.

It gave her a sense of satisfaction—perhaps, at the moment, her *only* sense of satisfaction—that her body was as much of an attraction as ever. After every session, she pored over the contacts and the transparencies with a magnifying glass, slashing big crosses with a crayon across the ones she didn't like. She even allowed a couple of the photographers, guys she really liked and trusted like Burt Stern, to shoot her nude for the first time since her famous calendar shots sixteen years before, though she knew they couldn't be printed. She wanted to see what she looked like, to test the limits, and she wasn't displeased with the results—she even let Stern keep his negatives. She wondered what he'd say if he knew she was pregnant!

All the same, despite the photographers and the interviewers (to all of whom she told the same sad tales of her childhood, with as much emotion as if she'd never recited them before), she felt as if she were in limbo, restless and miserable. She called Bobby constantly, but increasingly she found herself talking to his secretary Angie instead, and when she *did* get through to him, he was rushed, slightly distant, the way a man might be if there was someone else in the room while he was taking a call from his girlfriend.

She needed to take a couple of Randy-Mandies after speaking to him, to calm her nerves, but soon she was taking them *before* she called him, to steady her nerves, with the result that she wasn't always sure what he'd said, and had to call back, right after hanging up, to ask him to say it again. . . . When he told her he was coming to Los Angeles, however, she heard him loud and clear. "When?" she asked.

"June twenty-sixth," he said.

She had lost track of the date, and it took a moment before it registered. She felt a jolt of discomfort. She had spoken to him yesterday, and he hadn't mentioned coming to Los Angeles. Usually his appointments and travels were fixed weeks in advance. "That's *wonderful!*" she cried, trying to sound excited enough for both of them. "How long do you have?"

"It's just for one night," he said, sounding a little cautious. "I'm having a series of meetings, cross-country, with law enforcement people, about organized crime, ending up in Los Angeles. Will you be there?"

It seemed to her an odd question. "Will I be here? Lover, I'll be wherever you *want* me to be."

"We need to talk."

"I know it." She ignored the tightness in his voice. "I'll get some food in," she said. "Can you spend the night?"

There was a long pause. He seemed to be thinking over the suggestion. Then he coughed and said, "Well, I promised Peter and Pat I'd have dinner at their house. . . . Why don't you come? They'd love to have you."

She was so hurt at the offhanded way he suggested it that she hardly knew how to react. He might, she thought, have been speaking to a total stranger. She decided there *must* be someone in his office with him. "Okay." She tried to keep the hurt out of her voice. "Then we'll get together, at my place?"

"Sure," he said, but he didn't sound sure at all.

"I love you, Bobby," she said, and waited for him to say that he loved her, but instead, he only said, "I know," so sadly that she felt like crying.

All the same, he *was* coming, and his arrival at least put an end to the lethargic routine of her days. Mrs. Murray was galvanized into getting the house spick-and-span, the refrigerator was stocked against the possibility that he might be hungry during the night, and she made appointments to have her hair done, her nails taken care of. She gave instructions for her makeup man and her hairdresser to come to the house six hours before she would have to leave for the Lawfords', and went through her closets to find something sensational that neither Bobby nor the Lawfords had ever seen before.

For all her careful preparations, the day of Bobby's arrival began badly. Trying on dresses, she spilled coffee on the one she had chosen, and turned on Mrs. Murray (not that it had been her fault) with a rage that gave her an instant, splitting headache and obliged her to spend the rest of the day apologizing. Together—Mrs. Murray responded to any demonstration of "togetherness"—they picked out a replacement, a white off-the-shoulder dress she had bought when Yves Montand admired it in the window of Saks, and by the time she had tried it on, and picked out a bag and a pair of shoes, she and Mrs. Murray were reconciled. The manicurist gave her false nails that reminded her of the Dragon Lady in *Terry and the Pirates* and made it impossible for her to pull a zipper or fasten a button, but she had never confused glamour with practicality, and it was her intention to be glamorous tonight.

Halfway through the process, however, she changed her mind. After all, she was a mother-to-be, was she not? It wasn't as a glamorous Hollywood sexpot that she was appealing to Bobby but as the mother of his child (or yet one more of his children, to be painfully accurate) and his future wife. She proceeded to undo everything that had been done, starting with her hair, which had to be styled in loose waves, softer and more flowing.

When she glanced at herself in a hand mirror, she instantly realized how stupid she was being. Bobby wouldn't want her to be mousy and ordinary. If what he wanted was a good mother in tame clothes, one who didn't wear much makeup or go in for glamour, he would have been content with Ethel, and wouldn't have fucked *her* in the first place. "Let's go back to what we had," she said. She shook her head hard, ruining her new hairdo.

There was a collective sigh. Mrs. Murray looked at her watch nervously. "It's six o'clock," she said timidly.

People ate early in Hollywood, their habits governed by the fact that performers who were on call had to be in the studio, ready to be made up, before seven in the morning, as well as the fact that executives had to be up at dawn to take calls when people reached their desks in New York at nine a.m. Her proper ETA for the Lawfords ought to have been seven or seven-thirty, and allowing the best part of an hour to get from Brentwood to Malibu, she should have been ready to go, instead of which she was sitting here, naked beneath a smock, with work on her hair and her face only just beginning again.

It was almost eight before she was ready, standing a little unsteadily on the very highest of her spike-heeled pumps, in a dress that showed as much skin as any dress could—all of it looked pretty goddamned good, in her own opinion, and who would know better?

Her hair was like gleaming silver cotton candy, her lips were a bright, shiny red. She giggled. *"This* ought to show him," she said.

She took a couple of pills at random to steady her nerves, and poured a few into her sequined handbag, in case of emergency— though she knew there was an unlimited supply of everything she could possibly want in Lawford's bathroom medicine cabinet.

When her driver helped her out of the car, for some reason the driveway blacktop seemed to have developed a life of its own, like a slow-motion minor earthquake, and she was grateful to him for steering her to the Lawfords' front door. The maid opened the door, and she swept past her into the living room, surprised to find it empty.

"*Señorita!*" she heard the maid cry, but she was already on her way to the dining room, and taking a deep breath, she descended the couple of steps, eyes fixed on the straight lines of the sliding glass windows so as to keep her balance.

There was complete silence as everybody turned to look at her, Peter rising with his usual grin, while Pat had the embarrassed look of any middle-class hostess at the late arrival of a guest she had decided wasn't coming.

Then she saw Bobby, sitting with an empty seat at his right, and her heart fell, not at the realization that he was already eating his dessert—was she really *that* late?—but at the sight of his eyes.

They were a pale, cold blue like ice on a pond, as unforgiving as a sentence of death.

———

"I'm so sorry I was late," she said.

"That's okay," Bobby said nervously. During what remained of dinner, they had talked like strangers, for after all, there were guests present who presumably weren't in on the secret, and she was always conscious that Pat, however easily she accepted the sex lives of the Kennedy men, was still something of a chaperon, at least as far as her behavior in public was concerned.

They left together early—after he put on a show of making a fumbling offer to drop her off on his way back to the Beverly Hilton—and sat in silence most of the way down Sunset, holding hands like teenagers, while she watched his Adam's apple bob up and down, an unmistakable index of his nervousness and, presumably, his unwillingness to begin a conversation in front of the driver, a Justice Department cop of some kind, for she had sent her driver home.

Once they were in the house, she waited in vain for Bobby to throw his arms around her, but if he felt that kind of passion, he did nothing to show it. She stood there in her living room, until he was shamed into giving her a quick, married-couple kiss. If he'd been a drinker, he would have poured himself a drink, but he wasn't, nor a smoker either, so she went to the kitchen, poured herself a glass of champagne, and turned on the radio, then came back to the living room and sat down on the sofa, exposing her thighs, kicked off her shoes, and patted the cushions until he sat beside her, with visible reluctance. "What's the matter, baby?" she asked.

"Marilyn," he said, "I've always tried to be honest with you, haven't I? Told you the truth?"

"Do I want to hear the truth, baby?" she asked sadly.

"Probably not. Practically nobody does. It's one reason why Jack is the politician in the family, not me."

"They say you're getting better at it."

He smiled grimly. "I'm not sure it's a compliment. Listen, I've told you I love you. . . ."

"And it wasn't true?" Her voice sounded small.

"It *was* true," he said. "It *is* true. I love you. And I think you love me."

"Mm," she said. "You *know* I love you, baby."

"Yes, I *do* know."

He took her hand in his. "Would you love me enough to do anything I asked you to?"

"Anything?" she whispered huskily. "Anything you want, baby. I'm yours, all of me." Her cheek was close to his, she clutched his hand so hard that her fingers ached.

"If you love me as much as you say you do, there's one thing you *can* do for me, Marilyn," he said.

"Name it."

He stared into the middle distance. "Get rid of the baby."

She sat silently, eyes suddenly blurred with tears. "Why?"

His voice was patient, as if he were talking to a child. "Because I'm not going to leave Ethel. . . ."

"You love her more than you love me?"

" 'More' isn't the point. She's my wife and the mother of my children—all seven of them. I have obligations toward her I can't ignore. I have obligations toward Jack I can't ignore. I have to do what's right."

"Are you saying it wasn't right for us to fall in love? That it wasn't right for us to go to bed together?"

"It *wasn't* right. It wasn't wrong either. We're both adults. It happens, we both know that. It was a small sin. Falling in love, having a baby, those are bigger sins, with bigger consequences. Too many people are going to be hurt."

"Maybe you should have thought of that before you fucked me the first time."

"You're right," he said in a low whisper, like a small boy admitting to some fault or household misdemeanor. "We were both wrong."

"No," she said firmly. "I'm not married. And I'm willing to have the baby. I don't have anything to be guilty about, except that I fell in love with the wrong guy."

"I'm not the wrong guy."

"Oh, yes you are, but that's not your fault, honey." She laughed. "Never fall in love with a married guy who has seven children—every girl ought to know better than that!"

"Do you need any help?"

"*Help?* Christ, I've been through this before, more times than you'd want to *know*. Don't insult me, okay? You want it taken care of, I'll take care of it."

There was a long silence. "You have a right to be angry," he said at last.

"Yes, I do." She looked him in the eye. "I should have known better. That's the problem out here. We believe in happy endings, and there aren't any in real life."

"Yes there are. Sometimes."

"Not for me. . . . Bobby," she asked softly, "can we still be—friends?"

"Well, sure. . . ."

"And lovers?"

There was a moment of hesitation. It was remarkable what a bad liar he was for a man who had spent most of his adult lifetime in politics. "If you want that," he said.

"What do *you* want?"

"I want it, of course. . . ."

The words "of course" didn't ring true at all—seemed to make his statement meaningless, in fact—but she let it go. If she had to hang on to him by her fingernails, so be it, she would hang on.

She had been humiliated by the studio, and now the man she loved was giving her the brush-off.

"Stay the night, darling," she pleaded. "Don't leave me alone tonight."

"Well. . . ."

"Please." She could feel how awkward and stiff he was. Was he, as she guessed, under orders to do the deed, get out of the house, and haul his ass back to the safety of the Beverly Hilton? "You don't have to fuck me if you don't want to," she whispered. "Just stay and hold me."

"Of course I'll spend the night."

She stood up, knowing that she had never looked sexier—that perhaps *nobody* had ever looked sexier—took his hand in hers and pulled his face close against her stomach, feeling the warmth of his breath through the gossamer-thin fabric. She said to him huskily, "Unzip me, baby."

49

A borrowed private airplane flew her to Tijuana, where a limo waited on the runway to take her directly to the *clínica*. It was a well-equipped, supermodern, specialized little surgical facility, safely across the border, beyond the jurisdiction of the state of California, where for the right amount of money a rich *gringa*'s own American gynecologist could perform the simple procedure he could go to prison for doing at home. Only the clinic's administration and nursing staff was Mexican, all of them chosen for their discretion.

All the same, as she lay there, the pills holding the postoperative pain down to a dull ache, she felt like crying. She had given up her baby, Bobby's baby, her last chance, she knew instinctively, for motherhood, for a new life, for all the things she had traded for fame.

She was back in Los Angeles forty-eight hours after the abortion. She had confided in no one—even Mrs. Murray thought she had gone to Tahoe with the Lawfords. The moment she was home, she called Bobby at the Justice Department to tell him it was done.

His private number had been changed, so she had to go through the switchboard.

———

Hoffa paced restlessly. He hated this kind of shit, all the guinea bullshit about respect and honor, instead of getting down to the nitty-fucking-gritty. Palermo, with his smooth tailoring and his slicked-back hair, wasn't his favorite kind of guinea either, but he didn't have a choice: Palermo was the mob's appointed messenger, and that was that. Giancana was hiding out in Cuernavaca with his singer girlfriend, dodging subpoenas and assassins, Moe Dalitz wasn't talking to anyone, not even Dorfman; and the Lansky group —Trafficante, Marcello, and Roselli—were lying low. Just when he needed help, when that little fuck Bobby Kennedy had finally nailed him with a serious indictment, everyone was running for cover.

"Look," Palermo said, spreading his hands, "it's tough. We know that."

"Tough? It ain't you who's going to the can."

"It'll never happen, Jimmy."

"Bullshit! This time Bobby's got a case, and he *knows* it. Just remind your guys, I go down, they go down."

Palermo shook his head mournfully. "You don't want me to pass that message on, Jimmy. You really don't."

"The fuck I don't."

Palermo inspected the toe-caps of his highly polished shoes. If Hoffa wanted to commit suicide, it was none of his business. Could he be dumb enough to think the law of *omertà* didn't apply to him? Apparently.

"You put your people on notice that they'd better not try to hang me out to dry all by myself," Hoffa said grimly.

Palermo nodded. That, of course, was exactly what "his people" had in mind.

"Mind you," Hoffa said, smirking, "Bobby's got his problems too."

"Yes?" Palermo couldn't think of any problem Bobby might have that was as serious as those facing Hoffa.

Hoffa leaned across the desk until his face was close to Palermo's —a closeness Palermo disliked, since Hoffa's tawny eyes and putty-colored face close up were almost as disagreeable as Hoffa's breath. Still, he didn't flinch.

"Marilyn's just had an abortion," Hoffa said, his voice husky with contempt. "Bobby's kid! If he don't go out to California and see her, she's gonna hold a press conference and tell the world, that's what she's telling everybody."

"Is this for real?" For once, Hoffa had genuinely surprised him.

"I got it all on tape. Bobby don't know about the press conference, not yet. She called him right after she had the abortion, and he tried to calm her down, you know? But Bobby, he don't have the guts to come right out and say, 'Fuck off, lady, it's over!' He just says he's too busy right now, all that shit. . . .

"He even changed his private number on her, the little prick, and when she asks him about that, he gives her a whole sorry bunch of bullshit about how they're installing a new phone system at the Justice Department, and this and that, which she don't believe a word of. . . . What the fuck, it's the oldest story in the book, right?"

"What do you plan to do with this, Jimmy?" Palermo asked with a certain amount of skepticism. His people weren't big on sexual blackmail—they were believers in the broken kneecap or the garrote.

"I'm gonna let Bobby know that Marilyn is gonna go public with the story he made her have an abortion. And if she don't do it, I will."

"When's he going to get the news?"

Hoffa smirked again. "Any luck, he's already got it." He swiveled his big leather desk chair around so that he was looking out over the Washington skyline toward the Justice Department, the windows on the top floor still lit in the hot summer dusk.

He lifted a can of Coca-Cola in a mock toast. "Have a good evening, Bobby," he said.

The Attorney General kept late hours—later than anybody else in government. The people who were close to him understood that the job came first—if you weren't prepared to put the rest of your life, your marriage, and your kids on hold, you didn't belong on his team. Once, he had left the office with one of his assistants after midnight, both of them exhausted, and as the driver turned down Massachusetts Avenue to take them home, the Attorney General had looked up and noticed that the lights in Hoffa's office in the Teamster building were still burning. "Make a U-turn and take us back to the Justice Department," he had snapped to the driver. "If Hoffa's still working, we should be too."

He still felt the same way. His enemy was still over there, in his office, instead of behind bars where he belonged. Robert Kennedy rubbed his eyes, picked up a thick sheaf of reports, and turned on his Dictaphone machine. He was about to slip a new belt into the machine, but he realized there was already one in it. He pushed the review button to see if it contained something he had previously dictated, and heard a familiar, gravelly voice. *Hey, Bobby, listen to this!* There was a gap; then a small breathless voice, distorted by recording and transcription but recognizably Marilyn's, began to speak in a whispery undertone, like a little girl telling secrets to a friend on the phone. It wasn't altogether a little girl's voice, of course, because there was a strong impression that she was drunk, or on drugs, or both, the clear panic signal of somebody out of control.

He can't do this to me can he, Doctor? the voice said. *He can't make me kill my baby, then abandon me? I thought we were going to be together, that he'd help me through all this shit, but then he changes his fucking number so I can't even reach him when I really need him. . . .*

What's done is done. You terminated the pregnancy. It's natural you should feel depressed.

Fuck "depressed." I'm angry! I want him here. I thought he was my friend. I thought I could trust him. He fucked me over, just like every other man in my life. If he doesn't come out here to be with me, I'm going to hold a press conference and tell the whole world what happened!

I believe that would be a mistake, Marilyn. . . .

I don't care. I'm going to do it. I mean it. . . .

He listened, his chin cradled in his hands, the tinny voice crackling from the dictating machine, vibrating with pain, anger, and fear.

There was a click as she hung up, then the sound of her dialing, and very soon she was telling the story of her abortion all over again, in a wild rush of words, to some woman named Dolores, who offered to come over and keep Marilyn company, and then to Aaron Diamond, the Hollywood superagent, who gruffly told her to forget about it and call him in the morning, at his office, then to her makeup man, who was horrified. . . .

He switched the machine off, took the plastic belt out, and carefully cut it into small pieces with the scissors from his Mark Cross desk set, a gift from Ethel. Of course, it was just a symbolic gesture. He knew where the tape had come from, although not how it had been placed in his machine. There would be other copies—Hoffa wouldn't have sent him the original.

He wondered how many other people Marilyn had called with her news, and more important, her threat. But it didn't really matter— one was enough, or rather, too much.

On the desk in front of him was a travel folder, marked "AG & Family—California." He stared at it and sighed. In ten days, he was taking Ethel and the children to the ranch of an old friend, near San Francisco, for an eagerly awaited long weekend, then going on to join Justice William O. Douglas on a mountain-climbing expedition in Washington.

There were things that never needed to be spoken of in any long marriage, that were just somehow, as if by mental telepathy, *known*. Ethel had never once mentioned Marilyn's name to him, but he could tell that she knew about the affair. She had made it clear enough between them that the trip to the West was something he *owed* her. She hadn't said so. She didn't need to.

Next to the travel folder was a call sheet, on which Marilyn's name appeared almost a dozen times, the calls sometimes only minutes apart.

He glanced at his watch. It was eleven p.m. in Los Angeles.

He was so tired that he closed his eyes for a moment. He opened them and rose at last from his desk, stretching. He decided to call it a night—he was simply too tired to do any useful work, and Ethel, he knew, would be waiting up for him. He looked at his calendar and sighed. He had a full day tomorrow, July 25; then the next day he flew to Los Angeles in the late afternoon to make a speech at the banquet of the National Insurance Association convention, then back to Washington on an Air Force jet, for a meeting at the White House on the Soviet buildup in Cuba. . . .

He looked again at the long list of calls from Marilyn, all of them begging him to see her, and shook his head. He couldn't—he knew that. It was too dangerous, "counterproductive" as the CIA spooks liked to say, not even fair to her. . . .

On top of that, God alone knew what kind of trouble she might make. . . .

He dialed Peter Lawford's number instead.

———

On July 25, though she couldn't have explained why, she cashed in her chips. She had saved up a whole sheaf of prescriptions from her many doctors and filled them all in one long pharmacy-hopping afternoon.

She knew she didn't *need* that many pills, but she was only able to relax when she had a supply on hand, plus a few secret hoards stashed away for emergencies. It was the thought that she might run out that paralyzed her with fear, that sent her from pharmacy to pharmacy in Brentwood and Santa Monica on a kind of shopping spree, until her handbag was comfortingly full of pill bottles.

It had been five days since her abortion. She had lost count of the number of times she had called Bobby Kennedy, but he had spoken to her only once. She had begged him to come to California to see her, even if only for a night, but he had pleaded work.

She had not expressed her anger to him, or her hurt—for she wanted him back. Besides, she knew Bobby. Like Jack, it was useless to threaten him. Late at night, when she was sleepless despite all the pills and champagne, she kept herself from going crazy by calling everyone she knew, letting go of all her rage and frustration, but she would never have said any of it to Bobby himself, nor did she always remember exactly what she said during those calls, let alone mean it.

She drove down Sunset to the Pacific Coast Highway, parked at the Sip-N-Surf, kicked off her shoes and walked barefoot along the beach, feeling better than she had for a long time. Maybe life would make more sense if she never thought about it, if she could simply sit on the beach and watch the waves, and let the breeze blow in her hair. . . .

She walked back to the Sip-N-Surf, slipped on her sunglasses, took a seat under the palm-frond canopy, and ordered a hamburger and a Coke. Most of the kids at the counter were in their teens, and for a moment she envied them bitterly, but then, if they had recognized who she was, they would have envied *her,* so perhaps it all evened out, she decided. . . . "Penny for your thoughts," she heard a familiar English voice say.

Lawford was sitting at the counter a couple of seats down, separated from her by two stunning girls in bikinis. He came over and gave her a hug. He was dressed for the beach in baggy shorts and an old tennis shirt, his hair tousled, his feet bare. He was genial, good-natured, grinning, and clearly a little drunk.

"Slumming, darling?" he asked, dropping down beside her.

"Since when is Malibu a slum?"

"Depends which end. . . ." He gave an admiring glance at the bare back of the girl nearest him. "Ah, youth!" he said with a sigh. "The older I get, the younger I like them. Odd that, isn't it? I suppose I'll end up a pedophile if I live long enough." He held his glass up toward the barman. "Another scotch, George," he shouted.

"His name isn't George."

"All barmen are George. Listen, when you saw me here, didn't you think, Fancy that! What a coincidence! Here's darling Peter!"

She shook her head. "No," she said. "It didn't occur to me."

"Oh dear. Because it *isn't* a coincidence, as it happens. I saw you walking along the beach, and since I've been trying to reach you for days, I thought I'd follow you and say hello."

"I've been at home."

"Really? I must have called *dozens* of times, darling."

"You can't have. . . ."

"Oh, yes, but never mind. Here you are. I was calling to ask you away for a long weekend. Rumor has it you need a change of pace. I say, what are you drinking?"

"A Coke."

"That won't do. Give the lady a glass of champagne, George."

When the barman brought her the champagne, he clicked his glass against hers. "Cheers! Listen, do say you'll come. We're flying up to Tahoe in Frank's new airplane."

"You and Pat?"

"Probably. Almost certainly." He hesitated. "Although Pat's plans aren't clear yet. . . . It's going to be quite a party—all sorts of people, really. . . ."

There was a sweaty insistence to his voice that made her nervous. He put his arm around her, as if they were the best of friends—which perhaps they *were,* she wasn't sure. . . . "It will do you the world of good," he said.

Why not? she thought. Maybe that was just what she needed—a little fun. It might teach Bobby a lesson too, that she wasn't just going to sit around calling him, or waiting for him to call. . . . She could hardly spend the rest of her life wandering around the house aimlessly, while Mrs. Murray sat in the kitchen like a bodyguard—or a nurse, which was nearer to the truth. "Okay," she said.

He gave her a broad grin, then a kiss. "Smashing!" he said. "We might make a nice long weekend of it, what? Go up tomorrow, if the plane's free?"

———

Thursday was one of those days that would have made her mind up to go to Tahoe even if she'd been undecided—a day of blinding, sultry heat, with gusts of wind that brought no relief, and had the same effect as opening an oven door. Even Mrs. Murray was cross and short-tempered, while Maf, normally the most cheerful of animals, huddled in the shade beside the pool, panting.

She spent the morning fretting about what she was going to wear and pack. In the end, she did what was most comfortable and turned up at the plane in an old pair of Jax pants, a man's shirt—one of Jack's, as it happened—with the sleeves rolled up, and a scarf over her hair. Lawford poured himself a drink and slumped beside her once they were in the plane. He lit a cigarette with trembling hands.

"No smoking on takeoff," the pilot said—the door to the flight deck was open.

"Fuck off," Lawford said.

The pilot glared at him, but apparently decided that it wasn't his job to quarrel with his employer's guests.

She noticed that Lawford hadn't bothered to fasten his seat belt either. She was about to do it for him, then decided she didn't want to touch him for fear he might misunderstand the gesture. The hell with him, she decided. It wasn't up to her to be his nursemaid.

"Where's Pat?" she asked.

"Ah," he said, opening his eyes and looking around the empty cabin as if he were surprised not to see her there. "She couldn't come. Not her scene, really."

He drained his drink and fell asleep, leaving her to her own thoughts. "Not her scene"? Of course, it was *true*—the Cal-Neva Lodge *wasn't* Pat's scene. It was a place for "the boys," given over to heavy drinking, gambling, and partying. It wasn't even *her* scene, if the truth was known, but it beat being alone by a mile.

She still thought so the next day and the next night, for it was like a twenty-four-hour-a-day party, where she was surrounded by people with whom she could let her hair down and relax. Her cabin was between Frank's and Peter's, the same one she had once occupied with Jack, and she felt at home in it. She could rise late, read in bed, go for walks by herself, and somehow here, away from Los Angeles and the feeling that where she *ought* to be was the studio, she found herself beginning to relax, able, for the first time in weeks, to enjoy herself.

She joked and danced with Frank and Peter and their friends, protected by a kind of all-enveloping spirit of masculine camaraderie, her spirits kept high by an endless supply of pills from Lawford's "overnight bag," as he called the black leather doctor's satchel he never went anywhere without.

It wasn't until Sunday that she realized she'd been conned.

They had all been up until three in the morning, so it was well past noon when she joined Lawford at the pool, where he was nursing his hangover along with black coffee and juice.

With his eyes closed, he didn't notice the approach of a bellboy carrying the Sunday papers, and by the time he saw them and shouted out, "No, no, we don't want any!" it was too late. The *Los Angeles Times* had already been placed at his feet on the chaise, right side up, so she could see the top half of the front page clearly, with its large photograph of Bobby Kennedy speaking at some convention, under the headline:

"Robert Kennedy in LA
Vows 'War Against Crime!' "

It took her all of a second to realize why Peter Lawford had been so insistent on her coming up here for the weekend. "You fucking bastard," she said to him quietly.

A good actor might have feigned innocence, but one of the more likable things about Lawford was that he knew he wasn't a good actor, and didn't pretend to be. "We all do what we have to do," he said. "It was for your own good as much as his."

"The hell it was! He wanted me out of town, that's all. And you did it for him."

"Yes, that's true."

"Why?"

"He wanted to avoid a scene, Marilyn. I mean, what did you *expect?* You've been calling him day and night, blabbing to everyone about the fact you two were having an affair—sooner or later, he was bound to react, you must have known that."

"He could have called me himself!"

"That would have made matters worse, he thought. Listen, darling, you're lucky he didn't use the federal marshals instead of me. You keep forgetting who it is you're dealing with, baby, and that's a big mistake."

He was sitting up now, pointing his finger at her, his expression serious, without a trace of the self-mockery that usually made him bearable to her even when he was saying something hurtful. Her hand was trembling, but she didn't hesitate. She picked up the coffeepot from the outdoor table between them and sent it flying at his head.

——

"Marilyn went bananas, is what I'm saying."

I felt the usual palpitations at the mention of her name. In the past few weeks, since she had walked away from me at Malibu and I had flown back to New York, neither one of us had phoned the other. There seemed nothing more to say.

"Where *was* she, did you say?" I asked. Marty Glim was a client, a nice enough fellow (for a multimillionaire) who had made his pile in the wholesale plumbing fixtures business in Cleveland, then fulfilled a lifetime fantasy by moving to the West Coast to start a whole new life as an independent movie producer, leaving Mrs. Glim behind. I was in the process of transforming his image into that of a serious figure in the movie industry.

"I was at the Cal-Neva Lodge," he said. "I took a girl up there for the weekend, and we were having a good time, when Peter Lawford, who's at the next table, starts to make a pass at my girl. . . .

"Well, I wasn't about to put up with that, so I told him to knock it off, and I'm goddamned if the drunken son of a bitch doesn't get up and put his hands on my girl's tits, right there in front of everyone. Then all of a sudden Sinatra and Marilyn Monroe appear, she apologizes, he leads Lawford away, they send us champagne, and everything's hunky-dory. . . .

"Anyway, Marilyn was terrific. She handled Lawford beautifully, she was swell to this girl, and really nice to me. . . . And she seemed *happy*, too. I mean, you hear such a lot of rumors about how she's miserable, or crazy, or whatever, but here she was, right next to us, having a *great* time. . . ."

Glim was continuing, his voice boring through my thoughts—he had already picked up the Hollywood custom of talking without interruption until he or the subject was exhausted. "That's why you could have knocked me over with a feather when we saw her at the airfield," he was saying, and I realized I had missed some essential turn or detour in the conversation.

"What was that?"

"The airfield," he said with some annoyance. "Jesus, I wouldn't have recognized her as the same woman who came over to my table the night before. She was being *carried*, literally, and maybe not even *willingly*, frankly, if you can believe that. . . ."

I could believe that.

"They had a doctor there. He was walking right behind them, with his black doctor's bag. And she was struggling, fighting not to get on that plane, or maybe just to get their hands off her, who knows?"

"Did she say anything?"

"No. They pushed her onto the plane. Just *shoved* her in. Honest to God, David, it looked like a kidnapping. A hell of a thing."

I hurriedly thanked Glim, and called Marilyn right away, but it was Dr. Greenson who picked up the telephone.

"How is she?" I asked him.

"Resting, at the moment," he said. He had a pleasant voice—a perfect bedside voice. It occurred to me that he might just possibly be the only therapist in the country who made house calls.

"Look," I said, "is she all right? I hear there was some kind of problem last night, when she was leaving Tahoe."

"She went there against my advice," Greenson said rather stiffly, as if I were blaming him.

"What happened?"

"I wasn't there, Mr. Leman. I would say that the weekend was too stressful for Marilyn. Which is not so surprising, given her condition. . . ."

Dr. Greenson put a world of meaning into the word "condition."

"Can anything be done to help her, Doctor?" I asked.

There was a pause. "Not a great deal, frankly. She feels abandoned, her self-esteem is shattered—it wasn't that strong to begin with, after all. . . ."

"Tell her I'll fly out there if she wants me to," I said, though I doubted I could do much good. I had flown out to California on one rescue mission that had ended badly—for me. I wasn't about to rush into another.

"I'll tell her," Greenson said. "But I don't think it's necessary at all." His confidence was reassuring.

I said good-bye to him with a certain amount of relief, and asked my secretary to send Marilyn flowers. I told her that the card should read, "I'm here if you need me, David," and then dialed Bobby's number at the Justice Department, on the theory that there was never any point in putting off what you didn't want to do.

———

Bobby's voice, when he finally came on the line, betrayed the obvious impatience of a man who already knows what the subject of the call is. We disposed of a certain amount of small talk; then I said, "I hear Marilyn is in a bad way."

"She's going through a tough time, poor kid," he said, as if he weren't the cause of it. His tone was sympathetic, but guarded. By this time, Marilyn's troubles must have begun to seem like a tidal wave, about to rise and engulf them all.

"I'm doing what I can, David," he went on patiently. I knew him well enough to guess what it cost him to hold back his Irish temper, but he must have decided that the calmer he was with me, the sooner I'd get off the phone and leave him alone. "I asked Peter to keep an eye on her."

"He can't look after himself half the time, let alone her. Did you know she had to be sedated and carried onto a plane last night, to get her back from Tahoe to Los Angeles?"

"The situation is under control, thank you," Bobby said. "Between Peter and Pat, Dr. Greenson and Mrs. Murray, and so on, half the city is looking after her. If you'd like to join the throng, be my guest."

"I may just do that."

"Fine," he snapped. "Do what you think best. I'll be on the West Coast myself this weekend with Ethel and the family, near San Francisco, but I'm planning to stay away from LA. And if you want *my* advice, so should you. She needs some time to pull herself back together again. Rushing off to see her won't help. That's her doctor's opinion too, by the way," he added, and hung up.

He was right, of course. It *was* Greenson's opinion, and exactly what all of us—certainly Bobby—wanted to hear, which Greenson must have known.

It wasn't until he had hung up that I realized Bobby hadn't once mentioned Marilyn's name himself. And that he had been speaking to Dr. Greenson.

————

It was Wednesday by the time she called me back, reaching me at the office just as I was about to go out to meet a client for lunch. "They were beautiful flowers," she said. "Nobody else sent me flowers."

"I'd send you flowers every day if you wanted."

"Oh, honey, that's an old line. Listen, I really behaved shittily to you and I'm sorry."

"That's okay." She didn't *sound* like a woman in trouble, I thought. Had Greenson brought about a miraculous recovery? Apparently so. My secretary tapped the face of her wristwatch significantly. I shrugged. The client could wait.

"I want to apologize to you," she said. "When are you coming out to LA again?"

There was a level of anxiety in Marilyn's voice. I put it down to the fact that she had just gone through a terrible experience. If there was an appeal to me to drop everything and fly out to see her, I didn't recognize it, to my shame. "In a week or ten days," I said.

"Oh." She sounded slightly disappointed, but she made no attempt to press me. "Can we have dinner again?"

"Sure we can. I'd like that."

"Maybe not at Romanoff's this time."

We both laughed. I thought she sounded remarkably like her old self.

"You'll let me know when you're coming?" she asked.

"Of course I will."

"Good-bye," she said. There was an eerie moment of silence, then the sound of something that might have been the wind, or a sigh.

"Good-bye," I said, but the line had already gone dead.

I rushed off to La Caravelle for my meeting. I had what remained of a very full week in front of me. I had to be in Washington to see the President on Thursday; then I was planning to stay for a formal dinner at the White House.

I made a mental note to call Marilyn back and tell her about the White House dinner—she was still interested in hearing about anything that Jack did—but I never got around to it.

50

The call came on the special telephone the Signal Corps had rigged up at the Gilroy ranch house for the Attorney General. They had not wanted to damage his host's handsome living room with their wires, so they put it in the hallway—an ordinary-looking black telephone without a dial, which was connected to the White House. Wherever he went, the Attorney General had to be able to communicate with his brother. Less august callers, like his brother-in-law Peter Lawford, could be patched through the White House switchboard.

He took the call standing in the hallway, shooing the children out of the way for privacy, cradling the receiver between his ear and his shoulder, his eyes dark and hooded.

"What do you mean, she's out of control, Peter?" he asked.

There was a long pause while he listened. He faced the front door, his back toward the living room, as if to emphasize that he wanted to be left alone. "No, no, I realize you can only do so much. . . . Really, you've done well. I'm grateful."

He moved back and forth, as far as the telephone cord would let him, unable to pace as he clearly wanted to. It was as if there was so much energy contained in him that he couldn't stand still. "I don't think she'll come up here." He spoke crisply, sure of his judgment, as always. "She might do *that*, yes," he said. "Poor woman."

There was a wealth of sadness in his voice, layer after layer of pity and shame, but not self-pity, for he was a man without a trace of it. "Get the doctor there," he ordered, "what's his name. . . . Right. . . . No, no, I'll tell her myself. It's the only way."

He said good-bye, hung up, sighed, then picked up the receiver again. "Daddy, Daddy, when are you *coming?*" one of the children shouted from behind him, and he turned and flashed a huge grin. He held up a finger—a minute, he indicated, for he hated to keep children waiting—then spoke into the phone, asking the operator to transfer his call to a number at Justice. He didn't waste time on pleasantries. "Find out how I can get down to LA tonight," he snapped. "Without being seen."

He closed his eyes for a moment, as if he were suddenly exhausted. "There's a Marine base up here, isn't there?" he asked. "They must have helicopters?"

He listened impatiently. "Well, I don't care. Just *do* it."

He hung up and made a dash into the living room, engulfed in the noisy delight of his children, every trace of fatigue and concern gone.

———

She had spent Friday evening with the Lawfords. She remembered that she had joined them at La Scala for dinner—a party of five, with her the odd woman.

By the time dinner was served, she was bombed, and once she was bombed, she had started to talk loudly about Bobby and how he had given her the brush-off, until Peter, equally bombed and sweating bullets from sheer nervous tension, finally had to leave the table before his guests even finished the main course and drive her home. She hadn't made it easy for him either, but in the end, despite a nasty scene in front of the restaurant (in full hearing of the car jocks), she had let him bundle her into his car.

She remembered kicking off her shoes and putting her feet up on the dashboard so the breeze could cool her crotch—it was a blazing hot evening. She remembered arguing with him bitterly and angrily, while he begged her to behave sensibly, to remember who Bobby was, to think about her own career and reputation—most important of all, to stop making trouble and *shut up.*

She remembered telling him to fuck off as they pulled up in front of her house. She also remembered threatening, at the top of her voice, to go public with the whole story if Bobby didn't get his ass down to LA and see her.

"He *can't,*" Lawford had wailed. There were actually *tears* in his eyes.

She threw a shoe at him, and caught him on the forehead. "I *mean* it!"

"It's over. Forget about it."

"I love him!"

"So what? He's married. He has God knows how many bloody kids. He's probably going to run for the presidency in '68. Leave him alone."

"He loves *me,* you snotty British motherfucker."

"Very likely. That doesn't matter either."

She threw the second shoe at him. It caught him on the mouth, splitting his lip. She was pleased to see that there was fear in his eyes. She wished she had something else to throw.

"Tell him I'm calling Louella, Winchell, everybody, tomorrow. I'm going to give them the whole story. Jack. Bobby. The whole thing. Tell him I have to see him, or else!"

There were lights appearing in windows all up and down the street. Dogs were barking. Lawford cowered in his car, waiting for the next missile, then he put it in gear and drove off, leaving her alone outside her front door.

In the morning, she woke early. By nine she was up, feeling curiously clearheaded, seated in the kitchen while Mrs. Murray made fresh coffee for her. During the night, she had somehow gained hope —Bobby would come, and once he set eyes on her, things would be all right.

She skipped lunch, and lay in the sun by the pool for an hour while Mrs. Murray went shopping, so there'd be something in the refrigerator for Bobby—for she was convinced he was coming, whatever Peter Lawford might think. . . .

She was so convinced, in fact, that she called a toy store on Santa Monica Boulevard and ordered toys for all seven of Bobby's children, asking the store to deliver them to her house as soon as possible. For Mary Kerry, the youngest, she ordered a big stuffed tiger, just the kind of thing she would have liked to receive herself at the age of three; for the others, a variety of stuffed animals and toy cars —she wasn't much good at knowing what kids liked at this age or that, and it seemed unlikely now that she would learn.

It had been an impulse—probably a wasted one, she thought— but she wanted Bobby to know that she loved all of him, even his family, and that he didn't have to choose between her and his children. . . . She had put too much pressure on him, she realized that now.

About one in the afternoon, a deliveryman arrived from the toy store and Mrs. Murray returned from Brentwood with the groceries. There had been no call yet from Bobby, and she was beginning to be nervous—all the more so at the sight of the toys piled in the hallway, as if it were Christmas. They reminded her of the orphanage—for as Christmas approached, there were always piles of toys in the hall, old ones, left by well-meaning donors. The thought increased her anxiety, as anything to do with her childhood did, and she was about to call Peter Lawford to ask when—if—Bobby was coming, when the telephone rang. She picked it up and heard the familiar voice. "I'm in town," Bobby said. "We have to talk."

"I know," she said, trying not to let her emotions show through. "Where are you? When did you get in?"

"I'm at Peter and Pat's house. Is it all right for me to come over?"

"Of course it is. Hurry. Please."

She rushed to her room and made herself up, as quickly as she could. She was torn between putting on a dress or wearing slacks, but she decided that a casual "at home" look would be more appropriate, as if she'd been lounging around the house of her own free will, not trapped in it, waiting for his call.

She was still dressing when he arrived. She opened the front door for him—Mrs. Murray had been sent away—and gave him a kiss there on the threshold. His face was grave. He put his arm around her, but she already felt chilled, despite the sultry heat. "You know why I'm here?" he asked. He didn't seem angry—just tired and preoccupied, but at the same time patient.

"Because you love me," she said. "Because I love you. Those are the only reasons you need."

"Yes. I love you. That's true. And I know you love me. That's why this has to stop, Marilyn."

She had made up her mind there was going to be a reconciliation scene, decided exactly how she was going to play it. She would give up the idea of his leaving Ethel, accept the role of mistress—none of that really mattered. . . .

If he wanted her to stop blaming him for the abortion, so be it, she would put it out of her mind. . . .

"You're back," she told him, running her fingers through his hair, kissing his cheek, holding on to him fiercely. "I'll do anything you say."

Gently, but forcibly, he pushed her away, guided her to the sofa, sat her down, then took up a position in front of the empty fireplace, from which he could look down at her.

"Anything? Okay. For a start, no more threats. That's number one." He held up a finger, like a schoolteacher making his points.

"Number two, no more calls to radio stations. . . . Don't deny it, please. The FBI has been taping them. . . . Finally, no more communications. I'm sorry, but there it is—it's become too dangerous."

"I haven't threatened you!"

"You told Peter you were going to go public. If that isn't a threat, I don't know what is, Marilyn."

She stared at him. She hadn't really *meant* to "threaten" him—not the way *he* perceived it, anyway.

"Peter misunderstood me," she said. "You know what he's like."

"I know." His voice was grim. "But what he said was pretty simple. If I didn't come down here and see you, you planned to tell everybody about our—ah—*affair.*"

He drew the word out with evident distaste, as if the whole idea disgusted him. *"Did* you say that? Or anything like it?"

There was still no anger in his voice—but no sign of affection either. Nothing in his expression or his manner suggested for an instant that this was a man whose body had become as familiar to her as her own, the man who had fathered her child. . . . He might have been a total stranger, his eyes hard, his mouth set, more like a judge than a lover—and, in fact, he *was* passing sentence, on their love: a sentence of death. "It's been a mistake," he said. "It's gone too far." He paused. "I blame myself, not you."

"There's no blame. . . ."

"Yes there is," he said sharply, eyes flashing, as if she had managed to pierce his defenses at last. "I'm to blame. I should have realized—"

"I couldn't be trusted?"

"Something like this couldn't be, ah, *contained,* is what I was *going* to say. Not in the long run. You're too famous. I'm Jack's brother. There wasn't a chance it would work, in the long run."

"There *was,*" she said. "I'm sorry."

"There's nothing to be sorry about."

"Yes there is." She fought hard for his attention, trying to get him to look her directly in the eyes, but he couldn't, or wouldn't. "When I was with Jack," she said softly, "I always thought you looked so sad."

"Sad?"

"Sad and envious. Like David, only more so. I used to think, He isn't loved, not *really* loved, the way Jack is. He's lonely, and so very, very sad. I wasn't in love with you. I just felt heartbroken *looking* at you."

He laughed uneasily. "You were wrong," he said. "Ethel loves me. The kids love me. Very few people get as much love as I do. More than I deserve."

"Oh, Bobby, that's not love. Not the kind I mean, and you know it. Except for the kids Ethel might just as well be another one of your goddamn *sisters*. All you do is worry about Ethel, and what she wants, and what she'll think. . . . I told myself the first time I set eyes on you, after Jack's back operation, He doesn't know what it's like to be loved by somebody who thinks about *him*, and worries about what *he* wants, then *does* it. . . . I told you once—whatever you want, whatever you've dreamed about in your wildest fantasies, that's what I'll do for you, lover, forever, and I meant it. I still do."

He sighed. "It's no good," he said quietly. "It isn't that I don't have feelings for you, Marilyn. I do. It isn't that I wouldn't like to go to bed with you. I would. Right now. It wouldn't take a lot for you to be able to talk me into it. But it wouldn't change anything. It has to be over. I can't see you again. I won't take your calls. If you write me, I won't open the letters. Maybe it'll break your heart. Maybe it will break *mine*. It doesn't make any difference. That's the way it is."

She covered her eyes for a moment. What *did* surprise her was the way he said it. His tone of voice was calm. It left no room for doubt —or more important, hope.

"And I'm to keep my mouth shut, of course?" She hadn't meant to sound bitter, but she couldn't help it.

"That would help," he said. "I'd be grateful. Jack would be grateful. Still, if worst comes to worst, if you don't, I'll deny it." He looked thoughtful. "It'll be your word against mine. And Jack's."

The truth was, it didn't matter to her anymore. She didn't want to destroy Bobby, or Jack, even if she could have. They had wives, children, lives, careers that mattered to the world. "Bobby," she said, savoring his name. "Is this your decision? Or Jack's? Or Ethel's?"

"It's my decision," he said. "Jack wants it, sure. Ethel's put a certain amount of pressure on me, as you can imagine. But I'm the one who's breaking it off, Marilyn. And it's final. We won't see each other again."

She fell forward to her knees for a moment, sobbing, but he didn't trust himself enough to help her up. "You're making it harder on yourself," he said. "You're making it harder for me."

There was a knock on the door, which surprised her, for she had told Mrs. Murray not to disturb them, under any circumstances.

She looked up and saw Dr. Greenson standing there, a hypodermic needle in his hand. He wasn't looking at her. He was looking at Bobby, who nodded.

She let out a cry of anger and betrayal—at Bobby for having drafted Greenson into acting as his backup, at Greenson, her own doctor, the person she trusted more than anyone in the world, for having agreed to be part of a sordid plot.

"Be reasonable—the doctor is just trying to help," Bobby said. His voice was calm—deliberately so, as if he were trying to pacify her enough so Greenson could give her a shot.

"It's just a mild sedative, Marilyn," Greenson said soothingly. He was edging into the room now, trying to get close to her with his needle, while she backed away from him.

She felt such a deep sense of disgust, at herself, at them, that she couldn't even *look* at Greenson, let alone listen to him.

She shook her head numbly, feeling sick to her stomach—though she hadn't eaten since breakfast.

"It will help you handle the stress," Greenson went on. He pressed the plunger in his hypodermic gently, to eliminate bubbles. "You'll rest," he said soothingly. "Then tomorrow, we'll talk about all this. . . ."

He reached into his pocket and produced a wad of cotton wool dipped in alcohol, the sharp smell reminding her of the hospital in which she had lost her baby—Bobby's baby—only a couple of weeks ago.

Bobby was close to the door, barring her exit, while Greenson slowly circled the room toward her. She grabbed the telephone from the floor, with its long line that allowed her to carry it all over the house. Both men backed off a little, and it occurred to her that they must have independently jumped to the conclusion that she was going to use the phone as a weapon.

She smiled at them grimly, challenging them to make a grab for her, but apparently they weren't prepared to go quite that far. "Leave me alone," she said, her voice surprisingly flat and unemotional to her own ears.

Greenson looked at Bobby, who glanced at him quickly and nodded. "You're not the man I thought you were," she said to Bobby quietly.

She walked to the far end of the room, the telephone cord snaking behind, and up a couple of carpeted steps to her bedroom door.

She was almost safe now. Greenson, she felt sure, wouldn't have the nerve to break down her door, nor would Bobby. She held the telephone up in front of herself, as if she were performing an exorcism. "Don't. Come. Near. Me," she said, very slowly, as if each word were painful to articulate.

They didn't. Greenson stood rooted to the spot, the hypodermic needle hanging uselessly at his side. Bobby stared at her from across the room.

She knew that the moment she went inside her bedroom, she would feel trapped there, but she couldn't stand looking at the two men any longer. She was determined not to cry, or to let them see that her hands were trembling. She clutched the telephone so hard her knuckles were white. All she wanted was to get safely to the other side of the door.

"You'll call me?" Greenson asked anxiously. "You'll come and see me tomorrow?"

She didn't answer. She didn't want to speak to him, and she didn't want to think about tomorrow. Her only concern was how she was going to get through today.

She slipped into her bedroom with the telephone, and paused for a moment, looking directly down into Bobby's eyes.

"Please go now," she said. "Both of you."

Bobby was pale, his eyes fixed on her, trying to assess, she felt sure, what the damage was, whether he'd done the right thing. "Are you going to be all right?" he asked.

Again she didn't answer. It was no longer his business. She felt desperately tired, but not sleepy. "Somebody's got to pay for this," she said, not sure why she said it.

Turning away, she locked the bedroom door behind her. She did not even hear the front door slam or their cars start up as they left. She was alone.

She undressed, dropped her clothes on a chair, put Frank's *Blues in the Night* on the record changer, then stacked five more of his albums on top. She lay down on the bed naked, feeling the breeze from the window on her body. She luxuriated for a few moments in the silence of the house, broken only by the monotonous buzzing of insects in the eucalyptus trees outside, and the dry rustle of the leaves —a sound she missed whenever she was away from LA for long. Then the record dropped, the turntable spun, and Frank's voice, mellow and sad, the sexiest voice she knew, filled the room. She sang the lyrics softly along with him—"Blues in the Night," she thought, might as well have been her theme song.

She would take a few pills and rest, she decided; then she began to dial the phone. It was going to be a long, lonely afternoon and she needed to summon up support.

She no longer had Jack's private line, but she had the White House number.

She grasped the receiver and listened to the ring, waiting for someone to answer. . . .

A PRAYER
FOR
NORMA JEAN

Two Secret Service men met me on the runway and drove me straight to Marilyn's house in Brentwood, at my request. I don't know why. There was nothing I could do there, but I somehow felt I needed to be in her home before I did anything else.

The Air Force jet had given me a fast but bumpy flight, most of it haunted by thoughts of my own guilt. Now that I was here, I realized I would have done better to go right to my office and start making calls to the media, gently guiding the story away from the Kennedys, but I couldn't. I needed a moment of communion with Marilyn first.

The little house was still surrounded by cops, but they made way at the sight of the two Treasury agents' credentials, though with visible resentment.

There was a large stuffed tiger on the lawn in front of the house. "What's that?" I asked one of the LAPD detectives, who was standing around in the hope of being photographed by the *Los Angeles Times*. He shrugged. "A toy," he said. "Brand-new. There's a whole bunch of toys in the front hall, like it was Christmas."

"I wonder why," I said. I knew Marilyn didn't collect stuffed animals.

"Beats me. You the guy from Washington?" he asked. "Leman?"

I nodded.

"Macready," he said. "I'm supposed to show you round, do the honors."

We shook hands and Macready, a large man in a rumpled seersucker suit, led me into the silent darkness of the house. "Her husband was here," he said. "Poor guy."

I raised an eyebrow. "Arthur Miller? Here?"

"No, no. Her *first* husband, Jim Dougherty. He's a sergeant in the LAPD, nice guy. I called him the minute I heard the news and told him she'd OD'd. 'Poor Norma Jean,' he said. 'She never had any luck.' I guess he was right." He opened a door. "This is where she did it."

I looked at that sad little bedroom and almost burst into tears. Marilyn's bed was almost bare—no dust ruffle, no fancy covers, just a plain striped mattress, a couple of twisted sheets, a blanket, and a pillow stained with her makeup. It might have been a bed in a cheap motel room, the kind that rents by the hour. The furniture, what there was of it, belonged in a motel room too—a cheap nightstand, a couple of chairs piled with old magazines and clothes, a telephone with its long extension cord snaking out through the door. "She was holding it when she died," Macready said. "We had to pry the receiver out of her hand when we took her away. Rigor mortis." He lit a cigarette. "She must have died while she was making a call. Hell of a way for her to go, all alone, trying to call someone. . . ."

"Did she leave any note?"

He gave me a detective's cynical stare—he knew now why I was here.

"No note," he said. "If that's what they're worried about in Washington."

"I don't know anything about Washington, Sergeant," I said. "I'm just a friend of the family."

"Which family would that be, I wonder?" He led me through the living room and back outside again. "Anything else I can do?" he asked.

I told him, and he looked at me with even greater distaste than before.

"You're the boss," he said. "I'm glad I've got my job, not yours."

———

Back at the hotel, I found Lawford waiting in my suite. His face was white, he was sweating despite the air-conditioning, and his hands were shaking violently.

"Jack doesn't blame me, does he?" he asked.

I shook my head. Jack wasn't blaming anybody but himself, and he could live with that. "What happened?" I asked.

"She overdosed after Bobby told her it was over between them."

"I know *that*. Why didn't Bobby stay? Why didn't Greenson calm her down?"

"Bobby decided they'd done all they could. Greenson felt the situation wasn't critical."

"Did she call you?"

He nodded miserably. "She called, yes. Her voice was slurred—the way it always was when she'd taken a few pills. I wasn't surprised, under the circumstances. Or alarmed."

"What did she say?"

"She asked if Bobby was at my house. . . . Actually it was—a little, ah, unfortunate. Bobby was right there, you see, by the pool, when I picked up the phone, and he said, 'If that's Marilyn, tell her I'm not here.' She must have heard him, because when I told her Bobby had gone, she said, 'You're a nice guy, Peter—say good-bye to Bobby for me,' and hung up on me, just like that." He snapped his fingers damply. "Then I tried calling her back, and the line was always busy, busy, busy. . . . Bobby was waiting for a helicopter, and after it came, I went back into the house and called her again. It was still busy, so I called Dr. Greenson, and eventually he went round to her house and found her dead. . . ." His eyes told me he was leaving a good deal out of the story.

He had helped himself to a tumbler of scotch, which he drank in great gulps. I had the impression his version of the events had been carefully rehearsed. "It wasn't my fault, David. Honestly," he added anxiously.

"No," I said—though in fact, I thought, he was the one person nearby who could have saved her, and he hadn't.

I poured myself a drink. "I've just come from her house," I said, as if I needed to explain to Lawford why I needed a drink.

"Ah, yes," he said. "It's depressing to see, isn't it?"

"You were *there?*"

"Oh yes, old boy. They called me when they found her, so I called Bobby, who told me to get over there fast, before the police, and see if she'd left a note. I suppose he didn't know who else to ask, and after all, I *am* family. So I went to her house and looked around. She was naked, you know, facedown on the bed with the telephone against her ear. I couldn't help feeling that if I'd made a loud noise, she'd have woken up, just like that, but of course, it was an illusion. . . ." Lawford was crying silently, tears rolling down his cheeks and wetting his shirt front. He didn't explain who "they" were and I didn't ask.

"And then?"

"I already told Bobby. No note." He sobbed. "Not a fucking thing."

I looked him in the eye. "I don't believe you."

He blew his nose. "David, it's the truth, so help me God! No note at all." He paused, snuffling. "Just a notebook full of poems."

I held my hand out. Lawford stared at me resentfully, but he probably thought of me as somebody who had been deputized by Jack, the one person in the world he was more afraid of than he was of Bobby. He reached into his pocket and produced a small notebook, the kind you can buy in any stationery store.

"Thanks, Peter," I said. "You can go now."

"You don't want to know any more?" he asked.

"No," I said. "I really don't."

And I didn't, not a word. I just wanted him out of my sight.

When he'd gone, still babbling apologies and self-justifications, I sipped my drink and flipped through the notebook. Some of the poems were familiar to me—things Marilyn had copied in her rolling, circular handwriting, because they'd captured her attention, a few of them old favorites out of the *Oxford Book of English Verse;* others were poems of her own. It was the last entry I was looking for, and I turned to the end of the book. The writing was distorted and clumsy, as if she had reached the stage when holding a pen was almost impossible for her, but it was still possible to read what she had written just before she lost consciousness.

It was not one of her poems, or even somebody else's. It was simply:

> *Dear Bobby: I loved you. That's not a crime, is it?*
> *I only wanted to be happy. Was that such a lot to*
> *ask?*
> *Wherever I'm going, I'll love you still.*
> *Take care of Jack—and yourself . . .*
>
> > *Marilyn.*

Below that, as if it were a business letter, she had written out in capitals, "HON. ROBERT F. KENNEDY, ATTORNEY GENERAL, U.S. JUSTICE DEPARTMENT, WASHINGTON, D.C."

I wondered if she had really supposed, poor woman, that the note would ever get to him. Then I thought about what the repercussions would have been if the police had found the note, and leaked it to the press. . . .

Very carefully, I tore the last page out of the notebook and shredded it into tiny pieces.

I put the book in my pocket, and left on my final errand, the one I dreaded most.

———

Macready was waiting for me at the morgue, looking as if he belonged there. "You *sure* you want to do this?" he asked.

I nodded.

"Up to you." In a city of palm trees, Spanish architecture, and bright colors, the morgue looked as if it had been designed by municipal architects for Cleveland or Boston a century ago. There was nothing to remind one of Los Angeles, whose citizens, when they died, were apparently fated to return to the grim, old-fashioned dampness, full of brick, vomit-colored marble, and grimy, peeling woodwork, of the cities they had fled to come here. Of course, Marilyn was *born* in LA, I reminded myself, her orphanage only a short distance from here.

Macready led me into an elevator and we descended. He lit a cigar and offered me one. I shook my head. "It helps the smell," he explained as the door opened. The smell *was* unpleasant, a combination of stale urine, formaldehyde, and decay. I didn't think it was improved by Macready's Te-Amo cigar, which smelled like a burning horse blanket.

He preceded me down an aisle between rows of stainless steel gurneys, each bearing a covered corpse, past a white-tiled room where a couple of men in surgical scrub suits were busily emptying the brains out of somebody's skull while listening to a ball game on a portable radio. I thought it was possible that Macready was testing me, but if so, he was wasting his time. I had been here before in my younger days, when I worked in the movie business—Marilyn was not the first star to commit suicide, if that was what she had done.

He opened a door and ushered me into a bright room with row after row of stainless steel doors at the far end. It was cold enough to make me shiver. There was a uniformed cop sitting against the refrigerator vault doors, his chair tilted back, reading a copy of *Playboy* and smoking a cigarette. "On your feet, Quinn, you lard-ass," Macready said. "She's got a visitor."

Quinn didn't take offense. Cops, as I well knew, always talked like that to each other, like large, dangerous animals that appear to be fighting when they are merely playing. "Fuck off, Macready," Quinn said amiably, and got up.

"Why's she being guarded?" I asked, beginning to be glad of Macready's cigar smoke.

"We get all kinds of sickos down here," he explained. "Photographers would pay five, six grand, maybe more, to take one picture of Marilyn Monroe in the morgue. That's why we put Quinn on guard down here. He's too fucking dumb to take a bribe."

"Up yours, Sergeant," Quinn said, opening a vault door and pulling out the tray.

Macready puffed on his cigar. "Christ," he said, "when it's a beautiful woman, we even get perverts who try to fuck the corpse. Especially if it's a star. That's another reason to put Quinn on the job. He's so afraid of his old lady he wouldn't try."

"There you go," Quinn said, ignoring Macready, and pulled back the top part of the sheet covering Marilyn.

She was as beautiful as ever—the pathologists hadn't done the autopsy yet—her blond hair slightly mussed, her face clean of makeup, her lips parted in what appeared to be a slight smile. She looked years younger, and except for a slight bluish cast to her lips, she might have been asleep.

"Could you leave me alone for a moment, Sergeant?" I asked.

Macready eyed me suspiciously, as if I might be one of the perverts he had mentioned. He didn't look happy about it, but after a moment's pause, he shrugged. "Whatever you say," he grumbled. He didn't seem in any hurry to leave, though. He reached into the pocket of his jacket and drew out a scrap of paper. "The family might want this," he said with a knowing wink, handing it to me. Then he left the room, taking Quinn with him.

It was an official-looking list of numbers, meaningless at first; then I realized they were telephone numbers. I wasn't an expert, but I didn't need to be to guess that this was the telephone company's record of Marilyn's long-distance calls the day of her death. The morning showed nothing more than normal activity. Then, in the afternoon, standing out so clearly that they could hardly be missed, there was a long series of telephone calls to the same number, dozens of them, some only minutes apart. I recognized with a sinking heart the number of the White House. Most of the calls were short, no more than a minute or two, presumably because Marilyn wasn't being put through to the President, but the last one in the series was long—almost half an hour.

All of a sudden I knew what had happened in that cheerless little bedroom. I could picture it as if I had been there. Marilyn must have taken all her pills after Bobby left; then, as she began to realize she was slipping into a sleep from which she would never awaken, she had started to call the White House, more and more desperately reaching out to Jack, until finally the switchboard or his long-suffering secretary had put her through to the President.

She and Jack must have talked for nearly half an hour as she lay dying! Had he realized how far gone she was? Did he understand that she was saying good-bye to him, and to life? He must have, of course. Yet he had done nothing. Had he lulled her deeper into sleep, knowing that with each passing minute she was less able to call for help? Did he decide that it was time to cut his losses, that his future and Bobby's were at stake? Was he protecting Bobby, keeping Mar-

ilyn on the phone as she slipped into oblivion while Bobby headed
back to his family?

Yes, I told myself, Jack was capable of that, even if it broke his
heart—for he had genuinely loved her, I knew that. But in the end,
he would have protected himself, protected his presidency, protected
Bobby. He must have had all this in mind when he called me into
the Oval Office to tell me the news—or as much of it as he thought
I needed to know.

Poor Marilyn! She never had a chance. She had sought out the
only world more glamorous than her own, but she never understood
that in politics, unlike the movies, people play for keeps.

I wondered how Jack was going to live with himself, but I knew
he would survive, a little more bitter, a little wiser, a lot harder. We
don't put a president into the White House to be squeamish, after
all. We expect him to make the tough decisions we wouldn't want
to make for ourselves, to do the things we don't want to hear about,
or even know about, and Jack Kennedy understood that better than
anyone. He probably understood better than anyone the price he,
too, would have to pay.

I wondered, more urgently, how *I* was going to live with myself. I
tore the piece of paper into shreds and dropped it into a wastebasket.
History would have to judge Jack Kennedy, I decided, not I.

Quinn had left his copy of *Playboy* on Marilyn's body, opened,
cover up, on her stomach so he wouldn't lose his place. I didn't
touch it, or her. I looked down at that perfect face for a long time.
Then, at last, I allowed myself to cry.

I leaned over and kissed her, not on the forehead, coldly, as one
might kiss a corpse, but boldly on the lips—the last kiss she would
ever receive.

"Good-bye, Norma Jean," I whispered.

Then I pulled the sheet back over her face, and left her to Quinn's
care.